THE GREATEST HUNT OF ALL

Swift as lightning the Hunter coursed his prey, but the Stag was a shooting star come to earth. Though every glimpse of the elk made Blackthorn more reckless, not a stone made him stumble, not a twig scratched his face. This night, this wood, this Hunt was his. Tireless, he raced on, while fog rose from the river and blanketed the hills.

Shadows sprang from under the oaks, subduing hill and forest in their sudden assault. Blinded, Blackthorn stopped. The mists drew a shiver from his sweat-drenched body and brought another curse to his tongue.

Even as he voiced it, light erupted from the surrounding dark. The Stag stood before him, regal head glowing beneath immense antlers, proud chest blazing white.

Hunter
of the
Light

Risa Aratyr

HarperPrism
An Imprint of HarperPaperbacks

HarperPaperbacks   *A Division of* HarperCollins*Publishers*
10 East 53rd Street, New York, N.Y. 10022

Cover illustration by Paul Wright
Map by Dave Smeds

First printing: April 1995

Printed in the United States of America

HarperPrism is an imprint of HarperPaperbacks.
HarperPaperbacks, HarperPrism, and colophon are trademarks of HarperCollins*Publishers*

❖ 10 9 8 7 6 5 4 3 2 1

for Roy,
mo mhúirnín

ACKNOWLEDGMENTS

I'd like to thank my husband, Roy Jimenez, for his abiding faith and incisive editing. Thanks also to my children, Bryn Aratyr and Neil Jimenez, Mother-Writers Linda Beth Freese and Garnet McClure, and to my ground crew, Liane Makiva, Charles Makiva, Janet Guastavino, Wendy Masri, Kassy Fatooh, and Blair Zarubick. I am indebted to Dave Smeds for his map of Éirinn, to Katie Keaton for her research, and to Dr. James Duran for his assistance with the spelling and pronunciation of the Gaelic. For their efforts and encouragement I'd like to thank my agent, Richard Curtis, my editor, Christopher Schelling, and my writers' group, *The Melville Nine*, especially Janet Berliner, James Killus, and Joel Richards. Finally, for his all-encompassing dedication to the quality and success of my work, I would like to express my deepest gratitude to Melville-Niner Dave Smeds, Éirinn's true Champion.

ULAIDH

Clochán na
bhFormhórach

An Earagail

An Bhanna
Sliabh
An Óir

Sliabh
Tuaidh
Dún na nGall
Loch
nEathach
Crom-
ghlinn
Béal
Feirste

Loch Dearg

Sliabh Slanga

Inis Ceithleann

Binn
Chuilceach

Sliabh Ailp

NA
CONNACHTA

MIDHE

Temuir

Tuaim

Gaillimh

Sliabh Bladhma

LAIGHIN

Aillte an Mhothair

Aonach
Urmhumhan
Ceatharlach

Sliabh Coimeálta

Sliabh Buidhe

Luimneach

Caiseal

MUMHAIN

Tráigh Lí
Sliabh Mis

ÉIRINN

Samhain

Nine long years he had awaited the return of the White Stag. Twelve days and as many nights he had trailed the beast across fen and field, lost the track in the mountains, and sighted his heart's desire at last on a raw, gray morning.

Now morning's promise seemed to the Hunter as empty as the twilit glade about him. As dusk gathered, he crouched unmoving by the banks of An Mhorn Bheag, no longer certain that thirst would lead his quarry to the stream that ran through the coomb. Almost he despaired as the sun touched the crest of the western hills and shot a pale farewell through the branches of the alders. Yet, even as it died, the light fell gleaming upon the Goddess's Stag at the top of the ridge, just entering the narrow defile.

A pale breath of white moving through the trees, the giant elk made his way down to where the rushing water slowed and swelled. Head nodding with every delicate step he took in the shallow rill, the Stag came ever nearer to his death. He paused, as the Hunter knew he must, and bent his mighty neck to drink. Blackthorn never stirred from his cramped position amid the bracken. A great ash Spear, a year and a

day in the making, rested lightly in his palm against the
moment the Stag should raise his head.

An owl glided under the alders' arms and sang out mourn-
fully before vanishing into the gloom. At her warning, a
shudder ran across the Stag's rump, spurring powerful legs to
flight. His crowned head lifted as he turned, his muzzle drawing a tenuous ribbon of water from the pool. A single leap
and he was away up the hill, a bright shadow darting
through the dark-woven trees.

The Hunter came to his feet cursing the bird that had
betrayed him. Plunging across the stream, he flung himself
onto the slope, heedless of the impending dark and the
White Stag's matchless speed. Nine years the flame of his
geis had burned in his heart. Now it possessed him, a fire in
his blood nothing save the elk's death could tame.

Loam and rotting leaves welled through the fingers of his
free hand as Blackthorn groped for purchase on the steep
hill. Instinctively, he found rocks that were steady, grasped
branches strong enough to hold his weight. He forced a path
to the crest, then peered into the dusk, hoping to spy a glimmer of white. Only a gust of dank, icy air greeted him, blowing his long hair back from his forehead and stinging his
eyes. He was still blinking back his vision when the White
Stag flew from the shadows of the trees. Blackthorn was after
him like a hound, teeth bared in fierce delight.

Withered leaves spun in the Stag's wake, marking his
trail. Following the brittle traces, the Hunter came to a high
oak wood, where the trees moaned in the wind, and stars
glittered through a tattered veil of clouds. Brighter than the
stars was the distant flash of a silver hoof in the dark forest,
the taunting flicker of a milk-white tail.

Swift as lightning the Hunter coursed his prey, but the
Stag was a shooting star come to earth. Though every
glimpse of the elk made Blackthorn more reckless, not a
stone made him stumble, not a twig scratched his face. This
night, this wood, this Hunt was his. Tireless, he raced on,
while fog rose from the river and blanketed the hills.
Gentled by the mists, the Stag's light beckoned still, a silver
jewel in a clouded sea.

Then it was gone, and with it the Hunter's fey mood.
Shadows sprang from under the oaks, subduing hill and forest

in their sudden assault. Blinded, Blackthorn stopped. His heart pounded, his lungs labored to swallow the thick, moist air. The mists drew a shiver from his sweat-drenched body and brought another curse to his tongue.

Even as he voiced it, light erupted from the surrounding dark. The Stag stood before him, regal head glowing beneath immense antlers, proud chest blazing white.

For nine years Blackthorn's every act, every thought, every dream had been to realize this moment. He felt the Spear's balance, pulled his arm smoothly back for the cast. He ran forward one step, two. A third and he was near enough. The power of his thrust lifted Blackthorn off his feet.

His fingers had barely loosed the Spear when he perceived his folly. There was no Stag, only radiance pouring madly from a widening rift in the fabric of the night. Not the wide sheets of the Stag's antlers, but the broad, meshed arms of two trees the Hunter saw before him, and they slowly pulling apart like doors opening. The elk's features, so distinct a heartbeat past, blurred, swelled, became a formless cloud of implacable white. Blackthorn would have turned and fled, as the Stag had turned at the stream, but the brilliance leapt toward him quick as fire, burning away sight and reason. Spellbound, the Hunter was hurled like his Spear, and with as much will, into the terrible, beautiful light.

PART 1

the púca

One

*Broken are they that break sworn word,
a mother's heart, the bonds of geis*

The Second Triad of Éirinn

The light was blinding, but not all-encompassing, as he had first believed. With a slight shift of his head, Blackthorn's vision returned. What was he thinking of, to gaze straight into the dawn? Even winter's sun could destroy a man's sight, and his must be as the hawk's if he hoped to mark the White Stag's hide against the snow-covered hills. . . .

The Hunter's rueful smile tightened to a frown. How morning? How snow, deep and drifted? The festival of Samhain was no more than an hour old when he had come upon the print of the White Stag's hoof on the wet side of Binn Chuilceach. Since then but twelve days had passed that he could count. Rains might fall in Samhain-tide and frost dust the fields before daybreak, but this—this hushed and snowbound forest belonged to the dark of midwinter, and midwinter was yet four weeks away.

His frown deepened to a scowl. Not dawn, surely, but midnight the hour. And himself, giving chase to the Stag he should be—indeed had been, not a moment since. The Hunter's fingers tightened on the Spear in his hand. Between hurling the sacred weapon into the light and staring into the sunrise, Blackthorn could find no memories.

Gray eyes hard as flint, he turned slowly, searching the horizons. He had a fine view in every direction, but it was the jet-black pillar stone he discovered at his back that told him the Name of his lofty seat. He knew the lands all 'round well as any man, though never willingly would he have surveyed them from this summit. Many the tales sung of the Mountain of the Black Stone, Mullach an Lia Dhuibh, that the Wise called Brugh na Morna. Some praised its wonders, others laughed at those fool enough to fall under the hollow hill's many enchantments, more in number than the trees upon its slopes. All warned of time lost, and hearts changed.

Blackthorn set his shoulder against the stone and faced the dawn. Now he had his bearings, he could see the sun was far to the south. Only on the shortest days of the year did it rise so. Six dark weeks lay between Samhain and midwinter, when the sun turns northward and the days begin to lengthen. Two of those weeks he'd spent tracking the Stag from Binn Chuilceach to the banks of An Mhorn Bheag. For the rest, it seemed he'd been all the while tarrying in the elven halls of Brugh na Morna. Midwinter's forest it was in truth stretching out before him to the mist-rimmed edges of the world, and the sun a child new-born of the year's longest night.

That time had passed he could not deny, but Blackthorn's heart was steadfast. Once every nine years the White Stag appeared on Éirinn's shore, and then only from Samhain, summer's end, to Bealtaine, summer's dawn. On Bealtaine morning, nine years past, the White Stag had called Blackthorn to the Hunt. From that moment to this, but one desire had burned in his soul—to find the giant elk and bring him down. Half a year had he to fulfill his geis, and an entire moon lost already to the Sidhe of Brugh na Morna.

He spat, and would have muttered a curse against his recent hosts for waylaying him were he not still standing on the roof of their dwelling. A fool he had been to pursue his quarry to their very door—though he'd have thought it exceeded even the audacity of the elves to interfere with the Goddess Éire's chosen Hunter when the Stag was running.

The stone at his back was cold as a pillar of black ice. He stood away from it, but felt no warmer. His cloak was sewn of warm wolf hides, and his boots were well oiled, but winter's wind had little trouble penetrating the Hunter's doeskin shirt and leather breeches. Nor had he gloves to warm his hands, but only a leather guard laced to his right arm from elbow to wrist, and his fingers were red with cold.

Running them through his black hair, he studied his surroundings again, this time with an eye for the best way down. Wishing would not turn the Wheel back a season, a moon, even a day. And the Stag's snow-covered trail would grow no plainer while he stood here shivering and cursing his ill luck.

Choosing the more gentle southern slope, Blackthorn struck out across the unblemished snow, passing from the open summit to a ring of white-mantled gorse, and then under the eaves of the forest. His first thought had been to get off the mountain as quickly as possible. By the time he reached the woods he realized he was heading toward An Mhorn Bheag to find again the pool under the alders where the Stag had come to drink. Doubtless winter had destroyed all traces of that night, but might not the white elk return to a place once favored? And returning, might he not leave a fresh trail to follow?

Sunlight filtered through the oaks, coaxing slow drops to fall from the icicles dangling at the elbows of the trees and prompting an overheavy branch to let slip its load with a muffled roar. The crystalline daggers would freeze again come night, but this morning there was a lightness in the eddies of mist that rose in the broad shafts of gold, a promise in the gentle thaw.

The Hunter's long hike to the river was made longer by the care with which he had to place his feet. He had stopped noticing the beauty of the woods about him, his concentration bent on his downward path, when he came upon two hawthorn trees growing side by side. Even in the light of day he had no trouble imagining a giant elk's spreading tines in the thorns' reaching arms.

Despite the anger he nursed toward the inhabitants of Brugh na Morna, the sight of the tree-gate to their hidden halls touched Blackthorn with a pure, abiding joy. He pressed on the feeling, but though it ran deep, it led nowhere. At last he sighed and again ran his hand through his hair. If the hawthorns were a key to his lost memories, he could not fit them to the locks in his mind.

Shunning the plain path that lay between the may trees, the Hunter forced his way around the pair. Soon the Brugh's living doorposts were far above him, yet still the joy he could not name persisted in his heart. Below he could see a thick band of trees curling like a gray snake about the foot of the mountain. Under their empty boughs lay An Mhorn Bheag, and further on would be the glade where he had nearly taken the Stag. Blackthorn slid the rest of the way like a child, falling his height or more with every step and laughing aloud when he arrived unscathed at the water's edge.

Winter had reduced the brook to a gash of ice caught between the roots of the frost-bound alders. Following the slippery road, he made his way upstream until he reached the coomb where, a moon past, he had crouched in the ferns awaiting the Stag. The broad pool was buried under a thick blanket of snow. Only a few brown stalks of bracken showed through the drifts lining the river's banks. The Stag had not returned, at least not since these snows had fallen. There was no new trail to follow, and the old one could not have been better hidden if the white blanket had been spread expressly to confound the Hunter's craft.

The joy Blackthorn had felt on the slopes of Mullach an Lia Dhuibh ebbed sharply. The day half-gone, and he only to An Mhorn Bheag! Even the sunlight streaming through the canopy of leafless branches and mistletoe did nothing to hearten him. Storm clouds were gathering in the sky. Though the day had been fair, the night looked to be foul, and worse for a man without shelter in the wild.

The Hunter bent his head, sifting through his knowledge of this part of Ulaidh. He could follow An Mhorn Bheag down through the pass at An Bearnas Mór, and from there strike out for Dún na nGall. Dear to him was the stone fortress overlooking the sea, for he had been born there, and only the forest was more his home. Still, it would be night before he left the mountains, and tomorrow before he reached the dún. He'd be wiser to take the shorter, if steeper journey to the river that led to Loch Dearg. For didn't Roe the Thatcher keep a cote on the north side of the lake to house him when the reeds were ready to cull?

Hunger began to gnaw as he set off again, the cold to stab his toes. Neither the fort's comforts nor sight of the Stag would he enjoy this day. He would be fortunate indeed, reflected Blackthorn as the first flakes dropped lightly from the sky, if the lakeside bothy were still where he remembered it, if the thatcher had thatched his own roof before departing, and if Roe had left him the makings of a fire to soothe the sting of winter from his flesh.

Roe's tiny cottage stood where it always had, and the roof was well laid. But by the sullen twilight that squeezed past his snow-caked body as he stood leaning against the doorframe, Blackthorn could see that the little room held not so much as twig to bring to flame. A bed of dry grasses lay heaped next to the empty hearth. He could burn that, but its warmth would scarce be enough to draw feeling back into his hands before it was gone. Better to lie on the straw in cold and darkness than sleep on the frosthardened earth.

No vestige of the good feeling that had come to him on the knees of Mullach an Lia Dhuibh remained as Blackthorn stepped under the hanging cloth that served for a door and let it fall against the night. All day he had succumbed to the snow's deceits, following its inviting paths between the trees only to find rocks and tangled vines hidden under the smooth white roads. All day his sling had been at the ready, but the woods were barren, or the game grown warier while he was away. When at last a scrawny rabbit appeared, Blackthorn's bloodless fingers were slow in setting his stone, clumsy in their throw, and the coney had scampered off. The wind and weather all day had daunted him, building up the drifts even as he plodded through them. Every step sent wet snow slipping over the tops of his boots. From An Mhorn Bheag to the shore of Loch Dearg he'd walked, his feet not touching the ground, but sloshing about in two pools of melted ice.

He pried his sodden boots from his feet, and wrapped his cloak about his shoulders. It was wet, but not clear through, and would do something toward warming his bones. So brief the light, so bitter the weather . . . Sad cruelty it was for the Sidhe to have kept him the while, only to release him into the very nave of winter. From his pouch Blackthorn withdrew a handful of sloes he had managed to gather while walking. He felt their withered, hard

skins dubiously. A bitter fruit when ripe, these few puck-
ered berries, ignored by both bird and beast, were like to
make a sour meal.

A soft scratching at the stones of the hearth caught him
midway between chewing and dozing. A mouse, he guessed,
by the delicate noise. It occurred to him that where there
was one mouse there were often more, and he had no desire
to share his pallet with a family of them. He reached carefully into his borrowed bed, searching for the mouse's nest.
The piled straw was empty, his visitor but a lone wanderer.

Blackthorn tossed his last sloe toward the hearth, a gesture that brought immediate silence to the room. A few
moments later the little creature seemed to reconsider the
gift. The Hunter dropped off to sleep listening to frenzied
scrabbling as the mouse boldly made off across the dirt floor
with his unexpected prize.

TWO

Sooner trust a thief with your silver, than a fairy's advice

Sayings of the Mothers

Green-gowned in the ghost-gray wood, she kneels by the stream kneading a stained saffron robe with long, bony fingers. Scarlet cords worm through the clear water, ribbons of blood her sharp nails are tearing from the tattered sleeve. Her white face is hung with grief, her black eyes red with weeping, her mouth an open sore, wide and keening, keening, endlessly keening—

Blackthorn's heart raced as he fought free of his dream. Even when his eyes were open and locked on the wall of the cottage, his ears continued to ring with the Bean Sidhe's blood-chilling wail. Gradually her cries merged with the howling of the wind. The Hunter began to breathe again. He shivered, partly from the cold, partly to shake off the innate fear his nightmare had stirred in him.

The oiled cloth in the doorway flapped like the Bean Sidhe's green kirtle, allowing some dismal gray light to enter. Blackthorn was chilled almost past feeling. Frost stiffened his wolfskin cloak. His breath made ghostly clouds in the air. He could either sleep again and die, or rise and live in misery until he found something to burn. Tempting though the first

choice seemed in the moment, the Hunter climbed to his
feet and stamped to bring the blood back to his legs. His
high boots of supple leather had become sculptures of ice.
He struggled into them and hobbled to the door.

Outside the wind raged. In its fury it warred with itself,
first driving one way, then whipping about to fling snow in
the opposite direction. Before lifting the curtain Blackthorn
had told himself he could hardly be less comfortable out in
the open than he was within the cote's wattle-and-daub
walls. One look and he knew the shuddering cold of Roe's
bothy was infinitely preferable. He pulled his cloak more
tightly about him, but as soon as he stepped from the cottage, sleet stabbed his face and hands and managed to prick
him even through his clothes.

The cote sat on the edge of the marshes at the base of a
low hill and looked south toward Loch Dearg. This morning
there was little to see, only angry gray waters heaving under
an angry gray sky. Not far from the cote a stand of white
birch lashed about in the savage wind, but birch burns too
fast to make a good fire. Blackthorn stepped around to the
edge of the bothy and squinted across the flatland toward
the west. Through blustering sheets of icy rain he glimpsed a
grove of trees on a far hillock—beech, most likely.
Beechwood should warm him well, if this bitter damp had
not rotted all the deadfall.

Head down, he ploughed toward the tree-topped knoll. He
could have wished the day colder, to crystallize the rain and
harden the ground. Underfoot the snows were turning to
slush, and his boots kept sinking into the soft bog beneath.

He raised his head to make sure he was still bearing
toward the trees. At the edge of the rise, his back to the
grove and his proud gaze turned full on the Hunter, was the
White Stag.

A trick of snow and wind it must be, Blackthorn thought
incredulously, an illusion of the light, born of hunger and
cold and desire. His eyes had deceived him once before, and
he was reluctant to trust them now though they showed him
his heart's delight looking down on him from the beech-
crowned hillside.

Long he squinted into the wind, but the Stag never
shifted. A whiter island in a sea of white, the gigantic elk

stood unmoving in the storm until at last he lifted his head in challenge. Then he was away, streaking to the left and toward the loch. Blackthorn's geis flamed white-hot in reply, consuming doubt and caution in its irresistible fire. With a glad cry, the Hunter gave chase.

When last his geis had driven him to pursue the Stag, the forest had yielded to Blackthorn's passion and smoothed his path. The marsh conspired against him, congealing the melting snows on the ground to slow his footsteps, hurling the wind in his face to turn him aside. Though he set his will against the wild's, insisting on his right to the Hunt, it gained him but grudging passage.

He came to an even patch of white and dashed across it, swift as a hare—but a hare is not so heavy as a man. The crusted surface cracked under Blackthorn's weight, and his leg slid into a narrow trench hidden in the bog below.

Thigh deep in mud and snow, he fought to free his leg, cursing the treacherous fens. He stopped, and cursed again, this time hurling his words against his own folly. Not his memories, but his wits the Sidhe must have stolen! Sheer madness it was to challenge the storm for his quarry. And even could he keep pace with the Stag in this bitter weather, he had gone for firewood, not game. His Spear was still in the thatcher's cote!

The bog was determined to hold on to Blackthorn's leg, or at least retain his boot. Unwilling to have one without the other, he set about prying them both loose from the muck. Thrusting his arm into the cold mud, he groped about for the top of his boot.

His fingertips had just touched leather when he heard hoofbeats coming from the lake, and rapidly closing. Looking up, he saw the huge elk fairly dancing over the ground his own legs were finding so difficult to traverse. It was beautiful to behold, an agony of bliss. Then the Stag's eyes like white stars fixed on him, and turned the flame of Blackthorn's geis to ash.

Nine years he had journeyed to meet the Stag here, at the crossroads of life and death. Nine years had he dreamt of the kill, but always he had believed himself the Hunter. Always he had thought 'twas the Stag that would die.

He would have been glad now to leave his boot to the bog

if he could have taken to his feet and fled. There was no time for flight, and nowhere on the open marsh to hide. The Stag's head lowered as he charged, his prodigious rack pointing silver daggers at Blackthorn's breast. Digging about in the mire, the Hunter came up with a stone. His other hand reached for the sling at his belt, but though his fingers touched the soft strap, he let it go. Slowly he brought his arms to his sides. No weapon but the Spear could harm the Stag. And if Éire would have his life, what could he do but give it Her? Not weeks, but years must have passed while he lingered spellbound in Brugh na Morna. His geis must already be broken. As he had failed to achieve the Stag's death, the Stag would now encompass his.

A moment before the lethal tines reached him, Blackthorn closed his eyes. He saw them still, spread before him like a hedge of knives, but the sound of the Stag's pounding hooves was suddenly gone. Only the wind whistling across the loch and the beating of the water on the cold shore could he hear, and the roaring of his own blood in his ears.

Time stands still in the presence of the Gods, or so 'twas often said. Blackthorn counted his breaths, needing proof that time was passing. When he reached three, he opened his eyes. Before him lay Loch Dearg, its gray, choppy surface clearer now the clouds overhead were beginning to break up. He twisted about, more angry than frightened, but the Stag had vanished utterly. Only a brown wood mouse was to be seen, daringly scampering across the snow-covered marsh toward a rotting tree stump.

Between the flush of terror and the numbing cold, Blackthorn's body began to shake. Spitting yet another curse through his gritted teeth, he tried again to free his pinioned foot. The mouse, having reached his destination, raised himself up on his hind feet and chittered vociferously for attention. Ordinarily, Blackthorn would pay little heed to what a wood mouse had to say, but this particular rodent sounded irritatingly derisive. The Hunter scowled and hissed like a cat to scare the beggar off. The mouse only became more animated. Indeed, the little pest was so preoccupied with himself, he was utterly oblivious to the blur of white fur closing behind him.

Why Blackthorn loosed his stone at the weasel, he could never afterward explain. He had no quarrel with the creature, and no fondness for the weasel's prey. Moreover, he was hardly in a good throwing position, still stuck in the trench and twisted 'round to see.

Gusts of wind off the loch buffeted his arm, but Blackthorn's stone flew true, striking the stump not a whisker's length from the weasel's black nose. The foiled hunter pulled back, then predictably sped away, across the low ground toward the hills.

The mouse's reaction was altogether astounding. He neither froze nor darted off, but started, much as a man might when caught off guard. Then he lost his balance completely and tumbled from the stump. He seemed to fatten and stretch as he rolled. By the time he came to rest in a mound of snow packed about one of the stump's dead roots, he had become a skinny, hairless, naked old man.

"Curse him! Help! He'll eat me, he will! What?? But you've missed him, you blind, lumbering gawk! Och, to be sure, 'tis the great Hunter you are, indeed! Can't hit a weasel at thirty paces!"

Too surprised to take offense, Blackthorn could only stare. "A púca!" he whispered.

"Arrah, the light dawns at last in the dark night of his mind."

The shape-shifter climbed out of the snow and began brushing himself off. His face wrinkled with disgust, and he shook himself like a dog that's been swimming. Somewhere between relief and rising indignation, Blackthorn realized the truth.

"Then, the Stag . . ."

Still rubbing himself dry with his hands, the púca climbed nimbly back onto the rotting stump and squatted on his haunches, the personification of indifference.

"Is it waitin' for the bog to spit out your foot you are, or do you relish a bucket of blackwater in your boot?"

It took a bit of doing, but Blackthorn forced an expression as indifferent as his tormentor's to his face and bent again to the task of dislodging his leg. It came up at last, a sizable amount of half-melted snow going down his boot in the process. Unhurriedly, he pulled it off, dumped out as much mud and water as he could, and set it back on his foot.

"Is it waiting to apologize you are," he said, "or to thank me?"

"Thank you?" The púca looked shocked. "Och, for the entertainment, you mean."

"For saving your malicious skin, you ungrateful—"

"Savin' me skin? Pure luck it was I escaped, Hunter of Sloes, what an' your stone falling so wide of the mark."

"Hunter of Sloes is it? Not too proud last night, were you, to eat my catch? And had I aimed to kill the beast," Blackthorn added darkly, "be assured, I would have."

The púca spat in disbelief.

A retort to the tacit insult was on the tip of Blackthorn's tongue, but he swallowed it, and turned away without another word. The fairy folk were perilous, and púcaí born to mislead unwary wanderers. If he had wasted his strength chasing a shape-shifter through the storm, he had no one but himself to blame. Well, the beeches still stood where they had this morning, and a few moorhens were seeking their breakfasts in the brightening day. He might do the same, when he had his firewood.

"I'll wager it's curious you are, how I took the shape of the White Stag upon meself."

Badhbh, Macha, and *Mór-Ríoghain,* the tricksy rascal was following after him.

"A pity you've nothing worth wagering, an' you so enjoy losing," Blackthorn replied.

"It's winning's my pleasure, but sure an' you've given me so much sport already, I'll not keep you wonderin'. For you've never known another púca can take more than one shape as I can."

"I've never known a púca, at all, at all," said Blackthorn, "nor ever cared to. Nor care to know one now."

He hadn't slowed his pace, and behind him he could hear the púca's breathing grow louder as he labored to keep up. Glancing back, Blackthorn almost laughed at the sight of the little man's skinny bowlegs churning the snow as he struggled along. He glowered instead, too wet, too cold, too hungry to be amused, and lengthened his stride.

"'Twas the White Stag I Saw cavortin' with the Bean Sidhe," the púca called after him, "and that's how I know who you are, Hunter of Éirinn. You'd do well to mind your dreams better tonight."

Blackthorn stopped. "Is it telling me you are that you spied on my slumber and stole from my dreams?"

His voice was almost gentle, but there was a dark fire in his eye that wiped the smug smile from the púca's face.

"'Tis a rare talent, it is," the little man protested, "and careless you were entirely. Sure, an' why shouldn't I reach into your dream while you're sleepin' and take a shape out, and yourself stealin' me very own bed?"

"What, is it putting the blame on me you are for your connivery?" Blackthorn exploded. "Be off before I find another stone, and you can feel for yourself if I hit what I aim at!"

The púca's face crimsoned with ire. "Go your own way, you witless bodach, and I'll go mine! But when you've worn yourself out seekin' dry wood in the forest, come back to the cote and ask me where the thatcher's store is hid. Ask, but you'll get no answer, not though you beg me on your knees!"

Blackthorn couldn't tell if the little man were trying to throw a curse or just being spiteful. Contriving to appear unconcerned, he swung a corner of his sodden cloak over his shoulder and smiled.

"You'll find me begging before you," he said, "when the goose carries the fox home for dinner," and marched off with as much aplomb as he could muster while sloshing over slippery ground.

At the base of the knoll, he risked a quick look back. His ears had not deceived him. There was no sign of Stag, or mouse, or man.

The beeches were damp with melted snow, the fallen branches crumbly and wet. He took his search farther into the hills, but in vain. Though the high woods came hard by the loch, winter had penetrated every bole, every root, every limb of every tree in the forest.

When he entered the cote, Blackthorn looked quickly away from the mouse by the hearth to hide the relief in his eyes. He crossed to the firepit and dropped the log he had brought, showering the creature's brown fur with old ashes and drops of water. Instantly, he was confronted not by a disinterested wood mouse, but by an irate little man.

"Whisht, you fool, isn't it enough that my bed is still rank with the wet you brought yesterday? What do you mean, spatterin' me with . . . Och, now darlin', what have you there?" he asked in an entirely different tone.

Blackthorn was taking great care in spitting a long, lovely trout on a willow wand.

"Supper," he answered.

The fish ready to roast, he stepped outside, returning with another green willow and a second trout. The little bothy was growing dark, and Blackthorn stood in the doorway, letting the sunset fall on his work.

"Och, you devious creature." The púca chuckled and shook his head. "I see your stratagem now, I do. I like a tasty morsel, I'll not deny. But it'll take more than a silver-bellied fish to loosen my tongue. Eat it raw, an' you will. I'll pass on my share."

"*A trout in the pot is better than a salmon in the sea,*" quoted Blackthorn, laughing in return. "And why would I share my fish with you? Two days I've gone with only a handful of sloes to fill my belly. I'll not find this meal too much to finish alone."

"Well, that's a fine . . . Sure, an' you can't be meanin' . . ." The púca knitted his brow and rubbed his bald pate. "You'll not be tellin' me you plan to set this waterlogged faggot to light?"

"'Tis a rare talent," said Blackthorn, mimicking the púca's earlier boast.

Unobtrusively he lowered his voice, deepening its timbre and allowing a gentle sing-song to carry his words.

"On the barren plain I was, and naught but rain-drenched grasses to burn. A rann I had, and have it still, and when it was sung, my heap of straw burst into flame. So potent the spell, the drops of water boiled away ere they reached the fire, the blowing gale could but fan the blaze. Nine nights it stormed, nine nights it burned, nine hares I cooked, and tender was their flesh."

"Och, indeed," interrupted the púca. "And if your fire was so hot, it must be burnin' still!"

"And so it would be," agreed Blackthorn, "had the giant of An Cnoc Maol not come down from his hill, for I had not the power to put the fire out. Brown would have been the green forests of Éirinn forever and aye, the voracious flames devouring all from one sea to the other. A blessing it was that the smoke from my fire choked the sky over the red-haired giant's home, making day night, and night unending. A boulder he lifted, high as three men and wide as four, and dropped it down into the heart of the flames. The rock sits there still for you to see, an' you doubt my tale."

The trout spitted, Blackthorn took the second stick to the hearth and set it beside the first. Kneeling over the log he had brought, he slowed his breathing and swayed slightly, like a priestess making an invocation. The púca's eyes were open wide in the dim room, watching the Hunter's every move. Blackthorn's sight was not so keen. The little man's face was hidden by the darkness, but when he spoke, the púca's new-won respect was evident.

"Marvellous," he breathed. "Marvellous." He clapped his hands against his bare thighs, then rubbed them briskly on his knees. "Dig beneath the mound of snow that lies between the two hazel bushes behind the cote. There you'll find more turf and kindling than you could use in seven winters, dry as bone beneath a tanned elk hide."

"Marvellous," he said again, as Blackthorn rose with a smile and headed for the door. "Had I known you were such an astonishing liar, I would never have used you so."

Three

The alp luachra railed on the shore,
But safe was Dorchaidh's daughter
From the monster's hunger, the joint-eater's teeth,
For he would not cross the water.

Diorbhal's Ride

Swollen, flaming eyes weep to see the dawn. Saliva drips from bared yellow fangs. Long, gray shadows hang like ropes from their meaty, sharp-nailed paws. Up, then, where the goblins cannot follow. The world tilts, loose rock underfoot slides away.

The snarl of his nightmare come to life jolted Blackthorn from sleep. He pushed himself violently up and back against the cottage wall, drawing his dagger even as he stood. The goblin took a step back. His grotesque, hairy features blurred and shrank, his menacing grin became the púca's gleeful smile.

Slapping his knee, the little man danced a quick jig before his stunned audience. "Oho, but I'll wager you've never moved so fast of a morning! Arrah, what a sight!"

Try as he did to clear it, Blackthorn's mind refused to provide him with a worthy retort. All he could think was how pleasant it would be to put his knife to good use in the shape-shifter's hide. Instead, he sheathed his blade, lurched to the door, and pulled the curtain aside. Drawing deep draughts of the crisp, cold morning into his lungs, he soon cleansed himself of his residual fear and pointless anger. If a man keeps company with a púca, what can he expect but insults and pranks?

Yesterday's melting snows had frozen in the long dark of the night. The world glittered in the early light as if tiny crystals had fallen like dew. Even were Blackthorn's geis not urging him on, it was a day made for travelling, a glorious day.

It took but a few moments to gather his belongings, dried by last night's fire, and secure his Spear across his back.

"To the dún you're off then?" the púca asked carelessly.

"Shall I rake the embers, or leave them banked for your next fire?" returned Blackthorn, ignoring the little man's question.

"Och, rake them, rake them. I'll not be stayin', and 'twould be cruel thanks to the thatcher an' we burned his cote for his hospitality."

Blackthorn absently stirred the glowing cinders with a willow wand, his mind already rambling down the paths his legs would follow that day. No good picking up the traders' road to the dún. The White Stag had no fondness for human dwellings. The wild was the Stag's domain, but what use in aimlessly roaming the forests, hoping to chance upon the great elk's track in the snow? By now the Stag could be anywhere in the five kingdoms of Éirinn, and Blackthorn might search till Bealtaine and never spy his quarry.

The ashes cold, the Hunter tossed the willow into the hearth and rose. South he would go, to Teach an Fhásaigh, where Scáthach the Poet dwelt. Scáthach would not deny him if he asked a poem of her. With a rann of power to put him on the Stag's trail, he would soon regain all he had lost in Brugh na Morna.

Only birds travel a straight road from the thatcher's cote to Scáthach's house. Blackthorn must take more winding paths, for Loch Éirne lay between Loch Dearg and Teach an Fhásaigh. He could go south and west, and ford Loch Éirne at Béal Leice. Then he must through the fens, over the hills, across Loch Dubh at Béal Cú, and when he had climbed high Binn Chuilceach and come down the other side, he would at last be at Scáthach's door.

Ducking under the oiled curtain of Roe's bothy, Blackthorn

turned his face toward the rising sun. There was another way from here to Teach an Fhásaigh, and far swifter—the traders' road as it ran from Dún na nGall down the eastern shore of Loch Éirne to Inis Ceithleann, the isle of the fisherfolk. If the weather held, he could reach Inis Ceithleann by nightfall. There he'd be given a hot supper, a warm bed, and whatever news the latest peddlers had traded with their wares. Tomorrow one of the fishing boats would gladly ferry him to the western bank, and he'd be but a half day's easy stroll from the Poet's home.

"Whisht, the great Hunter's lost his way already," chuckled the púca behind him. "West, you want to go, you fool, an' you hope to see the dún ere night is upon you."

He should simply keep walking, Blackthorn knew, but he'd already taken one cut without parrying, and it went against his nature to accept another.

"An' it's lost I am, and a fool, then yourself a fool twice over to be walking in my footsteps."

"But maybe it's not Dún na nGall you have in mind." The púca rubbed his bald head. "A fair stretch of the legs it is to An Ómaigh, but not so far as to daunt a long-shanks like yourself."

Blackthorn laughed. "You'll have to stir your thoughts a good deal harder an' you mean to guess my road, little man. And move your feet faster an' you mean to follow it."

That last one hit the mark. The púca was practically running already in his attempt to keep up.

"An' you'd a scrap of mercy about you, you'd slow down, you heavy-footed clod. My short legs can't keep up with your long ones!"

"I don't mean that they should," Blackthorn answered pleasantly.

"Och, now, yourself wouldn't be so cruel-hearted as to bear a grudge for yesterday's bit of fun?" Though his breath was coming sharp and quick, the púca was doing his best to be cajoling. "And this morning, 'twas only a jest, and no harm done."

"A grudge is it? Why, it's grateful to you I am! For nothing pleases folk more than that a guest should bring a good tale with him when he comes. Everyone's heard of a man chasing a púca, but tonight I'll tell them how a púca chased a man, and fell behind, and lost him entirely, and is likely still traipsing about Loch Dearg, hoping to find him again. Now there's a jest will set us laughing."

The crunch of the púca's bare feet in the crusty snow stopped abruptly.

"So it's too grand you are to share the road with me!" he shouted indignantly. "Then may your three geasa grind you to meal between them, Hunter of Éirinn!"

It wasn't the curse that worried Blackthorn. He doubted the spiteful creature had the will to hurl a curse a stone's throw. Nevertheless, the púca's words rankled, and slowly brought him to a halt. As if against his will, Blackthorn turned to face the little man.

"One," he said.

The púca's scowl dissolved into a look of pure delight. He began to laugh, clasping his arms over his belly, and whooping like a demented swan.

"One is it?" he said when he could speak again. "Well, three geasa I See and three geasa there'll be, but I'll say no more an' you don't take me to An Ómaigh."

Blackthorn tossed a fold of his cloak over his shoulder and spun on his heel. He marched off at a good pace, but the púca neither padded behind, nor sent any more words after him. The little man whistled a sprightly air, and when Blackthorn did stop and turn back, he found the púca wasn't even watching him, but studying the clouds in the sky.

"Och, 'tis the witless fool I am, entirely," Blackthorn exclaimed, clapping his hand to his brow. "How could I be forgetting that rare and fine talent of yours? Why, you need only take on a horse's shape," he said with an ingratiating smile, "and yourself can bring the both of us to town, and that much sooner."

The little man shifted his gaze to Blackthorn. "And *when the sky falls we'll all catch larks*," he said dryly.

"And by that, do you mean you won't do it? Or you can't?"

"Can't? To be sure I can! Is it here you'd like to take your rest, or would you be more comfortable havin' a bit of a lie-down in the thatcher's cote?"

"Take my rest?"

"And didn't I tell you only yesterday," the púca said, making a great show of impatience, "'tis from dreams I take shapes? From dreams, I'm sayin', not wishes, or fancies, or the empty air!"

"I've seen you shift from mouse to man and back again, and not a soul slumbering nearby," Blackthorn argued.

The little man sighed. "A soft heart your mother must have had," he observed, "to have put such a daft and simple-minded idiot as yourself to the breast. I am a mouse, you fool, and to my own shape I can shift whenever I please. But to—"

"But to shift to a better one," Blackthorn went on smoothly, "you must take care to steal it while those you rob are bound in chains of sleep. Och, 'tis the bold thief you are, little mouseen."

The púca reddened to the top of his bald head. "There's not another púca in all the five kingdoms can take as many shapes as can I!"

Blackthorn clucked his tongue consolingly. "I doubt it not," he said. "Yet, an' you'll with me, your own two legs must bear you all the long way. Come," he said, brightening and opening the mouth of a small leather pouch at his belt. "Tell me of the three geasa, and I'll give you a ride."

The little man stared at Blackthorn in astonishment. "Whisht, you must think I've the wits of a goblin. Give me a ride, and we'll have a bit of a crack over a bowl of ale—after we reach An Ómaigh."

Blackthorn's mouth tightened into a thin line, but he nodded curtly to the little man. "Done," he growled.

Dropping swiftly to a mouse, the púca scuttled across the snow and climbed up the Hunter's leggings to his belt.

"Still, it's only fair to tell you, it's not to An Ómaigh we're going, little mouseen," Blackthorn said lightly as the púca squirmed into the leather sack. "'Tis Inis Ceithleann I'm bound for."

The púca's squeal of dismay brought a slow smile to Blackthorn's lips. A small revenge, but a satisfying one. No doubt the guileful creature would think better of his bargain when it came to crossing the deep waters of Loch Éirne.

Four

Luck threefold
On your journey be—
Good weather, good roads,
And good company

The sun dipped below the rim of the world while Blackthorn gathered dry grasses for his flint to kindle. Fading light still tempered the darkening sky with gray when he had his small signal fire leaping and crackling on the flat rock over the loch. Someone on the island was bound to see it, and come to fetch him. He squatted down, hunching into the warmth of his cloak, and ran his hand through his hair. A few moments later he undid the thong that held his pouch to his belt, opened its mouth, and set the sack gently beside him.

"Colder in there than it is out here. Come and enjoy a bit of warmth," Blackthorn coaxed.

The mouse's whiskers poked out of the pouch's opening.

"Before the currach arrives to take us across the loch," the Hunter added.

The whiskers began to twitch.

"Och, 'twill be a hard journey for you," said Blackthorn sympathetically. "Across the rolling water, black now the daystar's gone, and those little boats never can stay dry as they bob over the waves . . ."

The púca groaned in unmouselike misery and withdrew into the sack.

"There it is! I knew they'd see my fire!" Blackthorn jumped to his feet, his excitement genuine. A pale echo of his yellow blaze was delicately bouncing over the inky loch.

"Is a bowl of ale worth the discomfort of the journey?" he asked, one friend to another. "Rise to a man, now, and we'll talk before the ferry comes."

A sharp gust of wind blew Blackthorn's cloak back and tossed his black hair about.

"Sure, an' you're no more pleased with my company than I am with yours," he went on. "'Twas a foolish bargain we struck, and no good to either of us. Besides, what of the meals I've shared and your life I've given you? Aren't they worth a few words? But tell me what you meant by saying there were three geasa on me. I'll be satisfied, and you'll not have to risk drowning in the lake."

From inside the pouch the púca let loose a long string of chatter, unintelligible, but unmistakably disputatious. Blackthorn cursed and scooped up the pouch, knotting it tightly and letting it swing and bounce against his hip as he tied it to his belt.

"An' I take you with me," he said testily, "you'll stay in my purse until I tell you to come out. It's little thanks I'd be getting from the folk of Inis Ceithleann for bringing a shape shifter into their midst."

The púca fell silent, but whether in accord or in protest, Blackthorn couldn't tell. The boat was near at hand, and he turned to climb down the rock and meet it.

"Stay by the fire, where I can see you!" called a woman's voice.

It was hardly the hail he'd expected. Blackthorn stopped, then slowly returned to the dying flames.

"Is it only to have a look you've come, then?" he asked. "I'd hoped for better."

"Did you, now?" The boat's torch was set in the stern behind the rower, and Blackthorn could not make out the woman's features. Her voice, laced with scepticism, rose clearly over the sounds of water lapping against the side of her boat. "Then you're either a stranger or a fool. What's your business with us?"

"Many a year has passed since I've come this way," he answered, "but not so many as I'd consider myself a stranger.

It must be the fool I am, and my only business, to find shelter from the night."

In the silence that followed, Blackthorn's amazement grew. Twenty-seven years he'd lived, and never till now known a simple request to gain a lodging render a woman speechless. .

"What reason have you to be wandering about Loch Éirne in the dead of winter?" she demanded finally. "An' you've good cause, you'll be made welcome in Inis Ceithleann, I'm sure."

Whatever honest reasons he might have for being where he was, the woman's inexplicable rudeness made Blackthorn determine to keep them to himself. Until the púca stole the knowledge from his dreams two nights ago, only Úna the Oak Seer knew he was the chosen Hunter of Éirinn, and he'd been the one to tell her so. Should he care to reveal it now to the ferry-woman, he doubted it would gain him her confidence. If she believed him at all, she would know he bore the Goddess's geis, and such burdens were feared by most village folk. The geis-driven often followed dangerous paths. It was no more than prudent to let them travel alone. Should he further confess he had spent the last moon with the elves of Brugh na Morna, his bed for the night would surely be the cold, wet banks of Loch Éirne instead of a dry pallet by a warm fire. An' the fishers of Inis Ceithleann were hesitant to honor the sacred bond between host and guest, they would doubtless break it entirely if they knew their guest came to them with the perilous spells of the Sidhe clouding his mind.

"What reason does a traveller need to invoke the laws of hospitality?" he answered. "And what cause drives a Bard to take his songs roving with him? Blackthorn I am, late of Dún na nGall, and I claim the Bard's Welcome of you, as is my right."

It was an easy lie, sure to be believed. If anyone was likely to be abroad in the dark of the year, it was a singer-of-tales, bringing the music of the season from one village to the next. And he had been a Bard once. Or nearly so. Ten years ago, when last he had visited Inis Ceithleann, he had been in the service of Larkspur, the Bard of Tráigh Lí. He left his master when the Stag called his Name, but if he had not become the Hunter of Éirinn, he might well have become a Bard.

"Blackthorn?" the woman echoed dubiously. "Well, tidings of the dún we'll be glad to hear, but still . . . Strange it is you should journey now, and with none for company. . . ."

Painfully conscious of the púca in his pouch, the Hunter smiled broadly.

"Are my eyes red, is my flesh gray that you take me for a goblin or a Scáil? Are your people so rich in storytellers that you scorn the wandering Bard?"

When the woman replied there was a conciliatory hint of embarrassment in her voice. "Our hospitality has indeed been ungenerous of late, but our reasons are good, as you know. Well, come along, come along. The wind is rising, and you must be cold."

Blackthorn not only didn't know, but couldn't imagine what reasons could be compelling enough to warrant Inis Ceithleann's breach of good manners. He climbed down to the water's edge as the woman brought her little vessel close to the shore, and stepped in while she held it steady. He took up an oar as she pushed her own against the bank, and together they brought the currach out into the loch.

"No one has dared the journey from the dún since Samhain," she commented when under way. She made it sound as if the paucity of visitors justified her earlier unfriendliness. "It's good of you risk it, just to bring a few tales to a small village like ours. We're glad of your kindness, I'm sure."

Glad she might be, Blackthorn thought, but he was keenly aware of her bow and quiver lying at the bottom of the boat. Likely she'd had an arrow trained on him all the while they had been talking. Though in the flickering torchlight he saw bands of white in the woman's dark hair, her eyes sparkled keenly. Had his answers to her questions displeased her, he was certain she quickly would have sent death winging to his heart.

Five

Men are like bagpipes;
No sound comes from them till they're full

Sayings of the Mothers

Lower Loch Éirne was formed like a funnel, broad at its mouth and tapering at its head. Upper Loch Éirne, a narrower, wilder body of water, ceaselessly sent torrents of her liquid wealth pouring into the lower lake's basin. Just beyond the cusp of the two, where the upper lake's rushing waters began to slow and spread into the great pool of the lower, sat Inis Ceithleann.

The uneasiness the ferry-woman's suspicions had roused in Blackthorn lessened as they drew near the isle. No natural island, the fisherfolk claimed the great Chieftain Ceithil herself had built the rocky crannóg to be her seat, causing huge stones to be cast into the loch until at last they were piled so high they rose above the lake's surface. Surrounded by a watery barrier, Inis Ceithleann had no encircling walls, no earthworks, no engineered defenses of any kind. Blackthorn remembered admiring the open invitation of the island's stone-lined streets and unabashed houses when he had visited with Larkspur ten years past. Then it had been broad daylight, but by night, he thought, Inis Ceithleann's welcome was more lovely still. A soft aureole crowned the isle, firelight from the village caught in the swaddling mists of the loch. If not for the weapon at his feet and the surly greeting he had first received, he could well believe Inis Ceithleann a haven for the weary traveller.

When the boat came near the landing, Blackthorn disembarked and helped the ferry-woman carry the currach to a stone boathouse. Then together they wound up the rocky path to the Chieftain's hall, passing on the way a heavily bundled man going down to the loch.

"So this is what you found at the fire?" he asked, nodding at Blackthorn.

"Where are you off to, Netter? The night's still young, and we've a guest."

Netter shook his head. "'Tis old Sedge. He's forgotten to draw in his lines again, and himself so drunk, he'd likely fall into the loch an' he went to do it now."

"Well, hurry back, mo mhúirnín," said the woman kindly. "I'm bringing Blackthorn the Bard to the hall, and you wouldn't want to miss his song."

"Fast as may be," called Netter over his shoulder as he continued on his way. "And you are welcome, Blackthorn!"

Inis Ceithleann's oldest and largest building stood on the island's highest point. Ceithil's Hall had once been many-sided, but over the years the wind and cold had worn away at the stones. Now it appeared almost round, but a fat, jovial roundness, with light streaming out where the thatched roof met the walls, and music and laughter echoing within. The door was thick and rectangular, made of water-resistant ash. Outside a few weapons leaned against the stones, a staff or two, and several nets. His companion laid down her bow and arrows, and after a moment's hesitation, Blackthorn set his Spear beside them. If the folk of Inis Ceithleann did not bring their own weapons into the hall, he would be ill-mannered indeed to insist on bearing his. Besides, he would look more a Bard an' he went unarmed. Odd that neither the ferry-woman nor Netter had remarked upon his silver-pointed shaft—but it was just as well they hadn't noticed it, or weren't inclined to question.

Stepping over the threshold, Blackthorn was instantly showered with the cordiality that up until now he had thought so strangely lacking. Faces turned to him in surprise and pleasure, conversations were swallowed by shouted welcomes and exclamations of delight. The music stopped while the piper added his hello, and a welcome cup of ale was pressed into Blackthorn's hand. By the time the crowd had escorted him to the Chieftain's seat, the woman who had ferried him across the water was there already, telling the Lady of what had transpired on the eastern shore. Despite a babe in arms trying to push aside her bodice to get at the breast, and another child clinging to her skirt, Jet, the Chieftain of Inis Ceithleann, rose to greet her guest.

"A hundred welcomes, Blackthorn," she said.

"Éire bless all here," he replied.

Jet nodded appreciatively at Blackthorn's courtesy, and a general murmur of approval reverberated through the hall. As if their exchange had been a signal, the music started up again, and conversations resumed, though many dropped their old business and made themselves comfortable within earshot of the Chieftain's seat.

"Bring our guest something from the board," Jet said, more a suggestion than a command, "and let him refresh himself before we speak the more."

Almost at once Blackthorn was presented with a bowl of fish stew and several oatcakes smeared with honey.

"*Men are like bagpipes . . .*" he heard the Chieftain murmur to a solemn, brown-haired woman standing near her, but Blackthorn only smiled, and gratefully accepted the hospitality.

Jet took her place on the only chair in the room, the chair of her mother, and her mother's mother, of all her mothers back to Ceithil herself, or so it was said. A few of the elders had stools to sit upon, but Ceithil's Hall was far fallen from its days of grandeur. Most of the island's forty-five or so people sat on the floor or, if they were young, climbed the posts to sit on the rafters. Chairs were little missed, for the ground was covered with straw, and the blazing fire in the central hearth would warm the coldest bones. Someone offered a stool, but Blackthorn declined it and found a cozy spot with his back to a post and his feet to the fire. Only when he had finished his meal did the Chieftain nod to him, and beckon him near.

"Few guests have we seen this winter," she began. "Indeed

you are only our second since Samhain, and I fear our last, unless you bring good news from the west."

To the people of Inis Ceithleann, all the towns and lands of Éirinn were either "east" or "west," depending on which side of Loch Éirne they lay. News from Dún na nGall she was expecting, but Blackthorn had none to give her.

"In truth, Lady," he said, at a loss for a lie that would serve him, "nothing can I tell you of the strife in the west. Though I call the dún home, I have not stopped there since before Samhain-tide. In the north I've been roaming, and would have said as much before, had I not feared it would lose me my welcome."

"It may have," someone muttered, but Jet smiled.

"A pity, Blackthorn," she said. "We'd hoped to hear tidings of our kin." She gestured to the brown-haired woman beside her. "Bryony, my sister's daughter, has returned to my house, but 'twas to Dún na nGall most of the people of Doire Eile fled to find refuge when the Scáileanna attacked."

"The Scáileanna attacked Doire Eile?" Blackthorn asked, amazed.

Bryony fixed her dark eyes on him. "The Scáileanna destroyed Doire Eile," she said sharply, "and now lay siege to Dún na nGall. Where indeed have you been since Samhain?"

"In the north," Blackthorn repeated lamely, wishing he had earlier pretended to have come up from the south.

"There is nothing in the north, save the Sidhe and the Scáileanna and the forest," retorted Bryony, as Blackthorn feared she might. She tossed back her fine, brown hair with a disdainful swing of her head. "A brave man must you be to dare the wild alone."

"Many times have I done so," said Blackthorn, "though I do not think myself bold. For never have I known the dark elves to war on any save the Sidhe, nor to harm any save the foolish wanderer who strays from the path."

"Know it now," Bryony said, her voice soft with bitterness. "In the night they fell upon us, and we in our homes."

"So also said Flint, the trader from Latharna," someone else piped up, "when he told of the goblin raid at An Baile Meánach. They came though the moon was full, and none escaped the axes of the red-eyes that night."

"And the Mothers?" asked Blackthorn. "Do they not defend their people? Do the Kings not ride to battle?"

"Do the Mighty share their thoughts with Jet of Inis Ceithleann?" the Chieftain answered him. "It is rumored the Queen of Midhe summoned a council to meet on midwinter morning, but that was only three days past, and news will be long in reaching us with even the traders and Bards afraid to travel."

Bryony peered at Blackthorn through narrowed lids. "Yet, even when they do, we give more news than we get, it seems."

Blackthorn avoided her gaze and studied the pattern the dried grasses made before the Chieftain's chair. Bryony spoke true, but he had no news he was willing to share, and that he had received was astonishing. Long was the time he spent in the elven hall, especially as it had seemed brief as a moment. Yet it was an appallingly short time for the goblins to lose their abiding hatred of light, and for the Scáileanna to turn their scorn of humans into bloody war.

Nodding to the piper to begin again, the Chieftain called for more ale for her guest. It was midwinter-tide after all, and the man a Bard. The somber talk had cast a pall over the gaiety in the hall, but if she could, Jet meant to dispel it, with music and dance, and with the Bard's song.

Smiling, the musician laid his instrument across his lap, already sure of what he wanted to play. When the pipes were tuned, an ethereal melody reached out to Blackthorn where he stood wrapped in thought. In an instant it had carried his thoughts away, and his heart, and his very soul slipped from his body to follow the song back to the halls of Brugh na Morna.

Hearthfires burning bright. Music from the pipes burning too, like whiskey, ruthless and gasping. Sheer bliss to drink deep, and yet—and yet . . . In the heart a fire far brighter burns, in Éirinn's fair forests rings a far sweeter song.

Let me go, gentle Lady. The Stag calls and I must away.

Ochone, mo mhúirnín, but stay awhile more. Come, listen to the pipers play.

It was a scent that brought the Hunter back to Ceithil's Hall. The cloying, heady perfume of Brugh na Morna was suddenly cut by an acrid, earthy smell. The elven pipes fell silent. The white-gold fire dimmed to ordinary red and orange and burned not in a magnificent fireplace, but in a plain stone hearth. Gradually Blackthorn became aware of a steaming bowl in his hands, and countless eyes watching. A few of the youngest faces were openly curious. The rest were wary and guarded.

Blackthorn recognized the diffident look the folk of Inis Ceithleann turned on him. It had been his own when he met with strangers beset by memories of elven lands or hounded by the burdens of geasa. And if the enchantments overtook the traveller's wits, someone would make a broth of rue and betony and other strong herbs . . . Blackthorn stared miserably at the bowl he held, uncertain whether he wanted to weep or laugh.

"That tune . . ." he said at last.

"Just a boy, I was," answered the piper, running a calloused hand along his white beard, "and never a thought had I given to music. We were journeying to the dún for the summer Games when we lost the trail and found ourselves beside An Mhorn Bheag under the oaks and alders of Mullach an Lia Dhuibh. There we spent the night, but I could not sleep and so rose and wandered a way up the mountain. Then I heard it, that wondrous air, but it was too much for my ears. Only a fragment could I ever recall of what the elven piper played."

"It seems our guest has heard the selfsame piper," said Bryony, "and not long since."

Blackthorn took a sip of the aromatic drink, relieved to discover it tasted sweeter than it smelled.

"Three mornings past," he said, "I stood before the black stone on Mullach an Lia Dhuibh's peak and watched the sun rise. It was midwinter's day, yet I could have sworn to you that but a moment before it had been midnight of the twelfth night of Samhain-tide."

Some clucked their tongues in sympathy. Others spat to ward off ill luck. Jet sighed heavily, but her eyes were kind.

"You must entreat the Mothers' aid, an' the elves' spells are upon you," she said. "Here we have but little knowledge of such matters. 'Tis said the Queen-Mother of Ulaidh is in Dún na nGall, and the Scáileanna would prevent you reaching her. But Liannan, Mother of Midhe, reigns over her lands in peace. We will ferry you back to the east in the morning, that you might seek the roads to Temuir—"

"West," said Blackthorn, but he got no further.

"The Sidhe have made you mad indeed!" cried a gray-beard, banging his stick on the ground, and a young girl whispered, "Left him witless they have, entirely!"

Bryony's words sounded above the others'. "Have you heard naught of what's been said? In Éirinn you will find no lands safe this winter, but neither will you find any more dangerous than those west of Loch Éirne. An' it's Death you're seeking, ask not the folk of Inis Ceithleann to ferry you to Him."

"Not Death am I seeking," said Blackthorn, beginning to feel more steady, "but Teach an Fhásaigh."

Understanding flashed in the Chieftain's eyes. "Arrah, I see. 'Tis Scáthach the Poet you wish to find."

Bryony's expression became troubled. "Scáthach," she repeated. "In the very shadow of Binn Chuilceach the Poet dwells, and from that mountain did the evil fall on Doire Eile. We should have sent to her, in her home under Binn Chuilceach, and brought her here."

"Me mother has the right of it, I'm thinkin'," shouted a lad from the rafters, but the graybeard who had called Blackthorn mad rapped his stick for attention.

"Scáthach's a Poet," he said. "None better in all Éirinn. Who would dare harm her? An' any should try, they could only come to harm themselves. There's naught in the world more powerful than a Poet's verse."

Jet considered the elder's speech carefully, then shook her head. "Before Samhain I would have been first in agreeing with you, Scariff," she said. "But since winter has come, think what the Scáileanna have done to Doire Eile, and the goblins to An Baile Meánach in the east. And how hard the winter, how heavy the snows! Even you have said in all your days you have never seen worse."

The graybeard frowned for a moment, disgruntled to hear his own words being used as an argument against him, then pursed his lips and nodded.

"And so we will send a message to Scáthach, and let the Bard bear it," Jet went on. "But one of us must ferry him to the west on the morrow."

She turned to Blackthorn, but spoke loud enough for everyone in the hall to hear. "In exchange for this favor, I would have you say this to the Poet of Teach an Fhásaigh. 'Greatly honored would Jet, Chieftain of Inis Ceithleann be, and all her people, should Scáthach the Poet accept our hospitality until these times of trouble are past.'"

After Blackthorn had repeated Jet's message word for word, an uncomfortable silence settled over the hall. Since the piper's tune had stolen his wits, every eye had been fastened on the Hunter. Now, suddenly, everyone had somewhere else to look—the fire, the floor, the roof, each other. He could hardly expect that they would be eager to ferry him across the loch, but they might at least be eager to be rid of him.

"I will take you west over the water," Bryony said, "though we have not dared that shore since Samhain. But in my heart I regret our thoughtlessness to Scáthach. I will be glad if our Chieftain's message reaches her."

"Well said, and well done," announced Jet with a proud smile. "But let us leave such matters for the day, and let this night banish our cares. An' the Bard has recovered somewhat, is it time, do you think, to hear his tale?"

If he had hoped the events of the evening would have sent people early to bed, Blackthorn was sadly mistaken. The Chieftain's proposal was accepted with resounding enthusiasm. For a time the hall bustled with activity. Drinks were poured, and fresh turf brought to the fire. A stool was set near the Chieftain's for the Bard to sit, facing the blaze so everyone could watch him. Had things gone differently, Blackthorn might have admitted the Bard's Welcome was merely an excuse to secure passage to the island. As it was he felt he would do better to be mocked as a poor singer than cursed for a liar.

Blackthorn came to the stool, and sat with the smooth, easy confidence that the best of Bards practiced. Larkspur's manner he had long ago mastered, but Larkspur himself had contended that Blackthorn had more love of the tales than skill with the music. Hurriedly he ran through what songs he could remember, searching for something he might carry off. Not a midwinter tale. Three nights into the festival they would have already sung every song, and piece of song, and half-forgotten scrap of song about mistletoe and sun and wintertime that anyone had ever known. Not a tale of magic. Those were filled with elves and sorcerers, and Blackthorn hoped to distract his audience from such thoughts if he could. What was needed was a song of love and daring. A song to make them laugh.

"Blackthorn I am called," he began, using the ritual form, "a Bard by trade. Listen and I'll tell you a tale of Turlach of Tuaim."

"Turlach of Tuaim" was the story of a randy, but ridiculously naive young man and his mostly erotic adventures on his way to the kingship of Mumhain. The song was merry, rhythmical, and the only hidden meanings in it were thinly veiled carnal jokes, all points that won Blackthorn favor from the crowd. His audience swayed, laughed, and clapped their hands as the lads of Tuaim, unable to get any notice from the maidens while Turlach was around, ran the boy out of town. Wandering down to the sea, the intrepid hero meets an alluring sea-creature by the strand.

> *The beauties of Tuaim were fair as the day,*
> *Clear as the morning, and bonny and gay,*
> *But the murúch sang sweeter than dew on the rose,*
> *'Bring the gift, bold Turlach, concealed in your clothes.'*

The leather pouch that hung at Blackthorn's hip suddenly moved of its own accord. Adroitly, he shifted his cloak to cover his side, and slid his hand around the sack. The púca had been so still for so long, Blackthorn had forgotten him entirely. Now the little rascal seemed bent on clawing his way out of the leather pouch. Blackthorn pinched the mouse gently, as a warning, but the púca squeaked and continued to roll about.

When he had secured the purse at the flat rock, Blackthorn had tied the thong with vexed excessiveness. He wondered now if the púca were wanting for air. His fingers worked the knot until it loosened, and his efforts were rewarded by the immediate quieting of the púca's frantic acrobatics.

> *The Giant's roar shattered the rocks into sand.*
> *'Fight with me now, upon the sea strand,*

Or be cursed as a coward, despised for your fear!'
Turlach had but one weapon — his prodigious spear.

The verses describing the pissing contest between Turlach
and the Giant of An Trá Mhór were usually the most popu-
lar. All eyes were on the Bard, all ears tuned to his rich and
pleasing baritone. Or, thought Blackthorn, almost all. His
gaze rested for a moment on a somnolent form at the back of
the hall. An aged grandmother dreamed quietly, her head
lolling against the post at her back, her mouth open in the
unembarrassed indulgence of sleep. It was sheer luck that his
eye fell on her just at that moment, for it took no more than
a moment for the shape of a tall, ruddy man to rise from the
straw beside her. The stranger caught Blackthorn's eye, then
quickly melted into the shadows. Immediately Blackthorn
reached to the pouch on his belt, but his fingers found only
his flint and his whetstone. The púca was gone.

The fountains of yellow reached to the skies,

Blackthorn sang, but his heart was no longer in his music.

Forcing himself through the next lines, he noticed that
the quiet of the audience was occasionally broken by admon-
ishments to hush and irritated grumbles. Unexpectedly, he
found himself at the end of a verse with no idea which verse
it was. Had Turlach already played his game of hurling?
Better to pass it by than sing it twice. He went on to tell of
the Queen's discovery of Turlach by the grassy banks of An
tSiúir, all the while seeking desperately through the crowd
to find the red-cheeked man again.

She found him asleep and thought the boy fair,
Midsummer's silver dew damp in his hair.
Her bathing forgotten, the Queen let her eyes
Stray to the naked lad's tumescent prize.

He had him at last, just standing in the crowd with a
beatific smile on his ruddy face. For a moment, it seemed the
púca was enjoying the tale as much as everyone else. Then
Blackthorn noticed the bowl of ale almost between the
púca's feet. By itself, the vessel was no cause for alarm.

Coupled with the fact that the púca's hand was surreptitiously sliding under his pleated skirt toward his groin, the waiting receptacle took on disastrous significance.

No one could fail to note Blackthorn's sudden pallor, or the hesitation in the rhythm of his song. A few people turned to follow the Bard's eyes to the red-haired young man. Blackthorn started the verse again with renewed vigor, but it was too late. His performance had been outshone by another's.

"Curse you, Netter," swore the man whose bowl had so nearly been polluted.

"He must be drunk."

"So drunk he'd piss in good ale?"

Blackthorn pushed his way through the tightly wedged shoulders. "A walk in the air, the man needs," he said. "And I, too. We'll go together."

Reaching the false Netter's side at last, he laid his hand heavily on the pretender's shoulder. The púca beamed at him—plainly he was immensely pleased with himself. Blackthorn steered his charge to the door as quickly as he could. The bar was up, and Blackthorn's hand was reaching to push the door open, when someone pulled it wide from the outside, letting in a startling rush of frosty air. The newcomer stepped inside and shrugged off his bulky blanket, revealing deep red hair and bright red cheeks.

"Came as fast as I could," said Netter. The real Netter. "Have I missed the song? The lines were tangled and I . . ."

Netter trailed off and stared openmouthed into the face of his double. In the horrified silence that descended on the hall, the Netter in Blackthorn's care shrieked with laughter. His features blurred, and he squirmed from Blackthorn's grasp, collapsing into the form of a small, brown wood mouse. With every eye on him, the púca ran up Blackthorn's leg and dived neatly into the open leather pouch at the Hunter's belt.

PART 2

the scáileanna

Six

May the road rise before you,
May the wind be at your back,
May the sun shine warm upon your face,
May the rains fall soft upon your fields,
And until we meet again,
May Éire hold you in the hollow of Her hand.

The cold of winter is as may be, but the cold of a midwinter's
night upon the open waters of Loch Éirne is desperate. Even
so, Blackthorn felt he was hardly in a position to complain.
Though Bryony's thin body in the prow of the boat was a
negligible buffer against the wind, if old Scariff had had his
way, he would be swimming the frigid waters to the west
bank, not rowing over them. It had taken much charm and
ingenuity to convince the folk of Inis Ceithleann to let him
leave in peace. It had taken a great deal more to soften their
hearts against the púca. Even kindly Jet had at first held that
drowning the shape-shifter in Loch Éirne would be none too
cruel a fate.

"Isn't it strange, now," said Bryony quietly, "how fresh air
clears the mind? In the Chieftain's smoky hall, I thought I
understood why 'twould be best for you to bring the púca
away with you. Here on the loch, hasn't the wind blown
every one of your reasons from me?"

Her thoughts were stalking Blackthorn's own far too
closely. Facing his oar, he couldn't see Bryony's eyes, but he
could feel them, boring into his back.

"Sure, an' the sooner we're both gone from your isle, the better," he ventured.

Bryony said nothing, but her son Curlew looked over his shoulder at the Hunter.

"Not so, neither," the lad whispered. "A finer midwinter's never been had in Inis Ceithleann, I'm thinkin'. Why, the look on Netter's face alone—"

"Is it laughing you are at poor Netter?" chided the boy's mother. "Though I wager you're right," she admitted with a sigh. "This tale will be told around the hearthfires for many a long year."

"And grow in the telling," Blackthorn murmured.

"Will the Bards make a song of it?" asked Curlew eagerly.

"There's songs enough already of púcaí and their like," Bryony declared. "Tongues are quick to wag when the fairy folk are mentioned, but when all's been said, nothing's been learned."

"But it's always someone else who's heard the murúch by the strand, always some far land where the *fear dearg* is roaming," Curlew argued. "Now we've all seen a púca for ourselves, and in our own hall—Sure, an' wouldn't it be grand, now, if Blackthorn were to make a song to tell the world what happened this night in Inis Ceithleann?"

Blackthorn smiled and shook his head. "Let the Bards take hold of the tale, and you'll soon be hearing how a score of giants waded through the waters of Loch Éirne with a hundred púcaí riding on their heads. There's truth in the tales we carry, an' you listen hard enough, but never was there a Bard wouldn't twist the truth to make a tale better."

"Twist the truth?" repeated Bryony. "Is that what you call it?" But her voice was laughing.

"'Tis Poets make truth into words," she said more seriously, "not Bards." Blackthorn could hear she'd turned away, and knew she was looking toward the shadows of the shore. "Give Scáthach of Teach an Fhásaigh your true Name, Blackthorn, and she'll weave a rann to break the enchantments of the Sidhe and set the Hunter of Éirinn back on his path."

Completely astounded, Blackthorn stopped rowing and turned to stare at the woman. The boat started to drift, for Curlew had lost his stroke as well, and neither of them seemed aware of it.

"*By the light that shines!*" the boy cried. "The Hunter of Éirinn, mother?"

"Do you mean the current to take us to the middle of the lake, or might we still try for the western shore?"

Chastened, Blackthorn and Curlew set to their oars, but Curlew's mouth was now hanging open, while Blackthorn's was pressed into a grim line. When the currach was again cutting neatly across the water, Bryony went on.

"I knew him when he stepped into this boat and his Spear in his hand. Before that I was as gulled by his smooth tongue as everyone else, never thinking to question that he was a Bard from the dún. I only questioned his wandering about the wild north in a winter that has everyone else afraid to stir from their fires."

"I am a Bard," protested Blackthorn. "Or was once."

"What matter? You're the Hunter now. Not a Bard's road, but one far more dangerous you tread, and it was thoughtless cruelty to take the turnings that led to Inis Ceithleann."

Blackthorn's frown deepened. "I meant no harm," he insisted.

She dismissed the notion with a wave of her hand. "Whisht, of course not. But harm might well have come to us through you."

Curlew turned again to gape at the man on the bench behind him. Rather than meet the boy's eyes, Blackthorn studied the heavens. Their beauty stirred his heart—a panoply of stars piercing the black skies with a brilliance only the coldest nights can inspire.

"Great things and terrible come to those in the service of the Gods," Bryony said softly, but it might have been the stars talking for the clear truth in her words. "And the paths of geasa lie not on this earth, but fall in the cracks between the worlds. My heart turns to you, Blackthorn, but I would not have the Hunter of Éirinn near those I love while the Stag is running."

"Your Sight is keen as a Cailleach's, Lady."

She laughed. "No priestess am I, only a poor fisherwoman. But I, too, bear a geis. It is not so weighty as yours, nor was it laid on me by a Goddess, but taken by myself upon myself. Yet, it has opened my eyes—though not so wide as I can take in the sound and color of the worlds that hedge about you, any more than you could take in the wonders of Brugh na Morna."

"True it seems the shutters of my Sight were flung wide in that place, and the light is blinding me still," Blackthorn agreed. "But as you know mine, may I not hear what geis it is you bear, Lady?"

Bryony was quiet for so long, the Hunter thought he had been answered.

"I have not spoken of it to anyone," she said at last, "but if you would know . . . When we fled Doire Eile, I looked back to see our hall in flames and the stiff shadows of the Scáileanna dark against the roaring blaze. I knew then I would return to my home, that I must return to it. 'Twas no rash promise I made, no mere longing for revenge. Something came over me in that moment, more binding than a vow, more compelling than desire. . . ."

"A need that burns like a fire in your heart," said Blackthorn half to her, half to himself.

"Yes. Sometimes a burden, sometimes a blessing. No power on earth or beyond can lift it from me. But to fail to achieve it will break my soul, and only its fulfillment will set me free."

They rowed in silence for a time, and then Bryony took her bow from the bottom of the boat and put an arrow to the string. She kept her weapon trained on the wall of ebony that marked the shore, but as far as Blackthorn could tell, nothing moved on the bank, and he could not find it in him to fear the forest.

"Dark are the paths before you," Bryony said over her shoulder. "Surely it is folly beyond imagining for the Hunter of Éirinn to share his road with a púca! No honor have the fairy folk of the wild, nor conscience, nor courtesy—only a love of mischief and the means to accomplish it. Before we reach the shore, I urge you, loose your pouch from your belt and cast it over the side."

Blackthorn kept his hands on his oar. "Much wisdom has the wild taught me," he said gently, "and 'tis there my quarry runs."

Bryony took her eyes from the bank long enough to send the Hunter a withering glance. "To the Cailleacha turn, to the Mothers and the Poets, an' it's wisdom you seek. Not wisdom, but lies you'll find on a púca's tongue. An' you must dare the wild to hunt the Light, you will do well to be more wary of such creatures as you bear in your purse. Neither good nor evil do they know, no more than the birds and the beasts that share the forest with them."

"Well, an' the wild is a place neither good nor evil, then must I dare it, for wasn't it your own self said my path falls in the cracks between the worlds?" Blackthorn smiled. "But I'm not scorning your counsel. I've no intention of sharing my road with this troublesome rascal. Too long already we've kept company."

His oar brushed against the bottom of the loch, and Blackthorn pulled it in. As the currach listed in the shallows, he took up his Spear, set his other hand to the edge of the boat, and jumped lightly over the side.

"Let me come with you," Curlew burst out. "Please," he begged, striving to keep his voice low. "At least as far as Teach an Fhásaigh? No trouble I'll be, but maybe some help, and so also for the Poet on the road back—"

"I forbid it!" hissed Bryony.

Curlew cast his eyes down, but made one more try.

"An' he is the Hunter of Éirinn, mother, sure, an' it must be wrong to send him away unfriended."

Bryony said nothing, but Blackthorn understood her better now.

"You've a good heart," he said to the boy, "but your mother has the right of it," and he gave the boat a push away from the shore.

"May your road rise before you," said Bryony, her blessing softer than the rustle of the willows that draped their slender black branches in the water.

Blackthorn climbed the bank, then turned to watch the currach as Curlew's long pulls drew it out into the loch. He'd miss a warm bed tonight, and knew whom to blame for it. Wrapping his hand around his pouch, he jostled the inert ball at the bottom, but the púca wouldn't stir. Like as not, Bryony had the right of this, too. His three geasa were almost certainly no more than an inspired invention of the púca's deceitful mind. An' it would do any good, he'd have the shape-shifter out at once, but plainly he'd learn nothing until the wretched creature had recovered from his voyage across the water.

When the currach was no more than a black dot that merged with and emerged from the surrounding darkness, Blackthorn left the bank and went by instinct and starlight through the forest. Everywhere the ground was wet with snow, everywhere the wind plagued him. Finally he hauled himself into the lower branches of a broad-limbed oak and made himself as comfortable as he could in the dry crook of one of the tall tree's arms. Tomorrow, the Hunter silently promised the púca, cradling the pouch in his palm. Tomorrow you will keep your part of the bargain, as I kept mine today. Tomorrow you will speak to me of the three geasa you claim to have Seen, and then you will return to Loch Dearg and never, never speak to me again.

Seven

A road that was in summer the peddlers' green delight,
Is cursed by peddlers one and all when wearing winter's white.

Wake, old Stone. Wake, and tell me why the Bean Sidhe sings by the streams of Eas Aedh-Ruadh.

The sun is high, White One. Let me sleep.

Wake, old Stone. Day is dark, cloud covered. Wake, and tell me why the goblins Hunt.

They are only hounds, White One. Let me sleep.

Wake, old Stone. A gift I bring. Hard bones to crunch, soft flesh to devour. Wake, and tell me why Shadow rises to cover my Light.

I wake, White One, smelling red blood. Goblin meat is it? Sweeter than a baby's flesh, and I am hungry. Give it me.

Tell.

Dead is the Poet, all Éirinn will mourn. Two give chase, but only one Called. The false hunter's Name? Hidden. Hidden from me. Now shake loose the gory feast from your tines. I am hungry.

He thought it a dream, but thirty paces from where Blackthorn sat curled in the branches of the oak, a massive boulder was waking. Granite shoulders lifted from the solid rock, a neck stretched, twisted, and brought a flattened head around to glare at him with baleful eyes. Pasty gray lips pulled back to reveal a formidable row of dagger-sharp teeth. When half the troll's body was liberated from the inanimate stone, the Hunter swung lightly out of the tree and strode purposefully over to the lithic giant. He came well within reach of the hammer-fisted rock arms and spat.

"Two mornings I have wakened to your tricks, shape-shifter," he said. "I am slow, but I learn at last. Now to a man, for we've a matter to discuss."

The troll's eyes dimmed, but his torso remained partly unfolded from the rock.

"Do you think me so simple I'd believe a troll rousing at daybreak?" scoffed Blackthorn. "'Tis the sun that sends them back to stone. Now to a man, or I'll be sharpening my knife on your rocky hide!"

The sun was indeed shining, but it was a transient light, fated only to last until the daystar rose high enough to meet the clouds. Blackthorn meant to make his business with the púca as short as possible. Even without this delay he would be hard-pressed to reach Teach an Fhásaigh before the weather broke.

When a little man was squatting where the great boulder had been, Blackthorn folded his arms in front of his chest and narrowed his eyes.

"Could do with some breakfast, I could," said the púca, not giving Blackthorn time to draw breath. "'Twas ale and fish stew and oatcakes for himself last night, but for me, nothing at all, at all! Not the tiniest morsel of hospitality did you think to drop down the pouch for me—"

"Tell me of the three geasa," said Blackthorn, his voice slow with impatience.

"Words for breakfast, is it? Then we'll both go hungry, for I've naught to say!"

"Naught to say, for it's naught you know."

"Och, well, it's plenty I know," insisted the púca, "but little inclined am I to share me wisdom with a scurrilous fool."

Blackthorn forced an indulgent smile to his lips. "'Tis right you are, entirely," he agreed. "Why share your precious knowledge with me? I'll only doubt whatever you say, knowing you, as I do, for a cheat and a liar."

"A cheat and a liar! A cheat and a liar!"

The púca was so puffed up with indignation more air than sound came out of his mouth.

"This from the bodach who boasts of a rann for to make wet grasses burn! This from the shameless cur who unrightfully claims the Bard's Welcome of simple, trusting folk—"

Blackthorn muttered an exasperated curse under his breath and ran his fingers through his hair. Expecting a blow, the púca ducked.

"Would you beat on a poor creature half your size?" he whimpered, cowering low and shaking like a leaf in the wind. "Have the tales taught you nothing? Treat my folk kindly, they say, and with good reason. Ill luck will plague your path an' you do me harm."

"Ill luck has plagued my path since Samhain, you fool," Blackthorn exclaimed, "and you being the worst of it!"

Realizing he was in no danger, the púca quickly regained his impudence. "Is it so?" he snapped. "And little wonder an unmannerly beggar like yourself is short of good fortune!"

Blackthorn shifted his cloak about his shoulders and shrugged. "I'll be off, then, that my discourteous ways need offend you no more."

He struck out immediately toward the southwest and before long was in sight of the bogs. Had he been alone, he would have gone due west and travelled the high ground, but he knew he would lose the púca far more easily in the waterlogged lowlands. At first the shape-shifter marched along beside him, keeping a furious pace. Blackthorn made his long stride longer, and soon the little man was lagging behind.

"But carry me in your pouch, and I might tell you of the three geasa after all," the púca offered breathlessly. "Och, to be sure, I might well relent after a bit of a ride."

Without slowing, Blackthorn began to laugh. "Didn't I say I learn at last? That was the pact we made yesterday, and what has it got me? A freezing, uncomfortable night, and the chance to strike the same bargain again this morning!"

Breaking into a rolling, bandy-legged run, the púca managed to close the distance between them.

"Bargain!" he retorted. "A crack over a bowl of ale was yesterday's bargain. But 'twas over me head was the bowl of ale, not I over it, and yourself the only one to ease your thirst!"

"'Give me a ride, and we'll have a bit of a crack over a bowl of ale,'" said Blackthorn. "Your very words. 'Twas yourself set the terms of the bargain, though only I've kept them. My part was taking you along, and yours to supply the drink and talk."

"Sure, an' there's no denyin' it's a Bard's memory you carry in that stubborn head of yours," the púca conceded, an adulatory note in his voice now he was falling behind again.

"What? Out of insults? You'll not be resorting to flattery so soon?"

Coming to the edge of a small, soggy gully, Blackthorn jumped it easily and went on, never looking back.

"Och, now, it's a hard man you are," the púca called after him. "Bad enough to make me struggle along on me two old legs. You'll not be makin' me cross more water as well?"

Though sore tempted to make good reply to the púca's query, Blackthorn kept his mouth closed and continued walking.

"A púca and a fool," the little man wailed after him. "'Twas a sorry meeting and one I'll rue forever and aye!"

His parting words were as good as any the púca had given him, and Blackthorn couldn't help admiring them. He was certain the little man would get across the gully somehow, for the shape-shifter was nothing if not persevering. Still, the marshes held scores of water-filled gullies, and countless streamlets flowed through the trackless wetlands down to Loch Éirne. Blackthorn intended to cut a path through the bogs that traversed as many waterways as possible. If he didn't shake the púca from his trail at this first crossing, he'd lose him by the last.

There was no clear road to Scáthach's house, but the way was well-known to him. Over the bogs first, until the broad shoulders of Binn Chuilceach appeared in the west. Its evergreen forests would be white now, at least on the mountain's heights, and a crown of cloud might obscure its lofty summit. He need only make his way around Binn Chuilceach's toes to come to Teach an Fhásaigh. There he could count on a welcome, despite what Bryony had said. True enough he was no longer fit company for the fisherfolk. In all Éirinn he doubted he could find a village where he'd not be greeted by wary faces and a bowl of bitter brew. But Teach an Fhásaigh was the house of a Poet, the greatest Poet in Éirinn. Scáthach was no stranger to the Brughanna of the Gods, the Sidhe's hollow hills, the temples of the Mothers, or the Sléibhte of the Wizards. There was no world her verses could not Name, no crack between the worlds her poems could not span. And she was his friend. Sometimes his lover, but always his friend. His geis had the power to change many things, but never his friendship with Scáthach.

By the time the ground rose in anticipation of the high mountain slopes beyond and the empty bogs had given way to hazel thickets and thin stands of rowan, the day had grown dark and the wind fierce. Blackthorn stopped to look back, more to take heart from how far he had come than to see if the púca was still following him. He truly did not imagine the shape-shifter would not by now have given up. Yet, there he was, a slight, hunched figure slowly plodding across the bleak flatlands.

Blackthorn set his back to one of the stouter trunks of mountain ash, too puzzled even to curse. 'Twas the beasts of the forest he knew, their ways and their cunning, the songs of the rivers, and the rhythms of the wood. The fairy folk had not been his study, but neither had he spent nine years in the wild without gleaning some wisdom regarding the unseen creatures who called it their home. Never till now had he met one face-to-face, but often enough he had listened while the Oak Seer took counsel with the whispering breeze in the whitethorns, or watched her dance with the swirling dust. From her he had learned where to step that he would not tread on the fairy folks' toes, how to court their favor with small gifts and praise, and how to fox the ones that would do him evil.

Even Úna might wonder at this creature, he thought. Púcaí were born to lead unwary travellers astray—it was common knowledge—and *never did wild goose rear tame gosling*. Yet, here was a púca could do nothing but follow, though waters deep and shallow, still and rushing lay in his path.

The púca would be a long time reaching Teach an Fhásaigh, but it was plain now he would come there at last, if Blackthorn did not stop him here. He waited by the rowan tree, passing his time by casting annoyed looks at the threatening sky and tapping the toe of his boot against a stone. At last the púca appeared, preceded by his whining, self-pitying voice.

"Wurra, wurra, wurra, but 'tis cruel I've been treated, entirely. Not so far for a long-shanks, is it? Not so foul the black bogwater or slippery the muck when your legs are so lanky. Och, it's a sorry—"

He noticed Blackthorn and stopped abruptly. His mouth opened and closed a few times, as if he wanted to speak, but the Hunter's cold glare daunted him.

"Why do you follow me?"

The ice was as chill in Blackthorn's voice as in his eye.

"Whisht, and what else can I do, an' you refuse me your pouch?"

"You can hie yourself back to Loch Dearg and wait for another careless traveller to torment. For myself, I've had enough of your guile."

"Och, it's quick with the insults you are. Do you think it's my wish to be trailin' after a merciless tyrant like yourself?"

"An' you've no wish to be here, get you gone!" Blackthorn ground out.

"Pleased would I have been to say farewell two days past in the thatcher's cote! But you had to go and—and—" The púca sputtered with ire.

"Is it putting the blame on me you are?" Blackthorn demanded. "Why, I've done nothing all day but try and be rid of you!"

"You can't be rid of me, you thrice-cursed fool! Not now you've saved my life, and that though your stone missed the mark."

Blackthorn brushed the encounter with the weasel aside with a shake of his head. "An' that's what keeps you on my tail, 'tis forgotten. Get yourself home now, and think no more on it."

The púca gave the Hunter a look of profound forbearance and sighed. "Would that I could, Blackthorn. Would that I could. For a man driven by geasa, you're unsympathetic indeed to the burdens of others."

"You'll not be saying a geis binds you to me?"

Blackthorn was about to laugh at the staggering enormity of the púca's cheek, when the little man's arrogance crumbled. His wrinkled face twisted into an expression of abject woe, he bowed his head and groaned.

"Och, wurra, wurra, wurra. Not a moment's peace will I have till I do something grand to save your miserable life, and myself the greatest coward in the five kingdoms of Éirinn."

Blackthorn ran his hand through his hair, trying to decide if the púca were truly grief-stricken, or simply the most gifted liar he had ever met.

"I laid no geis on you," he said sternly.

"'Twas sent by the Gods," the little man answered hopelessly. "An Daghdha's geis will fall on any of my folk should someone save their life as you did mine. The Good God made it so because on occasion our little deceits bring your people to your deaths, or so Úna says. I'm not one to gainsay the Oak Seer, but sure, an' there's no more than hurtless mischief in my sport—"

Blackthorn tried to break in, but the púca was too deeply engrossed in his own sad tale to allow an interruption.

"How could a mouse do any great harm?" he asked. "Bears, some of my people are, and wild boars, and cats of the mountains. But I? A mouse! And well it suits me, coward that I am! Though I'll not be boastin' to say that to take shapes from dreams is a rare talent indeed—"

Blackthorn took a menacing step forward and the púca took a hasty step back.

"Tell me of the three geasa," Blackthorn commanded.

Looking as if he was about to be ill, the púca muttered in a barely audible voice, "One by the Goddess, two by the spell, three by your own choosin', and any or all may be the death of you."

Squinting into the Hunter's solemn face, the shape-shifter suddenly laughed. "Now you'll be wishin' I hadn't told you."

"It's wishing I am you had more to say," Blackthorn answered. "Only the first is clear, one by the Goddess. Nine years past, on Bealtaine Day, Éire's geis fell upon me." His voice grew soft with remembered astonishment and continuing awe. "Her Stag called my Name, and when I answered, leaving my lover's arms for the dew-wet morning, I saw not the dawn, but the wellspring of starlight. I saw the White Stag. He leapt away, and when I reached the place he had stood, not a trace of him could I find, not even his hoofprint on the ground. Yet, the bond between us was forged. The first sun of summer rose not upon Blackthorn, but upon the next Hunter of Éirinn."

He shot a calculating look at the púca.

"Nine years have I labored to be ready for this Hunt, making the forest my home and every creature in it my teacher. A year and a day I spent fashioning a weapon worthy of the White Stag's death. This brief time when the winter sun shines is all I have to find the Stag and take his life, if I can, and already I have lost the trail and an entire moon to the Sidhe. What means two by the spell? Who would cast it? And how can I believe you when you say I will take another geis willingly upon myself? This one may be more than I can accomplish!"

"Do you think the Sight makes the future clear?" the púca flung back at him. "A curse it is to whoever possesses it. Supposing I See a fog-covered path and yourself at a crossroads. Two ways before you, but which should you take? Which leads to glory and which to disgrace? Perhaps either one will bring you joy. Perhaps both will fail you."

"All I'm asking—" Blackthorn began, but the púca would have none of it.

"You say you bear one geis. I look at you and See a soul fair bent to breaking under thrice the load you claim. I'm no Oak Seer to ask the wind what it means, nor a priestess with Éire's wisdom to bring to bear, nor a Poet to interpret the vision. I've told you all I can. Is my honesty worth nothing to you? Have you no pity in your heart for the weight upon my soul?"

Blackthorn considered him gravely, but the little man could not long meet the Hunter's eyes. Only lies he'd hear from a púca's tongue, Bryony had warned him, but Blackthorn wasn't so sure. A surpassing liar himself, he had always thought he could tell when the truth was missing from a tale. The púca was slippery as an eel, but if the bonds of geis were not driving him on, what could explain his extraordinary behavior? What less compelling desire could overcome the shape-shifter's natural loathing of the roiling waters of Loch Éirne and the cold blackwater bogs? He would prefer to disbelieve the rascal and have no more to do with him. To his surprise, Blackthorn discovered that though he trusted the shape-shifter not at all, he believed the púca's story.

"Swear by the God of your geis that you will steal no shape from my dreams or anyone's dream," he said at last. "Swear to stay a mouse, hidden in my purse, unless I let you out. Swear you will leave the moment your geis is fulfilled and bother me no more. Swear all this, and I'll take you with me."

The púca turned to the Hunter with wide, innocent eyes, causing Blackthorn's suspicions to resurface immediately.

"Would you rob life of all its pleasures?" asked the little man, then flinched from Blackthorn's stony stare. "But I see that you would.

"Gladly I'll leave as soon as I may," he said sourly. "I'll remain a mouse, when other eyes are watching, and take no shape from your dreams or any dream . . . unless it be to save your life or mine. By An Daghdha, all this I swear. Are you content?"

Blackthorn frowned, but the púca's oath seemed straight-forward enough. He nodded. With a final disgruntled sigh, the púca dropped to a mouse and chittered irritably until the Hunter had picked him up and he was once more settled comfortably in the pouch.

Eight

Know where you're going, and mind where you step,
Keep to your road, or your journey you'll rue.
Once astray from your path in the dark elves' domains,
Only magic or might will deny them their due.

A Bardic Lore-Song

The road did indeed rise before Blackthorn, but as the day
wore on, it was of little help against the implacable wind.
Every step became an act of defiance. The shrieking air
caught at his cloak as if to tear it from his shoulders and
relentlessly tried to force him to turn back to Loch Éirne.

When at last he came under the shadow of Binn
Chuilceach, the Hunter discovered that the mountain, too,
was against him. In Blackthorn's mind Binn Chuilceach was
a place of poetry and love, but the mountain above him
seemed determined to shun any connection with either.
Gathering speed on the curving slopes, the wind lifted handfuls of the deep-lying snow and flung them, stinging, into
Blackthorn's face. The branches of the firs that covered the
mountain drooped under their oppressive loads or displayed
their needles like dark wounds against the white hillside.
The lulling hush of the wind in the pines had risen to a wailing moan, and instead of the cloud crown Blackthorn had
envisioned, Binn Chuilceach wore a fierce, gray cowl of lowering wrath.

In his heart Blackthorn knew that more than the weather

was amiss, but he denied he knew it until the sight of old Jackdaw's cottage ripped his denial from him.

Blackthorn had been friends with Jackdaw as long as he'd been friends with Scáthach. The old man had been living in the little home he had built for himself on the far side of Scáthach's fields since long before Larkspur ever brought Blackthorn to the Poet's door. Seven years ago now, by the comforting warmth of the old man's fire and over a mostly full jar of whiskey, Jackdaw had told Blackthorn his tale. As a lad he had been too wild for ever a woman to have taken him into her home. The roving life was all he wanted, until his beard whitened, and his gait stiffened, and the long roads began to look more lonely than inviting. Then he had made his way to Scáthach, hoping the Poet would help him to a wife. He begged a rann of her, glad to give her his Name if she would put it in a verse that could secure him a woman's heart. In return for this favor, he offered Scáthach the only treasure he had in the world, a small piece of amber wrought into the likeness of a hare.

Jackdaw had laughed, and Blackthorn with him, at his description of Scáthach listening to his humble request from the comfort of her carved chair, more magnificent than many a throne, a gift from the Mother of Na Connachta. Then the great Poet had risen, her rich, saffron gown flowing like silken sunlight about her, and walked across the tapestried carpet, payment from Dubhghall of An Cnoc Gorm for his poem, until she stood directly before Jackdaw. She had reached out an arm gold banded from shoulder to wrist with the offerings of suppliants, and taken Jackdaw's simple stone in her many-ringed hand. Yes, she said, considering it thoughtfully, she would give him what he wanted. But it would take some time. Let him keep his lovely amber until the poem was ready, and in the meanwhile, would he be so good as to go out to the meadow behind the house and gather wild oats and barley for her porridge?

Though not a day went by the old graybeard didn't tease the Poet about the verse he claimed he was still waiting for, Blackthorn never doubted Jackdaw was content with the role Scáthach had bestowed on him. Not a wife, but company and purpose he needed, and found both bringing in the grain for the Poet of Teach an Fhásaigh and shortening her long winter nights with tales of his rakish youth.

Coming or going, Blackthorn always stopped where the youngest trees encroached on the edge of the meadow, to peer between their slender trunks for a glimpse of Jackdaw's little house across the field. He paused there now, stepping out of the wind for a blessed moment to find the familiar landmark. Thicker stands of pine beyond the cottage hid Teach an Fhásaigh from view, but Jackdaw's home he saw plainly, stark against the darkness of the framing woods. The roof was gone and the door as well, and the lintel stones were blackened by fire. The soot-smeared shell called to the Hunter, but his own foreboding cry was louder in his ears. He turned from the burned cottage and set out for Scáthach's house at a run. The chill of winter and wind was on his flesh, but the cold that gripped his heart turned the very blood in his veins to ice.

The cottage may have burned through Jackdaw's carelessness, he told himself as he forced his weary legs through the snow. Even now, the old man might be entertaining the Poet with another tale, safe and warm before Scáthach's hearth. He might, Blackthorn insisted, but in his mind the fate of Doire Eile whispered insidiously against his hopes.

He rounded the clump of broom that marked the beginning of the footpath to Scáthach's dwelling. A hundred paces further on it curved, and the house came in sight. There Blackthorn stopped, all his hurry changed in a moment to terrible reluctance. Like Jackdaw's cottage, Scáthach's home was missing its roof. Scarred windows stared out with empty eyes, and the east wall was reduced to tumbled stones and cracked, coal-black beams.

He approached slowly, then stepped through the gaping doorway and surveyed the ruin. The wind howled through the drystone walls like the voice of the Bean Sidhe he had heard in his dream. It seemed a fitting lament for all that was once wondrous and fair in this place and was now broken and misshapen rubble. He made no attempt to sift through the debris for Scáthach's fire-bleached bones. One such as she would not have stayed inside to die. If he did not find her body outside, he thought, hope rising tentatively in his breast, he might believe she had escaped with her life. The Poet of Teach an Fhásaigh would not easily be killed while she could defend herself with her verses.

He went swiftly back over the doorless threshold and began searching for some sign that she had come outside, had stood, or fled, or perished. It was behind the house he found an answer, but it was a cruel one. A murder of crows sat on a low mound of snow, picking greedily at something buried within.

With a wild shout he raced forward, sending the carrion eaters to the trees to protest the outrage. Protruding from the snow where the rooks had perched, and almost matching it in color, was a human leg.

Blackthorn knelt in the snow beside his lover's corpse, unable yet to brush the snow aside and see what death had done to her. As his eyes travelled almost idly along the bloodless white curve of her calf, her words came flooding back to him, words that had once wounded his pride. Long ago he had asked her to marry him, knowing in his heart she would refuse. She was much older than Blackthorn, of an age to marry when he was still clinging to his mother's skirts. She was a woman of power and wealth, and could wed far better men than he, if she desired. None of these reasons did Scáthach give him, but a tender rejection, and a selfless excuse. As he listened to her answer, he had kissed the dimple behind her knee and drawn his fingers down her leg and up again.

Dangerous enough for you to love a Poet. I'll not flaunt our affection before the Gods in a wedding. But, oh, you have touched my heart. I will give you a poem, though I cannot give you my hand.

It's you I want. I've no need for your verses.

Not now, perhaps. But there is a time in everyone's life when the right words mean everything. Come back to me then, mo mhúirnín, and I will give them to you.

Blackthorn dug some of the heaped snow from Scáthach's frozen limbs, and turned her onto her back.

"Scáthach," he whispered. Blood hammered in his temples, and his stomach heaved with revulsion.

"Scáthach!" he said again, shouting this time. He had known the rooks were feasting on her flesh, but the snow had disguised the ragged, red stump of Scáthach's neck that had tempted them.

He stumbled to his feet looking wildly about for the head that had been so crudely severed from Scáthach's body. When his eyes could find nothing, he crawled through the snow on his hands and knees until his fingers were numb with cold and running with blood where he had cut them on the rocks.

"It's no good, no good," said a tremulous voice. "They took it, I'm sayin', and they'll take ours as well an' we stay here."

Blackthorn whirled on the púca. His eyes, bright as the flames must have been, fixed on the little man where he crouched near to Scáthach's remains. The shape-shifter quickly dropped his own gaze and set it on his two hands, which were knotted together and held tightly against his chest.

"They took it, don't you see, and paraded it on a pike, or brought it home to adorn their dirty hole under the mountain." The little man's voice shook, but he went on as bravely as he could. "Gather your wits, now, and let's be gone. It's only sense I'm speakin'."

Blackthorn turned from the púca, and cast his eyes again over the ground, searching. Frustration and fear twisted the púca's face into a mask of desperation. He crept furtively to where the Hunter stood and tugged on a corner of the wolf-skin cloak.

"A Poet she was—'twas to still her tongue they did this. There's nothing to find, no good to be done looking! *Badhbh, Macha, and Mór-Ríoghain*, are you listenin' to me, at all, at all?"

When Blackthorn turned back to the púca the savage brightness was gone from his gaze, leaving only dull pain in his gray eyes. The little man's face lit with eagerness, and he tugged even harder on the Hunter.

"No point in goin' back. We'll go on, we will, to Béal an Átha Móir—"

Blackthorn didn't bother freeing his cloak from the púca's grasp. He simply walked away, and the shape-shifter let go of his own accord when he saw the Hunter was headed for the house. Blackthorn went without haste to the fallen wall. There he stopped, took a weighty stone in his hands, and brought it back to Scáthach's body. Setting it beside her, he returned to the house for another. The púca let out a pitiful moan and followed the Hunter with a mouse's mincing steps.

"Wurra, wurra, wurra. A finer fool I've never seen in all my days. Are you blind to the storm brewin'? And sure, an' there'll be worse to fear from the dark than the gale. Will you build a cairn only to lie on it yourself?"

Blackthorn brought the second stone and set it by the first.

"Och, wurra, wurra, wurra," groaned the little man, lifting a smallish stone and staggering over to Scáthach's grisly form. "Wurra, wurra, wurra, wurra."

After a time, the monotonous task had a soothing effect on Blackthorn's sorrow. He worked quickly but carefully to construct a place where the Poet could return to the earth and not fatten the crows.

Though he was cheating them of their meal, it was the rooks that alerted the Hunter to his danger. Their hoarse voices had bombarded his ears with a raucous carol since he first surprised them, and by the time the base of the cairn was laid he barely heard them anymore. It was the silence that caught his attention when they suddenly stopped.

Blackthorn lifted his eyes from the cairn and for no conscious reason looked toward the house. A fleeting streak of gray darted past one of the windows, swift as a bird's shadow, but the rooks were all sitting silent in the branches of the nearby pines, and not a one had taken wing. Blackthorn's stomach tightened, and his breath came quicker.

"Right you are," said the púca, sitting back on his heels. "We've marked the place, and that's something . . ."

He trailed off, and lowered his voice to a whisper. "Och, now, there's a terrible Seeing in your eyes, bodach. Don't tell me, don't tell me what it was—"

"Fear only feeds their power," said Blackthorn, rising from the snow. "So says the King of Ulaidh, and my brother's faced enough of them to know."

"Och, help us, help us," sobbed the púca.

Shivers of fright danced down his naked body, but he made a peculiar, mouselike jump and landed right in the Hunter's path.

"Listen to me," he said, and Blackthorn could hear wild hope mixed with his dread. "Listen well, and you'll have a whole skin and be free of me, both. Leave now, takin' the straightest way to the nearest village. You're the Hunter of Éirinn—who wiser in followin' the forests' paths? An' you do as I say, I'll be savin' your life, I will, as well as me own."

Blackthorn shook his head, but kept his eyes on the house. "Is it true, then, that the Scáileanna can do us no harm an' we keep to our path? But a path is more than a trail through the forest," he went on more quietly, almost to himself. "A path is the way of doing what must be done."

The púca didn't move, but Blackthorn stepped easily around him, crossed to the fallen wall, and selected another stone. The sooty interior of the house was open to his scrutiny, but he saw nothing within save the burned remains of Scáthach's possessions.

The púca had been but little help before. Now he was useless. He alternately wailed and pleaded with the Hunter as a man, then dropped to a mouse and tried to hide among the stones of the cairn. Finally, Blackthorn picked up the shapeshifter while he was brown and furry and thrust him back inside his pouch.

The daystar was nearly done its journey when Scáthach's tomb was finished. There would be no sunset. The clouds lay heavy over Binn Chuilceach, bringing an early, false night to Teach an Fhásaigh. Blackthorn knelt once more by the body of the woman who had been . . . he could not bring himself to name her with paltry words like "friend" or "lover."

"I came for my poem, Scáthach, mo mhúirnín," he whispered to the stones, so quietly even the mouse in his purse could not hear him. "Do you remember? You promised me, and now my time of need is come. The Stag runs free and all I have to follow is scattered pieces of his history that visit me in dreams. What words do I speak that will show me the world, and the White Stag in it? And what have they done to the sweet mouth that would have told me?"

Blackthorn stood slowly. When he raised his head, he looked full on a Scáil standing motionless by the diminished heap of stones that had fed the cairn.

He was beautiful, Blackthorn realized. He gazed almost without willing to on the dark elf's flawless accoutrements and perfect features, trying to understand what made the

Scáil so utterly repellent. The haughty, serene face was faintly reminiscent of the loveliness he had Seen and could almost remember in Brugh na Morna. Yet, while the light had enchanted the senses, the dark oppressed them. If the imposing, angular being before him was beautiful, it was a superficial design of beauty, an edifice that neither touched the passionate splendor of life nor reflected any kinship with it. And the eyes . . .

Blackthorn looked away, but he felt the Scáil watching him still, through lidless slits of darkness. The Hunter's hair was black. So was a rook's wing, and the night sky, but these had sheen, and lustre. The Scáil's eyes were colorless, opaque, without shading or hue. They held neither love nor hate, pleasure nor pain, but looking into them, Blackthorn felt he had looked beyond, into a realm of evil and despair.

He turned his back on the Scáil, his mind clear. To Béal an Átha Móir he would go, and if he kept his thoughts on his goal and his feet on the path, he must believe there was nothing the Scáil could do against him.

The wind blew snow across the footpath, but this was a track he could follow blindfolded on a moonless night. He reached the curve, and there, waiting at the broom, was a towering, unbending shadow. It was too tall for the wildly blowing bush to have cast it, too small to belong to the tossing pines, and besides, it was absolutely still. Only the Scáil's cloak moved, flapping in the wind. The mantle was slate-gray, and merged with the dark air, bewildering Blackthorn's eye. He hesitated, unable to fathom how the Scáil could have reached the broom before him. The truth was harder to bear. A second Scáil waited ahead. The first was still behind him, his presence betrayed by the scrape of metal on metal as he drew his sword.

Blackthorn's instincts raged at him to turn and face the weapon at his back, or to run from it. His reason insisted that a dagger was no match for a Scáil's naked blade, and that to flee would bring the dark elves down on him all the sooner. Forcing himself to go easy, he walked past the second Scáil, then turned south and west, toward Béal an Átha Móir.

The wind had been fierce before. Now it was brutal. It took nearly all Blackthorn had to set one foot in front of the other. His legs had carried him no more than a stone's throw from the broom when the menacing clouds over Binn Chuilceach burst open, and their pent-up fury plunged to earth like God-driven spears of ice. The wind sweeping through the trees across the fallen snows was bitterly cold, but the air in the monstrous blackness above must have been warmer. What fell from the skies, flying east in long lances of translucent gray, was sleet. Full of its own power, the storm pounded the mountain's slopes and scoured Teach an Fhásaigh with its ruthless, half-frozen rain.

Lightning shouted from the top of Binn Chuilceach. Glancing up, Blackthorn saw the clinging darkness under a moaning pine unfold from the tree and draw sword before him. A sudden, wicked blast of wind caught him before the Scáil had taken a step, nearly knocking him down. As he struggled to get his feet under him, another gray shadow lifted from the dark hump of a fallen tree, and rushed toward him with a hiss that cut through the howling wind. Blackthorn stumbled back, flinching from the attack, and was lost. Quickly, he realized his folly and moved forward again, but it was too late. He had stepped off his path. Without hurry, the Scáileanna moved in to claim their own.

PART 3

the dancer

Nine

A Sliabh to house you, a servant to tend you,
Poets to sing your praise,
If you'll swear by Éire to serve Her people,
And come when the Mothers call.

The Wizards' Charge

The trouble with the Mothers, thought Meacán, jamming her foot into her boot, was they always made her feel like a child.

"I'm coming, I'm coming," she grumbled under her breath.

Briar handed Meacán her cloak without so much as a raised eyebrow. Three Wizards had Sliabh Mis housed since first Briar had come here to dwell. Her long years of service, from the last days of Fearchar the Flyer, through the brief time of his successor, Eochaidh the Stone-Eye, to these seven years with the mountain's current occupant, Meacán the Dancer, had enured the older woman to the odd ways of Wizards. If the Dancer demanded her travelling cloak but an hour after returning home, if she conversed with the empty air, what of it? Not that Briar wasn't curious to know whom Meacán addressed, or where the girl was off to now—but she knew better than to ask directly.

"Do you wish Dúr saddled?" she inquired politely.

Meacán's brown eyes flashed. "An' I ride to Temuir, I'll have Liannan's voice in my mind for weeks! Not a moment's peace does she give me. Last night her calling sounded even in my dreams!"

So it was Liannan, Mother of Midhe, whispering in Meacán's mind, and to far Temuir the Dancer must now go. Briar allowed herself a small smile. During the last three moons, Liannan's messengers had twice made the journey from Temuir, the Mother's seat in Midhe and the heart of Éirinn, to seek out the Wizard Meacán Iníon na Caillí in the kingdom of Mumhain. South and west they had travelled, to the very edge of Éirinn, where four rocky, windswept toes of land jutted out from the coast into the sea. Sliabh Mis sat on the first joint of the most northerly toe, a high peak looking down from a cautious distance into the bay of Tráigh Lí.

Though the emissaries had arrived safely at the Wizard's Sliabh, they had returned to Temuir unheard. Meacán the Dancer had departed her home before midsummer, to attend the fair at Aonach Urmhumhan. Where she had been travelling since then, Briar could not begin to guess, but it was only this morning, the fifth of midwinter-tide, that Meacán had returned to Sliabh Mis, apparently driven there by the power of the Queen of Midhe's far-reaching thoughts.

Briar's smile faded. 'Twas well-known from the mind of one High Priestess to another thoughts travelled fast and sure, and clearly could a Mother hear the secrets in the hearts that beat in their presence. But to call to Meacán, and not even knowing where the Dancer tarried—why the Mother of Midhe must be wearing herself out sending her summons the length and breadth of Éirinn! And though Meacán was a fine Wizard, she was no Queen to send a message back in kind. Not until Meacán knocked on Temuir's gates would Liannan know her call had been heard.

"Why doesn't she send for Reochaidh an' she desires a Wizard to attend her midwinter feasts?" Meacán grumbled, fumbling with the cloak's catch. "His mountain stands in Laighin, and near to Midhe, as does Fionnghuala's Sliabh Buidhe. Seven Wizards of Éirinn, and she must send for me!"

"Likely she has sent for the other Wizards, as well," Briar answered, gently taking Meacán's angry fingers from the cloak and fastening it for her. "Has my Lady spent these many moons in climes more mild and peaceful than we enjoy this year in Éirinn? Our harvests were poor. The winter came early and sits hard. The talk in Tráigh Lí and Coill na n-Áirní is of fighting in the north and goblin raids east of the great river An tSionainn. 'Twas a council the messengers came to announce, and all the Mighty to attend."

It was as close to a reprimand as she dared go, but Meacán seemed unaffected by it. The Dancer wasn't done pouting. Briar suppressed a sigh. Temuir would be as gay as any place in Éirinn this winter, its welcome as warm as anyone could desire. It wasn't the invitation that so annoyed Meacán the Dancer, Briar knew, but simply that she was being forced to accept it.

Upon arriving at Sliabh Mis as a young woman, Briar had been surprised to find the aged Wizard Fearchar such a petulant little boy at heart. Discovering the same perverse obstinacy in Eochaidh the Stone-Eye, she began to suspect all great Wizards bore the same trait. With Meacán's succession to the Sliabh, Briar no longer had any doubts. Of course, Meacán had been a child in truth, just a girl of fifteen, when the Mothers had made her a Wizard of Éirinn. Yet here she was, a grown woman of twenty-two, and still full of sulks and temper.

"'Tis the Wizards' arrogance gives them the will to rule their gifts," she often told her friends in Tráigh Lí when they wondered at her patience. "Besides, they're not hard to manage, an' you have the trick of it."

Aloud, to Meacán she said, "Mistake not, darling. If the Mother has summoned you, it is because what the Dancer of Sliabh Mis can do, no other of the Seven Wizards of Éirinn can equal."

Meacán's frown melted like ice over fire.

"Then I'll there at once," she said, a mischievous smile lighting her face. "And may the Mother be pleased to see me coming up the high road to Temuir."

She stepped back with a delicate lift to her step, raised a graceful arm, started into a spin, and disappeared.

"Willful children these Wizards are," Briar remarked to the empty room as she bent to pick up Meacán's discarded garments. "Give them a task, they will refuse it. Tell them their gift alone can accomplish it, and they will stop at nothing until it has been achieved."

Spinning gracefully out of the frosty air onto the high, crowded way that led into Temuir, Meacán set the dogs to barking, badly startled several horses, and so distracted the hawkers they lost the rhythm of their haggling and had to begin their bargains all again. Some cautious folk spat, suspicious of anything so sudden and unexpected. Children shrieked and ran up to touch the Dancer, doubting their eyes, but trusting their fingers to prove her real.

Meacán shook her hood back, uncovering her long, loose, chestnut hair, and started toward the gates of Temuir's village. With a living train of curious children and yapping dogs, and to the accompaniment of a chorus of astonished voices, Meacán strode up to and under the wooden arch. She looked over the tops of the close-built wattle-and-daub houses to the high stone rampart that surrounded the Queen's halls. The few warriors on watch upon the wall could certainly see the saffron of her gown flashing beneath her cloak as she walked. Even if they had missed her dramatic appearance, they would know by the color of her skirt that one of the Mighty of Éirinn was come to Temuir. News of her arrival must already be speeding to Liannan's ears. In a moment, surely, that unquenchable voice in her head would stop importuning her to come to Midhe.

The temple that crowned Temuir Hill was a dance of nineteen door-wide menhirs, most of them half again as tall as Eoghan, a few almost twice as high. As the temple was open to the sky, its paved floor was often swept, but today the stones were neglected and covered by a thin carpet of snow. In the very center of the temple, about fifty paces from the menhirs, lay a deep, flame-blackened hole. Liannan stood beside it, her arms raised over the firepit, but it was not fire she was calling. The Queen-Mother of Midhe had been nearly two days in the temple, calling to Meacán the Dancer of Sliabh Mis.

"She is come," said Eoghan.

The radiance that streamed from the High Priestess's head and hands was doused as the Mother let Éire's presence leave her. It was rare that Eoghan saw his Queen so, completely untouched by divinity. Everything seemed to waken the Goddess within her, from the simplest pleasures to the most difficult tasks. Seeing her dispossessed of commanding strength and surpassing gentleness, of awesome anger and irresistible beauty, seeing her as a mortal woman with strong, wide hips and full, milky breasts, and eyes the color of a clear autumn sky, Eoghan loved her all the more. He took off his cloak and wrapped it about Liannan's shoulders, knowing the Queen would now be feeling the cold. His fingers gently brushed back a few of her straggling ash-blonde tresses, but Eoghan's face was one great scowl. Curses the Wizard Meacán deserved, not the gracious welcome awaiting her. It was the Dancer's obstinacy had forced Liannan to send her thoughts searching the five kingdoms for her wayward Wizard, and great good luck the Mother had reached her at all. Eoghan was new to the circles of the Mighty, but not so naive that he did not know how difficult a thing it was Liannan had done, and how much it had cost her.

Her King's umbrage spoke in the Mother's heart, weary though she was.

"Musha, my darling," she said, reaching up a cold hand to stroke Eoghan's downy cheek. "If she were not so stubborn, she would not make half so fine a Wizard."

It was back already, that luminous glow in her eyes, that touch of a smile beyond human understanding. Four moons had Eoghan been Midhe's King, four moons basked in her light, and still he found it incredible that he was wed to Liannan, Queen-Mother of Midhe, Priestess of Éire. He picked her up in his arms and kissed her, anchoring his extraordinary good fortune in the deep seas of her love.

Ten

Five are the Mighty who use their true Names;
The Mothers, guarded by Éire and fame,
The Sidhe by their bright eyes, the Kings by their swords,
The Wizards by craft, and the Poets by words.

Meacán had arrived in Temuir at noonday, but days are short in the dark of the year. She had barely time to be shown her apartments and take a drop of wine before she was being ushered to the temple for Liannan's council. Already as she climbed the winding path to the temple the sun was setting.

The walk warmed her somewhat, but atop Temuir's hill there were only the tall stones to hinder the driving wind, and they made a poor job of it. The circle was full of saffron-robed Poets and Wizards, all hunched in their cloaks and shivering. Only Fionnghuala the Deceiver greeted Meacán, and then with the briefest of nods. All eyes were on the cold firepit in the temple's heart, and the Mother of Midhe standing before it.

The Cailleach, her features hidden by the hood of a voluminous cloak of black sheep's wool, came to stand at Liannan's left. White hood thrown back and red hair gleaming in the last light of day, Brí, the Maiden of Midhe, stood on the Mother's right.

"*Tine,*" the Queen said clearly.

She seemed to be calling to a friend, not commanding a power, yet at her word, fire leapt from the dark hole in the heart of Temuir's temple, and burned gladly, though there was nothing to burn.

Smiles eased the Wizards' and Poets' pinched, red faces. As one they moved toward the light and warmth.

"Let me greet you, Dancer," said a gentle voice behind Meacán, and a cold hand took her arm.

She turned to Tadhg of An Chluain Thiar and kissed the Poet on both his whiskery cheeks.

"Och, your beauty alone is almost enough to warm me," he smiled. "Almost. My old bones shake too easily these days. I'd have spelled a fire with a verse in a moment, an' the Mother of Midhe had not lit this one when she did."

"You'll not get me believing you an elder just by complaining about the cold," Meacán laughed. "Why it's younger you look today than half a year since at Aonach Urmhumhan's fair."

"The Dancer, at least, is cheerful," Feargna Óg remarked stiffly, elbowing past Meacán and lifting his thin hands toward the flames. "I for one find it irksome to be summoned to a council before Samhain only to be forced to wait until sundown on the fifth day of midwinter-tide for it to begin. And atop the hill of Temuir no less—"

Meacán regarded the young Necromancer evenly. "Blame me for the season and the hour, if you must, Feargna Óg, though I answered the Mother's summons as soon as I was able. Yet, it is not my fault, but Reochaidh's that we must convene on a high, bare-headed hill within an open henge."

Feargna Óg sent a sidelong glance up to Reochaidh towering over him, over them all. The Destroyer of Sliabh Bladhma was far too tall for the circle of stones to give him respite from the northwesterly blow. The giant could only turn his face to the southeast and bring his enormous shoulders up to his ears in an attempt to shield his thick neck from the bitter wind.

Catching Feargna Óg's look, Reochaidh inclined his boulder-sized head in greeting, but said no word. The giant was always careful in his speech. It was his voice that gave him his title.

Mac Ailch the Conjuror of Sliabh An Óir walked slowly

past them, his face drawn into lines of deep concentration. One hand stroked a solitary white lock in his silken, black beard. The fingers of the other were busy manipulating the frosty air. Gray gloves covered his hands, and both boasted five dark beryls, one set over each knuckle. Firelight glinted from the stones as Mac Ailch conjured comfort from the winter wind.

A soft cushion appeared at Meacán's feet, and another near Feargna Óg, and rugs, and a stool for Tadhg. The Conjuror made a complete circuit around the assembly. When he was done, the firepit was wreathed with his art. Liannan nodded her thanks.

"It is cold," she said, "and night is nigh. I will be as brief as I may, but there are words that must be said. It is plain that since Samhain much has happened to upset the balance, and we must act swiftly now, an' we are to right it."

Liannan opened her hands, and showed the palms to the sky, empty and waiting. At first Meacán thought she was waiting for someone else to speak, the Cailleach, perhaps, or a Poet. She turned to Tadhg, but a glimmer of light drew her eye past him, to the edge of the stone circle.

Gliding through the broad spaces between the standing stones came five figures, tall and proud, and burnished by the sunset's ruddy glow. When stationary the Sidhe filled every human sense to overflowing. In motion they were too much for Meacán's eyes to behold. She saw a glint of elusive silver, a gleam of gold stolen from the daystar's orb, a swath of deep, fir-green borrowed from the forests far below and carried to high Temuir by the rushing wind. The Sidhe seemed to walk in a gentle cloud of light and color, and only a soft mist marked the place where winter's air met elven flesh.

"Were the Sidhe summoned to Liannan's council?" the Dancer whispered aloud.

"Even if they were," said an amused voice in Meacán's ear, "would the Tuatha dé Danaan heed the Mother's summons unless they had reasons of their own for coming? I have attended many more councils than any of you, except Creathna, of course. But the Name-Sayer would say the same as I. Only twice in living memory have the Sidhe taken part in the Mothers' councils, though often enough they were invited."

With some effort Meacán pulled her gaze from the Sidhe and set it upon Seamair the Weather-Worker. Seamair was frowning, an expression difficult for the big, ebullient woman to make and hold.

"Their presence bodes ill for Éirinn, I fear." Seamair clucked her tongue worriedly. "Whether summoned or no, it must be the evils that trouble the five kingdoms this winter trouble the realms of the Tuatha dé Danaan as well."

And great the council Liannan has called to challenge these evils, Meacán thought to herself. Fionnghuala, Seamair, Feargna Óg, Mac Ailch, Reochaidh . . . yes, and there sat aged Creathna the Name-Sayer in a cushioned chair at the far side of the fire. All Seven Wizards of Éirinn had left their scattered Sléibhte to answer the Queen's call. The Poets were also come, Tadhg of An Chluain Thiar, and surely the saffron-robed woman on Tadhg's left was a Poet as well? She might be Scáthach of Teach an Fhásaigh herself. The Queens of the other four kingdoms were present in Liannan's thoughts, for as the Wise have said, *speak with one Mother, and speak with them all*. With Eoghan to stand for the Kings, and the Sidhe in attendance, all the Mighty of Éirinn were here met.

"Look you what a glittering assemblage the Mother has gathered to Midhe," she whispered under her breath to Tadhg as the Sidhe seated themselves around the fire.

Before Tadhg could reply, Liannan clapped her open palms together for attention.

"The first sign of our current troubles was Laochail's death," Liannan began, "on Bealtaine, the first day of summer. Alone the King went riding along the banks of An Bhóinn and was thrown from his horse. The beast fell upon him, killing him."

"Yet, Kings are born to die," said one of the Sidhe, a statuesque, golden-haired warrior clad entirely in silver mail. Meacán's heart raced just to look at her.

"Truly speaks Cessair of Cnoc an Eanaigh," answered Liannan gravely.

Meacán's eyes were not the only ones to widen, nor was hers the only chin to drop in surprise. Tadhg repeated the Name as if reciting a rann, and Feargna Óg cried out in amazement. Snatches of song ran through Meacán's mind,

tales of triumph wrested from the jaws of defeat, tales of battles won by the might of the enchanted sword Airgead, and
the courage of she who wielded it. An' the Bards sang true,
this sky-eyed, sun-haired elven woman was one of Éirinn's
greatest warriors, and had been since time before memory.

". . . only now becomes clear," she heard Liannan insist.

With a great effort of will, Meacán shifted both her sight
and attention back to the Mother.

"For Midhe, without a King, the summer was long and
luckless," Liannan was saying. "Rains fell heavily in the
moons of Hawthorn and Oak. Blossoms were stripped from
their trees before the bees could visit them, foreshadowing the
meager fruits of fall. Nor could the sacred marriage be celebrated at midsummer, and this, too, seemed to me misfortune.

"Not until Lughnasadh could a new King be chosen." The
Mother indicated the man beside her. "Victorious over all
others in the Games was Eoghan of An Mullach, now
Eoghan Rí na Midhe."

Eoghan endeavored to keep his face solemn, but his eyes
brightened and a small, proud smile touched his lips.
Meacán had heard that Laochail had died, but it was news
from far away, and soon put out of her mind. He was comely,
Laochail's successor, she admitted grudgingly, though truly,
he looked no more than a lanky, fair-haired boy. Still, there
is no telling on whom the mantle of Kingship will fall.

"Good luck and bad," said the Poet Meacán had guessed to
be Scáthach. "Both are woven into the patterns of our lives.
Times of hardship are not unknown in the five kingdoms."

"I agree, Saileach," said Liannan, smoothing her long, red
skirt against her leg, "and would not have been uneasy, had
this been all, or Midhe the only kingdom to suffer.

"Sometimes the songs do not bring the fish to the nets.
Sometimes sickness takes a child or a mother. Sometimes a
hunter is mauled by the bear. Sometimes the harvest is not
enough to see us through the winter. The gifts the Goddess
sends, whether of joy or sorrow, we must accept. But is it
Éire's hand weaving the strands of fate when goblins fight
though the moon is full? Is it Her will that the Scáileanna
drive their swords into human flesh?"

At her words the Sidhe rose in a dazzling sweep of color.

"It is for this reason we have come," cried one, a tall man

with an achingly lyrical voice. His hair was black as a raven's wing, but had a sheen that was pale moonlight on midnight waters, and his eyes burned like the stars.

"I speak for us all," he said more softly, "though I am no warrior myself. Fiach is my Name, and I am the harper of Cnoc an Eanaigh."

As he spoke, he cast his bright eyes about the circle.

"Always the Sidhe of Cnoc an Eanaigh have answered when battle called. Always our enemies have been the Scáileanna. Yet, since Samhain, our foes have scorned to meet us, instead casting their shadows over your villages. And the goblins who never before could abide the light of our eyes now strike at us when we ride, raid our hills, and despoil our groves and rings. Though we have bested them at every encounter, it is poor sport they offer us. We sicken of sullying our blades in their black blood."

Cessair came to stand beside Fiach, but still it was the harper who spoke.

"The elves of Cnoc an Eanaigh are come to Temuir to offer our service to the Mothers in this war," he said.

"War?" cried Seamair. "Is this a council of war, then?"

"If war," asked Mac Ailch quietly, "who is our enemy?"

Reochaidh shifted and bit his lip to keep from speaking, but Feargna Óg had a swift answer for the Conjuror.

"The Scáileanna, the goblins! Haven't you been attending? The Mothers may have Seen signs before Samhain, but we in the north learned of our danger then, at summer's end. First our forests filled with wild animals fleeing some terror in Cromghlinn. Next the Scáileanna attacked Béal Feirste, and still the battles rage. Then I learned through my art that goblins had destroyed An Baile Meánach."

The Necromancer made little attempt to quell the swelling pride in his voice. "And so I spoke to them, the shades of those that had fallen in the town. Though the night had been clear, and the moon bright and waxing, the goblins had come. The red-eyes indeed twined them of their lives, but not every last one, as the tale has been told. Dying, some saw their loved ones bound and dragged away."

"What?" exclaimed Meacán, and several other voices added their surprise to hers. "When have goblins ever taken prisoners?"

"When indeed?" said Liannan coldly. "Nor have the souls of An Baile Meánach's captured yet found their way to Tír na nÓg, the Land of the Young, though Feargna Óg has searched many times at our request. Either they live, prisoners of Shadow, or . . ."

Liannan hesitated, the words she had come to speak bitter on her tongue. "Or they have died under Shadow, and their souls have sated the Dead Lord's hunger."

No one spoke. No one had words to lessen the horror Liannan had evoked. Meacán shivered, the cold suddenly sharper, more penetrating than a moment before. "Eater of Souls" the Dead Lord was called, because of his incessant craving for the light of life to fill his dark, voracious hunger. Though the Goddess's black heavens were blessed, and the impenetrable depths of her seas, and the sweet, soft shades below the forests' boughs, yet the dark of Shadow, the world seen but unreflected in the Scáileanna's lidless eyes, was a realm beyond the Goddess's reach.

"But, only through the blindest ignorance or grossest folly can an unbroken soul be lost to the Dead Lord," Meacán said, somehow keeping her voice steady. "And those that serve Shadow have only the dark-moon nights and the roots of mountains to call their own, or so the Mothers have always said."

"So has it always been," answered Liannan, "but it is so no longer. We have been casting the omens since before Samhain, hoping to learn the nature of this evil. What we saw in the stones, in the waters and the fires led me to send my first messengers out from Temuir before winter was upon us."

Meacán felt a pang of guilt as she remembered that some of those messengers had come to Sliabh Mis. Had she understood the danger . . .

"What did the portents say, Mother?" Fionnghuala asked.

"They spoke of Light and Shadow," said Liannan, her voice suddenly deeper, wiser than a moment before. She was speaking not as herself, Meacán realized, nor even as Midhe, but for all the Mothers together. She was speaking as Éire. "In the spiral of every year, Light and Dark vie with each other. First one has the mastery, then the other. Though Light triumphs, still evening comes and shadows fall under the trees. Though Dark is victorious, still the new sun is born in the longest night, and the silver moon always returns. Both together, Light and Dark, making each blessed."

Night had crept quietly up from the east as Liannan spoke, but to Meacán it seemed to fall suddenly over the temple, purple and threatening. In its bruised light, the Queen's red gown appeared to stain her body with blood.

"Someone has called Shadow forth from under the eaves of the forest, from the dark caves and the hidden ways. Someone has bowed to the Dead Lord, and is even now serving his ends. Someone has opened a gate to the Shadow King's realm, and through it the Scáileanna and goblins pour out upon Éirinn."

"Who?" whispered Reochaidh.

Reochaidh's question swept like the wind through the temple. The standing stones groaned with the effort of staying upright and whole.

"Reochaidh the Destroyer has asked that which I cannot answer," said Liannan.

"Then Creathna," said Seamair, but she sounded unsure.

The old Wizard lifted his head, his eyes bleary from age and cold, and looked about. For a moment Meacán believed he had been dozing, and only roused when he heard his Name spoken, but it was an unworthy thought. Creathna was far from young, but he was no dotard.

"I must look upon a thing to Name it," he said mildly.

"Without a true Name to direct it, the most potent verse will not daunt the Darkness." Liannan turned to the Poets. "If our enemy's Name is hidden behind veils of Shadow, then you will make a poem to rend these veils. Show Creathna evil's face in the waters of my cauldron, and then will our good Wizard give us a Name, and a weapon to our hand."

Tadhg and Saileach bent their heads together. With every moment the two saffron-robed Poets sat conferring, the hope Liannan had briefly sparked flickered and waned. At last Tadhg looked to the Mother and shook his head.

"Like Creathna, our skills are best when our Sight is keen. In our own people's ears our words are mighty, and even the Sidhe honor and fear our ranna. But we have not the strength to part Shadow with our words, not an' we must pit our verses against the Dead Lord's will."

"There is one among us who may have the power to do this thing," said Saileach, "and I wonder that you did not ask her here. Scáthach of Teach an Fhásaigh is the greatest Poet in Éirinn. Ask Scáthach for this verse."

"Messengers were sent to the Poet of Teach an Fhásaigh, as they were to you," the Maiden of Midhe answered. "Those riders have not returned to Temuir, and we fear their message was never delivered."

"Can you not summon Scáthach as you did me?" asked Meacán.

Liannan shook her head. "Only with another Priestess, possessed of Sight and trained as I am, could I converse mind to mind at so great a distance. I would never have attempted so uncertain a means of reaching you had I known where to send my riders. 'Twas luck indeed you heard my message, Dancer, and only the speed with which you answered me prevented my complete exhaustion. It is folly to send messages so, with no surety that they have been received, and no means to hear the answer given."

"Yet, you must send some message to Teach an Fhásaigh," said Tadhg, "an' you will have a verse of Scáthach."

"And so I will," said the Mother thoughtfully. She turned to the Sidhe. "An' your service is truly mine, then I have a task for you."

"Ask, Lady," said Cessair, the music sweet in her voice. "My sword is at your feet."

"Ride, then. Ride tonight to Teach an Fhásaigh. No horses are faster than the Sidhe's, no one bolder in the dark of winter than Cessair of Cnoc an Eanaigh. Ride to Scáthach and beg of her this poem. Any boon, any gift she desires is hers. Will you be my messenger?"

"Five nights we have seen since the new sun was born," said Cessair, "and the Birch moon is new. Look for me again when midwinter is past, and the moon grown old. I will ride at once, and those of my folk who will come with me."

Cessair and her companions rose, and passed at once from the hill. When they were gone, Meacán found the firelight harsh and glaring, and the shadows that played against the massive granite stones taunted her with mockeries of familiar forms.

As if the Sidhe's departure had the power to break the

Conjuror's spell, the cushions and chairs that supported the Mighty of Éirinn suddenly disappeared. Tadhg sat down hard on the stone paving, but Meacán caught her balance and came quickly, if ungracefully to her feet. Feargna Óg, though unscathed, was never one to miss an opportunity to draw attention to another's failings. He rolled his eyes and sighed loudly.

"My gifts are what they are," said Mac Ailch. To his credit he sounded neither apologetic nor defensive. "I am afraid we must accept their limitations. What I bring into the world is fated to remain but a short time. I doubt I could conjure so much so soon again, but I will try, an' the Mother commands it."

"No need," said Liannan with a smile. "Cessair has her task, and we will soon hear the thunder of their ride. For the rest, I have told you what we know of Éirinn's danger. Go now, find ease and merriment in the comfort of Temuir's halls. Accept Midhe's hospitality until we have found a means to know Éirinn's enemy and our battle plans are laid. Then I will take you with me to war."

"But surely, Mother, you do not expect us to stay in Temuir all the winter?" sputtered Feargna Óg. "Let us use our spells as we see fit, against the bands of goblins and the Scáileanna that threaten Éire's people! Would we not be of more use in our homes, protecting the lands about our Sléibhte?"

A trace of anger laced Liannan's usually unruffled tone. "And when we know our enemy, and I need your craft, shall I waste days and weeks and even moons gathering you back again?"

"Yet, I will beg a boon for myself, Mother," said Mac Ailch. "The goblins in the north run rampant. Already An Baile Meánach has fallen, as the Necromancer has said. Let me go now, but I will swear to you to return by Imbolc, the Feast of Brighde."

The Queen of Midhe bent her searching gaze on Mac Ailch. Reochaidh broke in before she could respond to the Conjuror's plea, not with words, but by putting his hands together in supplication.

"Yes, I see. You all claim special privileges, you all have compelling reasons." Liannan sighed. "I should have expected this out of my Wizards. So be it. Reochaidh can be

comfortable nowhere but Sliabh Bladhma, for what other
house can hold him? Fionnghuala dwells near to Midhe, and
I will trust her to make the journey there and back again.
Yes, you as well, Feargna Óg. But I will have your word of all
of you that you will return to Temuir by Imbolc, when spring
begins to stir in Éirinn's womb, and I would have you
remember that Brighde's festival is but six weeks hence.
Seamair, I hope will stay, and Creathna. Your Sléibhte are
far, and the ways fraught with danger."

Seamair nodded. Creathna gazed into the fire abstract-
edly, but Liannan did not press him for a response. There
was no question but the Name-Sayer would remain as the
Mother's guest.

Liannan dismissed the council with a gesture toward the
lights at the base of the hill. "Go down to Temuir. Warm
yourselves in the great hall, and refresh yourself with what
food is on the board. All but you, Meacán. To you I have
more to say."

One by one the Wizards and Poets took their leave. At
last only Mac Ailch was left, and oblivious Creathna still
studying the fire.

"Come on, old man." Mac Ailch laid a gloved hand on
the Name-Sayer's arm.

Creathna turned his head and looked at the Conjuror
with child-wide eyes. "Mac Ailch?" he said, his quavering
voice turning it to a question.

"Time to go," said Mac Ailch kindly. "There are warmer
fires than this below."

Matching his step to the aged Wizard's slow shuffle, Mac
Ailch led the Name-Sayer down the now dark path to the
firelit halls of Temuir.

Eleven

The Mother to the temple, the watch to the keep,
The hunter to the forest, and the baby to sleep.

a lullaby of Laighin

Alone in the temple with the Mother of Midhe and her King, Meacán moved closer to them, feeling strangely light, remarkably balanced. It was between pride and fear she was poised, she thought, as surely as her face was hot from the fire, and her back nearly numb with the cold. She was honored to be singled out, and confident of her craft. Still, the possibility that Liannan would command her to dance to the lands of Shadow gripped her heart with suffocating strength.

Liannan looked at Meacán with an inscrutable expression for a moment, then left the fire. She wandered around the circle of stones, touching the ancient monuments with a delicate hand. It was only by following her movements that Meacán noticed that the Cailleach of Midhe had remained within the temple as well. The Old Woman stood looking into the wind with the unaffected stillness of the stones beside her.

"How old are you, Dancer?" Liannan asked.

The question took Meacán by surprise. What bearing had her age on the dire events unfolding around them?

"Twenty-two summers have I seen," she answered dubiously.

The Mother nodded. "Twice before has the White Stag run since you were born."

The White Stag. Meacán felt a fool for not thinking of the Stag before, a fool twice over for not understanding the Stag's importance even now. She waited for the Mother to go on, not wishing to sound as ignorant as she felt.

"A thread . . . a silver thread," said the Mother, almost too softly to hear. "It shimmers and weaves through the fabric of the year, and yet, when my eyes try to follow it, it twines below the dark tangle on the loom and my Sight is bewildered."

She turned from the stones and faced Meacán directly.

"Once every nine years, Éire sends Her Stag to us. From Samhain to Bealtaine he roams free in the forests and hills, invisible to most, glimpsed by a few, truly Seen by only one—the Hunter of Éirinn."

"How can the running of the Stag be part of the evil in the omens? Surely the Stag is a creature of the Light?"

"More than a creature of the Light, Meacán, the Stag is a bringer of Light. Did you never learn the Hunter's Rann as a child? . . . *The world awaits the White One's end/ At your hand*."

"I learned it, of course," Meacán began, then went on more truthfully, "but I paid little heed to it. I doubt I could recite it all now. Why does the world await the Stag's death? And what do the raids of the Scáileanna and goblins have to do with the Hunt?"

"For the first question I have only a facile answer," replied Liannan. "The killing of the Stag ensures that Éirinn will know a balance of Light and Shadow for another nine years—but in what way? I cannot say. Only the Hunter has ever witnessed the sacred elk's death. As for the connection between the rising of the Dark and the Hunting of the Light—"

She sighed wearily and leaned against a stone. Eoghan quickly spread his cloak on the ground and, smiling her thanks, Liannan came to sit beside him. She gazed into the fire, nestling her head against the King's shoulder.

"I cannot See it, I cannot comprehend it, but the connection must be there. I cannot believe this time was not deliberately chosen by the servants of the Dead Lord to call forth Shadow upon Éirinn. In the year of the Stag, when the balance of Light and Dark flies on swift hooves and hinges on the silver point of the ash Spear, someone is seeking to tip the scales to Shadow. Is it no more than that the gates between worlds are ajar while the White Stag runs between them, and evil has slipped through? Or, as my heart urges, is there some other, darker purpose hidden behind the goblins' daring and the depredations of the Scáileanna?"

"Why do you not call the Hunter to your council, Mother? Then might you find the answers you seek."

"No one can call the Hunter," said Eoghan softly, almost whispering in his Queen's ear. "He is already called."

Liannan's expression changed as she glanced at her King, as if she hadn't expected him to come up with something so apt.

"It is as Eoghan has said," she nodded to Meacán. "Do you know who this Hunter is? I do not. Eighteen years ago the Hunter of Éirinn passed through my village, and I knew her, though I was only a child. I could See the magic on the Spear she carried, and her burden, heavy on her soul. She passed on quickly, but I was brought to the Cailleach of Midhe because of what I had Seen and recognized. No, Meacán. Only by chance might we meet the Hunter of Éirinn, if our paths are fated to cross. Only by chance."

"If you do not wish me to dance through the worlds seeking the Hunter," said Meacán, allowing her impatience to show, "then—"

"Úna," said Liannan.

It was perhaps the one thing she could have said that could have silenced the Dancer.

"I sent to her already, before Samhain." Liannan sighed again, more deeply this time. "My messenger found her, but my messages did not. A whole morning my rider stood in the pouring rain humbly entreating the Oak Seer to come to Midhe, or if not to Midhe, to any Mother, to Na Connachta's Queen or Caireann in Ulaidh. Úna replied to the trees and grasses, and shared a jest with a raven, but would not hear the words I had sent. Becoming suddenly angry at some unintentional affront my messenger had given her, she stepped into a tree and would not step out again."

"Into a tree?" repeated Eoghan, saving Meacán the trouble.

"I sent to her a second time, but was even less successful than the first. Two messengers I sent out from Temuir together, one to seek Teach an Fhásaigh and the other Oak Seer's mountain, but neither did return."

"Mother," said Meacán gently, sympathetically, "why—"

"The Stag is a creature of the wild," said Liannan, an edge of determination in her voice. "Who better to ask of the wild than the Oak Seer? In this all the Mothers concur. Éirinn herself, her bones that are mountains, her blood that is the waters, her body that is the greenwood, Éirinn is in danger. The Mothers can speak for our lands, can feel for our kingdoms. But Úna speaks to the trees and the birds. Úna can See the wind."

"But, Mother," said Meacán, trying again. "Úna is mad."

Liannan's expression relaxed as if Meacán had just resolved a troublesome problem. "Mad?" she said. "Indeed she is. That is why I am sending you. What is madness to Meacán the Dancer but another world to journey in? Go to the Oak Seer, and enter her world. She will know what we cannot, of Shadows in the forest and Light on the hill. She will know of the Hunter and the Stag. Will you go?"

The Cailleach of Midhe at last turned her white head from the windy world and cast her keen gaze on Meacán. She said not a word, but Meacán felt unaccountably disconcerted. With one sharp look the old Priestess had offset all the Dancer's studied poise.

"Yes, Mother," she answered carefully. "I will go to Úna and knock on her door. But do not blame me if the tree does not open to my summons."

Twelve

Be careful with your wishes—
they may be granted

Sayings of the Mothers

Not even the cocks were awake when Meacán climbed the frosted steps that led to the top of Temuir's inner wall. The fortification had once been Temuir's outer defense, but long years of peace had seen a sprawl of cottages and stalls take root in the rich earth beneath the battlement, and generations of children grow up and old in the wall's shadow.

A stockade of sharpened poles encircled the wattle-and-daub village. The fence was more a show of pride than a necessity—Temuir had endured not only unconquered, but unassailed since time out of memory. The wooden enclosure embraced goat pens and pig sties, tiny huts and a sizable hostel. Only the linden tree in the midst of the village rose higher than the palisade, but then, it was far older and still growing. The protective stone rampart had become nothing more than a lonely balcony arbitrarily set between the Queen's halls and the villagers' crowded cotes. Meacán doubted there was a living soul in Temuir could recall when it had last been guarded by more than a token watch.

Spreading the edge of her cloak upon the time-smoothed stones, she leaned out to look upon the world. Slender tendrils of bone-white mist lifted from the shallow rivers of fog flooding the silent streets.

Her breath whistled out in a sudden cloud that matched the color of the cold mists. So careless of attack was Temuir, it had built the gate of its stockade in a direct line with the great doors of the older stone battlement. Though she had always known this was so, it was only this morning Meacán saw the folly of it. Friends entering the village were presented with a breathtaking view of the Queen's halls rising behind the high fortification, and the menhirs crowning the steep hill beyond. But should enemies pass the wooden arch, they would be presented with a straight, unhindered road to the Queen's own gates. The village would be swept away, and the folk of Temuir would be forced to trust to the forgotten strength of this cold, stone bastion to keep them safe. If evil came . . .

Through the cloth of her cloak Meacán could feel the deep chill of the weathered wall, but still she leaned upon it, shifting her gaze to study the woods beyond the village. There the mists were more animated, rising high off their winter-white earthen bed. They draped themselves on the lindens' long arms, and all but covered the thin, bare saplings in translucent, weightless gowns.

Her eyes lingered upon them, but Meacán's thoughts travelled on past the line of shrouded trees, to Cessair and her companions on their way to Teach an Fhásaigh. The noise of their departure last night had reached her as she came down the path from the temple. A rumbling, hollow sound, fierce as the wings of wild swans beating across the sky, lonely as a single cygnet's cry, swept up from Temuir, and broke like thunder upon the hill where she stood.

The rush of fear had faded almost at once, but left the exhilarating thrill of its touch. Down the broad avenue that led from Temuir's ancient stone rampart to the wooden gate the Sidhe had galloped, an untamed rush of might and magic. As they passed through the gate and rode on toward the forest, glints of silver and sparks of brilliant color had leapt from the ebon gloom of the dark woods to swell Cessair's train. Though she could not hold on to the fleeting images, Meacán's heart knew them—Cessair's companions from Cnoc an Eanaigh joining her ride, their eyes or clothes or spirits gleaming in the night.

In a moment the Sidhe had become a jewelled serpent that slithered into the black-curtained forest and disappeared. The parted wind hissed as it flew after the elves, and snapped like a whip as it came together over spiraling swirls of snow the horses' pounding hooves had tossed into the air.

Meacán frowned, envying the Sidhe their plain road through the forest. Her way was not so well marked. Liannan's messenger had journeyed to distant An Earagail mountain to find the Oak Seer, nearly as far to the north and west as one could travel in Éirinn. To Meacán, An Earagail was no more than words, a marked rise on an age-blurred map she had pored over in the grianán last night. Even had it been day and the dark room filled with sunlight, it would not have made An Earagail any clearer to her Sight. When she knew her destination, when she could See it plainly in her mind, not even the horses of the Sidhe could match the Dancer of Sliabh Mis for speed. Without a clear vision of place, without a holdfast to cling to as she danced, Meacán's feet might lead her anywhere. Or nowhere at all.

A cock crowed at last, summoning the dawdling sun to the rosy skies, and the first strand of blue smoke rose over the thatch of the village. Meacán bit her lip in annoyance, and pushed herself away from the wall. "Will you go?" the Mother had asked, as if the Dancer need only wish it and it would be accomplished.

Liannan doubtless expected more of her, but the nearest holdfast to An Earagail Meacán could envision was Dún na nGall. Her home from birth almost until she was made a Wizard of Éirinn and took up residence in Sliabh Mis, the dún was easy for Meacán to imagine in exacting detail. She brought to her mind a picture of mussel-carpeted rocks on the shore below the fort. Often she had played there, often sat on the coarse sands watching the swells. Slowly she turned in her thoughts from the sea to the land. The tides constantly shifted the line of the strand, but the dún was more permanent. She Saw the ditch that lay under morning mist in the shadow of the fort's walls, then raised her inner Sight to the pale stones of the rampart angled ever so slightly inward. Now to bring a single warrior to the wall, keeping a quiet vigil on the rough, winter seas . . .

"You will miss your time, an' you dance to that place, child."

Jarred from her spell, the Dancer spun indignantly toward the voice. Beside her on the high wall stood the Cailleach of Midhe. At once Meacán schooled her features, but cursed to herself, knowing the Old Woman had already sensed her anger.

The Priestess was a frail wisp of a woman. Deep lines etched her face and unerringly precise Sight glittered in her pale brown eyes. Her thick cloak fell open over her thin saffron gown, and the wrap's fur-lined hood was back, revealing the Cailleach's tightly knotted, pure white hair.

"Last year, perhaps, the dún looked so at midwinter, and for many years before that. Now scores of eyes watch the harbor, and the battlements all round the fort are crowded with warriors night and day."

Meacán put her hand to the wall and drummed her fingertips on the stones.

"I wish I could See the dún as you describe it, Cailleach. But my memories of the place are far different. Things have changed greatly since last I was there."

The Cailleach's gaze did not waver, and Meacán's cheeks reddened under the Old Woman's scrutiny. She dared a smile, and it was daring, for a Cailleach's Sight is keen, and it was presumptuous to try to evade it. In a Cailleach's eyes, most people stand naked, but Meacán's mother had been the Queen of Ulaidh, and now was the Cailleach of that land. With a Priestess's Sight upon her since childhood, Meacán had learned younger and better than most how to dissemble the secrets of her heart.

The Old Woman met Meacán's smile with a laugh, a girl's laugh, uninhibited and bright. She took Meacán's hand from the wall, linked arms with her, and began to stroll along the rampart.

"When I rendered the office of Mother to Liannan, I told her though my ears were growing deaf, yet I could hear everything." The Cailleach of Midhe shook her head, and her eyes seemed to cloud. "But, it's not true, my dear. Much there is I cannot hear, or See, or understand. I did not come to pry into your thoughts. I would not have spoken to you at all, but that the strength of your vision made the dún clear to me, and I felt I must caution you."

"I will heed your warning as best I can," Meacán assured

her. "But you were at the council last night—you know the journey Liannan has set before me. Where can I begin but in Dún na nGall?"

"Your journey begins here," the Cailleach corrected gently. "And from here can go in any direction. Is the dún truly your best choice, or is it that having learned of the strife surrounding the fort, you long to see for yourself how your brother fares?"

Meacán felt her cheeks warming again, and turned her face away from the Cailleach's penetrating glance. It was truth the Old Woman spoke, but a truth Meacán had tried to keep even from herself. The Old Woman laughed again, and Meacán found her resentment slipping away. Her pride was simply unequal to the Cailleach's genuine mirth.

"Why squander your worries on Niall?" the Cailleach asked peremptorily. "Your brother is a King. He glories in his battles with the Scáileanna, and should he die, a King's death can be no sorrow to his people."

She turned her eyes to the west, and Meacán looked also, though she could not begin to guess what the Cailleach Saw there. The Priestess was long silent. In the quiet Meacán considered once more the words Liannan had spoken last night. She tried to find in them another path to the Oak Seer, but if they were guideposts or directions, Meacán was not wise enough to ken them. Surely Úna, the madwoman of the wild, dwelt in no world her dances could reach.

The morning's silence was broken by the bleating of some goats wanting to be milked, and from the linden came a wren's cheery song, a breathless jingle of high trills and strident melody.

"These thoughts you pull through your mind like threads through your fingers, these are the tangled strands I brought to the wall this morning, hoping the light of day would help me See the pattern." The Cailleach shook her head. "Instead the dawn shows me a new snarl. Meacán the Dancer must find her way to An Earagail, that the Oak Seer's gifts might help us unravel the knots."

As she spoke, the Old Woman's eyes paled still more and glistened. It seemed to Meacán the Cailleach's eyes were suddenly filled with drops of pure, saltless tears that were washing away all the colored feelings that cloud the Sight.

"Need I journey at all?" Meacán whispered. "What can Úna See that the Cailleach of Midhe cannot?"

"Much," said the Old Woman shortly. "The mole I See, curled asleep in the roots of the linden, but not what day he shall awaken. The elves of Cnoc an Eanaigh I See, pausing at the ford of Áth na dTrom to refresh their horses, but not what lies ahead on the path to Teach an Fhásaigh. Shadow I See, seeping out of the dark places and crawling across Éirinn, but not the hand that has beckoned it forth.

"Midhe I See," she said, more softly, "and hear Her voice. But not the Midhe that is gone, nor the Midhe that is to come. Bring Úna to us, Dancer, for the Oak Seer's eyes look before and behind. Bring us the Sight not bound by time."

Meacán sighed, but quietly, so as not to attract the Cailleach's displeasure. The daystar now risen, the village astir, songs of morning flowing faintly down from Temuir's hill, and she unable to make even a good beginning to the unpromising journey before her.

The Cailleach no longer studied Meacán, but shifted her eyes to look over the younger woman's shoulder. Meacán turned, following the Old Woman's gaze to the steep, snow-white curve of Temuir Hill. A long while the Cailleach seemed to stare at the slope, but when she spoke, it was evident what she looked upon was far beyond the sacred mound.

"Midhe is always clear to me," she said. "The other kingdoms less so. Yet, An Earagail is high and our need great. An' I look to the wild north . . . yes, I believe I See the Goddess's breath rattling the tops of the bare-branched oaks on that broad mountaintop. Dark are the limbs, but blanketed in white. A peregrine wings by on her way to the hunt, calling out to Úna in her thin voice."

Meacán's eyes were still fixed on Temuir's hill, but it was another slope she Saw, not treeless, but thick with oaks. She heard the falcon's cry and looked up—the peregrine's ruthless, knife-sharp gaze flashed at her from a gray, cloudless sky.

"Between the aged, cracked trunks of two old oaks I look."

Another image filled Meacán's mind, the boles of deeply creviced trees. The forest the Cailleach was making her See lay far to the west of Temuir. Sunrise had not yet reached

An Earagail. The brown oaks looked nearly black in the pre-dawn shadows of the forest.

"Do you See them, Dancer? Their roots are hidden, but not all, for the snow is held back from the earth by the many arms of the trees. And there, prints in the snow, a squirrel's, yes? There he is, talking away . . ."

The Cailleach must have been speaking still, but Meacán was no longer aware of her voice. A living, moving wealth of detail filled her Sight, an image far more complex, more real than any her own mind had ever conjured. She stared through the trunks of the far-distant trees at a little, red-brown squirrel, and clucked her tongue disapprovingly. What was the foolish creature doing awake on such a cold winter morning? And not even morning yet, where he stood conversing with a snow-dusted, mossy green and gray lump of earth.

Spontaneously, Meacán shifted her weight, then stepped off onto the ball of her free foot, coming up into a smooth spin. She had finished her turn and left Temuir far behind before she thought to thank the Cailleach for the holdfast the Old Woman had given her. Too late now. The Dancer kept her eyes on the squirrel, taking three short steps forward and a quick dip.

As she rose again, onto her toes, the earthen mound beside the squirrel abruptly shifted. Its face, for it had one, turned to her. Sharp, hazel eyes regarded her with an expression so like that of the peregrine, Meacán gasped and missed her footing. As she fought to regain her balance, the Dancer glimpsed a mass of wild hair, black and white and tangled as bramble vines, escaping from under the confines of a decep-tively earth-colored shawl, an impishly pointed chin, full red lips, and a longish, straight nose. At the last moment, Meacán flung her weight forward and somehow managed two long, sliding steps and a leap. Instead of the gradual tip-toe into Úna's forest she had intended, the Dancer soared into the dark woods of An Earagail mountain, her arms stretched behind her like the wings of a stooping bird, her cloak and hood blown back, her piled hair streaming in the wind.

Thirteen

In the forest find wisdom
In your heart hold it fast
Until the time of trial comes,
And the Stag runs

The Hunter's Rann

The Dancer landed gracefully enough, and held still, allowing her vision time to adjust to the change in light. When it had, she was relieved to see her abrupt appearance had not frightened Úna away. She took a deep breath, and smiled her most charming smile in greeting. The Oak Seer watched Meacán intently, the glittering hardness of the peregrine's gaze still in her eyes.

Even as the comparison crossed Meacán's mind, the Oak Seer's look changed. She glowered, and rose with a movement more like a toad's hop than a woman coming to her feet. Her clothes swirled about her in a clash of colors, a skirt the yellow-brown of old fallen leaves, a bodice pale green as peat moss, a voluminous brown-and-black shawl shot with snow-white threads. Úna was taller than Meacán had thought, as tall as the Dancer herself. A gnarled oak walking stick was in her hand, but the Oak Seer did not lean on it even slightly.

"Well?" Úna demanded. Her voice hissed angrily, like a strong wind through the reeds. "Well? Aren't you coming to visit me?"

Meacán endeavored to keep her tone as amicable as her smile. "Yes, I have come to visit you, Oak Seer. I am—"

Úna crumpled into an irritated heap on the ground, losing much of her human appearance and taking on something of a hedgehog's prickly roundness.

"She's not coming," she said grumpily to the squirrel, who had inexplicably remained where he was during Meacán's unexpected arrival and the Oak Seer's brief outburst.

"I have come, Úna," said Meacán, more patiently. "I am here."

"The goose won't be able to hear a word I say from that distance." The Oak Seer looked suddenly forlorn, and sounded like she was about to cry.

"I can hear you perfectly," Meacán assured her. "But I'll come even closer if you wish me to."

The Seer looked up, and now her face was crafty, like a ferret's. "Will you?" she asked. "Och, do come to me. Do."

"Of course," said Meacán, pleased to have found a way to make friends.

She had taken only one step forward when Úna threw her head back and howled like a wolf. Exactly like a wolf. Though Meacán could see the sound came from Úna's throat, still her heart beat faster and the hair lifted on her arms and at the nape of her neck. The Oak Seer's warning descended into laughter, and Meacán was left tense and flustered, unsure whether to try to move forward again or not.

"You've missed the path," said Úna, stifling her mirth with great effort.

Taking the Seer's taunt as an invitation, Meacán dared another step. She was treated to the same blood-chilling performance as before.

"If you want me to come nearer, you must stop trying to scare me off!" Meacán exclaimed, forgetting her resolution to be polite.

"Nearer, goose. Nearer. But you're going the wrong way."

"I'm not. I'm coming right toward you."

As if Meacán hadn't heard her the first time, Úna raised her voice. "You're going the wrong way!"

"*By the light that shines!* Look where I am! I'm—"

"Not a word," said the Oak Seer sadly. She was speaking to the squirrel.

Meacán clamped her lips together. A waste of time entirely to try to reason with the madwoman. Best deliver

Liannan's message as quickly as possible and hope some good would come of it.

"I am Meacán Iníon na Caillí, the Dancer of Sliabh Mis," she began. "I am come from Liannan, the Mother of Midhe—"

"We all come from our mothers," Úna nodded sagely.

"—with her wish that you—"

"Have I all morning to wile away in gossip? How she dallies!" the Oak Seer whispered loudly to the squirrel. She patted her lap, and in a streak of red fur, the creature came to sit upon it. "Tell her what you told me, darling," Úna coaxed. "Go on. Don't be shy."

"—her wish that you might come to Midhe—" Meacán faltered.

Rising up on his hind legs, the red squirrel began declaiming his own message in short, agitated barks. He made a great racket, and Úna gave the little beast her full attention, even nodding and making sympathetic noises when the squirrel occasionally paused. At last the squirrel fell silent. The Oak Seer turned to Meacán with an ingenuous smile.

"You see?" she said. "Now hurry along, goose. No more dawdling."

Meacán's own smile had long since vanished.

"I don't see," she said flatly. "I don't understand the language of squirrels. And it's not to hear them I've come, but to beg you hear me."

Úna cocked her head, like a dog listening. Meacán entertained a fleeting hope that the Oak Seer was finally ready to concentrate on the Mother's words. The next moment the sound Úna was really attending to reached Meacán's ears. A rustling rose from the thickets on the slope below them, and quickly grew as loud as distant thunder. Coming suddenly up between the trees, a small herd of fallow does ran across the top of the hill, surrounding Úna in a pounding blur of dusky brown. When they had passed over the rise and down the far side of the mountain, the Oak Seer was gone.

The squirrel was still there, perched on an overgrown stump. Meacán stepped close to the furry creature, but her eyes were on the old broken trunk. Hesitantly, she reached out her hand to it. Her fingers confirmed what her sight told her. A tree stump now sat where the Oak Seer had been. What was it Liannan had said? That her messenger had given

up when Úna had stepped into a tree and refused to come out?
Meacán had thought the Mother meant that Úna had opened
some sort of door into a tree and walked through it, but that
wasn't it at all. The Oak Seer had truly "stepped" into a tree,
and now had "squatted" into a stump. Úna was a shape-shifter.

"Oak Seer," she called desperately, "I've come as near as I
can to you. Won't you hear what I have to say?"

A broad shaft of golden light broke through the trees and
spread a smooth path between the heavens and the mountaintop. Dawn had come to An Earagail, but the new day brought
Meacán no cheer. Liannan's previous messenger had managed
to spend a whole morning engaged in incoherent, aimless dia-
logue with Úna before the Seer had ended their meeting by
taking another shape. As an embassy from the Mother,
Meacán was proving even less successful than the last.
Meacán was tempted to dance up the sunbeam road and away
from the mute and motionless stump, but it galled her to
admit defeat so soon. Not the service she owed the Mother,
but her own stubborn pride kept Meacán where she was.

"Úna," she said again, then stopped.

Liannan had said something else, something about Úna's
madness—a world for Meacán to journey in? Why, the Seer
herself might be saying precisely that when she urged
Meacán to come nearer, and faulted her for going the wrong
way! But in what world do stumps of rotting oak become
human? What dance could take her to a place where Úna's
words would make sense? And what could she make her
holdfast in a realm she had never Seen?

As the sun rose higher, the long swath of daylight thinned
and disappeared. Meacán stood unheeding, pondering her
dance. An image of Úna could not guide her—Meacán might
well become lost if the Seer shifted her appearance again.
Yet, for an instant, when she had stepped away from the
Cailleach on Temuir's wall and toward the squirrel on An
Earagail's peak, hadn't the mound of earth turned to look at
her? Hadn't Úna's remarkable, birdlike glare fallen on her
even as she danced? How had Úna Seen her, unless they had
somehow shared a world for that moment, in the dip and spin
and soar of Meacán's journey to An Earagail's woods?

Slowly, carefully, Meacán began to move around the stump,
seeking again the path that had brought her to the Seer. In her

dance to An Earagail she had of necessity kept her Sight trained on the mountaintop. Now she tried to recapture the images that had flowed by as she danced, images of field and forest, loch and stream, of bird and beast, flower and fern, hoping to See the place where she and Úna had touched and met.

Meacán's foot scratched the hard dirt like a magpie's claw, her chin jutted forward like a tusked boar's. One arm swatted the air like a bear cub pawing a sibling, the other lay flat against her side as her torso swayed in the swift shimmy of a fish through water. She completed one circuit around the stump and began another, changing her steps and her gestures with every moment. Her hands opened like blossoming buds, she shook her head so her hair swayed like sea moss, then swept her tresses back so they flew like the wind. By the end of her third circle around the stump, Meacán no longer felt ridiculous in her dance. She no longer cared that her patchwork of movement must make her seem some fabulous monster, a storyteller's bizarre concoction of familiar creatures invented to shock an audience. She became so engrossed in weaving the disparate qualities of animal and plant, of weather and earth into an harmonious pattern, she nearly forgot the reason for her dance. An autumn leaf, blown from its tree and turning in the wind, Meacán spun away from the stump, her smile wide as a fox's grin, her eyes closed tight as a mole's. Next instant she faced the stump again, but it wasn't the stump. It was Úna, sitting on her haunches and studying the Dancer with deep, tranquil eyes.

The red squirrel was perched on Úna's shoulders, but he was just one of many creatures, fluttering, slinking, peering from the living folds of the Oak Seer's garments. Not the colors of the forest, but the forest itself clothed Úna in a cloud of yellow grasses and bare wood, fur and feather. Fairy folk dressed in red and green peeped out from behind her leafy skirt. Úna's gentle doe eyes never left Meacán, but the Dancer's gaze followed a fairy woman's pointing finger, down Úna's arm, wreathed in almost leafless bramble vines. Eventually her sight came to rest on Úna's fingers. They were long, and seemed old, for they were knotted as twigs where they lightly caressed the huge, living trunk of a great oak tree. Meacán looked fully on the tree, and moaned.

It was the mother of oaks, the Queen of the forest. With

the vision of it came the song of the broad-branched, earth-drinking, heaven-piercing giantess. Meacán longed to hear nothing else, but the mountain rang with the voices of the oak-mother's many tree-children, and those beasts living on Úna made so much noise! Meacán reproved them all, commanding them to be quiet; they laughed at her, and the wind carried her words away, and hung the syllables of her sense on the forest's brown-barked, white-cloaked arms.

"They're coming, they're coming," cried the squirrel worriedly.

The creature's voice cut through the deep singing of the oak and the sighing wind. Meacán's ears hurt from the din. She covered them, but the unceasing riot of life and death made her very fingers throb. Pungent scents of wet and rotting mulch, of wind-cleansed snow and tree-blood burned in her nostrils and flamed in her lungs. And the earth beneath her was spinning, spinning—

Meacán flung out her hands, grasping frantically at the chaotic world for something to cling to, for something that would keep her from flying off the mountain. Her fingers touched the oak tree, and she dug her nails into the bark. Long branches embraced her, deep roots anchored her. She was safe, she was safe. Gratefully she laid her head against the tree-mother's trunk. The oppressive weight of the heavens slipped from her shoulders to the sturdy tree, and the fire within the earth moved away from the soles of her feet as if the oak had called the flames to its buried roots.

". . . too close," one of a myriad of voices said in her ear. "Step back, silly goose. Now you've come too near."

"They're coming, they're coming," repeated the squirrel. "Soon here."

Meacán heard hysterical laughter, and thought it strangely out of place in the unbounded carol of the wild. The laugh ended abruptly, and suddenly she was crying and her cheek hurt.

"Step back, Meacán Iníon na Caillí, Dancer of Sliabh Mis," said the voice again, a beautiful voice, patient and comforting, a terrible voice, merciless and commanding. "You are too near."

Meacán looked furtively about. At first she could see nothing but the oak. Slowly her eyes focused on a woman, tall as a young sapling, proud as an antlered stag, ageless as Éirinn. Untamed Sight glowed in the Lady's eyes. Meacán cried out when it fell on her, for it scalded her heart like

steam and burned like ice in her thoughts. Looking down
she saw a fox darting away from the Lady, stealing the red
and white of his tail from her skirt.

"Can't step back!" Meacán said earnestly. "Can't let go.
The rolling world! I must hold on!"

She pulled herself closer to the oak, hugging it, trying to
wrap her arms around it. Unsympathetically, the woman
pried Meacán's fingers loose, and pulled on her shoulder to
separate her from the tree.

"Stop!" wailed Meacán.

Suddenly she had nothing to steady her, nothing to shield
her from the terror and ecstasy of the world. She fell away
from the tree, blinded by the colors of the forest, deafened by
the power of its voice. She fell, and screamed, and uncon-
sciously, instinctively began to dance.

Her fall became a smooth spin on the solid earth. The
doors of her senses, thrust fully and unwillingly open, now
closed, not entirely, but enough that she could take in the
colors and sounds of the world without losing her reason.

Trembling from head to foot, and flushed and hot despite
the cold winter air, Meacán looked around with extreme caution, moving only her head. The Oak Seer waited a few paces
away. She had shrunk once more to human size and was
clothed again in unliving garments. Even so, there was something not quite human about the Oak Seer and something
excessively alive about her attire. Her clothes were not sewn
from woven cloth, but pieced together from plaited grasses,
furs, and hides. Her shawl was made entirely of feathers, and
there was a rope of vine about her waist. The creatures Meacán
had seen crawling and fluttering about the Seer were gone, but
the squirrel remained, curled against the Oak Seer's neck. The
thing chittered. Though Meacán understood the warning in the
squirrel's tone, she was glad to discover she heard no words.

The magnificent oak tree that had stood beside Úna was
gone as well, and so too, the walking stick that had been in
the Seer's hand when Meacán first arrived on An Earagail.
Úna now held a tall, oaken staff. Whorls of growth from long-
forgotten seasons when it had been the heart of a tree stood
out like dark threads against the blonde grain of the wood.

Gradually Meacán shifted her hips and shoulders to align
with her head.

"Is this . . . Am I . . ." Meacán took a deep breath and forced herself to ask a coherent question. "Will we understand each other here?"

Úna shrugged.

Though her eyes could now take in her surroundings without sending her mind reeling, Meacán was clearly not in the world where she had first met Úna. The colors of sky and wood were deeper, clearer than she had ever known. The crisp air was laden with scents and sounds, and all of them were gravid with secrets. If only she could catch their meaning, she was sure she would know where the wild hare was hiding, where the merlin meant to stoop . . . but she must gather all her wits, all her craftiness and stealth, for there were others abroad in the wood, creatures with eyes to spy her, and ears to hear—

"In your Éirinn I am a madwoman," Úna said softly. "In mine, it is you who are mad. Now you stand between the worlds, upon a threshold only the hunters dare cross. And if they are cunning and canny and wise in the ways of the forest, then they bring death to the wild, and return to their own kind with life. But if they are clumsy and careless, if they are fools, then the wild brings death to them, and takes their life. This the only dance I know—has Meacán Iníon na Caillí, the Dancer of Sliabh Mis, come to join the ring?"

Answer her, Meacán told herself sternly. A whole speech, all of it sensible. Answer her.

"I've come at the Mothers' bidding, Oak Seer, to seek your wisdom and entreat your help in these times of trouble."

"In the forest find wisdom . . . so the Rann goes. But you are no Hunter. My wisdom is not for you."

"No hunter." Meacán stumbled over her words in her hurry to find the ones that would keep Úna talking. "No hunter am I. But it is of the hunter, the Hunter of Éirinn, the Mothers would know."

The Oak Seer looked at the Dancer with the veiled, disdainful look of a wild cat. "The Mothers would know? You know. But you know only this one. I have known them all."

"I? I know what? The Hunter?"

The fragile lucidity that had linked her to the Seer was rapidly crumbling. As it fell, Meacán's awareness of her danger grew. Let the hunters come to this threshold an' it pleased them. Let them cross to where their lives depended upon their daring and craft, upon the sharpness of their eyes and ears, upon their strength and swiftness and silence. Let them join Úna's ring, where the slightest misstep could mean their deaths—Meacán wished only to dance on safer ground.

"Come to the Mothers, then," she begged, speaking quickly, but articulating carefully. "Tell them of the White Stag and the Hunter. Let them See, as you do, how the Hunting of the Light is tangled in Shadow's designs. I entreat you come, Úna, and bring the wisdom of the forest to the Queens' councils."

"To the Queens' councils!" spat Úna, striking the end of her staff on the ground. "To walk on enslaved stones, to eat butchered meat, to listen to the drivel of domesticated beasts!"

Meacán stepped back from the Oak Seer's vehemence, then caught herself, afraid of where movement might take her. Simply keeping her balance on this narrow threshold demanded all her concentration, all her strength. Like a wild wind, the power of Úna's domain beat on her, wearing her down. She mustn't weaken—she must heed every sound, every scent, or the wind would pluck her from this gate and toss her into the heart of the forest. There she would surely die, for she was like the harnessed beasts and the walled towns Úna so loathed. She was tame, and the Wild would devour her.

She met Úna's eyes, and they were red as a raging boar's.

"This your reply, Oak Seer? Can you believe the evils that threaten the five kingdoms will leave the wild in peace? An Earagail, and all the mountains and forests of Éirinn will lie under Shadow if—"

While Meacán was speaking the red squirrel ran to the lip of the hilltop. Suddenly he turned and barked three times, whipped his tail anxiously, then darted away down the far side of the mountain.

"They are almost here," whispered Úna. "So listen well, goose. But one evil threatens Éirinn. Two pursue the Stag, and only one is called."

Meacán's mind raced. "Who is this false hunter, Úna?"

"When Spell-Maker's star shines / When silver bites stone—"

The Oak Seer broke off and shot a glance to the edge of the hilltop swift as a spider's pounce.

"Yes?" Meacán urged. "What will happen? How will these things come to pass?"

"That's what I told her."

"Told whom?"

Úna laughed and shook her head as if Meacán had asked her question in jest.

"The magpie. The magpie, silly goose."

It was gone, that brief moment, that window of clarity through which Meacán had discerned the meaning of the Seer's words. Standing in the hunters' footsteps, she could hear the squirrel's alarm and the wind's song in the trees, she could feel the tension in the wood, and faintly smell the sickly odor that inspired it—yet, for all she could understand, Úna's speech was senseless, her partial prophecy and disconnected intimations just so much noise. Meacán's last shred of patience shriveled like a wood shaving tossed onto glowing embers.

"Can you be a stump?" Úna asked conversationally. "No? Reaching roots and feeding mosses are tricky. A stone, then. We'll be stones and they'll never see us."

Even as she spoke a slow change came over Úna. Her body remained a woman's, her face and hands and hair all maintained their form and structure. Yet, a stillness, a solidity seemed to come into her limbs, starting at her feet and spreading slowly up through her torso.

"Let them fall," said Úna, her tone deeper and sleepier than before. "Let them all fall. Only the Hunt matters. Yours and his."

"Let what fall, Úna?" Meacán asked hopelessly. "Mine and whose?"

A stillness at once wholly unnatural for human limbs, yet completely natural for granite or marble stiffened Úna's arms and shoulders. She spoke once more before the magic consumed her utterly, in a voice soft and crooning as a lullaby.

"A little bay there is where the moon sets over the Mother of Lakes. A low ridge, and beyond it, the glen, where tall were the pale-leaved beeches and bright the stars they wore in their hair. But no more, no more. Dark are the nights and empty the woods. They have all fled, the children of the forest, fled the thorns that would have trapped them.

"We'll meet at Márrach," was the Oak Seer's final word before dull curtains of gray fell over her open eyes.

At that same moment the faintest drumming of hooves echoed below. The sound faded, and all was quiet again. Meacán began to wonder if she had imagined it when the rippling snort of a winded horse reached her ears. More warnings—feathered wings taking flight from the branches above and the scent of fear emanating from the wood—Meacán was suddenly sure riders were nearing, and was equally sure she should be terribly afraid of them. The messages of the wild were plain to her as they had never been before, explicit and compelling.

"Seer," she whispered, "your skin is gray, you are hard and quiet and breathless as stone. But you are Úna, the Oak Seer still. I can see you. They will see you!"

Not a hint of expression glinted in Úna's unblinking eyes. Her skin and clothes blended perfectly with An Earagail's hues, her feet seemed embedded in the cold earth. With a chill that reached deep into her soul, Meacán realized that however long she stood pleading with the Oak Seer, she would receive no human response, but only a stone's answer. She had been wrong to think the Oak Seer a shape-shifter. It was her blindness had made her see Úna differently. In truth she was always Úna, but only the eyes of the wild could always perceive her so.

The riders were close now, the thunder of their shod horses on the mountainside louder than the hooves of the fallow deer had been. Meacán could no longer delay. She looked quickly about and her eyes fell on a thick yew bush. The deep green needles seemed almost to beckon her, promising the best concealment the mountaintop could offer. In two smooth steps she had crossed worlds, off the hunters' threshold, and into the Éirinn she knew best. The yew stood in this world too, and there she hid, curiosity winning out against her fears.

Black horses topped the rise. The dark elves on their backs drove their heels into their foam-streaked, wild-eyed mounts. Swiftly, as swiftly as Meacán saw them, the Scáileanna's empty eyes flew to the yew. Before the scream in her chest could reach her lips, Meacán brought an image of the storeroom behind Dún na nGall's kitchen to her mind. Clinging to her holdfast with her thoughts, she danced away from An Earagail while the Scáileanna were still turning their horses' heads.

What stuck with her as she fled, nearly nudging aside the image she had chosen, was not the slate-gray, emotionless faces of the Scáileanna as they beheld her. It was the small boulder they looked past, not sparing it a glance. Tall as a squatting woman it sat, green lichens mottled its gray surface, and a net of brambles topped it like a mop of unruly hair.

PART 4

the sidhe

Fourteen

A limb of lightning-struck ash
A point of pure-wrought silver
Such the Spear to slay the Light
And no other

The Hunter's Rann

Blackthorn ducked as the Scáil's blade, gray as the hand that wielded it, parted the air over his head, then returned for his throat. Stumbling back, he felt a thin line of fire sting his neck below his left ear. The dark elf stepped carefully through the deep snow, attacking with an air of mild impatience, as if Blackthorn were already dead, and his attempts to deny it mere insolence. The second Scáil kept at a slight distance, leaving his companion ample room for his swordplay, but his own weapon was drawn and his imposing height always between the Hunter and the path to Béal an Átha Móir. Steadily his attacker's vicious, gray blade forced Blackthorn up and under the dark firs of Binn Chuilceach. He had no choice but to retreat, though he knew the Scáil would soon have him with his back to a tree and nowhere to run.

The dangling needles of a snow-bent branch brushed the top of the Hunter's head. He cursed his thoughts for coming true, but did not dare take his eyes from the threatening sword before him. Again the Scáil lunged. Jumping back, Blackthorn reached to the overhanging limb and pulled it

violently down. Mounded snow tumbled from the branch,
covering the Scáil in a cold shroud of white.

With an angry hiss the second Scáil leapt forward.
Blackthorn had already turned and was fleeing the only way
open to him, up the steep slopes of Binn Chuilceach. He
climbed as swiftly as he could, but the storm made the
woods treacherous, and in their treachery they allied with
the Scáileanna. The firs bent near to breaking in an effort
to block his path and swept their sharp-needled arms
painfully against him. The wind roared in the tossing pines,
hurling snow from the treetops to mingle with the falling
sleet. If the hard earth of the mountain could have reared
up and bucked the Hunter off its slippery incline, he had no
doubt it would have done so.

Blackthorn again turned west into the wind, trying to
make his way across the face of the mountain. If he could
get past the place where the Scáileanna had attacked him
and then return to Binn Chuilceach's base, he might set his
feet once more on the path to Béal an Átha Móir. Not that
he could be sure the track to the village would protect him
now he had fallen from it. Certainly no tale told of dark
elves daunted by a path regained. The Lore-Songs taught
that once in the Scáileanna's domain, only might or magic
could deny them their due. A King's strength or a Wizard's
sorcery he needed to save his life, but Blackthorn possessed
neither. Sanctuary was the best he could hope for. Binn
Chuilceach's corrupted heights offered none.

The gale tore deadwood loose from its moorings and
hurled it in the Hunter's path. Sleet hammered through the
forest's rolling green roof, blinding him and scoring the flesh
of his face and hands. And the stiff shadows of the
Scáileanna were ever below him, threading easily through
the tangled trees. Descent was impossible—he forced his
way up once more, though his feet slipped on the unkind
ground, and growing darkness deepened the shadows of the
storm-blackened woods.

Faintly at first, almost too faintly for him to credit his
ears, the Hunter began to hear words on the howling wind.
He struggled on, unheeding, until the voices were as loud as
the groaning trees. His weary legs slowed, he leaned, gasping, against the unwelcoming trunk of a larch to listen.

Rhythmic, continuous, what he heard was a chant—strange syllables wrapped in weird, discordant harmonies. The language was unknown to him, but the message was clear. *Wait,* sang the Scáileanna. *Wait for us. Nowhere can you flee, nowhere can you hide. There is no hope for you. Wait for us,* they called, and the Hunter's racing pulse beat in time to the spell.

A sudden, brilliant streak of lightning illuminated the southern face of the mountain and Teach an Fhásaigh nestled against its foot. He saw the Scáileanna creeping sure as spiders up the slope behind him. Their gray skin and dark raiment would have made them indistinguishable from the sleet-thickened air and the boles of the trees, but while the trees could only lash about in their efforts to pursue him, the Scáileanna's long, angular outlines rose unerringly up the mountainside, and their voices never faltered.

Just before the light was gone, the Hunter turned to look ahead. He was near the edge of the trees and within sight of a rocky ledge hanging like an open cockleshell on Binn Chuilceach's slope. Brief though the vision was, it lifted Blackthorn's heart. He knew the place.

As the thunder rolled, the storm-hidden sun fled the world, bringing unrelieved darkness upon Binn Chuilceach. Even so, the Hunter dared the slippery ground between the trees and the spur of rock, running, for he could still see the ledge clearly in his mind—an uneven stone floor jutting out from the steep angle of the earth, and rising above it, a vertical granite wall wedged into the slope. Commanding the ledge from the top of the high scar, a blackthorn tree sent sinuous roots cascading down the exposed rock face. Sweet grasses Blackthorn had once brought to this very spot, and newly opened flowers and supple willow branches to build a bower for Scáthach. Here they had come, here celebrated the amorous rites of Bealtaine night and welcomed summer in. Here he had heard the Stag call his Name, and here become the Hunter of Éirinn. Magic and power had once filled this place under the blossoming branches of the fairy tree. If any yet lingered, perhaps all was not lost.

He came to where the rocky bones of the mountain lay exposed to his touch, and the shelf jutted over his head. Slush and mud ran off the stony floor, but Blackthorn ignored the icy rivulets and hauled himself onto the ledge. Rising, he took five quick strides to the stone wall at the back of the shelf. There he stretched out his hand, seeking the blackthorn's roots, or purchase for his fingers. The rock face was smoothed by a glaze of ice, and he knew the tree's winding roots only by the shape of the hardened crystal sheaths that encased them.

Lightning dove down to Binn Chuilceach from above, striking somewhere on the far side of the mountain. Lifting his eyes as the harsh light again showed him the world, Blackthorn beheld an apparition of death at the top of the wall, the stark skeleton of a lifeless tree, a few bare limbs still reaching into a black sky, the rest broken and hanging in defeat from the tree's splintered trunk.

Thunder and grief broke over him together. Both shook him to the marrow of his bones. He had been a fool to hope. Doubtless the fairy tree had been the first to suffer when the Scáileanna overran Binn Chuilceach. Doubtless its spirit had been the first to die.

When the echoes of the thunder had disappeared down the mountain into Teach an Fhásaigh, the dark elves' song came to him louder, stronger than it had before. The rhythm beat on Blackthorn like drums, the warped harmonies twisted his disappointment to despair. It was madness to believe he could elude them, but certain death to wait for the Scáileanna here, with his back to an insurmountable wall. He felt his way along the rock face, trying to remember how far it was from the open ledge to the comparative cover of the trees.

Another burst of flame from the furious heavens destroyed Blackthorn's last fragile hope of escape. Five Scáileanna stood on the edge of the shelf, surrounding him in an impassable semicircle of shadow. Untouched by the lightning's sudden fire, five pairs of dark eyes gazed at him in cold, pitiless triumph.

A chill breath, not of wind, but of defeat, caressed Blackthorn. Its touch was brief, but under it he passed from desperation, through terror, to a singular, dispassionate relief. A willingness to make this storm-wracked ledge his place of death took hold, and steadied him. Only his unfulfilled geis brought any reluctance to Blackthorn's heart, but even this was more a passing regret than a reason to go on. Full circle he had come. Born the Hunter on the high slopes of Binn Chuilceach, here he would die the Hunter, and stain the pale stones red with his blood.

Idly, he dropped his hand to the pouch at his belt, but was not surprised to find it empty. Often it was said, and truly, that Death must be faced alone. The cowardly shape-shifter was wisely fled, though his geis, too, would now never be fulfilled. The púca would someday bear a broken soul into eternity, as this night must Éire's Huntsman.

Taking his fingers from his pouch, Blackthorn undid the strap that held his Spear to his back, and took the sacred weapon to his hand. No longer did he strive to close his ears to the dark elves' chant. He listened intently as Death sang to him with the Scáileanna's merciless voices. The chant drove up and on like a scream, then dropped suddenly as if into an unfathomable abyss, only to climb again. Once, long ago, watching a falcon stoop to a dove, the Hunter had imagined his own death would come winging, swift and beautiful and wild as the hawk. He smiled now, remembering his innocence.

A few graceful notes trickled through the tortured melody of the Scáileanna's spell and caught Blackthorn's ear. He had dreamed them, surely. Or worse, they were some cruel deceit his enemies had devised.

Lilting, unadorned, yet achingly deep, the song persisted. Words sprang unbidden from Blackthorn's mind to marry themselves to the tune, and suddenly he knew what magic it was flowing from the worlds beyond the terrible threshold before him to keep him company on Binn Chuilceach. No dream, no new cruelty, the music was a gift. His Death-Song had come to him, unexpectedly, for all that Larkspur had promised it would be there waiting when he reached the final gate. More than once Blackthorn had thought himself near death, but never had inspiration come. Now it burst upon his heart, its power drowning out the Scáileanna's insistent litany of hopelessness and surrender.

Quietly and evenly, Blackthorn began to sing. The song flowed from him and carried on the wings of the gale to the ears of his enemies.

I loosed my hope like a desperate arrow
To Éirinn that I love.

My cry was lost in the sea that greets the cliffs fiercely,
Caught by the wind in the bare-branched thorns,
Flown on rooks' wings over the hills.
It fell with the mists, and burned in the fires.
Oh, Lady, send a sad song,
Sing me Home, Sing me Home.

The Dead Lord is come with his hounds about him.
They ring me close and bay
To Gods of fear and despair. They chant my doom darkly.
I am lost in a land rife with pitiless foes,
But high is the road that leads to life's end.
To Death must I yield, but not to defeat.
Oh, Lady, send a glad song,
Sing me Home, Sing me Home.

Silence, save for the wailing wind, greeted the end of his song. Blackthorn smiled into the dark promise of the night. Having sung his Death-Song, death no longer frightened him. He welcomed it as he would a brother, as he would a lover.

His eyes could not help him, for sight was possible only when bolts of lightning ripped through the clouds. It was instinct, honed over the years to sense the shifting of the sparrow in her nest in the high branches of the elm, the pale eyes of the wolf watching from the autumn-browned ferns, instinct told him of the Scáileanna's approach. Drawing his dagger with his left hand, Blackthorn shifted the Spear until it was balanced in the palm of his right.

Had the Scáileanna come swiftly, he would have hurled the Spear at the first glimpse of a gray-skin his night-poor vision detected. They came slowly, savoring their victory. The weight of the shaft in Blackthorn's hand nagged at his spell-clouded mind, bringing forth the geis he had already consigned to the past. Not for these, not to pierce the dark heart of Shadow, but for the White Stag's heart had the Spear been made.

With a cry even his own ears could not hear above the storm, Blackthorn cast the silver-pointed shaft, but not at the Scáileanna. Turning his back to his nearing death, he hurled the Spear toward the blackthorn tree.

Double blasts of fire streamed from the sky, one striking

Binn Chuilceach near its peak, the other diving into the valley below. Blackthorn was still staring upward, following in his mind the Spear's final flight, when the lightning turned the blackthorn tree white. He saw no shaft winging to the sky, but instead a long, heavy branch of the fairy tree hurtling down. Into his waiting palm it fell, and the darkness closed again over Binn Chuilceach.

As the thunder died away, Blackthorn heard the whisper of metal against leather, a sword slipping its sheath. He sent his knife flying through the night before the Scáil's blade was fully drawn. A high-pitched moan like a woman's sigh answered the dagger's blind journey, and the Hunter brought the blackthorn limb into both his hands.

The wood was unusually straight and smooth for blackthorn, and one end substantially thicker than the other. It should have made a perfect club, but when Blackthorn grasped its tapered length, it felt wrong, as if the branch were slipping from his hands. Beyond reason, without time to consider, he gripped the heavier, knobbed end of the limb and swung with all his might at the close night.

The blackthorn rent the empty air, then struck against flesh and bone. The enveloping darkness erupted into light. The Hunter shied away from the sudden, blinding brilliance, and a terrible cry sounded in his ears. He saw three armed shadows standing near the edge of the shelf, frozen in the flash. The light flickered, dying, but the Scáileanna came no closer. Waiting for the dark, Blackthorn guessed, but the thought did not dismay him.

A smile played about his lips, more rapturous by far than the serene expressions that touched the dark elves' mouths. Bound in a spell of his own making, he yearned for the death that threatened him and revelled in the blood shed achieving it. Hurling a curse into the Scáileanna's masklike faces, he dared them on.

Again darkness engulfed the shelf. Blackthorn waited, too fey to question his enemies' hesitation. The scrape of a boot on stone brought his tree limb arcing to the right. This time it struck metal, and both wood and sword rang as they came together. Again and again the Hunter swung into the darkness, each blow countered by the Scáil's keen-edged sword and keener vision.

The dark elf's blade whistled as it descended toward Blackthorn's head. His wooden club met and held it, but a searing pain cut across his side. He thrust back on the sword that pressed against his blackthorn, felt the Scáil behind it stumble and his weapon drop. In a haze of pain and fury he spun about, swinging blind in hopes of striking the enemy who had wounded him.

Lightning split the heavens directly over Binn Chuilceach as his weapon drove into the Scáil's side with jarring impact. He did not see the heaven-born fire plunge to earth, but it must have, for his foe was flames one moment and smouldering bones the next. The thunder clap was immediate and deafening, and shook the rock floor beneath Blackthorn's feet. He turned unsteadily. By the afterglow of the Scáil's charred remains, he saw a dark elf on the ground with a dagger in his throat, and but two others still standing. Both were backing away.

"Come," he invited, trying to put welcome in his voice. He failed, unable to sound anything but menacing through his clenched teeth. "Come to me. I am waiting as you asked."

The stink of burnt flesh fired Blackthorn's bloodlust still more, but his Death would not be lured. The Scáileanna continued to retreat, their dusky features mingling with the encroaching darkness.

"Curse your evil eyes, come and fight!" he shouted.

Reeling like a drunken man, Blackthorn staggered after his inconstant foes. Though his side was warm where blood was flowing, the rest of his body felt cold as the death he sought. He came to the edge of the shelf, but the Scáileanna were gone. Roaring his frustration, he set out after them.

As Blackthorn slipped and fell down the mountain's precarious slopes, another song came to him. Not a Bard-Song of power, just an ordinary song, a warrior's lay. He sang it to the storm as he hunted his elusive Death through the forests of Binn Chuilceach.

Fifteen

The Bard of An Dubh-Linn mourned her love
Keening her death
In a voice like a dove's.
But each note sung was a piece of her heart,
Broken by Bard-Song
By grief torn apart.

The Bard's Lament

The shadows that pulled back from the shell-shaped ledge had little in common with the natural darkness of storm cloud and night. As they passed by the púca, a huddled ball of wet fur in a rocky niche not ten paces from the protruding lip of the spur, the mouse whimpered, though he was striving with all his might to be silent. Then they were gone, and only the black gale remained. After the terror of the dark elves, the púca found himself quite willing to endure the howling winds and thrashing branches of the pines. Alive, whole, he would gladly have come out of hiding, if not for the Hunter.

"Curse your—" and "—fight!" were all that had recently reached the púca's ears, but it was enough to keep him cowering in the stone's hollow. Arrah, the fool should have stayed with the simple tunes, an' he a Bard. Himself of all humans ought to have known what would happen an' he sang a true Bard-Song. It was in the tales, it was, what becomes of Bards who drink from the Poets' cup. There was the Bard of An Dubh-Linn who sang a lament so sad, didn't

it break her heart and she die? And the Love-Song so potent
it sent its singer into a frenzy that put a stag's rut to shame?
When the púca had heard that tale sung in An Ómaigh,
he'd laughed so hard the tinkers had gaped at the mouse in
the corner of the hall, and would have spat at him had they
been less drunk or he slower in slipping away. But the
Hunter, he was nothing to laugh at. His Death-Song he'd
sung up there on the ledge, and now death was all he longed
for.

A handful of wet snow sprayed into the púca's face. He
pressed himself further into the cleft before he realized it was
Blackthorn's boot had sent it flying. Sputtering, he wiped
the freezing slush off his whiskers and peered out from his
hiding place. He could barely see the Hunter, just a dark
shape moving swiftly down the mountainside, but he could
hear the man.

Brighde's Fire, the poor bodach was mad entirely. Singing
he was, and no Bard-Song this time. A warrior's chant rose
patchily through the screaming wind to the mouse's ears,
sung with a ferocity that withered the púca's frail courage in
his breast.

> *The wolf will howl*
> *The raven sing*
> *When the Mór-Ríoghain calls my Name . . .*

The púca shook his furred head weakly from side to side,
but there was no help for it. No matter that the Hunter was
spellbound in love with his own death. No matter that he
was bent on throwing his life upon the gray edge of a Scáil's
blade. Even so, the púca would have to follow him.

Calling to An Daghdha to make sure the Good God's eye
was on him in his moment of bravery, the mouse stuck his
nose out into the night and rose to a man. If his boldness
gentled An Daghdha's heart against him, still the púca felt
no easing of the weight of the God's geis on his soul.
Shuddering violently as the wet storm drenched his flesh,
the púca forced his skinny bowlegs down the mountain after
Blackthorn's raving voice.

*   *   *

All night the Hunter stalked the Scáileanna, seeking a shadow that would take shape again, would cut him again, would release him from this life he no longer wanted. All night and into the day he hunted, until at last the storm's fury and his own were spent. The gale moved east toward the dawn, a dismal, unwilling sunrise only just bright enough to drive the darkness from the storm-tattered woods.

As the colorless half-light crept through the forests of Binn Chuilceach, Blackthorn paused in his hunt and leaned against a pine's creviced trunk. One hand still grasped the blackthorn branch, but he wrapped his other arm around his ribs and pressed his fingers against the wound in his side. It was small enough that his hand could cover it, but was still wet with blood and burned like fire. He found himself longing for the numbing dark to return. In the night he had not been troubled by pain or weariness.

A soft footstep brought the Hunter's head quickly about. It was no Scáil, but only the púca coming near. The wild hope in Blackthorn's eyes dimmed to disappointment.

"By the light that shines, you've stopped singin' at last!" exclaimed the little man.

He hurried to Blackthorn's side and reached up as if to take the Hunter's arm. Thinking better of it, the púca settled for a corner of the wolfskin cloak and tugged gently.

"Och, now, it's hurt you are, bodach. Sure, an' you'd have come to your senses before now, we'd long ago have left this cursed mountain. No matter, no matter. We can leave now, can't we? Morning's upon us, and the way to Béal an Átha Móir clear before us—"

Blackthorn pushed himself away from the tree and shook his head. "That is not my path," he said.

There was a scratch in his voice, the rasp of harsh resolve and long hours of bellowing his war songs into the night.

"It was your path," insisted the púca. "It will be again."

He pulled harder on Blackthorn's cloak, and swept his arm in a broad arc, indicating the forest.

"Look about you. Are your enemies anywhere to be seen? Whisht, no creature but yourself is fool enough to be out on Binn Chuilceach this morn!"

Blackthorn frowned, but he looked as the púca had bidden him. The grim light of a sour day shone through the trees. Cheerless though it was, it was driving away the shadows of the night. It might also have banished the dark desire of Blackthorn's heart, but he was not yet willing to let go his death-yearning.

Encouraged by the Hunter's compliance, the púca stepped closer and spoke with conviction. "It's off to their black holes under the roots of Binn Chuilceach the Scáileanna have gone, and not even the Hunter of Éirinn will flush such cunning quarry from so dangerous a den. And best you don't try with only a blackthorn wand to serve you."

The púca's words dispelled the last of the Bard-Song's magic, but the little man would have caught them back again if he could. Blackthorn spun on him, surprising the púca into an involuntary squawk of alarm. The Hunter's madness had returned, but altered, more terrible. Not joy in death, but despair in life burned in the man's gray eyes.

"Softly, lad, softly," the púca pleaded. "Last night I wouldn't have wagered so much as a whisker on your chances. But this morning, sure, an' you should bless the good fortune that's saved you."

"Saved me?" Blackthorn spat his words like venom, and the púca dodged every one. "Saved you from An Daghdha's curse, you mean. An' the Scáileanna had killed me, it would not have been Blackthorn, but yourself left alive with a geis on your soul and no hope of fulfilling it."

He shoved the púca away from him, though the little man was already hastening to save the Hunter the trouble, and at once started up the mountain. After only a dozen steps he paused, breathing heavily, and considered his wound. In the night and storm he had run through the woods never feeling his hurt, but now he had no magic to stave off pain and exhaustion.

"Slack-witted, simpleminded fool that you are!" cried the púca. The little man had not yet mustered enough courage to follow the Hunter, but had found sufficient boldness to hurl a few insults after him. "You've only just come down these slopes!"

The snow was littered with deadfall and thick with slush, but Blackthorn took a handful of the cleanest he could find and washed his cut. Binn Chuilceach's woods boasted only pine, fir, and larch, and thickets of broom near the mountain's crest. None of these would speed the healing of his hurt, or keep infection from it. In this weather he'd not even find cobwebs to bind the wound.

He took the long leather strap that had held his Spear to his back, and wrapped it carefully about his ribs. It made a poor bandage, but at least the edges of the cut were pressed together. If he had cleaned it well enough, and it did not fester . . .

His side was still throbbing, but Blackthorn set his jaw and continued up the slope. Having finally decided it was safe to approach, the púca was just catching up to the Hunter when the man strode off, leaving the shape-shifter behind once more.

"You purblind oaf! Take me in your pouch an' you will insist on climbing Binn Chuilceach yet again!"

The púca glowered at the Hunter's receding back. "Sure, an' it's still death you're after—you mean to break your neck fallin' down the mountain, since the Scáileanna's swords proved too difficult to find.

"Doesn't even hear me," he muttered, lifting his arms to heaven and letting them drop against his bony shanks. "Wurra, wurra, but the man's gone both deaf and blind. An' what with all the blood he must have lost, and the wet and the cold—"

The púca's thought that the Hunter might still die and leave him cursed with a broken geis spurred the little man's tired legs to struggle along in Blackthorn's footsteps. The Hunter's stride was longer, his pace swifter, his need more urgent. He reached the spur of rock well before the shape-shifter. Lifting the blackthorn limb over the lip of the ledge, the Hunter's hand went into a half-frozen puddle of mud, water, and blood pooled in a depression on the uneven shelf floor. He grimaced, and climbed over.

The pale gray stone was blackened by the fires that had burned there last night, the ledge covered with muck and debris. Pausing only to pick up the blackthorn branch, the Hunter stepped past two piles of cinders and twisted metal, not thinking what they were or what they meant, and over the body of the Scáil his dagger had killed. The knife was still embedded in the dark elf's throat, a perfect smile fixed on the Scáil's lips, and the pits of his black eyes had turned

white as old ivory. None of this did Blackthorn see, but only
that the sheet of ice that had covered the rock wall was
gone, melted away.

With a glad cry he began climbing. The fairy tree's roots
gave him easy purchase—even with the blackthorn staff in
his hand and the stabbing pain in his side, he scaled the wall
in a moment. When he could not see his Spear in the tree,
he climbed into the bare limbs as high as he dared and cast
his eyes over the surrounding hillside. There was no sign of
ash wood or silver on all the broad slope.

Perhaps it was hidden by the snow, Blackthorn thought
wildly. Perhaps the Spear was just beyond that withered
broom, perhaps hidden by the shadow of that rock. He
dropped from the tree and scrambled up the hill, searching
everywhere on the heights. The snow displayed only storm-
cast refuse from the trees and the tops of pockmarked
stones washed bare by the sleet. The ground was untrodden, clear of any spoor of bird or beast, unspoiled by hoofprint or pawprint. Nowhere could he see the mark of a dark
elf's boot.

Turning, he slid back down the rise to where the fairy tree
stood gripping the top of the rock wall. The blackthorn was
not dead, then, as it seemed. It lived, and some mischievous
sprites lived in it. The fairy folk had taken his Spear and
thought the bargain fair, for they'd given him the blackthorn
wand in exchange.

"A fine weapon," he said clearly, "but I like my own better."

He laid the blackthorn branch at the foot of the fairy tree
as a warrior might lay a sword at a Chieftain's feet. A sound
from below made him catch his breath, but it was only the
púca, clambering onto the shelf.

"The Scáileanna have cheated me of my death," he said,
his voice rough with impatience. "Will you cheat me of the
Hunt because death has denied me?"

The Hunter's every sense, every instinct was open for a
reply, but the gentle clacking of the tree's leafless branches
in the wind was the blackthorn's only and indifferent
response.

"It is mine!" he shouted. "By Éire who compelled it, by
Brighde's Fire that forged it, by the Stag who must die by it,
you will give it back!"

Nothing. Nothing from the wind or the cold, wet earth. Nothing at all from the blackthorn. Were there no unseen ears listening, no hidden eyes watching?

"Give it back!" he raged, but no longer hoped for an answer.

From the depths of Blackthorn's despair came a sound, a moan that rose to a hoarse, barely human cry and tore free of his throat, shattering the forest's silence.

Long after the echoes of the Hunter's anguish faded into the wood, the púca remained motionless where the sound had caught him, halfway up the wall clinging to the rock and a twisted knot of tree root. Pure folly to go on. If that wasn't the cry of a soul near breaking, he'd no ears to hear with. Not much chance in getting back down to the ledge without the owl-eared Hunter noticing him, neither. And likely he'd slip and fall an' he hung on here much longer. The púca shook his head, wishing he were safe enough to voice his misery. What hope had he at all, at all . . .

Unless the Hunter was as hopeless as he! To be sure he was, he must be! For hadn't he failed entirely to find the Spear he was looking for? And a man without hope—what could he be thinking, but to do away with himself? Wouldn't it be saving the man's life, now, to give him some words of comfort and help the poor beggar to Béal an Átha Móir?

Even with his good reasons to urge him up the scar, the púca climbed so slowly a snail could have raced him to the top and won. When at last the little man peeked over the rim of the wall, he found the Hunter sitting slumped against the trunk of the fairy tree. Strength seemed to have drained from him as life had drained from the fairy thorn—indeed, if not for the swift, shallow rise and fall of the Hunter's chest, the púca would have thought Blackthorn dead already. He was pale as a corpse, certainly, and though his eyes were open, they saw nothing and never blinked. 'Twas a pitiful sight, and it was pity as well as his fond desire to free himself from his geis that brought the púca to squat by the Hunter's side.

"Hard it is, and hard you're takin' it," said the little man sympathetically. "But what's done is done, and *there is a sweetness in every sorrow.* And won't it be sweet, now, to have your wound tended in Béal an Átha Móir, to sit by a fire, warm and dry, to drink good ale and eat—"

Blackthorn's head came up, but more swiftly his arm shot out and his hand closed on the púca's throat.

"Who has taken it?" he demanded, his voice a raven's croak. "And where?"

"Don't hurt me! Don't hurt—"

The fingers on his windpipe tightened and the púca became frantic. He flailed about, his arms and legs waving uselessly in the air. His eyes rolled back in his head as if he were fainting, and only a high, choked whisper emerged from his constricted throat.

"Help! Help!! Och, save me, save— Murder! Mur—"

"Who has taken it?"

Seeing the dull look of a man betrayed in Blackthorn's gray eyes, the púca changed his strangled plea.

"Innocent I am—innocent, I'm sayin'! Can you—think it was me?"

The clamp on his throat eased, but did not open, and the gray eyes narrowed.

"Not you. But your kind."

"My kind? My kind!"

Suddenly understanding the Hunter's suspicions, the púca lost his fear in a moment of righteous pride.

"Unjust! Unjust you are! Because you lose your Spear near a fairy tree, you name the fairy folk thieves! Do you imagine my people such fools as to make their abode in a dead black-thorn? Do you think us so thick-witted we'd carelessly tarry on the Scáileanna's doorstep?"

Anger flashed again in the Hunter's eyes, but it was cold and dark, and made the púca afraid again.

"Who then? Who has taken it?"

"How can I know?"

"Where were you hiding last night, little mouseen? What did you See with your beady eyes?"

"Loose me," the púca begged. "Loose me an' you wish to know."

Abruptly the shape-shifter found himself flying through the air, and just as suddenly sprawling on the snow-covered ground. Slowly he picked himself up and began to brush the offending wet from his body.

"Och, wurra, wurra, wurra," he mumbled under his breath. "It's a terrible hard man you are, entirely.

"No true Sight had I," he said, raising his voice, "not in this evil place and the foul night. I saw as you did, when lightning lit the sky. Two bolts shot from the heavens when you cast the Spear, and unnatural they were, for when have you known lightning to strike a valley's heart an' a mountain in easy reach? I saw the Spear's silver point shine like a shooting star as it flew into the blackthorn's arms. Then it was gone, and the branch you now hold I saw tumblin' from the sky into your hand."

"Gone?" Blackthorn grinned savagely and came unsteadily to his feet. "This is all you can tell me?"

"An' it is," said the púca stepping back nervously, "there's else I can say of the blackthorn wand you'd so readily part with. 'Tis far more than a tree branch—but only remember the death it dealt the Scáileanna!"

Blackthorn tried to look back to the battle. Last night the intoxicating spell of the Bard-Song had put confusion on him, and now his memories were clouded by pain.

"They burned," he said vaguely. "Lightning struck them, and they burned."

"Oho! They burned indeed, you fool, but 'twas no lightning's fire. Burst asunder they did, when your blackthorn cut into them. Cut them, I'm sayin', like a sword, and that's why the rest fled you."

His expression thoughtful, the Hunter bent to pick up the branch. He gasped softly as his movement brought a fresh stab of fire from his wound, but rose again smoothly enough. Drawing his hand gently down its length he studied the wood, then sighed and leaned wearily against the fairy tree.

"Even so potent a blackthorn will not bring down the Stag," he said bitterly.

"Neither blackthorn nor ash should you be worryin' over now, but only your own life."

Though the púca's expression was sour as a dry sloe, his voice was honey-soaked.

"Death looked fine to you last night," he went on, "but sure, an' He seems less handsome in the light of day. Yet, He'll come again, I'm thinkin', an' you stand here waitin' for Him."

The Hunter didn't argue. The púca took a daring step toward him.

"Last night you fought like a King, I'm not denyin'. But you're wounded, bodach, and you'll not fight so well again without some healing. We'll not live through another night on Binn Chuilceach, not unless a King of Éirinn comes in truth to fight for us, and a host of Sidhe at his side. So gather your strength, and we'll down to the path—"

The Hunter lifted his head and smiled, but so grimly the púca knew at once his words had been to no avail.

"The Sidhe," Blackthorn said. "First at Brugh na Morna, now on high Binn Chuilceach. 'Tis the Sidhe are having cruel sport with me, the Sidhe who have taken my Spear."

"'Tis mad you are, Hunter of Éirinn, and your words the proof of it!" the púca exploded, then softened at once, seeing that Blackthorn was starting to lower himself onto the wall. "Och, well, an' it's down you're goin' at last, wait just a moment and I'll into your—"

Blackthorn's head disappeared over the edge of the scar.

"Curse you for a pig-stubborn, unheeding—" the púca shouted after him.

The Hunter never felt the curses raining down on his head, nor thought again of the púca who hurled them. His mind was on his climb down to the ledge and the bolts of agony shooting through his side. It felt like a dagger twisting in the wound, but he did not complain of it, even to himself. The pain would feed him. The pain would keep him sharp.

"Wait," the púca called, doing his best to get more than one foot on the wall. "Wait till I'm in your pouch, you empty-headed fool. Wait, and I'll take you to the Sidhe."

The Sidhe, he grumbled to himself, getting both legs over the edge and grappling about for a handhold. As if it would do any good to seek the Sidhe at all, at all! Would the elves have come last night, and none seen them, and they not staying to fight their mortal enemies, but only to steal away the Hunter's Spear? 'Twas madness, this, but sure, an' what save madness fills a fevered man's mind? And what could that hard light in the Hunter's eye and flush in his cheeks be if not fever—

By the time the púca reached the ledge, the Hunter had already left it and was headed down the mountain toward the thick trees.

"It'll not slow you greatly to give me a ride, you heartless, witless—"

The púca stamped his feet, one after the other, and rolled his eyes heavenward. There was a commiserating gloominess about the sky, but it did not soothe the little man's ire.

Dropping his gaze, the púca inadvertently let it fall on the still body of the Scáil that had died from the Hunter's dagger. Wrinkling his nose in revulsion he edged quickly away, but the more he thought about the knife stuck in the Scáil's throat, the slower he went.

"Och, wurra, wurra, wurra," he moaned. "Wurra, wurra, wurra, wurra . . ."

Forcing himself to go back, the púca knelt by the dark elf's corpse. The Scáil's sightless, white-eyed stare seemed fixed on him as he wrapped his knobbly fingers around the dagger's hilt. The púca closed his own eyes and pulled with all his strength, but the dead body was reluctant to part with the weapon. The Scáil's dark blood had congealed around the wound, his stone-gray skin had closed about the deeply embedded blade.

Opening his eyes, the púca stood, placed a bare foot on the dark elf's chest, and drew a long, shaky breath. Grasping the hilt and grunting with the strain, he heaved for all he was worth. The dagger stayed caught, but the dark elf's body rose up, and his black boot scraped on the stone.

With a gurgle that never quite made it to a shriek, the púca hopped away. He was a mouse before his feet were on the ground again, and had run, rolled, and fallen a good way down the mountain before he realized it was his own actions had caused the Scáil to shift.

Stopping to look back at the stone ledge, the púca roundly cursed Bards and Bard-Songs forever and aye. It was a ridiculous curse, and he knew it. No God would listen to such a poorly aimed malediction, but the púca was not such a fool as to speak ill of the Scáileanna while trespassing in their domain, and didn't have the heart to call down more misfortune upon Blackthorn. The Hunter was so thoroughly cursed without the púca's ill wishes, it would be too cruel entirely.

Sixteen

Deep the wounds Donnchú bears,
His life a red river flowing.
He lies upon the lonely hill,
No more to rise. Mourn people
Of Éire, Donnchú is dead. Weep
Na Connachta, no more your King returns.
An Leacán Ruadh now let it be called,
That hill of sorrow, stained with blood.

The Death of Donnchú
(a rann made by Ruairc,
the Poet of An Fharraige)

Three days of clear weather followed the night of storm, but Blackthorn hated the daystar for the spears of light it drove into his aching head, and he travelled slowest when the sun was highest. He was fonder of the night. Night matched the black despair within his heart, its numbing cold soothed the fire that was consuming him.

Three times the sun rose and twice set while he wandered aimless, seeking the Sidhe who had robbed him of his Spear. By the third nightfall, Blackthorn had lost count of the succession of days. He no longer knew that west was where the sun was sinking, or realized the gnawing in his belly was from hunger. He was only aware of looking down from a high, windswept knoll past a wooded slope of ash and oak to a narrow defile, white with birches, but graying in the twilight. He found no beauty in the sight, though it was beautiful, nor heeded the wolves' hunting songs ringing below, though no music did he love better. Only the broad, high plain on the far side of the birch-filled ravine did he find beautiful, and he heard only the thought of his own mind endlessly repeating—I have found them. I have found them. The pavilions of an elvish encampment dotted the not-too-distant upland, shining with their own light as if a rainbow had shattered and fallen as varicolored jewels upon the white snow of the high field.

"I have found them," he said aloud.

He had forgotten there was a reason he had taken to voicing his thoughts, and did not remember even when his words brought the púca's head from the pouch at his belt. Two days the shape-shifter had ridden thus, but though he had gained the Hunter's purse, he had yet to gain his ear. Perceiving the glittering camp on the plain, the púca sighed with relief and made no attempt to draw the Hunter's eyes away from it. When Blackthorn started down into the defile, the mouse dropped silently back to the bottom of the pouch.

The Hunter moved swiftly under the forest's leafless canopy and through the dusk-veiled furze and bracken, a sense of dizzy elation making his progress almost effortless. He felt as if he were not walking, but flowing like water between the close, shadowed trees. For once the wound in his side did not hinder him. For once he felt strong and light, almost invincible in the near achievement of his desire. I have found them, he thought. His feet touched the pale thread of a deer trail leading into the birches, and he followed it instinctively. I have found them at last.

He had nearly reached the base of the hill when his boot struck hard on a stone hidden in one of the long shadows darkening the narrow track. Searing pain erupted in his side, flamed across his chest, burned the sight from his eyes. He did not know he was falling, but cried out against the agony that shot through his body when he hit the ground. Gritting his teeth, the Hunter held still, waiting for the fire to abate.

As the pain ebbed, he became aware of the snow beneath him, a mere sprinkling on the hard earth, but soft and cool on his burning flesh. He sank down into the cold bed. His eyes closed. Oh, sweet Áine, giver of gifts, he prayed, let me lie here and never rise. Let me wrap the senseless, careless dark about me and sleep forever in its undemanding shade.

"What, have you come down the mountain and through the marshes and over the hills, only to tarry now, an' the Sidhe in your reach?"

It was not the answer Blackthorn had hoped for, and the voice was no Goddess's.

"Come daybreak, the pavilions will likely be gone, and you'll think the memory of them but a dream. Such is the magic of the Tuatha dé Danaan. Not far now, bodach, not far. Just through this dell and up again. Come, get your feet under you. You're too great a weight for me to lift."

Blackthorn knew the voice, though he couldn't remember who possessed it. He found it hard to attend to. The words it spoke were full of concern and fear, and their meanings eluded him. The voice itself was nothing, a whisper lost in the echoes of the other voice, the relentless, commanding voice of his geis. Nine years the Stag's call had spoken in Blackthorn's heart, belling like a hound on the path before him, like a stream murmuring even through his dreams. Now it cracked like a whip, stinging him for his laziness, goading him on. He must rise again, must hunt his Spear until his legs refused to carry him, then crawl along the trail until he could crawl no more. As long as his lungs drew breath and his heart beat, he would hear that imperious, imperative voice, and when he failed to obey it, the geis that had governed his will in life would break it in death.

He opened his eyes, and saw the half-moon shining through the slender branches of the birches in thick sheets of silver. Pain made all the world dark again as he rose, but when he had got to his feet the Hunter found himself once more in moonlight. The deer path was before him. Though each step hurt more than the last, he followed it into the heart of the glen.

Still squatting where the Hunter had fallen, the púca waited, a contented smirk on his lined face. A fine thing he'd accomplished, and it hadn't been easy. A great deal of pleading and a good bit of prodding and pulling he'd done before the Hunter had roused from his deathbed in the snow. Yet, Blackthorn had roused at last, and now he'd saved the madman's life, An Daghdha must lift this loathsome geis from his soul.

The púca waited another moment, feeling puzzled, then another, becoming truly worried.

"An' I'd left him to lie here, wouldn't he have died, now?" he asked the birches. "Well, wouldn't he?"

The trees, slim and white as the ghosts of young girls, swayed gently, but gave him no reply. The púca had his answer from the oppressive weight in his heart, growing heavier by the moment. He shook a puny fist at the sky, but his voice belied his angry gesture.

"Is it tellin' me you are he got up on his own?" the púca wailed. "Is it tellin' me you are that all me help was no help at all, at all?"

Dismayed, the púca turned to the shadows where Blackthorn had vanished. "And himself gone, and his pouch with him! In his sack I should have stayed, and not wasted me efforts on such an obstinate fool. Och, wurra, wurra, but there's not a drop of kindness or luck to be had in all the wide world."

The stars were disappearing into the brightening sky as the Hunter staggered to the top of the rise. He laughed at the sight before him, a town of brilliantly hued cloth tents rising from a vast plain of pristine white. His laugh was mirthless and almost without sound, just a harsh exhalation and a ruthless grin.

He ordered his legs to hurry him nearer to the glimmering vision. They were rebellious and would only shuffle slowly through the snow. Nor would his eyes fix on his goal, but lifted to the waving banners at the tops of the tent poles or wandered between the now starless heavens and the shining white plain. When the first gold of day struck the green and scarlet and saffron pavilions, Blackthorn felt it like a blow. Rocked off his feet by the explosion of color, he fell, and the snow-covered world with him, both spinning down and down into a lightless, soundless, endless void.

Seventeen

Time stands still in the presence of the Gods,
And idles with the Sidhe,
But in the wide and rolling world,
Time passes unceasingly.

Long before Blackthorn's eyes were open the rhythms of pain returned, pulsing agony, deep in his muscles, drumming between his temples, a throbbing ache in his wounded side. The dark, the blessedly insensate dark enticed him to return, luring him with promises of banished pain and unconscious slumber. How tempting, and oh, how easy it would be to slip back into that dreamless sleep, that unmindful, uncaring, unmoving state that was not quite death but not nearly living. His will alone could not have brought him awake, Blackthorn was sure, but then, his will was never alone. Nine years it had kept company with Éire's. Her insistence and the geis She had laid upon him forced the Hunter's lids to part, forced his eyes to focus.

Emerald veils filled his vision. For a while that was as much as he was able to take in, but gradually he became aware of gentle voices singing in harmony. Though the music was muffled by the green curtains and he could not make out the words, Blackthorn was rapt. The melody was soothing, warm and indolent, and somehow reassuring. Like all great songs, its end seemed naturally to compel a new beginning.

It was in recognizing that he'd heard this part of the tune before that Blackthorn realized time was passing. A thrill of fear wakened in his belly—he tried to guess if it had been moments or hours he'd been listening, but for all time meant to him, it could have been both, or neither. No ordinary music, but the magic of elven voices was in his ears, and the green veils about him the walls of an elven pavilion.

Hurriedly he tried to rise. His body protested his rash attempt, and punished him for his haste. Pillows soft as thistledown cushioned the Hunter's fall, and the sheets he collapsed upon might have been woven of gossamer threads.

Once again, and with considerably greater care, Blackthorn pushed himself from the comfort of his bed. This time he went only as far as his knees, and waited there until his dizziness passed. It was then he discovered he was half-naked. Instead of his shirt he wore a bandage over his ribs, and though they had left him his breeches, his hosts had taken his belt and his boots, his wolfskin cloak, and his blackthorn staff. He looked about, but as far as he could tell, the green tent held only himself and his bedding. Still, he'd be a fool to put much trust in his eyes. Human sight is easily deceived by elvish enchantments.

Climbing to his feet hurt more than Blackthorn hoped it would, but less than he imagined it might. He stood, and stayed standing, and a rush of confidence bolstered his strength. He had found them. He was among them. He would have his Spear of them, and have it now.

"Soft, friend," said a voice lovely as any Blackthorn remembered ever hearing. "You will bleed again."

He spun toward the melodious words with ill-considered speed. Before his eyes gold and silver and a black deep as the midnight sky over Loch Éirne flamed against a wealth of green.

The blaze of light and color swiftly took on new shape and hue, like a bonfire burning in a moment to glowing coals. The Hunter found he was in the presence of two startlingly beautiful beings. They were of Tuatha dé Danaan. One was a woman dressed in silver mail. She stood within the pavilion, yet Blackthorn could have sworn it was sunlight glinting on her white-gold hair. The other wore only black, not armor, but a finely sewn tunic and leather vest. He gleamed, his

clothes and hair like polished jet, and his eyes so brightly
Blackthorn could not guess their color.

Human eyes reflect the soul within, but in the eyes of the
Sidhe Blackthorn saw his own self mirrored. The image of
his madness and folly was not a pleasant sight. It was suddenly plain to him how sickness and pain had driven away
his reason, how fever and the shadows of Binn Chuilceach
had darkened his mind. Now he was healed, and reason had
returned. Now his mind was clear, and the clearest thought
in it was that these glory-clad and mighty Sidhe were no
thieves. The one truth revealed another—his Spear was lost
beyond hope of recovery.

"Look how you tremble." The woman's wondrous voice
rang in Blackthorn's ears, rich and resonant, like a bell heard
from far away. "You have risen too soon. Rest now," she
urged, coming nearer, "and when you wake again you will be
stronger."

Blackthorn shook his head and took an uneven step back.
An utter fool he'd been to come to the Sidhe for his Spear.
A worse one he'd be an' he remained with them any longer.

"I am grateful for your care, Lady," he said, "but I will not
ask more of your generous hospitality. An' you will accept
my thanks and return to me my few belongings, I'll be gone
from here and trouble you no more."

His voice was coarse as a goblin's after the music of hers,
but the Lady only smiled.

"'Tis rare to find one who prefers his own pain to elven
pleasures," she said, but to her companion, not Blackthorn.

"Yet 'twas he came seeking us, not we him, and he arriving at our camp all unlooked-for," the raven-haired Sidhe
answered her.

Sweat beaded cold on Blackthorn's skin and his muscles
began to cramp with the effort of keeping him on his feet.

"I was hurt and ill," he said. "I knew not where I was, nor
where I was going. I will leave now I am able."

The tall, dark Sidhe answered mildly, but his eyes flashed.
"Either you lie or you are greatly mistaken. You are not able.
Your own wound will prevent you leaving an' you are fool
enough to try. My Lady speaks true. You have risen too soon.
We have done what we can for you, but time is the better
healer."

"'Tis said time idles with the Sidhe," Blackthorn replied, a spark of anger in his own eyes, "and I have none to spare. A moon I lost when last I was in the company of elves. Another might pass while I lie here senseless."

"What errand can be so urgent as to prevent you taking rest or refreshment?" the Lady demanded. "What duty so pressing you must repay our hospitality with this discourteous farewell?"

"A geis," Blackthorn answered simply, then looked away lest he see his grief reflected in her glittering eyes.

"A geis?" she echoed. "But then you must stay with us until you are healed, for what chance have you to fulfill this geis an' you go wounded into the world?"

Blackthorn laughed bitterly. "What chance have I at all, at all without my Spear? Better to go wounded into the world and be broken by death than to sleep heedless in this pavilion waiting for time to shatter my soul."

He listened to himself with a kind of helpless horror. His words must surely offend his hosts, and worse, they revealed far more than he intended. He needed some device to throw the Sidhe off this trail he had laid them, and quickly. Not a lie, for 'twas said the Tuatha dé Danaan never lied, and so were impossible to deceive. A truth he needed, but one that would turn their piercing Sight from his sorrow. If only he could empty his mind of the color and sound of this place, if only the soreness of his body would ease and let him think. . . .

"An' you require a spear to fulfill your geis, this is not a hard thing to come by," said the Lady, but her tone seemed to ask more than suggest.

"No other spear. No other spear is like mine."

The words seemed to spill from him without him willing them go. Whiskey loosened his tongue this way, if he took enough to get him drunk, but by then his drinking companions were usually snoring on the floor. In this place the beauty of the Sidhe and the music of their voices was like whiskey, the very air intoxicating.

"How did you come to lose this unmatched weapon, this remarkable spear?" the black-clad man persisted.

The Sidhe's question drove everything from Blackthorn's mind save the dark memory of his night on Binn Chuilceach.

He didn't mean to tell his tale, didn't want to tell it, but he was too weary, too worn to guard his secrets anymore.

"In the shadows of Binn Chuilceach I thought I Saw my death," he said aloud. "But I was loath to soil my Spear in the blood of the Scáileanna, and so I threw it into the arms of the blackthorn tree. I went back. I searched. I searched everywhere, but my Spear was vanished entirely, and the fairy thorn was dead."

"So 'twas a Scáil's blade that marked him." There was respect in the Lady's voice, and a kind of eagerness.

"But his words are strange. 'Soil it in the blood of the Scáileanna' he says. Only one Spear I can Name would not gladly drink the wine of a dark elf's life."

Though the Sidhe spoke to each other, it was Blackthorn who answered.

"Of ash is the haft," he said quietly, "the unmarred branch of a lightning-blasted tree. In Éirinn's womb I found silver for the spearhead, and the sacred fires of Dair na Tintrí were my forge. With pine pitch, with elk sinew, with my own blood I bound spearhead to spear, and when it was done I had a weapon worthy of the Stag's death."

Blackthorn's breath came sharper, faster, as if he were running, not standing still. The pain behind his eyes grew as he struggled to hold himself erect. When he looked on the Sidhe, they had blurred again to clouds of sun-gold and silver, and shining black against a sea of green.

"The chase has led you to the pavilion of Cessair of Cnoc an Eanaigh," he heard the Lady say. "I and my harper Fiach do bid you a hundred thousand welcomes, Hunter of Éirinn."

The familiar greeting spurred the proper response in Blackthorn. He managed to gasp, "Éire bless all here," before the profusion of light and color burst into intimate, solitary darkness.

Blackthorn came awake more willingly the second time, and found he was leaning back upon soft pillows, an exquisite golden goblet pressed to his lips. A tantalizing scent rose from the cup and reached out to bind him in an aromatic web of delight. He drew back, lifting his hand to push the goblet away. Knotted designs ran around the rim, precious gems adorned its sides, and strong, white fingers were wrapped about it.

"Drink," said Cessair of Cnoc an Eanaigh, "and we will talk the more while Fiach plays."

Blackthorn drank, but of her resplendent beauty, not the mead in his cup. It was sweet like the honey wine, with a definite, yet indefinable bite. The Sidhe had features more precise in symmetry, more flawless in detail. The Lady's face was no more perfect than Scáthach's or Bryony's. Her cheekbones were high, her smile broad. She was impossibly lovely.

A shimmering note trembled off a harp string, graceful as a kittiwake's flight over the sea. Blackthorn fought against it as if it were a stone pulling him under the waves to drown him.

"Cessair of Cnoc an Eanaigh," he began.

He got no further. To speak of so famous a warrior was a simple matter. To speak to her was not so easy.

"You have heard tales of me." It was a statement, not a question, but the Lady sounded pleased.

"Myself have sung them," said Blackthorn. He tried again. "Cessair of Cnoc an Eanaigh. You know my burden. Let me bear it hence."

"A Bard," said Fiach quietly as he played, but Cessair frowned and the flash of annoyance in her crystal-blue eyes was unmistakable.

"'Tis your wound holds you here, as Fiach has said. Not myself, nor the refreshment I offer."

She thrust the goblet toward him. Blackthorn took it, but set it down beside his pillows and did not drink.

"Leave now, if you think you can walk even so far as the edge of the plain," Cessair challenged. "And when your legs fail you, look not over your shoulder to see the pavilions of the Sidhe, for we will be gone. One night we thought to rest here on An t-Ard Achadh, the high field. One night, to rest our horses and view the stars, for we ride not for pleasure, but in the service of Liannan, the Mother of Midhe."

Cessair's gaze softened, and her voice as well. "But with the dawn came a man nearer death than life, and mad with pain and fever. 'Twas luck led you here, and in luck our people place great store. We took you in and saw to your hurts, and lo! when you wake we learn 'tis the Hunter of Éirinn we have tended these many days."

Blackthorn sat forward. "Many days?" he repeated.

"'Twas sunrise of the eighth day of midwinter when you came unlooked-for to our camp. Tonight is twelfth night, and the Birch moon is nearly full. Do you begrudge your time with us?"

"I fear when I leave your camp I will find time reckoned differently in the world beyond," Blackthorn replied. "A moon I dwelt in Brugh na Morna, though it seemed to me no time at all, for I can recall nothing of my stay. Nor can I believe my own will kept me there, for the Stag was already running."

Cessair nodded, but the motion conceded nothing. "The Tuatha dé Danaan are not the only folk to make their homes in the hollow hills. It may not have been the Sidhe who desired your company."

From the rippling refrain he was playing Fiach moved smoothly into the lilting melody that Blackthorn had first heard in Brugh na Morna and had later spellbound him in Inis Ceithleann. For some reason in the Sidhe's green pavilion the tune did not confuse his mind, but made Cessair's words more plain.

"A God?" he whispered. "Wintering in the Brugh? This a greater madness than the one that drove me to you! What reason could any of the Gods have to hinder the Hunt?"

"To a Cailleach go, an' you would know the Gods' motives," said Cessair, "to a Mother, or a Maiden. I have no answer for you."

"Yet, a Mother it was sent you to this place you call An t-Ard Achadh, and here you found me."

"Here you found us. And not to An t-Ard Achadh did Liannan bid us go, but to Teach an Fhásaigh where Scáthach the Poet dwells."

Blackthorn's face darkened. "The Scáileanna you will find in the shadow of Binn Chuilceach, if battle you are seeking, Lady. But the Poet of Teach an Fhásaigh you will not find. The Scáileanna burned her house, and slew her before it, and took her head from her shoulders that she might not speak against them."

It cut his heart to give the news, but Cessair smiled, a

terrible smile, fierce and vengeful. Fiach merely changed
his tune. From his harp came a lament, deep and wild as
the sea. Blackthorn wept to hear it, but he would have
wept had he never known Scáthach of Teach an Fhásaigh,
so mournful was the song.

When the harper ended, Blackthorn bent his head and
watched light play on the rim of his cup, but Fiach set aside
his instrument, and turned to Cessair.

"I will to Liannan with the Hunter's tidings," the harper
said. "Take your sport among the Scáileanna of Binn
Chuilceach if you must, Lady, but forget not Midhe's council
when the Feast of Brighde is come."

"Be not so downcast," said Cessair to Blackthorn. "Scáthach
will be avenged."

"I doubt it not, Lady," he replied. "But I bear a geis I can
no longer fulfill, and all the world seems dark to me."

"A warrior am I, not a hunter, and I cannot advise you.
But if it will lighten your heart, know that I do not believe
elves took your Spear. Though the ways of the Tuatha dé
Danaan are not the ways of the Tuatha dé Éireann, nor does
time treat with the Sidhe as it does with your people, still
the Hunt is sacred to us both. The elves are neither so bold
nor so foolish as to call down Éire's anger by stealing Her
Hunter's Spear."

"Your words only darken my hopes more," Blackthorn
said. "'Twas reckless enough for me to seek the Sidhe. Now
it seems I must seek the Gods, and if I must do Them battle
to regain my Spear, I will surely fail."

Cessair regarded him with clouded eyes, but Fiach rose
and came to stand before the Hunter.

"You might well wish for an easier path," he said.

Blackthorn lifted his gaze from his cup, but he could not
read the harper's meaning in his shining eyes. "So do I wish,"
he answered.

"But I am no wish-bringer."

Following the harper's words was like crossing a rushing
stream by leaping from one unstable rock to another. Even
when he had arrived safely at the far bank, Blackthorn was
uncertain where the path had led him.

"The Wish-Bringer," he said slowly, "is surely no more
within the circles of the world."

"'Tis said of the wizard Róisín Dubh that she will refuse no one her hospitality," Fiach went on as if Blackthorn had not spoken. "And if a desire springs from an open heart, she will grant it by the magic of her many pools."

Blackthorn came to his feet without thinking, but his excitement overrode his hurts.

"I know the tale once told of Róisín Dubh," he said, "and in it she is Named the Black Rose for her beauty and the Wish-Bringer for her gift. But that song is no longer sung, and now the tale runs thus; three years ago, Breac the Mariner died, leaving Sliabh An Óir wanting a Wizard. 'Twas on Róisín Dubh the Mothers' Sight fell. Hoping to make her one of the Seven, they sent messengers to seek her home in the western seas, Inis na Linnte, the Isle of Pools. Yet, the Mothers' Sight failed them, for though the ship set sail, the messengers found no welcoming shore, and all but one perished in the rough seas. With Róisín's death the tale ends, for no one since has seen the Black Rose, no fond wish has her magic granted."

He took a step nearer Fiach, and dared look straight into the harper's star-bright eyes.

"But I am a Bard, or was once, and I know how the truth can run in and out of a tale. If this wizard lives, tell me, for I have a boon to beg of her."

"Wizards are proud and stubborn, and little inclined to caution," Fiach replied. "Whether this one yet lives, I cannot say. But since you came to An t-Ard Achadh, I have Seen Inis na Linnte in every one of my dreams, floating unanchored upon the western seas. When I slumber, it seems to me I stand upon a high head to the south of Aillte an Mhothair, and my Sight is drawn west over the waves. There on the far horizon, cloaked in mist, time and again I have beheld the Isle of Pools."

Blackthorn's gratitude burst from him in a glad cry. "My cloak I must have, and my boots and my—"

"Soft, soft," Cessair chided him. Blackthorn followed her eyes down to his side, where the white bandage was dotted with red. "Fiach's dreams have given you an easier path— will you not now consent to heal your wound that you may follow it to its end?"

"But, Lady, I must—"

Cessair shrugged, but it was not an unsympathetic gesture. "All Éirinn will suffer an' you fail to fulfill your geis, Hunter. Drink the draught I have poured you, and sleep, but a little while, I promise you. When you wake we will be gone, but I will leave a horse for you to speed your journey to the sea. Eocha he is called, and he will find his own way home to me, an' you set him free when you reach the western shore."

Blackthorn could only stare, and wonder if he had heard Cessair aright.

"Hah!" cried Fiach. "You have won the Lady's favor beyond question. Was it that he has sung your tales, or that he bested his Scáil?" he asked her.

"You are openhanded indeed to an ungracious guest," Blackthorn said. "I would I could give thanks as great as the gift; but Conall mac na Caillí has little to offer Cessair of Cnoc an Eanaigh."

"The true Name of the Hunter of Éirinn is no small thanks," said the Lady. "I will keep it a treasure in my heart."

"But I cannot take your Name, and give you nothing in return!" Fiach protested. "A rann I have, and it will be my gift. As the Lady's steed will carry you across the land, this song may bring you safely across the water. You will need your Bard's memory to have my gift of me, for the tune is elven, and difficult for human ears to remember."

When Fiach spoke, it was music. When he sang, it was almost too poignant to bear. Blackthorn closed his eyes to listen, and drummed his fingers on his leg to mark the rhythm.

"Do you have it?" asked Fiach when he was done.

Blackthorn nodded, not wishing to dispel the magic of Fiach's voice with sounds from his human throat. He opened his eyes, immediately, he thought, but to his surprise, he was alone in the green pavilion, with no one to thank.

Lowering himself carefully onto his bed, Blackthorn took up the goblet he had earlier set aside. His geis growled at him like a hungry cur, but he threw it a tasty bone—the promise of an elven steed that would carry him to the sea swifter than ever two legs could go, and to the wizard Róisín Dubh, and to his vanished Spear.

He sipped the honey mead in his cup. Though it was sweet and warm, and completely delicious, Blackthorn was asleep before the liquor was half-gone.

*   *   *

Fiach looked deep into the setting sun, but Cessair's eyes
were on the blackthorn branch in her hands. She stroked
the long, nearly straight wood with the loving gentleness of
a mother smoothing her child's tousled hair.

"You will stay with him, then?" Fiach asked.

The púca nodded his head reluctantly. "So I must," he
replied. "But, the long and the short of it is, the Hunter is
mad since he lost his Spear."

The púca shot a glance at Cessair, but no reaction to his
words crossed the warrior's face. The blackthorn staff
absorbed her attention. Though there was no envy, the púca
was sure he Saw a great longing in the Lady's bright eyes.

As if hearing his thought, Cessair looked up suddenly, and
handed the blackthorn to the shape-shifter, not releasing her
fingers until the little man had it firmly in his grasp. The sun
had departed the sky, and both elves turned to see the
evening star flame low and blue on the horizon.

"The Hunter has lost his Spear," agreed Cessair. She
smiled, and her gaze returned to the wand in the púca's
hand. "But he knows not what he has gained."

Eighteen

The murúch's Name she found in a shell
And spoke it within the rann's weave,
Then the Sea-God himself came to stir the swells
And the fuath was drowned in the sea.

The Voyage of the Green Heron

The third time the Hunter woke was the easiest of all. Without reticence or pain he left his dream of the White Stag hurtling through the shadows of an ancient wood, opened his eyes, and looked uncomprehendingly about him. He was warm and well rested, and so he knew it could not have been long since he had been asleep on the silken bed Cessair had given him. Yet, he was growing colder by the moment, for now he was lying on An t-Ard Achadh's untrodden, unblemished snow under a clear, early morning sky. Not a trace of the elven pavilions remained visible on the high field, but only long streams of mists low to the white ground, his blackthorn staff by his side, and twenty paces off, a horse so splendid even a God might consider it an honor to mount him.

Coal-black was Eocha. His mane rippled like a midnight stream, his chest was deep, his shoulder high, and silver bosses adorned his bridle. He stepped regally nearer when Blackthorn rose, and nodded encouragingly, but the Hunter could find no fit words to greet the magnificent animal. He could only close the distance between them, lift his hand to

stroke the horse's velvet nose, and smile with pleasure when
Eocha let him do both.

"Look at himself, now! Like a randy, red-faced boy you
are, too eager to say 'I won't' but too shy to say 'I will.'"

Blackthorn looked quickly down to see the púca crouched
at his feet. He could not have missed the little man on the
open field, and indeed, only his own footprints and Eocha's
marked the snow. Catching the flash of surprise in
Blackthorn's eyes, the púca cackled with delight.

"It's well the white elk stands such a terrible height above
the ground," he said, "or I wager the sharp-eyed Hunter of
Éirinn would be as likely to overlook the Stag as he is a púca."

"Och, well, it's lucky I am the Stag is neither so small as a
mouse nor so artful," answered Blackthorn, "or I'd have no
end of trouble with him taking cover in the folds of my cloak
while I'm hunting."

"Truth you're speakin'," the púca agreed. "It's that under
your very nose you've no eyes for at all, at all. Not for the
boots on your feet, nor the new shirt on your back—"

Blackthorn's gaze followed the púca's words; first to the
new boots, soft as butter and so well oiled the snow slipped
from them like water from a teal's back, then to his shirt.
He'd never have believed cloth could rival doeskin, yet the
finely woven green-gray fabric had a rich feel against his skin
and a suppleness he could not help but admire.

Lifting his eyes, he looked west to the moon. It had gone
three days past full, and was just setting, but though it
brought the tally of days he'd spent with the Sidhe to more
than a week, it did not dishearten him.

Bringing his lips close to Eocha's ear, Blackthorn asked
softly, "Will you bear me west, that I might follow Fiach's
dream to the sea?"

The horse's whinny was all but lost in the púca's outraged
protest.

"The sea? West to the sea? The stinking wet river An
tSionainn lies between here and the sea, and the sea itself
the wettest, foulest place of all! Do you imagine you'll find
the White Stag runnin' over the waves? A fine Hunt that
will be! 'Tis dry land you should be seekin', and high ground
at that!"

"'Tis my Spear I'm seeking, and west the path to it."

Blackthorn thrust his fingers into Eocha's silken mane and vaulted into the saddle. "Do you ride in my pouch or run behind? Swift are the horses of the Tuatha dé Danaan—none swifter—but do as you will."

The púca grabbed hold of Blackthorn's stirrup and peered up into the Hunter's face. "It's sense on me tongue, an' had you any, you'd listen. Fine clothes they've left you, and a horse better than Cearnach Caoch mac an tSeanchaí's, and didn't that filly leap Dún an dá Éan in a single bound?"

"Is it singing me the tale of 'Mac an tSeanchaí's Mare' you are, or have you something to say?"

"A horse they left you, I'm sayin'," insisted the púca, "but no weapons, now, did they? Not even a knife for to cut your meat. On Binn Chuilceach in the throat of a Scáil is your dagger, and you're a fool to ride to the sea without it, or without another in your sheath to take its place."

Satisfied he had made his point, the púca took his hand from the stirrup and folded his arms across his thin chest. Immediately he regretted it, for Blackthorn nudged Eocha forward, and the huge animal seemed to go from a dead stop to a flying canter in a single, smooth stride. The Hunter leaned out of the saddle and swept his blackthorn off the ground as they passed it, and then the two of them were riding for the edge of plain.

"Wait! Wait, you goblin-spawned idiot! I'll ride an' I must!"

Blackthorn wheeled at once, and in an instant had Eocha standing calm and still before the púca.

"I'll ride," the púca repeated, as Blackthorn lifted the little man up into the saddle before him, "but you'll remember my words when you need a dagger and you've none to hand."

"Or you'll remind me of them, an' I forget," Blackthorn laughed. "But what's a dagger to me, an' I have my Spear?"

The púca didn't answer, or at least gave no answer Blackthorn could understand. The sounds he made as he dropped to a mouse and burrowed into the pouch might well have been complaints, but the Hunter paid them no heed. As soon as the little creature was safe in his purse, Blackthorn urged Eocha on again. This time they did not stop, not for the slope at the edge of the plain as it dropped into the birch-filled dell, or the knoll beyond, or the wide stream on the far side of the hill. Eocha's hooves pounded on the white earth, and Blackthorn sang to the rhythm of the horse's drumming. The tale of "Mac an tSeanchaí's Mare" he sang, and it seemed to him that while most of the words went as great a distance beyond the truth as they could safely go, the ones that told what a wonder it was to ride upon an elven steed fell far short of the mark.

Below Aillte an Mhothair, where the western edge of Éirinn rises jagged from the sea, the world was a stinging, blinding squall of salt and wet and smothering fog. With a terrible speed born of its uninterrupted passage from the ends of the earth and a damp, bone-cracking cold gathered from its journey over the frigid waters, the wind blasted the land that dared look west. Waves hurled themselves against the rocky headland as if each believed it could bring the cliff down. The barren limestone resisted the assault, and sent sea spray leaping halfway to its summit. Nothing lived here. Nothing could endure the bitter, incessant, salt-laden air. And the sooner the pig-stubborn Hunter gave up trying to spy anything through the gray wind and came down off this horrible, perilous cliff, thought the púca, the better.

Head scrunched between his narrow shoulders, the little man crawled back and away from the lip of the head. The ground sloped steeply, and soon he came upon tough little mosses clinging to the wind-riddled rock. The blow was merciless, the limestone beneath his hands unmercifully damp, but the púca found if he pressed himself flat and laid his cheek against the mosses, the driving air skimmed past him and on into the east.

Once he felt confident the wind would no longer pluck him from the rock and toss him into the sea, he crept farther from the western rim of the head, and nearer its south face. Below him, in the protected lee of the limestone crag, kittiwakes dove from the cliff face to sing their plaintive songs to the bay. Herring gulls soared with them, or bobbed between the sea troughs, and a trio of slim-necked shags sheared like dark arrows over the waves. Halfway down the beach, their stink lost in the distance, the púca saw seals lording over the narrow strand, wreathed in mists like royal robes.

Lifting his head, the shape-shifter faced the west once more in order to glare at Blackthorn. The Hunter was poised on the very edge of the crumbly cliff, not even leaning on his thorn staff for balance. He was heedless of the gusting wind that whipped his cloak and his black hair about, heedless of the freezing wet waves surging over the sharp rocks beneath him, heedless entirely of the púca's hostile stare.

"Thanks be the pouch was wet through and through," muttered the púca as he ducked back out of the wind and laid his face once more against the brownish mat. "An' I'd been dry in the leather sack, sure, an' I'd have stayed there, and even now be danglin' out over the cliff, waitin' for the wind to tear me from the Hunter's belt and destroy me in the deep, cold sea."

The thought reminded him of the last deep, cold waters he'd known, and the púca shivered. Nearly drowned he'd been that day but a few days past—

A black boot crunched near his ear, and the púca looked up to see the Hunter looking down. His hair and clothes were dripping wet, but a reckless grin was spread across his fool face.

"My eyes are not keen enough to see Inis na Linnte through the winter winds," he said. "But I wager the Isle of Pools has drifted near to us, and the fog guards its privacy."

"And if it has," argued the púca, "do you mean to swim to its shores? Haven't I been tellin' you to make for Luimneach or Gaillimh where currachs are to be had? Did you think the ghosts that haunt the ruins of Lios Chanair yonder would have a vessel to lend you? Or is it thinkin' you are you've loosed Eocha too soon? Sure, an' I've no doubt that cursed animal would have offered to ferry you over the waves. 'Tis plain to me the elven steed was no better than the *each uisce*, the fairy horse that lures poor souls onto his back with a promise of passage over the river, then drowns them halfway across!"

A look of genuine concern crossed Blackthorn's face. "Now, how was I to know what Eocha had in mind at the riverbank? I almost lost my own seat when he plunged in, and what with An tSionainn tumbling along in such a hurry, and the waters up to me chest, well sure, an' 'tis no wonder it slipped my mind you were in my pouch."

"Slipped your mind?" demanded the púca, delighted to have discovered an advantage to himself in the Hunter's pangs of conscience. "Killed I was nearly, and your only excuse that it slipped your mind! Why, you can't have seen a less likely crossing in all your life, yet you give Eocha his head, never pausin' to consider your passenger! And meself, trapped in your purse with icy death pourin' into me lungs, and you laughin', laughin' you were—I heard you even under the swells—as if swimming An tSionainn on horseback were a rare pleasure to be savored!"

"Well, your lungs have recovered somewhat it seems," Blackthorn pointed out with a trace of amusement. "And it was a rare pleasure to me."

"An' murder's a pleasure to you, I'm through with you, I am. Sure, an' next you'll be leapin' off the head flappin' your arms, intendin' to fly to Inis na Linnte. Och, an astonishing pleasure that will be."

Blackthorn laughed, but the winds picked up the sound and broke it into pieces. "I've a song to carry us over the waters," he said. "Come to the strand, and I'll sing it for you."

Stepping over the prostrate púca, Blackthorn began climbing down to the beach. For a long while the little man didn't move, but only twisted his head to look over his shoulder and stare after the Hunter.

"A song?" he echoed. "A song? Did the wind freeze his wits, or blow them away entirely? There's not a song he's sung yet hasn't brought ill luck upon us."

When he did follow the Hunter, he went like a crab, scuttling sideways along the uneven rock, all the while muttering against the joint follies of singing aloud and trusting the Sidhe.

"Their advice, like their ford across the An tSionainn, is best taken by their own kind," the púca warned when he caught up to the Hunter. "Risky both are for humans. Arrah, and púcaí, as well."

"Quiet, now," Blackthorn answered, not unkindly. "Let me think."

Sanderlings hunting at the water's edge scattered when Blackthorn and the púca walked out upon the sands of the bay. The seals heaved their awkward bulks away down the strand, but kept their dark, liquid eyes on the two strangers. Blackthorn didn't mind the audience, nor the raucous cries of the curious seabirds swooping over his head. The music of the deeps was made by such as these. They could not hinder the magic of Fiach's rann, only enhance it.

Blackthorn stopped where water met shore, but the púca halted a good deal higher up the beach, where even the most daring wave could not hope to wet him.

"Be wary, me darlin'" he shouted. "A song you boast of, a song to hurl into the teeth of the wind, to toss to the poundin' white breakers. An' you sing it wrong, then woe betide us both, for *magic miscalled will find its own way in the world, and do great harm ere it is spent.* An' you sing true to the spell, the danger might be greater, or has the Hunter already forgotten what happened the last time he let a song of power loose from his throat?"

Blackthorn paused long enough to look back at the púca, and the little man groaned at the expression on the Hunter's face. Neither caution nor care could he see, but only the cunning glad look of a fox after a partridge.

Turning back to face the waves, the Hunter began to sing. Though the wind had been far worse at the top of the head-land, the rushing air distorted Blackthorn's voice and carried much of his melody away. Even so, the verses reached the púca's ears clearly. It seemed to him the wind tore Blackthorn's words not to mar the spell, but to add percussive punctuation. A mournful chorus of fisher-birds soared over the Hunter's deep voice and danced around the haunting, perfect tune. The voices of the waves were more constant, soft at the start of every line, then rising to a roar before breaking at the end.

On the threshold he stands, thought the púca, where land meets sea, and the watchers at the gate are pleased to join the Hunter's song.

I sing of wind, and white it blows
Across the crested foam.
I sing the tossing tide that flows
And speeds the sailors home.

I sing of shores and ships appear
On dark and dingled seas.
I sing of Manannán mac Lir
And Manannán sings to me.
The Sea-God sings to me.

At first Blackthorn thought the sudden deepening of the day natural, no more than the sun setting behind the clouds of fog at the rim of the world and bringing darkness upon Éirinn. But with the dark came a stillness, a breathless quiet that pierced the heart with keen expectancy. The wind dropped to nothing. The sanderlings stopped chasing the waves that came meekly lapping to shore, and pointed their slender black beaks toward the calming sea. The seals silently turned their long-lashed gazes to the west. Circling still, the gulls flew voiceless, but the kittiwakes beat to their homes in the limestone's craggy heights. The shags came to perch on a jagged rock in the midst of the bay and lifted their wings into the unmoving air. Blackthorn's own breath caught in his chest to see the rann's magic at work, and his pulse beat madly.

A wave slid quietly onto the strand. By the time it had come as high as the tips of Blackthorn's boots it had thinned to a transparent sheet of bubbly froth. While the white foam sank into the sands, the rest of the wave started home to deeper waters. Blackthorn unthinkingly followed the receding wave with his eyes, anticipating the next, the one that would meet the spent swell, disrupting its swirling retreat, and merging the departing waters with its own.

No second wave came. The first drew back and back, rippling softly over time-smoothed pebbles, then more loudly as it fled the land. Cascading stones rattled and tumbled in the vanishing wave's haste to return to the deeps.

Blackthorn lifted his gaze up and out over the line of the ebbing water. For when the sea pulled back so far, so swift, it meant another wave was coming, an exceptional wave, a wave that was gathering to itself all the stray currents and aimlessly drifting eddies of the lesser swells the land had already tamed.

Far past the headland he had to look before he saw it, and then he doubted his eyes. The horizon was blotted out— Brighde's Fire, the horizon itself was now a green-gray wall of water! So distant no curl or crest was yet upon it, the monstrous wave rose higher and higher as it rolled toward shore. This moving mountain would not be broken in the shallows, but break them. Sand and stone would rise weightless in its churning grip, would pummel the shore and smash the limestone crags, would wash away the empty ruin of Lios Chanair as if it were a castle made of sand.

Some part of Blackthorn's mind tried to reckon his chances of reaching high ground and safety if he turned and ran with all his strength and will, but it was an idle exercise. He would not run from the magic he himself had called. He stayed where he was, once the boundary of earth and sea, now the edge of a shell-strewn, stony valley, watching the wave until it came even with the jutting headland. Then he fell to his knees, yet still he watched, and so saw the wave change.

Since the bay that had sheltered below the head was gone, by rights the wall of water should have broken at the rock tower, crashing down into naked seabed. Instead it stopped, as if the air before it was a wall stronger than itself, or time had forgotten to turn and held the wave in an unending instant. Then the seawall moved again, but it came no nearer. It gathered up its reaching length and stretched narrow and tall, and taller still. High as the clifftop it grew, but it was not formless. The waters flowed, as waters do, but they flowed in the shape of a gigantic man.

Waving seaweeds and mosses blackened the gray-green limbs. Swiftly swimming fishes and murúcha darted up the huge legs and around the thick torso. It was the ocean still, teeming with life, but the ocean come as a God because the rann had bid Him come. Blackthorn looked with astonished awe into the white-bearded face of Manannán mac Lir.

A long time he must have gazed at the Lord of the Waves, but time stands still in the presence of the Gods, and Blackthorn did not feel its passing. It occurred to him he might try to speak, to beg a boon of safe passage to Inis na Linnte, but without a sense of time to spur him, he felt no urgency in summoning his wits and voicing his request.

As he waited, or knelt without waiting before the Son of Lir, the sea returned to the drained bay. Not all at once, nor with dangerous speed, but merrily the waters swept through and around the Sea-God's massive legs, children running out from behind their mother's skirts. Whether it took only a moment or as long as a day, Blackthorn could not say, but the bay had been empty, and now it was full, and the breakers were rolling in as they had before.

Where Manannán stood, near enough to the headland to reach out a long watery arm to touch the point, the deep sea reached only to the giant God's knees. He had to bend before He could scoop up a handful of seawater. Mac Lir's body undulated like a wave against the clouded sky; His hand was one with the ocean's expanse. Blackthorn's sight was bewildered, he only knew what he saw when Manannán was once again standing, and letting the drops He had captured trickle down through the sea mosses that dangled from the ends of His fingers. Even then, Blackthorn could not mark where the drops fell, for a pale mist rose about the Sea-God's legs and out of it sailed a swan.

As Manannán dwarfed Blackthorn, so did this swan dwarf all the wild swans of Éirinn. Yet, until the magnificent bird struck the shore before him, Blackthorn believed he looked upon a living creature. When it slid smoothly into the wet sands, and listed slightly, the Hunter had to rise and touch the craft to convince himself that the graceful arch of the neck was a boat's prow, the glittering eyes were sightless, the snow-white sheen of the feathers was divine craft, not animate perfection. Without hesitation he dropped his blackthorn into the boat, then stepped in himself. Immediately the vessel began to move away from the shore.

Unlike Blackthorn, the púca had done his best to escape the death he saw coming in the terrible wave. He turned and ran for the cliffs. The strand was narrow, a mere ribbon of sand that appeared when the tide was lowest, but the sands were soft and deep, and the cliffs far. No matter how he tried he could make no headway. Looking back, the púca saw the sky-raking water ready to fall upon the headland. With a gurgling cry, he threw himself upon his belly and buried his face in his arms.

It seemed a year and a day he waited for the wave to come and drown him, long enough, anyway, to pull a bit of courage together and glance toward the sea. The baywaters were unaccountably back in their bed. That was all to the good, and made the púca quite bold. He sat up and turned, an action that broadened his range of vision considerably. He suddenly had a fine view of the Sea-God, a mountain of moving water rising higher than the highest of the limestone cliffs.

Not since he had swallowed half the river An tSionainn had the púca fought so hard for breath. He would have hidden his face again, but the sight of the Lord of the Waves towering over earth and sea, his body writhing with currents and the unnatural creatures that breathed water like air, filled the púca with a fear so absolute he was transfixed.

It proved a blessing in the end, for out of the corner of his eyes, frozen wide in horror, the shape-shifter saw Manannán's swan drift into shore. And, still staring aghast at the giant Sea-God, he also caught sight of Blackthorn climbing onto the swan's back, and, curse both boat and man, they were setting out to sea!

"Wait, you worthless fool!" he shouted.

The gulls answered him with long, derisive cries, and well they might, the púca thought miserably. He could barely hear himself over the wind and water. The Hunter would never hear him at all, at all.

"May the Sea-God swift send you to a watery grave an' you leave me behind!"

Quite sure there could be no worse torture in all the wide world, and equally sure that he was entirely undeserving of such a fate, the púca staggered to his feet and began to stumble toward the sea. Though he kept his head down and his eyes averted, he felt Manannán's gaze like a pounding wave upon him. When the sea-foam touched his bare toes, the púca squawked like a chicken and ran with great, hopping bounds, trying to lift his feet out of the water with every step.

A blur of white, a strong hand on his arm, and suddenly the púca was lying on planks of dry wood, looking up at a most peculiar sky. Gray clouds swept across a purpled dome, making and unmaking, massing together and attenuating in long, smoky strands. The thought entered the púca's mind that if he watched the sky for many days, he might see patterns like this. He let the notion pass, for the clouds were always tinged with the rose and violet of sunset, and always he could glimpse beyond them the deeps of heaven where stars shone palely, like a dream of white moths flitting through the shadows of the forest.

PART 5

the cauldron

Nineteen

Blood-madness covered the lad like a cloak,
His eyes burned like fires, his hair filled with smoke.
The maidens ran to him, all Mumhain did sing;
O'er Turlach was fallen the mantle of Kings.

Turlach of Tuaim

Though a blanket of snow still covered the earth, the fires of life were stirring beneath it, kindling hunger in the bellies of the sleeping moles and bears, bursting the husks of the dormant seeds, rising as warm sap into the hearts of the trees. The wheel of the year was turning—this night would begin Imbolc, the festival of Brighde, and this the day the Wizards had sworn would see their return to Temuir.

For her holdfast, Meacán chose the village linden tree. Though Imbolc marked the end of true winter, as yet spring was no more than a quickening promise in Éirinn's womb; hidden, unless one had the Sight. The linden would have changed little in the six weeks since the Dancer had seen it last.

She loosed her vision almost as soon as she had it clearly in her mind, and looked instead on the real world about her, at Dún na nGall. Its rampart rose gray and somber into an empty sky, for the moon had set and the stars fled, but the sun had not yet risen. Though the watch upon the walls was tripled and the courtyard where Meacán stood was crowded with tents, the dún was a lonely place at this hour. The watch looked outward, the tents sagged under the weight of frosted dew, and shadows hung like grief from the cold stone walls.

She should have said her farewells yesterday. Indeed, she would have, knowing she must depart on the morrow, but yesterday Niall Rí Uladh had cloaked himself in his royal mantle well before daybreak. Covered in battle-madness, her brother had driven his chariot out beyond the walls and remained there until the sun went down, meeting any Scáil who dared accept his challenge. The Mother of Ulaidh, big-bellied as she was, Meacán had not even glimpsed, though she had pursued rumors of the pregnant Queen about the dún all day. Neither Caireann nor Niall had come to the meager night meal in the hall, for when the dark did not bring battle, both were glad to take their rest. It would be rudeness itself to disturb them now, and yet to attend on their slumber simply to take her leave of them when they awoke—it was more than Meacán could patiently abide.

Thin streams of smoke wafted from the kitchen chimneys. Someone besides herself was astir. The air grew redolent with burning turf, tempting Meacán to stay and see what was cooking over the fires. Little enough, most likely. Who dared hunt, with the Scáileanna lurking in every tree's shadow? True, she had availed herself of the dún's impoverished hospitality these last weeks, but had repaid it by daring to dance through time to rich fields of summers gone by and bring back grain for the pot and herbs for the healers. Sure, an' the scant rations she'd taken were no more than her due, for though it was no great trial to fix a holdfast in memory, yet to find the present again, an' time having rolled on without her, was no small risk to herself. Now she must needs be gone—why tarry when she could dance to Temuir and break her fast at Liannan's board? More food there would be and less hunger in Midhe. Arrah, 'twould be a kindness to slip away, and no harm done. In these troubled times who would take umbrage at such a slight breach of courtesy, or even much notice if the Dancer left without farewell?

Meacán lifted her heels and set her weight onto the balls of her feet, again conjuring the linden's thick boughs and bare branches to her Sight. The steps to Temuir made a simple dance, a matter of distance, not time or perspective. A single stride and Dún na nGall was behind her. Another and she was gliding over loch and stream. She leapt from a high hill, spun past a scroggy, ice-crusted fen, threaded her way quick as light through the vast forests. The linden loomed ahead; Meacán came to a smooth halt before it, gently placing her feet on the soft, damp ground between two of the tree's gnarled roots.

She ended her dance facing the linden's trunk and gazing up into its splayed limbs. The tree was exactly as she had envisioned it. Nothing else was as it should be.

The earth trembled beneath Meacán's feet, the wind was acrid and heavy with the sounds of thudding hooves and clashing metal, with roars, shouts, cries, and moans—

In the instant of arrival, before she had straightened her knees or taken her Sight from her holdfast, Meacán could have escaped. It would have been as effortless as a thought of home and a turn on her toes for the Dancer of Sliabh Mis, but Meacán hesitated, and the moment passed.

She never doubted the din in her ears was the strident voice of the Mór-Ríoghain. These last weeks in Dún na nGall she'd heard precious little else. Day and night the Goddess of War had called the champions to fight before the fort's high walls, and crowed as they twined their foes of their lives or themselves died under the Scáileanna's fell swords.

It was not her ears Meacán doubted, but herself. If this was battle, this could not be Temuir. Her eyes were deceiving her—she must have lost her holdfast and strayed to besieged Béal Feirste or the strife-torn Silvermines. Or she had failed in her dance entirely, and was still in Dún na nGall, for when had the Crow of Battle ever sung her harsh songs from Midhe's fairest hill? Meacán turned away from the linden tree, determined to clear her Sight and learn where she was.

The heavy fogs would have made the day a dark one, but the sooty clouds rising from the smoking ruin that surrounded Meacán made it cousin to night. Warriors in studded leather rode through the murk, some waving long, blood-spattered swords over the heads of their wild-eyed horses, others thrusting their thick spears into the bodies of the foes before them. Black-haired goblins met the warriors' blades with gleaming axes, or grasped the defenders' javelins with their long arms and pulled the riders down.

A horse raced madly by, ears laid flat against his skull, saddle empty and loose reins flapping against his foam-streaked neck. Meacán pulled back instinctively, feeling the undeniably real trunk of the linden scrape against her shoulder. Her hand reached to the tree like a frightened child's reaching for her mother, but the Dancer's gaze flitted among the scattered fires that lit the shadowed day. Though the flames were blue and sputtering, they cast enough light for her to see that what fed the fires were the remains of cottages. She had not missed her holdfast, but come to it in truth. She had not failed to find Temuir, but in finding it had found disaster. Evil had come to the heart of Éirinn, bloodthirsty, red-eyed evil, and like a blind fool she had danced into the midst of it.

A gust of cold wind ripped into the fog and smoke. Through the rent it made in the thick curtain Meacán spied Temuir's gray stone wall standing pale and defiant. She drank in the sight, drank it in and made it hers. The high battlement was crowned with gold—fires must be blazing there, and the glints of silver against the stones were surely arrows catching the light as they flew from their bows. Torches then, set all along the walkway, and archers shooting from every slit—

Meacán brought her arms, her legs, her whole body forward into one frantic leap, a driving, desperate dance for the safety of the rampart. For less than an instant the blaring noise of the battleground receded, she saw clear and close before her the battlement, crowded with archers.

Like a hammer to stone, a goblin's howl smashed against Meacán's holdfast. The foul breath that had made the hideous cry blasted hot into her face, and her vision of Temuir shattered into a thousand pieces. In place of Temuir's wall Meacán saw a goblin's broad face leering into her own. Red eyes glowed with hate, and a gash of a mouth pulled back into a wide grin over yellow, knife-sharp fangs.

Meacán groped after the images that had been her holdfast, but they slipped from her numbed mind and faded into the dark before she could gather them up and bind them together. Only the nearing curve of the goblin's axe was real, only his searing gaze was unwavering. Meacán threw herself to the ground, deaf to her own cry, but hearing plainly the wind's whistle of pain as it took the blow meant for her. Clawing through the slippery mud, she drew herself back toward the linden, sobbing, screaming—her lungs ached for more air, but fear bound her chest and her raw, dry throat strangled her cries.

A root under her hand! The linden's root, and a path to the tree—

Meacán dared not rise, but crawled to the linden, then quickly around it on elbows and knees, trying to get its great girth between herself and her death. Pressed against the tree's rough skin, she dared a look over her shoulder only to see a black-haired arm swinging, a blood-smeared blade slicing through the dark to kill her. Again she flung herself flat, scratching her cheek on the base of the tree. The axe drove past, brushing by her light as a spring breeze, and bit deep into the linden.

The wood was tough, but the tree shuddered, and a grip of iron closed on Meacán's hair. She fought the goblin with all the outraged, terrified strength in her body, kicking, crying for help, scratching at the paw that held her. The red-eye barked angrily, or it might have been laughter. For all her struggles, Meacán felt herself pulled from the tree as easily as if she were a sack of grain, then dragged out into the open where the goblin could use his axe more freely.

She fought him till her scalp was ready to tear away in the goblin's hand, but she couldn't stop him, couldn't even slow him. She glimpsed a longsword stuck into the trampled ground, but too far away for her arm to reach. Fires flickered blue and red on the burning cotes—fire was the weapon would free her from this filthy beast. An' she had fire, he would fear her, for goblins burn, and she would burn this one till his oily black hair burst into flame. She would burn him till his stinking, greasy flesh was charred cinders. She would burn him to ash.

But Meacán was no Mother to call Fire at will. The goblin had her well clear of the smoking wreckage, in a place all darkness and cold. The light of the too-distant flames only mocked her helpless anger.

Tightening his grip, the goblin hauled Meacán to her knees and pulled her head back to bare her neck. Here, too, was mocking fire, red as wrath in the goblin's eyes. It sickened her to look into them, but Meacán could not look away.

The goblin howled again, in triumph and eagerness. Even in her utter horror and despair, Meacán wondered at the sound, so full of murderous joy. It seemed to hang on the air forever, swallowing every other noise, the crash of weapons, the pounding hooves, her own unwilled scream. It stole all power from the world, that howl, all will, all resistance.

The goblin's paw dropped from Meacán's hair, his head lolled weirdly forward, his dark, greasy body began to fall.

Meacán watched the goblin go down and become a rank, unmoving corpse in the mud before her, and still the unearthly howl rang in her ears.

Slowly she lifted her eyes to the terrible sound. A warrior was standing where the red-eye had been. Though she gazed full upon him, at first Meacán did not recognize the man who had delivered her. His bloodshot eyes bulged from under his brows, his hair stood up from his head and smoked as if on fire. The jagged edge of his broken sword was running with fresh black blood, the fierce smile on his lips was as wide as the goblin's had been and just as gleeful. It was from his throat the inhuman cry came.

Reaching down with his free hand, the warrior grasped the goblin's half-severed head, set his boot against the goblin's body, and wrenched the two apart. Smoke curled from between the champion's fingers where they twined in the red-eye's long, oily hair. In a moment, Meacán knew, the heat of his grasp would set the ghastly thing aflame.

The man looked like a monster and fought like a God, but Meacán recognized him now. It was Eoghan. Draped in his royal mantle, the mild, fair-haired lad of An Mullach had become unmistakably and entirely a King.

Flames leapt from the goblin's head. The stench of rancid, sizzling meat made Meacán retch. Tossing his trophy aside, Eoghan's blazing eyes fell on the Dancer.

"Och, Mór-Ríoghain," Meacán moaned fervently, "Great Queen, Crow of Battle, call the King's Name that he will turn to You, and keep his scorching hand from me."

She crawled back and away from Eoghan as she had from the goblin, but it was useless. She had lost all sense of direction and no longer knew where the linden stood. Even if she could reach it, a tree was no protection against a King's rage. Curse their foul hides, where were the red-eyes, now she needed them? A whole village full of enemies, and Eoghan's fury about to fall on her!

She had been a fool to pray to the Mór-Ríoghain. Curses the Crow of Battle liked better, and She gave Meacán's a swift answer. A clatter of harness and bridles, the groan and creak of rolling wood, and four dark horses plunged suddenly into view behind Eoghan. They were foam-flecked and panting, but battle-eager as the King, and they drew a chariot, gold-rimmed and cunningly carved. The hand on the reins was the Maiden of Midhe's.

"Eoghan Rí na Midhe! Eoghan Rí na Midhe."

Not the Mór-Ríoghain's croak, but the voice of a younger Goddess, brave and fair, cried the King's Name through Brí's lips.

The Maiden's eyes fell on Meacán, and for a moment both a surprised girl and a reproving deity looked out of them. What folly has brought you out upon the field of battle? both seemed to ask.

"Eoghan Rí na Midhe!" the Maiden called again.

The King turned toward her and loosed another blood-curdling howl.

"More worthy foes await you, brighter glory to cover you! Battle calls! What is your answer?"

The horses shied as Eoghan bounded toward them, then reared as the King leapt behind his charioteer and Brí shouted to the team to be off. Meacán saw Eoghan's arm brush the young Priestess, but the girl only laughed. Under his mantle a King's flesh was like burning armor, hard and searing as red-hot iron, but he could do the Maiden no harm, not when she and the Goddess were one.

The chariot's wheels spun, spraying Meacán with mud, then lurched forward and the chariot thundered away, its polished rim drawing streaks of gold in the clouded dark. No, that must be wrong. A chariot cannot thunder on muddy ground. The thunder must be within her, her heart's terror. Meacán staggered to her feet, clenched hands pressed against her breast. Her heart was pounding indeed, but not with the rolling rhythm of the rising thunder.

Shivering with cold, Meacán cautiously turned her head and surveyed the battleground. Plainly she saw the devastated village, for the day was lighter now, much lighter—how long had she been kneeling on the cold, wet earth? Plainly she could see Temuir's gates. The fogs were lifting and the smoky fires dying, and the battle had retreated from the wall. Temuir's huge oak doors were open, and a storm, neither of dark nor rain, but of riders was breaking from them like sunlight pouring through a crack in the clouds. This the thunder she heard—the thunder of the Sidhe charging into battle, and their eyes flashed like the stars of heaven, and their swords were silver.

Twenty

Cold the comfort of Canar's hall
Sour the ale he sets on the board
Greasy as goblin the game put before me
Fit for flames, the foul repast

a rann made by Ruairc
the Poet of An Fharraige

Dismayed by the day and daunted by the elves' bright eyes, the goblins broke and ran. They surged over the splintered posts that had been the stockade, an ebbing black tide fleeing the lightening field for the shadowy wood.

A glad shout sounded from the top of Temuir's walls and was taken up by the warriors on the field as they harried the foe from the ruined village. It was a cry of victory, but it made Meacán shiver all the more. The Sidhe were everywhere, streaks of light and death flying through the smouldering dark debris. They were too swift, or Meacán's eyes too stung by smoke and tears to see the elves clearly. The more she looked, the more they seemed to ride into nothingness, to fade away like the pieces of her demolished holdfast. The red-eyes were disappearing too, vanishing into the sheltering gloom of the forest.

My bones will come loose, she thought. I'm shaking so hard, they'll come loose and I'll fall.

She closed her eyes in hopes of banishing the gory confusion and bringing a vision of safe haven to her Sight. The Mór-Ríoghain's music followed her behind her lids, vengeful cries and pitiful moans. Even in her mind Meacán could see nothing but grisly images of war.

Love awaits the hero
A soft sheath for your spear . . .

The Dancer's eyes flew open at the gentle words, the ancient, coaxing melody. The maidens were come. And if the Mother had sent the maidens forth, the battle must be over, the killing done.

Follow the fair white flowers
To the Lady's garden . . .

the girls of Temuir sang, and Meacán almost wept to hear the high, sweet chorus.

They were at the gates, a cold and miserable group of girls, hurrying to calm the King's blazing fury. Their breath veiled their naked beauty in puffs of white cloud. As they began their barefoot trek through the muck and mire of the village, their song faltered. The dead and dying lay all about them. Meacán saw the girls huddling closer together, avoiding the corpses as if they were curses. Older women followed the maidens from the gates, and older men, but they were not seeking the King. They were looking for their kin among the slain.

Meacán drew her hand across her brow, unaware of the dark smudge it left behind. Her head was spinning, and the world whirling around with it. She tried to follow the maidens with her eyes, but instead found her gaze drawn toward the woods. The dark tide had withdrawn from Temuir's ragged shore. Another was flowing in, grimy, bloody waves of drooping horses and haggard warriors, splintered chariots and tattered banners.

The maidens . . . where had they gone? Meacán found them at last, being carried toward Temuir like white foam on the crest of the waves, and with them the King was drawn in with the tide.

In time to their song the girls danced before Eoghan, slipping within his reach, then darting away when he lunged for them. Though each time they lured him a step nearer to the

gates, their rhythm was limping, their dance almost grace-
less. Brí was there, but even the Maiden of Midhe seemed
drained, exhausted, just another cold, uncomfortable girl.
She was as careful as the others to elude the King's hand.
The Goddess must have left her, Meacán thought. The
Maiden's immunity to Eoghan's burning touch was gone.

I can walk as well as they, Meacán scolded herself.
Though I cannot clear my thoughts to dance, still my feet
can walk the path to the gates. But where the high road that
will lead me there?

A hissing like a thousand spitting cats—Meacán shuddered at the sound, but looked up to see the maidens in a
circle by Temuir's walls and a cloud of steam rising above
their heads. They must be drenching the King now, pouring
tubs of cold water over him to douse his fire. Again the
white steam, the awful noise, but less this time. Meacán
imagined Eoghan's eyes turning blue, his hair lying plastered
against his forehead. Dripping wet he strides through the
gates and into the close. Liannan awaits him, naked as the
young girls, but no maiden she. She stands before all Temuir
as Midhe Herself in the fullness of Her beauty, the rich fruit
of ecstasy that is only a promise in the flowers of youth.

How many times had Meacán rejoiced to see Caireann
welcome Niall so? But then she had been safe within the
walls of the fort. Then she had witnessed the mystery, had
seen the embrace that turned a King's bloodlust to desire,
had felt the Queen's love enfold the King's madness. The
fire that brought death to his enemies would now bring life
to his people—this the magic of the hero's welcome, this the
Mother's gift to heal the wounds of battle.

But here outside the walls, where she should never have
come, here was no welcome, no healing. Where Meacán
stood the passions that filled the air were not of love, but
grief, not of life, but death.

They had gone in without her, she thought sadly. The
sky-clad maidens, the King . . . left her outside amid the
creaking, soiled panoply of war. Only a few living souls yet
wandered among the blackened bits of the village, some
hauling enemy carcasses into heaps for burning, others keening over the broken bodies of their sons, their daughters,
their lovers. Black-feathered ravens began to alight on the

goblin pyres, to pick at the untended dead. Red-eye or human, Scáileanna or Sidhe, it was all one to the birds of the Mór-Ríoghain. They supped as greedily from Éire's children as from the Shadow King's slaves.

The skies, so briefly light, were darkening again. For a moment Meacán feared her own black thoughts had invited Shadow's return, but when she looked up, she saw it was the mists thickening, sinking toward the earth. Invisible hands had set a crown of gray upon Temuir Hill. Soon the halls would be buried in cold, wet clouds.

She was facing the gates. All she need do was to take the steps that would bring her to them. She managed one, but it was shaky, and then she stopped.

An old woman stood in the middle of the ruined village, between the Dancer and the open gates. Her back was to Meacán; the Dancer could see only her long, white hair gently moving about in the wind, a black woolen shawl drawn tight and a gray skirt reaching to the ground. It seemed to Meacán she could see age and grief also, rounding the old woman's shoulders, and something else, something rigid and callous as stone hardening the old woman's body. Two ravens swooped over her head and two more hopped about near her feet, calling out vulgar thanks for the bloody feast. It might be the Mór-Ríoghain Herself she looked upon, Meacán realized, and the possibility was somehow frightening and comforting at the same time.

The old woman turned. Though her face and features were those of the Cailleach of Midhe, Meacán was more certain than ever it was a Goddess she beheld. Maiden, Mother, and Crone had come to Temuir this day, one to do battle, one to soothe its hurts, the last to survey the slaughter with a sovereign mien, to mourn the dead and bury them.

Walk, Meacán told herself sternly. Leave this dreadful place, where sorrow flows like rivers over the bloody ground. One foot before the other to Temuir's gates. Walk, she insisted, but her legs were rooted to the earth and would not obey her.

"Meacán! Meacán Iníon na Caillí. What folly is it has brought you here, Dancer?"

The voice that spoke in Meacán's ear was deep, silken, and reassuringly worried. She knew it. Turning toward it, a Name sprang into her mind.

"Mac Ailch," she whispered.

His answering smile was a little uncertain, but it was her own strangeness made the Conjuror uneasy, Meacán was sure. His strong hand took her elbow. As her arm was pulled forward, Meacán's feet naturally followed. Relief and gratitude flooded her heart and nearly broke from her eyes in tears.

"I saw you as I looked out from the wall," Mac Ailch said, steering her surely across the ravaged field, "but barely. You are the same color as the trampled sod, Lady, or likely you would have been gathered in long since."

Somehow the Conjuror managed to sound as if he were commenting on the weather or the day's hunting. Meacán leaned on his voice the way she leaned on his arm. Both supported her, both were bearing her to Temuir.

"Things are not so bad within," he promised. "Though the village is swept away, Temuir itself has not bent under this dark wind."

The tall gates were suddenly before them, and there Meacán hesitated. She could hear entreaty in the crows' voices. They invited her to return, at least to look back, to partake once more of the battlefield's lurid mysteries. She closed her eyes.

"Take me in," she begged.

Mac Ailch's eyes narrowed at the urgency in Meacán's voice. Tightening his gloved fingers on her arm, he led her quickly under the stone arch and into the close.

"Are you hurt?" he asked.

Opening her eyes, Meacán took her first good look at Temuir. Mac Ailch had spoken true; it was not so bad within the walls. There were tracks of mud all through the close and it reeked of horses and sweat, but all in all, the Mother's halls were one of finest sights Meacán had ever seen.

"Unscathed," she said, meaning both herself and the place.

A laugh bubbled up inside her at her small jest, but she swallowed it, afraid of what it might become if she let it out.

"Only my pride is wounded," she said soberly. "And my courage."

Mac Ailch raised his eyebrows. "What possessed you to test them so?"

"That was not my intent," she replied.

Her laughter spilled out with the words, and, just as she feared, it turned immediately to sobs. Mac Ailch's already grave expression darkened to one of such deep concern Meacán laughed harder, but she hadn't stopped crying, and between the two she felt torn apart.

"I'm all right. I'm all right," she gasped, trying to make herself believe it. "But take me to my own apartments, Mac Ailch. I need to sit down."

"That was my intent," he said amiably.

"Then why do you lead me on? There the hall where the Wizards are housed—behind us. Can we not—"

"Our rooms are changed," Mac Ailch explained. "There is the entire village to house now, and the warriors must be closeted near to the stables and armory. This is our way."

The path he chose climbed steadily, first along Temuir's broadest, busiest streets, then up an older, narrower road. At the end of the stone lane was an old hall, a wide, low building, sitting with its back wedged flat against the hill. Thick granite formed the walls, but the once-gray slabs were now black-veined and green with moss and had weathered to the irregularity of unwrought stone.

"So far from the gates," Meacán murmured.

"So far from battle," Mac Ailch answered mildly. "You are to share your chamber with Fionnghuala and Seamair, yet you will have some privacy for an hour or so, I think. The Deceiver and the Weather-Worker are hungry after their night's labors, and both are taking refreshment in the great hall below."

Mac Ailch kept his hand under Meacán's arm until they reached the building's metal-banded doors. There he let her go and pulled on the rings. The doors were well oiled and swung soundlessly open. The Dancer stared past them into the hall. The air from inside carried the scent of old fires, though a new one was burning in the central hearth. The long tables were bare, the room empty.

"I don't know where I am to go," she said.

Mac Ailch went past her, preceding her through the hall and guiding her to a flight of stairs. He took her arm again to steady her up the stairway, and drew her through a door at the back of the gallery into a low-ceilinged, windowless

corridor. The doors along the hallway were far apart, but
they had only to go to the second before Mac Ailch
stopped. He put his hand to the thick door, a smooth block
of wood polished by age and years of oil, and pushed it wide.

Meacán moved into the room on her own. The first thing
she saw was a low-backed, bowl-shaped chair set before a
cold fireplace. Without even a glance at what else the apartment held, she dropped into the chair and stared at the
empty hearth. Mac Ailch followed her in, found a woolen
rug and spread it across her lap, left her again, and returned
with a handled goblet. As she reached for it, Meacán
noticed her sleeve was rent, her fingers were caked with
mud, her hand was shaking.

She took the drink and brought it to her lips. The wine
was spiced, would have been better warmed, and it burned
just slightly as it went down.

"A hundred welcomes, Meacán Iníon na Caillí, Dancer of
Sliabh Mis," the Conjuror said.

There was a dubious edge to his voice, though the greeting was polite enough. Meacán lifted her cup to the
Conjuror, pleased to see she was already able to hold it
steady.

"Éire bless all here," she replied.

Twenty-one

Speak with one Mother,
and speak with Them all

Sayings of the Mothers

"When did the goblins—" Meacán began, then stopped. Her hand was steady, but her voice was not.

Mac Ailch knelt by a stack of turf piled near the hearth and began to mound the dry bricks in the empty fireplace. "Sundown three nights past they first attacked," he answered.

Meacán took another sip of the wine, and found on second try its sour taste was more to her liking.

"And the moon waxing? The weather was clouded, then?"

"The night was clear," Mac Ailch said, "though 'tis true the red-eyes fought the fiercer between the moon's setting and the dawn."

He had his fire laid, and took up the flint from its place by the piled turf.

"Yet, this good has come of it." He struck a few sparks from the stone and smiled grimly as one fell on the turf and caught. "We need no longer guess at Shadow's design. From Binn Chuilceach and Cromghlinn in the north, from the Silvermine mountains in Mumhain and the Blackstairs in Laighin, the Dark reaches out, and for what? For the jewels of Éirinn's kingdoms, for the seats of our power. For Dún na nGall and Béal Feirste, for Caiseal and Ceatharlach, for Tuaim dá Ghualainn, even for Temuir herself."

Meacán shook her head. She was actually feeling remarkably good, much stronger now and quite clear.

"But Doire Eile was destroyed," she argued, "and no smaller, less powerful village could you have found in all the five kingdoms. And An Baile Meánach—"

"They were in the way," Mac Ailch pointed out. "They lay between the strongholds of Shadow and our own."

"It may be as you say," Meacán conceded, and shrugged. Rain was falling; she could hear it tapping on the stones.

"Meacán the Dancer has travelled wide in the world," Mac Ailch said, rising from his fire, but studying it still. "What have you seen, Lady, what have you heard that makes you doubt that Temuir's downfall is Shadow's fondest hope?"

"Little of Éirinn have I seen since midwinter," Meacán answered. "Through time I've been journeying, back to the days when the fields were summer-blest and fruitful, when healing herbs were to be found in the forest glades. In Dún na nGall I've dwelt, serving the Mother of Ulaidh, for that place has been besieged since Samhain, and the war goes not well."

"So, 'twas to the dún Liannan sent you?"

Mac Ailch took Meacán's cup, though it was not quite empty, and refilled it from a ewer on a sideboard. Hardly the breakfast she had thought to enjoy in Temuir, Meacán thought wearily.

"'Twas to An Earagail she sent me," she told him, "and from there did I dance to the dún."

The Conjuror handed Meacán back her cup, but he was frowning.

"An Earagail? Is it telling me you are Liannan sent you to seek out Úna the Oak Seer? Desperate the Mothers must be an' they beg counsel of that madwoman. A fool's errand, I'm thinking."

Meacán looked sidelong at Mac Ailch. The wine was heady, but she'd not yet taken so much that she couldn't hold her tongue.

"What?" Mac Ailch said, folding his arms before his chest. "Could you not even find the Seer?"

There was just enough amusement in his ice-blue eyes, just enough scorn in his voice to override Meacán's prudence.

"I found her, I spoke with her, and to Caireann, Queen of Ulaidh, have I told all I heard. From her have all the Mothers learned Úna's answer. The Mothers have trusted the Seer's words to a Bard, that they'll be remembered in full and can be recalled at will."

Mac Ailch's eyebrows lifted and he nodded with grudging respect. "Good on you, then. Few are they can speak with the Oak Seer and make sense of what she says."

Meacán frowned with annoyance. "I said I spoke with her, not that I understood her." Rising from her chair, she came nearer to the warm fire. "Perhaps the Mothers have made sense of the messages I brought back from the wild. They are meaningless to me."

"Would they be to me?" Mac Ailch wondered quietly. "What—"

A knock on the door interrupted the Conjuror, and brought Meacán's head around. She called to enter, thinking to see Fionnghuala or Seamair come in, but when the door swung wide, it was the Cailleach of Midhe who stepped into the room.

"Tine," the Old Woman said absently.

A ring of candles in a carved wooden stand on the sideboard burst into flame, and thick yellow tallows in a wrought-iron ring hanging from the ceiling blazed with light. The fire Mac Ailch had set leapt with new life, driving Meacán away from its sudden heat.

The Cailleach bent her pale, bright gaze on Mac Ailch. The Conjuror shifted and dropped his eyes like a boy caught with his fingers in the butter urn.

"Then I will to my own chamber for a time," he said, and Meacán realized the Cailleach must have spoken in Mac Ailch's mind, asking him to leave them alone. "I and Feargna Óg have the rooms beside yours, Meacán, if you have need of anything."

Meacán started to thank him for all he had done, but he was gone before she had barely begun. The Conjuror's haste made her smile, but she understood it well enough. The Cailleacha had a way of making even the bravest, wisest, boldest heart beat like that of a frightened mouse.

"You were at the dún," the old Priestess said shortly, her sharp eyes now on Meacán. "Did not the Mother warn you what to expect at Temuir?"

A stern look and a reprimand, and now Meacán's heart was pounding just as she had imagined Mac Ailch's had done.

"I acted on my own counsel," she said as stoutly as she could, "thinking only of my promise to return to Temuir by Imbolc. The dún was still asleep when I left. It seemed inconsiderate to awaken the Queen. Just to tell her I was leaving," she added lamely.

"So you departed without farewell and found yourself between King and goblin on the field of battle."

The Cailleach lowered herself into the hearthside chair and sighed. Tiny droplets of rain netted her white hair and glimmered like clear gems in the firelight.

"I suppose there is always risk when you dance to a place Seen only in your mind. And how could you expect such danger as now we face? Who has ever dared to bring battle to Temuir's gates?"

Feeling almost forgiven for her ill-considered act, Meacán went to the sideboard, poured the Cailleach a cup of wine from the ewer, and added a drop more to her own.

The Old Woman looked up when Meacán came back, and took the cup, but did not return the Dancer's smile.

"Sit with me for a moment," she said. "Soon I will send for a servant to bring hot water and clean clothes, and you will bathe and rest and dress. But rest well. Though we do not look to see the goblins attack before tomorrow, yet we will not find time for sleep tonight. Liannan has called a council. And before it meets, we must talk."

The Dancer obediently seated herself at the Old Woman's feet, but her pulse had quickened again. The Cailleach of Midhe was no messenger to come with news Meacán could have had of Mac Ailch. The tidings must be grave indeed, an' the Cailleach saw fit to bear them herself. Meacán glanced at the Cailleach, then away, then back again, but if the Old Woman had secrets to tell, she was slow to share them. A long while the Cailleach stared into the fire, then she sat back in her chair, sipped from her cup, and sighed again.

"His mind is always so empty," she said.

Puzzled, Meacán asked, "Is it Mac Ailch you're speaking of?"

"It is." The Old Woman's frown deepened. "The Oak Seer was in your thoughts when I came in, and in my own as well. But the thought foremost in the Conjuror's mind? 'Does the Dancer need more wine?'!"

"But I did need his wine, Grandmother. And his arm to lean on and his conversation to steady me."

"And glad I am he was there to help you, child. But 'tis not willingness to serve that is wanting in that one. 'Tis a Wizard's pride he lacks, and ambition, driving purpose, and clarity of thought. Even a babe like Feargna Óg or an unanchored cloud like Fionnghuala possesses greater will than does the Conjuror of Sliabh An Óir."

"An' he is so poor a Wizard," Meacán ventured, "why was he made one of the Seven?"

It was a bold question, but the Cailleach did not seem angered by it. Rather her gaze softened, as if the Old Woman were turning her keen Sight inward.

"Three years ago, when Breac the Mariner died, 'twas not to Mac Ailch the Mothers hoped to offer Sliabh An Óir, but to Róisín Dubh," the Cailleach answered quietly. "The Wish-Bringer could not be found, and so the Mothers' messengers were sent to Ruairí the Fire-Worker. Ruairí was found indeed, burned in his own fires, his charred body almost unrecognizable. Only then did the Mothers' Sight fall on Mac Ailch the Conjuror."

"But surely he has proved a worthy Wizard?"

"Worthy? What has been asked of him? What has been asked of any of you until now?" snapped the Cailleach. "Can a worthy Wizard weather the storms of war?"

Meacán felt her cheeks flame, remembering this morning and the pitiful figure she had cut on the field of battle.

"No, Dancer," the Old Woman said more kindly. "Of your worth I have no doubt. You have done well, and will do better, I think, now you have had a lesson in caution."

Her expression eased and a small, conspiratorial smile touched her lips. "I am a fool to fret so. A turn in the fire but tempers the blade, is it not so? And Meacán the Dancer is not the only Wizard to have found herself unexpectedly thrust into the flames."

Sight gleamed in the Cailleach's brown eyes. "Mac Ailch was the first to return, four days since. His tale of strife in the north was not good, but his own journey was uneventful. Feargna Óg arrived the next day, just before sundown, riding through the gates as if the Dead Lord himself were after him, babbling so no one could make sense of what he said. But I Saw it in his mind, heard it in his rattling heart. Red eyes he'd seen filling the shadows of the woods, hundreds of red fires glowing in the dark. And the eyes had fallen on him, black throats had howled for his blood. Barely had he eluded the reaching arms and sharp axes, barely had he escaped to bring the news to Temuir that she was surrounded by enemies, that with night's coming the goblins would fall upon us—"

"How could it be?" Meacán whispered. "How could you not have known?"

The Cailleach's eyes seemed to darken. "How do I know Shadow? By the prayers in the hearts of my people when they glimpse red eyes in the night. By the birds and beasts that fly from goblins as they do before a gale. By the destruction left in the goblins' wake, the torn saplings and trampled grasses and dirtied streams. By the corpses of Éirinn's creatures, wantonly murdered and left to rot. But though I listened, I heard no voices calling. Though I looked, I Saw them not.

"Who has tutored these black-hearted beasts?" the Old Woman hissed, and Meacán flinched at the pain in the Cailleach's voice. "Who has taught them to walk lightly on the land, to be stealthy and cunning? Who rules their will, that they curb their bloodlust until they are before our walls, and dare the moonlight to bring us down?"

"But Feargna Óg's warning—"

The Cailleach took a deep breath, gathering back the anger she had released, drawing it deep within her until Meacán could see no more of it than a hard gleam in the Old Woman's eyes.

"We had barely enough time to bring the folk of the village behind the rampart. We had not enough time to see to their belongings or their animals. The sun set swiftly, and was barely down when the goblins attacked. The moon was waxing and the night clear, but still they fought, and fiercer in the dark when the moon had set and dawn not yet come."

"So said Mac Ailch. Yet Temuir stands firm."

"We have a good King."

Meacán smiled into her cup. The Cailleach sounded as proud as if Eoghan was her own son.

The Cailleach must have been listening to Meacán's thoughts, for she laid her hand on the younger woman's shoulder, and laughed softly.

"We were not sure how well he would wear his mantle, when true battle came," she said. "At the festival of Lughnasadh it is a blessing for all when a King kills his rival, or a rival kills a King. Then all may see the madness come upon them, and see who bears it best. But Laochail was three moons dead when Eoghan was made King at the Games of Lugh. We could not let the mantle fall fully upon the boy, for there was no sacred blood for him to spill. 'Tis a wonder and an inspiration to our people to see such glory covering our King in the battles he has fought these last three days. But for you, perhaps, the sight was not so fine."

"Terrible, indeed, but not unfamiliar." Meacán found she could speak of it now without her voice quivering. "Often have I seen the royal madness fall upon my own brother Niall."

"Yes. Your brother," the Cailleach murmured.

The Dancer looked up, baffled by the Old Woman's remark. Were her tidings of Niall, then? But Meacán had seen him but yesterday. The feeling that there was a question she should be asking pressed on the Dancer, but the only one troubling her mind had nothing to do with Kings.

"Why were the Sidhe so long in joining the battle?" she said.

"The Sidhe? But they did not join the battle. They have not yet returned to Temuir."

"But I saw them!" Meacán insisted. "'Twas they routed the goblins from the field!"

The Cailleach shook her head. "The Deceiver you have to thank for that rescue. A finer illusion I have never seen."

"Fionnghuala! Och, good on her! But why do the Sidhe not come? Cessair swore to return before the Birch moon was old, and the Sidhe do not lie."

"The Birch was only three days past full when Cessair's harper Fiach came to us with the news that the Poet of

Teach an Fhásaigh was dead and Cessair gone to Binn Chuilceach to avenge her."

Something nagged at the edges of Meacán's mind, something amiss in what the Cailleach had said. "These grave tidings I heard from Caireann," she said slowly. "A great Poet is worth many warriors, even those of the Sidhe. A terrible blow, that has brought down Scáthach of Teach an Fhásaigh."

Wait. She had it now. Meacán sat straighter, and looked into the Cailleach's eyes.

"'Gone to Binn Chuilceach' you say? But the Sidhe were there already, for how else would Fiach know Scáthach was dead?"

The Cailleach's eyes took on a brightness that was like sun on snow, glittering, but cold.

"'Twas on a high empty plain far south of Binn Chuilceach the Sidhe learned of Scáthach's murder, and 'twas the Hunter of Éirinn brought them the news. This much Fiach told the Mother, but one thing more I alone learned from him. I learned the Hunter's Name, for the sound of it echoed in the harper's heart when he chanced to look on me."

The Cailleach was speaking gently, too gently, as if a baby was sleeping nearby. Meacán felt a tightening in her chest and Úna's words sprang suddenly into her mind; *You know. But you know only this one. I have known them all.*

"True it is. You know him." The Cailleach rose. "The Hunter of Éirinn is Conall mac na Caillí. Your brother, Blackthorn."

It was well, thought Meacán, she had not risen with the Old Woman. As it was her cup had only a short way to fall, and her wine made only a small, garnet puddle on the floor.

Twenty-two

Infinite are the reaches of heaven,
the deeps of the sea,
the secret places of the heart

The Sixth Triad of Éirinn

Liannan reached out her hand to stroke the rim of the great, black cauldron, tracing its familiar, grainy edge with the tips of her fingers. The empty vessel was set in the center of Temuir's temple, resting over the firepit in the rigid embrace of a heavy metal tripod. As yet the Mother had called no fire to burn below. Time enough for Sight and blazing purpose. Now she desired only cold clarity and iron strength.

You will need both, the Cailleach said in her mind.

The afternoon's brief squall had left copious mists crowding between earth and sky, but Liannan Saw the Old Woman clearly, and watched her as she climbed the winding path to the temple. The white-haired Priestess's step was sure, though below in the town the people were saying to each other, "On a night like this you can't see the stones under your feet!" and in their hearts they fretted, *On a night like this, the goblins grow bold.*

They need not fear, Brí said in the Mother's mind. *The red-eyes will not attack tonight.*

Though she had looked already, many times, Liannan once more sent her inner gaze speeding through the forest to

assure herself that the Maiden spoke true. Thick as porridge
the fogs were there, but they were nothing to the Mother's
Sight, not now she knew what to look for. Besides, the surprise of their attack sprung, the goblins had abandoned their
new-learned subtlety. The path they had cut through the
woods as they fled the field was well marked—axe-scored
tree trunks, trampled ferns, and shrubs torn out by their
roots showed where the red-eyes had gone. Liannan found
the foe huddled deep in the woods, licking their wounds and
cursing. No, the red-eyes would not attack tonight.

Yet, they will come again, the Cailleach cautioned.

Liannan brought her attention back from the fogbound
forest and placed it on the Old Woman. The Cailleach came
between the stones into the temple, and the auburn-haired
Maiden just behind her. Swiftly the elder Priestess and the
younger joined the Mother at the cauldron and at once they
began to sing. In a moment out of time three voices twined,
three hearts touched, stopped, then beat again, but together
now, a single rhythm, a single voice. Maiden, Mother, and
Crone were one, and Her Name was Midhe.

When it was done, Liannan bent her Sight on those she
had called to her council. They wound carefully up the steep
hill, their heads bent to spy the twisting path, their torches
lifted to burn away the blinding fogs. The wet mists pressed
against their fires, molding them into faceted spheres,
golden-amber jewels adrift in a sea of dark cloud.

Liannan spoke a word. Fire waked in the pit, brighter,
stronger than the feckless flames creeping up from the halls.
She bade her fire bend around the cauldron's ebon bottom
before letting it reach up with tapering fingers into the
clinging mists. The tongues of flame ruffled along the sides
of the vessel, beating against the air like diminutive banners
in the wind. Liannan watched her fire, but she Saw only the
Wizards and Poets ascending to the circle of stones, and
heard them as well, though not a word was spoken.

Feargna Óg's thoughts were loudest, his slighted pride
knowing no discretion. *So Liannan deems us ready at last to hear
the news she has for a moon and more kept to herself,* he fumed.

An ill day that Scáthach died, Tadhg the Poet moaned to
himself. He walked with head bent nearly to his chest, for
his heart was hung with doubt, and it weighed upon him.

Seamair trudged slowly behind the Poet of An Chluain Thiar. She held no torch, both her hands busy with her skirts and her long cloak. Liannan called to her.

Make haste, Weather-Worker. I would have the fogs lift, and so lift my people's hearts.

With an unvoiced sigh, Seamair obeyed, lengthening her stride and edging by Tadhg with a mumbled apology. Slightly out of breath, she reached the top of the hill and stepped cautiously between the stones. With the Mother's firelight to guide her, the Weather-Worker made her way briskly to the center of the temple and began her spell, chanting words she alone in all Éirinn could speak. Obeying her will, the fogs abruptly spun up and away, vanishing into the evening sky as if some God had scooped them up and swallowed them whole. Sudden and low on the eastern horizon, the Rowan moon appeared in her fullness and drenched Temuir in soft, ivory light.

Meacán was nearly to the stones when the mists lifted. Looking up, she saw a few pale stars flickering valiantly against the brighter, bolder moonlight, and frowned. So might her brother struggle to fulfill his geis against the will of a stronger, fiercer foe. So might he fare against Shadow.

Meacán.

The Mother's call was imperious, but Meacán stayed where she was. She was not yet ready to join the circle.

You have told her. Liannan allowed the Cailleach to feel the depth of her surprise.

Yes.

And so she fills her thoughts with him, and closes her mind to me!

Let her thoughts dwell on the Hunter. To help her brother, she will freely bend her will to yours. Not so the rest of your council. Listen to their hearts. I speak true.

An elder's advice should never be taken lightly, and a Cailleach's least of all. Liannan listened to the hearts of the Mighty of Éirinn, each in turn. Mac Ailch's pounded with tension, but it was sourceless and undirected. Fionnghuala and Seamair lent their arms to support old Creathna, and of the three hearts only the Name-Sayer's held more curiosity than trepidation. The giant Reochaidh stood between two of the standing stones, leaning heavily on both. The wound he had taken in the goblins' first attack troubled his heart. Though the hurt was slight, it was uncomfortable, and he feared it would not be healed before the red-eyes came again.

All her council were uneasy, Liannan admitted to herself. All nursed a chary guardedness that was ready to rouse to defiance at the smallest provocation. All but two. Redwing the Bard, and Meacán the Dancer.

Listening to stout Redwing's heart, Liannan's own was eased. Here was one not bent on challenge, but bursting with eagerness and pride. To Redwing the Mothers had entrusted Úna's words, and the Bard yearned only to show how well his skilled memory had served to hold them safe.

But Meacán . . . To listen to her heart was to hear a hundred voices, like the voices of a hundred rooks startled from the trees and crying out in alarm and consternation as they beat to the skies. Overfull was the Dancer's heart, with worry and dread, with irritation and astonishment. Meacán was heartsick over her brother, Blackthorn.

My Wizards are wary, Liannan told the Cailleach. The Poets are filled with grief. An' the choice were theirs, they would face Shadow's armies and shun Shadow itself. But the choice is mine.

"I have called this council," she said aloud, "but no counsel do I ask of you." She waited until all eyes had fixed on her. "Counsel I will give, and I expect you to heed it." Though you dig in your heels to resist me like the stubborn goats you are, she added silently.

"Attend to me," Liannan went on, "and learn what must be done to combat the Shadow King's design."

Her statement brought the expected murmurs and gasps, the expected stiffening of hackles along the Wizards' spines. And, as expected, it was Feargna Óg who first gave voice to his resentment.

"Is our counsel worth nothing to you, Mother? Are the Mighty of Éirinn no more to you than common warriors to be ordered into battle? When last we met, Shadow's designs were hidden from us. An' they are now clear to the Mothers' Sight, I pray you make them clear also to mine, ere you will command me."

"Think you your Sight is keen enough to match the Mothers', Feargna Óg?" said Liannan, her voice soft and sharp, like a switch cutting the air before it reaches flesh. "Yet, listen, an' you will," she said more loudly, "listen all of you, and hear the words of Úna the Oak Seer."

Though Meacán had closed her mind to the Mother, her ears were open. Liannan's voice filled them, luring her to the standing stones. Peering between the tall menhirs, she saw a stocky, red-haired, broad-shouldered man nod to the Mother, then lift his head and begin to recite. With the first syllable he uttered, Meacán knew him for a Bard. The words the Oak Seer had given her poured from his throat in silver tones, and so too what she had given Úna back, grandly proclaimed, unerringly exact. With the passage of time, without understanding to fix them in her heart, Meacán had forgotten the order of Úna's ranting tirade, which insult she had chosen in place of another. Tonight, if she had been asked to recall what the Oak Seer had said, she thought ruefully, all she could have sworn to was, "You know only this one. I have known them all."

The Bard's voice was high and sweet, not rich and mellow as Meacán remembered Blackthorn's to be, but still it cut her to the quick of her heart. Sorrow rose to her throat and she tightened her jaw against the swelling ache within her.

Three children had her mother borne, and two of them had added much to her fame. Niall Rí Uladh and Meacán Iníon na Caillí the Dancer of Sliabh Mis were renowned throughout the five kingdoms, but Muirne's second son . . .

If mendacity could bring a man honor, sure, an' Conall mac na Caillí would even now be Named with his siblings among the Mighty of Éirinn. Easy as a smile and sly as a dog-fox was he, and though Meacán loved him dearly, she'd had cause many a time to curse him for a rogue and a liar. For where Niall wore the mantle of Ulaidh's kingship upon his shoulders, Blackthorn wore trouble like a second skin. And as Meacán herself, a Wizard trueborn, had won great praise for her gift, Blackthorn won naught but wagers, and likely those dishonestly. In Dún na nGall folk used to say of him he could coax a salmon from the stream to the pot, and make him think he was lucky to be there—and it was not always said kindly. Loud had been the sighs of relief when Blackthorn had left the dún to serve Larkspur of Tráigh Lí. 'Twas honest work for his dubious talents, though few believed Blackthorn would long be content to be a Bard, and none were greatly surprised to hear he had left his master without word or warning, or so the story was told. Nine years ago, it must have been, and himself but rambling since—

Her own thoughts stopped her. Meacán whispered them aloud. "Nine years ago . . . *Badhbh, Macha, and Mór-Ríoghain!*"

A flash of anger burnt away whatever sympathy she had been feeling for her brother. Why, wasn't it only last midsummer she'd seen Blackthorn at Aonach Urmhumhan's fair? And hadn't he invited himself to share her supper, charming away the afternoon with idle talk and never a word about hunting or stags? Then off he'd gone to bet on the horses, blithe as you please, wagering as grandly as if he'd all the Sidhe's silver in his purse, and himself clad only in rough-sewn deerskins and—

She stopped again, and considered. What a fool she'd been. 'Twasn't poverty clothed him so, but the spoils of his hunts. Nor had he spent nine years an aimless rover, but nine years with Úna, hunting in the wild. Meacán's anger was gone, and her sadness returned. You could have told me, she thought to herself.

I have told you. I hope I shall not regret it.

The Cailleach was in the middle of the temple on the far side of the cauldron, but her voice seemed to echo in Meacán's ear.

You will not, Meacán assured her. *But how can we help him?*

As Úna bade us. We must hunt the false hunter, and keep Shadow from covering the Stag's trail. Bend your will to Liannan's. Your brother's success is her greatest desire.

Meacán felt the Cailleach's touch withdraw from her mind. Suddenly too much alone outside the circle, she took a deep breath and went to join the council.

"'We'll meet at Márrach,'" the Bard was saying, and then in a slightly different voice, "'Seer. Your skin is gray, you are hard and quiet and breathless as stone. But you are Úna, the Oak Seer still. I can see you. They will see you!'"

Meacán thought her final words to Úna a weak ending to a tale, but the Bard gave a satisfied nod and smiled as broadly as if he'd just sung the thousand verses of "Niamh of the Golden Hair" without a flaw. Even the fact that his audience only frowned at him and mumbled amongst themselves did not seem to diminish his pleasure.

"I am glad the Oak Seer's counsel has enlightened the Mothers," said Tadhg in a worried voice, "for it makes very little clear to me."

"It is clear that she will not come to help us," said Seamair. "Clear that the Hunting of the Light is at the root of this evil."

"Úna perceives only the evil that threatens her domain," Mac Ailch disagreed gently, and Feargna Óg was quick to support him.

"The Oak Seer thinks only of the wild. She cares nothing for the goblins at Temuir's gates, or the Scáileanna that assault Dún na nGall and Béal Feirste. Indeed, an' I understand her aright, she would be glad to see our towns in ruins."

Meacán drew nearer to the fire, suddenly aware of how cold she was.

"'Let them fall,'" she murmured. "'Let them all fall. Only the Hunt matters.'"

Mac Ailch turned to her, and half smiled.

"Only the Hunt matters to Úna," he said. "An' it were the Dead Lord's sole concern, why would he send his servants against us? The Hunter cannot be found in Temuir, nor the Stag. An' the goblins meant to join the chase, in the wild they'd be, not before our walls."

Feargna Óg stuck his narrow nose in the air.

"Perhaps the Mothers give too much credence to Úna's mouthings," he said.

"Perhaps the Necromancer gives not enough," the Cailleach answered crisply.

There was an uncomfortable silence. No one dared contradict the Old Woman of Midhe, but Meacán didn't need a Mother's powers to sense Feargna Óg had but spoken what all were thinking.

"Enough." Liannan cast her eyes about the circle. "I have said I will take no counsel, and neither will I."

She lifted her arms, palms to the sky.

"When the cloth is woven by mortal hands, it is not hard for mortal eyes to discern the pattern," she said. "When the Gods lay Their fingers upon the loom, who but the Mothers

can describe the intricate designs? This has been made clear
to our Sight—our kingdoms are attacked, but we are not the
prize the Shadow King seeks. Or if we are, he need not bring
down our walls to defeat us. Though our might be arrayed
against the Dead Lord's armies, though we stand fast, yet all
Éirinn will fall under Shadow should the Hunter fail to kill
the White Stag by Bealtaine Day."

"Then it is the Hunter you mean to seek in the waters of
your cauldron, Mother?" asked Saileach of Glas an Mhullaigh.

Meacán's sudden alarm drew the Maiden's gaze, but all
others looked to Liannan.

The Mother brought her arms to her sides again. "Not the
Hunter," she replied.

A wordless sound of frustration broke from Feargna Óg's
lips. "But have you not just pronounced the Oak Seer's
words truth?" he exclaimed. "If it is to be the Hunt above all
else, then let us see the Hunter and how he fares!"

"But the Dancer has seen him already," said Mac Ailch.

"I?" Meacán responded, a little too hurriedly.

The Conjuror looked puzzled and turned to the Bard.
"Did Úna not say the Dancer knew the Hunter?"

Redwing beamed. "'You know. But you know only this
one,'" he declared. "'I have known them all.'"

Every eye was on her, every ear waiting for her reply.
Meacán stared at the fire, listened to the quick, bright flames
dancing about the base of the cauldron. They warmed her
not at all, and their voice was gentle laughter.

"The Oak Seer's words have been a mystery to the Dancer
from that day to this," the Cailleach said evenly.

Meacán lifted her eyes to the Old Woman and filled her
thoughts with heartfelt thanks.

"Yet, 'tis plain more is known about the Hunter than is
being said," Seamair ventured.

"The Sidhe have seen him," the Cailleach replied. "'Twas
the Hunter of Éirinn brought Cessair and Fiach the news of
Scáthach's death."

Feargna Óg leapt into the breach.

"Well? And what more did they learn? Who is this
Hunter? How goes the Hunt?"

"The Hunter of Éirinn is not one of the Mighty,"
Meacán broke in. Too late she thought to cover her flus-

tered interjection with an air of affected haughtiness. Oh, would that she possessed Conall's gift of making deceit sound utterly convincing!

"'Tis folly to discuss the Hunt as if we were discussing the weather," she went on with a little more composure. "And worse folly to Name the Hunter in our speech."

"The Dancer speaks true," said Creathna. "A Name is a door to the soul. An' you will thrust it open, it is well to have a King's madness to guard the threshold, or a Poet's rann, or a Wizard's spells."

Meacán could have kissed him.

Feargna Óg scowled with annoyance. "Who among us would seek to harm the Hunter? But an' we are to help him fulfill his geis, we must have his Name! How else will our Poets make a verse to strengthen him? How else will the Mothers call Éire's blessing upon him?"

"You attend too little, Feargna Óg," said Liannan coldly. "And presume too much."

The Necromancer stiffened at the Mother's rebuke. Liannan never spared him a glance, but once more lifted her arms. When she spoke again, it was with an authority only the bravest or the most desperate could oppose.

"What has Úna told us?" she said. "'But one evil threatens Éirinn. Two pursue the Stag, and only one is called.' Not the Hunter must we seek in the waters, but his enemy and ours. The false hunter."

She Saw her words fall on their hearts and, like sparks from a flint, kindle the doubts harboring there.

"The false hunter, Mother? Is it a man we seek? A Scáil?" Mac Ailch's eyes were lowered, but his voice carried as well as the Bard's. "And if the false Hunter is the Shadow King himself?"

Fear, horror, anger, confusion, a score of emotions shot across the circle like threads from a spider's belly, tangling the Mother's intent. In a moment she was caught in a web of defiance.

"Are we to follow a madwoman's ravings to the Dead Lord's realm, and his servants fighting before our walls?" demanded Feargna Óg.

Tadhg nodded. "An' we peer into shadows, only darkness will we See."

"An' the Mothers will turn their Sight on these hunters, false and true, who will look to their people?" asked Seamair, her round face drawn and tight.

"The Weather-Worker speaks wisely, Mother," urged Fionnghuala. "How can we think to attack Shadow when we ourselves are under siege?"

They did not all speak out against her, but Liannan heard refusal in all their hearts. Reochaidh was ready to fight the red-eyes in the woods, but what good his gift against the empty Dark? *Names I know*, Creathna was thinking, *but the Dead Lord has none.*

"'Only the Hunt matters,'" whispered Meacán. "'Yours and his.'"

The Cailleach's gaze flew to the Dancer, but Meacán didn't find it daunting now. She found it heartening.

"The Dancer sees only what Úna has shown her," said Feargna Óg scornfully.

"While you see only the danger Shadow has set before your eyes." Meacán's cheeks warmed from the Necromancer's insult, but she answered it with studied calm. "You are blinded by the Dark, Feargna Óg, and all who look with you. I will trust to the Oak Seer's words, and the Mothers' vision. I gladly bend my will to Liannan's purpose, but you—you serve the Dead Lord, for you would cloud the cauldron's waters with the shadows of your fears."

Did I not speak true? the Cailleach said in Liannan's mind.

Reochaidh stirred, and lifted his weight from the stones. "Bend," he whispered, and the Mother's black cauldron rang like crystal.

Liannan accepted his concession without a word, and waited for the rest. Tacitly they had submitted to her already, but she would have them yield their will aloud, before the Goddess within her.

"I know little of the Hunt," said Creathna. "Names I know, and their lore. Show me the face of evil, Mother, and I will Name it, unless it be the Dead Lord's, for He is Nameless."

"I also know little of these mysteries," said Fionnghuala. "But I will honor my oath to serve the Mothers."

"I do not wish to look upon this false hunter," said Tadhg. "But if I must, I will, and search my heart for words to use against him."

"And I also," said Saileach.

Feargna Óg was floundering, but in Mac Ailch Liannan sensed a peculiar strength. It seemed to the Mother of Midhe that this night had wrought a profound change in the Conjuror. From a reticent adversary he had become a man who had taken up a challenge he long had dreaded, and was glad.

"As you have said, a Wizard's Sight is nothing to a Mother's," he said slowly. "But I have felt in my heart that evil will befall an' we do not keep our eyes always on the danger before our walls. I feel it still, but I am content, and will look upon whatever your cauldron may show."

Liannan gave the smallest of nods and turned to Feargna Óg. Feeling utterly betrayed, the Necromancer still could not bring himself to relent.

"If this false hunter is dead, I will speak to him," he said sullenly. "If not, my art is of no significance to you."

Youth and pride, said the Cailleach to Liannan. *Endearing alone. Intolerable together.*

Liannan let entreaty fill her voice, that Feargna Óg could surrender to her with some dignity. "It is your will I ask of you, Necromancer, not your gift. Willingly give me that which you have set against me, and I will make of it a weapon even the Shadow King might fear."

Feargna Óg bowed his head, and Liannan at last smiled. Her right hand reached to the Maiden's, her left to the Cailleach's. In one voice the three Priestesses spoke a single word.

"*Uisce*," they said. Water.

A soft tapping echoed in the depths of the cauldron, like the patter of rain upon stone. The sound grew louder, became the hammering of heavy drops falling into a waiting pool.

The Wizards drew closer, edging together to look into the black bowl. Already it was a third filled, the water plunging down and leaping up as an invisible shower danced on its surface. Meacán watched for a time, then lifted her gaze from the cauldron to the heavens, where the scattered stars were drowning in the radiance of the rising moon.

Twenty-three

At the Mothers' word
the winds must rise
upon Ard na Gaoithe down.
At the Mothers' word
the stones must rise
and dance on Temuir's crown.
At the Mothers' word
the flames must rise
and burn both warm and bright.
At the Mothers' word
the waters must rise
and fill the cauldron of Sight.

"It may be we must look among the shadows to find what we seek," said Liannan when the cauldron stood full. "But our search begins at the place Úna described. . . ."

"'A little bay there is where the moon sets over the Mother of Lakes,'" Redwing recited, picking up where Liannan left off. "'Then a low ridge, and beyond it, the glen . . .'"

When first the waters of the cauldron had stilled, Meacán was struck by how perfectly they mirrored the sky above. As the Bard spoke, wisps of cloud formed just below the surface of the water, marring its clarity. They thickened, swirled, lifted and rolled, until the water was hidden, changed entirely into seething, gray-white mists. Suddenly, as if Seamair had again cast her spells to banish them, the clouds were gone, the waters clear. No, Meacán corrected herself. Not clear, not quite. Waters within waters the cauldron revealed, silver-sheeted waves skimming past as if Meacán were a kingfisher flying low over the restless swells. In the distance, so it seemed, a meandering shoreline appeared, and reedy marshes deep in shadow under a silver moon.

The images flowed easily by, like a lullaby. Like a dream. Before Meacán was aware that her mind was wandering, a demand sharp as a questing arrow darted through her, winging after her faltering attention. It was a novel sensation, exhilarating and a little disconcerting. Fleetingly, possessiveness rose in her breast, a desire to keep her will her own. Instead, Meacán opened her heart, and let the arrow pierce her, that her will would flow from her soul, and the Mother could do as she would with it.

"Loch nEathach," murmured Creathna.

The aged Wizard stood on Meacán's left and so she heard him plainly.

"Loch nEathach," she echoed. Of course. How could she not have known? What other loch could be the Mother of Lakes but east Ulaidh's great basin of water, the largest lake in Éirinn?

"Loch nEathach!" To her right, Feargna Óg pressed against Meacán's shoulder in his haste to peer over the rim of the cauldron. "But Sliabh Slanga is but a long day's ride from Loch nEathach! Often have I hunted the red deer from the beech forests that border my mountain to these very fens!"

Reochaidh's shadow fell on Meacán from above, but it did not dim the images hurtling past in the cauldron.

"And I know of a bay," Feargna Óg went on. "Yes, but we are too far north, I'm thinking."

Instantly there was a shift in the scenes before her. We've turned to the south, Meacán thought, unable to feel surprise as the change was so smoothly accomplished. Boggy lowlands gave way to spindly black alders, and the great loch became a blue-gray ribbon running alongside the scroggy woods. Away from the undulating waters of Loch nEathach Meacán felt not so much a kingfisher, but a merlin, soaring over the world.

Thin forest became tufts of broom and gorse sprouting from irregularities on the side of a rising cliff. Abruptly Meacán found herself above a high headland that stuck out into the loch like a long, pointed nose. Below her lay an open bay, its far end ragged and indistinct in the mists and moonlight, its narrow beach glistening under the protection of the cliff.

"'Then a low ridge, and beyond it, the glen, where tall

were the pale-leaved beeches and bright the stars they wore
in their hair,'" said the Bard, but his voice had lost some of
its polish and had deepened with wonder.

The waters seemed to spin to the right, and a dark rise
appeared to the east of the bay. At once Meacán's Sight was
racing toward the hills. With her falcon's vantage, she could
peer over the crest of the ridge well before they reached it.
The slope fell steeply on the far side, dropping into thick,
winter-dead woodland. Briefly she glimpsed the roof of the
forest beyond the crest, tangled empty branches, and something gray . . . a far, bare knoll in the midst of the valley?

As if she were a dead leaf, Meacán felt herself suddenly
caught in a gale wind and swept roughly back into the dark
vale on the western side of the ridge. She gasped, and heard
Brí moan and Saileach cry out.

She looked up bewildered, but everyone was confused,
every face blank and shaken save Liannan's, and Meacán
had never seen the Queen look so stern. Remembering aged
Creathna at her side, Meacán turned to lend him support,
but Fionnghuala on his left had already linked her arm with
his. The Name-Sayer was standing quite steady, blinking his
age-bleary eyes and squinting into the cauldron.

"What was it, Mother?" whispered Tadhg.

Liannan did not answer, but the Maiden frowned. "Did
you not See the Shadow rear up from the crest of the hill?
And a will behind it—strong enough to throw us back."

"Again," said Liannan.

The forest once more flowed through the cauldron's waters,
but the Mother was not racing now. Cautiously she advanced
the council's Sight, keeping low, weaving up the slope
through the trees. Silver-gray streaks of light fell through the
leafless canopy, not lighting a path, but randomly illuminating
bits and pieces of the wildwood—rocks and boulders, patches
of dusty ground, the pearl-gray boles of smooth-skinned
beeches and an unbroken net of stiff branches above.

As they crept through the wood, Meacán's feeling
returned that she was dancing through dreams. Its silence
made the forest unreal; the woods at night are alive with rus-
tles and calls, scrabbling and snuffling—

Brighde's Fire, it wasn't only the sounds were missing! Life
itself had abandoned these slopes. Though Úna was right in

saying Meacán was no hunter, still she was not so sightless she could walk through a beechwood under a full Rowan moon and see neither mouse nor vole, beetle nor bear! Where were the luminous eyes, the owl-shadows cutting across the moonbeams? And where the brackens, the grasses, the toadstools and mosses? Meacán cast her Sight over all the cauldron showed her, yet not a sign of life could she See, either in shadow or by the moon's soft light.

"Do you know this place?" she whispered to Feargna Óg. "Has it always been so barren?"

"Did I not say that at Samhain the beasts of the forest fled some evil in Cromghlinn?" answered Feargna Óg, not as quietly as Meacán. "Over the top of this ridge we climb is that valley, but where are the streams that ran so clear all through this land?"

"'. . . and bright the stars they wore in their hair,'" quoted the Bard. "'But no more, no more. Dark are the nights and empty the woods. They have all fled, the children of the forest, fled the thorns that would have trapped them.'"

"The thorns?" Seamair repeated.

They topped the rise, and suddenly a hedge was before them, frozen in the deep bowl of the cauldron as if caught in clear ice. Glinting like old silver, curved, dagger-sharp thorns covered the convoluted branches, and no rose's thorns these, uniformly arcing from the stem. A crazed web of knives thrust out at every conceivable angle from the warped maze of wood. The top of the hedge was easily high as three men, and was moored among the beeches by its thorns and grasping branches. Looking on it, the Cailleach groaned as if she were in pain.

The long sleeves of Fionnghuala's saffron gown fell back toward her shoulders as she lifted her arms and began to speak in the silent, elegant hand language of Ogham. With her palms facing each other, she used the fingers of her right hand to touch lightly specific points on the fingers of her left—a fingertip, the first joint of the third finger, the second joint of the thumb—her gestures were so swift Meacán's eyes could not follow them. Letters of light traced in long lines, thin as spider's silk and transitory as if they had been drawn by a breath of wind on a still pool, appeared about the Deceiver's hands, glowed, and vanished all in an instant.

Mac Ailch edged between Fionnghuala and Creathna,

and took the old man's elbow as Fionnghuala worked. The Name-Sayer acknowledged this kindness with a tentative smile, but his gaze never left the cauldron's waters.

The last of the Deceiver's runes faded into the night. "The hedge is no illusion, Mother," she said, "though truth be told, never have I seen such thorns as these in any wood I have journeyed in."

"Can we go no further?" Tadhg asked, and there was more than a trace of hope in his question.

"We cannot overlook it," Brí answered slowly. "Our Sight cannot pierce it . . ."

"It is but a hedge," said Mac Ailch. "However thick, however long, however tall, it is only a hedge. There must somewhere be a breach in this wall."

He had not finished speaking before the image of the hedge seemed to slide to the left, and keep going, as if the council were striding along beside it. Hours it seemed to Meacán she travelled so, her Sight constantly scrutinizing the unending mass of knotted branch and thorn.

"Arrah, here is an opening," sighed Liannan with relief, and finally the images in the waters held still.

The hole the Mother had found would have made a poor gate had the council brought themselves to the ridge and not their Sight only. But three of them might have passed together through the break in the thorny wall, and Reochaidh would have had to go alone. The breach was slightly wider at the top—along the ground, twisted, dagger-laden arms reached for each other across the gap.

"On," commanded Liannan.

Immediately their view plunged through the hedge and into the forest. For a moment, a mere blink of an eye, Meacán Saw an immense shadow flying through the tangle of thorns. Then the hedge was behind her, and her heart was pounding.

"Did you see it?" whispered Feargna Óg in Meacán's ear, and his voice held all the terror the swift image had stirred in the Dancer's blood.

The forest west of the ridge had been dreary. East of the hedge it was a nightmare. No moonlight played with the night, but everywhere were shadows, some dark giants towering over them, some sluggish black rivers spreading gloom through the empty woods. The thorns that had formed the hedge grew all down the slope to the valley; a low bush before them they could easily skirt, a looming clump of sharp blades that slowed them as they made a path around it, a long barricade that daunted their Sight and forced them to turn left or right and seek another way down into the glen.

Meacán looked up from the cauldron to the bright moon overhead, needing the true vision of the world she was standing in to stay the thought that she was lost in these dismal woods. When she looked down again, they had reached the midst of the glen, and an image of a bald hill lay still in the waters. Its desolate arc filled the circle of the cauldron. Nothing at all moved or grew upon it, neither creature, nor weed, nor breath of wind.

"When I was a girl," said the Cailleach quietly, "I rode once with the Sidhe of An Cnoc Leathan to An Bhrí Mhaol, the bald hill of Cromghlinn, and there danced upon the sweet green grass. Fond is my memory of this place, but hardly would I have known it now."

No living hill, this, thought Meacán, but a gray sore on the body of the earth. Even the moonlight could not heal it, but fell dully on the barren mound, turning it the color of a Scáil's pallid flesh.

"This is what we have come to see?" asked Feargna Óg, his earlier enthusiasm withered by the sight of the naked rise. "This the danger the Oak Seer deems greater than red-eyed goblins at Temuir's gates?"

Fionnghuala looked up sharply at the Mother. Without a word she began again to touch finger to finger, and ethereal lines of Ogham script brightened the air. Though they lasted longer than before, and their light was more brilliant, each symbol eventually broke apart, crackling and sizzling as it exploded about her hands. At last she stopped, and lowered her arms.

"Och, truly, Mother," she sighed. "There is illusion here, and well cast it is, I vow. The spell is spread like a veil over the hill. Were it only by someone's will this was done, then might I break it, for in illusions my will is as great as any. I can but think that the spell is bound in some sorcerous thing, and if that be so, I cannot dispel this enchantment until I have the charm in my hand."

"Illusion?" Feargna Óg scoffed. "But always An Bhrí Mhaol has stood in Cromghlinn."

"No more Cromghlinn." Creathna's voice was tired, and

everyone hushed to hear him. "No more An Bhrí Mhaol.
Márrach."

Liannan lifted her chin and filled the temple with the
true Name the old Wizard had given her.

"Márrach!" she cried.

A ripple coursed over the cauldron's surface. Beneath it the
wasted hill began to waver, to dissolve. Tadhg drew back, and
Meacán as well, but Feargna Óg shouted and Mac Ailch gasped
and leaned over the cauldron, briefly obscuring Meacán's view.

"Look! There upon the hill!" the Conjuror exclaimed.

Suddenly he stood erect, and the fingers of his free hand
danced. Able to see past him once more, Meacán peered
into the cauldron and beheld not the dead, gray hill, but
soft, grainy mounds—heaps of white sand. They remained in
her Sight less than a moment when they darkened, and a
broad, hairy, brutish face imposed itself upon them. Like a
goblin's it was, but where a goblin has only bloodlust and
hate in his red eyes, the fires that burned in this creature's
skull held more—cunning and cruelty and a rapacious
hunger. Had the goblins a King, this would be he.

"The Gruagach," whispered Creathna, and it was plain
the Name was bitter on his tongue.

"Gruagach!" Liannan said, command in her voice.

The red eyes bulged, the creature's fanged grin widened
until it nearly split the Gruagach's hairy face in two.

"Hah!" breathed the creature. "You cannot command me!
I have a master, and only him will I obey."

His voice was low and growling. Distance and the cauldron's waters made it sound as if it came from far away.

A black blur swept around the cauldron's inner edges, like
a tiny bat swimming just under the water's surface. In truth
Meacán supposed it was the Gruagach's arm drawing a circle
in the air. Tiny bubbles seethed about the rim of the cauldron's black bowl, following the path of the dark shadow. A
spell it must be, and certainly an evil one.

Meacán looked quickly away, and was instantly assailed
by a wave of nauseating dizziness. She reeled and flung out
her arm to find something to support her. Everything, everyone her eyes lit upon was hideously distorted—Liannan's
face bloated and pale, the Maiden stretched thin as a
beanstalk, the Cailleach squat as a dwarf. Even the standing

stones would not be still, but swayed on the hilltop, their shadows leaping across the paved floor of the temple, though the fire burned before them in the pit.

Finding nothing to hold on to save the cauldron itself, Meacán grasped it, clung to it, and looked down again, into the cauldron's depths. A bastion of stability in an inexplicably chaotic world, the Gruagach smiled up at her with gleeful satisfaction.

"A pretty little spell," said Liannan coldly, "but not your own."

Courage, calm, the Cailleach whispered in Meacán's mind, in everyone's mind. *Give Liannan your strength, and keep your patience . . . patience . . .*

"Not mine," agreed the Gruagach smugly. "My master's."

"The Mother of Midhe treats not with servants," Liannan said peremptorily. "Summon your master."

For a moment the Mother's unruffled confidence seemed to daunt the bold creature. His wide smile dropped into a snarl.

"Treat with me," he said, and his overwide grin returned.

How Liannan would have answered him, Meacán never learned. All at once Mac Ailch leaned over the edge of the cauldron, his long black beard almost brushing the waters.

"Midhe has told you to fetch your master, slave!" he said in a voice dripping with contempt. "Obey her!"

Without warning, a long, hairy arm shot out of the center of the cauldron. The paw at the end of it grabbed hold of Mac Ailch's dangling beard and the shirt of his tunic. The Conjuror had not even time to cry out before he was hauled bodily over the rim of the crucible and pulled headfirst into the water.

As Mac Ailch was dragged forward, Creathna staggered against the side of the vessel. Meacán reached out to the old Wizard, and saw with horror Mac Ailch's gloved hand was still locked on Creathna's elbow.

"Creathna!" someone shouted, a woman—Seamair?

"Mac Ailch!" Meacán cried. "Mac Ailch! Let go!"

Feargna Óg was yelling so loud in her ear she couldn't hear her own voice, but she found Creathna's free arm and closed her hand upon it. Immediately she felt herself pulled forward. She nearly tripped over the black tripod, and slammed into the side of the cauldron while Creathna, wailing for help, followed Mac Ailch over the side. Water sloshed over the lip of the vessel and onto Meacán, soaking her bodice. The

Name-Sayer's arm began to slip through her wet fingers.

"Mother!" Meacán cried, but made the mistake of looking up from the cauldron to seek Liannan's help. A blur of sickly colors met her eyes, and she lost hold of Creathna entirely.

Desperately she returned her gaze to the steadiness of the cauldron, but it was steady no longer. The waters were a roiling, violent mass of fury, the cauldron itself heaved and rocked over the fire. Creathna's face looked up at the sky in blind terror, his free arm flailed above the churning waters. Once more Meacán reached out to grab him, and other hands reached with hers, Redwing's, Feargna Óg's, Brí's, and Seamair's. Many fingers brushed the Name-Sayer's wildly waving arm, but none closed around it, not even Reochaidh's. The giant's huge hand struck the rim of the teetering cauldron, and it began to fall.

"Mac Ailch!" Creathna screamed. His voice, muted by thrashing waters, was a terrible thing to hear.

The cauldron broke from the tripod and struck the stone paving with a deafening crack, drowning out the council's horrified cries. Water washed cold over Meacán's feet and swirled swiftly down into the firepit, smothering the flames. They died with a sibilant gasp. Darkness swallowed the temple.

Darkness? Meacán raised her eyes to the sky. A cloud shadow was drifting across the moon's bright face. Long, ragged claws were closing like a cage, and a thick, dark palm swiftly covering the silver orb.

"*Tine*," she heard Liannan call. And again, with outrage and absolute authority. "*Tine!*"

A spark answered the Mother, then a fountain of fire tore from the damp hole in the temple's heart and spewed its flaming challenge into the heavens. A dragon's tongue, long and lashing, it spat its blazing poison into the shadowy hand. The dense cloud shriveled, the grasping fingers broke into powerless black pebbles and fell away into the silver sky.

With infinite control, the Mother brought the roaring flames down until they stood only twice as high as the dance of stones. They burned without sound, and no one else dared break the appalled silence, but only stood and stared at the cauldron where it lay in pieces on the temple floor. The warm amber glow of the fire turned the black metal the brown of dried blood, and moonlight poured down upon the shattered bowl like the balm of a mother's tears.

PART 6

the talisman

Twenty-four

Warily enter an unknown hall
And look both left and right —
Unwelcome the warrior late arriving
An' foes have found welcomes early

The Warrior's Rann

There were times, Blackthorn thought, when twilight lingered long past expectation, when imperceptibly darkening shadows mingled with the last light of golden day and held the rolling world timeless in the dusk.

This was such a twilight. All during the sea voyage evening was poised on the brink of night. Yet even as the swan boat passed through a ring of mist and dug into the welcoming sands of an island, a last whisper of light shimmered in the deepening air, illuminating the white strand and silhouetting the trees at the top of the island's lone mountain.

The Hunter leapt from the craft into a shallow swirl of water and foam, his eyes scanning the narrow white beach, then lifting to the forested slope beyond. The gently swaying trees were already wrapped in umbered gray, but a blacker shadow in their midst revealed a path leading from the beach up into the woods.

Turning his back to the forest, Blackthorn laid his hand on the carved wing of Manannán's boat and peered within. The crossing had taken its toll on the púca—a pathetic ball curled against the boards of the deck, the shape-shifter wouldn't be standing on his own feet until he'd had a long rest on dry land.

"To a mouse, now," Blackthorn coaxed, "and I'll carry you. It's Inis na Linnte at last, and my pouch is dry as bone—"

The púca made no response, but another sound, one Blackthorn's ears never missed, brought the Hunter's head around. Though the noises emanating from the shadows of the wood were faint, their message was plain. A creature was forcing a swift passage through the undergrowth, and to hear it at all at this distance meant it was no small one.

Training his eyes on the nebulous blackness of the wood, the Hunter caught sight of the animal as soon as its dark shape separated from the reaching shadows of the trees. By his size alone, Blackthorn might have thought the creature bounding across the sands was a small bear, but his wiry grace and deep voice, thick with threat, were that of a great wolfhound.

His welcome looked to be a poor one. Blackthorn was sore tempted to climb aboard the swan boat and head for the safety of deep waters. And yet, to cede the shore he had come so far to find without so much as setting foot upon it—

A stone might give the beast pause. Blackthorn's sling hung at his belt, but the strand was made of pure white sands. Not even a pebble marred their fine, fluent beauty. A dagger would do him as well or better, he thought, and immediately the púca's words, given him three mornings past on An t-Ard Achadh, came back to rankle. As the scamp had promised, he needed a blade, and having none to hand, he could but rue the day he had been mad enough to leave his dagger to rust in a dark elf's throat.

Hurriedly turning to the boat once more, he reached past the shape-shifter and took up the branch of fairy thorn. Gripping it tightly, he spun back just as the hound reached the edge of the water. The light was fading, but there was brightness enough in the air to make the dog's eyes glow red and his fangs shine white as he paraded stiff-legged just beyond the edge of the surf, not five paces from where Blackthorn stood. His barks had become low growls, but the dog's stringy hair bristled along his rigid back and his hostile stare was an open invitation to contest.

Blackthorn kept his eyes down, careful not to accept the hound's challenge, but careful too, not to display any fear. Though his boots were soaked and his feet beginning to ache with the cold, he dared not take the few steps that would carry him onto the beach. He couldn't even shift his weight without that the dog would stop and front him and his growl rise in warning.

Sands grated together, crunching softly under someone's foot. Blackthorn raised his eyes, praying they'd be filled with the sight of a dark-haired, saffron-robed wizard hurrying to call off her dog. He made his movement as slow and subtle as possible, but at once the hound leapt forward, heavy jaws opening wide and a bark almost like a roar pouring from his throat. Blackthorn brought his staff up and pressed his back against the side of the boat, but the hound's attack was only a feint. Satisfied with his adversary's quick retreat, the beast pranced back to his place, growling happily. He need not guard me so closely, Blackthorn thought. Having seen what was coming toward him across the sands, the Hunter was no longer so eager to gain the shore.

The wizard Róisín Dubh he had hoped to find here, expected to find, what with the surety of Fiach's dreams to guide him and the Sea-God's gifts to bear him over the waves. And finding her, he would not have been surprised to learn the Bards had oversung her beauty, that the Black Rose was in truth but an unremarkable, commonplace flower. Tales fall often wide of veracity's mark, as Blackthorn himself was quick to attest, but none could fall so wide as this. Were the bent and hideous woman hobbling toward him in a cloud of dust and dirt indeed Róisín Dubh, no storyteller in the world but would have delighted in saying so, for there could be no end to the tale of her ugliness. Where had he landed, if not on the Isle of Pools? And why had the swan boat brought him here—unless Manannán Himself meant to betray the Hunt?

In his heart Blackthorn thanked the winds for blowing from the sea, for as the old woman came steadily nearer, it carried most of her stink inland. A cloud of filth swirled about her grimy clothes, and by the smell it was plain her body beneath them was as unwashed as the rags she wore. Sparse and matted hair, as stringy as her hound's, only partly covered her misshapen skull. Her right eye was slack, and almost invisible behind a sagging lid and swollen pimple. The left was small and fierce, too small for the surrounding white, which even in the dusk looked yellow as bile. Her ill-formed face was pocked and warty, black hairs sprouted from her long bent nose, her mouth was a dark gash with a single greenish tooth protruding. Her skin was covered in boils and open sores, and the flesh peeled from her cheeks and gnarled hands, leaving dry tatters hanging about her oozing wounds. Age Blackthorn had seen, and disease and disfigurement. Never before had he seen the rot of death walking about in the guise of the living.

The old woman came to where her hound stood guarding her shores, and stopped. It was too close for Blackthorn's ease. He took a step back toward the stern of the boat. Though it brought him farther from the beach, the dog let out a short, harsh warning, and his muzzle drew back from his teeth.

Laying a bony hand on the hound's head, the old woman spoke.

"Step out of the water, and Dearg will tear out your throat," she said. "I brook no trespassers here."

A shudder ran down Blackthorn's spine, an instinctive reaction to the woman's hoarse, rasping voice.

"Grandmother," he began, coating the word with honey despite his gritted teeth, "no trespasser am I. Only a sailor who's lost his way."

His politeness gained him nothing.

"Across the waves or under them—there lies your way," she snapped. "Begone, and at once."

Dearg had quieted under his mistress's hand; now he began to growl again, and he trembled slightly.

"'Twas Inis na Linnte I was seeking, Grandmother," Blackthorn went on easily, as if he'd been asked, "the Isle of Pools, where 'tis said Róisín Dubh the Wish-Bringer dwells. An' you will steer me straight—"

The old woman's grotesque body shook as she laughed. It was all Blackthorn could do to keep his hands on his staff and not bring them up to cover his ears.

"Inis na Linnte these shores are called. But as for the other Name on your tongue—" Abruptly her laughter ceased. "I said begone, you witless worm."

"But tell me only this then, and I'll trouble you no more. Is the Wish-Bringer dead, or lives she still? Has she left this isle for another or left the world entirely? Strange it seems that the Sidhe and the Gods should have sent me so far an' no good to come of it."

The old woman seemed to grow taller, and her rags billowed about her.

"Ochone, mo mhúirnín," she hissed, "have you a fond wish? Does some fair maid disdain your company? Would you make a great Chieftain if only you could fight? Or are you a selfless idiot—is it health for your dying mother you're after, or do you come to beg for game in Cromghlinn that your village will not starve?"

The wind failed for a moment, and the odious creature's stench assailed Blackthorn full force. Before he could stop himself, his nose had wrinkled, his head turned, he had backed yet another step from the shore. The Hag's one good eye fixed on the Hunter, and she laughed again.

"Listen well, hapless fool that you are. You'll find no Black Rose blooming on Inis na Linnte. Only this withered weed, and I'm in no mood for to be granting wishes. Be off, or you'll leave less whole than you came."

The dog bristled, and slaver dripped off his fangs. Never doubting Dearg's sincerity, Blackthorn kept absolutely still.

"What would sweeten your mood, Granny?" he entreated. "For if, indeed, you could grant my wish, sure, an' there's nothing you could ask in return I'd not gladly give."

The creature spat through the line of her cracked lips. The spittle sizzled and boiled on the sands, and reeked like old eggs, but this time Blackthorn held still and kept his winning smile fixed on his face.

"Boastful words. I doubt you know your own heart's desire, and cannot begin to dream what mine may hold."

It had been a boast, but born of desperation, and in desperation Blackthorn persisted. "Then tell me, Granny, that I need not dream. Tell me what would soften your heart toward me."

A sharp gesture with her ravaged, sharp-nailed hand, and

Dearg lay down on the sands. He didn't drop at once, but lowered himself deliberately, bending a joint at a time, and growling all the while. Blackthorn's smile was genuine now. The foul old crone was going to bargain.

"What has a bodach like yourself to offer?" she asked, a crafty gleam shining in her good eye. "The vessel that brought you here? The life of that worthless sack of bones cringing within?"

A pitiful whimper came from behind the swan's graceful wing.

"The craft is Manannán mac Lir's," Blackthorn answered. "An' I steal his boat for you, and earn his wrath, no skiff in the world will ever bear me safely from these shores. Nor will I bargain with the life of another."

He met the old woman's eye. "My own you may have, if it's blood you desire. But first you must grant my wish, and also my life until Bealtaine is past. With the first sun of summer I will return, and pay you your due."

"So."

She sucked in her breath, a slobbering, disgusting sound. Dearg took it as permission to rise. He thrust his massive head under her clawlike hand. Absently the old woman began to scratch behind the huge hound's ears.

"Still," she said, "how can we bargain, an' I know not your own desires? What is this wish worth more than your life?"

"A Spear I wish for, my own back again, for I cannot Hunt the Stag without it."

He had supposed she would be amused, but that did not make it easier to bear. He clenched his teeth and weathered the gale of her laughter as he would a storm. When at last she ceased cackling it was to the dog she spoke, and not to him.

" 'Freed but spell-bound/ Both call their last hope,/ The Hunter, to Summer's Door.' Those her very words. Yet, here he is already, and many the days till Bealtaine is upon us. Though truly, so few, so few. Ochone, my darling, the Hunter of Éirinn it is, come begging the Hag for his pretty Spear."

"Was I expected?" demanded Blackthorn.

The old woman's blind eye seemed to glitter for a moment beneath its wrinkled cover, and her long tongue played about her single tooth.

"A Spear for the Hunter, and what for me? Bealtaine is too long to wait for such a meager prize as an idiot's life." She leered at him. "Yet there is a gift that would please me. Please me mightily, and win my favor."

In her croaking voice Blackthorn heard the echo of a yearning long held and long thwarted. His smile became wary, for he could imagine nothing but dark desires in a heart that could suffer to beat in a body so vile.

"But name it," he said.

"The Talisman of Domhnall the Spell-Maker I would have for my own. Bring it me, and I will do what I can to grant your wish."

Blackthorn neither frowned nor laughed, though either would have been a reasonable response.

"The Wizard Domhnall has been dead these countless years," he answered mildly. "His tales are all that remain, for his treasures are stolen, his magics destroyed, and even the place he dwelt lost to all knowledge."

"Thieves have not taken all of the Spell-Maker's treasures, or I would not ask you to steal this one for me. Nor are all Domhnall's spells broken, as you shall discover when you find his ancient home. And find it you will, or get no help from me."

"An' things of magic are to your liking," Blackthorn said smoothly, "look you, Grandmother." He lifted the blackthorn branch and stroked its polished wood. "Five Scáileanna I faced with this in my hand, and they could not stand against me."

"A fairy wand!" The Hag spat again, and the wad struck the water. The shallow wave gasped and hissed, and a fetid odor rose with the steam. "What use blackthorns to me?"

"What use to send me after that you can obtain for yourself? Wish this Talisman to your hand, and strike a fairer bargain with me."

"Do you mock me?" screeched the Hag. "What do you know of wizardry, you snivelling beggar? An' my magic could grant my own wishes, do you not think I should have had the Talisman long ago?"

The Hag blossomed in her fury. She swelled up, broad as an ox and taller than Blackthorn, and a baleful light began to glow in her withered palm.

"In your folly you lose your Spear, then come crawling to me to make amends for your unforgivable negligence. All I ask in return is this trinket, this trifle, this little silver pentacle upon a slender chain." Her voice grated like a blade on stone. "Bring me Domhnall's star, Hunter, an' you wish ever to hold your Spear again."

His eyes on the dully luminous sphere in her hand, Blackthorn answered the old woman carefully.

"I meant no offense, Grandmother. But an' this be the only bargain you will strike with me, then let these be the terms of it—help me to my Spear now, this night, nor keep me from fulfilling my geis, and by Éire and An Daghdha and my mother's heart I swear I will seek this lost Talisman, this plaything of a Wizard long-dead, nor cease in my search till I've found it or my life is ended."

"Lies are often told," the Hag said shortly, growling like her hound, "and oaths often broken."

"Lies are often told, Grandmother," Blackthorn agreed, "but oaths rarely broken, and never my own."

The Hag's good eye flamed. She tossed the yellow-green light in her palm not at Blackthorn, but close enough that he staggered against the boat as it burst into a sour, sulphurous cloud.

"Bring me the Talisman of Domhnall the Spell-Maker and I will do all I can to return your Spear to you. This my bargain, and this the last time I will offer it."

The Hag spat into her malformed hand, and held it out to the Hunter. "Done?" she asked.

Blackthorn stared at the revolting mess, unable to mask his disgust. Yet, it was fitting, somehow, that the first bargain he could not manage to twist to his own advantage should be held out to him in such a repulsive manner.

Only this Talisman would she bargain for, and only now would do for her to have it. His charm had endeared him to many an aged grandmother, but on the Hag he had wasted it entirely. And how could he coerce her to do his will, what with her magics to defend her and her wolfhound at her side?

It had grown too dark for Blackthorn to see the expression on the Hag's face, but he knew without seeing there was no leniency in her eye, no compassion in her smile. It was a bad bargain, and himself with the worst of it, but what could he do but return to Éirinn and try to make it good?

"Done," he said at last, but he did not take the old woman's hand.

Peals of cacophonous laughter erupted from her wrinkled throat, and another strangled whine rose from the bottom of the swan boat.

"Then go," she ordered, "and do not return unless you bring the Talisman with you."

Blackthorn did not wait to be asked again. He climbed back onto the boat and at once it slipped gently into the current. In a moment it had carried him away from the acrid fumes yet lingering from the sour and explosive ball of light, away from Dearg's unwavering hostility, away from the Hag's utterly loathsome self.

Just before he reached the mists that ringed Inis na Linnte, he looked back toward the receding shore. The old woman was turning gracelessly toward the forest, and in turning, melted into the night as if she had taken wings and flown. Her hound remained on the shore watching the Hunter's departure, his eyes glowing red as a goblin's by heaven's muted light. When the swan boat reached the fog-bank, Dearg, now no more than a dark shadow, rose and loped away up the beach.

Past the wreath of cloud, the mists were light. Breathing deeply of the sea-cleansed wind, Blackthorn ran his hand through his hair and glanced down at the púca. The shape-shifter lay on his side, his legs tucked up toward his belly, his head bent toward his knees, his eyes squeezed shut. Likely the little man wouldn't move or speak again until they reached land. Just as well. When the púca found his voice again, doubtless he would have plenty to say about the worth of the bargain Blackthorn had made, and the worth of the man that had made it.

Alone with the sea and his heavy heart, Blackthorn sat down with his back against the smooth boards of the stern. Wrapping his cloak tightly about him, he looked to see what stars he could spy beyond the veils of mist until the rolling waves lulled him to sleep.

Twenty-five

Through winter's wan light
To summer sun's crowning
Doors of doom and death open
To worlds of glory

The Hunter's Rann

On each of the thirteen nights of Brighde's festival, the people of Luimneach set balefires to burn high atop Woodcock Hill. Bright the flames, and quick, but not half so wild as the talk blazing through the town below that season, and for many more to come.

The first guests arrived more than a fortnight before the feast was to begin—folk from Cathair Cheann na Leasa and Cluain na Lárach, from villages west as far as Seanghualainn—and all had tales to tell of the goblin raids that had destroyed their homes and driven them to seek the protection of Luimneach's high stockade.

Next came the great warrior Chieftain of An Clár, him they called the Bear, the Ó Briain himself, riding through the gate, and a hundred warriors behind him. All the lands north and west of An tSionainn and south of Na Connachta were in his care, but 'twas east of An tSionainn his sight was set, on the goblins' stronghold in the Silvermine mountains hard by Aonach Urmhumhan. Glad was Wren, the Chieftain of Luimneach, to welcome the Ó Briain, but angry was she at his departure. For the Bear of An Clár brought away with him the flower of Luimneach to fight the goblins at the Silvermines, leaving mothers and uncles and lovers behind to fret for their darlings' lives.

And then, on the eve of the festival itself, the Bard arrived.

The sun was just setting when he appeared at the gate, out of the misted air it seemed, for though the watch kept a keen eye on the road to Aonach Urmhumhan, they had not seen the Bard upon it, nor spied him crossing the scroggy fens. Himself, he claimed at first to have been sailing lost upon the sea, then up An tSionainn until he made a landing on the shoals below the town. Wren knew that for a lie, and said as much, for who could scull against the current all the way from An tSionainn's mouth to fair Luimneach without rest, and only his own arms to row? Where his currach, then, an' he so fine a sailor? And was it that stout blackthorn was his oar, or didn't it serve him better as a staff for walking? At that he smiled, and admitted his was a story hard to believe, but as he was himself a Bard, he would rather a good tale than a true one.

Well, an' hearing he was a Bard, Wren forgave his deception at once. She spoke him a hundred welcomes, and thanked him for daring the dangers of the road. No singer-of-tales had stopped in Luimneach since before Samhain-tide, she told him, and here it was Imbolc, and winter gone by.

And did the Bard return her Éire's blessing for her hospitality, as courtesy and custom would have him do?

"Imbolc!" cried he, as if Wren had told him his mother was dying.

Then he laughed, but it was a bitter sound and full of despair.

"Time stands still in the presence of the Gods," the Chieftain heard him mutter. "Och, Mac Lir, how twilight lingered on your smooth seas. How long my journey over the waves."

Wren might have turned him out then, but he came to himself, and asked Éire's blessing on all there, and Brighde's too, for good measure. So, they let him warm himself by the hearth, and when the fire was lit upon the hill, they feasted him in the hall. And at last they asked for a song. He took his place, and everyone hushed, for they knew what to expect, and this night sacred to Brighde—stirring rhythms, a melody that leapt and danced like the fire itself, words aflame with beauty, poetry, and love.

The tale of "Máirín the Thief" he gave them, the song of a bold robber and her looting of the spellbound treasures of Domhnall's Keep.

The folk of Luimneach listened politely. At least, no one actually threw anything at him, though even Wren was heard to grumble. When the tale was finally done, they gave him ale in hopes it would inspire him to something better, and asked for a song more fitting to the occasion.

"The Spell-Maker's Bane" he began. Of goblins it told, and the Wizard Domhnall again. To make matters worse, he hardly knew the tale, and lost his place in the middle of it. Nor did he blush for his performance, but took up Otter's goatskin drum, and beat out the rhythm while Gannet Graybeard, Luimneach's most respected elder, sang what verses his long memory retained from the many times he had heard it sung rightly before.

At last they prevailed upon the Bard to give them a carol of the coming spring. He obliged with but a single tune before taking himself off to a quiet corner. There he drank his ale and exchanged barely a word with anyone the rest of the evening.

'Twas after the Bard went to his bed in the loft that Otter remarked that the stranger was surely mad, for with his own eyes hadn't he seen the man dropping bits of bread and even a few drops of ale into the pouch at his belt? Marten remembered not bread, but hunks of cheese going into the sack, and Shell related how the Bard had poured an entire bowl of ale under the table, yet when she looked, not a drop had wet the rushes on the floor.

By midnight it was casks of ale and a whole roasted kid the pouch had devoured. Scores of wagers were laid regarding the Bard's magic purse, though there seemed little chance of their ever being settled.

Waiting for the starless hour before the dawn, Marten and Otter crept stealthily to where the Bard rested, planning to win their bets by securing the ensorcelled pouch for themselves. The lads found the Bard risen earlier still. His pallet in the loft was cold and empty, and neither the man nor his pouch were anywhere to be seen. Wren won her wager, nonetheless, for she had bet the pouch gave its owner the power to walk invisible to mortal sight. At first some held against the Bard having come unseen to Luimneach, but when it was learned he had vanished as abruptly as he had appeared, and as the watch swore by Éire and An Daghdha and Brighde Herself that none had passed the gate, it was plain the Chieftain had the right of it.

"Fairy led or touched by the Gods," remarked old Gannet when he heard the Bard had fled. "Ill for him, and better for us that he is gone. Mind you that young man's fate," he warned his listeners, "and stray not from the safety of your own hearths until these times of trouble are passed."

Since before morning Blackthorn had been walking, across the lowlands surrounding Luimneach, through the marshes, into the scrubby woods. Now the sun was high, and the trees behind him, and when he looked up, the shadowless slopes of a tall peak filled his sight. Green and gray they were, with larch and ash, but the mountain's crown was white as an elder's beard, and pierced the cloudless blue sky like a spear. From the peak, a bony spine ran south and east down the mountain's back, rising again into An Driom Fiodhach's ridge in the distance. Far to the north towered a third mountain, snow-laden as well, but straighter and steeper, and flat-topped, as if a giant's axe had swept its head from its shoulders. Blackthorn considered all three with an expression closer to a scowl than a frown, and ran his hand through his hair.

The púca climbed out of the pouch, shinnied down the Hunter's leg, and came to a man. Following Blackthorn's gaze, he considered the mountains in turn. His face drew into a scowl the image of his companion's.

The day was as fair as any they'd yet seen, the púca thought to himself. Cold, maybe, but the streams were in spate, the music of melting snow trickled about them, the pungent promise of spring rose from dark patches of moist earth where the seeping waters pooled. And sweetest of all, breakfast was singing from the sky, rustling in the thickets, leaping in the swollen waters.

"Is it the Hunter you are, or a mewling babe that waits to be fed?" he asked. "Look!" he cried, pointing. "Look there! Two coneys, scamperin' 'cross the open! Get a stone to your sling, you gawkin'—"

Blackthorn made no move, neither taking his sling from his belt, nor even turning his eyes from the mountains before him.

"Och, sure, an' 'tis witless I am entirely," said the little man apologetically. "Arrah, but what's a púca's stratagems to the Hunter of Éirinn's? Now, meself, I'd a notion 'twould be grand to eat those coneys at once, scrawny as they were. But himself now, he'll wisely wait until spring greens have sprouted and the rabbits have fattened themselves on the bounty, never minding that we go hungry a moon and more."

Without a word, Blackthorn started on his way again, picking a path through the furze and broom that dotted the high mountain's broad base. Sending a quick curse after the Hunter, the púca followed more slowly, plodding along on his bare, bent legs and talking all the while.

"Is there a fool in all the five kingdoms the equal of your-self?" he complained. "Not forty paces behind us are hazels thick with wood pigeons. An' I beat those bushes, and you ready with your sling—"

"The hazels thick with birds, are they?" Blackthorn asked. The púca's eyes narrowed at the excessive gentleness in the Hunter's voice. "Yes, and the sap rising in the trees, and the ice beginning to melt from Sliabh Éibhlinne's stony crags."

"Am I to blame for the rolling of the world?" the púca demanded. "But a single night it seemed to me we sailed upon the seas, and you as heedless as I that three weeks were passing here in Éirinn. And 'twas myself told you, I did, as I lay upon the strand below Luimneach, tryin' to gather me strength together, I told you then that the wind was too southerly, and the northern geese gone from our shores too soon."

"Two seasons the White Stag runs," Blackthorn growled, "winter and spring, and the first now gone never to return."

"I bear a geis meself!" the púca exclaimed. Trotting until he came alongside Blackthorn, he delivered the rest of what he had to say red-faced and short of breath. "It's brought me no end of trouble, my geis, but unlike the Hunter of Éirinn's, my burden doesn't prevent me takin' breakfast in a town or supper from the woods!"

Suddenly the púca stumbled, caught himself, then stood still as stone. His eyes widened, and he looked up at the mountain as if it were an angry giant looking down.

"Sliabh Éibhlinne, you say?" His voice was barely more than a whisper. "But Sliabh Éibhlinne is nigh unto the Silvermines."

Blackthorn stopped as well, and a small smile touched his lips. "'Tis indeed."

The púca stared at the Hunter aghast. "Sure, an' you've lost your reason entirely. Were you dreamin', then, when the talk was all of the Ó Briain and how he'd led the brave youth of Luimneach away to fight the goblins not far from this very place?"

He glanced about nervously and lowered his voice still more. "Slaughtered the miners the red-eyes did, and took the mines for themselves, or so they were sayin' in Luimneach town. Fools enough we be on the Hag's errand to seek Domhnall's star. Dead fools we'll be an' we tarry here."

Acting on his words, the púca began to slink away in the direction they had come. At least, that was his intention. Ferrets slink. Even foxes can slink, an' the goose is fat enough. The púca's attempt at stealth resulted in something closer to a hedgehog's rolling, bent-backed amble. Despite himself, the Hunter found himself laughing at the creature's comical gait.

"There's not a red-eye in Éirinn could look out a day bright as this!" he called. "Come, there's not even a shadow to fear with the daystar high above us. An' we hurry on, we'll see the Wizard's Keep before sundown."

"And *when the sky falls we'll all catch larks*," the púca said sourly, but he stopped where he was, and looked back at the Hunter. "What can you mean, we'll see it ere long? 'Twas yourself told the Hag Domhnall's Keep was lost to all knowledge!"

"Well, so it might have been, though few things are. And if the Hag were half as easy to gull as your own sweet self, sure, an' I'd have talked her out of this foul bargain."

The púca smiled broadly, and clapped his hands. "Och,

you audacious darlin'! 'Tis a marvellous liar you are indeed—
and you knowin' all along where to find the Wizard's Keep!"

Blackthorn returned the púca's gleeful look with an
ingenuous one of his own. "Knowing? I'd no knowing at all,
at all where Domhnall's Keep might be." Cunning crept into
the edges of his smile. "But Gannet Graybeard the elder of
Luimneach knows where it lies hidden, and didn't he tell
me, too?"

The púca's face fell back into its familiar melancholy
lines. "Now it's lyin' you are for certain, and poorly, too. My
ears were as open as your own last night, and not a word
reached them from old Gannet's lips that might point you
on your way."

Blackthorn sighed heavily. "'Tis the curse of being such a
matchless liar as myself," he said. "An' I speak false, I'm sure
to be believed, but I'm ever doubted when I'm speaking true."

"The Hag never believed you," the púca argued, but
Blackthorn ignored him.

"Were you dreaming, then," he went on, gently mocking,
"when Gannet sang of Domhnall's death '. . . *by black beast
and axe/ on a winter's wild night/ 'twixt streams silver running/
and spear stained white . . .'?*"

The púca blinked. "From four lines of ill remembered song
you build Domhnall's Keep?"

Rolling his eyes, the little man let the air whistle out from
between his pursed lips. "Whisht, but hasn't all the drownin'
I've done gone and drownded me wits as well? Why, even a
goblin could ken the meaning of Gannet's song! Black, silver, and white. Sure, an' what could be more plain? What
could it be, but Sliabh Éibhlinne? 'Twas deaf I was and blind
entirely not to have realized it ere now."

Blackthorn grinned admiringly at the púca's elaborate
sarcasm.

"Well, an' you've a goblin's wits about you, likely the red-
eyes will take you to their black hearts as one of their own,
an' we chance to meet any. So let's be off."

The púca didn't drop to a mouse, but he did drop to the
ground, and made himself as small as he could.

"Hard-hearted you are, hard-hearted entirely," he whined,
"draggin' a poor innocent creature like meself to a dark and
ugly death, and I still sickly from the sea."

"Many things you are, little mouseen," Blackthorn said evenly, "but innocent, never."

"To the red-eyes you'd deliver us, and all the reason for it but a few lines of garbled verse!"

"What reason do I need, an' a geis driving me on?" Blackthorn answered. "Still, I have reason enough, at least to hope. I wager the Hag could have killed me, an' it would have pleased her to see me dead, and it's certain she could have refused to help me to my Spear. Yet, she—"

"She has refused you, you pea-brained idiot," the púca interrupted. "Or are you such a fool as to believe that reeking sack of old bones will keep her part of the bargain even an' you live to keep yours?"

"I hope," said Blackthorn deliberately, fastening his gaze on the púca, "I hope the Hag truly covets this Talisman, and will honor our pact an' I return to Inis na Linnte with her heart's desire."

A spark of the dark fire that had burned so fiercely in him that night on Binn Chuilceach glinted in Blackthorn's eyes. The púca cringed a little lower, but the Hunter took his gaze from the little man and turned it north, toward the distant, white-topped tower of rock.

"The old tales may be ill remembered," he admitted, "or the Bards that made them may have cared as little as I for the truth. Even so will I hope that the silver of Gannet's song is the Silvermine mountains, and the white is winter's snow adorning Sliabh Éibhlinne's narrow peak."

"Hope as you will," the púca muttered. "Meself, I'll hope 'by black beast and axe' doesn't mean goblins, and little hope there is in that."

"Little enough," Blackthorn agreed. "For 'twas only mid-summer last I stopped in Aonach Urmhumhan to take my pleasure at the fair, and wasn't the town all astir with rumors of trouble at the Silvermines?"

He let his voice drift into a storyteller's lilting cadence.

"Closemouthed were the miners at first, answering neither 'so it is' nor 'so it isn't' to the questions put them. But I wagered with them, on the fine-blooded horses, and careful was I to let them win. When the races were done, why sure, an' they were only too glad to help me soothe the sting of my loss with a jar or two. And didn't I drink the health of the stout folk that delve the hard rock, those that coax the moon's gleaming metal from the silver-veined earth? And didn't they drink to mine? And didn't the clear whiskey loosen their tongues at last, and they tell me their tales?"

Blackthorn faced the púca once more, and found the little man's narrow-eyed suspicion had given way to wide-eyed attention.

"Goblins they'd seen," he pronounced ominously, "blood-red coals flickering in the furthest reaches of the deepest pits. Who knows no fear, an' they spy the angry fire of a goblin's eyes, and the dark all about them? Only a King, little man, only a King fears them not. The miners, now, they feared greatly, feared for their dear ones and their own dear lives."

The púca shivered, but it was the contented shiver of a delighted audience.

"Since first human hand lifted stone from the soil, the goblins have hated us," Blackthorn continued, unable to resist embellishing his tale, what with such a willing ear to listen. "Yet, many the mountains we call our own, many the hollow hills filled with light. Took the miners too much from the silverlodes? Drove they their shafts too deep, waking the shadows that should never be disturbed?"

He paused, and was rewarded with breathless silence.

"Neither greedy nor careless were the miners," he answered himself. "'Twas no folly of theirs brought the goblins down upon them."

He paused again, and the púca responded exactly as a good audience should.

"Then how did the red-eyes find their way into the miners' tunnels?" he asked.

"Not across the open meadows," Blackthorn assured him. "Bright with summer were the fields stretching from the mines north to the town and west to An tSionainn, too bright for a goblin's eyes. Not along the broad, sunlit gap that runs eastward between the hills, for how could a red-eye see to travel it?"

"Well?" the púca urged.

Blackthorn shifted his gaze to the mountains, and a fey smile played about his lips. "'Twas from the south they came, from as far away as Sliabh Éibhlinne, so the miners said.

Under the black earth the goblins had made their roads, or found again winding passages mortal memory had long ago forgotten."

Without turning the Hunter opened his sack. "And so, little mouseen, an' you will hope at all, hope with me that the Ó Briain's war keeps the goblins busy in the north, and away from the rock tower that stands between the Silvermines and Sliabh Éibhlinne. Away from Sliabh Coimeálta, the mountain the miners call 'Keeper Hill.'"

The púca lifted his eyes despondently to the flat-topped peak.

"All the hope I have left in the world," he replied, "is that I've a chance for to hear another stunning lie drop from that terrible quick tongue of yours before a goblin's axe ends your prevaricatin' forever. Or closes me own ears against your grand, false tales," he added as a mournful afterthought.

Giving the Hunter a few moments to appreciate his look of bitter resignation, the púca dropped to a mouse without more complaint.

Twenty-six

I am a door always open
I am an old woman of the night
I am a dark pool under the willows
I am a stone in the hunter's hand
I am a tongue of bright fire
Who but myself knows the secret of the grave?

a rann made by Scáthach,
the Poet of Teach an Fhásaigh

Keeper Hill was misnamed, Blackthorn thought wearily, digging the end of his staff higher onto the slope and pulling himself up to stand beside it. "Keeper Mountain" it should be called, for such it was. Like the tallest tower of a giant's castle, the steep-sided, conical peak rose high above the blue battlement of the Silvermines to the north and the lesser heights to the south and east, the watchtowers of Sliabh Éibhlinne and An Driom Fiodhach. And like a true keep, the mountain protected its store well. Too well.

Not far to Blackthorn's right, an outcropping of weather-worn boulders offered a welcome rest. He looked carefully among its shadows before accepting the invitation, but he could see nothing to fear. On this side of the mountain the sun was shining still, and the pockets of gentle gray that lay among the mounded granite were far too small to harbor any evil.

He sat with his foot on one rock and his back against another, frowning. The daystar was lower in the sky than he, and himself little more than halfway to the mountain's flat peak. It wouldn't be long now and shadows would rule the heights—the base of the mountain was already wrapped in purpled dusk. Hours he'd wended his way up and around the rain-eroded, windswept slopes, careful to miss nothing in his search. Yet, no path had he found, no gate of trees, no cave leading in, no sign at all that mortal feet had ever walked on Keeper Hill. He had still the table-flat top of the tower to see, but should he not find a door to the mountain's heart on the exposed, snow-covered summit, bitter the night that would close on him there.

Blackthorn felt his pouch move as its occupant clambered from it, then a light tug as the mouse jumped from the purse to his cloak. Dragging his tiny claws along the wolfskins to slow his downward journey, the púca slipped to the ground. The next moment a wizened, worried old man stood before the Hunter, shaking his head slowly from side to side and clucking his tongue.

"Wurra, wurra, wurra, an' look at himself now. A Wizard's Sliabh the prize his vaunted cunning was to gain him, but what has he to show for all his guile? Naught but an inhospitable, unclimbable mountain. Och, a fine meal your boastful words will make, and greatly I'll enjoy servin' them up to you. But not here, not here," he added quickly. "Get up, bodach, and let's be gone, before the goblins start sniffin' about for the heavy-footed clod's been trippin' and fallin' all over their roof this day."

Blackthorn shot the púca a dark look, but the little man only wrinkled his nose scornfully.

"Och, you'll not be intimidatin' me, neither. 'Tis right I am, and you wrong entirely, and whether 'tis fire or ice in your eye, I'll be right just the same."

Blackthorn came to his feet in one swift motion. Unprepared for such immediate compliance with his wishes, the púca jumped back, startled, and lost his footing. Heels over head he rolled, into an overgrown thicket of leafless gorse, driving the long-tailed tits that lived there to the sky in a small, but vocal, cloud of agitation.

"Curse your limbs for their haste and your wits for their slowness!" the púca railed from the bushes. "Curse you twice over for laughin' at me, you heartless worm!"

Still laughing, Blackthorn slid down to the gorse and reached carefully into its thick mesh of wood to haul the púca out.

"Ow!" the púca howled. "You clumsy—may An Daghdha see you someday learn for yourself what it is to be slashed and torn by sharp branches! Ow!"

"A little louder, now," suggested Blackthorn, "and I'm sure the goblins will hear and come running to ease you of this trouble."

At once the púca fell silent. Dropping to a mouse, he scrambled through the netted branches to the ground, and swiftly made his way under them. Blackthorn stooped to pick up the púca, but when he looked under the bush, he saw the shape-shifter scurrying away, deeper into the thicket.

"Come back, you little coward!" he cried, laughing again. "'Twas a jest only, and no goblins in earshot!"

Using the blackthorn wand to hold back some of the gorse, he peered after the vanished púca. Suddenly his other hand shot out, he grabbed a fistful of brittle twigs, broke them off, threw them aside, and closed his fingers on a stout stem. He pulled, but the shrub refused to shift. Dropping his staff, he laid both hands on the stem, and pulled again. Some of the roots tore free from the thin topsoil, and a part of the plant came away in his hand.

A terrified squeak erupted from the branches he held, stopping Blackthorn just as he was about to fling the piece of uprooted gorse down the slope. Looking into the tangle of wood, he saw a little, brown wood mouse clinging to a thin twig. The púca set his beady eyes on the Hunter and let out a long string of furious chatter. Blackthorn listened a moment, then brusquely shook the mouse loose and tossed the empty branches away. Reaching back into the thicket, he began once more to wrestle with the prickly bush.

"You utterly daft and dangerous fool!" the púca swore behind him. "Have you gone mad entirely?"

For his answer, Blackthorn yanked another great clump of gorse out of the ground, and sent it down the mountain after the first. Heedless of the thorns, he next laid his hands on one of the main trunks. When it proved too deep-rooted to come loose, he bore down on it until the wood snapped and bent.

"Och, an' there's the mark of a clever man! Faced with nightfall on a goblin-haunted mountain, what does he do? Get off the cursed hill? Build a fire warm and high? Not a bit of it! Why, he spends his time and strength destroyin' a thicket of gorse! What else, and what better? Sure, an' you'd think . . ."

The púca trailed off.

"By the light that shines!" he whispered.

Shredded trunks and broken branches still masked some of the stones, but where Blackthorn had torn away the gorse, a well-laid section of wall stood plainly revealed. The Hunter cleared years of covering growth, the rest of the gorse, then bramble vines and a blanket of earth from around the piled stones. At last he stood back, wiping sweat from his brow, and surveyed the results of his efforts.

Two crumbling walls jutted out from the almost-vertical slope. Between them ran a dark, narrow corridor. Creeping quietly to the front of the passage, the púca peered into the shadowed recess of the ancient grave and shivered.

"I know what you're thinkin', bodach, but your thinkin' is mistaken. A Wizard renowned as Domhnall the Spell-Maker would have a finer tomb than this. Best leave it alone. Imbolc it is, and on days like this, who knows what might be crossin' gates like these?"

Blackthorn smiled strangely. "Gates like these," he repeated.

"Sure, an' there's no keener-eyed huntsman than yourself in all Éirinn," said the púca, changing his tune and singing praises with adulatory fervor, "nor a stronger. You've opened the mountain with your bare hands, you have. Not a moment to lose, me bold champion. Why, we'll off to Aonach Urmhumhan this very minute," he said, keeping the flattering tone, but backing discreetly from the grave, "and when we've found someone with knowledge of the secrets Domhnall kept within, why back we'll come—"

Blackthorn bent and picked up his staff. "Gates like these," he said again.

The púca grasped the corner of the Hunter's cloak and tugged. "Not a gate—not a gate for a livin' man! Och, look you, just a hole it is in the side of the mountain, and the mountain itself at its back." He paused and shivered again, then tugged even harder. *"Badhbh, Macha, and Mór-Ríoghain,* don't be stepping in there, I'm sayin'."

"Don't be a fool," Blackthorn replied easily.

He pulled his cloak free of the púca and strode to the mouth of the tomb. The passage angled slightly downward. The sun, casting a last golden light from the rim of the world, could barely reach the first stones. The end of the passage was lost in deep shadow.

"Are you blind, then?" the púca cried, forgetting he had reasons for being quiet.

Blackthorn stopped, then turned and fixed his eyes on the púca.

"Well, and blind I must be, little mouseen," he said softly. "So suppose you be telling me what it is you See within."

The púca squirmed under the Hunter's unblinking regard. "A star I See—no! Not the one you're hopin' for," he amended frantically, seeing a glitter of triumph in Blackthorn's stern look. "Not a little silver pentacle. Huge the star I See, and all glowin' with lights of every color. 'Tis the second one, it is, in there, waitin' for you. The one by the spell."

Blackthorn stood straighter, more astonished now than distrustful. "You See a geis past this door? A geis meant for me?"

The púca nodded miserably.

The sun dipped below the horizon, and shadows leapt up from the earth to cover the mountain. Blackthorn's eyes gleamed in the sudden twilight.

"'One by the Goddess, two by the spell . . .'" he murmured, running his hand through his hair. "So. The three geasa you cursed me with are more than a crafty lie to keep you in my company! What is this spell, little man? How will I know it?"

"Didn't I tell you once before, the Sight makes nothin' plain? I've said all I See and all I know. And if your wits fill more space in your head than a barleycorn, you'll have sense enough to come away from this perilous gate."

"And if you had wits at all, at all, you'd know better than to ask me."

Though his back was to it, Blackthorn could feel the cool, clammy chill that hung in the corridor between the grave's stone walls, and smell the sour odor of mould that rose from the dampness within.

"Come," he said, inclining his head to invite the púca

nearer. "Come along while we've still some light to guide our first steps."

The púca answered with a strained whimper, like a dog's submissive whine.

"I'll carry you, an' you fear to walk beside me," Blackthorn offered sympathetically.

He flashed the púca an encouraging smile and stretched the mouth of his purse wide with his fingers. The little man scrambled back quickly, as if afraid a goblin would leap out of the sack.

"Wurra, wurra, wurra," the púca groaned. "The long and the short of it is, 'tis a coward I am, and that terrible doorway more than I can dare."

Blackthorn shrugged and pulled the pouch's thong tight. "How will you ever be free of your geis, an' you run away whenever there's danger before me?" he asked.

"I might be free of it now, an' you'd heed my warning and strike a path for Aonach Urmhumhan," the púca pleaded.

Blackthorn smiled gently. "This is my path."

Turning, he stepped down into the passage and moved forward into the shadows.

"But an' the Hunter of Éirinn finds his way out of the darkness," the little man whispered after him, "Reathach the púca will be here, waitin' for him."

Fine words were the thanks usually returned for the gift of someone's true Name. For all that he tried to find a few, Blackthorn could think of nothing to say, but only turn and stare at the shape-shifter in quiet surprise. The twilight was swiftly deepening to night—the little man was no more than a thin, pale ghost, and when he dropped to a mouse, it was the delicate sounds of his paws hurrying over the littered ground that told Blackthorn he had gone off to seek a hiding place among the remaining patches of gorse.

When no further noises came from the torn bushes, Blackthorn faced the passage once more, and let his feet carry him down into the grave. His step was brisk and confident, and spoke not at all to the wild drumming of his heart.

Twenty-seven

When night upon you falls
And far from home you're winding
Heed no whispered calls,
Or death you will be finding.
And stray not from the road,
Seek for no abode,
Set your heavy load
Aside, and cease your longing.
Then build your fire warm,
Fear and trembling scorn,
Cut a stout blackthorn
To banish ghosts and goblins,
When night upon you falls.

Peddlers' Lore Song

Slightly dank, slightly chill, the mildewed interior of the grave was no more than a tomb should be, save that the passage was so long. Blackthorn's determined stride slowed, became a cautious step. The cool, close air pressed lighter on his flesh, and he stopped, sure that he had come to a widening of the corridor, or an intersection, or perhaps an inner chamber. The darkness was complete. He could see absolutely nothing.

He stood a moment, debating what to do, but when another had passed, the choice was taken from him. An almost imperceptible shifting underfoot was all the warning he had that the soil beneath his boots was crumbling into insubstantial air. He hadn't even time to cry out—his was a silent and sickening plunge into the empty dark.

As a child he had sometimes dreamt of falling. Not quite awake, not quite asleep, suddenly he would feel himself plummeting into a bottomless crack between worlds, and wake with a start. Only now there was no waking, just the rush of air up and away where his heart and his breath and his stomach still hung, abandoned when his body dropped like a stone into the pitch-black abyss.

How fast, how far can a man fall, and nothing to stop him? Blackthorn had only a single instant to wonder, while his blood froze and his mind screamed, and as quickly as it had begun, it was over. He didn't catch himself, nor did the hard earth break his fall. He simply found himself standing again, and on solid ground.

The unexpected reprieve unbalanced Blackthorn almost as much as his anticipated disastrous landing. Though the world beneath him was steady once more, he reeled under a wave of dizziness, lost his footing, and sat down, hard.

He stayed down, letting his pulse quiet and his breathing slow. Illusion, he thought, then dismissed the idea. Under his hands was not damp earth, but dry and polished stone paving. Reaching farther into the darkness, his fingertips touched the glazed surface of tile.

He rose at last, and turned slowly where he stood. No sounds came from the darkness, no scents to describe the place or betray a hidden watcher. There was nothing at all, no warm or cold drafts to point a direction, no drip of underground water, not the faintest echo to keep him company.

Whatever dangers awaited, he thought, it would make little difference which way he went to meet them. Keeping his staff slightly before him, and using it to test the ground, Blackthorn took three cautious steps into the lightless air.

"Dr-r-r-ead . . . Comes-s-s . . . S-s-s-train . . ."

The words grated painfully, like rough stones ground tediously together. Blackthorn held still, but the voice seemed not to come so much from before or behind him, but to rise from the floor and surround him.

"Dre-e-ed . . . wel-l-l . . . comes-s-s . . . s-s-tranger-r-r . . ."

The words came smoother this time, and seemed less ominous, but even so, they gave Blackthorn no ease. A thin

band of sweat dampened his brow, and his heartbeat quickened. What though he thought he heard a civil greeting in
the Mothers' tongue, still the voice that gave it was not
human, and his blindness made him reluctant to trust it. He
had half expected to find death in Domhnall's Keep, but he
would like to see his end, an' it was before him. In this
gloom he could not even be sure his eyes were open.

"Éire bless all here," he answered carefully.

Light flared behind him. Blackthorn spun about, but by
the time he faced the flash, it was gone, swallowed by the
dark. He waited, tense and alert, and fire shot again from the
blackness. At first he recoiled, unable to withstand the brilliance, but when the flames steadied, he almost smiled.
Another flash, to his right. This second light died as well,
but returned again almost immediately and held, a small
fountain of fire at the top of a cobwebbed torch. All about
him other torches burst into wakefulness, and sporadic
tongues of yellow and orange spurted into air.

When the display was done, four thick torches of bundled
twigs blazed in iron stands along the perimeter of what
Blackthorn could now see was a small, circular chamber.
Two more burned erratically and with much smoke, one
refused to light, and a last stand's socket stood torchless and
empty. Already the rising smoke had formed a small dark
cloud against the chamber's domed ceiling, and the ceiling
itself arced to a point only thrice Blackthorn's height at its
apex. The soot filling the air was reason enough to leave this
place, but though it was no more than ten paces from the
center of the room to any of the blue-tiled walls, Blackthorn
never moved. In all the chamber there was no door.

His relief at regaining his sight was mingled with distaste
at the scene spread before him. Bones did not frighten him,
but the tale these told was an evil one. A warrior's helmeted,
hollow-eyed skull grinned mirthlessly at the granite roof of
his tomb. The bones of the neck lay in a tidy line below the
head, and a golden torque at their base, but the rest of the
man's skeleton was not so neatly arrayed. Pieces of his hand
lay scattered around the jewelled hilt of a bronze sword. The
blade was notched and broken, and the tiles on the wall
above the fallen warrior were scored with the weapon's desperate attacks.

The flesh and sinew that had bound the body together had long ago succumbed to the years and the scavengers of the dark. Even so, Blackthorn could see the man had contorted in death, for his clothing lay strangely twisted around his bones. His shirt and breeches had endured, but were faded and frayed, save for a perfect knot embroidered in gold holding one corner of the shirt intact. The leather vest had once been lined with badger, but the fur was eaten away, the leather had hardened and cracked, and the vest's copper studs were green with age. Though time could not veil the richness of the man's attire, it had cast a fine layer of dust over the warrior's remains, dulling the sheen of his high boots and bronze helmet. Beneath the dust on the stone floor, the stain left by the corpse as it had rotted away spread like a rusty carpet around the dry bones.

That his own bones might soon lie with the ones before him was a thought Blackthorn could not stave off. The cobwebs and cleaned corpse attested to entrances and exits that some could use, but none for a man his size. The sealed walls of the chamber were covered in painted blue tiles, and upon these were set mosaics of sacred symbols, a spiral of jet, a triskelion of amber, an amethyst labyrinth, a garnet sun disc, and a crescent of white quartz that shone like the moon.

One thing else the room held worth study. A fallen statue lay an arm's length from the warrior. Squat figurines of the Goddess in her pregnant divinity, a carven Síle na gCíoch at Dair na Tintrí's gates, amber likenesses of the creatures of the wild dangling at a hunter's belt, all these had Blackthorn seen. Never till now had he seen a sculpture the height and shape of a living woman, translucent Na Connachta marble worked so cunningly as to capture all the grace and suppleness of the female form.

He shivered away the notion that this could once have been a real woman, preferring to believe the statue the expression of a master hand. Long, milky white robes, veined in the palest of greens, each fold perfectly delineated, flowed illogically upward, for the statue lay on her side. Her right arm was smashed from shoulder to elbow, reduced to a splay of powder and needle-sharp shards where it had struck against the stone and tile floor. Her hands had been outstretched, welcoming, or offering, or perhaps even taking

power in—Blackthorn could well imagine this lady under
the moon, drawing down power through her upraised palms.
Her elegant gesture was marred; the thumb of her right hand
had shattered in the fall.

What most disturbed Blackthorn about the sculpture was
that it brought back memories of Scáthach. Not in feature,
or height, or shape were the two alike, but in death the marble woman bore a marked resemblance to the Poet of Teach
an Fhásaigh. The statue's head was no longer attached to her
swanlike neck, and where it had broken off, the marble
looked rough and wounded.

The left side of her face evoked a sense of living flesh with
flawless craft, in the wisps escaping from her piled hair, ready
to stir in the faintest breeze, in the subtle creases near her
eye, in the smooth curve of her cheek. Her right side that
had borne the brunt of the fall was partially crushed, forcing
her head to rest at an unnatural, flattened angle. Her mouth
suffered the most. Only the upper lip remained. Below it the
polished stone deteriorated into uneven, primal rock.

"Hun-n-n . . . wel-l-l comes-s-s . . . mo-r-r-re . . . for-r-r . . .
courtes-s-s-e-e-e . . ."

No longer did the gravelly voice rouse unease in
Blackthorn. Seeing the slight lift of the statue's lip as she
tried to speak from her broken jaw, he was moved instead to
pity. Would she have come to life for him if she'd been
whole? Had her voice once been sweet and high? "A hundred welcomes, stranger. And a hundred welcomes more for
your courtesy." Not malicious intent, Blackthorn decided,
but age and accident were to blame for the alarming and
unpredictable nature of his reception. Domhnall's spells had
been too long unused, too long asleep in the masterless
mountain.

"Oo-ooo-ai . . . come you-u-u . . . nall's-s-s . . . Ke-e-e-ep?"

Blackthorn's heart leapt within his breast. "Why come
you to Domhnall's Keep?" Could it be so simple as to ask and
be given?

"I seek the Talisman of Domhnall the Spell-Maker," he
said clearly.

The lump of stone that had been the statue's head lay
silent for so long, Blackthorn began to question whether the
spell that had brought it to life had finally lost all power.

Though his throat began to chafe from the acrid air and the dead warrior's well-dressed bones pressed on his awareness, the Hunter kept his eyes and his hopes on the statue's scarred face. At last a delicate eyebrow raised and the torn lip fluttered once more.

"In . . . s-s-sanctum . . . upon . . . s-s-silver . . . tre-e-e-e . . . Talis-s-s . . . you-u-u s-s-e-e-ek."

Blackthorn kept his voice slow and calm. "How do I reach the sanctum?"

Again his wait was long, but the Hunter had found his patience.

"Oo-oo-uhn . . . thr-r-read . . . leads-s-s . . ." grated the voice. "Only . . . f-f-friend . . . may pas-s-s . . . portal-l-l-l."

"A friend am I," Blackthorn assured the broken marble. "But where is the door?"

"Before you-u-u . . . . s-s-stands . . . portal-l-l . . . No weapon-n-n . . . better tha-a-an . . . oo-uhn . . . you bear-r-r . . . un-n-nlock . . . do-o-or."

Blackthorn ran the slow, tortured words through his mind, filling in the gaps. "Before you stands the portal. No weapon is better than the one you bear to unlock the door." Was that it? Then the egress was hidden before him, so cleverly concealed as to be invisible. He let his fingers play along the length of his staff. Sure, an' what better key to a magic door than a magic wand?

Striding past the fallen statue, he raised his staff to the wall, choosing the spiral design for his marker. The solidity of the barrier did not alter at his gesture, but Blackthorn's confidence was undiminished. Gently, but with determination, he touched the tip of the wood to the gemstone pattern. There was an unresonant *tap* as the blackthorn came in contact with the wall, but no other change in the room.

Blackthorn frowned, then moved slowly around the edge of the chamber, examining the cracks in the stones for a latch or hinges, tapping the wall with his staff, touching the blackthorn wood to every mosaic symbol. He passed through the lights and shadows cast by the torches, tested their iron stands, studied the flow of soot above the smoking flames. Halfway around the room Blackthorn paused and glanced back at the statue with narrowed eyes.

"-fore you-u-u . . . s-s-tands. . . portal-l-l . . . "

He turned again to the wall, and rapped smartly with the branch of fairy thorn, but the stones were unimpressed.

"No weapon-n-n . . . better-r-r . . . than-n-n . . . one you-u-u . . . bear-r-r . . . un-n-nlock . . . do-o-or."

Jaw set, he continued his circuit around the room until he came to where the skeleton lay. His eyes were drawn to the pieces of white fingers, to the ruined blade. No doubt the once-noble sword had also been named a perfect key to the hidden door. No weapon better. Had his predecessor died slowly of thirst and starvation, or did the torches smoke even then, thickening the air with unbreathable darkness, as they were doing now? Had the statue fallen, or had the warrior toppled it in his dying fury, decapitating the animate stone in an attempt to silence the lady's mocking words?

Mocking words.

Blackthorn turned to stare at the half-crushed marble head. Immediately the statue began to grind out her message once again. The Hunter listened, hearing her as if for the first time.

Not an invitation. A riddle. 'Twas a game of wits the Spell-Maker had in mind for his guests. To win brought them into the Wizard's Keep. What Domhnall had intended for his visitors should they lose, Blackthorn could not begin to guess. For him, it would mean his death.

He stood still, as still as he had been that long evening past by the banks of An Mhorn Bheag, and the White Stag before him. Nine years he had readied to hunt the sacred elk through Éirinn's forests. Ill prepared was he entirely to follow a Wizard's canny mind down intangible paths of thought. The answer to Domhnall's riddle was an elusive quarry, yet Blackthorn was sure of one thing. A riddle's answer lies always in the riddle itself.

"'Before you stands the portal to Domhnall's Keep,'" he said aloud.

But the chamber was round, and the statue's message the same whether he stood at one end of the room or another. Not one door, then, but many? And would all open to the same key?

"'No weapon is better than the one you bear to unlock the door.' 'No weapon is better than the one you bear to unlock the door.' 'No weapon is better . . .'"

The smoke was heavy in the air now. Blackthorn felt he was drawing a little more of his harsh death in with every breath. He repeated the phrase again and again, trying to wring their secret from the deceptively simple words until they became meaningless syllables on his tongue.

From the chaos he had created the riddle was reborn, its order the same, its sense transformed.

Deliberately Blackthorn faced away from the fallen statue, waited a moment, and with heart pounding, slowly turned back. Instantly the statue spoke.

"Before you-u-u . . . s-s-stands—"

"Arrah!" Blackthorn's voice was a whisper, but it reverberated in the soot-filled dome above. "No longer do you stand, Portal, but I have your meaning nonetheless."

The cracked and broken mouth continued on without acknowledging Blackthorn's interruption.

"No weapon-n-n . . . better-r-r than . . . oo-uhn . . . you-u-u bear-r-r . . ."

"If no weapon is better," said Blackthorn quietly, "I will bear none."

Crossing to the lady, he knelt down on one knee. It was awkward, placing his blackthorn into the woman's palms, but now he could plainly see the statue's hands were not open to welcome or to give, but to receive. With short, stiff movements nine marble fingers curled, bent, closed around the fairy branch.

A faint rumble heralded the opening of Domhnall's door. Blackthorn looked toward the sound, but already he had missed the magic. A tall archway and a flight of stone stairs had appeared where a moment ago there had been only blue tiles inlaid with an amethyst labyrinth. At once a rush of air swept into the chamber, cold and rank, fanning the torches' flames, and a thin stream of smoke snaked under the arch and up the stairway.

The sour air was unappealing, the dark passage unwelcoming, but Blackthorn rose at once.

"One thread leads," the statue had said. He could have wished it had been the spiral—a single thread winding up and around—but the labyrinth too was a single thread, and likely matched better the Spell-Maker's convoluted mind.

The foul odors on the air grew stronger as Blackthorn

neared the doorway. Urine and rancid oil he smelled, and cursed under his breath. An' there were red-eyes and axes awaiting him above, he would prefer to meet them with a flaming brand in one hand and his fairy thorn in the other.

He turned back to the chamber and ran his fingers through his hair. Fire he might manage. With luck, the flames of Domhnall's spelled torches would burn long and well—and better to be running with light than stumbling through the darkness. An' the goblins had wits enough to turn their red eyes toward him, they'd spy him as swiftly either way.

Hurrying to the nearest torch, he lifted it from its stand. More slowly he started back toward the stairs, cursing as he went. An ill death he wished on any host who would deny a man his weapon, and enemies stalking the hall. It was a worthless curse—the Spell-Maker had already died an ill death, and at the goblins' hands—and speaking it did little to mollify Blackthorn's anger at losing such a potent staff.

Anger turned to alarm as he passed the statue. Her fingers suddenly sprang open and his blackthorn clattered to the floor. Sweeping the fairy wand from the ground, he raced to the doorway, fearing lest the spell that had opened the arch suddenly close it now that his weapon was no longer in the statue's grasp. His fear changed to hope, and hope quickly grew to elation as the arch remained open and he reached the stair.

The spell that had moved the statue's limbs might have broken at last. Or the Wizard might only have wished a token gesture from his guests, never meaning to keep their weapons from them. Whatever the reason for it, the Hunter was profoundly grateful to be holding both fire and blackthorn in his hands as he started up the shadowed stair.

Twenty-eight

A chest of gold she found within,
But neither lock nor key.
A harp appeared where none had been,
Jewels graced a silver tree.
A spell was laid, unfelt, unseen,
On every treasure rare,
And woe betide the bold Máirín
Unwarily treading there.

Máirín the Thief

The stairs wound tightly up into the mountain, allowing the light from Blackthorn's torch to reveal but a few steps at a time. Tall, narrow niches were cut into the stone wall, but whatever they once held, the malodorous recesses now boasted only cobwebs, rat dung, and unrecognizable scraps of tarnished metal.

After a long climb, the stairway leveled off into a corridor wide enough for four to walk abreast. The passage was curved, but the arc so gradual his torchlight leapt far ahead of his footsteps. The better part of an hour he stole along the corridor, finding no doors, no intersections, yet sensing that the passageway's constant curve was bringing him full circle. It had nearly closed with itself when at last it bent sharply to the right and rose steeply in a second flight of stairs.

At the top of the stairway stretched another corridor. This second passage curved like the first. If it had not been carved higher in the hill, Blackthorn thought, it would have nested perfectly against the lower, for its arc was marginally tighter.

Though he kept his eyes on the darkness beyond the golden pool cast by his torch, watching for red fires in the shadows, he missed nothing his light revealed. This floor had once been painted, and tapestries once adorned the walls. Among the years of accumulated dirt and debris Blackthorn saw a table's broken leg, the back of a chair, shreds of soiled cambric. There were signs that others often used this corridor, though there had been none below—heavy, bootless feet had scattered the litter and layered dust. His torchlight illuminated a dark gash in the gray stone wall, a doorway looming just ahead and to the left.

He retreated quickly, until the entrance was again lost in darkness. Setting his torch against some rubble, he crept forward once more. Not a sound came from the room. Though the smell of the place was musty, it had no more goblin in it than the passage. Still, the doorway gave the Hunter pause. An' Domhnall's Keep was in truth a labyrinth, and every chamber to be found along a single companionway, the red-eyed hounds who made it their home would have little trouble running this black-haired fox to ground.

He went back for his torch, then returned to the chamber for a better look. There was no door, only a dark threshold, which he hurried over, lifting his torch higher as he stepped into the room. A large iron ring lay in the center of chamber. It sported twelve sockets, all empty of the candles that had doubtless blazed there in Domhnall's day. The rusted chain that had held it to the ceiling now stretched across part of the floor. On either side of the ring were hunks of rotting wood—what was left of couches, long benches, and tables. Fungi sprouted from smashed and splintered boards, and veins of mould were creeping up the tiled walls.

Heaped in a corner of the room, untouched by the damp, unsullied, though surely goblin paws had many times caressed them, gold and silver treasures glittered with pure, abiding beauty. Blackthorn smiled, but listened long for any sound in the passageway before going nearer to the goblin hoard. Though the platters and urns, the goblets and bowls looked as if they'd been tossed heedlessly over someone's shoulder with no mind to where they might fall, Blackthorn knew each piece had been deliberately set, each gleam was precious to the goblin who had put it there.

Making his way carefully over the ruined furnishings to avoid contact with the evil-looking growths that were devouring them, he padded silently to the goblin's store. He set his blackthorn aside and quickly but quietly ran his hand through the mound, spreading the goblin's prized possessions into a pool of shining disarray. From the varied choices before him he selected a lady's copper armband, well and recently burnished, and a gold-rimmed finger bowl. Then he stood, lowered his breeches, and pissed into the booty.

Satisfied, he took up his blackthorn and turned to leave. Goblins were mad as dogs about who watered their ground. Now he need only see that their fury drove the hounds to seek the fox where the fox wasn't hiding.

He paused at the doorway before daring the passage, but it was empty. He went swiftly out and back the way he had come. He left clear prints in the deeper piles of dust and grime, dropped the copper ring at the top of the stairs, the bowl at the bottom, then hurried a short way down the lower passage making sure his cloak brushed against the rock wall. Finally, he let a last drop of piss fall to the stone floor.

His false trail laid, Blackthorn raced back up the corridor, this time with impeccable care, touching nothing, disturbing nothing, leaving no trace of his passing. An' his spoor led the goblins down the stairs, and the strong reminder of his scent in the passageway below goaded them on, they might well track him all the way to the chamber of the statue. Once there, the torches would daunt them for a while, but the smoky air would smell of him; they would wait until the fires had burned low, and it was dark enough for their red eyes to see. When they looked, they would find him gone, but bronze they would discover, and copper, and rare jewels, and all would entice them to tarry in the room they had never been able to open, or perhaps never known was there to loot.

He returned to the feasting hall and sped by, went on, and on, and at last reached another turn, this time to the left, and another long stairway leading up. Beyond the landing stretched a third corridor, the mirror of the last two, but the arcs were growing tighter—this curve was plain to his sight. A labyrinth indeed was Domhnall's Keep, each passage doubling back on itself, but each set higher in the granite tower than the one before. Most likely he'd find the Wizard's sanctum in the mountain's peak, after the last turn of all. He sighed, but saved his curses, sure he would need them before this journey was done.

The next chamber he encountered was blocked by an ash wood door. One of the hinges had broken and the door hung slightly off kilter. Though the wood was thick, sounds filtered through the angled crack where the door leaned wide from the wall, sounds he recognized, but did not fear. The room was not empty, but neither were there goblins within.

As if to prove him right, a rat scuttled out from beneath the door, froze when it saw Blackthorn, then spat a fierce challenge at the Hunter and darted off. The beast bounded away down the corridor, and Blackthorn relaxed, knowing the lower passages were clear of goblins. Red-eyes were more likely to eat a rat than listen to it, but he would rather no messenger at all than a black-furred one to tell tales of intruders in the Keep.

He pushed the door ajar as quietly as he could. It creaked dismally, but the sound it made was instantly overwhelmed by worse noises from within the chamber. The floor of the room seethed with scores of beady-eyed rodents, far more than the smell and scratching he had heard through the door had led him to expect. The torchlight and his own presence sent the rats into a frenzy of nervous chittering and panicked flight. They squirmed past him, waves of black vermin breaking over his boots and spilling into the corridor. A few got tangled in the folds of his cloak, a few more he had to strike from his legs with his blackthorn staff.

He sent a curse after them through his clenched teeth, knowing it would do him no good. So pleased he had been to see a single rat running down the corridor, now thirty and more of them were squealing up the passage, and in all haste!

Tightening his grip on the fairy thorn, he went on into the apartment, but as he had guessed, it was no Wizard's spell-room. Whatever it had been, bedchamber, most likely, now it was only a rats' nest. The stink, the gloom, the destruction were oppressive. It had been easier to look upon Scáthach's burnt dwelling, though a charred and gutted hulk, than to see this mouldering ruin of grandeur. Damp had seeped into the room below—here a sickly stream wove unevenly down the far wall and made a brownish pool on the floor.

He hurried on, certain his time to himself was growing short. Broken pots covered one section of the corridor, and countless twigs of gnawed wicker were strewn across another, forcing him to slow if he was to pass without disturbing them. Jutting slabs of granite rock threatened to trip him, and he had to take care that the spiderwebs, spread thick and white as sheets, did not catch on his torch.

He made it to the end of the passage, up the stairs, and to the next chamber unhindered. Here again he found no door, but the broad threshold spoke of a huge portal or double doors that had once led inward. The sound of heavy drops falling into a pool echoed inside, and water trickled out into the companionway.

Careful to keep his boots from the wet, Blackthorn looked through the gaping doorframe. The hall was immense, surely a place once reserved for the greatest entertainments, music and dancing and poetry to delight Domhnall's guests. Now the walls wept, the ceiling rained, the floor was flooded. Three hearths had been laid in an intricately tiled floor, but the colors and design were obscured by a sheet of dingy water, and the hearths themselves were now dark and ugly pools. Flecks of rusted iron floated on the water's gray surface, dislodged from two rotting candle rings that had fallen into the firepits from the roof above.

He went on, in a hurry to leave before the damp could cling to his boots and betray his step. Avoiding the rivulets that wormed down the walls and along the edges of the passage, he sped down the corridor, coming eventually to the turn. There he slowed, listened, and tasted the air.

Since he had left the open slopes of Keeper Hill and entered the stone-lined grave, he had been waiting to hear their voices and the stamp of their heavy feet—sooner or later, he knew, he would choke on the powerful and unmistakable smell of goblin. Even so, when he did, it was like a shock of cold water on a sleeper's face. For a moment his surprise held Blackthorn motionless. Then he turned and ran, retracing his steps to the great hall, to the chance that was there . . . that must be there . . . why had he looked so briefly and seen so little?

Reaching the doorway, he lifted his torch and peered within, his eyes searching upward to the chamber's roof. Huge drops of brown water hung from the ceiling, letting loose their loads one fulsome tear at a time. But there also was the chance he had looked for—three large smoke holes hewn into the rock, one above each hearth, and hanging just below the last chimney by a heavy black chain was the third iron candle ring, still fixed in the ceiling.

Blackthorn let out his breath in a brief prayer of thanks, and stepped quickly into the room. If he could reach the ring, if he could climb from it into the chimney itself . . .

Inside the chamber the trickling water became a dozen wavering rills, but now Blackthorn sought out the streamlets. Even dirty water is a friend to a hounded fox. When the ribbons widened to a foul wet pool he went faster, setting the torch in his teeth as he walked, and using his hands to bind his blackthorn staff once more across his back.

He found a rope, but it was sodden and fell apart in his hand. He came upon a broken chair, but that would serve him no better. A few steps more brought him to a broad table tipped on its side. The oak board was enormous—it must have seated thirty if it had ever seated one—and though the length that lay in the water was decomposing, still the rest of the wood was solid. Setting his shoulder against one of the table's narrow ends, he shoved with all his might. The slime feeding on the waterlogged edge aided him, and sent the massive board sliding toward the far hearth.

When he had it set where he wanted it, he paused and listened again. Faint but plain he heard them. On the stairs he guessed the goblins were from the muted sound of their rough voices, but as yet there was no alarm in their guttural speech, no urgency in their tread.

He would have preferred to balance on the table and leap to the candle ring, but he would never make it—he needed a running start. Both hands he'd need, too, and the torch nothing but a burden in his teeth. Still, without it how could he see where to jump, or where to climb an' he reached the iron ring? And should he miss the ring, and the goblins catch him here, he would want the fire all the more.

He stepped away, then ran forward, springing onto the

edge of the board and off again with all the strength in his legs. The table crashed down, sending water leaping to wet his breeches even as he flew toward the iron ring. His hands reached, grasped, closed, one on the outer band of metal and one on the thin iron crossbar. His weight made the thing groan and sway, but though it complained of him, the ring held. Immediately he pulled himself up, got a knee on the center of the crossbar, and a foot braced on a candle socket. The socket was rusted through—it broke off and fell into the water below. Choosing another toehold, Blackthorn took the torch from his teeth, and raised it toward the chimney hole. A few drops of water splattered down, making his flame sputter.

Cursing silently, he cautiously straightened his legs and stood on the shaking ring. He thrust the torch into the smoke hole and pressed his forearm against the wet rock, then quickly brought his other hand within the shaft and shoved against the opposite wall. The stone was smooth, and slippery with years of dripping water, but he was too close to safety to let a sheath of slime and a few drops of wet daunt him. Pushing his strength outward through his arms he lifted himself up, dug his knees into the side of the chimney to bear his weight, then shifted his arms higher along the shaft.

His body was hidden, and he trusted his body hid the light of his brand as well, when he heard the goblins' muted growls rise to a hideous howling. He glanced down between his legs, but saw no glowing red fires peering up, only blackness. Likely the red-eyes had only now caught his scent in the corridor, or had just reached the doorway and seen the changes he'd wrought in the great hall's decor. He crept another arm's length up the shaft, fervently hoping three things were true; that the iron ring had stopped swinging, that his fire was too far from the base of the chimney for its light to spill out, and that the goblins hadn't the wits to look up.

Looking up himself, he was faced with the grim fact that there was not a lot of flame still coming from the torch. A blessing at the moment, but an' he foxed these hounds, he'd need light to go on.

The goblins' howling lessened, but there was much barking and grunting and splashing from below. They were after him now, sure and certain. An' they couldn't flush him from the flooded hall, they'd hunt him on the lower levels, for hadn't they themselves just come down through the Keep with their red eyes and keen noses, and found all well? Now, while the goblins followed his trail to the roots of Domhnall's mountain, now he must make for the sanctum in its peak.

His shoulders were screaming, but Blackthorn forced himself higher, and higher still. For the first time he considered where the shaft might end, and how long his muscles would allow him to continue to climb. With doubts in his mind, the rock seemed twice as slimy, his torch twice as dim. High above, just visible in the outer fringe of light cast by his brand, he saw the long, dark outline of a section of black stone. It was an attainable goal, and promising himself a rest when he got there, Blackthorn worked his way up the chimney as quickly as he could.

By the time he neared the dark rock, he thought his arms would surely break. Once more he lifted them, once more pressed hard against the curving walls, hoping this time to find himself even with the patch of black stone. His right forearm scraped against solid granite. His left hand shoved toward the wall and went right through, through empty space where the side of the shaft should have been, and on into a narrow, black cleft.

With no opposing pressure to balance his right arm, it did nothing to hold him up. His legs were already shaking with strain when his weight suddenly rushed back into them. Both failed him. Blackthorn slipped from the shaft as if it was slick with oil, not water.

He fell only a matter of an arm's length or so, but by the time the fingers of his left hand had caught hold of an uneven hump of granite at the very lip of the black cleft, his heart was racing and a cold sweat covered his body.

Astonished to find his right hand still wrapped around the torch, he lifted the light into the crack, bent his arm around the little mound of rock, and hung there, willing his legs to move. At last they obeyed. Bracing his feet against the chimney wall, he climbed once more, finally squeezing himself into the relative safety of the cleft.

He sat sideways, one leg dangling down into the shaft,

and wiped the sweat from his eyes. His hand stung where it touched his flesh—he had managed to scrape a good deal of the skin off his fingers, but it seemed a small loss, considering how near he had come to losing his life.

If his flames weren't so low, he'd have rested there longer, but when this bundle of twigs died, he wasn't likely to find another. He leaned out to look up the shaft, then frowned and sat back to study the torch once more. The flames fluttered, barely, but distinctly. Now he could feel it, too, a whisper of air drifting outward from the dark interior of the crack.

The cleft was not tall enough to allow him to stand, nor broad enough for him to crawl. He could only lie on his side and pull himself along, and so he did, until the cleft widened and he came to a solid rock face. Or seemingly solid. A steady draft blew through a narrow fissure in the stone, fanning the torch's flame and chilling the sweat on Blackthorn's brow.

Turning around was awkward, but when he had managed to get his boots pressed against the rock face, he gave a sharp kick. The stone grated horribly, and shifted only a hair's breadth. He kicked again, harder, and a broad, rectangular section of rock slid noisily forward. He kicked a third time, and the slab dropped neatly away, falling to the ground with a crash Blackthorn felt sure could be heard as far away as Aonach Urmhumhan.

He grimaced and held still. When the considerable racket he had made brought no immediate response, he quickly followed the shattered stone out of the cleft. Lifting his torch, he looked about for the door, wanting only to be gone before any curious goblins arrived. His firelight reflected from two glittering piles of hoarded treasure. One was a few steps away, the other near the doorway, partly hidden by a circle of tall wooden posts in the center of the room.

As he wound through the pillars, Blackthorn wondered at their purpose. There were thirteen of them, all pine, all carved with long lines of Ogham script. The inscriptions were indecipherable; goblin axes had marred the runes beyond kenning.

He passed the last pillar. Standing behind it, still as the carved post and as silent, was a goblin.

Stumbling back, Blackthorn thrust his torch before him

and reached for the weapon at his back. Even as he loosed the strap and swung the staff into his hand, he realized he was in no danger. The goblin had not moved. His red eyes stared blank and sightless. His oily black hair was gray, and looking closer, Blackthorn saw that the beast was covered with a fine coat of dust. The goblin neither breathed nor blinked, and his rigid paw was wrapped around something bright and blue as a robin's egg.

Spitting to ward off ill luck, Blackthorn stepped quickly past the spellbound goblin, never looking back. As the Hag had promised and the púca had warned, not all Domhnall's spells were asleep. He shuddered to remember how carelessly he had run his hands through the goblin hoard he had found below, never stopping to think there might be some ensorcelled work from the Wizard's hand among the fair trinkets.

The door he came to was made of thick ash. Neither smell nor sound would get by this barrier—there was no way to tell what lay beyond. Taking a deep breath, Blackthorn thrust the door boldly open. His torchlight shot forward into another chamber and straight into the glowing red eyes of two living, and suddenly howling, goblins.

They had been creeping toward the door when he burst through, and though their heads turned from the light Blackthorn bore, their axes glinted in welcome. The larger of the two swung blind, but missed. The Hunter had already leapt forward, his own weapon ready. His staff cracked over the goblin's head. The creature groaned and toppled, his axe clattering to the floor.

Blackthorn swung again, catching the smaller goblin hard on the ribs. The red-eye staggered back into a mound of bright treasure, lashing out wildly with his long arms. His axe sighed as it cut the air. Blackthorn held back his staff and thrust his torch under his enemy's guard. Sparks caught on the goblin's greasy hair. Smouldering flames climbed slowly up his arms and down his chest. Baying like a mad dog, the beast dropped his weapon and turned to flee. Blackthorn bent to the axe—a clean throw and he'd bring the goblin down before his shrieks reached any more ears.

Blackthorn's fingers closed short of the haft as sharp claws snapped around his ankle and dug into his leather boot. He kept his balance, but barely, and brought his torch swinging down to scorch the sinewy paw that had him hobbled. He was rewarded with a feral snarl. The lock on his leg only tightened. Before he could try again, his foot was yanked from under him.

He came down hard into the hoard of metal. He twisted about to face his foe—the goblin's fangs were bared to bite, his free hand groping for the axe he'd dropped. A raised lump over the goblin's red eye showed where Blackthorn's first blow had fallen. His staff struck again in the same place, and black blood gushed from the wound. The goblin loosed his grip. Blackthorn kicked the beast from him and came to his knees. Sweeping the axe from the ground, he drove the blade deep into the red-eye's chest. Blood spurted from the goblin's mouth with his rattling breath. He did not draw another.

Listening to the echoes of the fleeing goblin's screams growing fainter, Blackthorn clearly and deliberately wished a slow death over a hot fire for any red-eye who heeded the cries. It was a well-worded and heartfelt curse, but did little to lessen the bitter sense of foreboding that had claimed him.

Twenty-nine

Hold your weapons high and laugh,
Boast of your valor, of victories won
Crash spear to spear, sword to shield,
Raise a din to daunt their hearts.

With deadly insults injure their fame,
Mock their courage, their mothers revile.
Many the foe felled by scorn,
Ere blow was struck or battle joined.

The Warrior's Rann

Before fleeing the room, Blackthorn spared a moment to examine the red-eye's corpse. The goblin was small for his race, and his companion had been smaller still. Goblin young, perhaps, left behind when the battle at the Silvermines began? 'Twas plain not all the red-eyes had deserted Keeper Hill to face the Ó Briain, but if the biggest, best-armed fighters had gone north, leaving only the whelps behind . . .

Taking the goblin's axe with him, he hurried to the door. The passage was deserted, but by the greasy odor of burned goblin hair and a few weaving footprints Blackthorn determined that the wounded red-eye had made off to the left. He turned to the right, hoping the goblin had fled down into the Keep, and that the right path would take him up. Another false step would surely be his last. The goblins would be hunting him all the more eagerly now. The enchantment that fed the flame of his torch was plainly weakening. And even should he find the Hag's coveted silver star, still he would have to get out of the Keep alive. Less care he took where his feet fell or what his cloak brushed against—speed would serve him better than stealth.

At the turn he found stairs leading up, and the tight arc of the next passageway delighted his heart. High he had climbed. Surely the sanctum could not be far ahead.

Running now, he passed a chamber bright with goblins' stolen treasure, overleapt a smashed cupboard blocking his path, and reached the next turning. Another long, straight flight of stairs led him to another corridor, shorter still, and more tightly curved. Then the same pattern again, a flight of steps, an acutely arcing passage. At the next turn the stairs did not rise straight before him, but wound in a close spiral. He took them three at a time, reached the next landing, and froze, gasping in amazement.

An archway, carved from the mountain's granite bones and tall enough for a giant to stride through, crowned the stairway. Beyond it stretched a chamber thrice again as large as the great flooded hall in the Keep below. As he stepped under the arch, the ebbing light of Blackthorn's torch shot to the ceiling, and the luminous dome of quartz crystals sparked and danced. A hundred prisms caught each tongue of flame, magnifying the light a hundred times before releasing it into the air.

The ceiling's beauty fell on Blackthorn like a spell, but the glamour was broken soon enough when he cast his eyes over the hall. The chamber was round, like the room of the statue, but instead of encircling walls of tile, this hall boasted five grandly arched doorways. Five slender marble pillars stood between the arches, but they alone in all the sanctum stood intact. "Upon the silver tree" the statue had promised the Talisman hung, but here was only rubble, smashed chairs, torn tapestries, shards of broken pottery. The ruin formed a low mound that dipped suddenly in the heart of the chamber, and there Blackthorn suspected he would find the soiled pit of the hearth. No silver tree rose above the refuse into the rainbowed air, no silver star dangled from enchanted branches, waiting for his hand.

Blackthorn waded through the heaps of wrecked furniture

and tattered cloths, moving toward the central hearth as
though through a reed-choked fen, pausing often to examine
the metallic glints that answered the erratic flames of his
torch. Broken weapons he found, chipped goblets, even a
few precious stones the goblins had missed, but no silver
until he reached the hearth itself.

It was the shape that caught his eye, long and tapering,
and branching at one end. Blackthorn bent to bring the
light of his torch over the length of smooth, dark metal.
New hope and a premonition of fear made his heart beat
fast; he was looking at the limb of a silver tree, aged to a
black like a raven's feather. All other silver in the Keep had
long ago been gathered to the goblins' hoards, yet the red-
eyes had not touched this huge branch in all the long years
since Domhnall's death. Did they scorn to take it because of
the spells it must have borne? Were there spells upon it still?
Nearby he spied more blackened pieces of the broken tree—
a thick trunk, a grasping root . . .

Setting down his staff and axe, he shifted some of the
heaped metal. Tumbled stones from the hearth lay below,
and each he carefully turned, a child looking under rocks for
treasures. At last one rewarded him with a treasure indeed, a
perfect silver leaf. It was the size of an alder leaf, and serrate
like its living cousin, but though it was black with age, this
one's edges would never curl.

Arrah, but it was not black entirely. Dots of silver like
white stars . . . but it was the stars and the clear night sky he
saw reflected in the delicate leaf! Patches of white now, con-
trasting with the dark . . . a magpie he saw, her unmistakable
black-and-white plumage stark against a blue-gold sky, and
there her pointed beak, like the point of a spear—

His Spear! Hurtling through shadowed air and past a gray
stone wall!

The leaf went dark again, and Blackthorn looked quickly
away. However compelling the visions, he had no time for
scrying in Domhnall's charmed leaves. Impatiently he rolled
over another rock, found nothing, and then another.

A feeble glint caught his eye. His fingers were reaching for
the spark of light before he had truly seen that what they
were closing on was a frail ribbon of silver, twisted upon
itself to form a five-pointed star. Then it was in his hand,

and the spell was loose, and neither will nor might, but only death itself could have kept it from him.

Light broke from the tiny tangle of metal with a crack like lightning before the thunder rolls. A fiery blaze of red, green, blue, yellow, and brilliant white burst into being, wreathing Blackthorn where he half knelt by the shifted stones of the hearth, an uplifted torch in his left hand and the Talisman's fine silver chain dangling from his right. Like spider's silk, the many-colored strands of light wrapped about his senses and held him fast. His very soul was caught in the writhing, crackling web, but so potent the magic that chained him, he could not break free, nor move, nor speak, nor even care that he was spellbound.

Long he knelt out of time, out of mind, and at last the spell began to close. Tighter the cords of power twined, pulling in over his head, legs, and arms, drawing deep into his body until they surrounded his heart. There the radiant threads knotted, and the spell was sealed.

Blackthorn stirred like a man waking from a dream. He remembered reaching for the star, no more than a moment since, surely. For all he could recall, the knowledge he now possessed of the Talisman and its powers had sprung on him in the instant of taking it to his hand. The gleam of red-eyes and axes at the periphery of the sanctum, and the diminished flame of his dying brand told a different tale.

The little star still dangled from his fingers, glittering like one of its heaven-born cousins. While it burned, its unmingled white brilliance was in itself enough to keep the red-eyes at bay, but it shone only a heartbeat longer before its light was doused. Abruptly, it was once more only a badly tarnished bit of silver, poorly reflecting the flickering light of the torch.

Shadows swelled in the gemstone roof as the brand in Blackthorn's hand sputtered. The more feeble the flames, the brighter gleamed the red eyes in the darkness, and the nearer they came. Smiling grimly, Blackthorn thrust his fingers through the Talisman's chain, then rose and reached for his weapons. The blackthorn he strapped quickly and loosely to his back, but he held the axe before him.

Fangs glistened as the goblins howled their disapproval. The fairy thorn was a wood they abhorred, his fire they despised, and the axe they knew for one of their own. Even so, the Hunter harbored no illusions that a single blade or a sturdy limb of blackthorn would keep so many from him. The fire would serve him best, though the torch's flame was faltering. Yet, he could call it back, an' he must. Like the goblins' grins, Blackthorn's own smile broadened, his teeth shone in the dying torchlight. Three weapons the goblins' eyes beheld; torch, axe, and staff. Four he held in his hands, and the last, a silver star smaller than his thumbnail, was the mightiest of all.

Quickly he glanced about the circle of enemies, looking for a weak link in the ring. His eye lit on a bantam goblin with only a knife in his hand. He was halfway to the red-eye before the lesser foe he had chosen disappeared behind a moving wall of broad black chests and sharp-edged axes.

He went on to meet them, using his fire against the first goblin to come within reach. The torch flamed in a rush of air as Blackthorn swung, striking the goblin's shoulder and releasing a shower of sparks and burning twigs. Howling, smoking, the red-eye dropped his weapon and pawed at himself. Blackthorn's fire sank down weaker than before, and the whistle and gleam of a half dozen axes filled his senses.

His own axe was swifter, sweeping in a broad arc before him and slicing open an unguarded gut. Holding his breath against the stench, he swung again. His axe bit deep into a goblin's flank, but there it stayed. The red-eye fell, wrenching the weapon from Blackthorn's hand. Too many the foe, too close, for him to stoop to free it.

With a quick, clean motion he drew his staff from his back, the tiny links of the Talisman's chain rattling lightly as the star was caught between his palm and the blackthorn. The goblins' red eyes burned sullenly at the sight of the wood, but they had enough wits to know that only a few would feel the stinging touch of the fairy thorn before its wielder was cut down and trampled beneath their feet. Blackthorn knew it, too, but the staff was not his only weapon. A single expiring tongue of flame was all that remained to the torch, but it would be enough.

"I call upon Fire," he said clearly, and hurled the dying torch into the red eyes before him.

Light flared briefly from the bundle of wood as it sped into the press of black, greasy bodies. Brighter burned the Talisman beneath Blackthorn's hand. Brilliant streaks of red shot from between his fingers, and then the red was fire, racing from his hand to either end of the fairy thorn.

The sanctum seemed to fill with blood as the white crystals above drank in the light and returned it many times over to the chamber below. A score of goblins roared their outrage, but others snarled and whined as they lifted their paws before their wounded eyes.

An axe glinted, arcing toward Blackthorn's side. He caught the blow on his staff. Fire ran from the fairy branch onto the haft of the axe, then down the goblin's arms. In a moment the goblin was burning as the Scáileanna had burned on high Binn Chuilceach. He died sprawled across the wreckage at Blackthorn's feet and beneath his body the flames rose higher.

Shifting his grip, Blackthorn swung the blazing staff left and right. Like living things, the flames ran through the sanctum, the bright red tongues licking, melting, devouring all they touched.

The goblins backed, slowly at first, then more quickly as the fires spread, for fire was their first enemy, their oldest enemy, the only enemy they truly feared. And this fire was voracious, like the fires that burned in their Dead Lord's eyes. This fire ate metal and stone like dry wood—it made rubies of the crystals of the dome and caused the sanctum floor to erupt into a blistering sea of flame.

Shrieking their pain and hate, the goblins turned and fled down into the darkness of the Keep. Curses filled their mouths, but Blackthorn stood easy, knowing their rage was nothing to the raging fires he had called to the sanctum. His magic would burn their words to cinders before they could do him any harm.

Still, the goblins' fury would long endure, while the flames must soon die. No good to follow the goblins down into the mountain, but the other doorways, now . . . Entrances they might be to antechambers or storerooms—but an' they led to passages, an' the passages leading out of the Keep . . .

The fire in the sanctum was gentling as he started for the nearest arch, and as well the flames consuming the blackthorn staff. Deep cracks ran like dark rivers up and down the

length of the wood. Even as he looked, a chip broke from
the blackthorn, blooming red as a peony as it burned to the
ground. He quickened his step, knowing that when the fairy
thorn had no more to give to the fire, neither staff nor brand
would he have to help him from this place.

Red eyes like dull embers glowed from the darkness
beyond the archway. Blackthorn stopped a safe distance
from the egress, debating whether to try for another. He held
a poor weapon for to face these red-eyes, but by the time he
could reach the other arches he'd have a worse one. Besides,
goblins were likely to be lurking in every shadowed doorway.

Spitting a curse between his teeth, he shouted insults to
draw his enemies out. Rat-spawn, he called them, swearing
that as he had beaten off their relatives with his blackthorn,
so would he deal with their dung-faced selves. Not red their
eyes, but white with terror at the sight of a single foe and a
single flame. Or was that glint he saw their piss flowing out
of them as they trembled in fear of him?

Three goblins answered his challenge, hurling their own
insults as they stepped from the archway and stood before it.
The Mothers' tongue suffers in goblin mouths, but
Blackthorn gathered they were either likening the pallor of
his skin to a maggot's, or promising maggots would feed on
his flesh, and then the largest of them charged.

Blackthorn grasped the fairy branch tighter. To his horror
the flaming wood began to crumble in his grip. If it did not
fall to pieces before he even struck a blow, still the fire-eaten
staff would never best three goblins, and they all with axes
in their hands.

The goblin's blade was descending—in despair Blackthorn
raised his staff to meet it. Blazing chunks of wood flew from
the branch of thorn as it struck against the red-eye's blade. A
flaming coal fell on the goblin's chest, bringing a roar of fire
to blaze above his heart. In an instant the goblin's howling
face was covered in a fluttering veil of flame.

Had the other two goblins not hesitated before the angry
fire, they might easily have cut their foe down. They
flinched, and turned their faces from the flames, and so did
not see that Blackthorn was standing as if he were spellbound once more, staring at the thing in his hands that had
once been a branch of fairy thorn.

Fire had destroyed most of his staff before it had met the goblin's blade, yet it was the axe had faltered at that meeting, not the blackthorn. And while his enemy's weapon was now a crackling, molten mass on the ground, the Hunter held his blackthorn still, though it was a staff no longer. The last few pieces of burning branch fell away, and in the Hunter's hands was a sword, a sword of exquisite balance and flawless beauty, a sword more splendid than any blade ever praised in the Bards' lying tales.

Black was the leather that bound the hilt, black the graceful, curving guard. Utterly black its long, lovely blade, but its three edges gleamed like the blue heart of fire, and flames redder than the dying sun's ran up and down its length. To look on the sword filled the Hunter's heart with joy, to grasp it brought new strength to his arm. What enemy would a man fear to face an' this blackthorn in his hand?

The fires were dying. The flames on the black blade jumped unevenly, and in the sanctum the blaze was low, the crystals in the dome darkening. As the shadows slowly swelled, the two goblins turned their heads back to the Hunter and lifted their axes. His gaze still on his prize, Blackthorn smiled.

"Much strife have you red-eyes given me," he said softly. "Now I will give you Strife in return."

The Hunter raised his sword. Blue-white radiance streamed from its edges, the red flames snapped in the air. Before the threat of the fiery black sword, the red-eyes retreated toward the dark archway. Dismayed by the sudden appearance of a fell weapon in their enemy's hand, they could not stand against him, but Blackthorn was unwilling to let the goblins regain the shadows.

Strife sang sweetly as she swept through the air. He had one goblin down before the other had thought to move against him. The last red-eye tried in vain to block Blackthorn's blow with his axe. As Strife cut through the haft in the goblin's paws, flames raced from the sword to the red-eye's greasy flesh, and there caught and burned. Blackthorn slew the beast with a single thrust to his black heart, granting him a quicker death than the Talisman's fire would have done. Springing over the goblins' corpses, he hurried under the arch.

A passage stretched beyond the opening, so narrow two could not have walked it shoulder to shoulder, but Blackthorn ran easily along it, hoping to reach its end before the fire on the blade of his sword was spent. For a time the flames lit his way, but the tunnel's gradual incline wound endlessly up and around in tightening spirals. Every few steps the reach of his light shortened. Finally, as the passage coiled so tightly on itself Blackthorn felt he was spinning in the mountain's heart, the last flame leapt, flickered, and died. Shadows swooped down on him, and Blackthorn stopped. His own harsh breath was the only sound in the empty dark.

Reaching one hand to the side of the stone passage and holding his sword before him, he forced himself to go forward. A blue-white glow still hovered around Strife's keen edges—not enough to see by, but comforting nonetheless. After a time his stride lengthened, and he went more surely, though his thoughts grew ever more uncertain. Suddenly, Strife's dim light shortened and spread, and the tip of the blade scraped on a wall of gray rock.

Pulling his sword back, Blackthorn thrust his hand before him. His fingers found granite. For a moment his heart faltered as his light had done. All this way, and in the dark, only to find the passage blocked? He laid his palm flat on the stone, and leaned wearily against the wall.

The granite shifted, gently, easily. Blackthorn jumped back. A thin line of brilliant white split the stone down its middle. Like two doors on well-oiled hinges, the rock swung soundlessly open.

The light beyond was too bright for Blackthorn to see where he stepped, but he stumbled blindly out, lest the doors close, and he still tarrying inside. A draft of shocking cold air struck him, lifting his hair from his neck and chilling his flesh where the sweat of fire and battle still clung.

He blinked, but already the light seemed less bright, the air milder. Like a blurred image in a pool that steadies when the waters are still, the world came into focus. Blackthorn smiled.

He was standing on the flat top of Keeper Hill, looking southeast into a cloudless lilac and primrose dawn. His back was to an immense slab of granite, two more were set in the earth nearby, and a capstone lay atop all three. The wind blew through the dolmen from the west toward the nearly risen sun, its voice rising to a fierce moan, then falling to a sigh, only to rise again.

Blackthorn listened carefully, though he'd never before thought he might hear what the wind had to say. He cast his eyes over the waking world, though he'd never before thought his Sight keen. The Mothers walked the labyrinth of Brugh na Bóinne to clear their Sight and sharpen their hearing. Sure, an' the path he'd just trod through Domhnall's Keep was as winding as any the Priestesses trod, and might do him as well.

Far to the north and low to the horizon a single star shimmered rebelliously, scorning to fade though the sun was peering over the eastern rim of the land. So long it lingered, Blackthorn's heart whispered that it was no star, but the Stag, and he longed to follow the glittering light. Instead, he turned his gaze west and set his eyes on the departing night. Mists hung in the distance, lying over An tSionainn doubtless, but to Blackthorn's mind they were like the mists that lay on the dark sea, the mists that wreathed the Isle of Pools.

At last he bent to clean his sword in the snow, but Strife had swallowed the goblins' blood, or the light that came from its edges had burned the black drops away. The blade was unstained. Carefully he secured the sword across his back, unraveled the Talisman's chain from his fingers, and fastened the clasp around his neck. Then he started down through drifts white as the sacred elk's hide to find Reathach the púca before setting out for the sea.

PART 7

the threshold

Thirty

Fools sleep. The Wise dream.

Sayings of the Mothers

The Ó Briain held back the tent flap with a calloused hand and squinted into the morning. More tents met his eye, three hundred cloth and hide bothies huddled just below his own on a low, mossy parcel of land, and beyond, a vast rocky range of mountains. The daystar blazed clear in a cloudless sky, nearing her noon, and glinted fiercely from the snow-covered peaks. Though the wind was crisp and the day inviting, hardly a soul stirred under the sun, only a pair of kestrels, circling high in a warm spiral of air. Safe asleep were the Ó Briain's warriors, while Oghma Sun-Face's unblinking eye kept watch on the shadowed entrances to the mines, and Lugh's bright spears penned the foe in their dark holes. Asleep the Ó Briain had been himself, weary as any after last night's skirmish, but sleep was far from him now.

"Curse their evil eyes!" the Chieftain swore, as he did every day upon rising to see the Silvermines before him, and not his own sweet lands of An Clár.

He set his thick neck even deeper between his broad shoulders and angled himself to pass under the tent flap. His posture gave him the look of a bull readying to charge, yet it

was a bearskin, not a bull's hide, he wore for a cloak, and the
dark curling hair covering his arms, chest, and back was
closer to a bear's dense fur than a bull's shaggy coat. The Ó
Briain's black eyes were small and sharp, his beard thick and
grizzled, the curling crop on his head, now shot with gray,
had once been dark as a bear's brown coat. Still, it was not
his appearance alone caused folk to call him the Bear of An
Clár. 'Twas the way he growled his war cries, and the foe
before him. 'Twas his smile when he fought, like a bear's
toothed grin. 'Twas the rage that possessed him in battle,
the wild fury that turned his lumbering gait into a swift,
unstoppable charge no enemy yet had withstood.

The Ó Briain breathed deep of the sweet, clean air and let
it out in a great rush of sound. "Ceallach!" he bellowed.

If the Poet of Tulach had been soundly slumbering at the
far end of the camp, the call would have roused him. As he
was tossing fitfully in his blanket in a tent not twenty paces
from his Chieftain's own, the towheaded lad was on his feet
before the echoes of the Ó Briain's voice had faded.
Hurriedly donning his boots, he stumbled under the tent flap
and stood blinking in the light of day.

"My Chieftain?" he asked.

The Bear of An Clár looked into the Poet's bleary face. "I
had a dream," he said.

Without another word, he turned and strode back into his
tent. Ceallach followed, blinking again as the dirt-darkened
cloths banned the morning's brightness.

The Ó Briain motioned sharply toward the floor. With
some trepidation Ceallach took a seat on a muddy rug. A
poem to stir the blood, a rhyme to praise the Chieftain's valor,
this was the service Ceallach had offered when he had laid his
sword at the Ó Briain's feet. His ranna alone would have been
enough to please most Chieftains, but the Bear of An Clár
trusted might over magic. Likely he would have declined the
honor of a Poet's service had he not known Ceallach to be as
skilled with spear as with words. A rare vision indeed must
have visited his Chieftain in the early morning, the boy
thought, an' he was calling for his Poet to interpret it.

"A Priestess possesses more keys than I to unlock the
meaning of dreams from behind the doors of sleep," he said.
"But I will do my best."

The Ó Briain grunted, and poured himself a horn of ale. He took a long draught, wiped his beard with a grimy sleeve, then passed the horn to Ceallach.

"Five women, beautiful as the evening and the dawn, beckoned to me," he began, after Ceallach had drunk. "At first I thought they stood upon a high, brown knoll, like An Chathair Dhonn that is our home, but suddenly I saw they were in a dance of tall stones on a lonely hill, and darkness was all about them. Storm clouds filled the heavens, black waters rose at their feet, red eyes glinted in the night. I lifted my spear to strike at the goblins, but as one the women called out to stop me."

Looking away from his Poet's troubled eyes, the Ó Briain frowned. The fear that had filled his dream rose again in him as he spoke, and to feel it in his heart stung his pride.

"A shadow rose from the empty air, darker than the overcast sky, deeper than the black waters," he said harshly. "Out of the shadow flew a black crow. Unlovely her cries, but well I knew the Name on the bird's tongue, for it was my own. The women turned from me, turned to face the terror looming behind them. 'Twas then I saw they were arrayed for battle, and their swords were drawn."

The Ó Briain moved close to Ceallach and took the drinking horn from the boy's hand. He finished what was in it, again wiped his beard on his sleeve, and bent his gaze on the Poet.

"I woke then, my heart pounding, my brow damp, as if true battle I had seen. Even now the sight of the glorious women and the shadow they faced is before me. And still the scaldcrow calls my Name."

For a time there was not a sound in the tent, save what came in past the oiled cloth walls from the meadow. The shrill, questing cries of the kestrels Ceallach heard, a blithe larksong, and the soft trickle of melted snow finding its way to the lowlands from the heights of the mountains. All belonged to a careless world far removed from the dark land the Ó Briain had conjured within the tent.

At last Ceallach spoke, slowly, choosing his words with care.

"Five the women, and five the kingdoms of Éirinn. 'Twas the Queens you saw, standing in the place yourself was born, that you might know them for your Mothers."

"But the standing stones?" pressed the Ó Briain.

Ceallach bent his head, and his pale hair fell before his eyes. "I have not seen it," he said uncertainly, "but is it not true that the temple of Temuir is built so, a dance of stones on a solitary hill? That shadows should assail the Mothers in that sacred place, this is ill dreamt indeed."

"The Mothers, the Mothers," growled the Ó Briain. "Would the Mothers have called back my blow that would have brought a goblin down?"

Ceallach raised his face to the Ó Briain's, and his eyes were clear, his uncertainty gone.

"The red-eyes in the night—that is the evil of the Silvermines, the enemy my Chieftain has led me here to fight. But the darker shadow that rose from the black and empty air . . . that is a greater peril, I'm thinking, an evil . . . an evil, my Chieftain, I fear to Name."

Ceallach's heart quickened at the Bear's glad, hungry smile.

"Long have they waited," the Ó Briain said, "long debated and held their councils and cast their omens while our people languished and our homes were burned. Folly it seemed to me, but my eyes saw only goblins in the night. The Mothers' Sight was turned on the Darkness itself."

The Ó Briain prowled about his tiny tent as he spoke. Ceallach drew his knees against his chest to make more room for the big man.

"This the meaning I take from your dream," the boy agreed. "Though the Mothers disdain to do battle with the lesser foe, they have resolved to war upon the greater."

The Ó Briain's teeth shone white. "And to that war they have summoned me. From there did the Mór-Ríoghain call my Name. By the light that shines will I answer Her."

He dismissed the Poet with a gesture, giving orders even as he sent the youth away.

"Wind the horns to wake the camp, and bring Cearbhall and the Ó Súilleabhán to me."

Alone, the Ó Briain stared into his empty cup, but the grin had not left his face. Too deep were the mines, too devious the tunnels, too thick the darkness for his warriors to take. Some success he had won here, some triumph. The goblins no longer emerged from the Silvermines like bats at sundown to prey upon village and town. Yet, still they emerged. Each night saw the red-eyes come forth to do battle, each day saw them beaten back to the mines. Sword and fire held the goblins in the mountain, axe and blinding dark forced the Ó Briain's host to bide outside. How many warriors must needs remain for to maintain this grim stalemate?

Cearbhall and the Ó Súilleabhán entered his tent already frowning, and what he told them did not lift the clouds from their brows. Only when they learned they would not be asked to follow the Bear of An Clár's sword to far Temuir did their eyes brighten. When together the three left the tent that the Ó Briain might speak to the gathered warriors, the Ó Súilleabhán was in truth smiling with the thought he would be facing red-eyes that night, and not the red-eyes' God some night hence.

If the Ó Súilleabhán's smile heartened any of the host, Ceallach could not see it. Set jaws and closed ears the Poet saw, and little wonder. None were pleased to be dragged from sleep by blaring horns, and few were likely to think much of the Ó Briain's reasons for sounding them. Quick had these villagers been to climb out of their pig sties and goat pens to follow the Bear of An Clár to battle. Quickly now most would climb back again, an' they could. The miners were fighting for their own, but the rest of the Ó Briain's band were far from home and family, and longed only to return to them. Not so sour the stink of swine after the gagging stench of goblin. What words could the Ó Briain find to fan the embers of honor and glory, courage and daring that were dying in his warriors' hearts?

"Wake from your dreams of cowardice," the Ó Briain began, "and look about you. Éirinn is your home, not the hearths you left behind. And what hearth will you have to return to at all, at all, an' you set your weapons aside? You must sharpen your blades, I'm saying, not sheathe them. Let them drink the blood of the beasts that would ravage your lands and kill your kin. An' the Silvermines are as far from your home as your legs will bear you, then remain here and fight the goblins under the Ó Súilleabhán's banner or with Cearbhall Broad-Hand."

The Bear of An Clár drew his sword. It glittered bright as his smile in the sun.

"But I—I go to strike a blow against the Shadow that spawned this red-eyed filth. The long road to Temuir is mine, and all who ride with me, for the Queens go to war. At their feet will I lay my sword, and by their leave will I taste the wine of a hero's cup, as sweet in death as in life. Drink with me, all who dare!"

Spears and swords clashed against shields, war cries from every corner of Mumhain rose into the air and hammered against the granite mountains. He had been a fool to doubt, Ceallach reproached himself. Dying embers of courage in the villagers' hearts? A fire the Ó Briain had made of them, a fire that would set all Éirinn ablaze.

Deep in the black tunnels of the Silvermines, the din raised by the Ó Briain's host echoed hollowly along the winding passages. The goblins snarled and cursed, and called upon Shadow's King, the Dead Lord, to blunt their enemies' weapons and rob the strength from their limbs. For what could they believe but that the Bear of An Clár's warriors were coming after them with fire and sword? And never before had they heard the Chieftain's army so glad to do battle.

With a thought Caireann dismissed the servant, and herself knelt to buckle Niall's sword. That done, she sat back on her heels, appraising her King. Long the winter moons had been, each filled with strife and trial. Yet, the towering, black-haired, gray-eyed man before her had not wearied under the strain, only hardened to it.

The Queen of Ulaidh nodded her approval, and caught Niall's flash of annoyance as he became aware she had been judging him. He turned to leave as she started to rise, but the child swelling the Queen's belly weighted her down. At once Niall turned back and proffered his arm. Caireann took it with a laugh and kept it after she had regained her feet.

"Coll must hold here." Niall spoke softly, but it sounded like a threat. "My Queen is too round and slow to be escaping to the hills or across the sea. Coll must hold the dún."

The Mother's smile gentled from her own merriment to a reflection of the Goddess's imperturbable serenity. Seeing the change in her, Niall felt his tension ease. Caireann and he so often quarrelled when the woman was without her

deity, but when Ulaidh was with her . . . son of the last
Queen, and King to the present one, Niall knew his kingdom's Goddess as well as any man. He smiled in welcome.

"Our safety rides with you," she said. "You must look only
to the battle before you, never back."

Niall nodded, but the Mother heard his thought, and
laughed again. "That advice you little needed. Eager you are
to fight this war. Eager to find a worthier foe than those you
destroy before our walls. No sadness is in you to be leaving
Dún na nGall. No, look not so rueful. Only good can come
of your joy. Desperate will be the battle, and the victory is
uncertain. Our people will need your madness to shine
before them in the Dark."

"Then give me your blessing, Lady, and I am gone.
Already Ulaidh's champions are gathered in the close, awaiting me."

Caireann pressed her mouth over his heart, against his
lips. He bent to her and she kissed his brow. When he lifted
his head, the Goddess gazed back at him. Niall hesitated
before the startling brilliance in her eyes.

"Is it my death you See?" he asked quietly.

He said it without fear of her answer. Kings are born to
die, and the thought of his death did not dismay him.

The Mother shook her head. Gently she stroked the hair
from his forehead, then laid her hand on his chest where her
kiss had fallen. "There is a dream weighing upon your heart,
my King, and though the tale of it is not on your lips, yet it
troubles your thoughts."

She started to take her hand away, but Niall grasped it,
pressed it harder against him.

"Then take it from me, Lady. 'Tis a burden I would not
carry into battle."

Caireann chanted softly, putting words to the images that
had plagued Niall's sleep and left him cold and irrevocably
awake in the long hour before the dawn.

"On and on you fight, fire all about you, but the red-eyed
and gray-skinned enemies are undaunted. Heads roll, bodies
fall. Corpses you see by the flickering light—not Scáileanna,
but men they are, adorned in kingly finery. And every
bloody brow bears a crown, and every frozen face is your
own."

The Mother looked up at Ulaidh's King, and she was Caireann again, and her eyes were wide. "Would that I could take this dream from you, Niall, or tell you what it means."

Niall's eyes narrowed for a moment, then he shrugged and gave his Queen a wan smile.

"No matter."

He released her hand and turned toward the door. Despite her girth, Caireann hurried forward, and was there before him.

"Wait," she said, and such unequivocal authority was in her voice, Niall knew at once it was the Goddess, not Caireann bidding him stay.

"Lady?" he asked.

"Hear this warning ere you depart, and heed it in the days to come. An' you bear your dream like a knife in your heart, what good will your mantle do you? You will be wounded ere the battle has begun."

A spark of fire waked in Niall's gray eyes. "How should I bear it, then?"

"Like the gift it is, my King," the Mother of Ulaidh answered simply, stepping aside to let him pass. "Like the gift it is."

The Sidhe sleep no human sleep, nor do they dream human dreams. Even so, Cessair had often heard tell of dreams from those who chanced upon Cnoc an Eanaigh when the gates were open. Traders, fishers, wandering Bards spent moons and years enjoying the elves' hospitality, and often and again they would speak of the visions they beheld without will or awareness while they slept. What I do now, Cessair thought, Éire's people would call dreaming. To visit the Gods of Éirinn—this is the dream of the Sidhe.

Her white steed, Fionn, paced proudly through the marbled gates of the Gods' dwelling. Trained for battle, he never shied when the noise and light assailed him, but went calmly on. Cessair herself was fair blinded. If the moon and sun themselves had come to dance in Brugh na Bóinne, the hall could not have been brighter. It was a world of coruscating silver and flaming gold and it spun about in reckless time to the screeling, droning pipes.

She looked down the length of a massive oak table heaped with viands and drink, alight with candles. The longer Cessair stared, the longer the board grew, until she could not see its end. Wisely she brought her gaze in, focusing her eyes on her own hand, and found her fingers wrapped around a cup of Guibhne's sweetest ale.

Cautiously she drank, and secretly she watched them, the celebrants at the table, but they seemed unaware of her scrutiny. Brighde sat in the midst of them all—the season was Hers, and the feast to honor it. Aengus Óg, shouting with laughter like thunder in a spring rain, sat beside Her. On the God's right, golden-haired Lugh the Long-Armed joined in the jest.

Not sitting, but suddenly standing Cessair was, and the deep and terrible eyes of the Gods were fixed on her. They knew her mind—all she wondered, all she wished to know, all she longed to tell. The harps were singing her plea even now. One question only passed Cessair's lips.

"Will you come?" she said.

"'Tis not our war," said Brighde, her thrilling voice laced with regret. "Scáil and Sidhe, goblin and human—these are the armies must fight for Éirinn and against Her."

"'Tis not your Hunt," Cessair returned, "yet you were quick enough to work your will on Éire's Huntsman."

A burst of merriment shivered through the burnished air and drew Cessair's eye to the far end of the banquet table. Áine, giver of gifts, was there, veiled in bright beauty. Hidden by the board, but visible nonetheless to Cessair's Sight, an ash wand lay in Áine's lap. Silver glittered like a star from the end of the polished length of wood.

"The Stag is Éire's," Áine replied. "But the Hunter himself, now . . ."

At her words laughter filled the hall. The Gods' amusement poured in on Cessair, deafening and irresistible. She did not laugh with them, for she could not unriddle Áine's words. Drawing a deep breath of the shining air, Cessair spoke against their mirth.

"Oath-breakers, mother-cursed murderers, rapists, those that die geis-bound—these are the Dead Lord's by right, these and the goblins and Scáileanna that have chosen to serve Him."

The laughter was gone as if it had never rung. The warrior Chieftain of Cnoc an Eanaigh hurled her challenge into the palpable silence.

"More than His due the Dead Lord takes—and more yet desires. You sit feasting while Éirinn's shadows are gathered to His will, while Shadow spreads over the five kingdoms. Have the Gods not delighted to dance on Éirinn's hills under the moon and stars? Have they not long taken their pleasure in the sweet shades of Éirinn's forests? Are they content, then, to open the gates of Brugh na Bóinne to Shadow's King, to sit at His board and feast with Him upon our souls?"

The sea of silence rose to a violent wave of outrage. It broke over Cessair, drowning her senses in a tumult of shattered light and sound. She felt herself shrinking, or Saw the Gods growing until they towered like giants over her. Oghma Sun-Face spoke into the subsiding roar of divine wrath, his words burning like fire in Cessair's ears.

"In Shadow still does the Dead Lord sit, awaiting the sacrifice his servant prepares for him. We say to you, Cessair of Cnoc an Eanaigh, and the Mothers and Kings, and the Wizards and Poets, and to all the Mighty of Éirinn, bring down the one who thrusts wide the gates to the Shadow King's realm. Bring the false hunter down, and we will fall upon his God like a storm, and redeem the Dark for Éirinn."

"Rend the Shadow King's mantle," challenged Lugh, "and my spears will pierce the heart of Darkness."

"Bring Shadow to Light," cried Aengus Óg, "and I will make glorious summer where spring could not come."

"Bring your war to Márrach," promised a croaking voice behind Cessair, "and I will come. Though the rest deny you, yet I will spread my wings over the field of battle."

No feast, no giants, but an empty chair was before Cessair, and beside it a blazing fire. On the polished back of the chair perched a scaldcrow. The bird tested the air in a flurry of black feathers. She landed and cocked her head to study Cessair with sharp, daring eyes. With a hoarse cry she lifted again from the chair, bewildering Cessair's Sight. 'Twas a crow rose into the air, but a black-gowned Goddess hovered there, tangled hair streaming behind her, lips red as blood, and face pale as death. She began to spin, and now there were three sisters embracing where one had been. Badhbh, Macha, and the Mór-Ríoghain whirled madly together above Cessair's head as drums pounded the march of many feet, the hooves of horses galloping.

Horns of battle, mournful and distant, reached Cessair's ears. She ignored them for a time, entranced by the dance of the Battle Goddesses, spellbound by the beating drums. There was a pattern in the chaos, something true and noble behind the wild gyrations, if only she could See more clearly. . . .

Again she heard the haunting summons winding from afar, and her heart turned toward it. What was the dance of battle to her, if battle itself was calling? She whistled for Fionn, and he came trotting to her. Leaping onto his back, she urged him on toward the marble gates.

A slight chill, less tangible than a breath of winter wind, swept from Cessair's toes to her head. Like waking from a dream this must be, she thought. Astride a motionless Fionn, she looked out at the morning from Brugh na Bóinne's wide portal. A sense of time passing from moment to moment was hers again, and with it, a sense of urgency. The battle horns blared, louder now and nearer, but Cessair smiled, remembering at last that she herself had ordered them sounded should she linger past dawn in the dwelling of the Gods.

With a light touch of her heel on his flank, Cessair brought Fionn out into the brightening day, then pressed her weight on him, stopping him again. Beside her, looking up with a smile glad as a child's, was the brown-skinned, green-haired God Tréfhuilgne. He put one weathered hand on her stirrup, and with the other held out a dainty shamrock.

"For luck," he said. And more quietly, "The Mór-Ríoghain will be at the battle, for so she said, but take not too much hope from that. An' swords are drawn and war cries heard, little she cares whose blood stains the field."

High on An Earagail, Úna the Oak Seer dreamed of things past and things yet to be. She dreamed as a stone dreams, unhurried and thoughtful, while the sun waxed to spring and the fire of life stirred deep in the earth beneath her.

She dreamed of a magpie, dreamed again the song that told the secrets of the future to the black-and-white creature.

When Spell-Maker's star shines
When silver bites stone
When the bell can ring no more . . .

But the bird listened with a woman's ears, and heard only the words, none of their meanings.

In the late storms of winter she dreamed of a mouse, dreamed the song that would tell of the gift he bore.

A mouse, a man, a mouse, a man,
Bearing a treasure in his hand . . .

When her song was complete, she dreamed on. Kings and Queens, and a green-eyed Poet were in her visions, and the goose-girl Wizard who had come too close. A black sword and a sword of smoke she dreamed, a star that was a door, and a beast that had no soul.

At last she roused from slumbering stone, and rose to her feet. Younger she was now than when she had hunched down on the mountaintop to dream. Her muddy brown skirt was brushed with new green, some of the white threads had melted from her shawl, her hair was all black, and shone red where the sunlight kissed her. Touching oak staff to earth, Úna started down the mountain. Far was Márrach from An Earagail, but many the meetings awaiting her there, many the dreams that would wake from tomorrow's shadows.

Thirty-one

Missed and mourned and márrach be
Till tears and time and toil are done.
A song of sorrow in silence heard
Wakens the way-weary heart.

a rann made by Scáthach,
the Poet of Teach an Fhásaigh

They had been bested.

The Priestesses might accept this truth with admirable calm, but the Poets were despondent and the Wizards plainly shaken to the core. In the sleepless hours between the cauldron's destruction and this morning's council, memories of Shadow's hand and the Gruagach's irresistible attack had festered. Every face was etched with lines of weariness and pain, every head bowed in humiliation.

Meacán looked slowly around the great hall of Temuir. Though sunlight streamed through the wide-open doors, the day was chill. The orange-tongued light of the fire in the central hearth played feebly over the Wizards' grim expressions. Never before had any of their wills been so completely overrun. Never before had any of them faced such unqualified defeat.

"We have lost Mac Ailch to them, and aged Creathna, too," Seamair grieved quietly.

Fionnghuala bit her lower lip. "What hope have we that our friends long lived in the Gruagach's grasp?"

An unreasoning anger filled Meacán's heart. How could

Feargna Óg so blithely have led their Sight to Cromghlinn?
How could Liannan so carelessly have pressed on? Where
was Fionnghuala's gift, that she was deceived by another's
illusions? Why did Reochaidh reach so quickly and clumsily,
and Seamair move not at all? What was Mac Ailch thinking,
the witless fool, to challenge the Gruagach? Where were
Tadhg's verses that might have drawn their comrades back
from the waters? And Creathna, curse him, could he not
have helped her, could his fingers not have closed on her
own when she touched his hand?

She flung her accusations silently, for of all the council,
Meacán was most profoundly disappointed with herself. The
Dancer of Sliabh Mis alone stepped at will from one world to
another. Who better than she to guess the truth about the
visions the cauldron revealed? She should have suspected it
was no mere image in the waters, but a tangible, reachable
reality they gazed upon. She should have known it was possible to cross through the cauldron from Temuir to Márrach.
Her gift had failed her, failed them all, and so had two of the
Seven been taken.

Feargna Óg puffed out his chest and lifted his chin. "We
must answer this outrage! Why does the Mother's army not
ride to Márrach? Why do we but sit and meditate on our
woes, and wait to see who next will fall under Shadow's
spells?"

Liannan's face disclosed nothing, and her eyes strayed to
the open door. It was the Cailleach who answered the
Necromancer.

"Wizards are wont to suffer for their lack of patience,
Feargna Óg, as well you might have learned last night. But
'tis yourself has been idle these last hours, not the Queens.
The Mothers of Éirinn have sent a call to every stout heart,
a summons to every great Chieftain in the five kingdoms.
Even now they come, walking, riding, swift as they may, and
hundreds following their banners. The host is gathering, and
when it is assembled within our walls, then will we march."

Liannan raised her hand for silence. Her eyes briefly met
the Cailleach's, then both women turned toward the doors.
A flash of silver and gold brightened the portal, and entered
the hall as a luminous cloud. It drifted past the thick pillars
of Reochaidh's legs and was weaving though the press of

Wizards before Meacán's eyes could make out the tall figure of Cessair of Cnoc an Eanaigh within the dazzling aura. The warrior came to stand beside the Mother's chair, and spread her arms wide.

"From Brugh na Bóinne I've ridden this morn," she sang. "Éire stands with us, for She is with the Mothers always, but it was my hope to win the warrior Gods to our cause."

How her hopes had been answered was plain in Cessair's bright eyes.

"They will not come," she said simply. "Only the Mór-Ríoghain vows to attend the battle, but who can say if She will bring glory or defeat to Éirinn's armies? For the rest, they charge us to bring down those that serve the Dead Lord, to part the shadows that guard his gates. Only when Márrach is fallen will the Gods come to humble the Shadow King."

"Shadows of illusion guard those dread gates," Fionnghuala reminded them.

"And guard them well," the Cailleach agreed. "Since Samhain the Cailleacha have been searching the five kingdoms, hoping to find Shadow's stronghold. Many times has the Old Woman of Ulaidh gazed upon Cromghlinn, yet never Seen more than an empty forest and a barren hill, and whose Sight is keener than Muirne ní Finne's?"

"Yet, when the Mother spoke the bare hill's true Name, its image vanished from the cauldron's waters," Seamair pointed out.

"True." Liannan's tone was bitter, her words clipped. "And so pleased was I at the sight, I was only too ready to believe my Goddess's power had brought it forth. But think you. Only a brief glimpse did we have of a high rampart and a round tower of stone before the vision faded, and the sands appeared with the visage of the Gruagach plain upon them."

She shook her head and sighed. "Not by my desires, nor even the council's together were these things revealed, but only by our enemy's intent."

Fionnghuala looked helplessly at her fingers. "Were the veil of invisibility like a cloth hung before the castle's walls, I could tear it down," she said. "An illusion of that kind is an act of pure will. It cannot persist through the nights and days, through the moons and seasons, for who is there that must not sometime sleep and their magic sleep with them? Even the

Gods must take their rest. I stake my Sliabh on it—this illusion is anchored in some work of power, some sorcerous charm."

She paused, and met Liannan's eye. "I must have this spell in my hands, Mother, an' I am to rip the shadows from Márrach's walls."

The Maiden's eyes flashed. "So, too, a spell it was made the temple buckle and quake, while in the cauldron the face of the Gruagach remained steady. Did you not see the hairy beast's arm, circling the sands before him? A tincture, a potion, a poison he poured, to hold our wills fast."

"But do they so rely on tricks and tools?" said Meacán. "Potions can be spilled, spell-stones can be crushed. Here is a breach in our enemy's wall!"

"Now who speaks o'er hastily?" demanded Feargna Óg. "Potent are their tricks and tools, Dancer. Because of them our friends were lost!"

"Lost?" The Cailleach lifted one white brow. "Perhaps. But was it vengeance that spurred the Gruagach to attack bold Mac Ailch? Or was it planned so? It may be the false hunter has some particular need for a Conjuror's skills. And had Mac Ailch's hand not been already locked on Creathna's arm, would the Gruagach's paw have returned for our Name-Sayer?"

"Not strategy, I think, but chance guided the Gruagach," said Liannan. "What use would Creathna be to Shadow? The Names of the Dead Lord's enemies he knows already, for we do not hide them. As for Mac Ailch, what he brings into existence endures but a short time. Even could the false hunter coerce Mac Ailch to conjure for the Dark, what treasure would he desire to possess for only a moment?"

The Mother's eyes widened and she looked at Meacán. The Dancer's face had grown deathly pale.

"Think you so?" Liannan whispered.

Meacán nodded miserably. "Not to destroy Temuir, remember, but to Hunt the Light is Shadow's aim. Creathna himself said the Hunter might be hurt through his Name. And could the false hunter face the Stag with the one Spear in his hand . . ."

"An' it will ease your heart," said Cessair, "I do not believe the Conjuror's skills can wrest the Spear from the hand that now holds it."

Meacán turned to the Sidhe. "The Hunter's, you mean?" Blinded by sunlight glancing off the elf's gold-white hair, she closed her eyes and persisted. "Has his grip become so strong?"

"The Hunter holds not his Spear. It has been lost to him since midwinter, and all this time he has been seeking it. Neither Mac Ailch's craft, nor the false hunter's desire, nor even the true Hunter's need will bring the Spear back into the world unless the Gods will it. For the Spear lies in the white lap of Áine the Blessed where she sits in splendor in Brugh na Bóinne."

In stunned silence everyone stared at Cessair, save Liannan, who brought a slim hand to her temple and bent her head.

"Every time I See a pattern in the weave, a new knot appears to mar the design," she murmured.

She lifted her eyes, and they were dark with resolve. "The Spear is not our concern. We will prepare for war."

"We have been fighting since Samhain," said Feargna Óg, "and to little avail."

Liannan answered him sharply. "We have been fighting shadows. Now let us strike against the enemy who casts them. Near the eastern shore of Loch nEathach beats Shadow's heart, on a barren hill in the midst of a once-lovely valley. We know where it lies and we know its true Name, for Creathna the Name-Sayer gave it us."

"A strange name," murmured Seamair. "A foreign name . . ."

"When I was a child, there was a man in our village, an old man. Once a trader of Alba," offered Eoghan. Though his deepening color proved he was aware of the attention suddenly focused on him, the King went on without hesitation. "Stories he told us of his homeland. In them he sometimes spoke of a 'márrach,' but it was not a word to fear. When his people wished to feast on the wild kine, fat from their summer grazing, they would drive them into a narrow defile where they'd built a márrach, an enclosure to capture and hold the beasts."

"Surely the Name-Sayer did not mean to imply that our enemy's stronghold is a cattle pen," said Feargna Óg.

He smiled as he said it. Only a fool angers a King.

"There is another meaning," he went on. "True you speak,

'márrach' is an Alban word. But if we may trust Muirdeach, the Sage of Cionn Tíre, it refers to an enchanted castle, a magician's lair. By this meaning the hidden fortress on the bald mound of An Bhrí Mhaol might well be Named 'Márrach.'"

Reochaidh bent forward and touched his thick finger to the carpet of ashes around the hearth. Swiftly he moved his hand, tracing a bold line through the pale gray cinders. It wove up and curved around, doubled back and arced again, weaving and twining like a coiled serpent.

"A maze," said the Cailleach quietly. Then louder, "Reochaidh tells us that a 'márrach' is a maze."

Reochaidh straightened and nodded carefully, his head once more among the rafters.

"Would Creathna were here," said Tadhg. "The Name we have, but the meaning is confused." The Poet of An Chluain Thiar cleared his throat. "'Missed and mourned and márrach be/ Till tears and toil and time are done . . .'" he recited. "Scáthach's poem she made when Róisín Dubh could not be found. Have you never heard it? 'Spellbound' she meant by the word, or so I believe, but truth be told, there are those would gainsay me. Many the Poets that contend she chose the word because 'márrach' alliterates so nicely in the line."

"The Name is my sword," said Liannan, "its meaning but my sheath. Nor will I wait till the host is gathered to draw my weapon. The Deceiver has wondered whether my good Wizards have survived in the hands of the Gruagach. Has Feargna Óg thought to seek their souls among the dead?"

The Necromancer nodded. "I have, Lady, but my search was in vain. Yet, I do admit my sojourn there was hurried, and many were the ghosts crowding 'round, for the toll of yesterday's battle was heavy. I will search again, and more carefully."

Liannan turned to Seamair. "Weather-Worker. The day is bright, but clouds are closing in the north, and likely will be here before day is done."

"My Lady, an' you will . . ." Eoghan smiled. "Yesterday the goblins fled at an illusion of the Sidhe. Should they return tonight, and find Cessair's warriors waiting, will they not believe them illusion as well? In their folly we may destroy them all."

A breath of wind stirred Meacán's hair. She looked up to see the Destroyer's arm sweeping before him as if he were gathering in grasses. His hand closed in a massive fist before his face.

"An' the Sidhe fight with us, we will surround the red-eyes and squeeze them till the field runs with rivers of blood," said the Cailleach, but it was plain the words were Reochaidh's.

"It will be as you say," the Mother said, and turned toward Tadhg.

The Poet of An Chluain Thiar lifted his shoulders. "A rann I could make, Mother, to hearten your armies that must do battle."

"A rann I desire, Tadhg," Liannan answered, "but not for my host. Make me a rann to dispel the clouds of darkness that veil Márrach in shadow. Give it not to me, but to Meacán the Dancer. And she will dance until she stands before the gray battlement we glimpsed in the cauldron, and speak your words."

"Mother." Meacán's voice was soft with regret. "I saw not the rampart. Mac Ailch was before me, covering the image in the cauldron. The bare hill I saw, and the white sands. The Poet's words would have to do more than lighten a shadow were I to speak them. They would have to shatter the spell-stone that hides the castle from sight."

Liannan's look became hard, and she shot a swift glance at the Cailleach. The Old Woman shook her head.

"A blurred glance was all I had," she said, "not enough to help the Dancer."

Liannan rose from her chair and paced slowly toward the door. She looked pale in the sunlight, and tired, thought Meacán, but unbent and unbending, a branch stripped bare, enduring winter's wind.

"An' they are not dead, we must help them," Liannan said, almost to herself. "Yet, they are prisoned within walls we cannot breach, much as we might dream of rescuing them."

She turned to Meacán, and she was smiling. "Yes. We would dream of it, and so would they."

Very cold Meacán felt suddenly. And keenly alert.

"You could not free them, but you could speak with them,

learn what they know, give them our messages of hope and succor."

Meacán ignored the uncomprehending looks on the other Wizards' faces. Liannan's meaning was all too clear to her.

"The world of true dreams is easier to travel than the one you wish me to cross, Lady," she said.

"Could their minds be reached in dream, would I not have already done so? Hundreds of dreams I visited last night, but when I bent my will toward the two that were taken, only shadows did I find. Not dream, Dancer, but daydream is the way. There Creathna himself is imagining the dark banished, there our Conjuror might well have escaped Márrach's power."

Meacán's voice was wooden, her jaw set. "I cannot dance to that place, Mother."

The Queen's Sight fell on her heavy as a blow. Though Meacán held still under Liannan's scrutiny, she bent her eyes to the patterned stone floor, and felt a burning warmth rise in her cheeks.

Having neither accepted Meacán's refusal nor denied it, Liannan addressed the council at large. "Go then," she said quietly. "Apply yourselves to the tasks I have set you, or rest, or offer your efforts to whatever work is at hand."

Meacán would quickly have obeyed the Mother, and fled the hall to find some task to keep her far from the Queen, but she was not given the chance. Liannan had barely done speaking, when the Cailleach called out to her.

"Yet, stay awhile, Dancer," she said. "Stay and have words with me."

Thirty-two

Come, come where sorrows must die,
Where beauty reigns
And love is for aye.

Dáithí Two-Winds

When the others had gone, Temuir's great hall seemed much larger. For two to stand where three hundred might dance . . .

Or perhaps it wasn't the hall's size, but the place itself. Host and witness to so many high and terrible deeds, to nobility and treachery, honor and disgrace . . . The ancient stones had surely heard Meacán's answer to the Mother's command—had heard and despised her for her cowardice. The fire spat scornfully, the alcoves and antechambers looked darkly upon her, the pillars could not hold the roof far enough from her shame. She glanced at her companion nervously, trying to see if the Old Woman was listening to her thoughts. The Cailleach's expression revealed nothing.

"No use looking to me," the Old Woman said. "I'm no Mother to kiss away your tears or brush your fears away. No sympathetic ear do I offer, but one growing deaf with age to listen to the reason why you will not dance. So speak true, Meacán Iníon na Caillí, and tell me why you are afraid."

"For good cause," she said quietly. "I have danced through daydream before."

The Cailleach tilted her head, as if trying to hear more clearly a far-distant sound.

"How old is this wound, Meacán, this hurt you have never brought to the air to heal? Why, 'tis a babe I hear crying in your heart!"

Like the hands of a harper plucking at the strings, the Old Woman's words played upon Meacán's feelings, making them tremble in her voice. "Just a child I was, four years old."

"On the strand you are," said the Cailleach gently, "sporting with the other children. 'Let's sail a ship to Tír na nÓg,' says the little boy with the oat-straw hair."

"A Bard had come to the dún the night before, and sung of Dáithí Two-Winds," the Dancer stammered. "Our minds were taken with his tale."

Meacán walked to the door as Liannan had earlier done. The sunlight fell on her, but did not warm her as she had hoped it would.

"So we climbed aboard a driftwood log," she said, forcing herself to go on, "and began to move our arms as if we were rowing. I stood to peer out ahead, dancing to the prow of our make-believe boat, the better to see. But it was make-believe no longer. We were upon the sea, I and my friends, and our craft was long and sleek, and the winds fair, and the western lands hidden in mists before us."

"And this frightened you."

Meacán looked at the Cailleach in surprise. "Frightened?" She laughed. "To Tír na nÓg I had desired to go, and so was I sailing, streaking over the waves to find it! How could I think I had left my friends behind on Éirinn's shore? How could I guess that my mates were frail colors on the wind, painted from my fancies? How was I to know I was lost in a realm where everything I imagined came into existence, and nothing at all was real?"

"The Mothers' Sight fell on Meacán, Muirne's daughter, because she travelled to Tír na nÓg when yet a child and returned," said the Cailleach quietly. "A true Wizard born."

"Yes." The feelings were too strong for Meacán's voice to hold. Her words came out dull and emotionless. "Easy it was for me to find the Land of the Young, for I never imagined I would not. My ship rode gracefully up on a white shore, and I stepped off with my companions. A lovely Lady was walking there, so beautiful I could not bear to look at her for long, but still I tried. All I remember now is her golden hair, not like Cessair's, white as noonday, but rich and glowing, the sun in the west."

Meacán's expression softened somewhat, remembering Niamh.

"'Not my idle thought, surely,' the Lady said as she looked on me. But I didn't understand what She meant. I showed Her my boat, forgetting about my friends in my excitement. And so they were gone. I missed them, and was afraid. I turned to the beautiful Lady, but She, too, had disappeared. Then I began to cry, and only stopped when I felt Her hand on my shoulder.

"'Why did you go away?' I asked. 'I was never here, child, only my thought,' the Lady replied. 'And lo, I have followed my thought, and find a little girl here in truth.' Her words baffled me, and so I was not comforted. I wanted my mother. I wanted to go home.

"'Leave whenever you wish,' the golden-haired Goddess told me. I looked for my currach, but before me was only the shell-strewn strand and white waves breaking. 'See your home in your heart,' I heard Niamh say, like birds' songs it was, 'and your feet will take you there.'"

The Cailleach raised her brows. "And did she not speak true?"

Meacán shrugged. "True enough. My longing for home made the dún clear to my Sight. I danced toward it, and came home at last. My mother embraced me, and wept, and said all these seven years she had believed me still to be alive."

"Seven years," echoed the Cailleach. *"Time stands still in the presence of the Gods."*

"It does indeed," said Meacán bitterly. "Five years my elder was Blackthorn when I returned, yet I left my brother a two-year-old imp still running to my mother's breast. A man I had never seen before was called King and slept in my mother's bed. My playmates had quite forgotten me— everything familiar was somehow changed."

"You are not the first to visit with the Gods, nor will you be the last. Seven years is not a lifetime, and in return you had your gift. Now Creathna and Mac Ailch are with our enemy. They may know his plans—they may have his Name to give us. Are a little girl's fears enough reason for a Wizard of Éirinn to refuse to serve the Mothers?"

"A little girl's fears," retorted Meacán wildly. "Had I not buried those fears, never would I have dared dance again." Unearthed, the helplessness, the terror the child Meacán had felt rose as fire in the grown woman's cheeks and venom on her tongue. "For all your Sight are you blind to what happened to me? It's not the years, it's not the journey! It's daydream, it's the world itself!"

She remembered to whom she was speaking, caught herself, and looked down at her feet.

"The steps to Tír na nÓg were not like any other dance, Grandmother."

The Old Woman nodded. "You had a destination, but no holdfast."

"Yes!" Meacán met the Cailleach's glittering gaze, inviting the Priestess to hear the truth she was striving to express. "When I make a holdfast, I build it in my mind. It is a vision, an image. A daydream."

"A daydream that becomes real."

"If it exists already. But if not? Och, Cailleach, can you See? When I first beheld Niamh on the shore of the Blesséd Isle, it was not Herself I saw. Niamh was far away, daydreaming, daydreaming about a stroll she might take along the strand. It was a daydream I looked upon, not Herself. In a world of imaginings, how can I know if I stand where I think I stand, if I hold a thing or only dream I hold it? Easy enough for me to cross into that world. But how can I ever leave it, if I cannot tell the difference between thinking I am dancing back to Éirinn, and dancing home in truth?"

"But, Meacán, you have been there, have stood in daydream with Niamh of the Golden Hair, and safely returned to your mother's hall."

Meacán shook her head and her lip quivered. "Three times I ran into my mother's arms, three times she welcomed me. Three times I thought myself home, but then the arms that embraced me melted away. I would find myself again with Niamh on the strand, or alone on the shores of Tír na nÓg, and once in my make-believe boat, sailing into Dún na nGall's bay. Lost in my hopes and visions, almost I despaired of finding the true dún, and my mother within. Pure luck it was that I crossed at last to the real world, the mortal world, and felt my mother's real arms around me."

The Cailleach shook her head sadly. "Forgive me, Meacán, but the Wise Woman of Midhe does not understand you."

"Can I find words for that my heart cannot show you clearly? In my thoughts, my mother was as I had left her seven years before. I did my best to dance home, but it was to my daydream of home I was returning, and there met time and time again with my mother's daydream of her daughter's return. By chance alone I stumbled into the dún, my eyes so blurred with tears I could barely See at all, neither her daydream nor mine. And then did she wrap real arms around me and hold me still until, when my tears were dry, I looked up at my mother and saw the gray in her brown hair, and the lines of care and worry the years had drawn on her face."

The Cailleach nodded. "And yet, you offered to travel the ways of dream for the Mother," she said thoughtfully. "Are the two worlds so different? Can we not dream ourselves awake, and yet be sleeping still? Are dreams not made of our imaginings as daydreams are?"

Meacán frowned. "I do not deny that the world of dreams is perilous. Many are the paths through that realm, some true, some false. The Gods are there, and great power, but also the deceits of our perceptions, and evils too hideous to face in the waking world. Still, I would gladly go dreaming, rather than dare the world of daydream."

Meacán turned away from the Cailleach and stared out into the fullness of the day.

"The world of dreams has a door, Grandmother, a gate between waking and sleep. Not even the Cailleach of Midhe, trained to journey there, not even you remember passing the dream-gate, for all the times you have done so. Only I remember, for I have crossed that threshold with my eyes wide open, and I tell you true, it is fixed as stone.

"But between waking thought and imagining? Daydream's threshold is impermanent as the boundary of earth and sea. As foam sinks into the sands, and sands are drawn out to the cold gray deeps of the ocean, so do the worlds of waking and daydream blend their borders beyond finding. Is your Sight keen enough to mark how far the next wave will reach, to

foresee the pattern it will draw upon the strand? Mine is not.
Once adrift in the sea of daydream, only chance can bring
me safe again to Éirinn's shore."

Meacán fell silent. She had opened her past and showed
her fears. Now she strove to bury them again, to lock them
away deep in her heart, where they could not darken the
world before her eyes.

A noisy group of children had gathered on the stone steps
of the great hall and were laughing and arguing. Meacán
watched a cheeky, snub-nosed boy snatch a ribbon from a
girl's curling hair and race away. With gleeful shouts the
whole pack bounded after the thief and in a moment were
out of sight.

Taking a slow breath, the Dancer turned back to face the
Cailleach's crystal eyes and sharp words.

The Old Woman was gone, the place empty. Only a waning fire and bitter memories were left to keep Meacán company in the vast and comfortless hall.

Thirty-three

O'er Na Cruacha's crest the night is creeping,
The wailing wind around us weeping,
Fair Suibhne sighs, uneasy sleeping,
Dreaming of goblins, dreaming of death.

Shearwater's Bard-Song

An hour before sundown, a shadow crept from under the
eaves of the wood and spread quickly across the open ground
between the forest and Temuir's wall. Like its cousins born
of the light, it lengthened and grew, but in truth it owed
nothing to sun, moon, or fire. The daystar was westering
behind gathering clouds, the moon not yet risen, and the
only fires burning were set in the hearths of Temuir's halls.
From the black womb of malice had this darkness come, a
shadow sprung from Shadow, where the Dead Lord reigns.

Alarms sounded urgent and challenging from Temuir's
walls as the goblins surged up the rise. An hour yet Temuir's
warriors had believed was theirs to prepare for battle—to
sharpen weapons, ready the chariots, light the pyres they had
built before the wall. The winding horns gave them not even
a moment.

Answering the summons, the Mother of Midhe sped to
the rampart and there looked out upon the enemy. Her eyes
lit on a score of red-eyes bearing in their arms a felled tree to
batter down Temuir's gates. Fivescore more surrounded the
battering ram in a living armor of black bodies and yellow

fangs. And five times that, a hairy, stinking swarm of darkness, pounded the earth with their heavy feet, dragged their weapons through the unlit mounds of wood and turf the folk of Temuir had built from the ruin of their village, all the while calling out a hideous invitation to Temuir's warriors to come and meet their deaths.

They dare the daylight, she told Brí.

Brí paused as the Mother's Sight filled her own vision, then turned again to the task of putting the King's horses in harness.

A bold move, she conceded. *An' they reach our gates before our warriors are armed, how can we open the doors without that the goblins will enter Temuir? Yet, an' we keep the gates closed, our hope is less. Though the gates stand for half the night, still, in the end they will fall. Either way we will end by fighting the red-eyes in our very streets.*

The nearing shadow had a fearsome voice that overpowered the strident call of the horns and chilled Liannan's blood. She turned her Sight to the armory and stables, but her warriors were still struggling to horse. Less than half her host had even taken their weapons to hand. One chariot alone was ready for the field, one warrior eager for battle.

All is not lost, the Mother told Brí. *Éire be with you.*

Aloud she called for all to hear, "Let the King ride!"

The Maiden leapt into the gold-rimmed chariot, but Eoghan was there before her.

"Eoghan Rí na Midhe!" she shouted, taking the reins into her hand. "The foe is upon us!"

"Eoghan Rí na Midhe! Eoghan Rí na Midhe!"

Every tongue in Temuir took up the cry. The halls shook with the sound, but beyond the walls, the goblins were undaunted.

"Open the gate," the Mother commanded.

The heavy iron bar was lifted, the high oak portals drawn back. Seeing the gates of Temuir widening, the goblins loosed a savage roar of triumph. Faster they came. In a moment the shadow of their army met and merged with the shadow of the stone battlement.

Into the darkness thundered a single chariot. Four great roans, matched for speed, power, and their coats, red and rusty as old leaves of autumn, carried the King to battle, and neighed their joy to have reached the field. Their harness

gleamed with the last light of day, the gilt edges of the chariot's rim caught the sun's rays and sent bright sun-spikes into
the goblins' red eyes. The black-haired beasts howled in pain
and hate. Brí urged her team on toward the battering ram.
The goblins called to her as if they knew no fear. Their axes
whistled a warning as they swept through the air.

The King's spear answered with a sigh, winging over Brí's
shoulder and between the heads of two of the horses. Silently
it plunged into a goblin's black heart, pierced through his
hairy back, and dug into the chest of the beast behind him.
Both fell, and those following stumbled over the corpses. The
front of the battering ram dropped, ploughing into the muddy
earth as the goblins at the rear ran mindlessly on.

With a steady voice and deft hand Brí turned the horses,
bringing the chariot around to cut across the goblins' charge.
Eoghan drew his sword as they wheeled, swung it once above
his head, then leaned over the side of the chariot, blade held
out before him. Howling his mad pleasure, the King of
Midhe mowed down the enemy, his sword reaping through
the goblins like a scythe through tall grass.

"Eoghan!" the archers cried from the wall. "Eoghan Rí na
Midhe!" and they loosed their first volley into the field of
darkness.

In the wake of the King's chariot the goblins closed, pressing on toward Temuir. The battering ram they left in the
mud, unneeded, for the doors stood half-open. Those in the
midst of the horde pressed hardest, feeling the power of their
numbers and the promise of the coming night. Only those
nearest the gates knew any caution. Though Temuir's pale
host was yet to ride forth, the fortress's open doors were not
unguarded. A giant stood in the gateway barring their path.
He was half as wide as the double-doored portal, and the top
of his head barely cleared the stone lintel. Sword or spear
would have been as useless as toys in the giant's massive
hand. He bore a great length of chain that reached from his
waist to the ground, each link the size of a goblin's paw.

An axe came spinning out of the darkness with a ululating
whisper. It was ill aimed, and harmlessly struck the stones of
the wall. Close upon the weapon's flight came the goblins.
When they were near enough, Reochaidh swung his length
of chain. Bones cracked, and howls of pain mingled with

bestial war cries. Challenges showered down on the red-eyes from the top of Temuir's wall, insults rose in answer from the sea of fangs and black, greasy bodies. Reochaidh alone was silent. His weapon spoke for him in a voice low and terrible, like a Bean Sidhe's moan. With three tremendous blows, the Destroyer laid low every goblin within reach of his chain.

The seething mass of goblin flesh wavered, but it was not fear made the beasts hesitate. The black horde parted, and up the uneven road more goblins charged, carrying the battering ram in their thick, taloned paws.

With a sharp twist of his arm, Reochaidh sent his chain whipping round his wrist, and held out his other hand as a shield. The goblins' tree trunk slammed into the giant's waiting palm. He staggered under the force of the blow, and the red-eyes drew the ram up to rush him again. This time Reochaidh was driven back a pace, but his fingers closed on the wood and held on.

Darting past the giant, a half score of goblins broke into the close. Reochaidh could but let them go. Gripping the tree with both hands, he pulled it toward him. His face reddened as he lifted the ram, and goblins still clinging to it, but never a sound passed his lips. With one arm he brushed the enemy from the right side of the tree, peas spilled from a pod. Then he hoisted the stout trunk higher, shaking howling goblins from the left. When the battering ram was his, Reochaidh swung the tremendous club as he had his chain, and dammed the tide of darkness surging by him.

The sounds of fighting at his back brought a grim smile to the giant's lips. The thirty or more red-eyes that had gained Temuir's close had there to face the Mother's army. Brief that battle would be, an' he could hold the rest of the goblins at the gate. With the tree he beat the goblins from the doors, but the dark horde returned again when the giant's club had passed. Once more he swept his weapon in a lethal half circle. Over the red-eyes' howls he heard a buzzing, like a swarm of furious bees. Feathered shafts sprouted in the dark wall of flesh before him, and at last the Destroyer was able to step forward onto the field.

Two great strides he took, his club swinging to the right and left, forcing the goblins back and back again. By sheer might the giant cleared a space before the gates, and the archers sent volleys of arrows to his aid.

The goblins' harsh voices rose into a single hate-filled curse. Temuir's walls no longer guarded the giant's flanks from their axes—empty air lay between his back and the rampart's stones. As one they attacked, spreading out to surround Reochaidh, to cut him down and storm the gates.

A second chariot rolled under the stone lintel and into the small clearing the giant had made. The charioteer turned sharply left, following Eoghan's lead, and a third team of horses stepped between the open doors. After this came another, and then warriors armed with spear and sword, and torches blazing with fire.

Having reached the end of the goblins' front ranks, Brí turned the King's chariot about only to find the way blocked by fangs and axes. The horses reared and struck out with their hooves. A spate of arrows sang from the wall and fell among the red-eyes. Eoghan's war cries blazed in the Maiden's heart and burned like fire in the ears of his enemies. Spear after deadly spear he flung at his red-eyed foes and his sword was ready.

Eoghan's every howl was music to the Mother, but she forced her eyes from the King's chariot, forced herself to order the battle with a Queen's wisdom and not a lover's heart. The fighting before the wall was a disordered contest of dark and light, a struggle without lines or strategy. Fearing the archers would wound their own, she commanded them to aim deeper into the goblin horde. Arrows hummed away into the black field. Alone of the watchers on the wall, the Mother could See goblins' red eyes grow dim in death and their black bodies drop. To the rest it seemed the feathered shafts fell into the darkness as harmlessly as into the sea.

Night is nigh, and Shadow gathering in the heavens, Liannan told the Cailleach. *The pyres must be lit, whatever the cost. And summon Seamair to the wall.*

Through the gate rode a dozen mounted warriors. They bore fire as well as spear in their hands. A few untouched mounds of turf and wood rose like small islands in a sea of pitch, but though the nearest of them was but fifty paces from the gate, for three of the horsemen the distance was too great. They went down screaming into the darkness. Using their spears like lances and their torches like clubs, two others broke through the goblins and put their brands to the pyre.

A second pyre was lit, and then a third. With light on the

field, Liannan's Sight was clearer. She Saw an axe bite deep into a horse's neck. The rider's sword swept the goblin's head from his shoulders before his mount was down, and then he was caught and trampled beneath his enemies' feet. Nearer to the wall, a goblin's bloodstained weapon sliced through a chariot's leather reins and splintered the horses' wooden harness. The animals shied, tipping the carriage onto one wheel. Both warrior and charioteer leapt clear as it toppled, but the red-eyes were all about them, and their axes were merciless.

Liannan's ears rang with the death cries of her people, her eyes wept with visions of blood and pain. Yet glory, too, filled her Sight, and shining courage. Eoghan's challenge echoed from Temuir's stones, his madness streamed like light from his brow, blinding the red-eyes that would have pulled him down. Reochaidh's tireless arms kept the gate clear— every sweep of his tree trunk brought another chariot or another thirty warriors onto the field.

More Liannan Saw, and she alone; patterns in the coming night, Shadow's dark designs, and the hidden glitter of the Sidhe's silver swords.

The sun was well down before Temuir's host was clear of the gate and the doors secured behind them. The goblins snarled when they saw the entrance barred, and their own ram still in the giant's hands. They gripped their weapons and shook them over their heads, swearing by Shadow's King that they would force the gates open again before this night was through.

The ruined village was a poor battleground for Temuir's chariots. The muddy earth, wheel-rutted from the last fight and soaked with yesterday's rain, was treacherous for the horses, and worse for the war-wagons. Refuse, charred beams, shards of pottery, forgotten helmets, and broken javelins hampered the goblins' flat feet, but snared the chariot wheels and made Temuir's warriors stumble as well. Darkness before them, beneath them, swelling over their heads, Liannan's host drove with all their strength into the goblin horde, trying to force the red-eyes back to the forest. Every blow was bitterly resisted, every step paid for with their own blood.

The Mother's army pressed the black-haired foe as far as they could, pitting everything they had against the evil that threatened their walls. To the limits of the old settlement, where the wooden stockade had once stood, their courage carried them, but there they stopped. Nothing could drive the goblins further, not the Queen's will, nor her warriors' might, nor even the King's royal madness.

Crouched behind a hastily erected barricade of old palings, debris, even the bodies of their dead, the red-eyes howled insults at their enemies, daring them on. The night was thick with smoke and shadow, the close air filled with darts and knives that flew from behind the goblins' defense. Beyond the red-eyes' makeshift wall the field was in darkness. No torchbearer had yet made it past the stockade to light the waiting pyres. None wished to try. An' they could but hold the goblins here until daybreak . . .

Even as Liannan wondered how she might feed her warriors' flagging hopes, the clouds burst, and the rains poured down. Water wept from the skies like blood from a gaping wound, as if a God's sword had rent heaven asunder. Stinging sheets of liquid ice soaked into cloth and leather, weighting already leaden arms and dousing the fires. Louder grew the howls from behind the goblins' wall. With only their victory cries as warning, the red-eyes broke from their cover and charged Temuir's host.

Against the blackness before them and the blackness above, Liannan's warriors could not stand. The storm, the dark, the night itself was in league with the goblins. Temuir's warriors began to retreat, slowly at first, more frantically as the red-eyes grew bolder. Like a dark wave the goblins came, each swell capped by a pale crest of axes. Eoghan roared in relentless fury, but his horses had not their master's madness. Battle-weary, with fang and axe flashing in their eyes and the stink of goblin in their nostrils, they fought Brí's hand, and strove to bear the chariot up the slippery rise and away from the horror of the field.

The goblins had fallen back with defiance. Temuir's champions were beaten back with little order and no quarter given. Death was in the rain-drenched air, despair echoed in the thunder. The only strength left Liannan's warriors was that of desperation, and it was not enough. The swift force of the goblins' assault cut Liannan's army apart, leaving isolated circles of men fighting back-to-back with no hope of succor. Chariots got mired in their own wheel tracks, and were overrun by black death. A red-eyed mob came against Reochaidh, forcing the giant to retreat to Temuir's wall. Though they still could not pass the tree-club he swung, yet they managed to drive a dark wedge between the giant and the rest of Temuir's host. Arrows flew from the rampart to Reochaidh's aid, but the fell wind defeated them. Mere shafts of wood and metal were as nothing against the might of the storm.

The warriors that were swift and did not stumble were borne back to Temuir's walls by the dark tide. There they pressed themselves against the stones and lifted their stained swords against the unstoppable wave of hatred and evil. They had not even their King before them to show them how to die, for Eoghan had denied his horses their escape until it was too late. Their coats streaked with rain, foam covering their sides and spewing from their mouths, the roans reared, neighing their terror. Their hooves came down on hairy bodies, then lifted again, unable to step forward, but only to trample the creatures that pressed against them.

To Liannan, the song of defeat was deafening.

"Seamair!" she cried.

The Weather-Worker looked up at the Queen from where she knelt on the wet stones of the rampart, her eyes wide.

"The will that brewed this storm, Mother—no mortal will, I swear it."

Swiftly Liannan turned to the close. Cessair patted Fionn's neck, and smiled up at the Mother in glad anticipation.

"Open the gate!" Liannan commanded.

The war cry of Cnoc an Eanaigh rang within Temuir's close, but was unheard beyond the walls, where the din of storm and goblin raged. Though the red-eyes knew the gates were opening at the Queen's command, they had no fear. What could the Mother do but unbar her gates that her beaten warriors might try to gain them before they were hacked to pieces? Let them run, an' their cowardly legs would carry them. Let them cringe behind their wall. On the heels of their enemies the goblins would enter Temuir. The streets would run with the humans' red blood—none would they spare, neither beast, nor brat, nor unborn babe. And before the Queen's head fell to their axes, they would pluck out her far-Seeing eyes that she might look full on Shadow's King. The music of her agony would sound their victory.

The goblins' howls rose to a roar louder than the storm.

They charged for the gates, cutting down the warriors before them and trampling the falling bodies in their haste to reach the widening doors.

Before a single splayed, black-haired foot could cross the threshold, a blaze of silver and gold filled the space between the gates. Behind the light, low thunder rolled. Even as they turned their eyes away, the goblins howled in derision. They had seen this vision but yesterday, and it had sent them running to the woods. From the shadows of the trees some had looked back. Scores of red eyes had seen the Sidhe turn to mist and vanish into the loathsome light of day. An illusion of elven warriors had deterred them once, and cost them the field. Never again.

Baying in disbelief, the goblins charged, their fervor carrying them into the Sidhe's countercharge, and onto the elves' bright swords. Only after the hundred warriors of Cnoc an Eanaigh had slain a hundred of the foe did the goblins credit their red eyes. Then they shrieked in fury, and lifted their bloodstained axes against the blinding cloud of elven light.

As she had despaired to See the high tide of darkness surge to Temuir's wall, so did Liannan now relish the Sight of the tide's turning. Over the sounds of battle, over the moaning wind came Eoghan's bellow to her ears, and there was laughter in it. Her eyes flew to her King, her lover. A huge goblin leapt into the King's chariot, axe swinging down toward Eoghan's smoking head, and already the beast was howling his triumph. Eoghan shifted to the side. The axe slipped by him, striking the rim of the chariot, cleaving the wood like kindling. Giving the red-eye no time to pull it free, the King seized the goblin by the neck. The fire of the King's rage was like lightning that sets the forest ablaze— the goblin's greasy hair burst into flame. Eoghan heaved the screaming, burning goblin from him and into the arms of his red-eyed kin. Sparks leapt from goblin to goblin, the screams from throat to throat. Brí turned the horses toward the smoking, stinking bodies, and rode them down.

A mighty blow of Reochaidh's tree trunk lifted three goblins off the ground. As he smashed them against the stones of Temuir, his well-used weapon splintered. The red eyes before him gleamed. A volley of arrows sang from the rampart, then fell silent as they sank into the massed darkness before the Destroyer. Dropping the tree trunk, Reochaidh clenched his

right fist and made three quick circles with his arm.
Whistling fiercely, the length of chain spun free from his
wrist. Closing his fingers on the last metal link, he swung the
chain in a brutal arc before him. Almost he cried out to see
the red eyes smoulder in surprise, but Temuir's walls were at
his back. He clamped his teeth together and kept silent, lest
the rampart come tumbling down in the echoes of his glee.

Cessair of Cnoc an Eanaigh rode her white steed scatheless
through the dark sea. Not a goblin could meet her glittering
gaze, and neither fang nor axe was swifter than the sword
Airgead. Tears of pain fell from the goblins' eyes at the flash
of the elven warrior's silver blade, and black heads rolled.

Almost as soon as the Sidhe began to rive the goblins'
hearts with their swords, glistening spears of moonlight
pierced the storm clouds, driving long shafts into the battlefield below. The more moonlight fell, the lighter fell the
rain. The clouds curled up into themselves, shrinking into
separate bundles, then scattered clumps, and then they were
gone. Light spread over the Mother's halls like a cloak of
pale gossamer, draped the rampart, blanketed the field in a
shimmering veil. The warriors of Temuir looked up to see a
perfect snow-white orb sailing clear of the trees in a cloudless sky. The goblins hid their eyes from the moon's round
face and broke from the battle, wailing in dismay.

High on the battlement, Liannan helped the Weather-
Worker to her feet that she could stand in the light her spell
had released. The tears of relief and exhaustion that ran
down Seamair's cheeks glittered like thin streams of crystal
under the moon.

"No longer does night ally with our foes!" Liannan cried
from the rampart. Her voice was Midhe's, full and rich. It
filled the air from Temuir's hill to the forest beyond the battlefield. "No longer does their God's magic hold against
ours! No longer will Temuir suffer goblins at her gates!"

The Mother's words were like a rann of power to her warriors. His chain singing a glad song of battle, Reochaidh
started forward. The red-eyes retreated before the whirling
menace of his weapon. The Destroyer quickened his pace,
shaking the ground with his tread. The goblins' retreat
became a rout. Their long legs were swift. Reochaidh's were
far longer and far swifter—he was on their heels, cutting

them down from behind, then in their midst, laying about with his chain.

Calling to her people, Cessair drove Fionn in behind the giant, but the path Reochaidh hewed through the goblins' ranks sealed shut behind him. Alone the Destroyer fought his way through the fleeing horde, then ran ahead of the goblins, coming before them to the forest's edge. There he choose a young sapling, uprooted it, and twined his heavy chain in its leafless branches.

As the first red-eyes reached him, he swept them back with his new club. More followed, their light-wounded eyes widening as their sight fell on the shadowy safety of the woods. Not even Reochaidh, broad as two men and tall as three, could stave off all the axes raised against him. A blade found his calf. He smashed the goblin who gave him the cut into a smear on the ground, but came down heavily on one knee.

"To me!" he said.

Though Reochaidh had spoken no louder than the soft edge of a whisper, his words reverberated with an immeasurable weight. The syllables struck his sapling first, making the wood crack and his metal chain crumble. The giant's weapon fell to the ground in a brief shower of splinters and metal. Next the edge of the forest felt the Destroyer's gift. Stout branches shouted with pain and broke away from their trunks, falling to form a solid wooden barrier before the forest's paths.

The words Reochaidh had spoken swelled when they reached the battleground. Like a great wind that makes the grasses bow and sway, his voice rolled over the two armies. Not a creature—mortal, Sidhe, or goblin—but bent before the sound. Horses screamed and panicked, throwing their riders or bearing them away over the field. Axes broke apart in the goblins' hands, poorly forged swords shattered into dust. On the rampart, the watchers covered their ears, but the echoes of Reochaidh's voice ached between their fingers, and made the stones under their feet shudder and groan.

The Destroyer's voice swept over the battlement and through the streets of Temuir. The words "to me" struck the walls of the Queen's halls, shaking thatch from the roofs, cracking stones that had been whole since time before memory. Up the dark lanes the magic rumbled, and to the farthest hall where it nestled against high Temuir Hill.

Thirty-four

No drink more bitter than the poison of defeat,
No wine so sweet as victory's cup

Sayings of the Mothers

First the shutters of Meacán's chamber window rattled as if some fairy were trying to pull them from their hinges. Quickly Reochaidh's potent whisper passed the frail wooden barrier and filled the room. Meacán dropped to her knees, pressing her hands to her breast, where her bones were thrumming with the deep magic that pulsed about her. The sense of the Destroyer's words were lost in Meacán's ears—was it the gale she heard? Or the Shadow King's voice crying victory over Temuir? The ewer fell from the sideboard and smashed to floor, the chair creaked and wobbled, the candle ring swung crazily overhead.

Meacán staggered to her feet and ran to the window. Thrusting back the shutters, she gazed out. 'Twas not thunder had shaken the room. The storm that had ruled the heavens was banished, by Seamair's gift, doubtless. Not even a cloud was in the sky, only stars, dimmed by the bright moonlight. Had Reochaidh spoken, then? In death, in pain, in defeat?

A chill wind, thick with smoke and burned oil, blew past the open shutters, lifting Meacán's hair from her shoulders.

"Let them all fall," Úna had said. And had Temuir fallen? Fair Temuir, the jewel of Éirinn?

Though the Queen had ordered her Wizards to remain in safety unless she or the Cailleach called them to the wall, Meacán could endure to wait no longer. She turned back to the room, swept her cloak from the chair, and hurried out the door.

The puddled streets of Temuir were crowded with people, but all had their urgent errands. None paused to mark the cloaked and hooded figure hurrying down from the northernmost hall toward the gate. Meacán marked them closely, and saw that though everyone was making great haste, no one was in panicked flight.

She reached the steps to the rampart without speaking a word to anyone, then sidled up the stairs past an irregular stream of people coming down. She found a space nearly wide enough for her body between two archers, noting that their quivers stood empty. Not fearing to hamper their aim, she squeezed in tighter and leaned out upon the wall.

Even with silver moonlight illuminating every detail of the field, at first Meacán could barely make out anything. A glittering line of fragmented light bordered the dark forest—but no. It must be the Sidhe Meacán saw, and their bright swords flashing. With them stood Reochaidh, or rather he knelt, but even so humbled the Destroyer was far taller than the mounted elves. Her eyes could more easily take in Reochaidh than the glittering warriors of Cnoc an Eanaigh. She saw the giant lift a hairy goblin high over his head in his mighty hands and hurl him down as if the beast were a bale of hay.

As he was nearer to Temuir, the King of Midhe was even clearer to Meacán's sight. A pitiful wreck of a chariot, splintered boards barely clinging together between two wheels, bore strange, demonic Eoghan across the field. Brí's horses were turned toward the forest, but they seemed unable to pass over the ground. They stepped high, rearing and kicking. A goblin's axe in Eoghan's hand danced with them, glinting as it rose and fell into the darkness. Temuir's champions fought beside him, driving spears and swords into the black shadow of the night. A long while Meacán studied them before she caught a gleam of metal in the dark pool.

She leaned even farther out over the wall, and squinted at the strange battle. At last she saw them—red coals glowing in the empty dark. Not black night, but a field black with goblins lay between the Sidhe and Midhe's King. Slowly the Mother's armies were drawing together, crushing into nothing the massed darkness that separated them.

Someone jostled her elbow, and a small boy's head popped up between her arms where they gripped the stones. Meacán looked around and nearly laughed. All Temuir had come to the wall to see the end of the battle, to see the goblins brought down.

At last the King's mud-stained, battered arm closed with the Sidhe's gleaming arm of light, and the dark between them was vanquished. A shout erupted along Temuir's wall greater than ears could hold. Mothers whose sons still carried their swords and mothers who had seen their sons fall cried out with one voice. Young and old, humble and Mighty—there was no meaning to the distinctions. One people stood on the wall and together sounded their victory. Meacán wasn't aware she was shouting with the others— there was no self, no feeling within or without, no world beyond the throbbing, glorious paean of victory. Temuir's triumph stole her senses, bore them up and away into the rising gale of jubilation.

Eoghan's chariot continued to rumble madly over goblin bodies and through the moon-colored pools of rain that covered the rutted field. Meacán had not heard the gates open, but the maidens were already beyond the walls and running to meet him. Cessair, unmistakable in her silver mail, urged her mount to match the King's wildly charging horses. At a full gallop she leaned over and caught their reins. They reared and tossed their heads, but under her hand they stopped. Eoghan's howl rose into the air, louder than the cheers from the wall. Leaping over the heads of his panting horses, the King landed on the bloody ground brandishing his stolen axe, and lunged for Cessair. The elven warrior threw back her head, laughing, and Fionn spun on his hind legs, bearing his mistress swiftly out of harm's way. Eoghan would have given chase, and in his royal mood might well have caught the white steed. But the King paused, forgetting his anger as the Maidens' Song began to turn his bloodlust to a lover's passion.

Not on the battlefield alone did the Maidens' Song ring. Half the women in Temuir joined the chorus, and not a warrior that rode through Temuir's gate but found a hero's welcome awaiting him. Meacán thought to join the women hurrying down the stairs, to open her arms to whoever came riding, striding from the field, but as the rampart emptied, an overpowering shyness possessed her. She should not be in Temuir at all, she thought uncomfortably, but away on the Mother's errand. This victory was not for her to have seen.

The archers had gone, but Meacán huddled against the stones, and pulled her cloak tighter about her. From where she stood she could see both the devastation outside the walls and the celebration within. Mingled with the shouts of joy were cries of grief—the long, keening lamentations of bereaved mothers and heartbroken lovers over the bodies of their darlings lying dead on the field. The maidens were laughing as they lured the dazed and smoking King to the wall, and so, too, the older women who began to douse him as they had the day before. Five tubs were needed to wash Eoghan's mantle from him, to cool his madness and make him sane.

Liannan passed Meacán by without a glance, and went down the stairs, dropping her clothing on the last step before coming to stand before the gates. Was it only this morning Meacán had looked on the Mother and thought her a barebranched tree weathering the cold of winter? Not a sign of weariness could she see now, nor worry, nor pain. The Mother's beauty was dazzling, victory incarnate, Midhe in the summer when the air is heavy with perfumes and the songs of birds. Meacán's blood thrilled as Liannan embraced Eoghan, and the cheers rose again, but then the Mother loosed her arms from Eoghan's neck, and spoke.

"Come, now, with your Queen." Her voice quieted the exuberant crowd to breathless anticipation. "Sheathe your sword, and lift your spear to serve Midhe's pleasure. Your mantle shall cover us both. Sweet this time of love, but brief. For greater battles await you, Eoghan Rí na Midhe, and greater fame. And greater honor is won by greater daring."

Liannan's words affected her listeners like a draught of honey mead. Some danced away, seeking their rooms in the halls or some private place, others embraced in the streets as if it were Bealtaine Day.

Only Meacán was chilled by what she had heard. True
Liannan spoke—honor was won by daring. And honor lost
by cowardice.

Meacán turned away from the close and gazed out over
the rampart. She saw without surprise that the Cailleach had
come to the field of battle. Surely the Old Woman stepped
across the ravaged ground where heroes had fallen, and amid
the pools and streamlets of rain, shining like unwrought
gems and veins of silver under the moon. For Meacán the
sight held no beauty. Corpse-covered the earth, and black
with blood. No more could Meacán taste the sweetness of
triumph. The wine of victory had been poisoned by the
shadow of her fear.

Thirty-five

"You are a bold gambler," says Aill of An Cnoc Gorm,
"And to settle our wagers will grieve my heart sore.
I'll take your right eye for the game that you've lost,
But the horse you've won from me you'll find worth the cost."

Mac an tSeanchaí's Mare

By the time dawn gentled the sky with rose and blue, the gaiety within Temuir's walls too had softened, to a dazed weariness, a brittle calm. People walked as if joy and grief were riding each on one shoulder, and a sudden move might bring the balance to tears or laughter. Only in the heart of Meacán the Dancer had fear found a home.

All the long hours since the battle she had watched from the rampart, no more able to accept the healing that victory had brought to the citadel than she was to deny the shadow that lingered over the battlefield. It was there Meacán's eyes were most often drawn, beyond the gate to the reeking pyres where the goblins had been heaped and burned. In the early light the deserted village was more horrible than it had been when its streets had run with blood, for now it was haunted. The dead looked out from the empty helmets, leaned on the broken pikes half-buried in the muck, sighed their death-songs in the wind that stirred the ashes.

Meacán looked out upon the battlefield for so long she stopped seeing it. Only when an unexpected lightness touched her heart did she realize her sight had lit upon a star

that had come to rest on the soiled earth. Slowly her eyes
focused. She saw not a star, but a glimmering figure astride a
white charger, motionless near the edge of the forest.
Meacán had only time to begin to consider why Cessair of
Cnoc an Eanaigh might tarry among the dead, when the reason appeared from the forest. Another horse, as black as
Fionn was white, walked boldly out from under the eaves of
the wood. In a single, fluid motion Cessair dismounted, then
strode through the mud and gore toward the beautiful animal. Light embraced darkness; Cessair's gloved hand stroked
the long, black mane, the horse's dark head pressed against
and nuzzled Cessair's silver-mailed chest.

"Eocha returns at last," said a deep, musical voice in
Meacán's ear.

She didn't turn, knowing the speaker to be elven, and
feeling already a little giddy from studying Cessair so closely.
The Chieftain of Cnoc an Eanaigh was leading both horses
in toward Temuir now, the white charger on her right, the
dark on her left. Eocha looked as fresh as if he had just
stepped from a stable, and Fionn fairly pranced across the
field, mocking the long hours of battle he had seen in the
departed night.

"All fire and spirit are the horses of the Tuatha dé
Danaan," Meacán said admiringly.

There was a deep laugh beside her, and Meacán dared a
sidelong glance. Her companion was Fiach, Cessair's harper.

"The spirit is life," he said, "and the fire is love. It was for
love of your brother Cessair gave him Eocha to ride."

Forgetting herself, Meacán whirled to face the harper.
"But Eocha has returned without him!" she gasped.

Fiach gazed back at her with star-brilliant eyes. Fighting
off the dizziness that assailed her with his look, Meacán
forced herself to go on.

"Is he dead, then, or hurt—"

"Calm yourself, Lady." Fiach laid a hand on Meacán's
arm. "I spoke without thought and have alarmed you without cause. Eocha was lent your brother, to bear him to the
western sea. He was to release Eocha when he reached the
shore, that the horse might find his way back to us. And so
the Hunter must have done."

"To the shore," Meacán repeated. "There to find the

Stag?" She frowned and shook her head. "But Cessair says he
has lost his Spear. What good to hunt the Stag, an' the fool
has no weapon for to slay him?"

The harper did not answer at once. When he spoke, his
answer was not at all what Meacán expected.

"Too much you dwell on another's path," he said, "and
look not enough to your own."

Was her shame common knowledge then? Meacán no
longer had enough pride to feel angry. She merely felt sick,
and tired, and scared to the depths of her soul.

A deep whinny drew her eyes to the courtyard. Cessair
had brought her horses in. An eager crowd of children
pressed as close as they dared to the magnificent creatures,
but none was so bold as to reach out a hand to touch them.

"It is good to have a friend like Eocha to carry you when
the way is perilous," remarked Fiach.

Meacán nodded miserably, then lifted her head as the
thought took root. "So must it be," she said wonderingly.

The harper smiled his farewell and went down the steps to
the close. He greeted Eocha warmly, and with Cessair made
his way through the crowd of small ones toward the hostel.
Meacán tried to follow them with her eyes, but it was too
painful, like watching sunlight upon water. The boisterous
and noisy children at the base of the stairs more easily drew
and held her attention.

"Thistle and Mallow, you be the goblins, and I'll be
Cessair and kill you with my magic sword," a red-cheeked
girl with long, dark curls directed.

"You are always the champion," complained the boy she
had addressed as Mallow, a stocky brown-haired fellow with
a turned-up nose. "I don't want to be a goblin! I want to be
King Eoghan in his golden chariot."

The children moved off from the steps, still arguing.
Softly, swiftly, Meacán descended from the rampart and followed at a discreet distance. She saw one child pick up a
long stick from the ground and swing it like a sword.
Another held her hands before her as if they were curved
around reins and bounced down the paved path at a trot.

"Och, as you please," she heard the apple-cheeked girl say.
"We shall all be warriors, and make-believe about the goblins. Mallow can be the King, and I am Cessair."

"And I the giant," piped up the littlest.

"And Cockle is the Destroyer."

The lad grinned and nodded happily.

The children reached the footpath that led to Temuir's kitchen gardens. Avoiding the walkway, they hurried to a place along the drystone wall that bounded the herb beds. The stones were tumbled and the wall in disrepair. Two of the older children straddled the broad rocks where the wall was lowest and lifted the younger ones over one at a time. An elder passed by, bearing a basket and headed toward the garden gate. She gave the children a stern look.

"Mind your feet in the Mother's garden. We'll have no medicines next year an' you trample the ground."

"We will, Grandmother," they all answered, but the looks they passed behind the old woman's back were sly ones.

By the time Meacán had climbed the low wall after the children, their game was well in hand. She sat for a time on the uneven rocks, watching stick swords smite invisible enemies and a tiny, adorable Reochaidh lift pebbles and hurl them to the ground with fierce glee. It made her smile, but it didn't make her feel any braver.

She jumped lightly down from the wall and began to dance into the children's game. The steps were graceful, but the timing odd, a quick jump to a place near as her own thoughts, a long extension of the leg, reaching to a place more distant than the future. Before her eyes the children's imaginings took shape. Cockle, the little make-believe giant, grew to a towering figure at once more enormous than the true Reochaidh and more ingenuous. A muddy battleground swarming with goblins superimposed itself on the patchwork of melting, muddy snow and the winter-worn yellow of the dead grass. The King was there in his chariot, pure gold it was, not merely gilt-edged, and Cessair dashed about on her white steed, felling five goblins with every blow.

It was Cessair that first noticed Meacán. An embarrassed, disappointed look sprang into her eye. The goblins hesitated, and Eoghan's spear started to melt into mist. Meacán called out to them quickly.

"My King! Cessair, Lady of great renown! It is I, Meacán the Dancer, and I must speak to you on a matter of grave importance."

"It's all right, Cockle," said Cessair to a shrinking Reochaidh. Immediately the giant came to full stature again, and flung goblins about as before.

A very young looking Brí with hair red as fire circled Eoghan's chariot about, and Cessair reined in her charger and dismounted. An impossibly gory battle raged about them, and storm-threatening night darkened the sky. Yet, the field was unaccountably illuminated, and the goblins considerably avoided the conference of King, elf, and Wizard.

"The Mother of Midhe has asked an errand of me," Meacán told them solemnly. "I must travel far, and the way is perilous."

"I will go with you!" proclaimed the King.

"No," Brí said firmly. "The King can't leave Midhe unless Midhe goes to war. Cessair can go with her."

"How your generosity eases my burden!" said Meacán. "But the long and the short of it is, Temuir must have your valor, an' she is to win this night. Not yourselves, but one of the Sidhe's noble horses do I desire. 'Tis Eocha I beg of you, Lady of Cnoc an Eanaigh. The steed that returned today."

Cessair knit her brows, but in puzzlement, not refusal.

"The black horse," Meacán reminded her, "the one you brought through the gate with your own."

Cessair's eyes lit. "Arrah, of course!" she said. "He will bear you well."

She turned and walked to a nearby tree that had not been there a moment before. From behind it she gathered reins and drew Eocha out onto the battlefield. He looked proud and fine, but by the time Cessair passed the reins to Meacán, the Dancer had fleshed the steed out with all the detail her more observant eye had noted. Eocha's eyes shone almost as bright as Fiach's, his coat was polished ebony, his step was both light and firm.

"I almost think you might speak to me," Meacán whispered in the beast's ear.

"And so will I, an' I've aught to say."

His voice was deep and throaty, and heartened Meacán still more.

"My thanks, Lady," said Meacán to Cessair as she mounted. "An' you will grant me your protection to the edge of the field . . ."

Cessair swung nimbly up on her own horse, and Brí wheeled Eoghan's chariot about with consummate skill. A dozen goblins attacked as soon as Meacán and her bodyguard started off, but all of them died without much resistance beneath her protectors' spears and bright swords. At the edge of the field the goblins lost interest in them, allowing a moment for a formal farewell.

"*Luck threefold on your journey be,*" said Cessair, "and safe home."

Eoghan howled ferociously, then both turned back to the fighting.

"Quickly, now," Meacán urged Eocha. "North to Márrach."

The elven horse leapt away from the children's daydream, and into Meacán's own thoughts. The rolling fields that bordered Temuir to the east and north passed swiftly under his hooves. At the crest of a far down, the last open knoll before reaching the oak and beech forest that stretched from Temuir's fields to An Bhóinn, Meacán rode suddenly into warm sunlight, and found wildflowers carpeting a green hill. Eocha slowed as he made his way down through the spring grasses on the far slope. A slim, fair-haired girl was there, gathering blossoms into her skirt. Her hair was loose, her feet bare . . . the maid looked up, suddenly aware of Meacán, and her eyes widened with surprise. Meacán had just time to cry, "Liannan!" and the girl was gone.

As soon as the Mother's daydream vanished, winter's flowerless cold once more gripped the hillside. 'Twas a pity to have disturbed so pleasant a vision, Meacán thought. Still, she couldn't resist smiling at the astonishment that had filled Liannan's eyes to see the Dancer come riding an elven steed through the imagined spring of the Queen's faraway youth.

Thirty-six

With owls' feathers and Poets' skulls
My nest is lined.
Nine my nestlings, harsh their calls.
Wingless I fly, songless I scream,
Unbroken, but bridled by morning,
I ride through your dreams.

a riddle

The geography of daydream was unlike any other land's. The world of dreams came closest, but in dream Meacán always knew that the earth under her was made of memory, imagination, and power. In daydream there were moments she forgot where she was—moments when it seemed the real earth was rolling beneath Eocha's pounding hooves, when the sun and air, the clouds and trees were solid and timely enough to be true.

Many times as she journeyed she crossed from her daydreams to those others had made and back again. She suspected she was travelling between the world as she envisioned it and the true Éirinn as well, but never could be sure where the borders lay or when she had crossed a threshold. Like the wind Eocha carried her from season to season, through forests and over streams, through lands familiar and strange. Day and night wrestled each other and passed rapidly by, hills turned to her with broad, green faces and called out, and a child flew over her head like a great bird.

"Not to someone's daydream of Márrach," Meacán said to

Eocha, suddenly concerned that they would miss their destination, "but the place itself we must find."

"An' you fear we will go astray, likely we shall," answered the horse with a snort.

"Sorry."

Meacán fell silent and set her will to controlling her thoughts. For a while it made things worse. The landscape faded in and out as she censored every idea that entered her head.

We're going north to Márrach, she told herself sternly. Eocha knows the way.

Abruptly she found they were in a forest hushed and empty, winter-bound, but without the beauty of snow or the scent of rich damp earth to soften its bitterness. Behind them the path disappeared into a thicket of furze, and before them it ended entirely, running straight into a tall, shadowed, sharp-thorned hedge. The cunning barrier rose like a low battlement, tall enough that even Reochaidh could not have seen over its top, tangled so that the forest beyond it was invisible beyond its thorns.

A murky cloud seemed to cling to the hedge and hold the surrounding air motionless. Meacán looked away, but the oppressive stillness of the forest persisted, as if a storm were brewing. She looked up, but no clouds filled the spaces between the bare branches of the overhanging trees. Neither was there any blue in the sky, only a peculiar murkiness that was neither of night, nor mist, nor any natural thing she could think of.

"Shadow's cloak is tightly drawn about this land," said Eocha quietly.

"We may not have to go closer," Meacán whispered. It felt wrong, somehow, to speak too loudly, to wake whatever dark mind was contemplating this evil dream of a wood. "Let us make our way around the hedge, and hope I can find my friends' daydreams beyond Márrach's borders."

Eocha did as he was asked. He stepped carefully through the pathless bracken and brambles, threading his way through the trees and putting some distance between himself and the hedge. Though they went on for some time, there was no change in the light, no breeze stirred under the forest's roof, not a sound echoed in the wood that they did not make themselves.

"Only a black heart would imagine such a place," said Eocha at last.

Meacán didn't answer at once, but she knew the elven horse was right. What good to have found her way into a daydream of Márrach, if Creathna's visions and Mac Ailch's were hidden behind Shadow's thoughts?

"Perhaps we are searching over the wrong ground," she said finally. "An' you were imprisoned in a place like this, would you not imagine yourself home, or in a time far removed from such sorrow?"

Eocha shook his head and his bridle jingled. "I would imagine myself tearing free of my bonds and o'erleaping this hedge. I would imagine my mistress bringing sword and light to release me. I would imagine trampling my gaolers under my hooves. I would not languish, idly wishing that my misfortunes had never occurred."

Meacán swallowed. "Then we must go in."

Eocha picked his way though tangled vines and over dry, fallen branches until he came to the hedge once more. He continued along it, while Meacán looked for an opening in the wall of thorns. She found one almost immediately.

"Like as not I made it myself," she muttered.

"'Tis useful nonetheless."

Three riders might have passed together through the gap, and though the hedge was dense, its width was less than the length of Eocha's body. Stiff-legged, the horse went on, easily keeping clear of the thrusting thorns. When he was exactly halfway through—his head clear of the hedge but his tail still beyond the thorn wall—suddenly the branches on either side of the gap began to twist and stretch, growing toward each other with incredible speed.

Meacán's breath caught in her throat, freezing the cry that strained to burst from her. She drove her heels into Eocha's side, but the horse's powerful legs were already propelling him forward. As Eocha shot through the leaping, twining trap, something rushed at them, slithering through the dark spaces between the woven branches of the hedge. At first it seemed simply a shadow, gray as a Scáil. As it neared, Meacán glimpsed flaming red, like the eyes of many goblins, and a flash of pale yellow, fangs or talons, opening to grasp and hold. The dusty ground churned under Eocha's hooves—the horse passed the hedge and wheeled to face the threatening thorns. Before them stood a gap, wide enough for three horses to pass abreast.

"I thought . . ."

Meacán stared at the hedge in confusion while her heartbeat slowed and the hairs on her arms and neck gradually relaxed against her skin. If the iron-dark branches of thorns were growing, it was at a natural, undetectable speed. Nor was there any Scáil-gray shadow mingling with the blacker ones the hedge already boasted.

"I thought . . ." she said again, but again found she had no more to say. She felt like a dreamer so badly frightened by a nightmare vision she had come awake, and dispelled the terror by opening her eyes.

"I also saw the hedge closing, and a wraith in the shadows," said Eocha. "But look you—'tis open, it is, and nothing stirs within. I can see the forest beyond."

"This is wrong," Meacán whispered fiercely. "Even if I only imagined the danger, why would it not become truth?"

Eocha shook his head, rattling his bridle, but gave no answer. With a deep, disturbed sigh, Meacán turned him from the hedge, and let him pick a path down into the defile.

At first the forest mimicked the visions the Mother's cauldron had shown the council. The usually smooth skins of tall beeches hung like birch bark from the trunks, sere sheets of peeling, curling wood. The trees looked wounded and sore, and near death from thirst. Thickets of brambles displayed vines withered and shrunken, but their barbs were no less sharp for that. Dense patches of thorny hedge grew all down the slope.

As they descended into the valley, the surrounding wood became less like the place Meacán had seen in the Mother's waters, and more a nightmare of Shadow's design. The dagger-bearing branches of the hedge grew high and dense, blocking the avenues between the trees. They wrapped themselves around trunks and limbs, anchored on rocks and deadfall. Only a short way into the valley, the hedge took complete control of the forest, turning it from a wood to a walled fortress with thorn-lined streets. Eocha no longer chose his path. The pattern of the hedges dictated his steps.

Winding left, then left again, the way was suddenly barred by an impassable barrier of thorn. Awkwardly, Eocha turned and doubled back until they came to a place where two paths divided. On they went, only to meet with similar choices, strange crossroads where hedge met hedge and opened new lanes, dead ends when they made the wrong choice.

"A maze," whispered Meacán to Eocha as they reached the blind end of one such turning. "'Tis the meaning of 'márrach' Reochaidh gave us."

Eocha whinnied sharply and laid his ears back. Meacán looked hurriedly about. There in the warped, leafless branches of the hedge she saw a tatter of gray slipping effortlessly through the mesh of thorns, and caught a glimpse of yellow curving out from the web of smooth wood.

"Can it get out?" she asked nervously.

Beneath her Eocha was as tense as she. He fretted and shied, bringing Meacán uncomfortably close to the hedge.

"Only a cold scent of fear comes from the hedge. Mind it not. The sour stink of goblin is in my nose. Do you not smell them? Goblins in the forest."

To Meacán the woods seemed empty, barren to the point of sterility. It had not been her thought that had brought the red-eyes, of that she was sure. This dream of dusty paths, soul-dead trees, thorn-choked clearings, and silence under the gray skies—this was Shadow's creation. Evil enough it had seemed without Shadow's creatures on their trail. . . .

"Where are they? Behind us? Can we escape them?"

Eocha managed to wheel and leapt away, backtracking until they came to another crossing of paths. He raced down a different passage, broader by far than the last. Meacán gripped the horse's mane, bending low over his neck. Above her the interlaced branches of the forest meshed like a wooden net. Below, the gray undrinking roots of the trees lay like snares in the dust. She glanced at the hedge wall, unable to stop her eyes from straying to its deep shadows, and saw what she dreaded to see—the shadow-beast keeping pace with Eocha. Black emptiness she saw also, and sharp, gray thorns, and—

Meacán gasped involuntarily as a brilliant, breathtaking glint of silver shone through the convoluted web.

"Eocha!" she cried, but the light had faded as quickly as it had sparked. Beside her the smooth, hard branches of the hedge swept by without a hint of light to relieve the shadowed gloom.

The elven horse galloped on, his hooves sure on the treacherous ground, the winding, thorny aisle before him wide and suspiciously welcoming. Meacán sat straighter and peered into the hedge walls. As she hoped, she was rewarded with another glimpse of glorious light, and not even the thought that it might have shone at her will dimmed her excitement.

"There! Eocha! Did you see? More than shadows and ourselves in these drear woods!"

The black horse slowed, then stopped under a high arch of branches. His ears were back, his nostrils flaring.

"True you speak. There is a light in the forest. It calls to me, calls to the wildness that ruled my soul in the days before the Sidhe's gentle hands brought the bridle, and tamed me to their service. But goblins are here, too," he said shifting uneasily, "and a beast in the shadows."

Meacán barely listened to him. Her ears were tuned to the sound of hoofbeats echoing hollowly through the trees, her eyes locked on the shadowy wood. There—the flash of a silver-white star amid the soot-dark web of thorns. Meacán held her breath, waiting, praying to see the light again.

When she did, it was no longer a flickering gleam, nor even a steady blaze. An explosion of white rounded the curve they had just passed. Hurtling down the corridor toward them was a gigantic white elk. Swifter than a stooping falcon he came, his huge, silver-tipped antlers grazing the dark mesh of thorns on either side. He gave Meacán no time to move, to think, to do anything but cry out softly in wonder and joy and sudden terror. Then the beast leapt, easily clearing Meacán's head. He landed softly some twenty paces beyond her, running even as his silver hooves touched the powdery ground. A hollow roar echoed in the domed and leafless canopy overhead, and tree limbs clacked uselessly together, grasping for the fleeing Light.

"Away!" neighed Eocha, digging in his hooves and sprinting after the Stag. "The goblins are behind us, and ourselves caught between hunters and prey!"

The elven steed galloped faster than before, but to Meacán, still breathless from the speed of the Stag's passing, he seemed suddenly slow and heavy-footed. She bent again over Eocha's neck, keeping her weight forward over his shoulders. The walls of twisted thorn spread shadows across the path, and cast confusion into Meacán's mind. Had her own thoughts brought the vision of the Stag to this nightmare forest?

A chill beyond the cold fear of the wood ran down Meacán's spine. The White Stag had not occupied the smallest corner of her mind, not even after she had seen the glitter of his rack through the thorns. It was the false hunter's daydream she was riding through, his evil purpose revealed in the Stag's magnificent flight.

Though their hairy bodies were still hidden by the winding corridors, Meacán could hear the goblins now. Their harsh voices made her shudder. She set her weight back in the saddle and squeezed Eocha between her knees.

"Running is of no avail," she whispered frantically. "'Tis as Eoghan said at the council. A 'márrach' is an enclosure to capture and hold. If the goblins are driving the Stag into a trap, we'll only be trapped ourselves an' we follow behind him."

Eocha whinnied but would not slow. The foul odor of goblin was too strong for him, the sound of their feet on the path too much for his keen ears. Meacán moaned softly, and pulled on the reins. Plain to her now was the design of the maze. This dark passageway, though the broadest of any they had yet tried, was only just wide enough for the enormous sheets of the Stag's spreading antlers. Nor was the passage walled—a thorn-lined tunnel it was through the tortured trees, and never a breach for the Stag to o'erleap the cursed thing and escape his pursuers.

Desperately, Meacán leaned forward again, and spoke in Eocha's ear. "This corridor is wider than the others. Do you understand? Wide, so that the Stag will choose it."

"Where can we go, that the goblins' noses will not sniff us out?" Eocha snorted.

Meacán glanced back over her shoulder. Though there were no goblins visible, she feared it was due to the twists and turns of the path, not the distance they were behind.

Their howls blared like hunting horns, terrifyingly loud and close.

"A real goblin could not miss our scent on the still air," she said, "but how can these imagined monsters be aware of anything their dreamer does not ken?"

She hardly believed what she was saying herself, but at the next turning Eocha wheeled, so suddenly a jutting thorn caught Meacán's skirt, sending a long tear down it and grazing her knee. The horse raced on until he reached the first bend in the new path, then stopped and edged around until he was facing the way he had come. Elven steed though he was, his sides heaved, and he trembled.

Meacán trembled too, listening to the tramp of goblins in the woods. The noise grew louder, then quieter, then louder again, nearly upon them. Eocha started at the sound and stench of the foul beasts, but Meacán patted him, urging him to be quiet. Only the width of the hedge was between the goblins and themselves, but the hedge was thick, and the black-haired hounds still following the Stag. Their red eyes had missed Eocha's hoofprints and the shreds of Meacán's skirt dangling from the hedge. Meacán had spoken true. Ruled by another's imagination, the goblins could but ignore any spoor that would take them from the Stag's trail.

When the sound of the red-eyes had grown faint again, Eocha stepped carefully back down the path to where it intersected the broad corridor the goblins had taken.

"I sense nothing behind us. Only before. Do we follow?" asked Eocha.

So deep into this evil daydream of Shadow's hunt, Meacán thought, surely she could not harbor any hope that here she would find Mac Ailch musing on freedom or Creathna envisioning rescue. Almost she told Eocha to find his way out of the cursed forest.

"Follow," she whispered. "Though I have failed to find our friends, I may yet learn something of value. An' this is the false hunter's dream, I may yet learn our enemy's Name."

Thirty-seven

Betrayal is the evil hardest to See, hardest to credit,
hardest to bear

The Seventh Triad of Éirinn

She kept a loose rein, trusting Eocha to keep a safe distance behind the goblins. He ran swiftly for a while, then slowed to a trot, and finally picked his way step by careful step, pausing before every turn.

At last he stopped.

"Dismount and look yourself around the next curve," he said, so softly it was barely audible. "I think we are come to the end of the path."

Meacán did as she was told, glad to be told, and not to have to think it out for herself. She would have liked to have pressed against the hedge for more cover, but feared to hurt herself on the lethal branches, or worse, to be cut by the shadow-thing that lurked within. Cautiously she knelt in the dust, and leaned forward to see around the turn.

"You are right," she whispered over her shoulder. "Here the forest ends. The bare hill of An Bhrí Mhaol is before us, and on it, a fortress of gray stone—a high battlement and a tall, round tower, a broch, rising behind the walls. The Stag is driven toward it, up the sloping rise. The goblins hound him toward the castle's gate—"

Meacán groaned, then bit her lip and fought to hold in her horror. "A gaping wound is the door to this place, empty, ugly, blacker than night—"

Meacán sucked in her breath sharply as riders came in view, galloping out of the forest from somewhere to her right. They were Scáileanna, cloaked and hooded in shadow-gray mantles. They rode upon black, wild-eyed horses, and among them was one bearing a silver-tipped spear. She could not see his face, for the hood of his mantle covered it. Even so, she knew at once he was no Scáil. Perhaps it was his height, less than that of the imposing shadows that were his companions. Perhaps the way he held himself, loose and relaxed, while the dark elves sat straight as blades in the saddle.

He stops, thought Meacán fiercely. She half closed her eyes, seeing already in her mind the images she wanted to unfold before her. He stops, and reins in while the others ride by. He turns to the forest, surveying his domain. He turns toward me, and I see his face, though he sees me not.

Meacán's will was as great as any of the Seven, her desire to see the false hunter's face a longing more intense than any she had ever held. Though this wrongful hunt through the forest's maze had doubtless been many times rehearsed in the false hunter's mind, still she thrust her own visions against the daydream she beheld, pushing at its edges until at last it wavered.

The man sat back in the saddle and pulled brutally on his reins. The Scáileanna began to pass him by, hurrying to intercept their quarry, but Meacán had no eyes for them, nor for the Stag, now nearly to the castle's gate. Only the false hunter did she see, the dull glitter of gems on his glove where it sawed on the reins, the one Spear glinting in his hand.

Turn, she insisted. Turn to me.

His heel dug into his horse's flank, he yanked the animal's head back and to the left. Then he stopped, stiffened, and held absolutely still. Suddenly he was turning again, and spurring his horse down the slope, but his hood had somehow fallen lower, keeping his face in shadow. He called out sharply to the Scáileanna to follow him. Meacán scrambled to her feet, and hurried to Eocha.

"He is aware of me," she said, swinging up into the saddle.

Eocha turned to flee back into the forest, then reared, pawing the air with his hooves. Meacán gripped him with her knees to keep from falling.

"Steady," she urged. "What—" But then she heard them, goblins howling their bloodthirsty challenge from the thorn-lined corridor.

"Curse their evil eyes!" she swore, and turned Eocha toward the open hill.

Eocha raced to the end of the path, but when he reached its end and the hill was before him, he turned sharply right and galloped along the edge of the wood.

"There!" shouted Meacán, shifting him toward a dark opening in the shadowy trees.

Eocha thundered toward the gap, but already it was narrowing. In moments their escape was choked with tangled, writhing, thorn-laden branches. Still Meacán urged Eocha on, hoping the breach in the hedge would reappear as it had done once before. When they were nearly upon it, Eocha lifted his front hooves and neighed shrilly. The entrance was locked by a wall of dead beeches and perilous thorns.

Eocha spun about, looking for another opening. There was none to be seen, and the Scáileanna were closing. There were more of them now than a moment ago, and goblins were spewing from the castle's dark mouth onto the field. Their backs to the closed wood, Meacán and Eocha were hemmed by an ever-tightening ring of foes. Foremost among them was the hooded hunter.

Fighting her panic, Meacán bent her thought on the man who held the Spear in his hand.

A breath of wind, she demanded. Just a small breath of wind. He makes it himself as he rides. The air catches under his hood and blows it back.

The effort of will drained Meacán's strength. She reeled in the saddle as a faint breeze drifted by her. It skimmed over the narrowing gap between herself and the false hunter, swept under his hood, and drew it gently back over his head.

The false hunter ground his horse to a halt and met Meacán's horrified stare with a mild frown. Every aspect of his appearance was familiar, from the jewelled gloves on his hands, to the straight, black hair falling to his shoulders, to the single white lock in his long, silken beard. Only the corrupt twist at the corner of his mouth and the chilling gleam in his frost-blue eyes were strange to her.

"Mac Ailch," she said, her voice flat with the bitterness of betrayal.

The Conjuror's frown evaporated. He laughed and brought his horse close to hers.

"I had prepared a welcome for you, Dancer. But at the real Márrach, I'm saying, not this imagined fancy of mine. Are you lost, then? What, has the Mother not sent you armed with one of Tadhg the Toad's paltry verses, in hopes that you had the will to tear the illusion from my walls? Sure, an' I would have wagered much on that being her strategy."

His composure was nearly seamless. Meacán was dismayed by how well he was handling the appearance of an uninvited guest to his private daydream. She might have despaired, but when he had done speaking, Mac Ailch's eyes narrowed for an instant, and took on a vague, distant look. Next moment they were sharp again, and blue as ever. Meacán kept her face still, but a frail hope bloomed in her breast.

"You'd have lost, then," she answered him. She tried to bring some arrogance to her tone, but wasn't sure how well she was succeeding. "Instead I came by less well trod trails. I am here in your thoughts, Mac Ailch the Traitor. You only think yourself here. Best wake from your daydream and prepare to meet the Mothers' host."

A flicker of doubt crossed Mac Ailch's face. It was quickly replaced by an expression of contempt. "I am not such a fool as you suppose, Meacán the Lame. You think you have uncovered my secrets, but you are far wrong, my darling. Almost I am tempted to let you return to Temuir, that you might learn to your sorrow how little this dance has gained you. But, alas, it is not to be."

His lips drew into a Scáil's serene smile. "As you say, Dancer, I am not here, only my thought. But you have come as a living woman to this daydream of mine. And if I imagine I have killed you, so must you die."

He lifted a hand from his reins and waved his gloved fingers—how many times had Meacán watched him conjure so, and thought it little better than a juggler's trick? With his movement the Spear vanished. In its place was a sword, stormcloud-gray and insubstantial as smoke. She should have doubted its ability to harm anything, but when he brought his arm back, the shifting, intangible shadow-blade moved through the air swift as a King's sword. Meacán sat paralyzed, watching her death descend.

Meacán was no warrior, but Eocha was a warrior's steed. As the blade arced down, he reared and spun on his hind legs. Instinctively, Meacán gripped his mane to keep from falling. Barely a hand's breadth from her clenched fingers the shadow sword fell, the dark-misted edge of the sorcerous blade vanishing into Eocha's neck.

The horse's scream wrenched Meacán's heart. Black mane, dark coat peeled back from the fell blade, red blood and muscle, and white bone erupted from the wound.

Meacán jerked her feet free of the stirrups and thrust herself out of the saddle as Eocha fell and rolled. She landed awkwardly, nearly falling herself. Yet, as soon as her feet were on the ground, Meacán was once more the Dancer. The horrible weapon was coming at her again, but she closed her eyes and Saw the stones of Temuir's wall, the archer's slit where she had watched the end of the goblins' attack. Her dance was swifter than the blade's deadly stroke—she whirled under Mac Ailch's arm, and out of his evil dreams.

Sensing the hard stones of Temuir under her boots, she took a shuddering breath and loosed the scream she had denied herself in Márrach. It was the voice of horror, the mate of Eocha's death cry. A wracking shiver swept through her body.

Opening her eyes, she leaned weakly against the wall and shook her head to clear the darkness from her sight. Had she come back before dawn, to the murky light before the sunrise? Shadows lay so heavy on the battlefield, on the bodies . . .

Meacán stared out at the village. Bodies, pieces of bodies were strewn everywhere under a voracious blanket of dark-feathered crows. Human bodies she saw, mortal remains. And there, a splintered wheel and part of the shattered rim of Eoghan's gilt-edged chariot. But she had seen it brought within the walls—

It's not real, she told herself fiercely, but she dared not turn, dared not look behind her to what the streets of Temuir might hold. The goblins are destroyed and Temuir safe. I have missed my holdfast. I have missed my holdfast, no more.

No more, her mind echoed. No more than I feared, no more than I dreaded. No more than the worst that could have befallen. Better to be dead than—

Clenching her teeth against her terror, Meacán drove the thought of defeat from her mind and put another image in its place. Her sanctum in Sliabh Mis, her home. So dear, so familiar, the beginning and end of so many journeys.

She stepped off lightly, but even before she arrived she could feel she was not on balance. She glided into a dismal ruin, long abandoned, long ago destroyed. With a cry of despair, Meacán fled the daydream, and found herself in another. She was on the shore below Dún na nGall, and though it was dark, neither night nor storm was the cause. Billowing smoke rose from behind the fort's walls and spread across the sky, suffocating the light.

Meacán spun wildly away, her thoughts in chaos. No matter the image she held in her Sight, every holdfast was rooted in the Dark, every threshold an illusion. For all that she might try to dance, she could only stagger blindly through the Shadow King's mind.

PART 8

the hag

Thirty-eight

Neither give cherries to a pig,
nor advice to a fool

Sayings of the Mothers

An icy drop fell from the cave roof onto Reathach's bald head. Before he could brush the culprit from his skin, a second drop followed the first. With an offended squawk the púca hopped away and ensconced himself in another of the cave's many nooks, furiously batting at his spattered pate with his hands.

"'Tis more than I can bear," he raged, "this dripping, wet, miserable hovel! What but a fish-eating fulmar would choose to abide in a hole on the seaward side of a limestone cliff? An' you are set on seein' the Hag again, a currach you need, as I've said oft-times before. That, or you must dare try Fiach's rann again."

A wry smile touched Blackthorn's lips. He was squatting before a smoky fire, a small pile of wood and straw set just within the mouth of the cave, and rolling handfuls of long grass between his palm and his thigh.

"And how many weeks will be lost this time, should Manannán's swan bear us over the waves?" He added a few more brownish stalks to his bundle and twined them with the others. "An' she wants her prize, she'll send for us, I'm thinking. If not . . ."

With a few more deft twists he tightened the strands of
his grass rope, looped the end, and secured the noose.

"If not you'll cast your rope out upon the sea, snare Inis
na Linnte, and pull the magic isle to Éirinn's shore," finished the púca dourly.

Before the Hunter had seen Domhnall's Keep, thought
Reathach, he'd have laughed to hear such dry, sarcastic wit.
Now the twice-cursed fool could only sigh and hang his head.

"Lift your eyes to the truth," the púca urged. "Is it your
fault the geis fell on you? She should have warned you, she
should, an' Domhnall's star so dear to her! Glad you'd have
been to fulfill your bargain and give the Hag her due. But
you can't part with the Talisman now, bodach. Nor can you
ever, not without destroyin' yourself entirely."

When Blackthorn had come down from the sunlit summit of Keeper Hill, his newly acquired geis had been plain
to the púca's astonished Sight. Though now huddled in one
of many dimly lit, wind-carved recesses riddling Aillte an
Mhothair, Reathach could See the spell as clearly as he had
ten mornings past—a flaming glory of light knotted tightly
about the Hunter's heart.

"You've a bond with the silver star 'twould shatter your
soul to break," the little man said in a hushed voice. "The
Talisman's a part of you now, there's no denyin', and will be
till death takes it from you."

The púca's eyes narrowed, and he went on more softly
still. "Sure, an' even could you put Domhnall's star in the
Hag's crooked claw, I'd wager a King's mantle the wrinkled
old woman has neither power nor desire to grant your wish.
An' you must break your bargain and keep the star for yourself, what reason is there at all, at all for makin' this loathsome voyage? Another way we'll find to your Spear, and a
better one."

The struggling flames of Blackthorn's pitiful fire smoked
in the wet and sputtered in the wind. Though its maker
stared intently at the feeble blaze, Reathach was sure the
Hunter was blind to it entirely. For once, the púca flattered
himself, Blackthorn was giving his words due consideration,
as well he ought. Sounder advice had ne'er been given.
Suppressing a smug smile, the púca watched his companion
out of the corner of his eye and held his breath.

At last Blackthorn rose, wound the rope at his belt, and nodded.

"I've had my fill of mussels, and the grebes have likely gone inland, what with the coming of spring. An' I find poor hunting at the shore, I'll over the cliffs to the scrogs beyond, and snare us woodcock or snipe for our supper."

Reathach's breath exploded from his lungs, followed by a well-aimed, if inadequately launched, wad of spit.

"You'd prefer hare?" Blackthorn asked calmly.

"I'd prefer you take your stinkin' black sword, your tarnished star, and your empty head, and throw each and every one of them off this filthy wet cliff and into the sea, I would! Was ever a creature ill-used as I? A pity it is, and unjust entirely I should be obliged to save your life, and yourself the saddest excuse for a mother's son it's ever been my misfortune to meet!"

The púca's tirade was delivered on a single breath. He paused for another to continue, but before he had drawn it fully into his lungs, a bright-eyed magpie darted under the roof of the cave. Swooping low, she settled neatly on Blackthorn's shoulder. Her white feathers were crusted yellow, the black ones damp and dull from the salt spray. She ruffled her plumage in annoyance.

"Hsst! 'Ware! 'Ware you great gawk!"

Blackthorn inclined his head toward the púca's frantic whisper.

"*One for sorrow*, don't you know," Reathach groaned. "Och, wurra, wurra, wurra, but it's from bad to worse, an' a púca must keep company with such a cursed and sorry fool."

The little man flattened himself against the rough, damp wall, pasted a sick smile across his face, and saluted the magpie with elaborate deference.

"Whisht, fairest of crows, sweet-voiced beauty," he wheedled. "Lost your way, you have, darlin'. Neither you nor I can find comfort here. Over the cliffs and into the woods—there you'll find your home. Off with you now, mo mhúirnín! Off with you!"

He waved a desultory hand in a vain effort to shoo the bird away. The magpie only blinked a sceptical eye, then turned her attention to Blackthorn. Cocking her head, she pecked lightly at the silver chain about his neck, let out an imperious *chuk*, then pecked at it again.

With one hand Blackthorn obediently withdrew the star from under his shirt. The other he presented to his guest, and when she accepted the invitation, brought his arm even with his chest, that she might study the Talisman to her heart's content.

"Hsst! Whisht, you fool!" said the púca, alternately mincing away from the wall to catch Blackthorn's eye, and scooting back to it when he feared he had caught the magpie's. "Biddin' her go, you should be, not encitin' her to stay! Think you when you've won her favor, you can climb on her back and she'll fly you to Inis na Linnte? Best save your wishes for a currach, and keep your star well hidden!"

As the magpie turned her head this way and that, examining the silver pentacle from every angle, Blackthorn stroked her sodden feathers with patient fingers, freeing them from the binding wet of the ocean's winds. She accepted his preening long after she was done with her inspection, but when the gloss had returned to her wings, she suddenly opened her mouth and made a stab at the Talisman. Blackthorn leaned back and stretched his arm before him— the magpie's beak clicked shut on the empty air.

Immediately she raised her wings, flapping them noisily, and chided her host with the rapid and varied flurry of chatter only a magpie can command. Next moment she was airborne, soaring from the cave into the cloudless day and out over the sea.

"Little thief!" Reathach shouted after her, though not so loudly that she might hear.

"And didn't I tell you?" he demanded, turning to the Hunter. "Didn't I warn you to keep the star under your shirt?"

Abruptly his mood shifted, and his brow furrowed into a field of worry. "Unnatural, unnatural entirely for a magpie to go winging west," he muttered, "and only the endless swells beneath her."

Prodded by a succession of drops oozing from the limestone onto his back, Reathach parted from the protection of the wall and crept to Blackthorn's side.

"Plain it is whose creature she is, Hunter of Éirinn," he whispered. "Sent by the Hag, sure and certain, to rob you of your Talisman—to snatch it from your throat and bring it to her mistress. Can you anymore doubt the old crone means to break her bargain?"

Blackthorn stood quietly, following the magpie's flight with his eyes.

"Birds of omen, magpies are," he said, not in answer to the púca, but to himself, "and as like to herald good fortune as bad." A smile touched the corners of his mouth. "And I've seen this bird before, I'm thinking."

For a moment the púca was too appalled to do more than blink.

"Good fortune?" he sputtered when he could speak again. "Is it good fortune you think the Hag will be sending you now her bird has failed to steal the star? An' you want the Talisman for yourself, we must away from here, you purblind idiot—"

Blackthorn turned sharply, and the púca stumbled back, trembling at the dark and terrible, and all too familiar fire glinting in the Hunter's eye.

"Want it?" Blackthorn rasped. "Want the geis-laden, ensorcelled thing? It's my Spear I'm wanting, and this to have been the price for it!"

He lifted the Talisman from his throat as if he would tear it from him and hurl it over the edge of the cliff as Reathach had earlier exhorted him to do. Slowly his fingers closed about the little star, and his burning gaze grew cold.

"'Then may your three geasa grind you to meal between them,'" he said, turning his face once more to the wind and sea. "Do you remember your words? Only two do I bear, yet their weight is crushing."

Reathach winced as the curse he had so unthinkingly uttered came back to reproach him.

"Is it puttin' the blame on me you are for the burdens you're fated to carry?" he blustered. "And didn't I warn you the second geis was lyin' in wait beyond the shadowed grave?"

"And so much good did your warning do me, here am I, my soul tangled in Domhnall's ancient spell, and myself about to break the bargain that would have won me my Spear!"

Blackthorn's lips twisted into an apologetic smile. "But I mean no offense," he said with mock contrition. "Eager I am

for your advice. Sure, an' a púca of your vast experience and
bold cunning must know a thousand ways to soothe the
Hag's fury and court her favor."

"Cherries to a pig," the púca replied. "But sure, an' I've
made up me mind to share me wisdom with you one last
time, for an' you go to the Hag, fool that you are, she'll kill
you for certain. I'll be savin' your life, I will, an' you'll listen
to me. Flee these cliffs before the magpie reaches Inis na
Linnte. That's my advice. An' you follow it, you'll be safe
from the Hag's vengeance, and meself free of this excruci-
atin' weight that troubles me soul."

An impeccable stillness came over the Hunter where he
stood gazing west, the coiled tension of cat ready to spring.

"You think we should leave?" he said softly.

"Now and at once."

"So," Blackthorn nodded, moving swiftly into action.
"Now and at once."

He stamped out the dull embers that remained to his fire,
swept Strife from where he had set her against the wall, and
bound the blade across his back. The púca watched the
Hunter's performance with a look of stupefied relief.

"By the light that shines!" he breathed. "And where to, me
champion? Lios Dúin Bhearna we could easily make by
nightfall, and where better to bide in these dark times than a
sturdy fort?"

"Lios Dúin Bhearna?" the Hunter echoed incredulously.
"Why 'tis the ruins of Lios Chanair we're bound for, and then
down to the bay, where once I sang Fiach's rann to the sea."

Reathach's delighted expression hardened into crisscrossed lines of suspicion. "It's curious I am to know why
you've a sudden longin' to return to that narrow, wind-
blown, sea-wet spit of sand."

"Because, my brave and clever mouseen, by the time we
get there, the answer to your question will be waiting for us
on the strand."

"What question? I asked no question!"

"Och, but you did! 'Is it good fortune you think the Hag
will be sending you now her bird has failed to steal the star?'
Your own words, every one. And my answer? Well, it's
thinking I am the Hag will be sending a currach for to take
us both to Inis na Linnte."

The púca looked where the Hunter pointed. To his profound and bitter disappointment, he saw a long, light currach scudding swiftly over the waves. A bit south of the cliffs the empty boat sailed, steering toward the high head. An' it kept to its course, and Reathach had no reason to think it wouldn't, the enchanted craft would surely come to shore below the ruins of Lios Chanair.

Too depressed even to bandy insults, he shifted to a mouse and drew himself into an apathetic ball on the cave floor. When another drop of icy water plopped onto his head, painting his brown fur black and plastering it against his skull, the púca didn't even bother to shake it off. By An Daghdha, 'twas a cruel, wet world. More than he could bear.

Thirty-nine

Never leave the fox
in charge of the geese

Sayings of the Mothers

All morning the Hunter rowed, and past day's noon, until his stroke brought them into a fogbank. The sun was stranded beyond a roof of cloud so low it touched the surface of the sea, and the color of the swells cooled from the green of Scáthach's eyes to a solemn gray. Blackthorn's arms and back were aching, his brow hot despite the cold ocean mists. He rowed blind through the clinging billows and veils, and at last his currach broke through the gray curtain into a world of high clouds and sunlight. Looking over his shoulder, he saw a white-gold beach glimmering in welcome, and a towering, green-carpeted mountain rising beyond.

His toil was eased as the currents carried his boat to shore, and the waves helped him draw the boat onto the strand. He took his sword from the craft first, drying it carefully, and securing it across his back. Next he lifted the púca out, and bore him higher up the beach. Gently laying the little man on the dry sands, Blackthorn knelt down beside him and started to chafe the shape-shifter's hands.

"I'm not cold, you daft fool," Reathach scolded weakly. "I'm wet. Through and through."

"Then open your eyes, and see the dry isle to which we've come."

One of Reathach's eyes cracked open just enough for a quick glimpse of white clouds and blue-gold sky, then quickly snapped shut again.

"Lovely," he croaked. "I'll enjoy it while I can, before the Hag kills us with one of her foul sorceries, eliminatin' my ability to take pleasure in the world."

"I'll strike another bargain with her," the Hunter said, but Reathach wasn't fooled.

"You've no idea at all, at all how to face her," he declared. "But I have, and if you've ears to hear with, you'll heed the advice I'm goin' to give you."

"I'll not be needing—" Blackthorn began, but the little man ignored the interruption.

"Destroy her with your Talisman, before she destroys us."

Blackthorn's brows lifted in feigned admiration. "A terrible fine plan, that. Kill the one creature in the world who can help me to my Spear! Now there's advice your wits must have labored over."

"Humble her, then," the púca argued, his voice stronger, though he lay as limp as before. "Call flame to her isle as you did to Domhnall's Keep. She'll grant your wishes soon enough. An' it's in her power. Which I doubt."

"You're an ignorant rascal," Blackthorn said pleasantly, "and your advice as sensible as putting the fox in charge of the geese."

Groaning with the effort, Reathach raised himself onto a bony elbow. "So, 'twas lyin' you were again, Hunter of Éirinn, when you boasted of calling magic fire to the Keep! And didn't I doubt your tale even as the words fell from your tongue—"

"Och, you're ever ready to doubt the truths I utter, ever ready to credit my lies! Fire I called, and flames answered me. But having so done, never can I summon that magic again, unless and until I bathe the star in the fires of Samhain, when the world stands once more at winter's gate."

The púca dropped back onto the sands. "Wurra, wurra, now there's a desperate pity. Here you must deny the Hag her due, and for what? For a glint of silver that's as worthless to you as a bow without an arrow."

Blackthorn's hand stole to the hidden star, and a sly smile lifted the corner of his mouth. "Well, not worthless entirely," he said.

Reathach's eyes slitted open and gleamed. "Och, you devious creature! Not such a fool as you look, then. And what other power can you call forth from that tangle of metal? Something fearsome, I wager, something to daunt the warty old woman who rules this place?"

Blackthorn's smile faded. Reathach groaned again, then suddenly opened his eyes completely and stared unblinking into the sun.

"Why, clear as a rain-washed sky it is!" he cried. "Give her the star, fulfillin' your bargain, and then"—the púca honked like a goose—"take it back!"

"The wonder of it all is," said Blackthorn thoughtfully, "that I stop to listen when you open your mouth. Sure, an' nothing but foolishness ever comes out of it. How am I to get the star back once it's in her hand? And should she take the Talisman to her hand in truth," he shuddered and spat, "how am I to bear her hideous touch on my soul? A gift I need, great as the one I deny her."

"A poem."

"What?"

"A poem, I'm sayin', for who in all the world is not pleased by the gift of a rann?"

Blackthorn laughed. "And where am I to find the Poet to make it?"

"Well, an' there's no Poet to hand," Reathach answered with excessive patience, "you'll have to make it yourself."

Blackthorn rolled his eyes heavenward. "A grand verse that will be."

"Quick you are to scorn my counsel," the púca fumed, hoisting himself back onto his elbow, "though little good you've done yourself by followin' your own!"

Blackthorn took a quick breath, but instead of using it for a sharp retort, he released it slowly, and turned to study the woods.

"An' you're fit enough to travel, to a mouse, now," he said, "and I'll bear you in my sack. It'll not endear me to the Hag an' I keep her waiting."

Surprised by Blackthorn's mildness, Reathach debated

whether it would be better to retire from the field having dealt the last blow, or whether he should follow up his advantage with a few choice insults. In the end he settled on the first and complied with the Hunter's wishes, meekly sequestering himself in the sack.

Best save me strength, he told himself, burrowing into the soft leather. I'll need it, I will, for the terrible battle to come.

As Blackthorn had guessed on his first visit, there was a path at the edge of the strand, leading away into the trees. Whitethorn and hornbeam, poplar and sloe vied with each other to cover the mountain's toes, but higher up the slope was forested in oak and chestnut, ash groves, stands of rowan, and thickets of holly, hazel, crab apple, and whortle-berry. The track was completely overgrown, sporting clumps of burdock and boneset, furled brackens, nettles, and spread-ing patches of pimpernel.

Eyes less keen than Blackthorn's would not have been able to pick out the path at all, but to the Hunter it was the best of roads, cunning, generous, kind underfoot. It imparted both the pleasure of roving and the challenge of stalking, though this was no idle ramble, and his only quarry was the path's end.

The song of a noisy stream was in Blackthorn's ears long before he could see plunging white waters between the sturdy trunks of the alders and the drooping limbs of the willows that lined its banks. Across a rushing, roaring, many-tiered cascade the path led, then up again, through a clearing rife with gentian and snowdrops already waking to spring. Then back to the stream and across it once more, where the waters swirled around huge granite boulders and pooled in deep cauldrons before flowing on down the mountain.

Once past the pools, the path kept to the right of the stream. The clean scent of the rushing water was his with every breath Blackthorn took, its roaring inextricably min-gled with the songs of the thrush, the whistle of the merry starling, the blackbirds' liquid trills and screeching chatter. With the sun still high, the path was a dappled wonder of emerald and gold. It twined through the quickbeams and oaks and under the chestnuts' spreading boughs. Mints clung to the stream's moist banks, and cress and sorrel, and early, silver-backed leaves of mugwort were starting to uncurl from their narrow stalks. The half-seen sweep of a hart's flank through the far trees made Blackthorn's pulse quicken, a glimpse of a gray-brown wolf in pursuit made it pound. Hearing the racket of a boar breaking through the foliage and his hoofbeats dully echoing on the forest floor, Blackthorn nearly gave chase. Were it not that he preferred to hunt boar with spear, the reason he had come to these woods would surely have slipped from his mind.

The path pulled briefly away from the stream, dallying for a moment in the deeper woods. Pausing within a circle of beeches, Blackthorn was instantly bombarded with the raucous complaints of a colony of rooks nesting in the tall trees' arms. Indignantly they contested his right to stop so near to their home, but he had to stop, to smell the rich earth, to fill his ears with the music of the greenwood, to rest his eyes on the shafts of light and sweet shades of the forest . . . here was a path to ease the heart, a path to walk away a man's sorrows.

Reathach poked his head out of the pouch, his nose twitching madly. He got free of the sack and clambered to the ground, rising to a man as soon as his toes touched grass.

"Marvellous," he crowed, and Blackthorn had to smile at the childlike glee in the púca's voice. "Marvellous it is entirely. And a great wrong that such a forest should be the domain of the foul and pestilent Hag. And isn't it truth I'm speakin'?"

"In Tír na nÓg," Blackthorn replied, "'tis said there's a hall where the greatest champions dwell. Everything is to a warrior's liking—chariots, horses, armor, arms. A great plain surrounds the dún, and there each day the battles rage. By night mead and ale overflow the hall, and the tables groan under the weight of the feast set upon them."

Glancing down, Blackthorn saw the púca gazing up openmouthed, caught once more by his love of a good tale.

"All the warriors of Éirinn hope their deaths will earn them a place in that hall. But an' death is kind to hunters," he said looking about him, "'tis here their souls will find welcome."

A distant thunder, water falling not in descending stairs but in a long drop to a deep pool, tickled at the back of

Blackthorn's hearing and grew steadily louder as they went
on. Unexpectedly the path broke free of the forest's undergrowth and deposited Blackthorn and Reathach at the base
of the falls, a jumble of rock almost hidden by incessant
sheets of plummeting water. A cistern spread out below the
stones. Silver trout slipped in and out of the broad bands of
tremulous light that fell in broken shafts through tree
branches and pierced the clear waters.

"'Tisn't possible, you know," the púca said offhandedly.

Blackthorn raised his brows.

"'Tisn't possible, I'm sayin', for a great river to be hurtlin'
off the top of a mountain, and not so much as a snowflake up
there for to be meltin'."

Blackthorn studied the tightly bunched waters as they
poured unceasingly through a narrow cleft in the mountain's
peak now not far above them. With his eyes he followed the
spreading veil until it folded onto the rocks, then leapt into
rainbowed fountains, and finally rained down upon the cistern in long, tattered, white ribbons.

"It's not a mountain," he said pointedly. "It's a wizard's
sliabh."

A sudden shadow grayed the white curtain of water, a
solitary cloud obscuring the sun. Saddened, Blackthorn
turned away. The afternoon was hurrying by, and every passing moment promised the Hag would be less likely to forgive
what he was about to do.

A fresh spoor upon the damp green of the path height-
ened Blackthorn's sense of impending disaster. The pawprint
of a large wolfhound he saw, and farther on, bent grasses and
scored earth made Dearg's recent passage all the more plain.
Despite his resolution to make haste, Blackthorn slowed as
the path climbed steeply beside the falls, then eased away
and ran level, hugging the side of a subtly curved and totally
unexpected meadow. The sodden brown of winter covered
the mounded field, but a fine dusting of new green lay
between the blades of yellowed grasses, and the wind was
redolent with the odor of moist, living earth.

The track led Blackthorn in a circle around the grassy
field, then headed back toward the water, keeping close to
the line of trees. As he made the turn at the far end of the
clearing, a small herd of dun deer stopped their grazing

among the thistles and lifted their heads. At his next step
they fled, scrabbling up the steep mountainside into the
sheltering firs and pines, and startling a pair of dippers from
the trees. The birds darted past the Hunter on their way to
the falls, calling out to him in their strange, clinking voices.

Blackthorn gave neither the deer nor the dippers a second
glance. With the rise of the meadow out of the way, the
long, low arch of a cave entrance on the wooded slope was
plain to his sight.

Keeping his footfalls soft, he went on until he spied Dearg
standing in the darkened doorway. The hound looked ferociously proud to be guarding the cave. His massive head was
high, his stance stiff and commanding. He put his nose in
the air and barked once. A strangled whimper answered the
hound, and a frantic rustling in the grass. Blackthorn guessed
that the púca had decided he would have a better chance
evading Dearg's notice as a furred mouse than as a naked old
man.

He was wondering whether he should call out a greeting
or wait to be greeted, when the dog suddenly pricked his
ears, wheeled, and disappeared into the cave. Cautiously
Blackthorn crept up to the entrance. More cautiously he
bent his head and walked under the arch.

He paused to let his eyes adjust to the change in light,
though he realized at once the cave was not as dark as it had
appeared from beyond the shadowed doorway. To
Blackthorn's left, the western wall was not bounded by
stone, but by torrents of water—the cataract Blackthorn had
studied from the trout-filled pool below. A jutting slab of
stone grazed the underside of the falls, diverting a small
trickle onto the shelf, where it pooled before running down
the slanted rock and rejoining the rest of the waters.
Daylight penetrated the translucent curtain and filled the
cave with a quiet, misted glow.

The pale scent of drying herbs wafted from the shadows to
his right—rosemary, sage, chamomile, and marjoram were
sweetest, but the mugwort and mint he had discovered on
the trail were here, too, their pungency muted and mingled
with the more bitter perfumes of boneset, horehound,
betony, and rue.

The greater detail his eyes took in, the more amazed

Blackthorn became. No barren shelter, nor even a cozy den, the cave was a dwelling to rival a Queen's hall. The chamber could easily host a hundred. Like the Spell-Maker's sanctum, it was round, and its ceiling was a high dome. Unlike Domhnall's Keep, the cave shunned opulent design, instead following the dictates of simple necessity and natural beauty.

The center of the chamber was a shallow bowl filled with white sands and surrounded by a slate floor. The stone-rimmed basin was a wonder of wizardry—it was round, the encompassing slate having been hewn in a perfect circle, defying the rock's natural bias. At the northern end of the circle, exactly opposite Blackthorn, a low-backed chair was set above the sands on a raised slate step. Perched on an arm of the chair was a bright-eyed, long-tailed magpie.

To his right, a hollow, chimney-shaped flute of rock rose to the cave ceiling. Looking closer, Blackthorn saw it was a chimney indeed. A quiet, amber fire burned steadily in the stalactite's open belly. The herbs scenting the air he saw dry-ing near the fireplace—bunches of leaves and stems heaped upon racks of latticed willow that were wedged between two small hiccoughs of stone. Nearby were a long table, and benches, and a sideboard littered with bowls, spoons, and an assortment of nuts and dried fruits.

A sudden fetor dispelled the herbs' sweet perfumes. Though she'd somehow masked her step, the Hag's stench announced her presence as loudly as if horns had been winded and drums beat. Blackthorn forced his eyes to follow his nose to the far end of the cave. The magpie was gone, and the Hag enthroned upon the chair. When she saw Blackthorn turn to her, she graced him with a grotesque smile.

"Give it me," she said.

Forty

The hart, he loves the high wood
The hare, he loves the hill
The King, he loves his bright sword
The Lady loves her will

A credulous fool he'd been, Blackthorn berated himself, to have thought the omens fair. What though the Hag's magpie had charmed his heart? What though her currach had been seaworthy? What though Inis na Linnte itself had welcomed him like a fond lover? Fixed in the glare of the Hag's good eye, forced to endure her voice and her smile, Blackthorn could no longer harbor even the faintest hope that the old woman might listen to him with a kindly ear.

He started slowly across the sands. With each dilatory step he discarded another of the stories he had considered using to soften the Hag's heart. He couldn't say he didn't have the star—she had sent the currach because she knew he did. An' she were easier to gull, he'd tell her the Talisman was cursed, but the avaricious glitter in the Hag's gaze made it plain that a mere threat of danger wouldn't move her. He could spin a tale of greater treasures to be had, and all to be hers, an' she'd leave him the Talisman. In his heart he knew that could he lay all the works of craft and power ever glorified in song at the Hag's feet, she would spit upon the lot of them.

Her good eye never left him, but the nearer he came, the more trouble Blackthorn had meeting it. His gaze strayed to right where a woven cloth hung like a door between two stalactites, to the left where the shallow pool of water swirled—anywhere but upon her hideous visage. He had not forgotten that she was ugly, but even the most vivid memories pale beside the immediacy of experience. Blackthorn's eyes, his nose, his ears betrayed him—he could come no nearer.

Though still a half dozen paces from the old woman, he unbound his sword from his back, knelt, and laid Strife on the ground before her. The Hag's all but toothless smile shriveled and her good eye flamed. She waited for Blackthorn to speak, but for once he was reticent to trust his tongue. All his lies lay strewn behind him in the sands—he had nothing left to tell her but the truth.

"Grandmother," he said quietly, "my sword is at your feet. I will carry it wherever you command, seek whatever gifts of might or magic your heart may desire, until death takes me. Or myself will place Strife in your hand to have my life of me, if my death will please you more than my service. Only let me fulfill my geis, and I swear I will serve your will the rest of my days. Not for myself do I ask this, but for the sake of all Éirinn I plead."

"Greedy beggar." The Hag's voice grated with frustration. "Give it me!"

Blackthorn looked straight into her eye. "I cannot," he said simply.

The Hag flew to her feet, her malformed body already swelling with rage. Her mouth opened. From the gaping, red-and-black maw came a sound of pain, of murderous fury. A yellow-green orb of sulphurous light was suddenly in her palm, then roaring through the air.

Though Blackthorn had started to his feet even as the Hag did, not even the Hunter of Éirinn was swifter than the old woman's sorcerous ball. It slammed into his side, exploding into acrid fumes. The blow lifted him from the ground and hurled him down, knocking the air out of him, but leaving him nothing wholesome to breathe. Gasping and retching, he struggled to rise, only to meet with a second blast of foul air. It hit him hard, like a giant's fist, throwing him against the slate rim of the bowl with such force the rock cut through his shirt and into his chest. Blood welled up from the long, shallow gash.

Ignoring the sting of his wound, Blackthorn tried once more to regain his feet. His eyes wept from the caustic fumes, but worse was the sour blackness from within threatening to overpower him. He pulled as much air as he could into his paralyzed lungs, fighting to stave off unconsciousness. When at last his vision cleared, he found himself near the edge of the sands on his knees before the Hag. A third sphere was glowing in her gnarled hand.

"Cannot?" she was screaming at him. "Cannot? Or will not?"

"Cannot." His voice was a hoarse whisper, and he feared she'd not heard him. He gasped in some air and tried again. "I cannot, Grandmother."

The Hag moved swiftly, smoothly toward him, skimming over the sands as if her feet were not touching the ground. Instinctively Blackthorn pulled himself back and away. He managed to scramble only to the rim of the bowl, and her fetid breath was in his face, her pocked and blistered fingers grasping his shirt.

"What hinders you, unfortunate man?" she asked, spittle foaming on her lips.

He arched his head back, but there was no air to breathe that was not tainted by her dirt and decay and the noxious ball. Coughing violently, he tried to pull her hand from his shirt, shuddering at the coarseness of her scaly skin. He felt her long fingers loosen, and hauled himself up onto the stone floor, putting as much distance between himself and the Hag as he could. Only an arm's length from the creature he felt warm breath on his neck, and heard Dearg's warning growl.

"Let me tell you," he entreated.

"Yes," she sneered, an evil light glinting from under the sagging lid of her blind eye. "Tell me why you must break our bargain."

Reathach's half-witted suggestion to give the Hag a poem looked no more promising to Blackthorn now than it had hours ago on the strand. Still, what else had he to offer her? An' a rann could bring even a drop of mercy to the Hag's pitiless heart, he'd be far better off than he was now.

Slowly, to give himself time to find words to fit the meter, and softly, as he was unable to bring much sound from his sore throat and ravaged lungs, Blackthorn began to chant.

> Dark was the door to Domhnall's Keep,
> Silent the stones and secret ways.
> Tales have told of treasures rare,
> Swords that sing and gleaming gold —
>
> Found I the fortunes the fables promise?
> Naught but a necklace beneath a stone.
> In haste, for I heard the howl of death,
> Bane of brave men, Domhnall's doom,
>
> Swift the silver star I grasped,
> Then froze, the foul foe unheeding,
> Unresisting, surrendered to spell of old.
> Ensnared, ensorcelled by Wizard's weird,
>
> Long I lingered in lands unknown
> Whilst magic molded man to charm.
> In time I returned. Terror awaited.
> Enemy axes, raised in wrath
>
> Glistened and gleamed in goblins' hands.
> One hope I had, one hurried call —
> Forth came Fire, fierce and bright.
> Destroyed was the sanctum, and free the wayfarer,
>
> But caught was Conall mac na Caillí, Blackthorn,
> By geis guarding the glittering prize,
> By Spell-Maker's song, sung from the grave,
> By a tarnished tangle, a silver star.

When he had finished, the Hag spat. The wad of phlegm sizzled offensively on the stone.

"I did not know what I reached for until my fingers were upon it," Blackthorn said. "I did not know my touch would loose the spell. I did not know that once I had lifted it from the ground, I could no more easily part from the Talisman than from the hand that held it."

"You witless, inept, ridiculous fool." The Hag's voice scratched like an axe blade on a grindstone. "The hand that held it! Oh, Gods, strike him down! With his bare hand he stole it from me!"

She threw her head back and screeched with laughter, then without warning, heaved her explosive orb. Blackthorn lunged away, but the edge of the blast caught him. He lost his footing and slid down onto the sands.

"The Hunter of Éirinn!" she mocked him. "And yet such a fool! What, had you no calling before Éirinn claimed you? Were you not a wizard, or to be a King? 'Tis plain you were no Poet!"

"I was a Bard, Grandmo—"

"A Bard! A wandering, whimpering singer-of-tales without the sense he was born with! A glove would have kept that spell from you! A fold of your cloak about your hand, and you could have brought the Talisman to me!"

"A fold of my cloak and I'd have brought you nothing," he said boldly. "Had the Talisman's fire not been mine to call, I would have died in Domhnall's Keep."

"A better death, perhaps, than the one you'll find here."

The Hag's hand shot out. This time she fastened her fingers not on his shirt, but around the Talisman itself. Blackthorn's eyes blazed, but he kept his voice even.

"An' you take it from me, still it will be mine."

The Hag sucked in her breath. It whistled sharply around her solitary green tooth. "You have angered me, Conall mac na Caillí. Angered me sore."

Bad enough the feel of her fingers on his flesh. With his Name on her tongue and his star in her grasp, he felt her loathsome touch within him, wrenching his insides, suffocating his heart. He writhed, but she had him fast. He groaned in agony, and the Hag smiled.

"Not for the likes of you did Domhnall fashion his finest spell," she hissed. Her tattered rags blew about as if a wind was stirring them. "Only the Mighty dare wield such power. You! You have neither the wisdom nor the will to command the star. Did you think to win my favor with the gift of your Name? With it, and the Talisman in my hand, I can destroy you."

Her thin face puffed out until the sores upon it looked like to burst. She grew grossly round, obscenely tall. Yellow-green light began to swirl once more in her open palm, but what took shape there was no orb. It was a shaft. Rapidly it grew longer, and one end narrowed, becoming sharp and pointed. In a moment, the Hag held in her hand a sorcerous spear, a travesty of the Hunter's lost weapon. Blackthorn looked at his death, and silently cursed the Talisman that had brought it upon him.

"What, no excuses, no promises, no more pretty lies?"

Let her kill me, then, he thought. But, Blessed Éire, let it be quickly, and let her not utter my Name while I live.

Instead of pulling back for the cast, the Hag leaned forward, thrusting her face into Blackthorn's. He turned away, but she dodged with him, compelling him to look at her.

"You bear Domhnall's star! Why do you not use it?"

Blackthorn shook his head trying to find an answer that would please. "I've broken our bargain," he managed to say. "My life is yours, Grandmother. I give it, if not gladly, at least without complaint."

She snorted derisively. "Such nobility! Half-blind as I am, yet plainly do I perceive your deceit. With verses and pledges and self-sacrificing humility you mean to beguile me. I hold death but a finger's breadth from your heart, yet still you connive to soften my anger, still you hope I will grant your wish!"

The reeking spear wavered, blurred, evaporated into nothing. Though he tried to dissemble it, Blackthorn was sure the Hag saw the relief in his eyes.

"You are bleeding on my sands," she snapped.

He watched her hobble away, walking this time, not gliding. She made deliberately for the black sword, bent, wrapped her fingers around the pommel, and lifted the weapon from the sands.

"Instead of a Talisman of power you offer me your paltry service," she said, shaking her head from side to side with deprecating slowness.

Blackthorn winced to see Strife in her diseased claw, but he set his jaw and said nothing. Though her words were scornful, in taking up his sword she had accepted his service—and that he had sworn to her only if she would let him fulfill his geis. An' she wished to have Strife at her command, first she must help him regain his Spear. He raised his hand to his slashed chest and mopped the blood onto his torn shirt, but his eyes never left the Hag.

Long she stood, studying the blade. Then she turned to Blackthorn, a forbidding smile on her face.

"My graciousness knows no bounds, Hunter. I will seek your Spear in my pools of magic. And if my powers are great enough to redeem it from wherever it lies, it will be yours again before this night is done."

She limped nearer, awkward and ungainly, and tossed him his sword. Blackthorn caught it by the grip, glad to have it in his hand, but wary of her sudden generosity.

"And what do you ask of me in return for your kindness?"

Her smile broadened. "Too great a task I set you before, not knowing you for a pitiful fool. An easy one will I set you now, something better suited to your simple skills. An' you agree to it, our bargain is made."

Torn between dread and hope, Blackthorn came unsteadily to his feet. It could not be so easy a thing, an' she desired it, but an' he could encompass her wish . . .

"Name it," he said.

"My bed is soft," the old woman croaked, "and my nights lonely. Lie with me this night, and stay with me till morning. This all I ask of you, and your service to me is done, your life your own again."

With great difficulty Blackthorn managed to take in some air, but he could make no answer. His breath whistled out again, empty and wordless. He could not even bring himself to consider the Hag's proposal—his thoughts leapt away, to his cut, burning now like fire, to the vanished púca—

"An' you refuse my bargain," the Hag did not sound greatly annoyed at the possibility, "you will leave Inis na Linnte now, at once. But no currach will I lend for to ferry you back to Éirinn's shores. Swim you must, and drown you will, surely. Do as you will, Hunter of Éirinn. Sleep forever in the cold sea's embrace, or one night in my arms. How do you choose?"

Better the sea, he thought, but his geis would not let him say it.

"A fool indeed I'd be to refuse your . . . hospitality, Grandmoth—Lady. But sure, an' I could never—I mean, I can't . . . I fear I'd not be able to please you, Lady."

"But you will so endeavor?"

Unable to hide his revulsion, Blackthorn bent his head and fixed his eyes on the blood-spotted sands at his feet. His Spear she was offering. His Spear, and his life, though the Talisman still hung about his neck.

It was not enough. He'd sooner die than lie with the Hag.

But an' he refused her bargain, he'd die geis-broken, never to reach the welcoming shores of Tír na nÓg, never again to be reborn. In the lightless realms of Shadow he would dwell forever and aye, or until it pleased the Dead Lord to sate His hunger on the shattered pieces of Blackthorn's soul.

Without raising his head, he nodded, agreeing to the Hag's terms as if he were agreeing to a thousand deaths.

"Then follow me."

She brushed past him, a griseous, foul-smelling cloud of filth. Dearg bounded after his mistress, glad to be off for a run. Blackthorn didn't stir.

When the falling waters had cleansed the Hag's stink from the air, he took a shuddering breath deep into his lungs. After taking another, he lifted his head. A third and his limbs regained their mobility. He bound his black sword across his back, turned, and slowly followed the Hag and her dog out of the cave. Not even the thought that his Spear might soon be in his hand had any power to quicken his step.

Forty-one

O bring to me my good yew bow
And my arrows one by one.
And bring to me my gray wolfhound
For truer friend have I none.

The Fallow Doe

Like a thief, dusk had robbed the colors from the greenwood and left the forest impoverished in shades of gray. The Hunter had little light to help him in tracking the Hag and her hound, and less with every passing moment. Tonight was the dark of the Rowan moon. Even if the skies remained unclouded, there would be only starshine to relieve the deepening shadows.

Still, little light the Hunter needed. The path was wide as a well-worn deer trail—better used than the one he had followed from the strand, and the forest had not so much claim upon it. From the cave mouth it led immediately up into the woods, then wound to the right, away from the falls, and began a gradual, curving ascent.

An owl's moaning cry sailed out over the trees, causing the night noises to cease abruptly—the scrabblings and rustlings, the chitter and munching. All was silent, save for the feather-light patter of tiny paws hurrying across the leaf-littered path behind him. That sound only became more pronounced.

"Less fear of owls have men than mice," Blackthorn remarked.

While the rest of the forest resumed their night songs, his solitary pursuer halted. Glancing over his shoulder, Blackthorn saw Reathach was taking his advice, and shifting his shape.

"*Brighde's Fire*, but its grand to see you alive!" the púca exulted. "What handsome lie did you tell her, me darlin', that melted the Hag's icy heart?"

"I told her my companion was King of the Púcaí, and if she'd let me live, he would fill her cave from floor to ceiling with silver and gold, and precious jewels."

Except for the pad of his bare feet along the trail, there was no sound from Reathach for quite a while.

"After all the kindness I've shown you," he said at last, his voice breaking, "to use me so! After all me fine advice and wise counsel. After all the loyalty I've given. After all the—"

"All the courage you've shown?" Blackthorn challenged, turning to face the little man. "All the danger you've dared on my account? All the times you've risked your life for mine?"

Reathach hung his head.

"And didn't I tell you, you were ever ready to credit my lies?" Blackthorn asked lightly.

"Lies?" The púca's head shot up, and his voice cracked with relief. "Then you didn't . . . well, and I knew 'twas only one of your false tales from the start," he went on, affecting indifference, "but sure, an' I'm too good-natured entirely to spoil your bit of fun, I am."

"True enough you are," Blackthorn agreed. "Why, it's your sweet temper and considerate ways that I so admire. But no need to tax your courtesy more. A warm fire burns below, and the cave is comfortable enough, now herself is no longer in it. Wait for me there."

The púca shook his head. "At your side, I'm stayin'. Between the hound and the Hag, sure, an' I'll soon have a chance to free myself from An Daghdha's geis."

"You've missed your chance already, you cowardly rascal," Blackthorn said, less patiently than before. "No good can you do me, so be off and leave me alone."

"Och, bodach," the púca shook his head sadly, "what bargain have you struck with the evil creature now?"

Blackthorn glowered at the púca, certain Reathach could

see his expression even in the darkness. Nonplussed, the little man sighed wearily and clucked his tongue.

"Well, that I'll doubtless learn to my sorrow soon enough. Best keep me with you, you soft-brained idiot, if only to stop you from strikin' worse bargains as the night wears on."

"Impossible," Blackthorn muttered, running his hand through his hair.

Before the púca could prick him with another well-aimed barb, Blackthorn turned and started up the path. Reathach followed behind, still clucking his tongue in dismay, and for once he had no trouble keeping up.

The path spiraled toward the mountain's top, but it had not quite circled around to the cataract when it veered left and climbed steeply, easing between two shoulders of rock. Standing in the cleft, Blackthorn looked down, and beheld a vision of wonder and beauty so irresistible even the bold robber night had failed to steal away its splendor.

He had thought the mountain's summit a narrow peak, for so it had appeared from the sea and shore. In truth it was a mountain of fire that no longer burned, and its peak a stone-rimmed cauldron where once molten rock had boiled. Now pools of water covered the basin floor and mirrored the fire of the stars.

Nine pools Blackthorn counted, and none like another. One was set in a garden of grasses and trees, one bounded by stone, one busy, one still. At the far end of the cauldron, a spring leapt and bubbled, its fountain ceaselessly tumbling into a dancing, crystal-blue pond. The waters splashed out on all sides, feeding two other pools.

The largest of these was both deep and clear, and ran around the edge of the cauldron to Blackthorn's right, then dropped away through a narrow groove in the rock face. The other was a flat, cerulean sheet of water, opaque and motionless under the shadow of a steep scarp. A long, branchless tree trunk held the wide pool frozen, save in one place only, where the wood had rotted away. There a pure white cord of water reached down into the next pool.

This fourth lay hidden beneath a blanket of mist. What its nature was, Blackthorn could not guess, but he marked its liquid treasure running away in a merry rivulet across the basin floor. Eventually, the rill gathered together and spread to form a pool so shallow its waters sang as they rippled over the stones that lined its bottom. Then it narrowed, became silent once more, and flowed on until it came to a jumbled pile of granite boulders. Over, between, around the giant stones the waters poured, and pooled at last in a gray-green pond crowded with rushes and stonewort where the banks were green.

As Blackthorn stepped down onto the narrow track that led to the cauldron floor, his heart began to pound. High enchantment filled this place, magics so potent they beat on him like the wind, pulled on his senses like the currents of the sea. Magic had filled the forest of Inis na Linnte, but the primal magic of life and death, of the hunter and the hunted. In those mysteries Blackthorn was well learned. The magic of the pools was more akin to the elvish spells that had bound him in Brugh na Morna and healed him in the pavilion of Cessair of Cnoc an Eanaigh than to the magic of the wild. They throbbed in the air and tingled on his skin, and set his hopes on fire.

He lengthened his stride, in a hurry now to find the Hag. Behind him the púca called imploringly, but Blackthorn was in no mood to be carting the impudent beggar about. Reathach had come uninvited—he would have to manage the journey on his own two legs. Or four.

The track wound down the crumbly rock of the inner slope, then forked into many paths at the base of the incline. Studying the pale, well-trod trails, Blackthorn found Dearg's spoor freshly marked upon one. He strode along it, and shortly came upon a tiny emerald pool adorned by an elegant stone altar on which sat a silver bell and a crystal cup of rose quartz. Beyond the pool and to his right he saw the limp branches of a willow caressing the waters of a teardrop-shaped, sapphire mere. His path led away and to the left. In a moment the farther pool was hidden behind a stand of tall birch.

The trail wound to the very heart of the cauldron, and ended at the banks of a circular pool. No willow stood near, nor any tree, but the still and nearly silent waters were wrapped in a green-gray kirtle of huge, mossy stones and tumbled piles of rock.

The Hag was precariously perched on one of these mounds,

on the highest point of a tremendous boulder. Dearg sat at the base of the heaped stones, head cocked, staring intently into the pool. Blackthorn came to the bank, found a comfortable seat on the stones a cautious distance from the hound, and, following Dearg's example, peered into the waters.

The edges of the pool gently lapped against the stones that lined the banks, though Blackthorn could see no ripples on its surface. Nor could he detect any life within, no fish, no reeds, no mosses, but neither was the pool empty. Stars flamed in the midnight-blue of the waters, making the pool appear as deep as the fathomless reaches of the heavens.

The barely audible sound of paws intermittently scratching on dirt caught Blackthorn's ear. Looking over his shoulder, he saw the brown wood mouse covering the last leg of the trail in short sporadic bursts.

Dearg's ears were as keen as the Hunter's. When the hound's head turned and his ears lifted, the púca risked everything in a frantic dash for the rocks. Arriving safely, the mouse scurried into a narrow niche between two stones. Dearg returned to observing the waters, but Blackthorn looked away from both púca and pool, and fixed his eyes on the Hag.

At first he thought she was muttering to herself, for her mouth was moving, though he heard no sound. Suddenly, she glared at him.

"Speak your wish," she charged.

"I wish my Spear returned to me," Blackthorn said clearly.

Lifting her arms, the Hag began to sing. Mating cats, howling goblins, and the croaking of toads was in her voice. It was only by telling himself she was singing the spell that would conjure his Spear that Blackthorn managed to keep his hands away from his ears.

As the Hag's caterwauling rose in volume, he started to imagine that some of the notes she screeched were coursing bearably, even lyrically through the air. Listening more carefully, he realized a melody of surpassing beauty was struggling to break free of the Hag's wrinkled throat. Despite the rude quality of the instrument, the spell itself was true. A woven song of power reached out from the rocks on which the Hag perched to the center of the pool, and there caused the waters to part as if a pebble had been dropped from above.

Immediately, the stars vanished from the dark mirror. The black waters became impenetrable, smooth and lustrous as a marten's coat. The wolfhound came to his feet, whining with excitement. The slight depression in the center of the pool deepened, and the surrounding waters started to turn.

The dance began with languid ease, a sunwise circle gradually widening about a gently sinking core. The rhythm quickened, the waters whirled and spun—dark wine swirled in a giant's cup. Another moment, and the ring was a racing vortex, reaching from the water's edge to its plunging navel, as if a God had reached from beneath the pool and pulled its center down to the roots of the mountain.

Gazing into the madly spiraling waters, Blackthorn was gripped by the terror that had assailed him in the passage grave of Keeper Hill, the fear of falling. His reason was overwhelmed by the sensation of hurtling over a precipice, but he dug his fingers into the stone beneath him and held on, refusing to turn his eyes away. Barking loudly, Dearg bounded about, putting his paws up on the rocks, jumping down again, leaping toward the waters, then away. Over the noise of the hound, the Hag's voice was barely audible.

"In your hand, Lady?" Blackthorn heard the old crone ask. "I beseech you, give it unto the Hunter's."

Whose hand? he thought wildly, but did not dare interrupt the Hag's spell.

Faster the waters whirled, deeper they bored into the mountain. Foam appeared where water met air, turning black to white, and a glitter of silver shone deep in the maelstrom's distant heart. Blackthorn nearly cried out with joy, but it was too soon yet to believe his eyes. A trick of the waters it might be, or illusion.

Gleaming still, the mote of silver rose from the rushing depths and grew—a spearhead brighter than the foaming white spray, bright as the stars above.

With a hunter's restraint Blackthorn held himself still, with a hunter's patience waited while his Spear was born into the narrow cup of air that lay in the midst of the whirlpool. First the point, then the elk sinews binding point to shaft, then the length of polished ash . . . Springing to his feet on the rocks, he watched his Spear come clear of the spinning waters.

As the maelstrom's fury had spread outward from the middle of the pool, so did peace move inward, starting at the mossy rocks and sweeping toward the center. First, the edge of the pool that lay against the stony bank calmed, then the waters a little nearer the hub—in ever-tightening rings the pool grew quiet and still. Soon it lay black and unruffled, as when Blackthorn had first seen it, and the Spear hung in midair just above the water's surface, its point to the sky.

The Hag ceased her song. Her eyes were closed, and she was breathing deeply, heavily with the effort the spell had cost her. Yet, her arms were still upraised, and as Blackthorn watched, her good eye opened. A grimace of satisfaction twisted her lips. She gulped down some air, and held it in her lungs.

A note, thought Blackthorn. A single note more, to call the Spear home. For a moment his gratitude was so great, he could almost forgive the Hag her cruel bargain.

The crone's gash of a mouth opened. What issued forth was no song-spell, but a shrieking wail enough to rive Blackthorn's hearing. Out of the corner of his eye he saw a long, hairy arm shoot out of the water. Clawed fingers reached into the air and closed around the end of his Spear.

The waters roiled in protest, Dearg howled and bayed. The Hag hurled curse after strident curse at the intruding limb, and a sickly green light began to glow in her hand. None of this did Blackthorn heed, but only that the goblin-like fist was tightly wrapped around its prize, and beginning to pull the Spear down into the water.

With a wild cry, he loosed his sword. Strife's edges had gleamed in Domhnall's Keep—here among the pools a light like blue-white fire streamed from the blade, running down over the hilt and Blackthorn's hand and blazing from the deadly point. His Spear would not be taken from him again, Blackthorn thought grimly, gathering himself to leap. Not an' Strife severed the paw that held it.

Even as he threw his weight forward, the Hag's lucid, malodorous ball exploded in Blackthorn's face, throwing him back. The force of the blast sent him sprawling to the ground, and Strife flying from his hand. The black sword seemed to sigh with regret as she slid across the soft grass.

"An' you touch the waters, all is lost!" the Hag screeched.

Blackthorn crawled to the rocks, choking on the poisoned air, and turned his stinging eyes toward the pool. The Spear was not yet under the water, though the creature now had two hairy paws locked on the ash shaft. The beast's hideous face bobbed beneath the surface of the churning pool, glaring up at his defiant treasure. Blackthorn saw a fanged, grinning mouth, a broad, flat nose, fiery red eyes. He engraved his enemy's features on his memory as if on stone.

"Master!" the beast cried. His voice was deep and harsh, and distorted by the heaving waters. "Master, it is in my hand! Master!"

Blackthorn stumbled to his feet. "Release it!" he shouted.

The thief's red eyes rolled about in his head, then lit on the Hunter.

"Gruagach!" screamed the Hag.

A yellow-green dagger tore through the air, grazing one of the beast's forearms before bursting into sour-smelling fumes. The beast howled in pain, losing half his grip on the Spear, and pulled his hurt arm into the water. The ash shaft began to slip through his other paw. Desperately, the creature groped after his fleeing prize, his claws scraping against the wood.

A second, sulphurous blade flew from the Hag's hand. This one was better aimed—it embedded in the beast's forearm and exploded, ripping apart the creature's flesh. With a bitter wail, the monster let go the Spear. His black and bloody limb disappeared into the pool.

"Master!" the Gruagach howled.

His face blurred and faded, but another was already taking shape under the seething waters, another arm breaking through the surface. Unerringly the fingers reached, unerringly closed. Blackthorn had a single glimpse of his enemy's arm—a hand gloved in jewelled leather, an embroidered saffron sleeve . . . It was more than he could bear. Turning from the pool, he reached for his sword.

"Dearg!" shrieked the Hag. "Hold!"

Her words didn't register in Blackthorn's mind until the hound tore into him.

He turned at the sound of Dearg's charge, instinctively raising his arm to ward off the attack. Sharp teeth clamped shut on his forearm, piercing the skin. With a savage growl

Dearg yanked back, digging his fangs deeper into Blackthorn's flesh and dragging him from Strife. Cursing the beast, Blackthorn wrenched his arm from the dog's mouth, freeing it but worsening the wound, and dived for his sword.

Dearg rammed into his side, and they both went down. Blackthorn twisted and rolled, trying to extricate himself from the tangle of legs and teeth and muscled fur, but Dearg was on top, and had the advantage. The beast roared his challenge and snapped his heavy jaws together so near to Blackthorn's jugular his fangs bruised the skin of the Hunter's throat.

Slamming his fist against the side of Dearg's head, Blackthorn shoved his other arm against the hound's chest, trying to shift the animal off him. The wolfhound's skull must have been made of stone—he staggered, but came back at once, swinging his massive head around and refastening his fangs on the wound he had already made in Blackthorn's arm. The Hag's sibilant whisper was all but lost in the sound of the Hunter's pain and fury.

"Trespasser!" she hissed. "Betrayer! Thief!"

"Fight me, my flower, and you must fail." The voice that answered the Hag was deep and seductive, despite the deadening weight of the water. "Why waste your gifts? What use this toy to you? Give it to me kindly, and even now I might relent."

The brilliant blue-white light that emanated from Strife's blade glowed at the edges of Blackthorn's sight. Desperately he swept his arm across the ground, seeking his sword. His fingers found only damp grasses and moist earth. Strife was beyond his reach, and he'd yet to put a dagger into his empty sheath.

Reathach.

He turned his head, searching frantically for the púca among the stones. He found the mouse almost at once, half-hidden in a crack between two rocks, beady eyes blinking nervously, forepaws clutched together and washing each other like the hands of a worried old man.

The Hag laughed, an hysterical note blending with her scorn. "Did I ever believe you? But I was a young fool. Older now, I know you for a liar. Speak again, that your folly will open the door to your doom. Lie again, that I might wrest this prize from your hand."

"Lies that gain my ends but feed my strength. See. It is mine.

"It is mine!" Blackthorn roared his denial in a voice deep and terrible as Dearg's. "You useless coward!" he spat at Reathach. "Help me get this hound—"

The púca ducked completely under the shadow of the stones.

Cursing bitterly, Blackthorn grabbed Dearg's ear and pulled hard. The dog's neck bent to the pain and pressure, but his teeth stayed fixed in Blackthorn's arm. Shaking the offending limb as if it were a rat he meant to kill, Dearg got his head free, leaving a handful of stringy, red hair in Blackthorn's fingers, then hunkered down, using his weight to hold his captive still. Thrusting his hand into the knotted muscles of Dearg's neck, Blackthorn strove to push the dog off him. He kicked, driving his knee into Dearg's balls. The dog jerked to his feet, digging his huge, heavy paws into Blackthorn's shoulders, and growled like a goblin, but he never let go the Hunter's arm.

"May the Spear be broken ere it serves you," Blackthorn heard the Hag say, "and your false lies open the door to your doom."

Hatred and contempt laced the old woman's curse. Bitterness, too, was on her tongue, the bitterness of defeat.

"It is mine," Blackthorn moaned.

The pool's angry waters quieted, the stench of the luminous weapons the Hag had hurled dissipated on the night air. Only Dearg's growling broke the terrible silence, and far away, the laughter of merry waters tripping over stones, careless of the Hunter's despair.

Forty-two

Bear your burden nobly
And honor Éire's Call
The world awaits the White One's end
At your hand

The Hunter's Rann

"Dearg."

For once the Hag's voice, rasping and sore, seemed to Blackthorn entirely fitting to the moment.

"Off."

Dearg brought his threat down to a low rumble and backed away, watching the Hunter all the while, a suspicious glint in his eye.

Blackthorn climbed slowly to his feet. What use to hurry? His Spear had returned to the world and been lost again while he lay felled by the Hag's magics and pinned beneath her dog. Neither speed nor sword could help him now. He was beaten. He was betrayed.

Averting his eyes from the pool, he took the two steps that separated him from Strife, and lifted the sword from the grass. His arm was bleeding badly. His chest and shoulders were stiff from holding off the wolfhound. He was cut and bruised, and his lungs were scorched.

Involuntarily his sight strayed to the pool, to the spangled deeps of the quiet waters and the empty air above.

"I had it," the Hag hissed.

She was sitting on the boulder now, one arm behind her, the other hanging limp in her lap. Blackthorn looked up at the old woman with eyes hard as flint.

"Yet, I had it."

A faint ripple coursed over the surface of the pool, drawing Blackthorn's stony gaze. Though the waters swiftly stilled, the stars did not return. In the dark bowl a solitary image appeared, the bowed figure of a young woman. Her posture was like the Hag's, half-reclining, shoulders slumped in dejection, a slim hand hanging limp against the saffron gown that covered her knee. Her head was bent, and masses of waving dark hair flowed over her face and down upon her breast.

Though the Hag's misery had not touched him, Blackthorn was moved to pity by the sorrowful lady's image. He felt a kinship with her, imagining that the burden that weighed upon her was like his own, a grief born of frustrated hopes and vain efforts.

Her head came up suddenly, as if she had felt Blackthorn's eyes upon her. Her black hair fell back, parting like a curtain to reveal the woman's features. They were exquisite. Wet with tears, her eyes glistened, and they were dark and deep as the pool itself. Fair skin, with a blush of high color in her cheeks, black brows, arched in surprise, a delicate nose, lips full and red as if they'd just been kissed—

Blackthorn's breath caught in his chest. The Bards had not oversung, but undersung the beauty of the black-haired wizard whose face was like a rose.

"Róisín Dubh," he whispered.

He would have caught her Name back again if he could, for as it left his tongue, the spell was broken. The waters stirred as if a hand had disturbed them, and the dark of Róisín's hair and the white of her skin fragmented in the broken mirror. For an instant they came together in an uneven reflection of a magpie in flight, but when the waves calmed, neither woman nor bird could Blackthorn see in the dark waters, but only the stars.

He spun back to the rocks to demand an explanation from the Hag. The miserable bag of bones was gone as well. He could hear her, though, limping about on the far side of the piled stones. A few strides brought him around the boulders,

and face-to-face with the old woman. Dearg prowled menac-
ingly at Blackthorn's heels, then bounded forward to place
himself between the Hag and the Hunter.

"Was it your spell conjured the vision of the Black Rose?"
Blackthorn demanded. The old woman's odor wafted toward
him, and he backed a pace. "Where is she then, and what
have you—"

"What have I done with her?" the Hag cackled. "Not I,
insolent puppy, but himself is to blame for the Black Rose's
sorrow."

"Himself?"

"He who defiled my waters and stole your Spear." The
Hag shrieked with laughter, and Blackthorn flinched from
the sound. "Feckless the Hunter that Éire has chosen. But a
glimpse of a handsome woman, and the Stag is banished
from his mind! Will you prove false to your ladylove,
Huntsman, as love has made you prove false to your geis?"

"You speak to me of falseness? You, who plied your sorceries to constrain me and ripped my sword from my hand?
You, who set your dog upon me, and my Spear in contest
over your waters?"

"Thanking me, you should be! Had I allowed you to leap
into the pool as you meant to do, you would have destroyed
my spell entirely, and lost your Spear to the Gruagach."

"Shall I thank you then, for losing it to the Gruagach's
master?"

"No, you blind and idiotic fool! Thank me for hiding you
from your enemy's sight!"

The Hag took a step toward him, but Blackthorn stood his
ground.

"The Spear was lost the moment your enemy's gloved
hand pierced the enchanted waters," she hissed. "You could
not reach him without breaking my spell, and I—" She
laughed again, and Blackthorn shuddered. "In my folly once
I trusted him. By my folly did he wound me, and by that folly
does he wound me still."

Her face twisted into a mask of spite. Turning away, she
hobbled to the edge of the pool. With a wave of her withered arm, the stars in the waters below blinked out. A long,
desolate mound, devoid of tree, grass, bird, or beast swayed
in the black depths.

"Here dwells your enemy, Hunter. Here stands his hall. Here he has taken your Spear, and cloaked it in Shadow."

A cruel smile touched her lips. "Little hope have you to steal it back again," she said. "Little hope have you to keep it even an' you do steal it from him, for he has held it. The jewelled glove he wears upon his right hand is a work of great sorcery—nothing that it grasps but that he can call to his hand again at will, unless it be a living thing. Little hope have you, I'm saying, but none at all, an' your enemy knows your face."

Blackthorn looked long and hard at the empty hill. "Yet the Gruagach saw me."

"Is it putting the blame on me, you are? 'Twas by your own rashness he beheld you."

She erased the pool's vision with another wave of her gnarled hand. "Do you wish your wounds healed?" she asked.

Blackthorn regarded her narrowly and nodded. "I would be glad of some healing."

"The teardrop pool where the willow grows. Bathe your hurts, then come down by the path. I suppose I must feed you as well. An' you are not too wounded, you will say you are too weak from hunger to fulfill your part of the bargain."

Blackthorn stared at her with ill-concealed disgust. "Bargain? Can you think I will lie with you tonight? I was to have my Spear in my hand ere I came to your bed!"

"Having broken one bargain, you care naught for breaking another!" the Hag flung back at him. "'Blackthorn' you are called? 'Blackheart' I Name you, for 'tis plain honor is as dear to you as it is to a goblin! Not your Spear did I offer, but only to do my best to regain it. So have I done, Hunter, or do you deny I did all in my power to help you?"

Blackthorn said nothing, unable to refute the Hag, unwilling to admit she had the right of it.

She came nearer, tilting her head and rolling her hips in a manner that would have been alluring in another woman. It repelled Blackthorn as nothing else she had said or done. Without thinking he raised his sword and pointed it at the Hag's heart to stop her advance. She laughed until he prayed to go deaf.

"Much I can tell you, an' you please me tonight," she croaked softly. "The land where lies the bare hill where your enemy dwells. How to breach its unseen walls . . ."

Blackthorn lowered his arm until the tip of his sword touched the ground. A bargain was not an oath. Still, it would do his soul little good an' he broke faith at every turn. And though he half believed the Hag was simply leading him farther down the path of shattered dreams and false hopes, the geis within him was adamant. He must follow the trail, no matter how faint—he must hunt his Spear, that he might at last hunt the Stag.

The Hag shivered and wrapped her tattered rags about her. Blackthorn's skin crawled as her gesture blew her stench into his nostrils and brought her arm close to his own.

"You will honor our bargain?" she demanded.

He clenched his teeth. "So must I."

The Hag shivered again and cast her shawl over her head.

"Then do as I bade you. Bathe your hurts and fill your belly. I will await you in my bed. Dearg," she called to her hound. "Time to go. Already the ground grows damp with dew."

Reathach was well hid behind the rosemary's green-needled branches. Whatever faint scent his small body possessed was completely masked by the resinous plant. And the púca took care to keep still—not so much as a whisker twitched as he watched Blackthorn rise dripping from the sapphire-blue waters of the Hag's teardrop-shaped pool.

The Hunter paused just short of the bank, the cold air raising bumps on his wet skin. Suddenly he turned, stooped, and struck the water with the flat of his hand. An arcing fountain went flying into Reathach's cover.

Squealing in horror and wet dismay, the púca scurried out from under the drenched rosemary. Suddenly finding himself in the open and unprotected, he stopped and glanced fearfully at his tormentor. To his relief, the Hunter was not looking his way, but had climbed onto the bank and was even now stretching out beneath the willow. Though Reathach could see small shivers running along Blackthorn's muscles, the man had made no attempt to dry himself. The fool will catch his death of cold, lying wet and naked in the chill night air, the púca told himself worriedly.

He had to repeat the thought many times over in his

mind before he had worked up the courage to shift to a man, and many times over again before he felt bold enough to say his thought aloud.

"A cool breeze weaves a poor blanket," he ventured. Blackthorn never stirred. "Wish yourself dry, I'm sayin', and it's warmer you'll be."

In a single swift motion, Blackthorn raised himself up on his elbow and threw a stone, then another, and another. The first clipped Reathach on the shoulder. As he dropped to a mouse, the second hit him on the thigh. Turning to flee, the third stone stung him on the rump, somersaulting him into the dirt. Protesting vehemently, the púca skittered off to find a safe hiding place.

When, after a while, he peered out from behind an auspiciously dry bracken, the Hunter was slowly donning his breeches. Slowly, he reached for his boot. Slowly, slowly he set it on his foot.

It was a pitiful sight, and full of pity, Reathach crept quietly closer to the melancholy man. His ear only brushed the tip of the bracken's leaf, lighter than the breeze it was, and the swish of his tail in the grass could have been the willow branches moving in the jewel-colored waters.

Blackthorn's head lifted, and the púca froze.

Without a word, Blackthorn bent his head again and reached for his other boot. Feeling reprieved, if not forgiven, Reathach rose to a man.

"Well, and look at himself, now," he said with unconvincing jauntiness. "Why, any pool could have washed the blood from your hurts, but sure, an' this one has healed them entirely."

The Hunter's wounds had closed to pale, white scratches, all save for the cut on his chest, and that was no more than a thin red weal. If his swim had eased his heart as it had eased his hurts, Blackthorn gave no sign of it. Without a word he stretched out his hand and selected a small pebble from the many that lay on the ground between the willow and the pool.

Reathach dropped to a mouse and began dashing about, frantically looking for shelter. The fern was too flimsy, the rosemary too wet—he began to chitter in agitation, feeling the Hunter's eye on him wherever he ran. Finally, he sat back on his haunches and shifted to a frightened man.

"And what good would it have done for me to be eaten by that huge, fearsome hound?" he argued desperately. "Would it have won you your Spear? Would it have freed you from the astoundingly stupid pact you made with the Hag?"

"Great good would it do me even now an' Dearg would rid me of your company," Blackthorn answered so coldly that Reathach whimpered.

"'Twould have done us no good at all, at all, I'm sayin'," the púca insisted. "Why, 'twas plain from the start you were in no mortal danger. 'Hold' the Hag bade her hound, not 'kill.' And I as helpless as yourself against the magics those sorcerers wielded."

Blackthorn sent the stone skipping over the surface of the pool, then bent and took his shirt from the grass. The fine, elven-green fabric was torn, front, back, and sleeve, its color mottled by the brown of dried blood. He sighed and tucked it in his belt, a rag to wipe his dagger with, an' ever he found a knife for his empty sheath. Shrugging his wolfskin cloak about him, he fastened the catch at his shoulder.

"A dark night for a walk," Reathach remarked. He tiptoed nearer and lowered his voice conspiratorially. "A terrible dark night," he repeated. "On a moonless night like this, why even the hawk-eyes of the Hunter of Éirinn might miss the trail, and wouldn't we be lost, then, in the woods of Inis na Linnte? Arrah, but wouldn't it be grand good luck now, an' our aimless rovin' brought us to the strand? For there's a currach sleepin' on the sands, an' my memory serves me— just waitin', I'm sayin', for someone to come along with arms to row . . ."

The púca couldn't help shuddering at the thought of the sea, but he nodded sagely at the Hunter and gave him a knowing wink.

Blackthorn took up Strife from where she leaned against the willow, and held her gently in both hands.

"My death I saw on a dark elf's blade," he said, ignoring the púca and speaking to his sword, "but the Scáileanna could not stand against me. Alone I faced a goblin horde, yet escaped without harm. By rights the Hag should have killed me, but though the sorceress is as forgiving as a wounded bear, still she spared my life."

He smiled ruefully and shook his head. "They could rest

from their labors, those that seek to do me hurt. What my enemies cannot accomplish with sword, axe, or spell, Reathach the púca will achieve by dint of his ready and estimable advice."

Speechless with admiration, Reathach nevertheless struggled valiantly to devise a worthy retort. Disgraced he'd be forever and aye, an' he allowed such a fine insult to go unanswered.

"Astonishin'," he said, at last. "Astonishin' entirely that a man who can cast such elegant aspersions and tell such audacious lies is such an utter fool when it comes to strikin' bargains."

"Astonishing," Blackthorn admitted wearily.

The wrinkles on Reathach's face deepened, and he dropped despondently to a mouse. Sure, an' what joy was there in havin' a tongue to speak his wit, an' the Hunter so downcast he could take no pleasure in the game?

Blackthorn lingered awhile by the pool, staring at the waters and seeing nothing. Reathach stayed by him, guessing correctly that the Hunter was too rapt in his own thoughts to notice whether the púca was near or not. Doubtless the sorry fool was wishing the earth might open and swallow him up, or the sky fall upon him. The long and the short of it was, the only one on this isle who might grant his desires had wishes of her own this night.

Blackthorn came to the same realization soon enough. Still, the púca was pleased, and not a little surprised, when the Hunter opened his pouch and himself set Reathach inside before setting off for the Hag's cave.

Forty-three

There is a sweetness in every sorrow

Sayings of the Mothers

Reathach poked his nose out of the pouch, drawn by a tanta-lizing scent that tempted him even through the leather. Free of the sack, the púca's short snout sniffed ecstatically as he inhaled the aroma permeating the cave. Quickly he wriggled from Blackthorn's purse and dropped to the slate floor, shift-ing to a man even as he fell.

Once on two legs he lost no time in scuttling over and peering into the pot hanging above the fire that burned in the stalactite chimney. With a gleeful chuckle, he dipped a finger into the pot, then scooped it quickly into his mouth.

"Marvellous," he gloated, waving his finger in the air to cool it.

Hopping over to the sideboard, he grabbed two bowls and a single large ladle, then returned to the pot.

"Marvellous," he said again, and filled both bowls to the brim.

"Barley grain, mostly, but herbs and honey as well, and hazelnuts, an' I'm not mistaken," he said, handing one of the bowls to Blackthorn where he stood leaning against the table. "Eat quickly, now," he cautioned. "No knowin' when the Hag will arrive to spoil our appetites."

Reathach slid onto one of the benches, set his bowl on the wooden table beside the Hunter's sword, and began at once to devour his meal. Blackthorn never moved, or took his eyes from the narrow curtain effectively blocking off a far corner of the chamber.

There wasn't much for the Hunter to see, Reathach thought to himself, what with the cookfire being the only source of light in the cave. Though the flames burned hot, all yellows and ambers, and the coals were the brightest red, the chimney jealously kept most of the firelight imprisoned behind its stone walls. The púca's sight was not as daunted as Blackthorn's by the dark, but even he could only just make out the cloth doorway, lost as it was in the shadows of the cave. The Hag's wolfhound, asleep before the curtain, was no more than a large, dark lump on the ground.

With a sigh, Blackthorn lowered his gaze. He seemed mildly surprised to find a bowl resting in his hands, but set the porridge down without tasting it.

"Eat, bodach," urged Reathach. "You'll be needin' your strength."

"More likely I'll be losing my stomach, an' I fill it now," Blackthorn told him.

Reathach glanced at the curtain. It fluttered.

Lifting a porridge-caked finger, the púca pointed to the door. Blackthorn's head spun sharply about.

"'Twas only a slight breeze ticklin' the curtain, I'm thinkin'," Reathach assured his companion, "or the hound stirrin' in his sleep. What else? An' it were the Hag, we'd smell her!"

Blackthorn scowled.

"Och, but wasn't I forgettin' the magpie!" the púca exclaimed. "Sure, 'twas the magpie, brushin' a wing against the drape as she darted past."

"And what would a magpie be doing awake at this hour?"

Blackthorn stood erect, his expression stern with resolve.

His resolution crumbled almost at once. His face took on the naked, desperate look of a fox run to ground. Reathach could See the Hunter searching his wits for a way out, and as plainly Saw the man's helpless anger when he failed to find one.

The púca gave Blackthorn a sympathetic nod. "Och, bodach, and what's worse than bein' ill-used?" he asked.

"Being caught," the Hunter answered grimly.

Looking more resigned than determined, he ran his hand through his hair and started across the sands to the Hag's bedroom. If he did not go swiftly, neither did he drag his feet, and his head was high. Dearg pricked his ears at the Hunter's approach. Reathach saw the dog's eyes gleam, but the beast didn't rise or growl, only watched.

The púca watched too, in respectful silence, until Blackthorn's hand was reaching for the cloth. Clear as crystal the woven strands appeared to Reathach's Sight, and behind the transparent veil a flower was opening, black petals blooming, ring upon ring—

"'Ware! 'Ware you blind fool!" Reathach gasped. "You'll not find the Hag past the curtain, but a geis—a geis, lurkin' there!"

Blackthorn's reaching fingers curled slowly back from the cloth.

"Of my own choosing you said the third would be," he said warily.

"And if I did? Precious little wisdom have you shown in your choices ere now!"

Blackthorn laughed mirthlessly. "A fool I may be, but not a madman. My soul is fair breaking under the two geasa I bear. Three would destroy me entirely. Doubt not I'll refuse the geis, an' the choice is mine."

Uncurling his fingers from his palm, Blackthorn took a last, long breath of untainted air, and lifted the cloth. Like a thin, pale mist, the glow from the distant fire seeped into the alcove and showed Blackthorn a three-legged stool set beside a huge mound of blankets and furs. Stepping under the door, he let the curtain fall behind him, blotting out the light.

She was there, wrapped in the bedclothes, waiting for him.

He couldn't see her. The Hag's thankfully lightless bed-chamber would spare him the sight of her, at least till the dawn. Nor could he smell her—not yet, not while he held the pure air from beyond the arras in his lungs. Neither could he hear her, for she lay still, without a rustle, or a whisper, or a sigh to reveal her.

Even so, Blackthorn was sure she was there. He felt her presence in the way a doe feels the pale eyes of the wolf upon her, and starts at her danger. He knew her as a swift knows winter is coming, and flees Éirinn's shores. His certainty rose from deep within him and was absolute. His own racing pulse measured the beating of the Hag's cold heart. In his blindness he felt her blind eye upon him. Her breath thickened the surrounding air.

He let his own breath out cautiously, expecting his next would be far less pleasant. What he drew in was fragrant and wholesome—a faint muskiness from the furs and a quiet incense of rose and lavender, mugwort and yarrow.

Puzzled, Blackthorn made his way to the stool. Sitting down, he loosed the catch of his cloak, unbuckled his belt, and set about getting his boots off his feet. He worked quietly, and the Hag was utterly silent.

He rose and stripped off his breeches, feeling flushed and embarrassed. An' it were a woman's bed he had been invited to, he would ease the awkwardness with words of affection, or a jest to set her laughing. This bed belonged to no woman, but a monster. No words at all were the kindest he could hope for, and himself the jest set to amuse his waiting lover.

A single step took him from the stool to the bedding. The mound shifted to accommodate him. He sat gingerly on the piled covers, anticipating the Hag's foul stink.

Only the scent of blossoms rose to meet him, rich and inexplicably potent. It was as if the Hag's bed were a Bealtaine bower and all the flowers of summer were there gathered. The heady perfumes mingled in Blackthorn's veins, sang to him of a woman's moist flower that opens to a man's passion. . . .

Blood rushed to his groin. His hand was already reaching toward the softly breathing darkness when he remembered the feel of the Hag's scaly skin, the rotting stench of her desiccated flesh. He froze, his heart still pounding. The bedding stirred again. A blanket bunched against his thigh. A small rabbit skin brushed his arm on its way to the stone floor as the Hag rolled over to face him.

Had he believed his instincts keen as the doe's, infallible as the swift's? Everything his senses told him wakened fire in his heart and desire in his loins—the sultry whisper of air drawn deeply in and slowly out, the voluptuous scents of a forest glade courting the lusts of the wild . . .

Only his reason and his memories fought to resist the Hag's spell, but they were enough. The one bespoke him of the cruel terms of the bargain he had made; the other conjured to Blackthorn's mind a truer vision of what lay beside him than his senses could conceive.

With an effort he extended his hand toward the inhabited dark. His fingers found flesh, the curve of an arm. The skin was smooth, and cool to his touch, but it burned him like fire, and like fire spread, running from his fingertips along every nerve in his body. His manhood blazed up, and he almost laughed, glad of the illusion, glad that his task would not be so difficult as he had feared.

His relief was short-lived, and swiftly gave way to resentment. How ridiculous she must find him, how droll his easily persuaded passion. A vision of the Hag's face floated before Blackthorn in the darkness—he imagined he heard her silently laughing at the reluctant lover who had so quickly grown hard and eager. What a fine entertainment of an evening was a randy and gullible fool. Better to endure the ordeal of her ugliness, than to endure the mockery of her false beauty.

"Would I could see you as you really are," he said harshly.

A pale light sparked and began to glow just above the bed. Had Blackthorn looked up, he would have seen a nest of clear crystals set in a niche in the stone, and in their heart, a moonwhite fire growing steadily brighter.

The Hunter would not have looked up if his Spear were stuck in the wall, and flames dancing upon it. His eyes were fixed on the flower of a woman lying beside him on the bed.

Her skin was fair, soft as rose petals and faintly blushing. She had long, lustrous, blue-black hair, and red lips, gently parted. And her eyes . . . black they were, and deep—pools of magic more mysterious by far than any enchanted waters the Hag could boast. The heady fragrance of Bealtaine faded away as he gazed on her, but he caught a whiff of perfume infinitely more intoxicating—the sweet, musky, long-missed scent of woman.

A wistful look briefly clouded Róisín's gaze, and she

reached out tentative fingers to the Talisman that hung at Blackthorn's throat. He caught his breath, and nearly spoke his Name, for he wanted hear it on her lips. He wanted to feel the wonder of her fair touch on his soul as he had felt the horror of the Hag's foulness when her clawed hand had closed upon the star, and her Naming him with her poisoned tongue.

With an inaudible sigh, the Black Rose took her hand from the star and let it stray to the weal on Blackthorn's chest. Her brows drew together into a frown, and she shook her head.

"'Tis no matter," he said, smiling at her concern.

She sat up and leaned forward, bringing her lips to where her fingers had been and pressing them tenderly against the mark. Her long hair flowed over his arm, her tongue flicked against his skin. He felt her nipples harden against him. Slowly, lightly, she let her hand drift down his body until it brushed against his thigh. Sliding her arm between them, she drew her delicate fingers along the side of his swollen phallus.

He throbbed under her touch, but held still, a hawk balancing in the wind. When he could bear it no more, he stooped to the dove. Thrusting his hand into Róisín's night dark hair, he pulled her head back and drank the nectar of her kisses with his own lips.

PART 9

márrach

Forty-four

Curses come home to roost

Sayings of the Mothers

Blackthorn had neither the intention nor the desire to sleep that night. In his heart he knew that if he took his sight from Róisín Dubh or let her out of his arms, the Black Rose would vanish and the Hag return.

When he did close his eyes it was unintended, a moment of carelessness in the blissful, damp lull of passion between climax and arousal. Rocked by the pounding of his heart as it slowed, soothed by the gradual quieting of Róisín's breathing, his face buried in the pillow of her dark hair, he drifted to sleep, and into a dream that had hovered at the edges of his slumber since midwinter's day.

Elven folk, all light and glory, dancing to the wild screeling of the pipes. Bright the hall, ablaze with red-gold flames and the glittering host. Brighter still, two eyes, two oceans of sky-blue fire, drowning, searing the heart . . .

Let me go, gentle Lady. The Stag calls and I must away.

Ochone, mo mhúirnín, but stay awhile more. Come, listen to the pipers play.

Sweet Goddess, open the gates of Brugh na Morna. My geis urges me be gone.

And so it will an hour from now. Refresh yourself from my cup, Blackthorn. My maidens will sing ere long.

He woke without a Name to put to his gaoler or a reason for his imprisonment, only an impression of blinding light and intoxicating joy, as if the sun or the stars themselves had held him captive in Brugh na Morna. Still, an' he had remembered this much, might he not believe that in time his memory would be whole?

His pleasure in regaining a piece of his past soured as soon as his eyes were fully open. Gray light seeped through the cloth curtain. Though it did a poor job of illuminating the alcove, it did a fine one of showing Blackthorn he was alone.

He bolted from the bed, shivering as his bare feet hit the achingly cold stone floor. His clothes were on the stool where he had left them, but his boots were nowhere to be seen. Pulling his breeches up with one hand, he tossed furs and blankets aside with the other, heedless of where they fell. Unearthing his boots at last, he grabbed his cloak and belt from the stool, ducked past the curtain, and stepped into the cave.

A quick look drew a muttered curse. The spacious chamber boasted but a single occupant, and it wasn't the one Blackthorn had hoped to see.

"Where is she?" he demanded, dropping one boot and jamming his foot into the other.

Reathach turned from the hearth, his mouth stuffed with nuts.

"Fear not," he said, fairly unintelligibly. "Out she's gone, and her hound with her. Your night of toil is over, me darlin', and breakfast's—"

Blackthorn got his other boot on and dashed across the sands toward the cave mouth, pausing only for an instant as he reached the arch, to throw on his cloak and toss a final remark over his shoulder.

"Your Sight was deceived," he told the púca. "Neither Hag nor geis did I meet with behind the door."

"Deceived?" Reathach nearly choked on his meal. "Deceived is it? An' it's deceived I am, what's that dark flower's taken root in your heart, and growin' now like summer is come?"

Though his final words were plain and clearly spoken, the only one to appreciate Reathach's indignant reply was the púca himself. The Hunter had already gone.

Blackthorn could find no trace of Róisín outside the cave, neither the soft press of a young, firm step nor the Hag's halting, uneven tread. Dearg's spoor he spied, leading up the path to the pools, but it was well Blackthorn knew the way. Heavy mists clung to the mountain's heights, dulling the forest's green, making ghosts of the pines, and obscuring the trail.

As he climbed into the cleft at the lip of the cauldron, he stepped out of the fogs and into a clear, bright day. The only clouds on this side of the slope were from his own exhalations and the few fragile trails of moisture that rose light as thistledown from the waters below. Though the basin lay under the mountain's shadow, the pools blushed emerald and ice-blue, gentian and pale amethyst, and he could hear waters singing as they splashed over stone.

Blackthorn hurried down the track, then bent and scanned the frosty ground at the base of the incline. Dearg's passage was well marked upon two footpaths, the one taken last night, and another, more recently travelled, that wound away to the left. He followed the fresher trail, his long strides bringing him swiftly across the basin floor and to the shores of the singing pool.

Dearg lay by the waterside, and looked up as Blackthorn neared. His tail swung grudgingly from side to side, but Blackthorn was oblivious to the hound's first friendly gesture. He had eyes only for Dearg's mistress.

The Hag was squatting on a shoal of mounded stones, one of many that divided the pool into a chorus of streamlets. A ragged, yellowish fog puffed from her mouth. Her warped hand was twisted around a tiny clay vial. Stretching her arm over the thin veneer of cracked ice lining the edges of the stream, she dipped the jar in the pool. She shuddered as the noisy waters filled the vessel, as if the wet were as repugnant to her as it would be to Reathach.

Blackthorn could have wished she were bathing more than her hand. She was a good ten paces from him, but even at that distance and in the open air, she smelled rank. Yesterday her stink would have driven him away. This morning pity stirred in Blackthorn as powerfully as revulsion. He stayed where he was, and called out to her.

"Spells can be broken."

The old woman went on as if she hadn't heard, stoppering the vial with a finger from her dry hand, tilting it, then taking her hand away and examining the damp spot on her finger's tip as if it were a bird dropping or a bit of goblin dung. She gave a short nod, quickly dried both the bottle and her hand on her filthy rags, and raised her head. Without thinking, Blackthorn averted his eyes, and almost turned away.

It was part of the curse, he realized, catching himself—her voice that was painful to hear, her appearance that wounded the eye, her unbearable touch. He forced his gaze back in her direction.

"Spells can be broken," he said again.

"So they can," she snapped. "Some by words, some by deeds. Some, like the one you stole from me, can only be broken by death."

Her truculence, her scorn—he knew them now for what they were—the work of dark magic, cruelly cast.

"And the one that binds you?" he asked.

He kept his tone affable, as if he were talking to a skittish horse or a quick-tempered King. He was talking to the Hag, and his care was wasted entirely.

"Had you given me that," she said, pointing a crooked finger at the Talisman, "then might I have learned how to lift this curse! Could I have taken Domhnall's star to my hand, then might I have kenned the meaning of Úna's words."

"The Oak Seer! What were her words, Lady?"

The Hag wrinkled her nose, as if it were Blackthorn, and not herself that stank.

"A sailor you claimed to be when first you came to this isle," she scoffed. "Then a Poet. Now you would have me believe you are one of the Wise! Think you because you are your mother's son you are possessed of your mother's wisdom, Conall mac na Caillí?" she said, painfully drawing out the last syllables.

Though her hands were far from his star, it sent a bitter chill down Blackthorn's spine to hear his Name on her tongue.

"A fool I think myself, many times over," he answered as

evenly as he could. "True you speak, that little of my mother's wisdom has come to me. But though I be a poor sailor and a worse Poet, yet I am the Hunter. And there is neither man nor woman in all the five kingdoms knows Úna the Oak Seer better than I."

"To know her is not to understand her," the Hag countered.

She glided over the rill, not touching the waters. When Blackthorn took an unwilling step back, her lips drew into a sneer.

"I shall try your boast, Hunter. Hear Úna's prophecy, an' you will, then tell me what it means."

Her rags settled about her, and the Hag began to chant.

> *When Spell-Maker's star shines*
> *When silver bites stone*
> *When the bell can ring no more*

> *White will fly*
> *Black take wing*
> *And bide on hidden shore*

> *Freed but spell-bound*
> *Both call their last hope,*
> *The Hunter, to Summer's Door.*

"'When Spell-Maker's star shines,'" Blackthorn repeated slowly. "Greater my grief now than before that I cannot give the star to you, Lady. Yet, Úna did not say you must have it for yourself—only that its power would wake."

The Hag grunted noncommittally, but Blackthorn took it that she was conceding his point. He frowned, and ran his hand through his hair.

"'Summer's Door,'" he went on. "Bealtaine that must be, surely. And 'white' might well be the Stag, for is he not called 'The White One' often and again? But 'black,' now . . ." He watched the Hag carefully. "'Black' is the Black Rose of Inis na Linnte, I'm thinking."

The Hag spat as if the idea disgusted her. Turning her eye once more to the vial in her hand, she brought a wooden stopper from the folds of her rags and set it into the mouth of the jar.

"Take it," she said, holding it out to him.

He frowned at the bit of fired clay in her hands.

"We were speaking of Róisín Dubh, Lady."

The Hag's face contorted, and her sallow eye gleamed. "You were speaking of her—not I. Not I. And if your mother left you any wits at all, you'll gather them together and speak of her no more. White is your calling, Hunter. Shun the Black, or doubt not you'll regret it."

"Then we'll speak of Úna's prophecy."

"What more to say? You tell me only what I have guessed myself, and nothing of value."

"I could tell you more, an' I knew how Úna looked when she spoke her words."

"She looked like a madwoman," the Hag replied. "She bounded all over the mountaintop like a distracted fool, then strutted about, clucking like a barnyard fowl—"

"Bounded like a deer or a dog?"

"A deer?"

"What was she saying when she looked like a bird—and was it a cock she reminded you of?"

"You're as mad as she! What matter the form her madness took?"

Blackthorn shook his head. "There's no madness in Úna—she but speaks a different tongue, and her words are the least part of her sense. It's in the creatures she shows you, in the way she makes you see the corn growing, or hear the wind blow that her true message lies."

"Then is the Seer's prophecy meaningless," the Hag said icily, "for I attended to her mouthings, and not at all to her bestial idiocy."

The Hag took another step toward him, pulling her tattered kirtle clear of the melting frost on the damp stones.

"And what manner of idiot are you, Mac na Caillí? I offer a gift that could help you regain your Spear, yet you spare it not a glance! But yesterday you cared more for your geis than your life. This morning you would break it for a kiss! Is it the Hunter you are, or a lovesick fool?"

Blackthorn started and froze, like a hare overshadowed by the hawk. Her question was absurd—surely Éire still owned his soul. He could feel Her geis even now, hammering a familiar litany into his heart's blood; to hunt the Stag, always and only, to hunt the Stag. So, too, could he feel the bonds of the Talisman's silver spell upon him, and the star itself the second geis he must bear.

But with these two geasa, there weighed a third.

He had not until now realized it was on him, for this last made no demands, issued no orders. It promised nothing, it forbade nothing. It was not a curse that had fallen on him, or spell cast over him—no one had laid it upon his soul. By his own will it was his, and having taken it freely upon himself, neither craft, nor might, nor even a Poet's rann could ever recall the geis love had wakened in his heart.

When he answered the Hag, it was without any trace of doubt or hesitation.

"I would hunt the Stag, and serve the Black Rose, too."

The Hag shrieked with laughter. "Serve her? Already the Hunter has served Róisín—lifting his spear to serve her pleasure!" She spat again. "Insolent beggar. Your service here is ended."

"Why do you say 'her,' when it is yourself you're speaking of?" Blackthorn asked quietly. "Let me wish again to see you as you really are. Let me wish all the world to see you so, and break the spell that binds you."

With a single breath the Hag swelled to twice her size. "A sailor, a Poet, a sage—now a wizard you fancy yourself! Think you the wish you made last night, born of vanity and petulance, was enough to banish the Hag from Róisín's bed? Arrogant fool. The dark night conspired to aid you, or did the Cailleach your mother never tell you that a wish made upon the dying moon will come true with the new one?"

"Is it telling me you are 'twas the changing moon brought Róisín to my arms?"

The Hag cackled shrilly. "Not even the moon's magic could have blessed you so, Hunter, had a far greater will not bent to your own. A Goddess decided to grant your second desire, having failed to grant your first."

"Which Goddess?" Blackthorn's mind raced. "She Who kept me by Her side a moon and more in Brugh na Morna, and the Stag running?"

"Stay the anger from your heart, fool, an' you would retain Her favor."

A dark fire burned in Blackthorn's eyes. "Is it Her favor

She's shown me by hindering the Hunt, and compelling Éire's Huntsman to Inis na Linnte to do the Hag's bidding?"

"Not for spite has She done these things," the Hag hissed, "but for love. And not for the Hag, but for Róisín Dubh."

Her voice grated into Blackthorn's sudden silence.

"What, have I doused the fire of your fury? Simpleton. Though She took your Spear, yet gladly would She have returned it to you. And when it was stolen again, 'twas the Goddess used your wish, and the moon's death, and Her own power to make amends by giving you a night of rare pleasure. In all She has done, She means you well."

"Who?" Blackthorn whispered.

"Who blessed Róisín Dubh with the powers of a wish-bringer? Who shaped this isle for her to dwell? Whose breath stirred the pools and woke the magic within them?"

"Who plucked my Spear from the storm when I fought the Scáileanna on Binn Chuilceach, and gave me Strife in return?" Blackthorn pressed. "Who has kept it from me all this while? Tell me, Lady, for long have I desired to know."

"I have told you all I care to tell. Take the vial and my counsel, or take your empty head and that whimpering shape-shifter back to Éirinn and fend for yourself."

Anger rose in him again, but Blackthorn kept it in check. "An' you'll not tell me of the Goddess, then again I beg you, tell me of Róisín Dubh."

"Tell a fool of a fool."

The Hag moved away from him and turned her yellow eye toward the rippling pool. A long while she was silent. Dearg rose and ambled over to her, and she laid her claw on his huge head. Gently, she scratched behind his ears, but when she spoke, her voice was brutal.

"Beautiful, they called her, the Black Rose of Inis na Linnte. Her wizard's gift would have won her a Sliabh—it was unsurpassed among the Mighty, and lavishly she used it. Wishes she granted without number, for she believed herself wise enough to know a good suit from an evil one. Fool that she was. Easily deceived, so did she deceive herself."

The Hag looked over her shoulder at Blackthorn. Her smile was heartless.

"A sad tale and a selfless request never failed to soften Róisín's heart. Many times he came, your enemy and hers, always with gifts, always with praises, always swearing his wishes would serve fair and noble ends. And when he had all he wanted, gem-studded gloves of power, scrying sands, potions, spells, then he turned on her, and called upon his master, the Dead Lord, to make good his curse."

A shuddering breath shook the Hag's withered bones.

"Three years has Róisín borne her affliction," she said, "three years sought to rid herself of it. Three years were hers to break Shadow's spell, and now her time is all but over. When the first sun of summer rises on Bealtaine Day, no more will a beneficent Goddess be able to grant the Wish-Bringer a night of joy. No more will a drink from the pool of the fountain give Róisín Dubh wings to fly. Never again will the Black Rose walk within the circles of the world."

"Then the curse must be lifted before summer's morn."

The old crone whirled on him, her good eye widening in astonishment.

"You are as greedy as she was trusting," she accused him. "What, do you hope to win Róisín's heart by breaking the spell that binds her? Have you not enough to do before summer's dawn?"

"Whether I win your heart or no," Blackthorn answered with a hint of a smile, "you have won mine. An' we cannot lift this curse by Bealtaine, then Shadow will have us both, Lady."

"Pig-stubborn idiot," she rasped. "Will you take Róisín's folly as a geis upon yourself? Of all men, you know the weight of such burdens—the peril they place upon the soul."

"No man better."

She threw back her head as if she would laugh, but only a gurgling hiss came out of her mouth. "And if the Hunt leads you north, and the Rose bids you go south? Will you tear yourself in two, and hope to sew the pieces back together when summer is come?"

Blackthorn folded his arms. "Yourself did say the same enemy that caused your sorrows did cause my own. Both geasa point to the same path, and Bealtaine marks the end of both roads."

"Bah!" The Hag opened and closed her toothless mouth, then spat a wad of slime onto the stones. "Take not this geis upon your soul, Conall," she said at last.

She made it sound more like a threat than an entreaty, but Blackthorn shrugged. "It is mine already."

"Then you are both doomed."

Blackthorn paced slowly to the water's edge. "Tell me of our enemy," he said.

"He serves Shadow. What more to tell?"

"Have you his Name?"

"A spurious Name have I, one he gave to Róisín. Ignorant of its falsity, she tried to use it against him when at last she knew him for a traitor. And so were the words she spoke mangled and distorted, and so did her curse come home to roost."

Blackthorn's eyes narrowed. "What kind of beast is he?"

"And haven't I just told you? He's a man, you idiot. The vilest beast of all."

"What kind of a beast is he, I'm saying—" Blackthorn ran his hand through his hair, looking for another way to form the question. "Is he a bear, ferocious and unappeasable? Then I must challenge him, showing no fear, and strike once and well to bring him down. Is he a fox, sly and cunning? Then I must be as the hound, swift and untiring on his heels until I drive him to ground. Is he a hawk or a harrier, ruthless and wild? Then I must lure him in, hood his sharp eyes, and with hunger tame him—"

"He is an eel," the Hag interrupted. Her voice carried a note of bitter conviction. "You don't even mark him, hidden in the murky weeds. Or if you do, you see but the tip of his snout, and think it no great danger—how can you guess at his true size, his true power? Then he strikes, an enormous, sinuous, evil worm, swift and inescapable. Jaws wide, he bites, his sharp teeth close and sink in."

Her tongue darted about her thin lips. "He is a hunter himself, Mac na Caillí, too smart to take the fisherman's hook, too quick for the net, too slippery for the spear."

Blackthorn's eyes gleamed. "Two ways there are to hunt eel," he said. "The first is to build a weir across a waterway and let the creatures entangle themselves in the net."

"So might a village catch eel," the Hag snorted, "but it takes more than one man to erect a weir across a river and drag it in again."

"The second way," Blackthorn went on, ignoring the

Hag's interruption, "is to set a narrow-necked basket in the eel's waters. All that's left is to wait for the eel to invite himself in."

The Hag shook her head. "Dark the pool where this eel bides. Pure waters you'll need to clear your sight, an' you would spy him in his lair."

She tossed him the vial. Blackthorn caught it and considered the gift, then looked straight into the Hag's good eye.

"You pretend to be cruel," he said, "but in truth you are nothing but kind to me."

From a squawk the Hag's laughter rose to a screeching howl of contempt.

"Is this a kindness I do you? Come Bealtaine Day your soul will break into a thousand pieces as many lifetimes cannot make whole! And if love has blinded you to the truth I'm speaking, then is the fair Róisín far crueler than the Hag."

Forty-five

Then he threw off his beggar's clothes,
And kissed her thrice and thrice again.
"Though I've gold rings, a thousand, thousand score,
And though I've silver worth a thousand times more,
And though I've a thousand jewels in store,
Will you love me, my brown-eyed darling?"

The Beggar of Baile an Bhothair

This is what comes of trusting the magpie, Reathach thought morosely. It was not long past midday, but though the patches of cloud overhead were white with sunlight, a deep shadow clung to the hedge before them. Peering right and left over the top of Blackthorn's pouch, the púca saw the thorny wall stretching unbroken along the ridge in both directions. The only sensible thing to do would be to turn their backs on the grim barrier, but Blackthorn was already stepping toward it.

With a squeak of protest, Reathach squirmed out of the pouch. He shinnied down the Hunter's leggings, then skittered away to a small mound of crumbled chert that lay wedged between the trunks of three spindly trees. The beechwoods that covered the hillside were unseasonally empty and late in greening, but far less frightening than the hedge's knifelike thorns.

Rising to a man, Reathach shivered as Blackthorn reached a tentative hand to the thick branches. Every gnarled limb was leafless and, except for the thorns, smooth as polished stone. Never had the púca seen its like. No mere bud would ever break through that iron bark, nor fragile flower endure upon it, not though Aengus Óg Himself willed it so.

The Hunter reached his other hand to the maze of branch and thorn, and the púca groaned. The reckless fool meant to scale the cursed thing.

"It's impossible to climb!" Reathach called out.

"Well, difficult, certainly. Perhaps not impossible, an' I'm willing to suffer a few cuts."

Despite his words, Blackthorn pulled back suddenly. Reathach saw it too, a formless patch of gray, flitting soundlessly through the hedge. As soon as the Hunter stepped away, the thing grew still and was lost to their sight. Blackthorn and Reathach matched the shadow's silence, waiting for it to move again, but the pattern of darkness and gray in the grim web of thorns bewildered their eyes.

The magpie darted between the hedge and the Hunter, and began to chide, but whether her raucous reprimands were directed at Blackthorn or the shadow-beast, Reathach could not tell. Circling gracefully, the bird folded her wings and stooped, then spread them and came fluttering to Blackthorn's shoulder.

Reathach's face crinkled like a dried currant as the Hunter reached up to stroke the bird's breast.

"Bewitched by that twittering pest, you are," the púca grumbled. "That or you're mad. And didn't I say as much, even before we left Inis na Linnte for Éirinn's shore?"

"Neither bewitched nor mad—" Blackthorn began amiably, but the púca wasn't listening.

"Sure, an' what save madness or spells could have made the Hunter glad to share the Hag's table for a fortnight? What save madness or spells could have driven him to cut turf and gather wood for the rotten old sow's fire, to bring fresh meat to her pot, and himself never receivin' a word of thanks, but only abuse for his kindness?"

"Only abuse?" Blackthorn challenged, raising an eyebrow. "And weren't we both well housed and well fed those fourteen days? And when I brought down my first game in the forest of Inis na Linnte—a fine, healthy buck it was, and myself with no tool to dress it—I went looking for our host to borrow a knife, and didn't I find instead a keen-edged dagger waiting for me by the still, quiet pool? And wishing for a shirt to cover my back, didn't the pool give me the one I now wear, and also a sheath for my sword when I thought to ask for it?"

Reathach squinted dubiously at Strife's new home, a black leather scabbard studded all down the edges with stones of jet. "Arrah, and that little clay bottle hanging from your belt—that you claim is a boon as well, though yourself did tell me the Hag gave it you with her own hand."

The magpie ruffled her feathers impatiently and flew from Blackthorn's shoulder, piping sweetly to lure them on. Like a spellbound fool, Blackthorn started after her.

"Wake from your dreamin', bodach," Reathach pleaded. He hurried along behind, but on tiptoe, not wanting to disturb the shadow he feared was yet lurking in the thorns to his left. "Can you be thinkin' the Hag means you well with her presents? Whisht, 'twasn't an evening's pleasure you bargained away, but your wits, sure and certain! You owe the Hag nothin', I'm sayin', and should trust her creature not at all."

Blackthorn laughed.

Brighde's Fire, but it wrung the púca's heart to see the man so ensorcelled. Blind the Hunter was entirely, and deaf to the sense Reathach was speaking. Sure, an' wasn't it plain the Hag meant them ill? But look where the magpie had led them!

Two weeks it had taken the floating Isle of Pools to sail up and around Éirinn's coast, until at last it lay alongside the rocky northern shore of east Ulaidh. When Blackthorn had climbed from Inis na Linnte's white strand onto the sea-washed rocks of Clochán na bhFormhórach, the Giants' Stepping-Stones, the púca had been glad, for spring had come full upon the world. It warmed the earth like green fire, flowed like lifeblood through the forest. A matter of days it must be, Reathach had told Blackthorn, before the magic that had quickened in Éirinn's womb at Imbolc would burst from the limbs of trees and cloak the branches in buds like pale jewels. A matter of days before violets scented the wood, before lupines and daffodils shone in the sun, before cowslips lifted their shy heads from the wet grasses. They had returned to Éirinn at the midpoint of spring, when the lengthening days and the shortening nights would meet in perfect parity. And to this happy news all the Hunter had answered was, "But six short weeks lie between this day and Bealtaine."

Reathach paid him no heed. Not an hour had Blackthorn carried him through the greenwood before the púca was as drunk as the rest of the wild, intoxicated by spring. Like the hares madly mating on the hills, like the swollen streams that roared with unabashed joy to be free of the bonds of winter, Reathach imbibed the liquor of returning life. So young it made him feel to be in the forest and spring come, he had abandoned Blackthorn's pouch for his own two legs, and kept pace with the Hunter without complaint.

But south the magpie had coaxed them, ever south from where they had come ashore. So they came at last to An Baile Meánach, or what was left of it. The Hunter did not pause to view the ruin of the town—one look at the empty-eyed cotes had been enough for him even without Reathach's begging to be gone—but neither did Blackthorn fail to point out the fresh prints of goblins' feet and horses' hooves in the mud of An Baile Meánach's abandoned fields.

They had shunned the traders' roads after that, the Hunter promising they would be less easily spotted in the woods than on the paths. The thick forest and spring-deep marshes slowed their progress, and they had difficult crossings at the rivers An Bhuais and Méan. To Reathach it seemed the Hunter slipped through the tangled trees with the effortless grace of a seal through the deeps, and traversed the wet lowlands almost as easily as the Hag's bird flew over them. His own feet plodded across the forest floor and sank into the bogs. Finally, he stopped dead in the midst of a soggy fen and cursed loudly.

"May your cup overflow with these brackish waters you're forcin' me through! Marsh or mountain, it's all the same to the Hunter of Éirinn! No thought do you spare for Reathach's old legs!"

Blackthorn turned at once and came back to the púca. "Hush, now," he said placatingly, "and don't be telling the world who we are. I'll carry you, then, an' it's your pleasure."

Reathach shifted, and Blackthorn lifted him up. "Truth be

told, I feel more a mouse than you," he remarked ruefully as he set the púca in his pouch. "Running low, hurrying from cover to cover, death's shadow always about us . . ."

That had done it. Bad enough spring's song had gone out of tune since An Baile Meánach. Bad enough that with every step south the colors of the season dulled the more, losing their brightness for the faded green of lichens and the brown of dying leaves. Bad enough that game was scarce, that the dinners Blackthorn did bring down were scrawny and tasteless. Worse now Reathach had no sleep at night for listening for the sound of goblins' feet, and each day lived in terror of the shadows.

From then on he rode in the Hunter's pouch, and thankful he was to be there when twice they were surprised by their enemies. The first time the magpie's shrill warning gave the Hunter time to find refuge in a thicket of cranberry. Peeping out of the purse to see what was about, Reathach caught a glimpse of half a score dark elves, mounted and riding north like the wind. He dived quickly down to the bottom of the pouch, and waited to hear the Hunter draw his sword, but Blackthorn held still, and the hoofbeats faded as the Scáileanna galloped by.

The second time it was goblins. Though Reathach had imagined he'd heard the beasts every night since seeing their footprints, he doubted his ears when he heard them in truth. The bird was no help at all, at all, sleeping as she was in the crook of Blackthorn's arm, as if it were the bent limb of a blackthorn bush. 'Twas the Hunter that woke, and killed his foes by the faint light that streamed from Strife's edges and by the baleful red glow of the goblins' own eyes.

Even before the attack, Reathach was doing his best to redirect Blackthorn's footsteps to the nearby towns, Bealach Cláir and An Dubh-Áth in the east, and Tuaim to the west, where the river An Bhanna ran north from Loch nEathach. 'Twas no more than any decent soul would do, he argued, to see if all was well, or if the villagers had suffered the fate of the unfortunates of An Baile Meánach. The Hunter would have none of it, but wended his way south to the loch.

Yesterday they had reached its banks, nearly a week after departing the Isle of Pools. The lake lay under clouded skies, dark and sullen, its waters empty of birds, its shoreline quiet.

Blackthorn and Reathach had gone the day hungry for want of game, and 'twas only this morning the Hunter had snared a meal in a reed-choked estuary—and the snipe had made a meager meal at that.

All the early hours they had walked hugging the loch's eastern bank, but near midday the magpie veered away from the water and called for them to follow her into the listless alder groves inland. She led them east, through the spindly woods, up a hill of pitiful beeches, and at last to this thorn hedge at the top of the ridge.

Casting a suspicious glance toward the cursed thing, then down the slope at the cheerless forest, Reathach sighed dismally. Sure, an' the journey they'd made across Ulaidh was a long one, but further it seemed they'd travelled in time—backward—from budding spring to a winter without promise.

Still what could he do, and his geis forcing him to follow the Hunter, and himself pleased to follow the magpie? All afternoon the same sight was before Reathach's eyes—the dreary wood to his right, the daggered hedge to his left. All the rest of the day, until day's end, and there it was at last—a passage through the thorns. The púca had never felt so wretched.

It was a sizable gap, broad enough for three horses to pass at once, but it was less than inviting for all its width. Thorn-laden branches stretched across the ground from one section of hedge wall to the other. Above, where the wall met the lowest limbs of the trees, the forbidding vines bunched together and formed an arch over the gap.

Peering through the gate, Reathach looked down into a narrow valley of dead or dying beeches. A sliver of gray, a clearing or a meadow, lay in the valley's heart, just visible in the midst of the leafless forest.

Returning to Blackthorn's shoulder, the magpie cheeped an inquisitive note and cocked a curious eye at the Hunter.

"Twilight," Reathach implored. "A poor time to pass so forbidding a door."

To the púca's surprise and great relief, the Hunter nodded. Turning away from the hedge, Blackthorn squinted down into the mass of indistinguishable grays pooled at the base of the slope.

"There," he said, pointing. "As hospitable a spot as these

woods can offer, and even water below, an' my ears don't deceive me."

The magpie dove down, a black-and-white arrow winging through the smoky dusk. Reathach hurried after her.

Blackthorn looked back at the gap before joining his companions. He saw a flicker of shapeless fog run along one side of the hedge. It seemed to thin, and worm upward, then wriggle across the branches that arched between the two portions of thorny wall. In a moment it had disappeared into the shadows of the other side.

He carried the evil vision with him down the hill and into the coming night, where it haunted his brief and fitful sleep.

Dead hearts, black souls fester in the evil-armed trees. Where, oh, where the flowers of Achadh na Liag, the spring-swollen streams racing to fill Loch nEathach? Where my death, the Hunter, with his bright Spear? Only red-eyed hounds behind me, and gray riders before me, and Mother Éirinn below me, deaf to the hammering of my silver hooves upon Her dying bones.

Blackthorn woke chilled and uneasy, and frowned at the bare-branched trees that so resembled the ones of his dream. Rising, he took his sword in his hand and let his ears lead him to where a pathetic trickle of brown water wandered away toward Loch nEathach. As he knelt to drink, the magpie settled on a half-dead sapling on the other side of the rivulet.

The water was cold in Blackthorn's palm, but acrid and bitter in his mouth. He spat it out, and followed the narrow waterway with his eyes up the slope to the hedge. In the pale morning light the thorn wall on the crest of the ridge cast a long shadow. The rill he had drunk from ran hard by the hedge, under the darkness, only finding the light again when halfway down the hill.

His pouch stirred as Reathach poked his head out. The púca climbed to the ground and came to the water's edge to drink.

"It's tainted," said Blackthorn, directing the shapeshifter's eyes up toward the hedge.

"All this land is tainted," Reathach grumbled.

Coming to his feet, Blackthorn moved his hand to his pouch as if to open it. Reathach dropped immediately to a mouse, but the Hunter's fingers froze on the purse string as his eyes fell on his own shadow. Reathach squeaked impatiently, but the magpie began to scold, and Blackthorn had ears only for her. Disgusted, the púca shifted again.

"Och, isn't that clever, now?" he said sarcastically. "Sure, an' why should the Hunter of Éirinn listen to words of wisdom spoken in his own tongue and by a friend, when he can hearken to a magpie's chatter? And what is the silver-tongued creature advisin', an' you don't mind me askin'? Whisht, don't be tellin' me now—I can understand her meself! 'Tis the straightest road to the nearest death she knows, and yourself fool enough to go where she bids."

"Not a bit of it," answered Blackthorn mildly. "Why, it's tellin' me she is that my enemy will know me, an' I come to him looking like this."

Reathach stared at Blackthorn, then turned his eyes slowly toward the magpie, then back again to the Hunter. "But you said the thief did not see you in the pool, that the dog had you down before your eyes met." His voice was hushed with uncertainty.

"And so the hound did. But my enemy has stolen magics that can show him much he desires to see. Though he has no gift of Sight, yet he may glimpse shadows in his scrying sands, and even that may be enough to betray me."

"*By the light that shines!*" Reathach whooped gleefully. "You do ken the magpie's speech! Is it only herself you understand, or is it any bird? Sure, an' what secrets we'll learn, an' you—"

"It's not only that you're the most cowardly beggar in the five kingdoms that makes you such fine company," Blackthorn said, kneeling again by the brooklet and unlacing his sleeves. "It's that you are the easiest to gull. All I've just told you, the Hag told me before we left Inis na Linnte."

He carefully washed his face and arms in the polluted waters, then ran his wet fingers through his hair. Taking one of the laces from his sleeve, he wrapped it around his dark mane, tying it into a tight knot at the nape of his neck. He shifted his cloak so that it fell open in the front, and last took his sword and bound it not across his back, but at his hip. Reathach studied the man, then the shadow on the ground.

"You're an ill-natured, flint-hearted, unmannerly rake," Reathach said. "But sure, an' when it comes to lyin', whether it be the smallest deceit or the grandest deception, you're fair astonishin'."

The magpie whistled, in agreement the púca thought, but Blackthorn knit his brow.

"Uncanny, it is." Reathach looked sidelong at the Hunter, as if mistrustful of his transformation. "Not Blackthorn do I see, but his twin, and he not so handsome as yourself. Look you," he nodded at the ground. "A small change in the man, but your shadow's a stranger altogether."

"I'll fool no eye that has ever looked into my own," Blackthorn muttered, remembering the Gruagach. He shifted his weight more to one leg and rested his hand on the hilt of his sword. "'Tis the best I can do. Let's be off."

"Then open your pouch, bodach, and put me in," the púca said miserably, "for truth be told, me own legs will never bear me through the gap at the top of the ridge."

Forty-six

*May your feet always lead you
away from misfortune*

Blackthorn half expected the hedge's warped limbs to rise from the ground and snare him as he passed through the breach in the hedge, but the twisted branches defied his expectation. They lay unmoving, and the fleeting wisp of gray he glimpsed far off in the tangle of wood and thorn may have been a true shadow. The magpie skimmed under the arch, then flew to Blackthorn and perched near his ear.

"*Bare is the companionless shoulder,*" he laughed quietly. "Stay with me, then. The path is clear."

Clear to some, thought Reathach. The púca, peering over the lip of the pouch, saw no path at all. Granite boulders he saw, and feared they might be trolls. The beeches with their peeling bark reminded him of the Hag and her withered flesh. He shuddered at the thickets of dagger-thorn bushes, and shook his head helplessly at the trackless, silty soil passing swiftly below him.

The Hunter's eyes were keener. Though they marked the same rocks, the same trees, the same ground as the púca, to the Hunter of Éirinn they told a tale. *This is the way*, they said. *Here goblins have pounded the earth with their flat feet, here torn dead leaves from a dying beech. Here a hoof tripped on a root, here did an axe once scrape the stone. A black goblin hair marks the turn at the clump of thorn, and the next turn almost as plain—the broken twig by the fallen tree. Now left again, avoiding the clearing where the sun dares shine, for a path trod by goblins will cleave to the shadows. . . .*

Like a hound with the scent, Blackthorn sped through the woods, sometimes bent low to the ground, sometimes running with head high and a strange, fey light in his eye. Unexpectedly, he paused, and his look became furtive. Before the púca could ask what was wrong, he had taken cover behind a rocky outcropping.

Reathach heard only a suggestion of hooves upon the earth, barely enough to alert him that horses were passing some distance from where the Hunter crouched. The sound of the Scáileanna's ride was little louder to Blackthorn, and lost to him entirely after a few moments. But when the noise had been swallowed by the wood, the púca had learned nothing, while the Hunter now knew where another trail lay, that there were five Scáileanna upon it, and that the dark elves were making all haste for the valley's heart. He moved on, keeping to the goblin-marked path under his feet, and if he went with greater caution, yet he went with even greater speed.

Reathach prudently curled into a tight ball at the base of the leather pouch, and stayed there until Blackthorn stopped a second time. Even then, he'd not have dared set whisker outside the sack, but for the Hunter.

Opening the mouth of the purse with a quick, ungentle hand, Blackthorn hauled the mouse out by the scruff of his neck. The púca tried to bite the fingers that grabbed him, failed, dug his claws into the purse, and hung on with all his strength. The supple leather slid out from under his paws. Reathach found himself on the ground beside a rough-barked beech, and the Hunter frowning at him with a finger set sternly against his lips.

"To a man, now," Blackthorn whispered, "and take a look."

Reathach shifted, then glanced about nervously. All that met his eye was the magpie as she dropped from Blackthorn's shoulder to a humped root. "What's to see?" he asked, as softly as he could.

Blackthorn inclined his head. "You've the Sight. You tell me."

The sun was high and bright as the day would allow, but the deep shadows of the trees made the world dim and indistinct. Reathach craned his neck, peering around Blackthorn. His initial alarm doubled as he saw that the malevolent-looking beech that hid them was the last of the trees before the forest opened unexpectedly onto a flat, grassless belt of land. This dropped away after a hundred paces or so into a broad, shallow ditch. Beyond the ditch lay a long, low, utterly desolate hill. There was no creature upon it now, nor could Reathach see any sign that life had ever visited the barren knoll. Just to view it made him feel exposed.

"An empty hillock," he whispered, "sportin' not so much as a blade of grass for to bend in the wind."

Blackthorn shook his head in annoyance. "That my own eyes could tell me."

"Use them, then, and let me back into your purse. Under these shadows my sight is no better than your own."

Reathach jumped as Blackthorn pressed himself flat against the ground. In another moment, the púca joined him on the dusty earth, for now he heard them—horses, at a gallop. At first the hoofbeats were as quiet as the shape-shifter's beating heart, but like thunder they grew louder as the riders neared.

Suddenly they broke from the woods to the right, five Scáileanna, mounted and armed with swords. They rode swiftly along the edge of the forest, heading toward the beech that hid the bird, the púca, and Blackthorn. Reathach tried to still his trembling, not daring to shift lest his movement draw the dark elves' eyes. When they were no more than a hundred strides away, they wheeled their horses to face the bare hill and halted. One of them called out.

Reathach trembled all the more when he heard the Scáil's voice, hollow and cold, like the voices of the dark elves of Binn Chuilceach. He heard no answer, but as one the Scáileanna spurred their horses on toward the rise. Not down into the ditch did they ride, but across it, onto the empty air. Their horses' hooves clattered as if they were riding over timbers. When they had crossed the ditch and reached the base of the hill, they disappeared.

Blackthorn lifted himself higher to get a better look. Not a breath of wind was upon the knoll, not a flicker of life.

Undoing the thong that held the clay jar to his belt, he brought the vial gently into his palm. As he worked the stopper out of its mouth, the magpie hopped to his knee and bobbed her head. At that the púca could no longer hold still.

"Stop it up again, you daft and witless fool!" he hissed, aghast at what the Hunter was doing. "Will you let loose the curses bottled in there by that foul and malevolent Hag?"

Blackthorn shot the púca a strange look. "I'll hear no more ill of her. Do you mark me?"

"Mark you? Do I mark you? Only too well, you poor, benighted fool."

Reathach's hands began to twist about each other as Blackthorn blocked the vial's narrow mouth with his finger, and turned the jar briefly upside down. The bird blinked her eyes, and Blackthorn obediently drew his wet finger over his own. Then he turned and looked out over the bare hill.

"*Badhbh, Macha, and Mór-Ríoghain!*" he breathed.

Reathach closed his eyes, as if his own blindness might block the Hunter's Sight.

"A broch," whispered Blackthorn, "rising behind stone battlements, and they surrounding the hill and standing as high as the walls of Dún na nGall—"

"Wurra, wurra," the púca moaned. "Spare me. I don't want to know."

"A wooden bridge stretches across the ditch where the Scáileanna passed," he went on, ignoring Reathach.

The púca was about to repeat his plea when he realized, with a twinge of irritation, that Blackthorn was describing the place for the magpie's benefit, and not his own.

"It leads to a wooden door, bound in iron bands and opening on black, iron hinges. The gate is closed, but I can see the gatehouse behind it—sturdy gray stones under thick thatching. Beyond that, pressed up against the backside of the gatehouse, stands the broch."

His breath quickened, but he kept his voice low. "A monstrous, conical tower it is," he said. "Smoke pours from its crown as if the fires that burn deep in the belly of the earth have here found a vent. Many eyes it has—windows looking out upon the forest. Yet for all the shadowed slits streaking the drystone wall, the broch is faceless."

He shifted position and looked again. Reathach whimpered.

"There's a close surrounding the tower, I'm thinking, but all I can be sure of is a few faint trails of smoke and the tops of two thatched roofs beyond the rampart."

He stopped there, before he could tell of the three Scáileanna in plain view upon the battlements. How many more might be guarding the rampart beyond the limits of his vision, Blackthorn was reluctant to guess. They were lax, these guards, turning as often to watch what was going on within the walls as without them. Plainly they expected nothing untoward from the forest. At least he might look to have the advantage of surprise.

Reaching a finger to the magpie, Blackthorn stroked her gently across the top of her head and down her back. "Home quick as you may," he told her. "Well you've guided us, but there is danger to you in these woods, and danger to me an' you are discovered."

The magpie jumped into the air and beat to a low branch of a nearby tree. There she stopped, and looked back before flying on and out of sight.

Blackthorn turned to Reathach. "Be a mouse, an' you will with me."

A terrified moan was all the púca could muster. He would have dreaded the invitation in any case, but since that morning the Hunter's every word seemed to promise disaster. This gate was a worse one than the grave on Keeper Hill— but to wait for Blackthorn here, alone in this horrible forest . . . *Brighde's Fire*, not even a forest. A forest's tomb it was, a forest's dark and empty shadow . . .

"A few more drops are yet within the bottle," coaxed Blackthorn, more softly still. "Let me clear your Sight, that you can look upon what frightens you, and so fear it less. Come with me for once."

Reathach shook his head, but to the bottle, not the pouch. Dropping to a mouse, he crawled up Blackthorn's leg and into the purse. Let the Hunter think him too great a coward to look upon the broch. 'Twas easier than explaining that what he feared to See, should his eyes be opened, was not the stronghold upon the hill, but his own geis beckoning to him from the shadowed gate.

The lightless eyes of the Scáileanna on the rampart fell on Blackthorn as soon as he stepped from the forest. He affected not to notice the guards, but swaggered slowly, arrogantly toward the gate. They must be calling out to him, he reasoned, but the magic that had cleared his sight did nothing to sharpen his other senses. Stopping at the edge of the wooden bridge, he looked quickly up to the top of the wall, as if his attention had been drawn there.

"I'm no more free with my Name than you are with yours!" he shouted to the Scáileanna, praying they had challenged him. But surely they had—what task had any watch but to demand the stranger's Name and business? "I bear tidings for your master, and none other."

Though not the slightest hint of interest crossed the Scáileanna's faces, two of them set arrows to their bows and drew back the strings. The third motioned to two other guards, who turned at once where they stood and cast their dark gazes out upon the wood. Blackthorn laughed, lacing his mirth with contempt.

"Why, I thought 'twas Scáileanna I heard challenge me, but sure, my thinking was mistaken. Goblins it must be, for who but red-eyes are so lacking in wits they would kill the messenger, his words unspoken?" He changed his tone, and his look darkened. "Present me to your master, or the Shadow King himself will curse you for the fools you are."

His threat hung for a long moment in the unnaturally still air. The Scáileanna did not relax their bowstrings, but Blackthorn said no more, certain that further words would only tempt them to let fly. He knew when to make the lure dance, and when to let it rest upon the waters.

Soundlessly, the gate opened, and a single Scáil rode out upon the wooden bridge. He wore a dark helmet, and armor the colorless black of his eyes. A sheathed sword was at his side and the butt of a spear rested against his stirrup.

"Deliver your message to me, little man," he said.

The Scáil's voice was more air than substance, and chill as a winter wind. The horse shied when his rider spoke, but the dark elf brought his mount swiftly under control. Blackthorn almost shied as well, but in his heart he gave thanks that the Scáil had come out from the silence of the fort's spelled walls to treat with him. He kept his smile by gritting his teeth, and shook his head.

"What good my news to me, an' its reward goes to another?"

The Scáil urged his horse on another step. "Death will be your reward, an' you try my patience. Give me your news, and I will judge its worth—but beware, bold intruder. An' I find your tidings worthless, it will go hard on you—and little there is in the world the master of Márrach desires to know, yet cannot learn for himself."

Márrach, thought Blackthorn. The Name itself casts a shadow.

"From An Lorgain I've come," he answered easily. "A day it took me to travel up from the south, and all this morning have I been wandering about in your fair woods, seeking a path to your gate." His eyes narrowed. "An' the master of Márrach's Sight is so keen, how came I here, an' none to welcome me? Can it be I arrived all unlooked-for? Perhaps my tidings have merit—perhaps none." His smile turned to a sneer. "Whichever it be, I'll not tell them to a doorward."

He had not thought to see the Scáil react to his insult, and so was not disappointed. The dark elf's expression was indifferent, but his horse was restless, disturbed by something the Scáil was saying too softly for the Hunter to hear. Turning his head slightly to focus the whisper into his ear, Blackthorn trained his attention on the words he was missing. In an instant he was caught. Like the spell the dark elves had made to slow him on Binn Chuilceach, the syllables that fell from this Scáil's lips were in a language strange and unlovely, yet their sense rang clearly in Blackthorn's heart.

Tell me, the Scáil chanted. *You long to speak, I wait to hear. Tell me why you have come.*

With an effort, Blackthorn got his hand to the hilt of his sword. The familiar feel of the leather-bound grip was comforting, but Strife could do nothing to stop the Scáil's spell unless he drew her, and that was already beyond him. His limbs felt weighted with heavy chains—soon he would be unable to turn his head or blink his eyes. Only his tongue was loose, and the words that threatened to spill from it weren't the lies he had invented for his enemy's ears. Of himself he yearned to speak, of his geasa, of his Spear, of his desperate plan. Only truth would unbind him, only truth rid him of the darkness that had invaded his heart.

A last scrap of volition kept his tongue still—a fragment torn from him in Domhnall's Keep and there spellbound to the dead Wizard's knot of tarnished silver. If the Talisman's powers served Blackthorn's will, so was his will entangled in the star, and the star untouched by the Scáil's sorcery. Blackthorn clung to the geis that linked him to the Talisman as a drowning man clings to a piece of drifting wood. For a time, it held him above the dark waves that threatened to overwhelm him. Each breath he drew waxed heavy with his secrets and hopes, but by his own will it lightened again as it left him, and passed soundlessly from his lips.

The Scáil's voice became more sibilant, more insistent. The chanted words tugged at Blackthorn's resolve, prying him loose from his fragile mooring, pulling him under the spell. If he could not silence the Scáil now and at once, he would be undone.

"Márrach's arrows do not daunt me."

Though the words were carried on little more than a whisper, they were of his own choosing, and in speaking them Blackthorn felt the shadow lift from his heart.

"Nor do Márrach's spells bind me." He kept his voice low, as if the softness of his interruption had been intentional, and added a note of scorn. "Either your master is poorly served, or his reputation exceeds his might."

The Scáil's song ceased. Blackthorn wanted to shake himself, to wipe the cold sweat from his brow, to look away from the empty eyes that held his own, if only for a moment. Instead, he raised an eyebrow, and shifted his weight to his back leg in negligent ease. The dark elf's face remained impassive, but when he spoke again, Blackthorn noted a harsh edge to the Scáil's voice that had not been there before.

"Come, then, an' you are so eager to enjoy our hospitality," he hissed. "But be warned. You will find Márrach's gate opens more readily in welcome than in farewell."

Forty-seven

Swiftest run a stream of fire,
a stream of water, a stream of lies

The Fifth Triad of Éirinn

A volley of noise and stink assailed Blackthorn as he passed through Márrach's gate, the clashing of metal, jeering and shouts from the close, the smells of acrid fires and goblin filth. The sudden attack on his senses was jarring, but he had time to gather his wits while the Scáil dismounted and passed his helmet and spear into the care of another guard.

By the time they set off again, Blackthorn's step was sure and deliberate. He was led through the gatehouse, a strangely spare building under an unusually high, slanted roof. At the far end, where the gatehouse walls abutted the outer stones of the broch, a second gate was hung. The two great wooden doors, their rounded tops snug against the high stone archway, stood open, but Blackthorn was certain they would be swiftly closed an' there was need to bar entry to the interior of the tower.

A dark, airless tunnel stretched beyond the doors—more a high-roofed cavern than a passageway. Its length was daunting. Scores of towers Blackthorn had seen in his wanderings, and many, like this one, were double-walled. But an' this tunnel began at the broch's outer wall and ended at the inner, then were the walls of Márrach's tower more massive than any others he could Name. Ceithil's Hall could be housed between them, so wide the gap that set them apart.

He went as smartly as he could through the unlighted entranceway, almost unable to make out the stiff shadow of the Scáil before him, hearing the footfalls of two other guards fall in behind. Not waking reality, but a nightmare it seemed—caught between Scáileanna in a dark passage, with the sound and stench of a goblin-filled hall before him. Márrach's hospitality made no pretense of courtesy. Not as a guest ushered to a Chieftain's seat did they bring him into the tower, but as a prisoner led to his doom.

His doubts were beginning to erode his disguise— Blackthorn set a disdainful look upon his face and willed the tension from his shoulders. Though only a semblance of confidence, his conceit eased his apprehension. *Only magic or might will deny them their due*, or so 'twas said. Should he win free of this place, he would make another line for the old Lore-Song, adding guile to the list of things of which Scáileanna need beware.

Stepping out of the corridor into what should have been the inner court, Blackthorn found the light little better, the air stale, the space choked with red-eyes and Scáileanna. The tower Blackthorn had seen from the forest, crowned with an edge of thatching and spewing smoke from its open top, that tower should have allowed daylight through to the courtyard. Yet, within the broch it was inexplicably night. Only the windows provided any relief from the blackness, but what passed through the narrow slits was clouded and cheerless, and revealed little.

With difficulty Blackthorn followed his guide, an elusive slip of gray, and threaded past goblins and Scáileanna, past shadows that only vaguely resembled tables and benches. Eyes better sighted in the gloom than his own marked his progress. Curiosity and anticipation sparked like fire and swept through the hall. Blackthorn felt himself on the crest of a wave of silence; as he walked forward, the sibilant whispers, the snarls, the clatter of bowls and knives, even the scrape of benches and creak of leather subsided into the dark.

Without warning, the nebulous shadow he had been trailing

vanished. Blackthorn stopped. The quiet was palpable, broken only by a few cautious growls. He strained every sense to its utmost, and used his wits to fill in where his senses failed him.

Mingled with the greasy odor of goblin and the musty tang of sour ale was the smell of burnt meat. The shadows of the Scáileanna were cast upon long tables—other boards were crowded with goblins, and one seemed reserved for a few savage-looking men. The inner court had been made into a feasting hall, and such repast as Shadow's servants might enjoy was spread before them.

Blackthorn assumed the stance he had practiced that morning by the stream and scanned the gleaming red eyes that hedged about him. They seemed no more than goblin eyes, burning with hunger and hate. The two he feared to find turned upon him—red fires aglow with sentience and cunning—were missing, as far as he could tell. It mattered little. An' the Gruagach were watching him from the surrounding dark, there was nothing Blackthorn could do to blind him.

A voice reached out from the shadows. Not the Gruagach's harsh rumble, but a deep voice, rich, silken, superior. The voice of the thief who had taken his Spear.

"Few men seek Márrach," said his enemy. "Fewer still find it, for men's eyes do not love the Dark. Better they love the light."

And light there was, leaping red and orange at the end of a torch in his enemy's hand. The goblins howled in pain and outrage, and even Blackthorn had to turn his head away from the sudden brightness. As he did he saw the reason behind the unexpected fire. Himself caught in the glow, Blackthorn's shadow fell back and lay plainly etched upon the ground.

Turning again toward the light, Blackthorn gazed full upon his foe. The hand that held the torch aloft was sheathed in a glove adorned with small beryls, and a richly embroidered saffron sleeve slid down the sorcerer's arm toward his shoulder. He was tall, his hair black and straight, and his beard also, but for a single lock of white streaking its purity. His eyes the Hunter could not see, for they were cast to the floor.

Surreptitiously, Blackthorn followed his enemy's gaze, and saw it rested not on his outline, but on Strife's. The sword hung at his side, and the torchlight caught upon the hilt and pommel, defining them clearly in shadow. With sudden, unequivocal certainty, Blackthorn knew his enemy had seen that image before, seen the sword's dark shape riding over his own shadow-shoulder. The master of Márrach recognized Strife for the Hunter's blade.

"How came you by that weapon?" A simple question, asked almost kindly.

Lies had always come easily to Blackthorn's tongue. Could he have been content to restrict his falsehoods to his music, his master Larkspur had been fond of pointing out, he would have made an incomparable Bard, but to Blackthorn the tales had been mere words, without the moment to inspire him. 'Twas in hunting his gift found its finest expression. There the art of deception was everything, and the stakes the highest. Life for a lie well told, death for one poorly delivered. *I am not here*, he would tell the roebuck. *I am the tree. I am the rock. I am a patch of long-leaved bracken. I am your brother*, he would call to the wild ducks. *Come to me, here in the rushes—I am one of you.* The grouse believed him the wind in the barley until the noose was about his neck, the hare knew him only as a lightning-swift stone.

Now he hunted eel, but it was far too early to be thinking about placing baskets on the bottoms of pools. An' he could not slip into the water without that the eel would be attacking him, he would be dead before he had a chance to set his trap. A lie he needed, one that would dull the eel's instincts, soothe his suspicions. *I am a meal not worth the hunting*, he must tell him. *I am not your prey.*

Blackthorn looked up sharply and stared into eyes blue and cold now meeting his own. This one lie, his first lie, must be his best lie.

"It is mine," he said sternly, and laid a possessive hand on Strife's hilt.

The corners of his enemy's mouth twisted. A dubious gleam shone in his eye.

"So thought I, until you spoke." The master of Márrach lifted a glittering hand to the white lock in his beard and stroked it lovingly. "Your claim betrays you. That blade belongs to the Hunter of Éirinn, and well he knows, if you do not, that no man's life do I hold less dear. Now tell me truly how you came by the Hunter's sword, or die his death."

Blackthorn scowled, masking the sweet rush of triumph that was coursing through him. His first lie believed, the rest would be all the more easy to credit. He relaxed his scowl and let a slow, crafty smile spread across his face.

"But I tell you true, 'tis mine, it is. A week or so past, I happened to be at Clochán na bhFormhórach, the Giants' Stepping-Stones, where the rocks of eastern Ulaidh meet the northern seas. Raining it was, and hard, and I poorly sheltering in the stones."

As he spoke, Blackthorn let his eyes stray down his enemy's board. Chairs were set before the master's table, not the benches crowding to the other boards, and the seats on the left were filled with goblins. The red-eyes were looking away, averting their faces from the torchlight. All wore golden torques and arm rings, and one an iron crown upon his bony brow.

"All at once, the rains stopped," Blackthorn went on. "The clouds lifted, and the birds sang out, as surprised as myself."

The Scáil who had challenged Blackthorn at the gate had a place of honor on his master's right hand. Márrach's champion he must be. His empty eyes were fixed on the Hunter, and his long, gloved fingers idly traced the design on his bowl. The rest of the seats were filled with stiff shadows— dark elves wrapped in their gray cloaks—save for the last place at the far end.

There sat an old man, and woefully unsuited to the company he seemed. Bushy white brows shielded his eyes, a long white beard flowed down his chest. His face was deeply lined, and his hands trembled slightly though they rested on the table. Something heavier than age seemed to bow the elder's shoulders, something blacker than dirt sully his once-fine saffron robe.

"I looked out, thinking to rise and go on my way, when I saw a strange, white mist sailing swiftly over the waves to shore." Best to tell his story properly, Blackthorn thought, like any good tale. But not too smoothly, not so sure as to seem rehearsed. "A sea fog I would have said it was, but the breeze could not lift it, nor the sun diminish it. No fool I, I stayed hidden, and kept my eyes open. At last the mists touched the stones of the Causeway, and out of them stepped a man and a woman."

He was interrupted by a hostile chorus of howls and whining. Blackthorn paused, but Márrach's master smiled indulgently.

"An' your tale is a long one, they protest the light," he explained.

He opened the fingers that held the torch, waving them in a brief dance. Instead of falling to the ground, the torch disappeared, and darkness again consumed the courtyard.

He should have guessed. When the Hag told him his enemy was a conjuror, he should have guessed his enemy's Name. Or a moment past, when the blazing torch appeared in the sorcerer's hand—but then his thoughts were only of his Spear that had been stolen. A rare breed were wizards, and more rarely still did two possess the same gift. Conjuring was the art of Mac Ailch, the Wizard of Sliabh An Óir, and was he not also reputed to be tall and black-haired, to have a black beard shot with white? But if one of the Seven—

"Pray resume your tale," his enemy's voice entreated, "unless the dark daunts you . . . ?"

"The man was close to my height—" Blackthorn continued, but his thoughts were distracted. Where had Mac Ailch sent the torch? Back to some Chieftain's hall whence it came? Or did he store the objects his gloves had touched, keep them in a private treasure house to conjure forth at will? "—dark of hair and grim-faced. The woman, now . . ." He shuddered and sucked in a breath between clenched teeth. "The woman was as foul a creature as ever I've seen, stringy and ugly. She had but a single eye and a single green tooth, and her voice was a trial to endure."

His eyes slowly adjusted to the darkness—he thought he saw his enemy nod his head. "Yet, you listened," Mac Ailch stated.

"And curious was their conversation. The way to this very glen the old woman tells the man, but swears he'll never see the broch. A fool she calls him. 'With the black sword in my hand,' says he, 'I fear no unseen enemy, and would dare face even Shadow's King.'"

Low hissing from the Scáileanna and howls from the goblins answered this challenge to their God.

"So you boldly made off with this perilous sword and hurried here before Éire's Huntsman, to warn us of our danger."

The goblins' howls turned to harsh laughter. Blackthorn waited for the clamor to die, not wanting to weaken his answer by raising his voice.

"Not a bit of it," he said easily, when the goblins had quieted. "An' the man who stepped from the mists was the Hunter of Éirinn, yet now he is a corpse rotting under the swells. Slippery the rocks of the northern coast, especially after the rains. The sorry fool met with an accident there, and too late was I to save him. Sure, an' it grieves my heart sore to tell you the sad news, but the Hunter of Éirinn will not be coming to Márrach at all, at all. I've come in his stead."

This time there was no laughter, only silence.

It was more than that his eyes were becoming used to the darkness, Blackthorn realized. The sun was lower, and came better through the slender windows than when the daystar hung above the tower. Thin, slanting partitions of pale light cut like gray axe blades through the black air, and fell on a long ladder of stairs set against the tower's stones and leading to an arching gap in the wall. Glancing up, Blackthorn could now see a high wooden ceiling blocking what light might have entered through the tower's roof. Or was it a floor he looked upon—the floor of a Wizard's sanctum, set in the highest reaches of the broch?

A bulbous, ebon shadow was caught in a dust-thick sheet of sunlight, partly obscuring the wooden beams above. Blackthorn studied it as long as he dared, but brought his eyes away still unsure. It looked to him like a massive bell, suspended over the courtyard by a heavy black chain.

Mac Ailch laughed, a single, explosive note of derision. "You are the poorest liar ever I have heard," he said.

Blackthorn's pulse quickened, but he allowed himself only the outward signs of alarm a guilty murderer might show—a narrowing of the eyes, a tightening around the mouth, a firmer grip on his sword.

"At the Giants' Stepping-Stones you say you killed him?"

"I said he died. I did not say I killed him."

The master of Márrach laughed again, longer this time, and with more evident amusement.

"But at the Causeway you say. Yet, less than an hour since you told Urchóid you are up from An Lorgain in the south."

Urchóid. The Scáil at the gate. Not his true Name—an appellation, like Blackthorn or Bryony—but the meaning of "urchóid" was "malice."

Blackthorn looked away carelessly and shrugged. "Did I, now?" he asked.

"An Lorgain is no more," said Márrach's champion. "We have destroyed it. You show us a sword and tell us an enemy is dead. Better had you brought us his head, an' you wished to be believed."

"But I do believe him," Mac Ailch said softly.

"Can you credit his lies?" hissed Urchóid.

"They are transparent," Mac Ailch replied, "and ill wed to the truth. He has seen the Hag, for how else could he describe her? He was at Clochán na bhFormhórach, for how else could he know of the mists that came ashore? Only I knew of them, having by my art spied the shadow of Inis na Linnte upon the Causeway, and I wondered greatly at the Hag's purpose. And he bears the Hunter's sword."

"No faith have I in this beggar's tale. I'll not believe he encompassed the Hunter's death, when the Scáileanna of Binn Chuilceach could not."

"Believe what you will." The master of Márrach turned to Urchóid. "But an' you anymore cross me, I will ask my Poet for a verse to silence your tongue."

An eerie hiss echoed within the round walls of the broch. Blackthorn struggled to keep the shiver that was running up and down his spine from making the rest of his body tremble. A rann that could seal Urchóid's lips would need his true Name, and the Scáileanna revealed their Names not even to each other. An' the master of Márrach had the dark elves' Names in his keeping, it went far to explain why they were content to serve a mortal man.

Mac Ailch's pale eyes caught his own. "What do they call you?" he asked.

Blackthorn cocked his head, as if to give the matter some thought. "'Blackheart' was the name last given me."

"By your master?"

"Master have I none. A woman so named me."

Some laughter and a few lewd comments were thrown Blackthorn's way, but Urchóid's hiss cut through them all.

"Blacker his heart than my master can guess."

Márrach's champion rose from his chair, raised his bowl from the board, and flung it to the ground. It shattered at Blackthorn's feet, splashing his boots with ale and littering the packed earth with shards of pottery. Blackthorn flinched, but did not stir from where he stood.

"Will you trust him because his Sight is Dark enough to see Márrach's walls?" the Scáil hissed. "Or because Shadow clings to his skin and hair? You do not See his cunning, master. Long has it taken even my eyes to spy it where it lies— the magic he carries beneath his shirt—but clear it is to me now how he defied my spell at the gate. And clearer still that with this work of power he means to defy the master of Márrach as well."

Mac Ailch gave his champion the slightest of nods.

Like a huge cat, Urchóid sprang over the table, drawing his sword as he came. Blackthorn's hand went for his own weapon, but where habit would have placed it—like a fool he reached first toward his shoulder. He cursed his error even as he made it, and masked his mistake by shrugging back his cloak as if freeing his sword arm. The delay was costly. By the time his hand closed on his sword, the Scáil was nearly upon him.

Strife sighed as she slid along the scabbard's jet-stone seams. A blacker sigh and screams of hatred greeted the blade's unveiling, for the Scáileanna Saw its power and the goblins' eyes were wounded by the sword's blue-white light.

Urchóid showed no surprise, and slowed not at all. Blackthorn barely managed to keep the Scáil's first cut from slicing open his chest. The dark elf's blade circled quickly around Blackthorn's and hammered down. Urchóid's gloved hand shot out—too late Blackthorn realized it was not swordplay Márrach's champion had in mind. The Scáil's fingers brushed against Blackthorn's neck, and his fist closed on the Talisman's chain, leaving the Hunter no choice.

"I call upon Earth," he said.

With the chain still in his grasp, the Scáil snapped his arm away, forcing open the clasp, and pulling the Talisman

out from beneath Blackthorn's shirt. The star blazed like a
tongue of emerald fire. With a satisfied hiss, Urchóid swung
the pentacle into his gray-gloved palm. He pointed his sword
at Blackthorn's chest, but the Hunter kept his blade low and
made no move to regain his treasure.

"A work of great power, this," Urchóid said, taking a
deliberate step back.

His arm began to tremble, and he stopped. His hand that
held the Talisman dropped suddenly, as if borne down by a
great weight. The Scáil staggered, his complacent smile
hardened. He loosed his sword and brought both hands
under the blazing green star, but still his arms shook.

Blackthorn watched coldly, his expression as dispassionate
as a Scáil's. Slowly, the Talisman's magic brought Urchóid
to his knees, relentlessly forced his clenched fists to the floor
and ground them against the pieces of the broken bowl.
Only when his gloves were rent and his blood mingling with
the spilled ale did the Scáil open his fingers and try to rid
himself of the enchanted star. By then the Talisman was too
heavy to shift.

"Take it," hissed the Scáil. "Take it off me."

Blackthorn glanced at Mac Ailch and received the same
barely discernable nod that had been the signal for Urchóid's
attack. Without a word he bent and lifted the Talisman from
the dark elf's open palm. Though it was his again, it brought
Blackthorn little ease. This he had not meant to reveal. This
more power than his enemy should know he possessed.

"Domhnall's star," said Mac Ailch. Suppressed envy deepened the Wizard's voice.

"It, too, is mine," said Blackthorn calmly, but his heart
was as heavy as the Talisman had been in the Scáil's hands.

Forty-eight

There are finer fish in the sea
than have ever been caught

Sayings of the Mothers

"Get up," Mac Ailch ordered his champion. "Get out, and bind your wounds."

It was some measure of Urchóid's might that he passed from the tower with barely a jeer or taunt coming his way. He left not by the gatehouse, Blackthorn noted, but by a side tunnel, narrower than the main passageway and doubtless leading to the close.

"In Keeper Hill did you find it?"

Mac Ailch's voice had regained its charm. Blackthorn nodded cautiously.

"Long have I suspected it lay in the Spell-Maker's Keep." Mac Ailch gestured to the goblins beside him. "But though I long ago ordered my servants to search well and surrender to me anything of value they might there find, I learn to my dismay that goblin eyes see not so well as your own, even in the dark."

The goblins protested with snarls. The one with the iron crown pounded his meaty fist on the table before him, and said something about surrendering a man's red blood.

Mac Ailch graced Blackthorn with a mirthless smile.

"Still, what can I know of events at the Silvermines, what with the Ó Briain's cursed band keeping my armies holed up in the tunnels? Yet, you found a way in, it seems, and a way out again. Black indeed must be your heart, an' you could enter Keeper Hill and leave it alive."

Was Márrach's master praising or mocking him? What answer would win Mac Ailch's favor and what words earn Blackthorn his death? The goblins' snarls grew louder, and the Scáileanna's hissing burned like ice in the Hunter's veins.

"They would have you sheathe your blade," Mac Ailch translated with excessive patience.

Blackthorn had been unaware that he was standing ready for more battle, his sword in one hand, the Talisman clenched in the other. He returned Strife to her scabbard, and refastened the star about his neck, staring down the eyes that watched him do it. He cannot conjure it from me, Blackthorn told himself. His glove has never been upon it. But the truth of that thought did little to lessen his unease. The Talisman flamed white against his throat, then lay quiet, a tangle of lightless silver.

"By this harsh light of Domhnall's star" Mac Ailch said, his voice carrying to the far shadows of the courtyard, "is Blackheart's tale of Clochán na bhFormhórach made plain. Had he stolen the Hunter's blade, never would he have reached Márrach, and the sword's rightful owner on his trail. Nor does the Hunter of Éirinn slip on damp stones, or fall by mischance from rocky heights."

As his enemy discounted his false tales, Blackthorn heard him affirming the lies that lay beneath them, the lies he was relying on to keep him alive though he stood in Shadow's Sight.

"At first you meant to bring the weapon to me, and thereby gain my favor," Mac Ailch went on. "Now you love it too well to part with it. An' you will not gift me with the Hunter's sword, Blackheart, then lay it at my feet, and serve Márrach's master."

For a blind moment Blackthorn believed the eel had snaked out into the open water and was swaying in the current before him, trusting and unwary. He thought madly, wanting to present an irresistible hook to his prey, but what promises could he make he would be willing to keep? To swear loyalty to Shadow would stain the blade that bore his oath, and once broken, his vow would rive his soul.

He would swear falsely, then, empty words with the ring of truth. They were ready on his tongue, his hand was drawing Strife from her sheath, he was bending the knee to go down before Mac Ailch, when he saw the snare.

With a start of fear, Blackthorn realized he was not the only hunter fishing these dark waters. So intent he'd been on setting his own hook, he had nearly trammeled himself in the line his enemy had cast. A false oath would never suffice to please the master of Márrach—'twas to draw such deceit from him Mac Ailch had invited his service. An' he took the bait, he was as good as netted.

Thrusting his blade back into its scabbard, Blackthorn stood tall and folded his arms before his chest. "I may be a poor liar, but I am not the fool you take me for. An' I lay my sword at your feet, sure, an' we both know I'd not hesitate to pick it up again. Myself I serve, in all things, and gold the only other master I'll consider."

With a smile that touched only his lips, Mac Ailch rose from his chair and strode easily along the table behind the seated Scáileanna.

"With your oath or without it, I will have your sword at my command." Stopping at the end of the board, Mac Ailch set his hands on the graybeard's stooped shoulders. "I am pleased to present my honored guest to you. Creathna the Name-Sayer," he said with mock courtesy, "late of Sliabh Ailp, Wizard of Éirinn. Serve me well, Blackheart, and your Name is your own. Serve me poorly, and you will serve no one. For an' you betray me, Creathna will render me your true Name, and I will curse your soul to Shadow to sate the Dead Lord's hunger."

Creathna seemed to wilt under Mac Ailch's grasp, but his gaze darted out from under his brows and met with Blackthorn's. Puzzlement glimmered in his age-bleary eyes, then a feeble glint of recognition. Blackthorn's breath caught in his throat. The aged Wizard had already fit a Name to his face, and knew him for the son of a Cailleach. He broke from the Name-Sayer's stare, glowering fiercely, but not before he saw a true spark of hope catch fire in Creathna's eyes.

Plain it was to him now the power Mac Ailch had over the Scáileanna. The sorcerer did not hold their Names in his keeping. An' he had made it a practice to compel all of his servants' Names from Creathna's tongue, he'd soon have had no servants at all. Before he had garnered a score of Names from the elder Wizard, the dark elves would have abandoned the broch for shadows, where their faces could not be seen. Wisely, the master of Márrach left their Names in Creathna's keeping, but displayed the Name-Sayer himself like a jewelled dagger at his side—a threat sharp enough to engender obedience, rare enough to evince admiration, but harmless enough, as long as it stayed sheathed.

"An' it's a false promise you're wanting," Blackthorn said, "glad I'll be to give it you—I've been forsworn ere now, and fear the perils of a broken vow not at all."

"You are a fool," Mac Ailch answered mildly. "Neither your oath nor your loyalty do I desire, for I hold both at nothing. Obedience I demand, and will reward."

He lifted one hand from Creathna's shoulder, and brushed his fingers through the air. A dull gleam appeared between them, then came ripping through the darkness toward Blackthorn. He put out his hand and caught it; a gold arm ring, heavy and warm to the touch.

"That for your tidings."

Blackthorn considered the gift, shot a dark glance at Creathna, then slid the arm ring over his left elbow.

"I will endeavor to see that my new master never need question his esteemed guest regarding me," Blackthorn said, his jaw tight.

"That would be well."

Mac Ailch released Creathna and returned to his chair. Blackthorn watched him, keeping his expression sullen, and was pleased to see his enemy smile.

"Find your seat," Mac Ailch commanded, gesturing to the tables. "Today we feast. Tomorrow we may hunt. Do you take pleasure in the chase, Blackheart?"

It was an idle question, requiring no answer. Márrach's master had already looked away and was beckoning for more ale. Turning on his heel, Blackthorn made his way to the bench where men were sitting. It was perhaps some measure of his own might that they moved quickly aside to make room, and set a full bowl in front of him before he asked for drink.

He stole a glance at Creathna the Name-Sayer, but lowered his eyes at once, finding the graybeard's gaze fixed eagerly upon him. Did the wretched fool think Blackthorn's true Name made him the Queens' champion, come to bring an old Wizard out from Shadow? The light in Creathna's eye was enough to betray them both.

There were too many snares in his enemy's shadowed waters, too many nets. Between himself and Mac Ailch, Blackthorn no longer could say who was hunter and who was prey.

Someone pushed a platter across the board. The roast was charred beyond recognition, but Blackthorn tore off a piece and put a bite down the pouch for Reathach, following it with a few drops of ale at the end of his finger. He doubted the púca would thank him for the meal. The burnt meat was gamey, and the drink as sour as the Hunter's victory.

PART 10

the bell

Forty-nine

Glory's the bright edge of war's hateful cloud,
The light in the elves' eyes, the dead's shining shroud,
More radiant by far than keen swords or gold rings,
The warrior's armor, the mantle of Kings.

The Billows of War

Meacán the Dancer did not return.

A week Liannan waited, while Chieftains arrived from nearby Laighin and east Ulaidh, and Magadh the Mother of Na Connachta came with her King, Cormac, and all their retinue. Liannan commanded her people to think on the Wizard when their thoughts were idle, to imagine the Dancer returning whole and well to Temuir. She spoke with the children, asking if in their games they might not play that Meacán was among them. She sent her thoughts winging to Caireann in far Dún na nGall and Queen Eimhear in Mumhain, that their daydreams too could turn toward the Dancer.

Another week passed, and Temuir's gates stood wide for the Kings Niall of Ulaidh and Aedh of Mumhain, for the Ó Briain, called also the Bear of An Clár, for the Sidhe of An Cnoc Buidhe, An Cnoc Glas, Cnoc na gCapall, and Cnoc na Fírinne. Bochna, the Mother of Laighin, and Longaire, her King, rode in on the twelfth day of Imbolc, and the trail of warriors behind them stretched from Temuir's gates to the forest's edge. The last balefires were lit, stores prepared, horses shod, chariots mended, swords reforged, spears sharpened, armor oiled for battle, and still Meacán the Dancer did not come.

Before dawn of the next day, the Queens met in the henge, and the Maiden and Cailleach of Midhe with them. Bochna and Magadh studied the pattern of the fire they had called, looking for portents of the battle ahead. Liannan stared long and deeply into the heart of the flames, hoping for some sign of the Dancer, but there was none.

Is she dead? Liannan asked. *Is she caught in the webs of her own mind, or trapped in another's thoughts? Does she bear tidings of Mac Ailch and Creathna?*

The other Priestesses heard her thoughts, but none had an answer for the Mother of Midhe.

"We can wait no longer," said Bochna aloud. "Éirinn's might is too great for Temuir's walls to hold, and the journey north will be slow with so many feet and horses to travel."

The Cailleach's thoughts were crisp and stern. *Time grows short. The Sidhe of Cnoc na Fírinne have Seen that when light and dark hold the year in perfect balance, that is the time appointed. Then will the battle of Márrach decide if the Wheel turns to the great sun of summer, or grinds to a halt by the Shadow King's command.*

Her brown eyes fell on Liannan and grew soft. "Did you think you would not suffer in this war?" she asked quietly.

"My suffering I can bear. The suffering I have brought on our people—" Liannan shook her head. "Midhe's folly has reduced our Seven Wizards to but four. By my own acts have I diminished our hopes."

"Our hopes can be made whole again by the death of a single Stag," the Cailleach answered. "Does Shadow's defeat rest with the Mighty of Éirinn or with Éire's Huntsman?"

The Cailleach turned her gaze back to the fire, and her eyes grew brilliant with the Sight. "It may be that you will find your Wizards again, waiting for you at Márrach's gate."

The Queen looked from the blaze to the Old Woman of Midhe. The elder Priestess frowned at the flames, and Liannan knew whatever vision had prompted the Cailleach's prediction had already burned to ash. The wind whistled up from the west, fanning the red and yellow tongues of fire.

Márrach, echoed the air as it moved among the standing stones. *Márrach*, as if the temple itself was lamenting the battle yet to come.

Niall's horse fretted, but whether because of the beast's impatience or the King's was difficult to say. Riding just behind the Mothers at the head of the column, the King of Ulaidh chafed under the pace the Queens had set. Hard enough to have endured the weeks of planning before the vanguard was allowed to set out. Harder still to be on the road to battle and compelled to fare with no more speed than a joint-sore palfrey could muster! The vanguard should be comprised of the Kings and the mounted Sidhe, and what Chieftains had come to Temuir on horseback. So had he advised, but the Queens, in their wisdom, had refused his counsel. What with the snail's crawl they maintained in consideration of the warriors marching on foot, and the time taken to make and break camp each day, the King's easily kindled temper was almost at the burning point. The Mór-Ríoghain had called his Name, but it seemed to Niall Rí Uladh his beard would be long and gray before he would be given a chance to answer.

Abruptly, the King of Ulaidh turned his horse, dug his heels into Racánaí's flanks, and raced him down the ranks. Racánaí had only a slender grassy channel under the trees to call his own—the Mothers' thirty hundred warriors filled the road from one side to the other, and stretched along it beyond the limits of sight. Though he was heading the wrong way, just to ride swiftly again eased Niall's heart. He did not let his horse slacken until they reached the end of the line.

There he drew rein, and turned Racánaí's head north once more. His mood much lightened, Niall started a marching song, and the warriors took it up gladly. The chorus swelled as Niall rode slowly back up the column toward his place.

"So great our host," Niall remarked to a Chieftain riding under a banner of Mumhain's blue with a bear fiercely displayed upon it, "and thirty hundreds more coming with the wains."

The Chieftain shrugged. "An' the Mothers have gathered so strong an army, it must be they expect a great many to die."

It was said without fear or rancor, and Niall was pleased. "No sad fate for a warrior," he remarked.

"Or a King," returned the Chieftain, and grinned.

Niall laughed. A bearskin covered the older man's shoulders, his graying hair was thick and untamed. His smile was ferocious.

"But I have heard tell of you," Niall said softly, his gray eyes narrowing. "For are you not the Ó Briain who has since Imbolc held the goblins captive in the Silvermines?"

"I am," the Ó Briain replied proudly. "And I hope they are prisoners still, though I am no longer their gaoler."

"The goblins of Mumhain are not meal enough to satisfy a Bear's hunger, I'm thinking."

Now it was the Ó Briain's turn to laugh. "A Bear am I no longer, but only a part of this huge serpent!"

Niall raised his brows.

"A notion my Poet Ceallach gave me," the Ó Briain said, indicating a young, fair-haired lad who rode nearby.

The boy glanced over, somewhat embarrassed. "'Twas just an idle thought, to fill the empty hours."

"My hours have been empty as yours," Niall said. "I would hear Ceallach's thought."

"The Mothers are the serpent's head," the boy explained, gesturing toward the front of the column, "the snake's unblinking eyes, deep thoughts, and lashing tongue. Then the Kings, with their swords like sharp fangs. Last the long body, two thousand armored scales."

"Do we wrap ourselves around Shadow's stronghold, Niall Rí Uladh," the Ó Briain asked, his small eyes gleaming, "and squeeze the life from it?"

Niall rose in his saddle and looked up and down the ranks.

"A snake think you? A dragon, I would call it. This worm has claws to grasp and talons to rend. And you have forgotten the Sidhe. Though they ride unseen, declining to travel our roads, yet they are here, spread out through the forest like great wings on either side of our host."

The Ó Briain's grin widened. "And the Poets?" He

inclined his head toward the saffron robes riding just behind his band, then to tall Reochaidh, striding not far ahead. "The Wizards?"

"The Poets are the spells upon the dragon's tongue." Niall's look grew stern. "As for the Wizards, the magic fire in the dragon's belly they are," he said. "But the flames burn low."

"Where magic fails, might oft prevails."

Niall's smile returned. "True you speak," he said, "for never yet have I found a spell that would not break beneath my sword."

He urged his horse on, then wheeled about and called to the Ó Briain. "Let the Bear of An Clár bring his band forward, and himself ride behind the Kings. If with our might we must daunt the Dark, let Shadow's Sight fall first on Éirinn's boldest."

Fifty

A tune is more lasting than the songs of the birds,
And a word more lasting than the wealth of the world

Sayings of the Mothers

Five days and nights, while the light waxed and darkness waned and the Wheel of the Year spun full into spring, Blackthorn dwelt in Márrach. He was given a lice-ridden pallet in a dingy cote he shared with the other men, a fretful horse from the stable, his choice of javelins from the armory. He stood his watches upon the wall and at the gate. He gambled, cheating the men of their purses and the goblins of their gold. He drank stale beer and brackish water, and forced down the meals that were served under the shadow of the great, black bell that hung from the roof of the Márrach's tower, but was never rung.

The first night he slept not at all, and so managed to cut off the hairy paw that reached for his Talisman in the dark. Though he was not troubled by thieves after that, still he slept badly, and dreaded the dreams that came to him when he closed his eyes. The sick fear the Scáileanna inspired curdled in the pit of his stomach, the rancid stink of the goblins caught in his nose and never left him. The endless waiting rubbed his temper raw, the endless dark embittered his sight. His grim, crafty look, an artifice when first he passed

Márrach's gate, was now a part of him; the name Blackheart began to suit him better than his own. A hunter knows patience, but Blackthorn's was near gone.

He had discovered the hidden doors to the windowless halls of the Scáileanna. He had crept down the frayed rope ladder that hung at the entrance shaft sunk into the floor of the broch's courtyard and leading to the pits where the red-eyes slept during the day. He knew his way about the close and gatehouse even when midnight deepened Márrach's gloom. He had ferreted though the storehouses, coaxed secrets from his companions' tongues, pried into every black and fulsome hole the fort could boast—save one.

Mac Ailch's sanctum could be reached only by climbing a long ladder of stairs from the broch's inner court to a high, open archway in the tower wall. From there, Blackthorn guessed, inner stairs wound up between the broch's double walls, but he could not be sure. The ladder-stairs were always in full view of the courtyard. According to Othras and Marfach, Scáileanna with whom Blackthorn had twice shared a watch, the Gruagach was installed in the sanctum, scrying for his master.

A man was a fool to believe what he heard from a Scáil's lips. At his meal last night, his fifth night in Márrach, Blackthorn had tried the dark elves' assertion on the men who shared his table. 'Twas common knowledge, they confirmed. The Gruagach was secreted above, nor was he expected to leave the sanctum until his red eyes descried two shadows in his master's ensorcelled sands. The first he sought was the shadow of the Mothers' host falling across the thorn hedge. The second was the pale shadow of a giant elk running in Márrach's woods. By the one Mac Ailch would know the Queens' armies had reached Márrach's borders, by the other that his goblins had driven the White Stag through one of the four gapped gates in the hedge wall. 'Twas rumored the Gruagach would See both shadows by the dark moon of midspring, the men told Blackthorn, and laughed, for tomorrow's sun would yield the heavens to the night of the dark Ash moon.

That his Spear was in the sanctum under the Gruagach's care, Blackthorn was now sure. Though the knowledge galled him, and his geis tormented him, and red-eyed hounds were coursing his prey, he did not dare try for it. Even should he gain the tower unmarked, even should he come to the sanctum unhindered, even should Strife prove a match for the Gruagach, still he could not see his way out of Márrach with both the Spear and his life.

Vainly, he tried to persuade Reathach to spy for him. A mouse could scurry up the ladder-stairs and none the wiser, he told the shape-shifter, but the púca was unconvinced. Reathach's cowardice was sound—both rats and goblins were real dangers to him should he leave Blackthorn's pouch. Even so, the Hunter cursed Reathach for a useless burden, and as well An Daghdha's geis that bound the púca to him.

On the morning of Blackthorn's sixth day under the shadow of the broch, the smells of fresh meat awakened him from uneasy sleep. Pulling aside the soiled cloth that hung in the doorway of the men's bothy, he saw fires burning in the close and pieces of butchered bear roasting on long spits. He grabbed the arm of a man hurrying past, a weasel-faced stableman they called Turnstone.

"What's to do?" Blackthorn demanded.

"Fresh game," answered the other, wincing at Blackthorn's grip. "Fresh game at last. Brought down in the woods west of Latharna—it's only two days old!" Turnstone licked his greedy smile. "Meat for us, and none for the starving of Béal Feirste. We'll feast this day, I'm sayin', you can stake your life on it."

"A wager not worth the risk," Blackthorn muttered to himself, but Turnstone had spoken true. All morning the cookfires flamed, burning high, but not hot. By midday those turning the meat shouted that it was done, though Blackthorn would have said otherwise. The bear's outer flesh was charred, but bright blood still ran with the juices. An' this was a feast, 'twas not to Blackthorn's taste, but he went with the rest to tables, trying to appear willing.

Though the sun was high, inside the broch it might never have dawned. Blackthorn sat with one foot upon his bench, dropping old ale down his finger to his pouch. Except for pitchers of stale brew, the tables were bare—the meat would be brought when Márrach's master assumed his chair, and Mac Ailch was late in arriving. The red-eyes, already enraged at being forced to wait for the Scáileanna's portions to be roasted before gorging themselves on the bear's raw flesh, growled with hunger and impatience.

Faint cries rose up from the goblin pits below, cries of pain and death. The goblins howled louder, pounded the tables, and stamped their feet. The dark elves sighed like a wind from the grave, then fell silent, rapt in the sound of human misery. Blackthorn clenched his jaw, and kept still. Such music was familiar entertainment at the master of Márrach's feasts. Nothing could he do for the doomed prisoners, and less for himself, an' he let his horror be seen.

A goblin Chieftain raised his full bowl to the assembly. Blackthorn's ear had grown used to the red-eye's mangling of the Mothers' tongue, and he had no trouble understanding the beast.

"May the Eater of Souls enjoy the feast the goblins have provided him," the red-eye snarled.

The goblins roared, and even the dark elves lifted their bowls and drained them.

"May it sate Him," added a Scáil that might have been Othras—the dark elves' whispers were ever hard to distinguish, and when they wore their gray cloaks, their forms and features merged with the shadows. "Not a village or town within two days of us but that we have destroyed, save Béal Feirste. Where will we find more captives?"

Urchóid smiled. "When Béal Feirste falls, we shall have all the blood we need and more."

Curses on Béal Feirste hissed like steam among the tables, but Blackthorn thought of the folk of Latharna, dying beneath his feet, and wondered what purpose their blood was made to serve.

Silence rippled through the hall as red-eyes and Scáileanna became aware of Mac Ailch standing at the top of the ladder-stairs. Blackthorn's gray eyes beheld him as well. Triumph covered the master of Márrach like a mantle.

Mac Ailch descended to the courtyard, and strode to his chair. Before taking his seat, he raised his cup as the goblin Chieftain had done. It was a pewter goblet set with quartz, but the gemstones had no lustre in the sombre darkness of the broch.

"A great day, long awaited."

Mac Ailch's voice shone with more than its accustomed polish. Blackthorn's pulse began to race.

"The Mothers' armies are but an hour from our borders."

He drank, set the goblet down, then lifted his arm again, his fingers manipulating the murky air. A gleam of silver shot through the gloom, making the goblins yowl. An ash shaft appeared below the glitter of metal, straight and smooth as the day it had passed through the sacred fires of Dair na Tintrí. Blackthorn leapt to his feet, unable to stop himself. The Spear—his Spear—was in his enemy's hand.

Blackthorn's folly was happily masked by the rest of Mac Ailch's company. Not a red-eye or gray-skin but did not leap to his feet as Blackthorn had done, the goblins stamping and roaring, the Scáileanna rising like swelling shadows and uttering piercing, blood-chilling cries. Mac Ailch held the Spear over his head as his host's hideous joy filled the broch.

"Patience . . . patience," he reproved them. Confidence filled his voice and carried it over the din. "An hour we have yet. While our God's Shadow lengthens, let us feast. And when we have done, it would please me to hunt."

Acknowledging the answering laughter as if it were a rann of praise, Mac Ailch set the Spear on the board before him and took his seat. Scáileanna and goblins returned to their places. Drink was poured, and the platters began coming in from the close.

Blackthorn was one of the last to take his bench. He could not take his eyes from his Spear, and as long as he beheld it, he could not make his knees bend. At last someone bearing a smoking dish of bear meat walked in front of him, breaking his gaze. He forced his eyes to the floor, forced his clenched fists open, forced himself to sit and cut a slice from the joint that had been brought to his board. I will have it, he told himself. I will have it before this foul feast is done. But if ever he would set his trap, it must be now.

"Your celebrations come over-early," said a feeble voice from the far end of Mac Ailch's board.

Most eyes turned to the Name-Sayer, though some few paid him no heed. Blackthorn set his gaze on Mac Ailch.

"The Mighty are not so easy to daunt as the unfortunate villagers whose souls you have cursed," the old graybeard went on. His words were bold, but his voice was unsteady.

"Kings are coming to Márrach. And the Sidhe, and the Poets, and the Wizards of Éirinn."

The man beside Blackthorn shouted for Creathna's silence, but Urchóid lifted his bowl.

"I drink to the Mothers who all unwittingly brought our master into their counsels," said the Scáil. "May they down the bitter draught of their folly at the Shadow King's board."

With an effort Blackthorn stifled the reflex that bade him spit to ward off Urchóid's curse, and pretended to drink to its fulfillment.

"*An elder is a child twice.*" Mac Ailch looked as if he were considering laughter, but only scorn issued from his bearded lips. "Old fool. You wave the Mighty of Éirinn before me like a wooden sword—I, who dwelt in the Mothers' Sight three years, and they blind to my true purpose! Shall I fear such enemies? An' the Kings dare my hedge, the wraith will destroy them for all that they are mad. Darkness will cover the Sidhe's bright eyes an' they look on Márrach's shadow. Poets? I have my own, and fear the Mothers' not at all."

Blackthorn attended upon every word his enemy spoke, listening for one that would reveal the eel's hunger, that would show him a lure enticing enough to hook the beast. All he heard were bitter truths. For three years the Conjuror of Sliabh An Óir had gone at will to the Queens' halls, and there played the fool with consummate skill. In his enemy Blackthorn recognized a master of deception the equal of himself—all Éirinn deemed Mac Ailch the least of the Seven, and who but did not believe that what the Conjuror brought into the world by his art must needs depart it soon again? Yet, the gold ring with which Mac Ailch had bought Blackthorn's service six days past still encircled the Hunter's upper arm. When he had remarked upon it, the other men had jeered him for a gullible fool. An' he doubted his payment, they said, let him look upon the bell that Márrach's master had conjured to the broch. Four days rest the sorcerer had taken after bringing the bell out from Shadow, yet for all that it cost him, it had hung in the broch on its thick iron chain since Samhain last. Plainly no power save the will that had called it forth would banish it again.

Mac Ailch's Poet, now, that was a riddle Blackthorn had yet to unravel. No Poet had he seen at the master's table, or walking about the close. No one save Mac Ailch ever mentioned the Poet, but an' the rann-maker were but another lie, why did the men quake with fear when Blackthorn asked them the Poet's Name? Why had Urchóid bowed to Mac Ailch's will when the sorcerer had threatened him with the Poet's verse?

And if a Poet had not armored Mac Ailch with words of protection thick as Márrach's walls, why was he not dismayed at the thought of his Name on the Mothers' tongues? The dark elves and men knew their peril, and hid their Names; the red-eyes were un-Named beasts. Except for Creathna, whose Name was known long before he was imprisoned in Márrach, Mac Ailch alone let his true Name be known, and that though the evil he had wrought must have left his soul unguarded, vulnerable to a Scáil's spell, or a goblin's curse, and most certainly to a Poet's rann. Blackthorn would have thought only the Dead Lord Himself could show such contempt, for Shadow's King was Nameless.

Creathna bowed his head, but Mac Ailch was not done. "As for the Wizards, my friend . . ." He smiled with honeyed disdain. "You are here with me."

"Five still will stand against you."

The gleam of Mac Ailch's smile disappeared. The master of Márrach was more than displeased at the Name-Sayer's insolence, Blackthorn realized. He was surprised.

"Five? Not so, dotard. Did I not tell you? Meacán the Dancer presumed to intrude on my daydreams half a season past. I nearly destroyed her there, but failing that, my heart was heavy, thinking she may have returned safe to Temuir. Imagine my delight when I learned that but four Wizards ride in the Mothers' train. The Dancer of Sliabh Mis is lost in Shadow, and lost she will remain forever and aye."

Mac Ailch's arrow was aimed at Creathna's heart, and his pale eyes were locked on his quarry. A wave of callous laughter washed over the Name-Sayer. The old man shook his head in useless denial, and brought his hands to cover his face.

Creathna's pain was Blackthorn's salvation. No one noted how he trembled, no one heard him whisper, "Meacán," as if his own soul were lost in the Shadow King's lands.

"A tale while we dine!" called Mac Ailch. "Where is that groom who fancies himself a singer?"

Turnstone rose a little unsteadily from Blackthorn's table and went to stand before his master. Without preamble, he began an oversung tale of the Alban Wars.

After a time, Turnstone's efforts penetrated Blackthorn's shock and prevailed upon his awareness. The stableman's voice was forceful, but unmusical. The fool was half-drunk. More than once he forgot the words and had to begin verses again.

Would the braying idiot would choke on his song, Blackthorn thought, and leave a man to his sorrow. The iron-crowned goblin at Mac Ailch's board said much the same thing, save that he offered to choke the singer himself. The man sitting next to Blackthorn called out that it was a shame to ruin a toothsome feast with a song to turn the stomach. Blackthorn shot a swift glance at Mac Ailch. His enemy was studying Turnstone with an expression of mild distaste.

Blackthorn sat a little straighter, listened more closely. Though Turnstone's poor rendition was a punishment to the ear, to Blackthorn it was a boon as well. Every misremembered verse, every sour note sung made it all the more likely the Hunter could set bait that would draw the eel into the basket.

The Scáileanna hissed for Turnstone's silence; the goblins achieved it by pelting the singer with bones. The stableman retreated ungraciously, matching his discontented audience insult for insult as they drove him back to his bench. By the time he took his seat, Blackthorn's lure was ready.

"A disgrace that the master of Márrach is so poorly served," he said. He did not speak loudly, but when he wished it, his voice could carry. "'Tis well for you he is inclined to show forbearance. Best mind your horses' tails, and leave the Bards' alone."

"Best mind your tongue, Blackheart," Turnstone flung back, reddening at the laughter that followed Blackthorn's remark, "or I'll cut it out. Quick you are with the insults, but I wager you could do no better than I."

"A goblin whelp could do better," Blackthorn replied easily.

Turnstone was on his feet in an instant, knife drawn, roaring for a fight. The other men goaded him on with gibes and taunts, the goblins pounded the tables, eager to see blood spilt. Blackthorn had ears only for Mac Ailch.

"Is our Blackheart a singer-of-tales, then?" he asked.

Blackthorn turned his head, as if surprised to discover that Márrach's master had been listening. "As good a way as any to gain a welcome in a strange town." He shrugged. "I've played the Bard before."

"I would have you play it again."

Blackthorn narrowed his eyes, feigning annoyance at being ordered about, then smiled and rose from the table. Turnstone lunged for him as he turned away, but others held the stableman back. Blackthorn never spared him a glance. Coming to stand where Turnstone had so lately been reviled, he lifted his head.

"Blackheart I am called," he said clearly, "a Bard by trade. Listen and I'll tell you a tale of Uisdeann Óg and the Scáileanna of An Dubhchathair."

Fifty-one

Silver-winged starlight petals the hall
Golden-stringed harp sings in praise.
Awake could you dream so pleasant a night,
Or dreaming, awaken the day?

Ochone, ochone, ochone oo-la-loo,
Sleep now and dream, Diurán Rí Uladh,
Sleep, Diurán, sleep.

Diurán and the Harper

Mac Ailch raised his brows. It was doubtful the master of Márrach had heard the tale. The Bards taught it to their own, keeping it in memory to honor Uisdeann's courage in the face of certain doom. Yet, it was a tale never called for, a doleful song of a brave lad's terrible death at the hands of the dark elves. The Scáileanna recognized the Name, and sighed longingly as Blackthorn began.

He sang as well as he could, holding thoughts of his sister from his mind, holding grief from his heart. His hand itched for the Spear that lay not five paces in front of him—he had to wrap his fingers about Strife's hilt to keep them from betraying him.

The goblins made known their pleasure even while he sang, howling with glee as Uisdeann was caught, his Name wrung from him, himself killed without honor, and his soul cursed to Shadow. When Blackthorn had done, the dark elves called out, praising his performance with voices that cut like cold knives.

All fell silent as the master of Márrach rose from his chair. With a gesture, he conjured a gold arm ring to his hand, and tossed it to the Hunter.

"Had I known how my master rewards a good tale," Blackthorn said with a laugh, "sure, an' I'd have given him Diurán's instead of Uisdeann's, and be wearing jewelled bands on my arm, instead of plain gold." He slipped the second ring over his arm until it lodged against the first, nodded his thanks, and started back to his place.

"Give it now," Mac Ailch said.

The goblins echoed Mac Ailch's command. The Scáileanna hissed their willingness to hear more. Blackthorn stopped, only half-turned toward the master's board, and shook his head.

"A better tale it may be, but a longer one, and I've yet to get any enjoyment from this feast. Later, perhaps, when my voice is not tired—"

The goblins began to howl in protest. Mac Ailch's response was more encouraging still—his cold smile assured Blackthorn he would not accept the refusal—but it was Urchóid who interrupted.

"At last you have found your place," he said. "Blackheart, the Bard of Márrach. Content yourself, master, and hear his next tale after the hunt. More pleasing to my ears would be news of our enemies and tidings of the Stag. How great is our enemy's strength? What magics do they bring against us? And how runs the Light?"

The goblins' objections lessened to snarls. The Scáileanna sat silent. Blackthorn stood appalled. He had played his lure perfectly for the eel of Márrach, but a great, black pike was muddying the waters with spite and jealousy. The eel was turning away without taking the bait. *Brighde's Fire*, he had given them Uisdeann only to win their ears and their hearts. It was of Diurán he must sing, Diurán's tale that would win him his Spear. He thought wildly, but invention failed him—he could devise no believable lie to draw Mac Ailch's interest back to his song.

"Diurán Rí Uladh," said Creathna loudly.

Every eye in the broch turned to the old Wizard.

"Name-Sayer?"

Mac Ailch's tone was gentle, entreating Creathna to continue. The aged Wizard shot a quick glance at his captor from under his thick brows, then a quicker one to Blackthorn, bright and crafty. This time Blackthorn dared meet it, showing his need to the Name-Sayer in a single thankful look. *An old fox is a wise fox,* he thought, and in his heart blessed the graybeard for his blind trust in the Cailleach's son.

"You spoke a Name," Mac Ailch persisted, "and Names from your withered lips bear consideration. Do you know this tale? Have you heard it sung?"

Yes, Blackthorn realized. Alone of this company, the Name-Sayer knew Diurán's tale. A young Wizard he must have been that Samhain so many years past when Larkspur the Bard of Tráigh Lí, then no more than a youth himself, stepped to his place before the Mighty of Éirinn to sing at their New Year feast. The honor was great, but Larkspur's nervousness greater—so much greater he had barely begun when he lost the thread of his tale. Desperately he groped for the song, but the words escaped his memory and the tune eluded him. In his confusion, Larkspur had caught hold of the magical ribbon of a Bard-Song and followed it blindly.

"Diurán Rí Uladh," repeated Creathna. And more quietly, "A Name to mark."

Blackthorn nearly groaned. Well meant were the old Wizard's words, but would Creathna were a better liar. He should have but whispered Diurán's Name, then met Mac Ailch's eye and refused to say it again. That would have brought the eel in for a closer look.

Mac Ailch stroked the white lock in his beard, debating. His curiosity was aroused, but so also was his mistrust of the Name-Sayer's motives. Blackthorn longed to ease Mac Ailch's uncertainty, but there was nothing he could do. He had made it plain he had no wish to sing. What credible excuse could he offer for changing his mind?

The master of Márrach turned a calculating eye on Blackthorn. Seeing it on its way, the Hunter fixed his own gaze on his cup, and endeavored to appear more interested in returning to it than in the outcome of Mac Ailch's deliberations.

"Time enough for another song," Mac Ailch said in a tone that brooked no argument. "Slake your thirst, an' your throat is dry," he said in answer to Blackthorn's hostile look. "I will hear Diurán's tale."

Blackthorn stalked back to his table, downed his ale, then returned to the singer's place, trying to present a mixture of resentment and confidence. His heart was pounding, his palms damp. The words to the song refused to stay in his mind—the first line was all he could remember. He prayed the rest would follow when he put it to the tune. If only he had once practiced the tale, but how could he? He had coaxed and pleaded, sulked and flattered until he was at his wits' end before Larkspur had consented to teach him the song, and even then his old master had insisted he learn it in pieces. First he was given the melody, and the words weeks later, after being strongly warned against ever putting the two together.

"Another tale I'll tell, an' you'll give me your ears," Blackthorn said, using the Bards' formula, "a tale of Diurán and the Harper."

He began as Larkspur had done, with the true tale, the unmagical tale. The verses did come back to him, for they were made to be remembered, complementing the tune with clear patterns of rhyme, meter, and alliteration. At first his audience was keen, expecting that the hall where Diurán Rí Uladh sat with his warriors would soon be attacked, that swords would be drawn and heads begin to roll. They became restless when he told of a harper come to the feast, and bored when the harper began to play.

'Twas here Larkspur had forgotten his verse, and the magic of the Bard-Song had come upon him. Blackthorn felt it too, an irrepressible allure in the poetry of the verse, a delicate, lulling harmony twining through the air where a moment before a simple melody had run.

Blackthorn ceased to doubt, ceased to worry whether the magic would echo in goblins' ears, or the enchantment blind the Scáileanna's lidless eyes. The Bard-Song took his voice and worked its spell—all Blackthorn need do was let it flow from him.

The sour expressions at Mac Ailch's table softened. Disinterest turned to drowsy indifference, impatient stares tempered to vacant ones. Heads nodded, lifted for a moment, then dropped again.

"*Ochone*," Blackthorn sang. "*Ochone, oo-la-loo*."

Like Diurán Rí Uladh, spelled to sleep by an elven harper, like the Mighty of Éirinn, spelled to sleep by Larkspur's Bard-Song, like babes rocked in their mothers' arms, the servants of Shadow listened to the lullaby, fell into a torpid daze, and slept. The ice-blue eyes of Márrach's master closed in slumber.

Blackthorn finished his song and stood barely breathing. Men and goblins lay sprawled across their tables, and some had tumbled to the floor where they lay blissfully snoring. The Scáileanna looked eerily awake, but not one dark-slitted gaze followed him as the Hunter slowly turned and surveyed the courtyard.

Last Blackthorn looked on Creathna. The long, white tassels that dangled from the aged Wizard's lip rose into the air with every slow exhalation. The Name-Sayer deserved better than to be left here among his enemies, but Blackthorn must go with all speed, and Creathna's old legs had none.

Swiftly, soundlessly, Blackthorn stepped forward. He reached out his hand, and closed his fingers on his Spear. His geis woke like a hungry fire, burning him with its need, feeding on his exultation. To have it again in his hand—

Barely containing his glad cry, Blackthorn turned from the table and raced through the shadowed hall toward the gatehouse. His step was long and sure, and his feet made no noise—he was halfway to the arched passage before any sound reached his ears save the rumbled breathing of the sleepers.

Only once before had he heard it, by the Hag's pool, and his Spear in contest over its waters, but Blackthorn knew the Gruagach's voice at once. Harsh, excited, and muffled by the stones of the tower, it emanated from the high archway at the top of the ladder-stairs and grew louder with every passing moment. By the time the Hunter had halved the distance to the tunnel passage yet again, words rang clearly in the quiet hall.

"Master! Master, the bell! The Queens stand at the southern gate! The Stag—"

Blackthorn heard the sleepers stirring in the hall, goblins at the tables nearest the ladder-stairs shifting, rousing. Larkspur had spent the night trying to wake his audience that Samhain Eve long past, but the Bard-Song's magic had been his, and he possessed of a high, fair voice. Blackthorn had but borrowed the magic of Larkspur's song, and the Gruagach's rough growl was already breaking the spell.

As he reached the dark tunnel, a single word exploded from the top of the ladder-stairs and rolled across the court-yard to hammer in Blackthorn's ears.

"Traitor!"

He turned, when he should have run on, turned and met the Gruagach's flaming eyes. They glowed with recognition, and burned into Blackthorn's with bloody promise.

"Traitor!" the beast howled again.

Blackthorn ran into the tunnel, the Gruagach's cry still echoing behind him. From the darkness of the passage, he shouted to the gatehouse guards.

"Open the gate!"

There would be two Scáileanna in the gatehouse, two more at the gate itself. When they saw the Spear in his hands they would know him for a traitor, but an' the gates were ajar before he burst from the passage—

"Open the gate by the Gruagach's command!"

Six days he had served in Márrach, six days rubbed shoulders with every gray-skin and red-eye in the broch. The guards knew him, and if they did not trust him, still they had no reason to doubt him. The Gruagach was bellowing in the courtyard—the sound of his anger would surely spur the Scáileanna to quick compliance.

The brightness stung his eyes as he tore from the black passageway, but he saw the gate's iron bar had been lifted, and a crack between the banded door and Márrach's wall just wide enough to slip through. He raced across the plank-board floor, hearing the hiss of the Scáileanna as they saw they had been tricked, and the whisper of swords coming clear of their sheaths. He stopped for nothing, but ducked under a descending blade and dove past the now rapidly closing gate. Then he was out and over the wooden bridge, and enveloped in sudden silence as Márrach's spelled stones caught the rising clamor within the broch, and locked it away behind the gray battlement.

In a moment he was under the trees. A blur of black and white swooped out of the branches and over his head.

Strife was in the Hunter's hand before he realized it was the magpie.

"Och, mo mhúirnín, what madness is this?" he said softly. "And didn't I tell you to get safe home?"

The whine of arrows spurred him on—the magpie darted ahead, making no sound. Resheathing his sword, Blackthorn took to the path that had led him to Márrach. Even knowing the Scáileanna were on his heels, he ran with a light heart and a fierce, glad smile on his lips. It was his again, it was in his hand. What though the Stag was being hounded by goblins—Mac Ailch would have no hunt without the Spear. The Hunt was his once again. He'd find the Stag's trail, destroy the red-eyed dogs that pursued his quarry, and himself bring down the Light. The master of Márrach he would leave to the Mothers, and Márrach to the Mothers' host. Though his enemy had scoffed, surely Creathna had the right of it—surely the Mighty of Éirinn would cast a light to humble Márrach's dark tower.

Thoughts of the Mighty brought Meacán to mind. Blackthorn's heart twisted in grief, but he ran steadily on, for now he could hear Scáileanna in pursuit. The magpie bobbed under the drooping branches of the trees, showing him the way to the ridge. He little needed her guidance. No matter how devious, a trail once trod was as good as a paved road to the Hunter. When he saw his way clear, he shortened the distance, making his own path through the dismal woods. Goblins might have come hard on his tail, smelling his fresh footprints on the earth, but the red-eyes were bound to Márrach's pits until the daystar set, and that was yet many hours away. The horses of the Scáileanna could go not so swift as Blackthorn along the trail he chose.

The pale sun became a beacon for him, glittering wanly through the somber trees as it rode slowly into the west. He lost the light at last, but was not disheartened. The sun was waiting for him behind the thorn-topped ridge, and already his feet had found the long, winding track up the slope.

He could hear the Scáileanna close behind him now—they must have guessed Blackthorn's goal and were driving their animals cruelly for Márrach's borders. Let them come. Though still below the crest, Blackthorn could already see the gap in the thorn hedge. They could never catch him before he was through, and beyond the hedge the woods were more generous, offering cover to a hunted quarry, and many more paths from which to choose.

Weary of the climb, yet Blackthorn pushed himself harder, no longer bothering about the tracks he left behind as he forced himself up the steep rise. He was less than fifty strides from the hedge, when he heard the bell.

He had thought no sound could penetrate the spells that girded Márrach's stone walls, but the mournful knell that rolled through the woods could have only one source. The huge, black bell that hung in the tower, the ebon shadow that had never been rung, was ringing now. Its tone was low, but insidious. Its throbbing peal caught in Blackthorn's ear and entered him, and shook his bones with its dreadful rhythm. The magpie came fluttering down to his shoulder; the wild beating of her heart made her whole body tremble.

A second peal followed the first, and then a third, an unbroken chain of ponderous sound reaching out from the heart of the glen to fill the forest. As each dark note left Márrach's broch and rumbled through the trees, it cast a shadow, as if the Dead Lord were spreading his cloak over the valley to blot out the day.

To his horror, Blackthorn found he had stopped—the bell's unearthly song was congealing in his veins, freezing his limbs to immobility. With a bitter cry he stumbled forward, forcing himself to run. Even as his legs dragged over the dead earth, he knew he could not outrace the bell's note to the hedge.

Another dolorous peal rang out and the dark closed about him, making him stumble. Blackthorn looked on the gate of his escape, and his hope failed him. The hedge was alive. Wood and thorn were writhing, twisting, weaving a net across the gap.

The shadow-thick air caught in Blackthorn's chest and clung to his limbs, slowing him, making him gasp for breath. A moment more he struggled, then stopped again, hearing the eerie cries of the Scáileanna mingled with the bell's hideous moan.

Stooping down, he set the Spear aside and untied the Hag's vial from his belt. Loosening the thong that held his pouch closed, he thrust his fingers into his purse. The mouse he came up with had his eyes squeezed shut, his hair was on end, and he quaked like a birch leaf in a gale.

"Quick, now. The gap."

Blackthorn looped the string of the vial about the púca's neck, then glanced up at the hedge. The gnarled branches were embracing, daggered limbs clasping each other like lovers' arms. Blackthorn was already sealed within Márrach's borders, but there were yet holes a mouse could get through.

"Past the hedge, then south," he told Reathach. "Find the Mothers. The bird will guide you."

Blackthorn's muscles ached with the sound of the bell, the shadowed air refused to feed his lungs. Setting the púca down, he took up his Spear again, and gave the mouse a shove toward the thorns. The magpie flew ahead, calling softly. Reathach scurried on for a few faltering steps, then stopped and looked back, his beady eyes beseeching.

"Go!" Blackthorn growled.

Reathach gave a pitiful squeak, and Blackthorn almost smiled.

"Go, little fool. They are no match for Conall mac na Caillí in the wild."

An' he could, Blackthorn would have gone with them as far as the hedge, if only to be sure the púca didn't faint from terror before he reached it. The thunder of hoofbeats drummed between the swells of the bell's evil song—the riders were almost upon him, and would have him, sure and certain, an' he tarried here.

The beeches near the crest were too spindly to hide him, but off the path were thick patches of dead bramble. He went as far as he could from the hedge, then crawled under the bushes just as the dark elves came in sight. From under his prickly cover he saw five Scáileanna riding like a storm up the track to the ridge.

When they had passed him by, he rose and crept down the slope to where the trees grew straight and close. Climbing into their arms, Blackthorn took the squirrel's road south, going carefully through the tangled, brittle branches. The bell continued to toll its dirge as he made his way down the valley, compelling Blackthorn's heart to beat in time. At last the mournful pealing stopped, and though the darkness did not lift, he was glad that his pulse was his own again, and his limbs more obedient to his will.

Without the bell's despondent song in his ears, he was better able to listen for sounds of pursuit. He heard them soon enough, more horses, more Scáileanna. They were hunting him in the lower woods, and like him, they were headed south.

Dropping out of the trees, Blackthorn laid a false trail down into the glen, then turned his feet northward. Another troop of Scáileanna rode by, and with them ran goblins. There was no wind, and the hunters were before him, not behind. The red-eyes did not catch his scent and the Scáileanna's empty eyes passed over Blackthorn where he lay under the dry bracken, pressed against the cracked earth.

Hard news that the goblins were abroad so soon, but no surprise. With the Dead Lord's cloak to protect them, the red-eyes need not wait for the night. Sure, an' it might be night in truth for all the help the day was giving him. The paths were difficult for Blackthorn to see—even the broadest were covered in darkness. He soon abandoned hope of using the trails even when he could find them. The bell was silent, but the forest rang with hooves and flat feet, with jingling bridles and creaking leather—he would be too easily seen on the open paths.

Skirting the thickets of thorn hedge that carpeted the slope, Blackthorn forced a path to the ridge, seeking another way through the daggered wall. An' the gaps had opened again when the bell stopped ringing, still they would be guarded—yet with Strife in his hand, he might win through.

He went along the ridge, finding no breaks in the high thorn wall. The stink of goblin rose up from the coomb on the unmoving air. Blackthorn slipped away from the crest and onto trails less easy for the red-eyes to follow. He sought a way to turn south again, where he had some faint chance of finding the Mothers' host. The darkness behind him sparked with glints of fang and sword, and kept him moving up the defile.

Despite the dark, the dismal wood, Shadow's servants on his trail, the Hunter's smile had returned, grimmer, perhaps, but no less fierce. His was a wolf's stealth in the darkness, a stag's fleetness through the trees. Though they filled Márrach's woods with their red-eyed hounds and gray-skinned hunters, still they would not catch him. And if Reathach was through the hedge, and if the púca delivered the Hag's magic waters to the Queens, then might those that chased him this day be themselves harried by the Mothers' armies when tomorrow dawned.

The Hunter's hope was less than he knew. To the hedge Reathach had run, dragging the vial along with him. Had Blackthorn been watching, he would have seen the púca dive under the thickening branches and disappear into the hedge, and at that his heart would have been glad.

As well he would have seen the magpie winging between the beeches' dead arms and the top of the hedge. He would have seen a sweep of gray as the shadow-beast rose from the wall of thorns, seen the magpie beat the air with her wings, desperately trying to back from the hedge. He would have seen the bird drop to the ground as if felled by a stone, and at that his heart might have broken.

Fifty-two

From the brows of the champions, the hero-light shone,
Their bodies now broken and sleeping in gore.
The battles of war are billows high raging—
They flow o'er the strand leaving blood on the shore.

The Billows of War

The Mother of Midhe had ordered the horns blown every morning before setting out, and every evening when they made camp. At first it had been a bold gesture, and inspired the host. Last night, the horns were as mournful as a Bean Sidhe's wail, and their eerie sound lingered long over the once-fertile fields of Achadh na Liag. And this morning, Liannan thought, their call was like goats pitifully bleating into the day.

No matter, Bochna, Mother of Laighin, said in Liannan's mind. *Márrach is before us.*

Bochna's Sight was undaunted by the dense fogs that had descended on them in the hour before sunrise. Liannan mounted, and melded her mind to the Queen of Laighin's. She Saw it now—a thorn hedge running the length of the valley's lower end, as it ran also upon the ridge to the west, and the hills to the east.

Less than a half day's ride, she thought, and her heart was lightened.

Beyond the thorn barrier she could not See, but together the Mothers sent their Sight skimming along it. There, slightly east of where they stood, a gap in the hedge, wide enough for three riders to pass together.

"Let word be sent along the ranks," said Magadh, the Mother of Na Connachta. "We will see Márrach this day."

They rode slowly, the entire army dependent on the Mothers' Sight to guide them through the cold, clinging mists. When Liannan turned to survey the winding might of Éirinn's host stretched out behind her, she needed to use the Sight to see Eoghan's face, and her King rode just behind.

Bochna sighed deeply and reined in her horse. Liannan and Magadh did the same, and Liannan heard Niall curse as he was forced to halt as well.

Seamair, the Mothers ordered.

The better part of an hour was lost while the Weather-Worker spelled away the fog. Though her craft made the day brighter, still it was cheerless. The mists thinned to translucent veils and lifted to the tops of the trees, where they clung to the highest branches, refusing to be banished.

Again the Queens set off, but it was past midday when they sat before the gap in the hedge and looked with their Sight into the valley they had known as Cromghlinn.

Na Connachta's Queen frowned. *The Dead Lord knows we are come,* she thought, *and is glad.*

Magadh speaks true. We are Seen, but not challenged, Bochna agreed. *Evil abounds in these woods, yet will not turn our way.*

Liannan frowned and shook her head. *Does our enemy spurn our challenge?* she demanded.

"Why do we delay, Mother?"

Had one of the Kings voiced the question, Liannan had no doubt she would have sensed frustration behind the speaker's words. It was Cessair who spoke, and in the elven warrior's heart the Mother could hear only eagerness.

"Let the Sidhe of Cnoc an Eanaigh be first to dare this gate. The light of our eyes will pierce the shadows and find the path to An Bhrí Mhaol."

"The elves of Cnoc an Eanaigh are not the only ones impatient to enter Márrach," said Aedh Rí Mumhan gruffly.

We must understand our danger, before we dare this gate, said the Mother of Na Connachta.

"No," Liannan answered Magadh aloud. "We cannot hesitate before our enemy's wall."

Liannan looked again past the hedge, sending her will

into Márrach with greater determination. The Mother of Midhe, she told herself, was not easily blinded by the Dark. Dying trees she Saw, their souls in torment, Éirinn's power prisoned deep under the barren soil, and dense shadows both under the trees and wrapped about the bald hill in the midst of the glen.

Help me, she insisted, and the Mothers of Na Connachta and Laighin joined their efforts to hers. At once it was clear—the shadows in the woods were some of them Scáileanna on black horses. They were riding in great haste, but in all directions, and not only toward the south where Éirinn's might was gathered.

What, are our swords so little feared, then? Magadh thought angrily. *Hardly a dark thought turned this way—*

Liannan bent her Sight again on the bare hill. Shadow's spells were there so thick, she could See nothing, but the intensity of her gaze drew her Sight through the emptiness, past the hill, and into the forest on the far side of the valley.

"Blessed Éire," she breathed, and the other Queens echoed her horror.

"On to Márrach!" cried Liannan, her mind, the mind of all the Mothers instantly clear. "I with Cessair, then the Kings Eoghan, Niall, and Aedh together."

Anticipating the furious objections of the two Kings she had not Named, Liannan turned to them sternly. "Our army is great, our warriors are many. Those who are not first through the gate may need the courage of Kings before them an' they are to dare it. Cormac and Longaire will stay with their Queens and order the passing of the host into Márrach as swift as may be."

Her voice lowered, but her words were heard and carried down the lines to the ears of every warrior.

"No more argument, but only haste. The White Stag is himself in Márrach's woods. An' we do no more than distract his pursuers from the hunt to war with us, we will have acquitted ourselves well this day."

She spurred her horse through the gap in Márrach's hedge, and Cessair was with her, and three Kings of Éirinn close behind. The Ó Briain rode directly behind Niall, and so passed with nine of his band through the hedge after. From the shadows of the trees, several more of Cessair's folk appeared. At a word from Bochna, the rest of the Ó Briain's warriors stood aside to let the Sidhe pass.

In rows of three the elves rode forward. The horses in the first row had each one hoof within the gap, when a solemn knell rolled slowly from the midst of the valley down to where the host was gathered at the hedge. The sound passed through the gap, and out over Éirinn's host. The note was oppressively low, the tone resonant to the point of pain. Barely had it begun to fade when its twin echoed from Márrach's dark heart. The dying beeches shuddered, the earth shook. Brave warriors of five kingdoms wailed and wept to hear Márrach's bell, and even the Mighty of Éirinn groaned and covered their ears.

Already past the hedge and within Márrach's borders, the Ó Briain, the Kings, and Cessair turned instinctively back toward the gap. Liannan was deepest into Márrach's woods, her Sight fixed before her on the barren hill, the birthplace of the hideous sound. The peals poured inexorably out upon the still air, and with them came darkness, a gray shadow that deepened with every aching note.

"Conmac!" Cessair cried, and her voice was fierce. "Corann! Maelgorm!"

The thorn hedge was growing, the dagger-laden limbs twisting, leaping across the gap. The iron-hard wood meshed, the knives on the branches whistled sourly as they cut through the air.

The Sidhe within the gap answered Cessair's cry by driving their heels into their horses sides. Two of the horses leapt forward, out of danger. The third shied at his rider's jabs, backing and sidestepping into the hedge. Before the next dull echo of Márrach's bell reached their ears, the gap had closed.

The trapped horse screamed as the grasping branches bound him. Thorns tore into his flesh, and flames deep blue and pure white lit the hedge from within. A ragged shred of gray flew through the animate wood toward the light and seemed to surround it. Then the fire was gone, and only the shadow remained. A trickle of red seeped from under the hedge and sank into the dusty earth.

Not the horse's death cry, but Eoghan's rising howl brought Liannan's eyes away from the far heart of Márrach.

"Soft, my King," she urged.

She rode her horse close to his, and smiled. "Musha, my

darling. Your fire burns too hot," she crooned. "No enemies are here, Eoghan Rí na Midhe. No glory to be won."

Could he hear her voice over the incessant tolling of the bell? Eoghan's reddening gaze caught and held her own. She felt Niall's eyes burn into her too, flaming eyes, already half-mad. Red hair smoking, sword drawn, Aedh was charging at the hedge. *Badhbh, Macha, and Mór-Ríoghain*, how could she control the fires of all three?

"Shake off your mantles. Listen to Éire's command, and you Her servants."

She made her voice sing, made her words mark the tune of the Maidens' Song, though they struggled to defy her and follow the bell's single note. The light was fleeing before the bell's sorrowful tolling, unnatural dusk was claiming the wood. Liannan reached her hand to Eoghan's arm, and felt it warming like an iron thrust into a blacksmith's forge.

"Soft, my King," she said again. "Vent your fury not at shadows, but at the enemies that cast them."

Eoghan's eyes paled to blue, but red still rimmed the edges. 'Twas the bell, Liannan moaned to herself, the cursed bell that was stoking his fire. Glancing at Niall, she Saw he had better control of his battle-madness, but was fighting hard to stay sane. Cessair was with him, her bright gaze bent on the King of Ulaidh. And Aedh, where—

"Éire, no," Liannan whispered, but the young, fair-haired boy rode his horse in front of the King of Mumhain's as if he had no fear.

Aedh roared, and raised his sword to strike. With an effort the lad kept his horse where he was, and began to speak.

> *Aedh rests his royal sword*
> *Not finding foe worth battle.*
> *His madness like a mantle falls*
> *Upon the patient earth.*

Slowly the King of Mumhain's gaze became mild, his blade lowered to his side. Liannan's relief poured from her heart in a silent prayer of thanks. The boy was a Poet. She could not speak in his mind—the bell's onerous tolling filled the boy's senses, overpowering her unspoken words. She shouted to him, hoping he would hear.

"Can you make a verse to stop the bell ringing?" she asked. "To bring back the day?"

The lad shook his head. Desperately, Liannan turned her Sight to the wall of thorns. Only barren wood and sharp daggers could she See, and a shadow lingering where the elf had died—nothing beyond. She reached her thought to the Mothers on the other side of the hedge, but if they heard her, she could not hear them.

Heat seared her hand—she looked back at Eoghan and saw the fire mounting, smoke rising from his hair. Again she bent to the task of cooling his madness, smiling at him, singing to him, while each knell sounded was a dagger of ice in her heart, another shadow before her Sight—

And, at last, the bell stopped ringing.

It took a moment for Liannan to realize it had done. The note seemed to be ringing within her, pounding against her bones, vibrating still in the branches of the dead trees. When she could hear only silence, she tried again to reach the Mothers beyond the thorn wall. Neither word nor vision came to her.

Though she heard not her sisters, yet the Mother of Midhe was not deaf to those who stood with her here. Against the tolling of the bell, the Ó Briain had growled words of courage to the warriors that had followed him through the hedge. 'Twould not be amiss, an' a few were given him as well. Cessair and her two companions turned their glittering eyes on Liannan, trusting the Mother's Sight to show them what theirs did not—where to seek their revenge. Their royal mantles were now loosely draped about their shoulders, but the Kings longed to wrap their madness tightly about them, to do battle and not suffer attack.

"Wise were the servants of Shadow to close their gates upon us," Liannan said, "but fools to have closed them too late. Let the rest of the host follow as they may. We will not wait to meet the foe."

They were brave words, but Liannan did not feel brave. Never had she felt so impotent, never so alone. The ground is still beneath me, she said to herself, the sky above me. She called with all her heart to the wind that it might bless her with clarity of thought, to the earth to grant her endurance. Neither answered her prayer.

Only fire was left her. Fire glistening in Cessair's eyes, gleaming in the Kings' fierce smiles, crackling in the Ó Briain's voice as he roared a challenge into the shadowed wood. Fire is still mine, Liannan insisted. Fire to burn away the shadows, and light the Dark.

Fifty-three

Mavis, magpie, merlin, thrush
Robin in the hazel bush
Wolf treads on the forest floor
Fly safe home through oak tree's door

a children's game

Meacán had stopped dancing long ago. Every leap, every glide, every turn only took her deeper into Shadow. Each time she danced, the strand, the town, the safe haven she was imagining transformed into a place of horror when she arrived, a burnt and empty ruin, a goblin pit, an abode of Scáileanna. At last she could no longer bring herself to choose a direction. She began to drift through the Dead Lord's daydream. Step after faltering step, Meacán's weary feet led her across an Éirinn in torment, where rivers of blood cut through haunted glens, and desolate, windless plains lay cracked as broken souls under a sunless sky. No longer did she seek a border she might cross, a gate between worlds. Sometimes she cursed herself for her suffering, blaming her imprisonment on her own thoughts of failure. More often Meacán sensed that another had bound her in this shadow-land, but it made no difference who was at fault. She was not strong enough to break free of the evil that held her will captive.

Time she could not measure, for there was no dawn, no day, no passing season. Cold there was, bitter as winter, bare as bone. Dusk crept to terrifying night, and night seeped away only to bring back the dusk. Weeks, moons must be passing in Éirinn, in the world beyond the surrounding shadows, Meacán knew, while she wandered aimless. How long had she carried in her heart the Name that could wound the false hunter? How long could she cling to the hope that she would find her way out of these Shadows and place her knowledge like a weapon into the Mothers' hands?

Many dark paths Meacán travelled. They led her at last to the shores of a great, stagnant mere. Only when she had followed another track away from the water, and climbing to the top of a treeless ridge, found the thorn hedge, grown taller now, and the daggers longer, only then did she know the dead lake for Loch nEathach. Only then did she understand why the Scáileanna and goblins had ceased to plague her footsteps. The cursed heart of Darkness was beating the dance her feet must follow, and in the end all the shadowed ways led to Márrach.

A few tears fell from her eyes as she walked, but Meacán had wept so much, there were few tears left in her. She was becoming hollow, as empty inside as the world was without. Nothing she touched was real, nothing she leaned on solid enough to hold her up. There was no succor in the Shadow King's realm. She fell to her knees, bowed by the weight of the vast and insubstantial Dark. An' she would rise again, she would need a staff strong as Úna's oak to support her.

Meacán stopped trembling. Could the Dead Lord See it there, in her mind? Would he bar that door, too, before she could reach it? Sweet Éire, was there any way out of this nightmare that was not locked and guarded?

Banishing all other thoughts, Meacán stumbled to her feet and honed her mental image of the Seer's oak. Not the branch the Dancer had first glimpsed in Úna's hand, nor even the stout wand the Oak Seer had held when Meacán stood in the world of the Hunters, but the great mother oak she envisioned—the huge, deep-rooted, sky-touching tree that had been her bastion of sanity in the chaos of the wild. She had not forgotten her madness when she stood in the world where the oak tree grew, but better to be mad in Éirinn than forever trapped in the Shadow King's dream.

Meacán filled the giant tree's branching arms with birds

and beasts, with sprites and fairies. Its rough-barked trunk she made three times as thick as Reochaidh's chest. Buds she set upon it, for the Dancer meant to return to Éirinn while spring yet reigned.

She had her holdfast, Saw it clearly, but Meacán was afraid to move. How many times had she brought the visions, how many times danced to them only to find herself come to a warped mockery of the place she had Seen? She couldn't bear to have this last door closed upon her, this final hope crushed. . . .

Her first step was unsteady. The Dancer caught herself as she tottered, and stepped out again. Slowly, dredging up from her bruised mind the bizarre and wonderful movements that had once made her one with the wild, Meacán danced as she had never danced before. She danced as Úna danced, and her feet carried her to the edge of Shadow, and onto the living oaken threshold of the Seer's world.

Patient as the sea that wears down the shore, Úna waited by Márrach's hedge. On high An Earagail she had Seen, but now she looked again, to behold the unfolding of her visions in time, for the patterns of fate were not immutable. What a rock had dreamed in winter, in spring might change, by the act of a single, mighty will, or by the whim of a capricious heart.

Looking through the thorns, Úna Saw the magpie soar into the air above the thorn hedge. Unblinded by the Dark, her eyes followed the shadow-beast's flight as it abandoned the mouse, a lesser prey, and rose out of the tangled wood to capture the bird, one far greater. She wept to See the magpie fall to the ground, to See the shadow-beast dive and batlike spread its shadow over the stunned bird. She moaned as the wraith stooped to drink of the magpie's soul, for an' the magpie was lost to Shadow . . .

Faintly to her ears came the cry of the Scáileanna as they topped the ridge and themselves saw the shadow-beast about to feed on the magpie's life. One of them spoke in his own tongue. Úna listened, for there was no speech of bird or beast, mortal or God that the Oak Seer did not understand.

"Begone!" cried the Scáil. "You come too soon from your

post. Foes are massed at our southern border, yet you would tarry over a single, feathered invader! Begone, and come not forth from the thorns again, until you are called!"

The wraith drew back, a cloud of smoke that melted into the shadows of the hedge.

"Yet, even so," the dark elf sighed darkly, "a magpie come where no creature has cared to linger since Samhain last—" and he lifted the limp bird in his hand.

Mounting again, he spoke to his companions. "I'll to our master. An' the bird is not what she seems, he will know it. An' she is but a magpie, doubtless a goblin will be glad to make a meal of her."

The dark elves laughed, and Úna smiled with them, but turned her Sight to her oak that was the gate of worlds. The Seer's smile broadened with delight. At last, at last, the lost goose was waddling home.

"Come, come, come, come," she called to the Dancer, a goosegirl calling to her flock.

Meacán was too far away to hear, but nearer she danced, and nearer still. A dark shadow fell across the oak tree's door. Úna spat at it. The shadow withdrew. The goose came on and placed her foot upon the threshold.

"Like a lapwing the girl crosses," said the Red Man who had been watching Meacán from a branch of Úna's oak, "dragging her limbs as if she were wounded."

The fairy brought the hood of his red cloak over his red hair to cover his ears. "She is wounded," he complained. "Listen to her wail."

Meacán was indeed wailing, but it was dismay, not pain. It had seemed so like a true crossing. She had Seen her holdfast so clearly. Madness, ochone. She had found the madness she sought, but she had not left Shadow. Madness had come to the Dark. It was soft in the doe eyes of the Wild Lady beside the oak, wide in the leering grin of the fear dearg in the branches, cold in the vicious web of wood and thorn that hung upon the gasping, dying beeches, and clouded the still, lifeless air.

Meacán collapsed beneath the oak and wailed again, sending a flurry of creatures into the folds of the Lady's clothes. Meacán's cry changed abruptly to a startled yelp. A bogan had rudely yanked her hair.

"Stop that," said the Lady of the Wild, shooing away the sprite as She might a naughty chick.

"Silly goose is frightened," the Lady crooned, nestling beside Meacán and stroking her as if she were not a goose, but a cat whose fur needed smoothing. The doves on the Lady's shoulders cooed consolingly.

Meacán giggled. She laughed outright, then wailed again as the fullness of despair possessed her.

Another tug on her hair, this one harder. Meacán's head jerked toward her tormentor, and somehow—was she pushed?—she found herself falling on her side, rolling away from the tree. . . .

By the time Meacán lay still upon the dusty earth, her mind had cleared, and her Sight had diminished. She looked up and saw the Oak Seer—not a regal, commanding Queen of the Wild, but a strange, ridiculous woman, her bright green and golden attire covered in budding twigs and just-opened leaves. Spring's early flowers were set in her pure black hair, snowdrops and daffodils, gentian and clover, and a crazed look glittered in her ageless eye.

The oak tree had shrunk to an ancient, worm-scarred staff in Úna's hand. The Red Man was gone, and there was no sign of the bogan who had been pulling her hair, unless it was the swirling dust at the Oak Seer's feet. The hedge was before her still. Meacán began to tremble all over again.

"This is not Shadow," she said firmly. "This is day, not dusk. I have returned in truth to Éirinn."

She waited for some response from the Oak Seer. A word would be enough, even a simple nod. Something to say, "This is Éirinn. I am real."

Úna spoke, but her words were not reassuring.

> *A mouse, a man, a mouse, a man,*
> *Bearing a treasure in his hand.*
> *Come to me, little mouseen.*
> *Come and tell me what you've Seen.*

"Úna," Meacán pleaded.

The Oak Seer opened her eyes wide and put a finger to her thin lips.

"Ssh," she whispered, standing straight and pointing

toward the hedge. "He's a great coward, you know. An' you start wailing again, you'll scare him off."

Still sprawled on the ground, Meacán turned her head to follow Úna's finger. Nothing but empty, winter-bare woods . . . or . . . what was . . .

A little, naked man shot up in the midst of a patch of yellow bracken. His bald head was scrunched between his narrow shoulders and he turned it quickly this way and that. Then he was gone, everything still again. A rustling in the dry grasses, and the man reappeared, nearer now, running, his scrawny legs turning like a mill wheel. He gave Meacán no notice until he was nearly upon her. With a gurgling shout of surprise, he slid to a stop and crumpled.

Meacán's eyes followed him to the ground, but when they got there, she saw only a brown wood mouse running frantic circles around a little clay jar and chittering shrilly.

"Och, not at all," said Úna decidedly. "Not for them. Give it to her."

Next moment the mouse was a man again. He scooped up the vial and thrust it at Meacán.

"Take it," he said urgently. "Take it, then."

Dazed, Meacán stretched out her hand, and the little man fairly dropped the bottle into her half-open palm. Immediately, he stooped to the ground and disappeared. A wood mouse scurried to the Oak Seer's side and climbed up her green skirts to her gold shawl, then up her shawl to her shoulder, and tried to hide in Úna's unbound hair.

"No match for himself in the wild, 'tis true," Úna whispered, putting her lips near the mouse's ear, "but in Márrach the wild is enslaved. Though they are not hunters enough to bring him down, yet they will snare him in their sorceries."

The mouse squeaked dismally, but let the Oak Seer pluck him from her shoulder. As she placed him gently on the ground, the little creature swelled in size, and became a man again.

"A shape-shifter," Meacán breathed, but she was utterly ignored.

"'Tis broken I am," the creature sobbed, "broken entirely. My courage you said, my courage I'd find in the thatcher's cote. Och, not courage, Oak Seer, not a drop of it. My doom met me by the shores of Loch Dearg. My doom, I'm sayin', in the shape of a fool, and I cursed ever since."

The creature sounded so forlorn, Meacán's heart was moved to pity. Úna was moved to laughter.

"He is your courage, little mouseen. You must go to him. 'Where is one to call you back?'"

"Go to him? Go to him?" The púca wrapped his bony arms around Úna's legs and hugged with all his strength. "I can't go. I would an' I could, but I can't go, I can't. 'Tis still the coward I am, for all that you promised me."

Úna's smile widened like a vixen's when she spies a plover's unguarded nest. "A coward still? An' the Hunter's gift in your keeping?"

"The Hunter?" Meacán was on her feet in an instant. "What do you know of Blackthorn, little rascal?"

The little man was a mouse again before Meacán had done speaking. Tears welled up in the Dancer's eyes, though she thought she had cried them dry, and a flush like fever warmed her cheeks. She was too tired to understand, too worn to be patient, too misused to bear any more.

"What do you mean by 'his gift,' Úna?" she demanded. "I entreat you, tell me of my brother, and then turn your Sight to the Mothers, for I must go to them with all haste."

The corners of Úna's mouth pulled down, making her look as glum as an old goat. She cocked a finger at Meacán. When the Dancer came near, she turned the finger to point at a small hole in a knot along her staff.

Meacán bent closer to the smooth oak wand, then peered through the tiny opening. At first she Saw only a ring of red, a circle of fire. All else was dark. A few glittering stars seemed to dart about the shadows within the circle. No, not stars. The eyes of the Sidhe. And there was Liannan, standing proud in the center of the flaming ring, while about her a small band of warriors fought . . . Niall! Niall was fighting, and Eoghan, the royal madness upon them, their swords slashing through the flames at shadows deeper than the night, at red eyes. . . .

Meacán staggered back and turned her face away. "Not him," she begged. "Not that brother. Blackthorn, I'm saying—"

The Oak Seer acted as if Meacán were not even there, but squatted like a frog, and began speaking to the mouse that cowered at her feet. Meacán could not comprehend a word of it, for Úna chittered and squeaked, but the púca listened intently, then chittered back.

The Seer smiled.

Loosing Úna's skirt, the mouse changed again, and came hesitantly to Meacán as a man.

"You'll have to carry me," said the shape-shifter, "as he used to do." When Meacán didn't answer, a look of annoyance added a few more lines to his already wrinkled face. "Sure, an' you're the sister to himself, and no mistake. As blessed with wits as he is."

Meacán looked from the púca to the Oak Seer. "You're mad, the both of you," she exploded. "Carry this creature? And where? To the vision in your staff? That place lies under Shadow, and from Shadow have I only just escaped! Show me no more images of night—let me See Liannan where she is now, walking under the sun. Show me this, and I will bring the Mothers a Name to banish the shadows before night comes."

"A Name worth nothing," said Úna carelessly.

"A Name—" Meacán's cheeks flushed with anger. "I nearly lost my soul to Shadow for this Name you so readily discard!"

"Mac Ailch fears not his Name on the Mothers' tongues," the púca said, siding with Úna.

Meacán whirled on the little man. He backed before her fury, and cringed against the Oak Seer.

"Mac Ailch!" Meacán hissed. "And how do you know of whom I speak, little imp? Welcome are you, to the lands beyond this hedge? Good or evil, Light or Dark, it is all the same to a púca!"

The little man flinched. "And didn't I say you were his sister?" he asked, his voice quivering. "Not only are you possessed of the Hunter's wits, but of Conall's fine manners as well."

Meacán's mouth fell open. *Badhbh, Macha,* and *Mór-Ríoghain,* could her brother have been such a fool as to treat with this creature? To have given an unscrupulous fairy his Name?

"I'll to the Mothers," she said, her voice shaking like the púca's.

"What can I do, an' she'll not take me through?" the little man whined.

Úna's eyes narrowed to slits, like a basking seal's.

"Where are the Mothers, goose?"

"Temuir—"

"Long gone."

"Dún na nGall, then. Caireann is with child and—"

"The child is born. Meat for the Shadow King's board."

Meacán shuddered. "I must take my message to the Queens!" she cried.

Úna clapped her hands and jumped up and down like a fawn who has just found her legs.

"Let me," the Seer begged, a child pleading for a treat. "Let me take the Name."

The Oak Seer kept springing off the ground until one of her jumps carried her far higher than the others. Her legs tucked under her, her arms spread into wings. In the blink of an eye she was a feathered raven, the oak branch a fragile twig in her claw.

Thrice she circled around Meacán, calling, "Mac Ailch, Mac Ailch, Mac Ailch." Her black beak closed. She beat her wings, climbing the air until she was above the branches of the trees, then flew away to the south.

Too much, too fast, no time to think . . . Meacán put a hand to her throbbing head. Did Úna truly mean to bear a message to the Queens? Would the Mothers understand her? And what was Meacán to do meanwhile? Dance to the battle-ground Úna had shown her? To what purpose? And what purpose had the little jar she now held?

That at least she might find out. Composing her features as best she could, Meacán fixed what she hoped was a mild eye on the shape-shifter.

"What is this present you have given me?" she asked as sweetly as she could.

The púca rolled his eyes to heaven and sighed as if Meacán were a great fool and not a great Wizard.

"Water," he answered, and spat in disgust. "But this water cleared the shadows from your brother's sight when in his folly he chose to look on Márrach."

The púca's face crinkled and he began to moan. "Wurra, wurra, wurra. An' you be his sister in truth, take me safely through the hedge, for both your brother's soul and mine will be broken an' I don't get to his side."

Only a fool would trust a púca's words, she told herself, but Meacán's heart ached with fear. "Get to his side." Her eyes scanned the thorn hedge as if she might find a peephole that would show her Blackthorn beyond. "Get to his side."

Meacán needed food and rest. She needed to look at a blue sky, and a sward of spring green grass. Clear visions filled Meacán's Sight, her home in Sliabh Mis, the dún, Temuir's wall . . . She could dance to any of them, would reach them this time, she was sure.

"To a mouse, now," she said softly.

The púca gave her a strange look, but did as she said. When she picked up the creature, she could feel his terror racing through his veins, tiny bubbles of fear under her fingers. She had no pouch or basket to carry the mouse, but wanted her arms free. Drawing up one of the long tatters that now hung from her skirt, she bundled and tied it into a little sack, and set the mouse within.

"Hold fast," she said, and did the same.

Taking a deep breath, Meacán started to dance. Her movements were slinking, liquid glides and her holdfast was rooted in darkness—Liannan, standing tall in a circle of red fire.

Fifty-four

One may be clever, and yet want wisdom

Sayings of the Mother

Úna Saw fading sunlight, pale gold and burnt orange, fall softly on the twisted web of enchanted wood, and disappear into its shadows. In her eyes, Reochaidh's voice was a gale of color, riding the dying light to the hedge. There the storm broke upon the unyielding wall of thorns, and rolled back over the ranks of Éirinn's defenders in volleys of thunder. Even Úna's feathers were ruffled by the noise, though she flew high over Éirinn's host.

"Enough! Enough!" she heard Magadh, Mother of Na Connachta cry. "We achieve nothing but our own deafness with this folly."

Folly, Úna croaked. And more to come.

"We cannot let them face night alone in Márrach's valley," Bochna, Laighin's Queen insisted. "An' we knew what sorcery strengthens this evil, an' we knew the spell that made it, then might we breach this daggered wall."

"The spell, or the Name of its maker," amended Tadhg.

"Mac Ailch," Úna called down to the Mighty of Éirinn. "Mac Ailch."

The Name caught in the leafless arms of the trees. Bereft

of meaning, Úna's harsh voice came faintly to the ears of those below.

"Look!" Feargna Óg shouted, pointing to the sky. "Look there!"

The warriors nearest the Necromancer took up his cry, their arms lifting with his toward the dark bird half-seen beyond the forest's roof.

"A crow is it?"

"A scaldcrow!"

"The Mór-Ríoghain come? Then battle is upon us!"

"The Mór-Ríoghain come to call us to battle!"

Folly and more folly. Úna crowed her amusement. She circled languidly over the trees, watching the false tidings spread like fire down the Mothers' lines. Folding her wings, she dropped gracefully through a hole in the netted branches.

"Not the Mór-Ríoghain," Magadh said with irritation. She gestured impatiently to her King. "Go, Cormac Rí Chonnacht. Ride down the ranks and quell that rumor before we must halt a charge we never ordered. 'Tis no scald-crow, but a raven, though 'tis true both dine at the same table."

Úna spread her wings for some lift, and glided to a perch in a beech not a half dozen paces from where the Mothers stood. As her feet touched the branch she let go the raven's dark feathers and was Úna once more.

"Mac Ailch," she cawed boldly. "Mac Ailch. Mac Ailch."

Like the thousand facets of an insect's eyes, the faces of all in hearing and sight of the Seer turned and gaped at the uncanny woman squatting in the high branches of the beech. Úna soothed her annoyance by drawing her head along her arm as if she were preening feathers. Where was their courtesy? A Name they had asked for, a Name she had given them. She stopped and peered brightly at Bochna as the Queen took a determined step toward the tree.

"Neither crow nor raven, but the Oak Seer is here," the Mother said in astonishment. "Seek you the Conjuror of Sliabh An Óir, Lady? Or have you news of him? To our sorrow, he is not among us. Yet, an' it's tidings you bear, I pray you, give them to me."

Úna hissed like a threatened owl. She had given her tidings. Twice. A raven was a bird of deep wisdom, but perhaps they doubted a message given by the black-feathered omen of the battlefield. Owls, too, were wise, and even the Mothers often called them Cailleacha of the night. An owl, then, and they would understand.

Úna's shoulders came up to hide her neck, her eyes grew round and yellow. She swiveled her head until it seemed to be looking backward, then quickly brought her golden gaze around to bear on Bochna.

"Who? Who?" she asked. Úna blinked one of her large round eyes knowingly.

"To me," Bochna said again.

"Wasting your words with that madwoman, you are," growled Longaire Rí Laighean.

Úna screeched with frustration, but not as an owl. 'Twas a marsh harrier's cry she uttered, one to freeze the hare to stillness and attention. But did they halt—did they cease their madness and attend? Bochna stepped quickly back, plainly alarmed at the change in the Seer, yet gleaning nothing from it. The King of Laighin's sword flashed. Almost as swiftly Magadh's hand covered his, but not before Úna had responded to Longaire's challenge.

A dark green oak leaf she became, then swiftly faded to red. Gently she wafted from the high branch to the dry earth at the Mother's feet. When she touched the soil, she was Úna herself, and a slim oak wand was in her hand.

The Oak Seer watched the Mothers with the hard, unblinking stare of a serpent's lidless eyes, but her upper body swayed in slow, graceful undulations, inviting the Queens to try again.

"How it strengthens our hope to have you with us," Magadh said. "Dark the day, darker the coming night—but Úna's Sight is not daunted by Shadow. Help us. Look beyond the hedge, and tell us what you See."

"Not S-s-see. Tas-s-ste. Taste the Name the Dancer found." Úna's forked tongue flicked the air. "Pois-s-son. S-s-spit it out."

Patient, then swift. That was a snake's advantage. Patient she had been with them, now swift to tell—and more Úna could tell than ever the goose guessed. Patient again, the Oak Seer waited for someone to understand.

"You speak of the Dancer," Bochna coaxed. "Can you tell us where you met with Meacán, Úna dear? How we would like to speak with her ourselves! Can you tell us where she is?"

Patience was wasted on such fools.

"Between day and dark she dances," the Oak Seer said, bending like the barley, "to the ring of fire."

"'The Name the Dancer found,'" Tadhg whispered.

"Treachery is her meaning!" Magadh cried. "Then is Éirinn's hope already betrayed."

"All our counsels." Feargna Óg's voice shook. "All the Mothers have Seen, all the Mighty have done—"

The lark's song burst from Úna's throat. At last the dawn! What else could she tell them, now their ears were open? Turning to Seamair, Úna tossed her unruly hair and stamped her foot, a bull's challenge.

"How many times need I remind you? Let the rains fall! Shall she fly to Loch nEathach for a mouthful of water?"

Seamair looked about as if a sensible response to the Seer's tirade were hiding in the trees. Úna ignored her and sidled up to Fionnghuala.

"To the sky, my dove," Úna cooed, gently patting the Deceiver's arm. "Only look to the sky."

Obediently Fionnghuala tilted back her head. Úna followed the Deceiver's gaze to the heavens. This dusk was eager to relinquish its brief reign to the night.

Úna laughed at the twilight and the impatient dark, her voice as light as water running merrily over stones. Stepping back, her face lengthened, her grin grew feral, her body became muscled and furred. A wolf, she bounded away in a sweep of silver, gray, and brown, singing the sorrows of the coming night to the black and dying moon.

PART 11

shadow

Fifty-five

An' a hunter's horse is sure
An' a hunter's hound is swift
An' a hunter's hawk flies eagerly
Ill luck for the hunter's quarry

At the far end of Márrach's curved valley, the two sides of the defile met in a steep, thinly forested escarpment. The terrain forced Blackthorn up toward the ridge—he climbed until he could see the sombre outline of the hedge lining the crest, by now too familiar a sight to dishearten him.

Not much farther, he came to good cover, and took refuge in the heap of stone and fallen beeches. The trees had long ago washed down from the ridge, lodged between the rocks, and caught the scree that had followed them down the slope. The loose stones, bleached wood, and smooth-sided boulders sat like the gray ruin of a fairy fort on the wasted hillside.

His back against a large stone, Blackthorn looked out over the sparsely wooded vale. His weariness told him it was near sundown, but the light would not swear to it. Since the ringing of the bell, time had stopped at the edge of dusk, scorning to mark the sun's journey. And dusk, it seemed, would deign to pass only to bring on the deeper shadows of night.

His thirst was fierce. It was some sign of water his eyes were most eager to see, but they touched ever and again on the half score Scáileanna and seven goblins that occupied a

broad, crumbly ledge some distance below him. The trees
hindered his view only slightly, and he saw his foes were just
now turning to see what his own ear had already noted—a
rider coming up through the thicker forest that lined the
base of the slope.

Under Shadow's cloak, Blackthorn had found his ears far
keener than his eyes, yet he recognized the mounted Scáil as
soon as his horse broke from the trees. Urchóid's dark
leather armor had a distinctive hue, a peculiar depth without
sheen. Márrach's champion swung from his saddle, and
opened a cloth sack that hung from his stirrup. He took
something from it, and displayed the object to those he had
come to meet.

An' it was some weapon, Blackthorn would have thought
to hear the goblins howl. The goblins gazed silently at what
Urchóid held, but the hiss of the Scáileanna's pleasure
washed over Blackthorn like death's chill.

Sorcery, then. Blackthorn glanced away from his foes to
study his escapes. Back he could go, the way he had come,
but the woods to the south were thick with enemies, and his
scent heavy enough on the western slope. Was there sufficient cover to slip past the hunters on the ledge and make a
run for the high end of the valley? The hedge doubtless
barred Márrach's border, but an' he could circle around the
glen, he might start down the valley once more, and this
time along the eastern hills.

He had been sitting, but now pulled his legs under him
and went into a crouch. The hardest step would be the
first—leaving his hiding place without rattling a stone, or
worse, sending one down the rise. Motionless, he listened,
waiting for sounds that would tell him when his foes might
be least likely to look his way.

For a long time the Scáileanna were utterly still, and even
the goblins made hardly a sound. Blackthorn cursed to himself. Every moment brought true night nearer, and 'twas
himself would be most disadvantaged by greater dark.

The Scáileanna began to chant. The spell fell clearly on
Blackthorn's ears, but it bore him no message. He did not
expect it would—the hunters were unaware their quarry was
in earshot. But an' the magic was not for him, then it must
be for the thing Urchóid had brought.

Blackthorn strained his eyes, trying to see the shadow in the champion's hand. A dark orb it was, a dark tear of stone. Every eye, red and black, was fixed upon it. Not slowly, but all at once and as one, every eye turned, looked up the hill, and fastened on Blackthorn.

Instinctively, he shrank back, deeper into the shadows, though it was plain his cover no longer concealed him. The goblins were already scrabbling up the slope, the Scáileanna mounting and fanning out below the goblins.

Keeping low, Blackthorn crept away from the rock and up the hill to a clump of scraggly gorse. He went stealthily, soundlessly, unseen. The goblins kept their red eyes on the fallen beeches, and would have missed him, had Urchóid not called out to them from the ledge below.

"Higher now. Behind that gorse."

With savage cries, the goblins were on his trail again. Blackthorn cursed, aloud this time. He could almost hear the laughter as his bitter words reached the Shadow King's ears. Pursued since he fled the broch, not until now had Blackthorn doubted his ability to elude his pursuers.

The goblins sped up the gravelly hillside on all fours, running swift as wolves on their broad, flat feet and sharp-nailed paws. The Scáileanna's horses were having trouble on the steep incline, but the dark elves steered their mounts to the left where the slope eased and, further on, a faint trail wound to the top of the ridge.

Shifting his Spear to his left hand and drawing his sword with his right, Blackthorn turned and raced up the hill. The ground broke under his boots like hardened sand, giving him no purchase. In a moment the goblins were at his heels. He spun, Strife taking the head from the nearest red-eye's shoulders. Another felt the blade pass through half his body before he was dead and falling down the hill.

The corpse slid into the goblins coming up behind, and its weight bore them back. Turning, Blackthorn started up the slope again. The loose rock tore away underfoot—he dug the butt of his Spear into the ground to speed his ascent and sent a hail of sharp, stony clumps of dirt raining into the goblins' faces.

The last bit was the steepest—the slope had dropped away from the crown of the hill in some bygone day when rain still fell in the valley. Blackthorn struggled up the concave incline. Still gripping his sword and Spear, he put his arms over the lip of the ridge and pulled himself up.

The crest was flat and barren, save for the tall thorn hedge, not forty paces on. He sped toward it, just as the first of the Scáileanna spurred his horse over the ridge to Blackthorn's right.

Sending another unheeded curse into the darkness, the Hunter stopped and faced the Scáil. The hedge was too far. The dark elf would cut him down from behind an' he kept running—but an' he stopped to fight, any chance he had of escaping over the thorn wall was gone.

He tossed Strife lightly into the air, caught her by the hilt, but in a spear grip, and hurled the black sword toward the Scáil's chest. Strife sighed with pleasure as she streamed through the air, then buried herself deep in the dark elf's heart. The Scáil burst into flames.

Scorched by the fire, the Scáil's horse screamed. Goblins echoed the animal's cry as they poured over the lip of the ridge. Blackthorn cursed at losing Strife, but turned his back on the Scáileanna and red-eyes, and sprinted for the thorns. Flinging himself onto the hedge, he began to climb, swift and sure as a spider, though his Spear was in one hand and the thorns stabbing him through his clothes.

He was more than halfway to the top of the hedge wall when his foes reached its base. Any moment he'd feel the agony of an axe stabbing him in the back, driving him against the thorns. Any moment he'd hear the whistle of a knife through the air. He kept climbing, and only the thorns cut him, and only the sounds of hissing laughter and baying reached his ears.

Out of the corner of his eye, Blackthorn saw a rush of gray flying through the hedge, like a banner of smoke borne by a strong wind. The shadow hurtled through the web of wood toward him, startling in its speed. He would have cried out, but cold gripped his chest, and he could make no sound.

Nearer it came, shapeless, silent. Blackthorn could see it clearer now—talons sharper than a hawk's, stretched out to grasp, eyes redder than a goblin's, burning like fire, a mouth, a black maw, opened wide, not for his body, but for his soul.

Blackthorn felt the wraith's icy breath on his hand as he

let go of the hedge. He landed lightly on his feet, his eyes still fixed on the shadow-beast in the thorns. The wraith glided on, disappearing into the weave of knives and tangled branches.

"An' you open your mouth to utter even a single word," said the soft, sibilant voice of a Scáil behind him, "you will be dead before you utter another."

The Hunter turned to face his captors.

Blackthorn could not say which pain was greater, when they took his Spear from his hand, or when they ripped his Talisman from his throat. The goblins bound his wrists with ropes and the ropes they tied to two saddles. He was made to run the long road back to Márrach, breathing the dust raised by the goblins' and horses' feet, dragged along when he stumbled, prodded, taunted, jeered by his enemies.

Night closed on the valley as they brought him back a prisoner to Márrach. Shadowy dusk thickened to impenetrable night, the blackened air was heavy in the Hunter's lungs. He never really saw Márrach, just a vast, inky presence lowering over him. Then his weary legs were pounding over the wooden slats of the bridge, and the horses' hooves thundering beside him. Too many goblins ran before him for Blackthorn to mark the gate, but when he was through, flickering torchlight briefly showed him the gatehouse before he was driven into the tunnel. The Scáileanna's horses went more easily than he through the long, lightless passage, but slowed as they came into the courtyard.

At last they stopped. There was some light, some few torches set against the broch's walls, but all he could see was a press of horses, goblins, and Scáileanna about him. Gasping, Blackthorn bent his head to his shoulder to wipe the stinging sweat from his eyes. He didn't notice the Scáileanna untying the ropes from their saddles, but suddenly felt his arms pulled down and back, and goblins made the ropes fast behind him. They shoved him forward until he stumbled and fell to his knees.

Red eyes flamed all around him, burning him with their hunger. Whispers shot through the shadows and clung to his body like spiders' silk. Nails scraped his scalp as a massive paw grasped Blackthorn by the hair and hauled him to his feet.

The Gruagach's eyes like glowing coals bored into Blackthorn's own, his wide, leering mouth pulled back over his sharp, dripping fangs. Blackthorn saw the creature's other paw balled and swinging toward him, but could make no move to avoid it. The Gruagach's hairy fist smashed down on the side of Blackthorn's head and sent him back to his knees.

"How pleased we are at Blackheart's return." Blackthorn recognized the sibilance as Urchóid's, but could not focus his eyes. "This time, let us welcome the Hunter of Éirinn as he deserves."

Rough paws seized him, forcing him to his feet and across the courtyard. Shaking his head to clear it from the Gruagach's blow, Blackthorn saw a single torch set above the passage to the close, and another by the tunnel to the gatehouse. The tables were gone, and the chairs and benches. The tower was transformed—no longer a feasting hall, the courtyard had become a stable yard. Horses were everywhere, being saddled and mounted. Scáileanna carried horns under their cloaks, goblins were milling about like huge packs of hounds. The master of Márrach was readying for his hunt . . . but an' he was hunting, and the borders of Márrach closed fast, then the Stag—

The rope ladder hung from the lip of the shaft that led to the goblin pits, but Blackthorn's hands were not unbound that he might use it. Snarling, the goblins dragged him to the edge of the shaft and pushed him over the side. He fell, unable to see the dark earth rising to meet him. When he landed, he hit hard, jarring every bone from his heel to his head, and staggered, scraping his leg and shoulder against the uneven dirt wall.

More goblins awaited at the base of the shaft. They growled at him to get his feet under him and move. He did not go fast enough to please them, so they used the hafts of their axes and their sharp-nailed paws to goad him along. The dirt floor sloped ever downward. The corridor was dark as pitch, and twisted like the branches of the hedge guarding Márrach's borders. The pits stank of rancid oil, piss, and goblin dung. Sightless, Blackthorn stumbled over goblins sprawled sleeping along the passage—firelight seeping from an open cell ahead fell on a mound of snoring red-eyes piled like rats against the tunnel wall.

When he came near the cell, he found the door hanging wide, nearly blocking the corridor. A heavy iron bar rested in brackets beside it. Below the bar was a raucously slumbering goblin. Above it hung a ring with a single iron key. Blackthorn must have slowed—the butt of an axe jabbed into his back. The goblins grabbed at him, hurrying him over their sleeping comrade and into the cell.

The fire was a smoking pile of hot coals behind a metal grate at the back wall. The light it gave was minimal, but enough to illuminate two wooden poles set slightly apart from each other in the center of the room, and to cast their long shadows to the door. A heavy chain was nailed to the top of each pole. Shackles hung from the ends of both chains.

The goblins hurried Blackthorn to the poles. His arms were loosed from the ropes, but not from the goblins' paws. The red-eyes forced him around until he faced the door, then brought his arms up, locking the shackles on his wrists. They worked quickly, snarling about the fire, now flickering only twenty paces from their backs. As soon as Blackthorn was chained they edged away from the meager red glow, and crowded at the door, as far from the coals as they could get and still watch the entertainment.

The cell was twice as long from door to fire as it was wide. Neither the walls nor the low ceiling were evenly made, but roughly hewn from the black earth and bolstered by soot-dark beams. Cautiously, Blackthorn tested his bonds. The bands of heavy metal about his wrists were coated with dried blood, and the chains themselves strong enough to hold goblins.

The red-eyes at the door moved aside. Urchóid came down the aisle they had made, with Márrfach, and a Scáil Blackthorn did not recognize. The dark elves moved easily in the gloom, their footsteps quiet and measured on the packed earth. The low ceiling made them seem even taller than they were, but though their heads nearly grazed the cell's dirt roof, the Scáileanna did not deign to bend. They came close to Blackthorn, set their lidless eyes upon him, and smiled their contentment.

They said nothing, nor hissed, nor touched him. Though the fire was at Blackthorn's back and the Scáileanna standing before him, their shadows fell on him, chilling his flesh and deepening the darkness.

Mac Ailch arrived soon after. It might have been a relief for Blackthorn to look upon a human face, but for the inhuman serenity in his enemy's expression. Though Mac Ailch's eyes were blue, they were a Scáil's eyes—two unreflective pools draining the light of courage and hope from all they looked upon. The sorcerer was not wearing his gloves. They were neatly folded and tucked into his belt. Mac Ailch's left hand was wrapped firmly about the Spear, and Domhnall's star glinted dully from his right.

"I had thought you a poor liar," said the master of Márrach, "but an obedient servant." His voice was impeccably smooth. "I find you a surpassing liar. 'Tis your service that disappoints."

He half turned his head to the door and nodded, the familiar, subtle signal. The goblins grinned, and howled into the corridor. There was scuffling, snarling . . . two red-eyes burst into the cell dragging Creathna the Name-Sayer between them. They hustled the old man to stand before Mac Ailch, then left him there and hurried back to the door, as far from the fire as their duty would allow.

Creathna would not meet Blackthorn's eyes. The boldness, the daring that had been his at the feast, tonight was gone without a trace. The aged Wizard's head was bent like a suppliant's. He wrung his hands.

The goblins brought Blackthorn pain, the Scáileanna inspired dread. For Mac Ailch, even now Blackthorn felt more hate than fear, but the obeisance the Name-Sayer made to the false hunter with his trembling hands and humble deference cast the cold shadow of despair over the Hunter's heart.

"Look on him, Creathna, my friend," said Márrach's master. He spoke to the old Wizard as if he were a child. "Look on the Hunter of Éirinn, and give me his Name."

Fifty-six

The King's blood seeped under the winter-cold ground
(Too-ra a-loo-ra a-lay)
Deep drank the oak,
Deep the apple's dead roots
Deep drank the brown, lifeless rye.
The oak blossoms bloomed,
Apples hung from the tree,
Made sweet by the death that he died,
And the grass a green cairn built around, all around him
(Too-ra a-loo-ra a-lay)

Muirgheach Rí Mumhan's Death
(a dance of Oileáin Árann)

Meacán felt the shadow-beast before she saw it, an icy chill gusting through the tangled web of thorns. Fear rose in her breast, but turned immediately to anger. Never again, she thought fiercely. Never again would she be at Shadow's mercy. She leapt away, swift as thought, Liannan's proud face still in her Sight.

A quick turn and she was past the hedge, the wraith's attack no more than a cold shadow on her back. Once through the thorns, Meacán stopped, and caught her breath before starting off again. Keeping her holdfast steady, she changed her dance. Knees lifting high, arms cutting the air with vicious precision, Meacán danced like a sword in a King's hand, grim and tireless. She tore through the shadows of the forest, through the dusk-colored day, through time itself, until she burst out of the night into a ring of red fire.

The Mother of Midhe stood before her in the center of the circle. No word of greeting passed Liannan's lips when she beheld Meacán, for the Queen was singing, but her eyes stared in surprise, and she spread her uplifted arms a little wider. Nor did the warriors who fought at the edge of the ring welcome the Dancer, or even seem to notice her arrival.

The vision Meacán had Seen through the hole in Úna's staff had been of a small band of Éirinn's brave. Now the Dancer saw how small—fifteen she counted defending the ring of fire, though there was room for twice that number. The warriors' spears and swords thrust through the waist-high flames and there met with the shadow-gray blades of the Scáileanna. Red eyes gleamed in the darkness beyond, but did not come nearer. Neither the warriors' courage, nor the roaring madness of the Kings, nor shining-mailed Cessair kept the howling, hissing Dark at bay. It was the Mother's fire that held it back, burning gladly though there was nothing to burn, burning because Liannan told it to, in a voice sweet and pure, and glittering as crystal.

> *Burning bright, Brighde's arms,*
> *Flame and fire, defy the Dark.*
> *Though goblin and grayskin growl and hiss,*
> *Their shadows shrivel to ash.*

The blaze danced to the Mother's music, fueled by the power of the rann.

"I have a Name, Mother," Meacán said clearly.

A look of anguish crossed Liannan's face—she shook her head and began her verse again. Meacán dared not interrupt a second time. Meacán was no Priestess, but she had sense enough to know that should Liannan's will fail or her voice waver, the protective ring of fire would not long hold back their foes. To distract the Queen from the magic of her song would be madness.

Yet, an' the Mother could not take the enemy's Name from her, still it would be of some use to a Poet. Meacán turned and surveyed the ring of fighters. She saw Aedh Rí Mumhan's sword pierce the flames to bring down a Scáil, saw Cessair fly to fill the gap as a tawny-haired warrior fell. Had Saileach of Glas an Mhullaigh or Tadhg of An Chluain Thiar been present, surely they would already be standing with Liannan in the heart of the circle. Some few other, lesser Poets Meacán knew, but none she recognized fought at the wall of flames. Useless indeed was the Name she bore, Meacán thought bitterly, a Name worth nothing, as Úna had said it would be.

Meacán pressed her lips together in a thin line and squeezed the clay vial in her hand. More than a Name had she brought to the ring of fire. She dropped her other hand to the pouch where she had set the púca. It was empty.

Finding him fled, Meacán immediately began to doubt. When had the shape-shifter left her? Was he here in the ring, or had he slipped out when she paused in her dance after passing the hedge? Were his words truth or tricks? Did the jar contain water to clear the Sight or a blinding spell of Darkness? Had he left her to find Conall, or to tell Márrach's master that Meacán the Dancer was again within the borders of his lands? She should never have trusted the shape-shifter at all, at all, and never would have had Úna not—

Meacán!

Liannan's cry was faint, as if the Mother were far away. Lines of strain drew the Queen's face into a mask of weariness, her upraised arms were knotted with tension.

"*Burning bright, Brighde's arms . . .*" the Queen sang.

Meacán's heart went out to her. How long had Liannan's voice carried the rann to the flames? Not Sight did the Mother need—the danger was plain before her eyes. Succor she required, the kind of succor a Maiden might give her.

Sure of what she should do, but uncertain entirely of her ability to accomplish it, Meacán moved to stand beside the Priestess. She raised her own arms toward the black, starless sky, and opened her mouth to sing.

Liannan's desperate need struck Meacán like a blow. The Mother's will plunged into Meacán's being and at once began feeding on her strength. Meacán's knees grew weak, she swayed where she stood . . .

Meacán!

Even in the Dancer's mind, Liannan's voice sounded frantic. Sweet Éire, could Liannan truly be so spent? Though away from her own lands of Midhe, still the magic that served the Mother must be no less than Éire's—unending abundance of air and earth, fire and sea. Were the shadows of Márrach mighty enough to imprison the Goddess's powers, to prevent them answering Liannan's call?

Taking another, deeper, shakier breath, Meacán tried again to blend her voice with the Queen's. She did better this time, holding almost steady against Liannan's overwhelming need. She made her voice as determined as she could and gave her strength unstintingly, that the Mother could make it her own.

Liannan took what Meacán had to offer, took it brutally, greedily, and the flames danced brighter. The Mother's Sight was dim, her hearing poor—she had not even the ability to pluck the gift Meacán had brought at such peril from the Dancer's mind. Yet, the Dancer had returned from Shadow's realm, and did she not carry with her the false hunter's Name? Liannan sought out Ceallach, the Ó Briain's Poet who had made the verse she now sang. With the weapon Meacán had brought, could the boy make a verse to destroy their enemy?

She found the young Poet, fighting bravely beside the Bear of An Clár, but sent no summons. Márrach's servants are here, Liannan thought to herself, but not Márrach's master. Deep in the heart of this darkness he lies, scorning to turn his Sight upon the Mother of Midhe. On the Stag did his eye dwell, Liannan knew, on the Goddess's sacred beast flying through these very woods, pursued by the false hunter's hounds. Without that she could pierce their enemy's ear with her voice, what good her curse? To send a rann past his shield of arrogance and disdain would take greater power than was now at Liannan's command.

And if she bade Ceallach dispel the shadows of night? Had the boy such skill with words? And should he succeed, would the Scáileanna and goblins hesitate while the sun lay under the earth? An' her people could endure till day, then might a Name rend the Dark and summon the Light . . . but the dawn was yet hours away.

". . . Flame and fire defy the Dark . . ." she sang. "Though goblin and gray-skin—"

The raucous cries of a scaldcrow split the night. Harsher than the Mother's rann was the Mór-Ríoghain's verse, and fully as potent.

"Kill," the Goddess of Battle called to the fighters. "Die."

Niall Rí Uladh grinned like a goblin to hear the black-feathered bird. As She had promised, the Mór-Ríoghain had come. The Mother's song of fire was good, but the Mór-Ríoghain's song of battle was better.

"Kill," Niall roared to his blade, and this time it did, sliding past the edge of empty-eyed Scáil's weapon and cleaving through the dark elf's gray-cloaked shoulder to his black heart.

"Die," he commanded, and the Scáil died, but another stood already in his place.

On he fought, driven by the Mór-Ríoghain's glad and terrible song, unaware of the passing hours, and his companions' growing fatigue. Two score Scáileanna lay dead and dying beyond the fire, but the Ó Briain's warriors could barely lift their swords for the ache in their arms. Corann of Cnoc an Eanaigh fell as his cut leg refused at last to hold him. Foxtail lay bleeding his life away at the edge of the ring. Meacán the Dancer sank to her knees. Her arms hung at her sides, her voice was little more than a scratched murmur.

The Mother of Midhe turned her Sight to the east and sent a prayer to the Light. Shadow denied it. Long the night that had passed in blood and darkness, but still the day refused to dawn.

Only Niall, and Aedh, and Eoghan, the Kings of Éirinn, warm within their mantles, did not feel the chill of defeat, and Cessair of Cnoc an Eanaigh, herself cool and keen as starlight. Ulaidh's King laughed and swung his sword over his head, daring the enemy on. Did the gray-skins think the shadows their ally? The woods were not dark, but bright with the red blood he had made flow.

"Come!" Niall bellowed. "Come and be killed!"

They came at his call, but not the unblinking Scáileanna. Red-eyes were nearing at last, creeping out from the cover of the trees.

"Come! Come die!" he cried.

He was not sane enough to see that the goblins were advancing because the Mother's fire was waning. He did not ken the meaning of the chant emitted in sour whispers from the dark elves' mouths.

Liannan's voice quivered, a solitary note faltered before the next soared sweetly again. So slight her hesitation, only a few tongues of fire dipped and vanished, a small patch of flame burning before Eoghan Rí na Midhe. The blaze rose again almost as soon as it had dropped; less than a moment did a dark gate open in the ring.

In that moment, the Scáileanna's chant swelled like the winds of a black squall. Goblins burst through the circle and threw themselves upon the King of Midhe. Six made it past the fire before the flames leapt again, and with them came a single Scáil. Swiftly the Ó Briain ran to Eoghan's aid, more swiftly still Cessair flew across the ring, a streak of silver lightning.

They were not fast enough. The goblins held back their axes and wrapped their long limbs around Eoghan, pulling his arms wide to bare his chest, hanging on his legs that he could not move. Eoghan's howl shook the trees. Two of his hairy captors burst into torches of shrieking flame.

Beyond the ring of fire, the dark elves wailed. Within the circle, the Scáil thrust once. His blade went straight into Eoghan's heart.

Before the dark elf could pull his sword free, Cessair was upon him. Eoghan's slayer was dead even as the body of Midhe's King hit the ground.

Niall tore into the fray, his eyes blazing, hewing down goblins as if they were weaponless against him. Three red-eyes died under his blade, and another, venturing too near the King of Ulaidh, was caught by Niall's hand, and burned to death.

His foes within the ring dead, Niall faced the flames and saw Scáileanna pressing close to the fire. Gray swords dared his own to dance with them, red-eyes howled for Niall's life. The King of Ulaidh howled back, promising only their deaths.

A cold shadow caressed Niall's cheek, blew past him, and on into the defenders' circle. He shivered, then gnashed his teeth at the outrage. Turning his back on the foes beyond the ring, he cast his bulging eyes about, seeking the foe that had dared dampen his fire. On Eoghan his burning gaze fell, on the dark shroud covering the dead King. In the wisdom of his madness, Niall knew the shadow for a mortal enemy, and lunged toward it.

"Ulaidh!" he roared.

The shadow-beast had no face to raise to Niall's, but eyes only, red as a goblin's, and talons that were digging into Eoghan's dead body, and a mouth, a black, gaping sore. Wordless in his wrath, Niall came near enough to swing. His cut was vicious, but his blade severed only the empty air above the fallen King's corpse. The wraith was gone.

Niall spun about, searching the darkness. He came full circle, and stopped. Eoghan had risen to his knees. His dead hand gripped the sword in his chest, and slowly pulled it from his heart.

Cold crept stealthily under Niall's mantle, making him shiver again. His madness started to slip away.

Anger would warm him. Howling his battle cry, Ulaidh's King wrapped his mantle tightly about him once more, denying the chill that had touched his heart. Not upon himself, but on the young King of Midhe had frost fallen. A sculpture of ice Eoghan seemed, captured in his royal mood. His hair stood stiff above his head, his eyes were wild, his grin wide. Yet, no smoke came from his crown, no fire lit his eye, no rapture formed his smile. The sword that had been his death in his hand, Eoghan advanced, opening his mouth as if to answer Niall's challenge. An empty, voiceless sigh issued from the dead King's throat.

Niall leapt to meet Eoghan's corpse, but the chill was with him again, a sliver of ice in his heart. The cold hampered his movement—his mind was too clear, his sight suddenly bewildered by the shadow-spelled night, his strength . . . what was his strength without his madness?

Eoghan's blade arced swift and high. Niall parried, but Eoghan's sword bore down irresistibly on his own. He dove under Eoghan's stroke, and rolled to his feet. Dead the King of Midhe might be, but his limbs carried him nearly as well as they had in life, and in his bloodless hand the Scáil's sword was deadly.

When Eoghan had fallen, the pain of Liannan's grief had poured into her voice with sorrowful beauty. Watching him rise again, her heart nearly stopped, her voice cracked and broke. The flames dropped to nearly nothing, but she could not take her eyes from her dead King.

Another voice struggled to carry the rann, but it was pale and hoarse after the Mother's sweet song. Goblins' howls rushed in to fill the air where the Poet's verse had rung. Like a gray wave, the Scáileanna swept against Éirinn's few. The defenders backed until they stood shoulder to shoulder, a ring of swords and courage facing the Dark.

"Sing!" Cessair's fair voice soared over the enemy's clamor. "Lady, sing the fire!"

Deaf Liannan had been to the goblins' howls of triumph, and blind to her folly. With Cessair's cry, the prayers in the hearts of her people rang in Liannan's ears.

"*Tine!*" she gasped. Her own tears brightened the Mother's eyes, and she called her summons again, louder, a Queen again. "*Tine!*"

The flames sparked at her command, caught on the red-eyes' greasy hides even as they were crossing the blackened ring. Hastily, the fire rose to burn. As Liannan's voice grew stronger, the flames joined her music, crackling with Brighde's power. Caught between fire and sword, those that had breached Liannan's wall found only death beyond it.

Eoghan turned away from Niall. With another soulless cry, he sprang at Liannan. Niall rushed to stop him, managing to deflect Eoghan's blow with his sword. Eoghan's arm shot out, his hand closed on Niall's throat. The cold of the dead King's fingers bit into Niall's flesh like hoarfrost.

Rage flamed desperately in Niall's heart. A haze of red again colored his vision, darkening the pallid face of the corpse-King. Eoghan's frozen grin became a grimace of pain, but he retained his grip on Niall's throat. Lifting his sword, Niall cut up and deep into Eoghan's belly. Eoghan didn't flinch. Close as lovers, Niall plainly saw the gash his sword had made in Eoghan's flesh, yet not a drop of blood flowed from the wound.

The red before Niall's eyes started to grow black. He could force no air past the band of ice on his throat, the muscles of his neck were rigid with cold. He pulled his sword free from the dead King's gut, but the world grew darker. He felt himself sinking, felt his knee driven down against the hard earth.

The dead King's fell blade lifted for the final stroke. Niall countered by driving the point of his sword between Eoghan's ribs. Taking one hand from his sword, he clawed at Eoghan's fingers, trying to wrest them from his windpipe, but the corpse had the strength of a King, and Niall . . .

"Niall Rí Uladh!"

His own chilled blood roared so loudly in Niall's ears, he heard the Ó Briain's bellow like a distant echo. Louder was the Ó Briain's sword, whistling through the darkness to fall on Eoghan's upraised arm. It bit clean through. The cold limb leapt, then fell to the ground, dead fingers still grasping the hilt of the sword.

The Bear of An Clár swung again, but with the speed of insanity Eoghan loosed Niall and turned on the Ó Briain. Eoghan kicked, his boot landing solidly in the Bear's chest. The Ó Briain staggered back. The corpse-King's fist hammered down on the Chieftain's sword, shattering it, then lifted, and smashed against the Ó Briain's temple.

The Bear fell back stunned, his breathing ragged, his eyes glazed. He struggled to pull himself away from Eoghan, but like some ghastly buzzard, the dead King followed, dropping to the earth to cover the Ó Briain with his body.

Niall lurched toward them both, lifting his sword as he came. His blood was half-frozen in his veins, his sight still clouded, but he swung savagely at Eoghan's body spread like a shadow over the Bear of An Clár.

Eoghan's fair-haired head flew from his broad shoulders. No blood fell from the stump of his neck. His torso remained poised over his prey. Niall reached out, hauled the thing that had been King of Midhe off the Chieftain, shuddering as his hand touched Eoghan's frozen flesh. He swept his sword across the backs of the corpse's legs, severing the hamstrings. The headless body fell like a tree, but Eoghan's arm waved wildly, fingers clawing the empty air.

A deafening roar, the sound of a royal death, made Niall lift his head and look toward the ring of fire. In his madness Aedh Rí Mumhan had followed his foes beyond Brighde's light. Gray swords were falling like rain upon the King of Mumhain.

As Niall watched Aedh die, Eoghan's arm dropped. A shadow, formless as a wreath of smoke, rose from the butchered body of Midhe's King and flew rapidly over the flames to Mumhain's. The dark elves stepped aside, and Aedh's corpse rose slowly from the ground.

The warriors who stood within the ring of fire held their weapons before them as the dead and walking King of Mumhain neared the circle of flames. Only Cessair dared stand before him at the edge of the fire, and her presence seemed to make Aedh hesitate. Niall knew better. It was the fire, the heat of the flames the cold corpse dreaded, not the silver-armored warrior.

He laughed, but not like a King. Madness was in his laughter, but no battle-fury, no joy. Niall Rí Uladh would have battled goblins and Scáileanna until the end of the world, and never cared if he lived or died, but only that he fought. Shadow's King he would have faced without trembling, and when Ulaidh's King had fallen to the Dead Lord, his soul would have gone flaming into the Dark.

They are men, arrayed in kingly finery, and every bloody brow bears a crown, and every face is yours.

Like a gift in his heart Caireann had told him to bear his dream, but it was no gift. It was a curse, the foreshadowing of the evil that would rob the King's death of glory, and turn the King's fire to cold ashes. Eoghan's head had rolled near to the reaching flames. His colorless eyes stared back at Niall, but it was his own face the King of Ulaidh imagined he saw, his own deathless doom watching him.

"Niall Rí Uladh."

On his knees, swaying weakly, the Ó Briain was calling to him.

"Not 'Rí,'" Niall answered him. "A King's blood is potent as his seed, a King's corpse a blessing upon the earth." He gestured to the bloodless pieces of Eoghan's corpse. "Kings are born to die, but in Márrach, death denies us."

"Never has Niall Rí Uladh found a spell that would not break under his sword," the Ó Briain insisted.

"Not 'Rí.' Only bones and madness break under my sword. I am King no longer."

"Niall Rí Uladh," the Ó Briain said again, but this time he spoke the Name as if lamenting.

"Niall Rí Uladh!" the Crow of Battle croaked from the high, empty arms of the trees beyond the ring of fire. "Niall Rí Uladh! Niall Rí Uladh!"

Liannan's voice wavered. She gasped for breath, for strength. At her feet, Meacán sobbed with exhaustion.

Two Scáileanna rushed forward as the flames bent, and engaged Cessair's blade. Aedh ignored the Sidhe Chieftain and the battle raging at the wall of fire, nor even lifted his blade until he was well within the ring. His unseeing eyes were fixed on a single foe. He had come for Niall.

Niall raised his sword. The tattered remnants of his mantle slid off his shoulders as if his body were made of ice, leaving him naked as he had never been before. He had no hope that he might live—and the King of Ulaidh knew at last what it was to be afraid to die.

Fifty-seven

'Gainst a knife, a sword
'Gainst a sword, a spear
'Gainst a spear, a shield
'Gainst a shield, a rann
'Gainst a rann—naught

warrior's salute

Creathna's white head lifted. His eyes looked sadly out from under his frosty brows and met Blackthorn's.

"Do not do this thing," Blackthorn whispered. "The Mothers' host is—"

Mac Ailch drove his fist into Blackthorn's midsection. He grunted and doubled over as far as his chains would allow.

"I have not forgotten your treachery at the feast," the master of Márrach told Creathna. "Give me his Name, and swiftly, an' you would have me forgive your indiscretion."

"What is death to dishonor?" Blackthorn ground out between clenched teeth. "How can you serve Shadow, when you—"

This time it was Urchóid that silenced him, with a sharp blow to the side of Blackthorn's face. Tasting blood, Blackthorn spat some of it in the Scáil's direction. Urchóid stepped back out of range, his perfect smile never leaving his face.

Creathna's mouth worked, but no sound came out.

"Death or dishonor, old friend?" Mac Ailch's voice was confidential, remembering a beloved secret only the two of them shared. "But death is not the reward for disobedience, nor can death's cloak hide your secrets from me. Do I take his Name from your dead lips, or will you give it me willingly?"

The old Wizard's eyes swam in tears of betrayal.

"Courage." Blackthorn begged him, but the tears dropped from Creathna's eyes, and Blackthorn's Name from the graybeard's tongue.

"Conall," the Name-Sayer whispered. "Conall mac na Caillí."

Rage filled Blackthorn, but it gave way at once to panic. He watched his enemy's fingers twine in the Talisman's chain, watched him draw the pentacle up until it rested in his bare palm. Experienced in the ways of magic, Mac Ailch had known, as Blackthorn had not, that gloves would keep Domhnall's spells from him. And so the sorcerer wore none.

"Conall mac na Caillí," the master of Márrach repeated, and closed his fist around the silver star.

A hand of iron gripped Blackthorn's heart, strangling his life. He stiffened and gasped in pain.

The dark elves' sighed their delight, the goblins howled with pleasure. Mac Ailch laughed. Contempt rang clearly with his triumph.

"Take the dotard away," Márrach's master ordered, "and bid the Gruagach come."

The pain in Blackthorn's chest slowly eased. He sagged against his chains, cursing the Name-Sayer under his breath. The guards that had brought Creathna started forward, but stopped when the Name-Sayer turned and began shuffling toward them, content to wait by the door for the old Wizard to reach them if they could avoid coming any nearer the fire.

Suddenly Creathna spun about. Swift as a beardless youth he ran back to Blackthorn and set his lips against the ear of the man he had betrayed.

"Máchail! Do you understand?"

The goblins barreled forward. Urchóid's gloved hand was already on Creathna's shoulder.

"Not Mac Ailch. Máchail," the Name-Sayer insisted.

Urchóid pulled Creathna roughly away. An old man again, the Name-Sayer stumbled back, lost his balance, and fell to the ground. At once the goblins were swarming over him. Their paws tore at his hair and clothes as they hauled him to his feet and stood him before Mac Ailch. Not Mac Ailch, Blackthorn corrected himself. Máchail.

Máchail's ice-blue eyes bored into Creathna's until both were sure Márrach's master knew what the Name-Sayer had whispered in Blackthorn's ear. When Máchail spoke, his voice was gentler than Blackthorn had ever heard it.

"Old fool. 'Tis yourself will suffer for this, not I. What good my Name to him? The son of a Cailleach is he—not a Cailleach himself, nor a Mother, nor a Poet. Did you hope he would curse me with his dying breath? I will cut out his tongue first! Back to your cell, doddering graybeard, and consider—your folly has earned you the fate you most fear."

Creathna's knees bent under him. The goblins held him up, and half dragged, half carried the old Wizard from the room.

Máchail. Máchail, not Mac Ailch. Blackthorn almost laughed. All his enemy had told the Name-Sayer was no more than truth. What use Máchail's Name to him? An' he tried to barter it to the Scáileanna, they would promise whatever he asked—his life, his freedom, his Talisman, his Spear—only to break their bargains when they had the Name from him. An' he were a Poet, he could he make a rann to destroy his foe. An' he were a Priestess, he could call down Éire's wrath upon his enemy's head—but he was the Hunter, and "Máchail" a useless weapon in his hand. With his Naming, Creathna had doomed them both.

Máchail came close, and set his lips against Blackthorn's ear as Creathna had done.

"'For an' you betray me, Creathna will render me your true Name, and I will curse your soul to Shadow to sate the Dead Lord's hunger.'" He stepped back a pace. "Do you remember my words? But so you must, and you possessed of a Bard's memory. Still, I will postpone the Shadow King's feast yet awhile, while I make the Talisman mine."

The coals hissed like Scáileanna's laughter. Not another sound stirred the soot-choked air of the cell. Even the goblins were quiet as Máchail's fingers danced and the pentacle glinted in his palm. The star's geis ached in Blackthorn's heart. An' it was kept from him long enough, the Talisman itself would weigh on him till it broke his soul.

"Conall mac na Caillí," said Máchail deliberately.

His own Name twisted like a dagger in Blackthorn's heart. He groaned, but the master of Márrach's expression did not change.

"Sweet as your pain is to me, sweeter are the pleasures of the hunt. Make your last moments easier—shorten the agony of your death. Tell me how to command the Spell-Maker's star."

Blackthorn said nothing.

"I will not be denied."

"But you will." Blackthorn words came out less smoothly than his captor's. His tongue was thick with hate. "Butchery, such as the goblins practice, that is the most you will enjoy. Only I was called to the Hunt, and its pleasures are for me alone."

"You alone!" Resentment dulled the gloss of Máchail's voice. "I am thrice the Hunter you are. I have preyed upon power, stalked it where even Éire's Huntsman fears to go. I have chased quarry greater than ever you have dreamed, brought it down, bled it, and gorged upon it. And so will I do until I am sated."

Blackthorn spat. "You have not stalked, but stolen. Not brought down, but fed like a carrion crow on others' kills. Not in the lands you boast, but in the wild does a hunter's quarry run, and in the wild Márrach's master is but prey to better hunters than himself."

The cold in Máchail's eye crystallized to ice. A moment he stood motionless, saying not a word. Then slowly, carefully, he spoke the Hunter's Name.

Pain ran like fire through Blackthorn's body. He cried out, yet, in that breath of silence he had spied it. In his torment he saw it still—the source of the hate in his enemy's eyes. He had it at last, the lure this eel could not resist. 'Twas not with the Mighty the master of Márrach contended, not their fame and glory he desired. 'Twas against the Hunter of Éirinn Máchail had set himself, and the Hunt the only bait he would rise to. Could Blackthorn but set that bait upon a hook, and tempt the eel until he bit—

Blackthorn forced a grim smile to his lips and nodded at the star. "Even this small quarry you could not catch, but had to rob from me. No hunter, you, but a greedy jay with a shiny stone in your beak. Though the Talisman be in your hand, you cannot command it."

Máchail's answer issued sibilantly from his lips. "No hunter I?" He lifted the Spear to the level of Blackthorn's eyes. "Yet, 'tis my hand holds the Stag's death, and the Hunt is mine."

"An' you hunt, you must dare the wild, even to the untamed heart of Éirinn where Her power is absolute, and there bring down your quarry. An' you hunt, you must be Death to your prey while eluding your own, you must find your way safe home again yet bearing your prize—for Death is ever generous. A gift of life He returns to the world with every life He takes. Do you pretend to be a hunter? A thief you are. And though you kill the Stag, yet never will you hunt him."

Máchail laughed, but it was hollow. "Jealous Éire calls only fools to Her service," he said, "cowards possessed of neither the sense nor the courage to claim the spoils of their own Hunts. You would bring down the Light only to watch others bask in it. I will have it for myself."

The eel was out of his muddy hole and snaking to the surface, revealing his whole, bitter length. Clearly now Blackthorn could see the ragged scar of an old wound on the dark beast, a wound that had closed, but never healed.

"You have seen him," Blackthorn whispered.

A malign light flickered for an instant in Máchail's eye. Its spark was soon doused, but its shadow remained.

"You have seen him," Blackthorn said again, certain now, "but he did not call your Name."

"How Éire will grieve at the loss of Her Huntsman," Máchail remarked, the edges of his words smooth once again. "How She will rue this night, the night Her Stag is brought down by a Hunter self-chosen, for I will not lay my kill as a gift at Éire's feet. To Shadow's King will I offer it. And though the Queens of the five kingdoms come begging for Light to lift the Darkness, I will part the shadows only an' it please myself."

"No hunter you, but a beggar at the Dead Lord's table," Blackthorn taunted him. "The Eater of Souls will feed on the Stag's glory, but toss you not a single scrap. Though you offer Éirinn to the Dark, the Dead Lord will not suffer you to rule it."

The Scáileanna laughed, and Máchail joined them.

"Éire's Huntsman affects to know the Shadow King's thought," he scoffed, but his hand was so tight about the Talisman, Blackthorn could feel his enemy's wrath like a scourge on his soul.

"More." Blackthorn masked his pain with a mocking smile. "I know His folly. 'Tis in trusting the Stag's death to so hapless a hunter. Not even mine have you accomplished, though I stand chained before you."

"Are you so impatient to die, Conall mac na Caillí?"

His enemy's hatred burned Blackthorn like ice. A moan escaped him, and drew a sneer from Máchail. Closer, oh Lady, let him come a little closer, Blackthorn prayed, and then must the eel bite.

"Conall mac na Caillí," Máchail said, taking excessive care with each syllable. "Release the Talisman to me."

Blackthorn shuddered, but clenched his teeth against the cry Máchail wanted to hear. Then he spat full into his enemy's face.

The hand that held the Spear lifted. Máchail's arm went up, and back, then drove toward Blackthorn's heart. Blackthorn's life swelled in his breast, eager to burst red and warm over the glittering death coming to pierce it.

A slate-gray shadow shot soundlessly toward the Spear. Urchóid's gray-gloved hand closed upon the ash shaft, halting the silver point not a finger's breadth from Blackthorn's chest.

"Where is his despair, master?"

Máchail's gaze narrowed. Some of the tension left his arm.

"I look deep, but cannot See his vanquished hopes. Where is his surrender, where his defeat? Not fear of death, but triumph blazed in his eyes as you raised the Spear against him."

Blackthorn watched helplessly as the quarry he had so cunningly courted grew wary and backed away. Máchail lowered his arm until the Spear's point touched the black earth. His smile was merciless.

"Hunting still?" he asked.

Blackthorn thrust against his chains, but it was useless. His death had eluded him.

"He would have welcomed a quick death, master," said Urchóid, "and almost achieved it."

"Think you so?" Máchail's smile hardened. "He was after worthier game, I'm thinking. Having drunk of his heart's blood, would the Spear have thirsted for the Stag's?"

Blackthorn was silent, but Máchail nodded, seeing the confirmation of his suspicion in the dark fire that burned in the Hunter's eyes.

"The greater fool he," remarked the Scáil. "What matter had you brought down Mac na Caillí instead of the Light? An' the Hunter fails to kill the Stag by Bealtaine Day, the Stag will depart, and the Light with him, and the Dark will cover Éirinn."

"The greater fool you," Máchail rebuked him. "What though the White Stag flees Éirinn's shores, and the Light with him—yet before he is gone another Hunter will be called. And though the Dark cover Éirinn, yet with hope alive, the Mighty will not bow to Shadow. They will wage war upon us until the Stag returns, and the Light with him. In nine years' time, who can say the next Hunter of Éirinn will not succeed where this one has failed?"

Máchail raised the Spear, turning it until it caught the coals' red light on its silver point.

"But an' the Stag dies by my hand," he said, "the Light will go to the Dark, never to return, and our victory is complete."

Máchail took his gaze from the Spear and set it on Blackthorn. "Arrah," he sighed. "I See it now. Even the fire of his hate is dimmed by the shadow of his despair."

The goblins at the door growled as they stepped aside to allow the Gruagach to enter. The beast came in cradling a black bowl in his long, hairy arms. It was small and deep, like a cook pot, but without handles or legs. Noting his master's eye fixed on Blackthorn, the Gruagach dipped a surreptitious finger into the bowl, then thrust it quickly into his mouth and sucked like a greedy child with a pot of honey.

"An' you relinquish the Talisman to me," Máchail promised, "I will grant you an easy death."

Blackthorn didn't bother to answer the lie. Máchail only laughed, and handed the Spear to his champion.

"Close the door," he commanded. "Stoke the fire. Begin the spell."

Few goblins lingered once the Scáileanna began to lay more fuel on the coals. In the red eyes of those that stayed, love of cruelty gleamed brighter than hatred of flame. A huge goblin with a scar over his right eye stepped from the shadows beyond the door and fought the tide of his companions to force his way in. Máchail nodded at the beast's boldness, and inclined his head toward Blackthorn. The goblin's grin widened. He moved toward the Hunter, lazily swinging his axe and letting the haft fall into his free paw.

"Don't kill him," Máchail cautioned, a tender warning to an impetuous child. "Only keep him quiet."

Though the fire was now hot on Blackthorn's back, he shivered as the dark elves moved to form a semicircle about Máchail. The Gruagach knelt before them, holding up the black bowl. No gesture or sign was given that Blackthorn could see, but with one voice the three Scáileanna began to chant.

The spell was meaningless to Blackthorn, but the dark sibilance wounded his ear. This chant was for Máchail. The master of Márrach drank it in as if thirsty for the terrible sounds. His face grayed. The white and black in his beard blended, his spine straightened into the blade-stiff rigidity of a dark elf's shadow.

When his blue eyes clouded and grew dark as the eyes of those about him, suddenly he reached out to the pot the Gruagach held before him and pulled something from it. At first Blackthorn could make no sense of the thing in his enemy's hand. It hung from Máchail's fingers by long, matted strings like a misshapen ball of sodden twine, and slowly spun. Not a ball, sweet Éire, it was a head, and black drops falling from the severed neck. It turned gently, revealing a slack jaw, a pallid cheek, spattered with blood—

Máchail lifted the head higher, brought the thing's ear close to his lips. The sorcerer spoke, but Blackthorn could not hear him, nor the snap of the fire, nor the hissing of the Scáileanna. He could hear nothing save his own horror, a wordless cry that racked his body, but stuck in his throat, choking him.

The head spun a quarter turn more, and a wretched face looked out at the Hunter.

"Scáthach," he whispered.

Her Name rose from his lips into the smoky air and died in the darkness.

Blackthorn wanted to close his eyes, to look away, but he watched as if he were spellbound. Máchail was speaking still, no, shouting into Scáthach's long-deaf ear. Blackthorn could feel the force of his enemy's will reaching into the unliving piece of woman he held, bending the power of the soulless Poet to his desires.

A dull gleam crept from under Scáthach's pale lids. Her lashes, caked with crusted blood, parted slowly. The whites were sickly yellow, but green as the sea were Scáthach's eyes still, and they gazed at Blackthorn and saw nothing.

Máchail fell silent. The Scáileanna chant ceased. It was the head was speaking now, though thankfully Scáthach's words did not carry to Blackthorn's ears. He could not have borne to hear her, to listen to the ghost of her voice chanting his doom. Her blue lips closed, opened again, her black, swollen tongue clumsily pressed against her teeth—her tongue that had taught him the language of lovers, the lips Blackthorn had begged to kiss, the eyes that had shone in the morning like sunrise on the hill—

"Scáthach!" he cried.

His guard dug the butt of his axe into Blackthorn's gut, but the Scáileanna never turned, and Máchail's attention never wavered. As slowly as they had opened, Scáthach's eyelids drooped, her jaw fell open. Máchail's hand was shaking as he replaced her head in the blood-filled bowl, but with the strain of his effort. His gray lips were twisted into a satisfied smile.

"No more for you," he scolded the Gruagach. Weariness tinged his voice, but there was elation in it, too. "We have no more blood for this pot tonight."

The Gruagach nodded to Blackthorn. "But, master, his life will soon flow—"

Máchail shook his head. "His I will pour into another bowl, one that will hold the Name-Sayer's head, and not even that will I do before the Dead Lord has devoured the Hunter's soul. No more for you, I say. Go. Watch the sands."

Wrapping the bowl gently in his arms, the Gruagach pushed open the door with his shoulder and disappeared into the tunnel.

"Your sword," Máchail said to his champion, and when Urchóid drew it, "There." He pointed to the doorway.

The Scáil plunged the blade deep into the wooden lintel above the door and stood aside. Máchail nodded, then held up the Talisman as if displaying it. Firelight stained the star a sombre red.

"Conall mac na Caillí," Máchail said clearly.

Blackthorn recoiled from his Name as if he had been stabbed.

"Conall mac na Caillí," he said again.

The Hunter's body arched and he cried out.

A third time Márrach's master Named him. "Conall mac na Caillí."

His breathing ragged, Blackthorn crumpled against one of the poles. Máchail turned to the door, lifted his arm, and hung the Talisman on the crosspiece of his champion's sword.

"Between heaven and earth," he murmured.

Máchail had said he preyed on power, and that boast Blackthorn knew to be true. The Hunter had often heard it in his enemy's voice, coaxing, commanding, disparaging. As the master of Márrach stood with his back to the Talisman and began to speak the curse he had compelled from Scáthach's lips, the power that came from him was beyond mortal ken, a malevolent hate that seemed to rise from the blood-soaked earth of the pit and flow through the sorcerer's body. From Máchail's mouth poured malice, malice that at his bidding the greatest Poet of Éirinn had woven into a rann. Out of his mouth the evil came, but the voice was his God's.

> *Cursed be Conall mac na Caillí, Blackthorn*
> *Hunt him, Hound him, Harry him, Bind him*
> *A desolate soul, doomed to wander*
> *Sunless, Moonless, Starless, Lost,*
> *For where is one to call him back?*

Only Blackthorn saw the summoned evil when it first appeared, a mote of midnight dancing below the dangling pentacle, but then, it had come for him. Swiftly the darkness pulsed and grew. Warmth and light were sucked into the swelling emptiness, and from the void came a vast and terrible cold.

The Scáileanna backed away, melted into the shadows by the wall. The goblins at the door bolted or hid their eyes. Blackthorn's red-eyed guard fell on his belly before the face of Máchail's curse. Even Márrach's master, who had called it forth, cringed against the doorframe and raised his arm like a shield before him. Blackthorn stood erect, but he trembled in his fear, and his eyes never left the dark shadow of his bane.

Almost imperceptibly it began to move, gliding noiselessly across the cell. In desperation Blackthorn flung himself against his bonds. He strained at the unyielding iron until his wrists ran with blood. One of the chains began to pull away from its post.

It was not enough. The curse had found him.

The shadow fell between the two poles, engulfing Blackthorn's body and blocking the light from the fire. He screamed as the cold spell met his flesh, but his cry was quickly stifled by the smothering dark.

A long while the Hunter was hidden by the impenetrable blackness. Gradually, the shadow began to fade. The flames crackled, pressing their light against the dark until they started to win through. The Scáileanna slowly separated from the walls of the room. The goblins dared to lift their heads from the dirt. Máchail lowered his arm and opened his eyes to looked on his enemy.

The Hunter of Éirinn hung unmoving in his chains. Though his body was edged by the fire's red glow, it cast no shadow upon the ground.

Fifty-eight

To the wildwood now let us go
To hunt the hart, to hunt the roe

The master of Márrach pulled Blackthorn's head up by the hair and looked into his prisoner's face. White as death it was, and his breath so faint it barely lifted the cursed man's chest. The softest of moans sounded in Blackthorn's throat. Máchail's eyes narrowed with pleasure. The Hunter had he been? Now the hunted. Long and difficult would be his death, and well deserved for his deceits, evasions, and scorn.

Máchail laughed quietly at his own falsehood. Lies, secrecy, disdain—these were the jewels of his heart, prized and admired. Not for his cunning would the Hunter suffer, but for the favors of fortune he had so unjustly enjoyed—for that Éire's Sight had fallen upon Conall mac na Caillí, and Her Stag had called his Name.

What blessing had crowned Mac na Caillí's birth? What great deed marked his youth? Why was this fool destined for glory, and Máchail's lot but to sing his praises?

A stray gleam left the fire and fell upon the beryls adorning the master of Márrach's glove. Máchail studied the stones, the source and wealth of his conjuring art. A thief, the Hunter had called him. A carrion crow feeding on others' kills. Carrion himself was the Hunter now. What had been Mac na Caillí's would be Máchail's, not by robbery, but by right. Fate had graced Márrach's master with neither a King's madness nor a Queen's Sight, neither a Poet's ranna nor a Wizard's craft. Yet even Fate must this night bow to Máchail's insuperable will.

The sorcerer's smile tightened, and also his grip on Blackthorn. Before this artful liar had dreamed himself a hunter, Máchail had made himself the best in Éirinn, striving with all his vast ambition to attain the one great honor an ungifted, unfamed man might achieve. By the ruins of Ráth na Saileach he had camped that Bealtaine Eve nine years past, confidently awaiting daybreak and the Stag's call. The moon had set early, and summer's sun was yet hours from dawning when a silver spark had glimmered in the birch woods hard by, and swelled, and brightened. Then light had filled his staring eyes—the White Stag bounded out of the woods and o'erleapt the tumbled stones of the ráth. Intoxicated by the sweet taste of triumph, Máchail had laughed like a drunken man, then wept to have seen his heart's desire.

Those were the last tears ever to fall from Máchail's eyes. The white elk ran on, mute and indifferent, his light fading into the shadowed woods below the ráth like a shooting star melting into black heaven. With the Stag's passing, winter's last night fled beyond the circles of the world, bearing with it Máchail's last hope.

When the dark elves stepped clear of the shadowed stones of Ráth na Saileach, Máchail had felt no fear. The cup of his heart was empty, and the dregs held only bitter desires for revenge. Besides, there was no menace in the Scáileanna's smiles—only welcome. He had not stepped from his path. He had followed it faithfully, and it had led him to Shadow.

"He yet lives, master."

Máchail loosed his fingers. The Hunter's head dropped to his chest.

"You do not appreciate the elegance of Scáthach's rann," Máchail reproved his champion. Taking his gloves from his belt, he pulled them over his hands. "This offering is not like the others, no placid kine to be butchered and laid upon the Shadow King's board. Mac na Caillí's heart is wild, his will untamed. Some sport he will give the Eater of Souls before the Dead Lord brings him down."

He turned to the cell door and lifted the Spear. "Shadow's King hunts this night. And so shall I."

Like eager hounds, the grinning goblins at the doorway barked and whined for their master to hurry. Máchail's champion held back, and inclined his head toward Blackthorn.

"I will remain, master, to witness your enemy's death. When it is accomplished, then will I bear the glad news to you."

Máchail laughed. Urchóid looked away from the sound of genuine human pleasure, but his expression was one of studied detachment.

"Do you think me such a blind fool I cannot See your ambition?" Máchail asked. His voice grew soft, became indistinguishable from a Scáil's aspirant hiss. "The star will be mine, as will the Stag, as will the Light itself. In my service is your place. Do not seek to exceed it."

Máchail nodded to the red-eye guard at Blackthorn's side. The huge beast came near to learn his master's will.

"Bolt the door when we have gone," Máchail ordered. "Let no one pass."

The goblin snarled and went to stand outside the open doorway, swinging his axe and catching it again in his broad palm. Urchóid's empty eyes showed no disappointment, but Máchail's gleamed. Chance had never been kind to him, and he left nothing to it. Domhnall's star would not want for guarding.

Márrach's champion led the way out of the room and up the winding passage. The goblins followed, and Máchail came last, delaying to watch the red-eye close and bar the door. When he had done, the tunnel was plunged into unrelieved blackness.

Máchail laughed again, shaking dark forms loose from the passage. Goblins sleeping in the corridor woke and followed, gray shadows separated from the earthen walls and walked beside their master as Scáileanna. Like a black spring, Shadow's host rose from the pits and flowed across the courtyard, the Scáileanna sweeping to their horses, the goblins pressing on toward the gates.

The hunting horns the Scáileanna winded sang like mourners at a grave. The goblins joined their guttural voices to the keening calls. Together dark elves and red-eyes flung a spell against the tower's walls. The gray stones thrust it back and tossed it up into the fathomless dark. Reaching their long arms into the resounding air, the goblins drew long, ropelike shadows out of the emptiness to swing at their sides. When the sorcery was done, every red-eye bore a length of darkness in his hairy paw.

Then they fell quiet, awaiting a word, a sign from their master. Máchail was as silent as they, savoring the moment. The Hunter was dying accursed in the goblin pits below. Beyond the broch the Stag was running, every silver-hoofed step he took tangling him tighter in Márrach's dark webs.

A third time Máchail laughed, and if the Scáileanna stiffened, it was with rapture, for in their master's voice rang the sweet sound of vengeance. Máchail spurred his mount. A gale of screeling voices surged through the courtyard, filled the gatehouse, and burst through the fort's widening gates. The dead trees of the forest moaned in the fell wind, their skeleton arms applauding hollowly as horses' hooves and goblins' feet pounded their roots.

In the fore of the bloodthirsty storm rode Máchail. Never had he felt more a hunter than this night, setting forth to capture the Light and bring him down to his shadowed death.

Fifty-nine

Dark is the deep sea, and dark is the night
Dark are my love's eyes when sorrow shades their light.
Dark is cruel bondage, dark grief and dole,
But the darkness of Shadow is the death of the soul.

Beannachán Óg's Lament

The goblin guarding Blackthorn's cell peered up the black corridor long after Márrach's master had passed from sight. His red eyes glowed in the dark, his own harsh breathing made the only sounds in the silent passage. Finally, he turned and put his heavy paw to the bolt he had just secured.

It grated as he slid it back—the goblin hunched his shoulders against the painful noise and glanced furtively up and down the tunnel. A moment he stood motionless, holding the heavy bar. Reassured that he had attracted no attention, the creature slowly set the bar to rest in the brackets beside the door. His clawed fingers awkwardly grabbed for the key on the wall and lifted the ring from its peg. Gripping it tightly, the goblin pulled the door just wide enough to accommodate his girth and squeezed his bulky frame into the cell.

The weave of red light from the dying fire was shot with thick threads of shadow. The Hunter's body hung black against the bloody air. Angling himself toward the door, the goblin listened intently. Gradually he straightened, puffed out his broad chest with a tremendous gulp of air, and took a single step forward. It brought him just under the treasure dangling from the guard of the champion's sword. His red-eyes burned as he gazed upon Domhnall's star. Reaching a long arm up, his fingers closed on Máchail's prize.

His meaty paw was barely upon the Talisman when the goblin loosed it again. The air he had swallowed to swell his chest escaped him in a startled bark, and he backed uneasily toward the door. His eyes were angry as he regarded the bit of silver, but he whined softly and edged a splayed foot over the threshold.

As he turned to leave, the goblin's red eyes lowered and caught on the Hunter. The sounds emanating from the beast's throat grew more pitiful. Slowly, as if forced against his will, he drew his leg back into the cell and slunk forward until he stood once more beneath Domhnall's star. Extending his paw, he wrapped his fist around the Talisman, shuddered, and carefully lifted the star from the sword.

With another hasty glance at the door, he shambled over to where Blackthorn was chained. His whining deepened to surly snarls as his big paws clumsily forced the key he held into the lock of first one, then the other of the Hunter's bonds. Blackthorn fell forward as his arms were freed, but the goblin caught him easily and laid him on the ground with extraordinary gentleness.

For a moment the goblin squatted beside Blackthorn's still form, prodding it gingerly and making vaguely threatening noises. With a last desperate look to the partially open door, the goblin seemed to dwindle into himself. His dark, greasy hair vanished, revealing an old man's pale, naked body. His unintelligible growls became coherent pleas echoing softly in the gloom.

"Och, can't you wake, you fool?" Reathach whispered. "What, will you tarry among the Shadows and the Stag runnin' hard by? Gone are your enemies, after your quarry they are, and haven't I your Talisman in my hand?"

In his hand, sure and certain, but cold as Blackthorn's flesh the star was. The púca pursed his lips, and shook his head. Stronger even than the Hunter's geis the Poet's curse must be, for 'twas plain Blackthorn was deaf even to the call of the Hunt, and he in the Shadow King's realm.

The call of the Hunt. The púca squirmed and looked away

from the Hunter. *"Where is one to call you back?"* the Poet had said, and Máchail after her, and weren't they both only echoing the Oak Seer's words? Reathach's beady eyes darted about the cell as if the murky air could release him from his task.

"Here is one," Reathach admitted, "but aren't I still the greatest coward in the five kingdoms of Éirinn?"

It had taken all his courage to reach this place, and double that to place himself in Máchail's sight, and thrice it again to endure the coming of Shadow's curse—

Yet, Úna had promised . . . "He is your courage, little mouseen." Her very words. Reathach forced himself to look at Blackthorn again. Close to death the Hunter was. The sorry bodach wasn't even moaning anymore.

Reathach's fingers held the silver star so tightly it bit into his palm, a flake of ice cold enough to freeze a fire. Reathach ignored his shivering hand. Tenderly he brought his most cherished possession from its secret place in his heart and set it upon his tongue.

"Conall," he called softly. "Conall mac na Caillí."

Curse the Hunter, the Seer, Márrach's master, all three. A spark to light the dark the Hunter's Name should be, but greater darkness it conjured, and greater fear. Shadows swarmed over the cell, blotting out the fire's embers, wrapping Blackthorn in ebon shrouds. Like a swift, unnatural night, the dark fell over Reathach. The púca cried out. The Hunter was vanishing from his sight.

"Conall!"

Reathach's arms swept blindly across the dirt floor. He found only empty air where Blackthorn had lain, but for a flicker of light—there—flashing again as his groping fingers floundered in the black sea of shadows. Reathach gasped, then laughed until he heard the near-delirium in his voice and made himself stop. 'Twas in his own hand the light was, glittering in his palm. Though still it burned him with cold, the Talisman, bright as the morning star, warmed the púca's heart.

He slid his fingers in and out of the slender chain, then stood and held the pentacle above his head. It gleamed, the lucid heart of a small glistening pool. Beyond the star's reach the púca was sure he Saw his dark and terrible death waiting, but he believed, he must believe, that within the Talisman's illumined sphere he would be safe.

"Conall mac na Caillí."

His voice seemed to stop at the ill-defined boundary between the Dark and the Talisman's light. *Badhbh*, *Macha*, and *Mór-Ríoghain*, was it not enough to call? Must he wander himself through the shadows, seeking the Hunter?

Reathach slid a tentative foot forward and dragged the other up to tremble beside it. He felt awareness turn toward him from the unredeemed dark, but though he had spoken, had trespassed, he was yet unmolested.

"Conall!" he called, and again, "Conall mac na Caillí!"

The púca's bowed legs shuffled through layers of shadow—gray upon black, ash upon sable, ink upon ebony. The dark pressed against his thin bones until he could barely breathe. Though the Talisman's light was steady, Reathach's hand was not. And though the star's halo comforted him, it showed him nothing solid to tread upon, nothing real to touch. His reluctant passage through the Shadow King's realm grew more faltering with every step.

"Conall mac na Caillí!" he shouted, or meant to. He could not be sure he made a sound. Loud or soft, the gloom swallowed his words. And if any ear heard him, he could but doubt the listener would be a friend.

Again Reathach forced his right foot forward, but this time his left refused to follow. He had travelled as far as he could in this dreary land, and wouldn't have wagered a whisker that he had gone anywhere at all, at all. The púca lowered his head, bowing to his fear and doom, and pressed the Talisman against his heart.

"Conall mac na Caillí," he whispered in farewell.

A single gleam of light broke from the surrounding dark and flew straight into the púca's eyes. By An Daghdha, there again, a flickering gem of white fire it was—the pentacle's twin, dancing among the shadows.

Three quick steps Reathach took toward the light. Then a fourth, and he nearly fell. Smooth and vacant had the shadow-land seemed when his footsteps were small and hesitant. Now his eagerness had wakened the sleeping dragon. Shadows swelled in the dark. They rose to form mountains of gray, sank into a seething black abyss at his feet. Knife-sharp the edges of darkness appeared in the star's silver nimbus, impossible the path leading through them—but beyond the threatening shadows the brilliant light beckoned. Setting his hopes on the distant glint, Reathach toiled toward it, continually calling.

"Conall! Conall! Conall mac—"

Not of sounds, but of wings the Hunter's Name must be made, Reathach thought wildly, for suddenly the púca was hurtling through tiers of pitch and veils of smoke-dark shadow. The glistening light grew brighter, bolder. Reathach's voice broke in astonishment. Immediately the púca was hemmed in by yawning pits and flint-hard walls. They daunted him less than they had before. He was near enough now to see clearly the light that shone in answer to his, and it was no tiny star such as Reathach bore.

The source of the light was Blackthorn himself. Bolts of blue-white lightning streaked down the length of the Hunter's body. Strands of radiance clung to his muscles and his long, black hair, streamed like rivers of silver fire along his limbs. He was running—sweet Éire, but he was running so swift and desperate the light of his soul could not match him, and was left lingering behind on the airless dark to fade and die. He was running like a stag with the hounds after him, but if hounds there were, they were shadows all, and bayed with silent voices.

Reathach's mouth opened and closed, but no sound came from it, not even the scream that heaved in his frail body and threatened to tear it apart. Falling to his knees, he closed his eyes. It did no good. He saw it still, the greater blackness in a world of black, the infinite, empty dark pursuing the Hunter across the vast and desolate land. Shadow's King. The Eater of Souls.

Reathach's eyes were open again, though he had not willed them so. He watched the Hunter dart and weave through the swirling dark, saw him balance on the edge of a void and leap beyond to a barren field of midnight. Shadows cut through the air like swords, wounding Blackthorn's light when they fell upon him. Mists congealed into gusts of soundless wind and beat against the fleeing man. And at the Hunter's heels, never farther from him than his own shadow should be, the Shadow King paced Blackthorn with unflagging precision.

Flat and featureless, the Dead Lord bent to the contours of his bleak lands. Like a true shadow he ran long behind, short beside Blackthorn, then stretched suddenly before, blocking the Hunter's path.

Blackthorn managed to stop, turn, and double back. His shadow followed. Unlike the man it mirrored, the dark outline changed direction easily, declining to mimic the frantic scrabbling for purchase that marked the Hunter's efforts, nor the superhuman burst of speed that carried Blackthorn beyond His reach. The Shadow King sped along the endless waste straight and stiff as a Scáil's shade, a black spear clasped in one hand and a sword gray as smoke in the other.

Admiration for the Hunter vied with the terror in Reathach's heart. A creature of the wild Blackthorn seemed, possessed of unconscious skill and passionate grace. Yet, for all his splendor, the Hunter was near exhausted—Reathach could see it in the fierceness of his exertion, like a salmon struggling in a bear's claws, or a fly caught in a spider's web.

The púca clutched the Talisman to his chest, but it consoled him little now. A creature of the wild himself, well he knew the three ways prey might elude the predator; by might, by flight, or by taking cover. How could Blackthorn fight Shadow's King, an' he weaponless? What good to flee an' the Dead Lord unerringly matched his speed? And where in all this dark realm could the Hunter hide his light?

As if day's noon had subdued it, Blackthorn's dogging shadow suddenly shrank away, leaving only an abbreviated mockery of the terrible God. The parcel of darkness slipped neatly under Blackthorn's feet, became for a moment a jagged, jet-black stone. Blackthorn stumbled, caught himself. The stone erupted into a black whirlwind. Blackthorn staggered, took to his heels, and ran. The dark storm raged about him, driving him to the ground. He staggered again, and fell.

All in an instant the gale was the Dead Lord once more, a giant looming over the fallen Hunter. The giant grew, His own profound shadow obscuring the lesser shades He ruled. So dark it was plainly delineated against the air, the Shadow King's spear lifted for the thrust. A corner of the Dead Lord's cloak brushed by Blackthorn where he lay panting, eclipsing a fragment of the Hunter's light.

"Conall!" Reathach wailed.

Blackthorn's head came up, his haggard face lifted to the púca's. Hope unlooked-for sprang into the Hunter's eyes. The star Reathach was clutching flashed in sudden sympathy, but the púca's faint heart nearly shattered into a thousand slivers of ice. Blackthorn's head was not alone in lifting to his cry. Featureless had he thought the Dead Lord's shadow? But the Eater of Souls had not then looked upon him as he was looking now. Eyes had Shadow's King, two savage fires burning in the pitiless dark.

Reathach could not move, could not think to move. Numbing cold blasted him, and the cruel fires of the Shadow King's Sight scorched his soul. A puddle of marrowless bones and shivering flesh, the púca held his hands before his eyes, unable to face the Dead Lord's hunger.

The Talisman flamed. Not his own will, but Blackthorn's streamed in blazing defiance from the little star, ripping through the dark to wound the Shadow King's Sight.

The Dead Lord bent his spear arm to shield his eyes. His sword thrust blindly, the blade overshadowing the Talisman's light. Reathach could only whimper, but Blackthorn had already regained his feet, and was racing through the shifting dark to where the púca knelt.

"Run," he gasped, but Reathach could not.

"Run, you bold, witless fool!" Blackthorn shouted.

The púca stumbled to his feet. With his legs under him, he found he could move after all, but what was the use? Though he had turned his back to the Dead Lord, he felt the fires of the Shadow King's Sight upon him once more, burning away his hope and his courage. Was the Hunter following behind? Reathach dared not look. His legs began to tremble, his lungs ached with sucking down the foul, cold air. Lost he was, lost forever among the shadows. . . .

Reathach stumbled again. Next moment his legs were churning, moving faster than they had ever moved in all his long life. They carried him toward a shadow—the bright shadow of a huge star—a shadow the Talisman in his trembling hand had cast in gleaming silver upon the lightless world.

PART 12

silver and stone

Sixty

Only fools and children reach for cups beyond their grasp

Sayings of the Mothers

As he passed the shimmering gate, the light in the púca's hand burst from the Talisman and merged with its own bright shadow. Darkness awaited Reathach on the other side. He felt the ground beneath him heave and thought he was falling, but there was no impact, only a kind of jolt as he or the world or both stopped moving. He twisted around, hoping to spy the star's glow behind him. He saw a black, rectangular doorway and the dull gleam of firelight on the edge of the sword protruding from the wooden lintel.

He was back in the pits of Márrach, back on his knees beside Blackthorn. The shadows had grown since last he was here. They thickened the walls of the cramped cell, swam about the sullen fire. They hung over the Hunter's body where he lay still as death on the cold dirt floor. Reathach longed for more light, but did not dare leave Blackthorn's side to feed the coals. He clutched the Talisman tighter, and it gave him some ease. Though its light was gone, the silver no longer hurt his hand with bitter cold, but lay warm in Reathach's shaking fist.

"Conall," he whispered.

In the dark, he could not even be sure the man was breathing.

"Conall mac na Caillí."

Blackthorn's eyes glinted as they opened and looked up into the púca's anxious face.

"You came after me." The Hunter's voice was weak, but the admiration and abiding gratitude it held made his words ring in the púca's ears. "All the dark places you would not face, then alone to dare the most evil of all. You're free of it, then?"

Free of it? Reathach sat as still and attentive as he knew how, listened with all his might. He heard not the faintest whisper of An Daghdha's voice in his mind, felt not the least weight upon his soul.

"Free of it," Reathach echoed, astonished. "Free of it. *By the light that shines!* Free of An Daghdha's geis your ill-aimed stone laid on me that miserable wet midwinter's morning long since! Free to go me own way and leave the perils of Shadow and Light to those who love life less!"

The púca scrunched up his face in puzzlement and rubbed his bald head. Glad he should be, his geis fulfilled and the Good God satisfied. Lighter his heart was indeed for the lifting of his burden, but emptier, as if there were a hole where his bond with the Hunter used to be.

Blackthorn raised himself onto one elbow. Hastily Reathach reached out and clasped his hand, pressing the Talisman into the Hunter's fingers as he helped him up. Blackthorn smiled—Reathach saw the quick gleam in the dark—then gently freed his hand and regarded the pentacle in his palm. Slowly his fist closed about the little star.

"To a mouse, now, Reathach," he said, "and into my purse."

The púca groaned. "I can't, you daft fool, an' 'tis your own fault it is. Until this moment, I'd have said there's no more dangerous place in all Márrach than the Hunter's pouch, but sure, an' now I must find me way out of these pits alone, aren't I full of praise for the sweet safety of your purse?"

"Avail yourself of it, then."

"Och, wurra, wurra, would that I could! For all your vaunted memory, you've forgotten the oath you compelled from me! By An Daghdha I promised to leave you the moment me geis was fulfilled, and isn't that moment now? An' I tarry longer, I'll be forsworn."

He crept toward the door as he was speaking, then peered out into the corridor.

"Empty as far as me eyes can see," he whispered, "but keep your ears open, bodach. Sure, an' I'll be givin' you a warnin' an' any red-eyes are lurkin' up ahead—just hearken to me screams as they devour me. Och, wurra, wurra, wurra," he groaned again, then dropped to a mouse and scurried out the door.

"Good luck to you, little mouseen," Blackthorn said quietly. "I'll miss your company."

Reathach was surely out of earshot. An' he had heard Blackthorn's fond farewell, he'd have been back already, if only to make good retort.

Securing the Talisman about his neck, Blackthorn climbed to his feet and moved unsteadily toward the door until his eye fell on Urchóid's blade. The thought of taking a Scáil's weapon in hand made him grimace, but he reached up without hesitation and freed the blade from the lintel. Sword in hand, he slipped into the passageway.

Though he had only his fingers running along the wall to help him find his way through the pitch-black tunnel, Blackthorn went as swiftly as if sight guided him. He knew the corridor from his journey down—a single passage, with many twists and turns, and many cells, sealed by wood and iron doors.

Stopping to listen at a bend in the tunnel, Blackthorn set his back against the dirt wall. There were soft drums echoing in the earth, and muted roars reverberating in the passage ahead.

He set his jaw and pushed his pace. 'Twas horses' hooves making the earth shake as they stamped in the courtyard overhead, and goblins' howls sounding in the tunnel. Blackthorn was not such a fool as to believe he had been cursed to Shadow and returned, and still Máchail's hunt had not gone forth. *Time stands still in the presence of the Gods*, and so must it have done for him, and the Dead Lord pursuing his soul across Shadow's realm. In the wide world, time had rolled unceasingly on. The sounds he heard meant the hunt had already returned—but returned empty-handed?

The Stag was alive. Blackthorn knew that to be true, for had the Spear taken the Stag's life, his geis would already be broken, and so too, his soul. But an' the Stag was alive, why had the hunters returned to Márrach at all, at all? And why was the call of the Hunt belling so keen and clear in Blackthorn's heart? He felt the Stag's presence as the hare senses the hawk above him. The hunters must have taken their quarry alive—like himself, the White Stag had been brought a prisoner to Márrach.

A cinder-gray pillar of light appeared at the far end of the passageway—the shaft to the courtyard faintly lit from above. In a moment, Blackthorn stood at the base of the shaft, his hand on the rope. Shadows danced ominously over his head, distorted shapes of horses, goblins, stiff-backed Scáileanna. Though the din from the courtyard was loud enough to drown any noise he might make, Blackthorn climbed the rope without a sound.

Only a few wild-eyed horses spied the Hunter as he crept over the lip of the shaft and into the deep shadows draping the nearby wall. They shied, but the Scáileanna never turned their lightless eyes from the center of the courtyard, believing it was the master of Márrach's frantic prey making their horses skittish.

Red-eyes and Scáileanna surrounded the giant elk. Ropes of shadow were caught on his antlers, encircled his neck, hobbled one milk-white leg. Goblins hung at the end of the dark cords. The Gruagach stood with them, roaring orders and goading them on. White and resisting, the Stag bucked and leapt. His silver hooves lifted, he reared, nearly tearing the ropes from the goblins' hands. The red-eyes dug their broad feet into the dusty ground, tightening the nooses.

Máchail had not chased, but driven his quarry through the forest—not run the Stag to ground, but penned him in this great stone márrach. On the barren dirt altar of Márrach's cursed broch the Stag would die, a helpless sacrifice to Shadow's dark King.

Length after length of tangible shadow descended over the Stag, snaring the Light. An army of red-eyes laid their paws on the ropes and pulled them taut. Blackthorn shivered, remembering Shadow's chill upon his own flesh, and the cold weight of the dark, like fetters of iron.

The shining Stag lowered his head and thrust, catching a tormentor on his rack. Black blood spurted over his silver tines. With a vicious twist, the giant elk flung the goblin against the wall. The red-eye left a dark smear on the gray stone as he fell to the ground, but for the one that died two came forward to take his place.

Máchail sat relaxed in his saddle, an easy spear's cast from his victim. His stolen weapon rested in his hand, his arm was high and poised to throw. The Stag roared, the sound of a great wave rising to bludgeon the shore. The Scáileanna replied, their hissing contempt the spray smashing upon the rocks, the hollow sigh of the spent wave drawn back to the jealous deeps.

Only Blackthorn heard reproach in the White Stag's call. He made no reply, but his answer was ready.

At last the goblins had the Stag fast. The white elk could move neither right nor left, neither charge nor turn and flee. In defiance he lifted his crowned head, baring his chest to the Spear.

Máchail pulled his arm back a hair's breadth more. The goblins ceased their harsh clamor, the Scáileanna drew a sharp breath. Though the Spear had not yet left his enemy's hand, Blackthorn knew now it must—it was already too late for Máchail to hold back his arm. With a grace and skill Blackthorn would have admired in another, Máchail loosed the Stag's silver death.

He did not speak loudly, but the Hunter's answer to the Stag's challenge carried to every ear in the hushed courtyard.

"I call upon Air."

At Blackthorn's throat the Talisman gleamed golden as the sun. The still air stirred, lifting the hair from his neck and ruffling his tattered shirt.

Swift flew the Spear. Swifter the summoned wind to meet it—no gentle breeze as caressed Blackthorn, but a fierce gust that plucked the silver-tipped wand from its path and hurled it at the tower wall. Twice might the Hunter's heart have beat as the Spear sped past the gray stones. His heart was still, and the flight of the sacred weapon an unhurried image that burned like molten silver upon his soul.

The Spear's point met the rock of the broch, pierced it, plunged deep and held, trembling in the wall. A savage blast of wind snapped the ash haft in two.

No goblin's howl could match Máchail's cry of outrage, yet even in his wrath the master of Márrach could not stand against the power Blackthorn had called forth. Roaring, the wind whipped about the broch's enclosing walls, then dove, beating the sorcerer back until his horse stumbled and fell.

Though red-eyes and Scáileanna had turned at once toward the Hunter, they were unable to move against him. The wind blasted through the yard, compelling Shadow's servants to bend and part. Like a scythe it cut them down, so many stalks of dark grass. Screaming horses bolted in terror, throwing their riders and trampling them. Shadow-ropes were ripped from the goblins' hands, shot out of reach, and blown back to nothing. Sweeping around the stone walls and up into the tower's heights, the shrieking air lifted clouds of dust, and sent them spinning into the bell's dome. With a single, glorious note, the massive instrument began to ring.

Blackthorn stood unmoving, the eye of the storm. He thought he was waiting for the gale to break his soul as it had his Spear. Instead his heart swelled with astonishing joy as the wind drove a song bright as day from the great iron bell.

The walls shook under the exultant peals, the stones of the tower groaned. Scáileanna clinging to the ground loosed their hands to cover their ears. Goblins crawled toward the pits and howled their dismay, but the unremittent wind caught their curses and wrung them into twisted fragments of sound, empty of threat.

As Márrach's host bowed to the wind's power, Máchail forced his arm up into the rising maelstrom of dust. His fingers danced, trying to mold the gusts to his will. The air refused to linger in his hand long enough for him to draw anything from it.

The grit-filled wind stung Blackthorn's eyes and caught in his lungs. It changed the cloaked Scáileanna and black-haired goblins to half-glimpsed shadows, and stole Máchail from his sight. Only the Stag's distant light could Blackthorn see plainly, a silver-white jewel dancing to the bell's glad song. The Hunter's geis blazed within him, blinding him to hope of escape through the gatehouse and safety in the woods. Though in all Éirinn there was now no weapon that could bring his quarry down, the Hunter gave chase to the Stag.

As he ran toward the Light, the surrounding shadows congealed into enemies. They moved to stop him, Scáileanna who had kept their swords from the robber wind, goblins who needed no other weapons to serve them but their claws and fangs. Urchóid's sword lay finely balanced in Blackthorn's hand, but he mistrusted it until he thrust. Eagerly the blade dove into a Scáil's hard heart, and came out dyed with the dark elf's blood. An ironic smile touched Blackthorn's lips. Made for treachery, here was a sword would not balk at taking a Scáil's life, even an' it was Urchóid's own.

He struck again, and again, and each time had the advantage, for the wind was his ally. Blasts tore weapons from his foes' hands, usurped their balance, pounded their flesh. Fighting always in the calm of the storm, Blackthorn kept his feet under him, and his sword fell where he meant it to fall.

He raced across the yard with the windstorm for his cover. What could the Stag smell but goblins and Scáileanna? What could he see save shadows in the dark? Blackthorn came nearer, pacing his prey. Nearer, and the brilliance he had been stalking coalesced into a towering white elk. The Stag was charging for the passage that led to the close. Blackthorn sped after him, saw the Stag rear, silver hooves pawing at the stones that marked the dark opening. Bending his great neck, the Stag suddenly bounded under the arch, and the black passage swallowed the Light.

Blackthorn was less than twenty strides behind his quarry. He had taken barely six when joy fled the bell's song. A succession of agitated peals filled the broch, almost loud enough to drown out the howling wind.

An earsplitting crack brought Blackthorn's head up. Peering through the turbulent dust, he saw the bell swinging dangerously off-center. The groaning complaint of over-stressed wood joined the bell's strident tolling. To a chorus of clanging metal and snapping, splintering beams, light plunged down through the roof, and Márrach's bell plummeted into the bedlam of the tower's floor.

Blackthorn had barely time to dive for the wall and press

himself against the broch's stones before the bell's enormous edge struck the ground. Dark earth leapt like water around the point of impact, and splashed high against the tower walls. The bell crashed to its side, splitting along its length. Two more cracks swiftly formed along its upper sides. The bottom pieces rolled apart, but a jagged plough of metal shot forward, gouging a great trough in the floor of the yard.

Blackthorn threw himself to the side. The iron wedge rammed into the tower wall where he had stood but an instant before.

The echoes of the bell's death song faded as the broken pieces of iron rocked on their bed of smashed bones and bloody flesh. A thunderous shower of crumbling stone fell from the arch over the passage that led to the close, blocking the tunnel and covering the Stag's trail.

Blackthorn had a curse ready for the bell that had cut him off from his quarry. He never uttered it. The Talisman's golden light changed to pure, brilliant white, and the wind dropped to almost nothing. Now he must run, or face death here.

Blackthorn picked himself off the ground, but instead of running, he looked up to the light falling through the rent in the ceiling. The brightness had fair blinded him as it broke through the roof, but in truth it was only a rose-colored, gilt-edged cloud of soft morning. Caught in the glow, a stream of pale sand poured into Márrach's heart from the floor of the sanctum above. Invisible for a moment as it left the sunlight and dropped into the gloom, the fine, glistening rain reappeared in the thin golden shafts edging through the broch's high windows. Leaving the light a last time, the white sands mingled with the settling dust, both coming to rest in a mottled blanket over the shattered bell.

Parting light and shadow note by note, the raucous and unexpectedly lyrical song of a magpie cascaded down with the soft sands and fell upon Blackthorn's ears. It entered him, echoed in his soul. Though a common and familiar tune, to Blackthorn the bird's call was as compelling as the Stag's. For all her sorrows, the magpie's voice was clear, and the song she sang a tale of love's geis—a song to break the Hunter's heart.

Sixty-one

To Name is to Know

Sayings of the Mothers

Bochna ordered the watch doubled that night, but though the host was camped on Márrach's borders, neither goblins nor Scáileanna came from the cold shadows under the starless sky to do battle. In all the long hours of darkness the camp had but a single visitor. Long past midnight, when even the stoutest hearts had begun to despair of the dawn, a maiden-warrior of Laighin, on watch near a dry streambed, was startled by the sight of the Bean Sidhe washing clothes in the waterless gully. She brought word of her vision to the Mothers, but they needed no telling. By then the wailing keen of the green-kirtled fairy woman was echoing on the unmoving air, and every ear in the camp listening to the message of death's harbinger.

The daystar's light was unable to penetrate the dark clouds and dense woods—only Bochna's Sight and Magadh's were keen enough to behold the dawn. Even so, the host required no call to wake. None had slept soundly, and all were glad to leave their dreams.

"We have other means," Magadh told the worried council, "to breach Márrach's defense."

And if other means fail? Bochna asked her, but Magadh had no answer for the Mother of Laighin.

"Úna's meaning is plain," argued Feargna Óg. "Treachery is poison, and so do we revile a traitor's Name—but we are fools not to use it against him!"

Magadh frowned. "And if Úna meant that the Name itself is poison—that it will harm us an' we invoke it? *Magic miscalled will find its own way in the world, and do much harm ere it is spent.*"

At Magadh's urging, the Mothers attempted to force entry with less potent ranna, Reochaidh's deafening words, and their own prayers. When all broke upon the hedge, swords and axes were brought to bear. None of their weapons could open so much as a crack in the thorn wall. Bochna felt Magadh's misgivings like an ache in her heart, but in herself, anger was stronger than doubt.

"Are we to be kept like beggars at Márrach's door, awaiting the Dead Lord's favor to be let in?" she demanded. "We must try the Name or admit defeat."

She shared a hard, glittering look with Magadh, and both turned to the Poets.

"We ask a verse of you," Bochna said, but her voice made her request a command.

When the rann was ready, Tadhg brought it to the Queens. Their minds one, their hearts steady, the Mothers lifted their voices in song.

> *Éirinn's host, armed and ready,*
> *O'erwhelms the wall of wood and thorn*
> *Through the breach thousands pour—*
> *Mac Ailch's shield breaks, evil is undone.*

Bochna joined her Sight to Magadh's, and together they watched the rann soar from them. Their verse flew swiftly to the hedge. In moments the words had caught in the thorns, and the thorns had stripped them of meaning. Darkness overwhelmed the poem, distorting it, then investing it with a new and dire purpose.

The rann has failed, Magadh grieved.

Worse, Bochna answered, for she Saw the spell returning. Impotent against Márrach's hedge, the mangled spell rebounded from the thorns transformed into a formidable curse. It swept past the Mothers and through the front ranks of Éirinn's host, breaking every shield into bits of wood and torn leather, losing its power only when it reached those who stood so far from Márrach's hedge they had not heard the rann spoken.

The Mothers slowly turned to face the fear and helpless anger of their warriors.

"'Poison,'" Magadh whispered. "'Spit it out.'"

Bochna's thought shot like an arrow through Magadh's mind. *Poison, because Mac Ailch is not our enemy, or because our enemy's true Name is not Mac Ailch? Brighde's Fire, what hope have we left?*

An answer came to the Queen's question, though she had expected none. Márrach's bell began to ring.

As the edges of the first note reached her ears, Bochna flinched, remembering the horror of yesterday's doleful song. Then she stood straighter, opened her heart to what she heard. Neither low nor mournful, the bell rang out gladly, the sound as bright as the light it heralded.

The host shouted with joy as a second peal followed the first. Long-awaited day broke through the overcast sky revealing a bold, blue sky beyond the clouds. Battle cries resounded in fierce reply to the bell's brilliant song. From the surrounding forest, glittering harmonies swelled under the warriors' challenges—a battle song of the Sidhe sung in their own jewelled voices.

The bell's clear notes beat against the hedge wall, cracking the branches. The tallest limbs shriveled, loosing the prisoned arms of the beeches. Daylight streamed through the rents in the Dead Lord's cloak and fell on the crumbling hedge.

"Liannan!" cried Bochna, not seeking, but having found. "Sister, we are here!"

The ecstatic song had barely begun when the bell's rhythm faltered and grew convulsive. The tolling grew wild as a beast's death throes, then abruptly ended. Damaged, but not destroyed, the hedge wall stopped shaking. No longer a solid barrier, still it offered only a grudging, prickly passage into the glen, a gap less than yesterday's through which Liannan had so bravely ridden. Morning hovered uncertain over the wood, caught between light and shadow. A word from either, and the balance would be broken.

Let it be our word, Bochna prayed, and sent a quick thought to Reochaidh.

The Destroyer of Sliabh Bladhma strode forward until he stood with the Mothers.

"To Márrach!" the giant said.

At his voice, the tall trees trembled and the hedge's smooth limbs burst asunder. A cloud of soot-black powder and gray dust billowed into air already thickening with dead-wood Reochaidh's words had torn from the forest's roof. Partly in pain, for his voice hurt their ears, partly in praise of his gift, the armies of Éirinn shouted the giant's Name as they spurred their horses.

"Reochaidh! Reochaidh the Destroyer!"

Tossing shattered shields aside, the warriors rode over the ruined thorn barrier and charged into the desolate woods. The ways were tangled, and the host's speed would have faltered, but for Reochaidh who strode before the host, and with his voice carved a broad avenue through the tortured trees, straight to Márrach's dark gate.

Aedh thrust, and blade met blade. Niall pulled back, darted to the side. His weapon came down on the corpse's sword arm, but only partly severed the limb—Aedh's skin armored him as if he were a living King.

Niall retreated, slow as any mortal man. Aedh turned, whipping his mangled limb in a wide arc. His blade sliced through Niall's embroidered shirt and across his chest. The wound was not deep, Niall told himself, and hoped he was right. It bled profusely and stung like fire. Aedh's blade swung wide on its return. Niall parried and backed again. Mumhain's dead King leapt after him.

"Niall Rí Uladh," cried the Mór-Ríoghain, swooping low over his head. "Day is come."

Niall never heard the Goddess. His ears were filled with the beat of metal on metal that meant his life was his own for one moment more. Aedh's possessed corpse lunged forward and cut high. Niall ducked and the blade missed, but barely. Before Aedh could strike again, Niall aimed another blow at the dead King's sword arm. He found only Aedh's sword, but the weight of his stroke overtaxed the half-severed tendons of the dead man's hand. Aedh's fingers unwillingly opened. His mouth formed a soundless howl as his blade slipped from his grasp.

Though weaponless, the corpse of Mumhain's King did not retreat. It charged. His maimed limb waved like a careless club, but it was Aedh's sound arm that smashed against the side of Niall's head and sent him sprawling to the ground.

The scaldcrow darted over the circle again, this time delivering her message to the Mother of Midhe. "Day is come," croaked the Mór-Ríoghain. "Day is come, but not to Márrach."

Liannan looked up to the sullen sky. This the dawn she had prayed for all this grim night? A Name Meacán had brought her, a weapon to her hand, yet in her folly she had kept it sheathed, thinking day would come to strengthen her blow.

Though the dawnless day brought Midhe's Queen no hope of victory, some measure of power returned to her in her acceptance of defeat. A curse from a Mother's dying lips might pierce her enemy's armor of anonymity.

With a thought she summoned Meacán. The Dancer reeled as she came to stand before the Queen, her grace eroded by exhaustion.

"These I have for you." Meacán's sore voice was painful to hear. With a trembling hand she held out the vial the púca had given her. "Water to clear shadows from the Sight. Perhaps. And a Name from Shadow. Mac Ailch's."

Liannan's lips still mouthed the rann of fire, but her shock echoed in the Dancer's mind.

Betrayal.

Liannan thrust her shock aside, and by force of will set hope in its place. Two gifts Meacán had brought, and the second unlooked-for. As her fingers fumbled to pull the stopper from the vial, Liannan saw Niall roll out of Aedh's reach and come to his knees, lethargy and desperation ruling his movements—

She bent her head and peered within the jar. Water, arrah, but barely two drops. She tipped the bottle, catching the water on her finger, then brushed her damp fingertip across her eyes. When she opened them again, they shone as if the unrisen sun had dawned in her Sight.

There, beyond the circle of faltering flames, not shadows,

but gray-cloaked Scáileanna, each one distinct, etched against
the gloom. Behind the dark elves, the goblins—only glints of
red a moment ago, now Liannan might count their strength to
every last beast, and far less it was than the impenetrable shadows of the forest had led her to believe. But twenty goblins
waited in the darkness for the fire to die, and the Scáileanna
now numbered no more than the warriors of Éirinn.

She looked beyond the circle of fire, looked far away, to the
barren hill in the heart of the valley. But, the hill was not
bare! A stone broch rose above the withered trees of the forest. Liannan's eyes widened, Seeing the first note of Márrach's
bell burst from the tower and roll out over the forest.

In a moment the sound had reached the ring of fire. The
bell's huge voice shook the defenders' bones like thunder, and
like thunder woke their souls to courage and awe. Covering
their ears, Éirinn's foes howled and wailed, but their protests
were lost in the bell's mighty song. Light streaked across the
sky in banners of yellow, rose, and azure, and left the Dead
Lord's gray cloak hanging in tatters against the dawn.

Of all the things Liannan now could See, it was the
White Stag that caught and held her eyes. While the bell
lost its melody and filled her ears with sounds neither Light
nor Dark could claim, the sacred elk raced through
Márrach's close to the wall, then to the top of the high rampart in a single bound. Daylight glanced off his silver tines as
the Stag leapt from the wall.

Blinking away tears of joy, the Queen set her Sight on the
battle at hand. Mumhain's dead King was armed again—he
grasped his sword firmly in his good hand. The goblins were
fleeing, the Scáileanna retreating, but Aedh fought on. Like
as not, his dead ears had not heard the bell, nor could the
sun's light reach the shadow that ruled him from within.

Liannan's eyes looked deeper, fastened on the wraith. She
had glimpsed it before, at Márrach's hedge, feeding on
Conmac's soul. From crown to heel the shadow-beast now
possessed the dead King of Mumhain, congealing the blood
that should be flowing from his wounds.

Ulaidh's King backed before Aedh, stumbling in his
weariness. A mantle of shadow draped Niall's shoulders, and
ice was lodged in his heart where fire once burned. In her
thoughts Liannan cursed Mac Ailch for taking Creathna

from her. Keen as her Sight had become, she could not See the wraith's Name—but the evil that had taken root in Niall's soul she knew, and its Name was Fear.

"Sing, Dancer," the Queen commanded. "Sing for me."

The flames dropped as she spoke and the burden of the rann passed entirely to Meacán, but Liannan had eyes only for Niall. She started toward him. Aedh's colorless, bloodless eyes stared at the Mother as she drew near, his mad smile broadened.

"'Ware, Lady!" the Ó Briain shouted.

Liannan heard the Chieftain's warning, Saw Niall's baffled look and his despair as he leapt to her defense. Nothing could stop her.

With a wild cry Niall threw himself upon the dead King. Aedh's blade was swift to counter, but with reckless agility, Niall lunged toward, then past his foe. He spun and drew his sword two-handed across the corpse's back. The blade parted flesh and muscle—a living King would have gone down under the blow, but Aedh whirled to face his opponent. As he turned, Niall drove the point of his sword deep into Aedh's right thigh, where neither weapon nor arm defended him. The corpse-King tottered, and dropped to one knee.

A moment she had, and in it Liannan flew to Niall. She pressed herself hard against him, set her palm to his bleeding chest.

"Tine!" she commanded, calling forth fire and bidding it flame in the mortal heart pounding beneath her hand.

At first it hurt, as numbed and frozen toes and fingers hurt when at last they begin to thaw. Then it was agony—not his limbs, but Niall's heart was warming, and not slowly, but in a searing explosion. His blood boiled. A paean of fire roared from his throat. His eyes grew red as dying suns.

Liannan felt the ice melt from Niall's heart, Saw the shadow that draped him reduced to charred cinders by the heat of his royal fire. Mantled once more in his fury, the hero-light burst from Niall's brow. Liannan laughed up into the King of Ulaidh's leering face, laughed to See his wild, ruthless joy.

He kissed her then, though Aedh's corpse was rising from the ground. He kissed her, and the kiss she returned him owed nothing to the cool waters of love, but everything to the fires of raw desire, fires kindled from the flaming heart of passion itself.

In a single motion Niall broke from Liannan's arms, raised his sword, and caught Aedh's descending blade upon his own. His free hand shot out and closed on the dead King's throat. Cold was Aedh's flesh, but Niall was afire. The heat of his grasp penetrated the chill of death that hung over the corpse-King and scorched the shadow-beast within.

Aedh raised his sword, but the blow never fell. Flinging his own blade aside, Niall closed his fist around the dead King's weapon. The full glory of his madness upon him, the sword could not wound him, but buckled and broke under his hand. Aedh sank slowly to his knees. Niall wrenched the mangled sword from his enemy's grasp and hurled it after his own. Bringing both hands to Aedh's neck, Niall shook his foe, trying to rouse more sport from his already dead prey.

"Niall Rí Uladh!" The Bear of An Clár bellowed the Name of Ulaidh's King as if it were his own war cry.

A narrow beam of sunlight broke through the clouds. Liannan's eyes followed its journey, Saw it fall on Aedh's back. She swore ever afterward that it was no stray gleam from the daystar's wealth of gold had struck him, but a golden javelin, and that it did not merely strike, but entered Aedh's body.

Mumhain's King arched. Blood began to flow from his many wounds. A second ray shot through the dark forest, and another and another, as if a mighty hand were hurling shafts of light from heaven to earth. Each found a mark in a piece of Eoghan's dismembered corpse, and his blood, too, poured out upon the earth.

"Behold!" Liannan cried. "Did not Lugh the Long-Armed promise us, 'Rend the Shadow King's mantle, and my spears will pierce the heart of Darkness'? An' we breach Márrach's walls, then will the Gods themselves come to humble the Dead Lord's might!"

At first only Liannan could See the shadow-beast burning, impaled on a weapon of starfire and light. Now the wraith rose from its host, flimsy as a spider's web caught in the wind. Niall loosed the King of Mumhain to snatch at the shadow that fled his corpse, but it was devoured by flames before his hand could close upon it.

Turning to Meacán, Liannan held her gently by the shoulders.

"Enough, Dancer. Enough. No more need we sing the fire."

Gratefully, Meacán fell silent. The circle of red flames sputtered and died. Those warriors still standing came to the darkened edge of the ring only to see their enemies vanishing into the woods. Within the circle Foxtail lay dead, and Linden, and Corann of Cnoc an Eanaigh. Four others were wounded, and Liannan went to them, bringing what healing she could. The Ó Briain was soon on his feet again, and Ceallach's arm no longer bled, though it pained him to lift it.

With a clear call Cessair summoned the horses. They came trotting from the now-empty woods, and though Fionn was first among them, Niall was first astride. He roared to be off, but Liannan paused a moment at the edge of the clearing, and looked long and well at the fallen Kings. Sweet the scent of the green grass growing around their bodies, already nearly tall enough to cover them. Feeder roots from the nearby beeches were drinking of the Kings' sacred blood as well, for pale emerald buds now adorned the gray branches over Liannan's head.

"Even to cursed Márrach, a King's death brings life," she said, and turned her Sight toward the gray stone tower in the midst of the valley.

Though open to the cloudless sky, the broch was wrapped in deep shadows. Magadh and Bochna looked with her, sharing her Sight, and they were not battle-weary. Strengthened, steadied by the company of the other Queens, Liannan urged her horse on. With a determined shout, her warriors followed.

Faintly Liannan heard Reochaidh's voice rolling through the woods as they rode, distance gentling its power to the sound of fading thunder. Louder were her own horses' pounding hooves, and louder still the Mór-Ríoghain's call as she shot over their heads, a black-feathered arrow pointing the way to combat.

"Márrach!" she cawed, and again, "Márrach!" summoning Éirinn's host to the battle she had Named.

Sixty-two

It is difficult to tame the proud

Sayings of the Mothers

Swiftly, while his foes had yet to regain their feet, Blackthorn slipped through the shadows that clung to the tower's stones, heading toward the ladder-stairs that led to Máchail's sanctum. They stood a long way from where he was, and a longer way an' he kept to the wall.

A dark elf turned from his belly to his back almost under Blackthorn's feet, but the Scáil had not time to call a warning before Blackthorn's sword whitened his eyes. The Hunter debated only a moment before yanking the cloak from the Scáil's corpse and casting it about his own shoulders. The gray mantles did a fine job of making the dark elves hard to see—and why should he fear a Scáil's clothing, and he with Urchóid's blade in his hand?

Weight the cloak had, but no warmth. Head down and hood up, Blackthorn sped through the carnage covering the floor of the tower, daring the shorter route to the ladder-stairs. The wind had pressed the wooden structure hard against the stones, broken several steps, and cracked much of the wood. Even without the wind, the scaffold creaked and rattled. A shred of encouragement, and it would come down entirely.

He looked quickly over his shoulder, but neither red eyes nor black met his own. Grasping hold of the ladder, Blackthorn started up. No amount of care would get him safely to the top—he trusted to reckless speed. The wooden frame swayed against the wall, the smashed railing fell apart under his hand. Ignoring the warnings, Blackthorn kept climbing, nor stopped to see if his ascent was marked. An' anyone saw him, he would know it soon enough.

His boot came down on the top rung, light as he could set it. The step broke beneath his weight. He threw himself forward, refusing to fall, and caught the ledge with one hand. Sending his sword onto the landing, he gripped the stones with both hands and hauled himself up. As soon as he felt the floor solid under him, he kicked back, hard, sending the ladder away from the wall, then rolled into the shadows beyond the opening. Wrapping his cloak tightly about him, he peered over the edge to watch the stairs fall.

They toppled into a heap of useless wood, sending fresh clouds of dust into the air. Heads turned toward the noise, and Blackthorn drew back into the shadows, praying his foes would believe the ladder-stairs' collapse an aftereffect of the windstorm.

Máchail's voice answered his prayer. It was taut as a drawn bowstring, controlled and deadly. He ordered the goblins to drag the corpses to the pits, and to inform him should they find Blackthorn's own. He ordered the Scáileanna to gather before the blocked tunnel to the close, and to weave a chant with their cold voices that would strengthen the arms of the goblins who would be clearing away the tumbled stones.

Blackthorn dared look out again. A horse had been brought to Márrach's master. Máchail mounted, and began waving his fingers, conjuring the murky air. Now the wind had stilled, the darkness was once again pliable in his hand.

Out of dust and shadow the Conjuror forged a blade. It wavered like smoke as Máchail passed it to his champion, but Urchóid uttered a piercing cry as he took the weapon to his hand, a sound of sated greed. The attendant sighs of the other Scáileanna were soft with awe, envy, and avarice. The blade Blackthorn had seen before, and recently, in the Dead Lord's hand.

Retreating until he was out of sight of anyone who might

chance to look up from the courtyard, Blackthorn started through the tower. No light penetrated between the broch's double walls—he went in darkness halfway around the ring, and came to stone steps leading up. He climbed them, went halfway around the tower again, and came to another flight rising. Darkness greeted Blackthorn at the end of each stairway, as deep and empty as the darkness he had left in the passage below.

His only guide through the shadows was the shimmering thread of the magpie's uneven carol, now no more than a trickle of disparate notes. The dark rock tower dulled the bird's song, and the melody grew no brighter, no matter how high he climbed.

Máchail was deaf to the goblins' complaints. Clouds the Scáileanna would call to darken the skies, but not now, not to spare their red-eyes while they worked to clear the courtyard and carry away the last of the stones from the passage to the close. When the Mothers' armies stood before Márrach's walls, then would he command that the Scáileanna bring shadows to banish the light.

His pale eyes strayed to the thinning stream of sand as it left the ruined floor of the sanctum and dropped in a perfect line to the courtyard below. Though the stolen white grains had never revealed more to his Sight than indefinite shadows moving over Éirinn's green hills, still the loss galled him. Sullied in the dust, now they would show him nothing at all.

Máchail smiled—were he a head taller and his skin gray, it would have been a Scáil smiling—and looked away. What could he learn from the sands that he did not already know? That the hedge was breached? Let it fall. That the Mothers' host was riding to Márrach? Let them come. That Shadow's cloak was torn? That the shades of the forest were fled to the deepest thickets or lay cowering under the bellies of rocks? Let the sun shine for an hour, let the Queens revel in their false hopes. Not victory, but war had the Hunter won for Éirinn. Its dark and bloody mantle would cover the five kingdoms for nine long years.

The goblins at the tunnel stood back from their efforts and bayed for Máchail's attention. They had cleared a path through the passage wide enough for the master of Márrach to use, though it would not yet permit the horses through. With a word Máchail sent Urchóid to the close to order the host for battle; archers to the wall and the gatehouse, fresh horses saddled and ready for the dark elves to ride.

Máchail himself was not yet willing to leave the inner court. Better the broch than the close for thought—nearer his God in the tower than under the sky. The daystar's intruding light but deepened the shadows, and the Dead Lord's bitter wrath filled them with cold.

He brought his horse well into the dark by the wall. His eyes followed the goblins as they pulled bodies from under the pieces of the bell, but his thoughts were on the spell the bell had cast, broken when the Hunter had made it ring a second time.

It was the wind, the Gruagach growled. His eyes burned like red fires in the darkness as he came to kneel before his master. It was the wind had bested him. The Hunter's scent was here, yes, but everywhere, scattered about the courtyard with the dust. There was no trail to follow.

"Drive out those that fled to the pits," Máchail told his servant. "Set some to seek the Hunter, the rest to repair the ladder-stairs."

As the beast went to do as he was bid, Máchail's gaze returned to the cataract of sand. Its source was drained; the white stream fell no more. A pity he could not scry in the scattered grains to discover the Hunter's hiding place. Still, the goblins might flush him from cover. Should the goblins fail, the Finding Stone would reveal his enemy in the end, as it had done yestere'en in the forest.

Impatience and no little trepidation nearly drove Máchail to conjure the orb from the sanctum at once. Pride and a keen sense of what would best serve his fame kept his fingers still—or so he told himself. In truth, bringing the Dead Lord's sword out of Shadow had cost him much. And it was no less true his reputation would suffer an' he displayed concern over the Hunter's escape.

A mere annoyance he must treat his foe, a fly to be swatted down. And surely Mac na Caillí was no more than that. The Spear broken, so must his geis be broken, so must his soul be in pieces. Fled to the forest he was, an' he had somehow slipped by the gate, or lying like a wounded deer in some unmarked corner of the broch. Were it not that the Talisman hung still at the Hunter's throat . . .

A fool he had been, overeager to feel the Talisman's power against his flesh. He had thought to make the star his by holding it in his hand, but had he held it in his glove, even for a moment—

But had a broken man the will to command Domhnall's star? An' the Hunter had the power to call forth more destruction upon Márrach, would he not already have done so?

Yowling at the brightness that had invaded the broch, goblins crawled unwillingly up from the pits. Behind them came the Gruagach, driving them in a voice so savage the red-eyes hurried to their tasks despite the morning light. Though his body had begun to ache with the cold of the shadows that sheltered him, Máchail never moved. Scáil-stiff the master of Márrach sat, drawing dark inspiration from his God's chill touch, laying his strategies in the tower's black, concealing pools.

The Mothers' armies were the greatest danger. Against them Máchail had fell weapons to wield. Names he would have from Creathna's easily coerced tongue, and ranna of battle victory were already his—extracted from Scáthach's dead lips weeks ago, when he first thought to humble nearby An Dubh-Áth and topple the wooden walls of Latharna.

Even so, when the ladder-stairs were in place, he would bid the Gruagach fetch Scáthach's head from the sanctum. Poets of Éirinn rode in the Mothers' train. To counter their verses he might need Scáthach's gifts. An' the Hunter had been taken captive by then, his blood would go into Scáthach's bowl to strengthen her curses, and Creathna would live a day longer. An' the Hunter still eluded the goblins, Máchail would wrest a spell from the Poet of Teach an Fhásaigh that would silence Conall mac na Caillí wherever he hid.

Máchail's body was ice now, to the marrow of his bones. Coils of darkness pressed against him, constricting, demanding, but the Shadow King's appetites were akin to the master of Márrach's, and Máchail did not fear them. Both he and his God had been denied the feast of Light, but soon their hungers would be appeased. Together they would gorge on Éirinn's blood running red upon Márrach's hill.

Sixty-three

The wolf will howl
The raven sing
When the Mór-Ríoghain calls my Name
Mother will weep
My darling mourn
When the Mór-Ríoghain calls my Name

Marching Song of Ulaidh

When the first hundreds came out from under the cover of the trees, ropes and grappling hooks in the warriors' hands and a banner of Ulaidh flying over their heads, Máchail laughed. At least his enemies had wit enough not to bring a battering ram from the woods. Blinded as they were by Márrach's spells, they could only guess where upon the barren hill the gate might stand. The rampart they could find, by running into it with their thick heads, but then the Queens' host must stand defenseless before it, as easy to kill as ducks on the water.

An' this tale were told by Éirinn's Bards, Máchail remarked to Urchóid, they would call the Mothers' charge desperate courage, and sing the praises of those that dared lay siege to a fortress they could not see. The master of Márrach called it folly, and ordered his archers to shoot them down.

The foe were easy prey, though they kept low behind their round shields and ran so close together they made a moving wall of leather-bound wood. Márrach's arrows stuck in Éirinn's shields thick as prickles on a hedgehog, and the dry soil sprouted straight-stemmed flowers in gray-feathered profusion.

Not only shields and sod did the arrows strike. Slipping between the cracks in the attackers' wall, the shafts found arms and legs, lodged in chests, and necks, and eyes. Only two score of the Mothers' first hundred reached Márrach's invisible stones, and though some stood erect long enough to cast their ropes, not one hook caught.

Even as they died, three hundred more came from the woods to take their place. Battle cries of Na Connachta Máchail heard on the still air. He welcomed Magadh's warriors as he had Ulaidh's champions. Na Connachta's bowmen knelt on the dusty ground, shooting their arrows blindly back to the heavens only to see their weapons break upon the air before their own deaths came winging out of nothingness to claim them.

Yet, still they came, warriors of Laighin, of Midhe, following hard upon their comrades' charge. Some bore hastily rigged ladders of twine and wood, and held their shields above their heads as they came on. Others took up the ropes and hooks of those that had fallen before them as they ran to the wall. Down the shallow ditch they raced, and up the rise to where Márrach's rampart was now marked by a ragged line of dead bodies.

Máchail's laughter ceased. Volley after volley his own archers sent into the ranks of the foe. Their corpses strewed the ground, their lifeblood soaked the gray earth. Márrach's quivers ran empty. More were brought to the battlements, and still Éirinn's brave dared the open to die upon Márrach's hill.

Máchail's lips twisted into a mirthless smile. "Och, Fionnghuala, clever darling," he whispered, and louder, to his champion, "We waste our strength on the Deceiver's illusions. Cease firing on these false foes, and sing me power enough to bring shadows to the skies."

Liannan stood as near as she thought wise to the edge of the wood—Scáileanna were keen Sighted. She had positioned herself opposite Márrach's gate, but her shining eyes were on the rampart, and the traitor Mac Ailch. Sharing her Sight,

Bochna and Magadh beheld Márrach's archers relax their bows. They Saw Mac Ailch turn from the field, more interested in his own army's preparations in the close than the insubstantial hosts storming his walls.

Now we strike, Liannan said. *The Mór-Ríoghain is calling your Names.*

Hidden among the trees to her left, two score and ten Sidhe drew the hoods of their cloaks over their glittering eyes. Their silver swords were sheathed, and their horses left behind, that the Scáileanna upon the wall would not know of their coming until it was too late. Beyond the elves of An Cnoc Buidhe, the Bear of An Clár, lying flat on the dusty earth, raised his hand and shook the grappling hook it held. Seventy of Mumhain's bravest mirrored him.

They will believe you are but another of the Deceiver's illusions, Magadh told them. *Be swift, and bold, and stop for nothing. May Éire guide your arms.*

As the Deceiver's mock warriors took shape under the trees and dashed toward Márrach's unseen walls, the Sidhe of An Cnoc Buidhe joined them, and the Ó Briain led his band forth. If only she dared bring a battering ram to the gate, Liannan thought. Or dared direct the assault to the section of the wall where Mac Ailch was standing.

How quickly would our enemy's strategy change, an' he learned Márrach's spells no longer daunt our Sight? Bochna argued. *We cannot afford to lose this advantage. Neither against Mac Ailch, nor the gate yet send our hosts. We can See their quivers stand empty. An' we gain a foothold on their rampart, then must they come from behind their wall to stop us—and we will be here to greet them when they open their gate.*

Meacán watched Fionnghuala where she sat under the arms of a dead beech, her fingers speaking the secret, silent language of Ogham. Light danced like sparks on the wind, following the Deceiver's every gesture. The beech was one of six forming a small circle around a bare patch of dirt, and the grove itself set far deeper in the woods than the trees that were the Mothers' protection. A fairy ring it must have been, Meacán decided, in the days before Mac Ailch had come to Cromghlinn.

Mac Ailch. She felt a fool to be calling him that still, and a fool twice over after hearing how that false Name had broken scores of shields at Márrach's hedge. *Badhbh, Macha, and Mór-Ríoghain*, but he was cunning. Not only could he have the Hunter's Name—by abducting Creathna he had made sure no one could learn his own.

Fionnghuala's fingers flew so fast the runes of light wove together into a shimmering cloud about her hands. Meacán moved away and joined the rest of the Poets and Wizards at the edge of the clearing. Squinting through the trees, she watched the Deceiver's art take to the field.

Many waves had Meacán seen break upon Márrach's invisible wall this last hour, but this one . . . this one might break the wall itself, for warriors of flesh and blood ran with Fionnghuala's illusions—

The Bear of An Clár roared, and Meacán's heart jumped within her breast. It was a fearsome sound, betraying none of the weariness the Ó Briain must feel from the battle he had seen already. Liannan had not wanted the Bear to risk himself again, but when she had said as much, the Ó Briain growled back that an' he didn't give the rest of his folk a chance to equal the deeds of those who had stood with him in the ring of fire, they'd no more have him for their Chieftain.

Was the Ó Briain's courage greater, she wondered, charging up a hill that seemed empty of threat? Or was it less, knowing an arrow might suddenly burst from silence and sky to whistle into his heart?

"Och, Mór-Ríoghain, hear me," she prayed. "Let them gain the wall. But let them gain it, and there will be bloodshed enough to content even You."

The Crow of Battle granted her prayer. Not a single shaft left Márrach's spelled walls. Not a single warrior of Éirinn fell upon the narrow field.

"They are to the rampart," Meacán told Fionnghuala in a cracked whisper.

"The fools scorn any longer to credit our attacks," Feargna Óg gloated, but the Deceiver's face was drawn, and the patterns her deft fingers wove began to fragment as the bare arms of the beech cast shadows upon her work.

The Ó Briain swung his arm round and round, easing

more length to his rope with every circle. A final spin, a mighty heave, and the hook was shooting up over the Ó Briain's head. Dozens more sang with his. Hands loosed the ropes, hooks like giant talons reached up to the heavens.

And then they vanished. Some were back in an instant, those that fell short, or struck the wall but did not catch. The hook on the Ó Briain's rope did not reappear, nor did a good fifteen others. Their thick cords dangled from the sky.

"They are climbing!" Meacán tried to shout, but her voice was too weak.

"The Sidhe first—whisht, the Ó Briain will not wait," Seamair told Fionnghuala. "The rest cast again, and still—no! A rope is cut! Och, Mothers! Our enemies are aware of us!"

Cú Ceat! The Mothers' summons was so loud it echoed in everyone's mind.

Cú Ceat, the Chieftain they called the Wild Dog of Ciarraighe, rushed howling onto the field, and with him ran Brónach, his mate, as fierce as he. Behind them, baying like their leaders, came the warriors of Dún na gCon.

"Hounds with the scent they are!" Feargna Óg shouted to be heard over the din. "Arrah, and with them, look! The Sidhe of An Cnoc Glas. They do not lower their eyes, and take to the field their silver swords drawn!"

The Deceiver's hands fell to her lap, and her shoulders sagged wearily. "I can do no more," she said. "Mothers, forgive me, my power is spent."

Liannan's reply was a gentle thought for Fionnghuala alone.

Rest then, darling. Your host has done all that is needed. For every rope our enemies cut, another catches on their stones. For every warrior that falls before their walls, two more scale them. An' they will stop us, they must come out from behind their gate.

Bochna and Magadh melded their will to Liannan's.

Reochaidh, they called, and another summons, *Tadhg of An Chluain Thiar.*

Rest, Deceiver, Liannan assured Fionnghuala. *Others will strike the next blow.*

The master of Márrach scowled at the clouds his servants were calling to the blue skies. The Scáileanna's chant was an impressive spell, but it was Máchail's will bade it blacken the heavens.

The storm clouds thickening above, Máchail lowered his eyes, and looked to see the reason for the piercing cries of the Scáileanna guarding the rampart on the far side of the gatehouse. His eyes darkened as the skies were darkening— hooks had caught on his wall, and living warriors were scaling the ropes that hung from them.

With a word he sent arrows flying into their bodies. With another he called for fires to be lit under cauldrons of water and oil, and stones to be brought to the wall.

"Shoot only those you know are not illusion," Urchóid ordered. "Waste no more arrows on the field."

Even as the Scáil spoke, the field changed. Hundreds of Éirinn's warriors grew pale as fading mists, wavered in the darkening day, and disappeared. Hundreds more poured from the gray trees to take their places. Márrach's master smiled with grim satisfaction.

"Fionnghuala extended herself greatly with this elaborate deception," he told his champion, "but at last the Mothers' host is come in truth onto the field of battle. The Deceiver has exhausted her gifts."

"While we have exhausted our arrows on bloodless apparitions!" Urchóid returned. "How are we to keep our foes from overrunning our walls, and the Sidhe already upon us, and the warriors of Mumhain?"

Máchail studied the enemies who had gained his wall. The Sidhe offended him with their bright swords and brighter eyes, the others with the insolence of their daring. Still, they had achieved no more than a place to die—their backs against Márrach's gray stones, they were hemmed in on all sides by the gray-skinned Scáileanna.

Flaming arrows arced over the stones of the battlement and rained briefly on the close. The Queens were striking blind, hoping their missiles would chance to fall on the thatched roofs—targets they could only guess at. None of the shafts hit a worthy mark, but still the volley gave Márrach's master pause. If an arrow did chance to find the thatch, or one of the wooden bothies . . . with fire in the close, the goblins would be ungovernable.

A fierce and terrible challenge echoed against Márrach's

walls, and Urchóid's smile hardened. "The dogs of Ciarraighe whine at our gate."

Máchail's smile was softer, a smile of contempt. "Is Márrach's champion so easily dismayed? An' the dogs will howl, then let our spears fly screaming from our walls to silence them."

Urchóid's voice was as chill as his master's eye. "Spears for casting we have yet a few, but not so many as to halt all the warriors in the Mothers' host. Our arrows we have already spent. Too much we trusted in the veils that hide our walls—even unseen it seems they can be scaled, and we are ill prepared to defend them. We must to the field, an' we are to have the victory."

Máchail scorned to look upon the field, but returned his gaze to black clouds now almost woven into a solid mass.

"These your orders. The Gruagach by now is on his way to the sanctum to fetch my Poet to me—have Othras bring Creathna to the wall as well. Curses will close this breach better than swords, and deadly my ill wishes will prove under a lightless sky.

"As for you—gather the best warriors, and lead them out beyond the gate. An' we have not enough arrows to daunt Éirinn's brave, they will learn to fear Márrach at the point of a Scáil's sword. Let the goblins run with you. Glad of battle they'll be, now dark has exiled the sun from the heavens."

"My sword alone would be enough to teach them fear," the Scáil answered. "But it will be as you say."

Barely can we constrain the Kings, Magadh told Liannan. *And Cessair is fair mad herself with waiting.*

But a moment more, Liannan urged. *The Scáileanna are to the gatehouse. What? Goblins with them! Has it grown so dark? Reochaidh, stand fast . . . Destroyer—now!*

Only the Mothers could See the gate begin to swing inward, but Reochaidh did not need to see, only to send his voice forward.

"Fall to me!" he roared.

Though he cupped his massive hands to direct his voice to the hill, the Mothers' hosts staggered back at the power of his command, and their ears rang with his voice long after he was silent.

Bochna's disappointment ached in Liannan's heart. *Less than we hoped for.*

Enough, the Mother of Midhe insisted. *It is enough. Too much to hope that the spells that guard our enemies' walls have no purpose but to keep them hidden. Shadow protects Márrach well, but though the gate stands, and the battlement, and the gatehouse, yet the Scáileanna are swept back. They fight to govern their mounts, and have yet to take to the field.*

They will ride through despite the Destroyer.

Liannan gasped, and spoke aloud in her excitement. "But look!" she cried. "Reochaidh has cracked the bolt that bars the gate! Look! In the Scáileanna's hands! A verse Tadhg, to break the beam, and they can no more lock the door against us!"

The Poet of An Chluain Thiar knit his brow and bent his head. Bochna, Queen of Laighin heard the verse in Tadhg's thoughts even as the words came to him, and the Mothers sang them out with all their power.

> *Wood nor iron, words nor spells*
> *Seal your door unseen.*
> *Your gate may close against our host,*
> *But barred it will nevermore be.*

The gatehouse guards held the great wooden beam ready to bar the gate as soon as the mounted Scáileanna were past it, but the Scáileanna were fighting to control their horses, and the door stood ajar. Like wedges, the first lines of Tadhg's rann fixed in the split in the weakened beam. Like hammers the last lines pounded the syllables deep in the wood. Liannan Saw the bar fall from the guards' hands in long, useless splinters.

An' we win the field, we may take the gate, Liannan said. *Yet from there, we must still pass the gatehouse, and the broch itself is the seat of Shadow's power.*

The Scáileanna have their steeds in hand, Magadh cautioned.

Let loose the Kings' horses! Bochna commanded. *Let the warriors of Cnoc an Eanaigh ride!*

The Scáileanna streamed forth from Márrach, a river of darkness. Out the gates, over the bridge they came, then wheeled their mounts to drive them into Éirinn's warriors gathered beneath the walls. Against Márrach's three hundreds, the Queens sent one—the Kings, Niall, Longaire, and Cormac, and the Sidhe of Cnoc an Eanaigh. The Kings' battle joy howled upon the air as they saw the battleground before them, and the war cries of the Sidhe were like a rann of hope to the hearts of those already on the field.

Even as the Mothers' champions rode forth, rainclouds banished all light from the sky. Liannan lifted her eyes briefly to the heavens, then fixed them on Márrach's gate once more. Goblins were passing through. Behind them rode a single Scáil on a black steed. A naked sword was in his hand, and the sight of it wounded Liannan's gaze. She looked away, but not before Bochna and Magadh had Seen what her eyes had beheld.

That weapon is surely made of the same darkness that roils in the skies above, thought Magadh.

That weapon, answered Bochna, *is surely the Shadow King's own.*

Seamair! Liannan ordered.

The Weather-Worker hurried to the Mother of Midhe, already shaking her head.

"Mothers, I know what you will ask, but think! 'Twas Úna cautioned me against dispelling the rain."

"The Oak Seer?" Liannan demanded.

"Yestereve, Mother, as a raven she came to us. To the Mothers she spoke, and they can tell you more, but words she gave also to myself, and Fionnghuala. Little sense made I of her angry speech, but—"

"And little time have we now to ponder it."

Liannan let her eyes wander over the battlefield as she considered Seamair's news, then raised them to the wall.

"Brighde's Fire," she moaned, and sent her Sight to her sisters.

Creathna! they called together, but the Name-Sayer, standing on the wall beside Mac Ailch, seemed not to hear.

Grief Liannan could See, bowing the old Wizard's shoulders. And fear, filling his heart. Mac Ailch drew closer to Creathna, inclined his head to speak in the elder's ear, and pointed at a young warrior who had gained his wall. Creathna's bearded lips moved. Mac Ailch straightened, and spoke again. The boy his finger had chosen dropped his sword. Clutching at his chest as if to pull his heart from it, he fell back against the stones. The Scáileanna heaved his body over the wall, but Liannan could See the child was dead before he hit the ground.

Her Sight lingered on the warrior Creathna had betrayed until a Scáil on the field distracted her eye—the champion who held Shadow's sword. The blade was dark as smoke and soft as cloud, and every living thing it touched was dying horribly.

"Forbid the rain, Weather-Worker," Liannan said softly.

Seamair started to repeat her protest, but the Mother cut her off.

"Forbid the rain—I command it. We must have the day, an' we are to win it."

PART 13

the white stag

Sixty-four

The sword that had dealt him his death in his hand,
He struck Conn a mortal blow,
Saying, "An' I a man, you'd have left here alive,
But you've murdered the Wolf of Dún na Bó."

The Wolf of Dún na Bó

His boot upon the first step of yet another long companion-way, Blackthorn paused and leaned his back against the inner wall. The gray stones sent a chill through his clothes to his skin. He ignored it as he ignored the cold of the sword in his hand, and considered.

An' the Dead Lord held the passing moments in his shadowy fist, he might well let them slip slow as hours through his fingers. But even were the hand of Shadow's King closed upon time, Blackthorn should by now have come at least to the windows of the tower. Enchantments must guard the broch's passages—spells woven for to bind trespassers like himself in an infinite ring of stairs and halls.

He bit off the curse he was about to utter before it left his tongue. All too certain in this place his words would fly to the wrong ears, and return to wound the speaker.

He spat instead, and ran his free hand through his hair. Had his enemy an amulet or charm to unlock the shadows— a ring, perhaps? Yet, the Gruagach's hand that had struck him down was unadorned, and Máchail's servant had no trouble finding the sorcerer's sanctum. . . .

Words, then? Were a few syllables all the darkness required before the tower's closed circle would spin into an open spiral? The passwords might well have been on the magpie's tongue all this long while, Blackthorn thought ruefully, but an' they were, he had not Úna's gift of understanding. Only entreaty could he hear in the magpie's voice, and though it was all too clear his attempts to answer her must be in vain, he started up the stairs once more.

Ten, twelve steps he passed. On the thirteenth, the world shifted, nearly sending him tumbling down the stairwell.

The stone risers beneath his feet shuddered as if the shoulder of earth under the tower had carelessly shrugged. Putting his hand to the suddenly visible stones to steady himself, Blackthorn saw he was not on stairs at all, but a landing. Cheerless light fell through a window slit to his left and marked the floor before his feet.

He ran to the casement, thinking the light would tell him how long he had been lost in the dark of the tower. The clouds were too heavy and told him nothing—but he could see a part of the battlement. The rampart was thick with Scáileanna. A narrow slice of the field beyond was open to his eye as well, and that was covered with hundreds of Éirinn's bravest.

Long enough he'd tarried. Blackthorn turned from the window and sped on through the tower. He expected no more obstacles to his ascent to the sanctum, though it seemed less likely than ever he would accomplish anything by reaching it. An' the spell that guarded the broch had broken, 'twas not his doing. Whoever had opened the way to the top of the tower was hard on his heels, and would scarce be pleased to find the Hunter of Éirinn there before him.

Blackthorn's soft footsteps awakened the quiescent sands heaped about the hole in the middle of the sanctum floor. Small landslides started on the miniature dunes, tumbling white grains into the ragged-edged abyss. When he had seen the sands from the courtyard below, falling through the gap and into the sunlight, they had sparkled. The pale grains were lustreless now, for light no longer streamed through the open center of the sanctum's thatched roof. Storm clouds had gathered so low about the tower they seemed almost to rest upon it, a seething, dark crown.

An air of precarious balance hung over the room, a legacy of the bell's demise. A small tripod sat at the very edge of a beechwood chest, ready to fall. A black pot rested in the tripod's wrought-iron arms, the shape and size of the bowl that had held the head of the Poet of Teach an Fhásaigh. Blackthorn turned his face away.

In turning, his eyes lit upon a long shadow clinging to the wall to his right. Smaller shadows played within the larger, shadows of cups, cloaks, torques, and torches . . . the shadow of a long, lethal blade. . . .

Blackthorn quickly drew his gaze in and set it before him, on his next footstep. From the top of the stairs he had first glimpsed Strife's shadow in the smoke-gray pillar, and had run to her, hoping to pull her from the dark. His grasping fingers had closed on nothing, only shadows, and his hand had swiftly grown numb in the cold and empty air. He would not be lured there again, unless and until he had found the key to Máchail's shadow-bound treasure chest.

Smoky shards crunched under his boots—the debris of the orb that had yesterday torn his cover from him, or perhaps another such stone. Two ornate chairs lay on their sides, one without an arm, the other's intricate design forever flawed by an uneven crack running through the carved knotwork. An upright oaken table to his left seemed unshaken, but varicolored gems that must have rested upon it now lay scattered beneath on the sand-covered floor.

Though the candles and vials, the grotesque bits of once living creatures, the brazier and tongs, the rune-carved wands, everything was perfectly still, it seemed to Blackthorn his enemy's possessions were only feigning immobility. Like the white sands, the slightest provocation would send them sliding down the angled boards to the gaping hole the bell had torn in the floor.

The Hunter's path across the sanctum tested the chamber's uncertain stability. He went as near as he dared to the center of the room, near enough to feel the floorboards bend with his weight and hear them groan in warning. Sands poured like water around his boots, passing him by in their

hurry to reach the courtyard far below. His goal still beyond
arm's reach, Blackthorn stopped and lifted his sword.

Suspended before him upon the unlit air was a tightly latticed wicker box. Its square bottom rose to a rounded top,
but neither door nor hinge could he see on any part of it. No
chain held the frame, no pedestal supported it. High above
the cage, beyond the tower itself, menacing clouds boiled.
Beneath it was nothing but empty air as far as the courtyard
floor.

The magpie's song thrilled in welcome. She flitted to the
very top of her prison and clung, her midnight eyes peering
through the crisscrossed wood. Taking Urchóid's sword in
both his hands, Blackthorn swung it across the base of the
cage.

The delicate wood took the blow with a loud crack and
the obdurance of granite. Pain shot through Blackthorn's
arms and shoulders. In his hands the Scáil's blade trembled,
giving out a sound like a moan. Abruptly it crumbled, raining down on the sanctum floor as a fine, gray powder, and
disappeared with the coarser sands through the ragged hole.

Blackthorn stood staring stupidly at the useless hilt he yet
held, then at the unmoved, undamaged cage before him. A
long moment passed before he realized the magpie was no
longer singing. As he missed her voice, he heard another.

A growl echoed in the stairwell, too terrible even for a
goblin's throat. Blackthorn knew it at once, and in knowing
it, knew also who had followed him up the tower stairs. The
knowledge gained him nothing. Still he must meet the
Gruagach with only the hilt of a broken sword in his hand.

Carefully he turned from the cage, his legs seeking more
solid footing, his eyes, a better weapon. He spied a stout staff
leaning with several lesser lengths of wood against the stone
wall near the top of the stairs, and longed to take it up. The
swiftness of the beast upon the stairway forbade him even try.

The Gruagach appeared on the top stair, his long, hairy
arm already reaching for the wand Blackthorn had meant for
himself. He was tall as a young giant and broad as an ox. As
his sharp-nailed paw wrapped around the wood, his glowing
eyes fastened on the Hunter, hatred burning in them like the
fires of Shadow King's Sight. His wordless threat rose to
howl, and he charged.

Hurling the hilt of the Scáil's sword at the Gruagach's ridged brow, Blackthorn darted to the left and up the sloped floor. The gray metal crosspiece struck dead between the beast's eyes, a blow that might have killed a mortal man. The Gruagach only roared to shake the tower's stones, wiped the blood from his sight, and came on.

Blackthorn raced for the table, intending to put the massive oak board between himself and his foe. He bent as he ran, taking up a fistful of sand to hurl. His fingers touched something smooth and hard among the white grains. Without thinking, without needing to think, his hand closed on the stone and he sent it flying toward the Gruagach's face.

Dark blood spurted where a red eye had flamed, and then the Gruagach was upon him. Clear-sighted or half-blind, it seemed to make no difference to the beast. As the staff came at his head, Blackthorn ducked, taking the brunt of the Gruagach's blow on his back. It brought him to his knees. Nails sharp as fishing hooks dug into his shoulder, piercing cloth and skin. His hold secure, the Gruagach hauled his captive to his feet.

Clasping his two hands in a single fist, Blackthorn swung as hard as he could at the Gruagach's side. The beast only snarled, and sent the agony lodged in the Hunter's arm deeper into his flesh.

Blackthorn drove his boot down on the Gruagach's flat foot, and when his enemy's weight shifted, jabbed his elbow sharply up into the Gruagach's face. The immense head snapped back. Drops of sticky, black blood flew from Gruagach's wounded eye, spattering Blackthorn's arm, and still the beast did not let go.

A blur was all Blackthorn saw of the staff before it landed again. The blow caught him on his ribs, and knocked him back to the sands. The Gruagach's nails tore through Blackthorn's shoulder as he fell, and raked along his arm.

For a moment Blackthorn couldn't see for the pain, couldn't think, or move. Sucking a lungful of air through his gritted teeth, his vision cleared on the sight of his own blood dropping onto the white sands between his hands. Another breath, and it struck him that the Gruagach's claws were no longer locked on his flesh.

Sand flowed through Blackthorn's fingers as he tried to get away—there was nothing to grip, nothing to push against. He heard the staff descending, flung himself to the side and rolled.

The floor took the blow from the heavy wand. The air sighed as the Gruagach brought it up, and whistled around the wood as he slammed it down once more. Blackthorn rolled again, onto his knees, got his feet under him. Half-running, half-falling, he scrabbled up the floor to the table, grasped the edge of the board, and vaulted over.

Pain lanced up his side as he landed and erupted into fire in his wounded arm. Gasping in enough air to stay conscious, he watched the Gruagach's stroke come down on the board. The beast's staff snapped in two.

Thunder drummed in the dark heavens above, but the roar that burst from the Gruagach's throat was louder and shook thatch from the roof. Tossing his splintered wand aside, the beast set his great paws to the table. He did not leap over as Blackthorn had done, but lifted the edge until the enormous slab rose like an oaken wave and overturned. Blackthorn staggered back as the board crashed onto its side, then staggered again as the weakened floorboards quaked under the table's impact.

Abruptly, the angle of the floor steepened. The table started to ease down the incline. The sands under Blackthorn's boots ebbed more swiftly, rushing to the sagging center of the room, and down through the ruptured floor. Blackthorn's feet almost went with them—turning, he scrambled for the safety of the wall.

The Gruagach threw himself flat and started slithering up the floor, a black-bellied salmon swimming up a waterfall. A twisting leap, and his fingers wrapped around Blackthorn's ankle. They closed like iron bands and brought the Hunter down so fast it seemed the floor leapt up to meet him.

A creature so massive shouldn't move so quickly, Blackthorn cursed to himself. A creature so wounded shouldn't be so strong. He grappled for purchase on the tilted floor, kicked wildly, and landed a blow in the middle of the Gruagach's chest.

For an instant Blackthorn was free, and again clawing his way to safety. Next moment, the whole of the Gruagach's weight drove into his legs, pinning him. His right shoulder buckled. A vise fastened on his right arm and wrenched it up behind his back. A heavy paw struck him on the back of the head and jammed his face into the sands.

His enemy heaped insults on him, but Blackthorn barely heard them for the roaring of his own pain within him. Blood poured from his shoulder. Sand filled his mouth. His right arm was breaking. He swept his left across the ground, groping through the sands for the Gruagach's splintered staff, another stone—

At the very limits of his reach Blackthorn's fingers brushed against something solid. His hand closed quickly. Levering his trapped arm down with all his might, he arched his back. It meant rolling onto his hurt shoulder, but he clenched his jaw and rolled, at the same time swinging his newfound weapon in a wide arc from the floor to the beast looming over him.

He held an old bone, the leg of an elk. Its knobbed, heavy end caught the Gruagach just above his blood-blinded eye. The beast grunted and reeled back. Blackthorn turned all the way over, shook sand from his sight, spat it from his tongue, and smashed his club into the Gruagach's jaw. A stained fang broke in the beast's grinning mouth, and his hold loosened. Pushing his legs hard against the slanted flooring, Blackthorn squirmed out from under the beast, a new fear gripping his belly as he saw that their struggles had brought them near to the edge of the gaping hole in the center of the room. Clasping his weapon with both hands, he swung a third time.

The bleached bone struck the Gruagach where his thick neck met his shoulder, and flew apart in a flurry of dried marrow and chipped yellow flakes. The Gruagach swayed, but even as he began to fall to the side, his arm shot out. His paw clamped down on Blackthorn's ravaged shoulder, and his nails dug in.

Blackthorn's cry reached his own ears as faintly as a shout from the battlefield far below. Sound and sight were overruled, every sense made to submit to the knives in his shoulder and the jarring blows that rained on him from the Gruagach's clenched fist. The beast paused and his fist opened, only to close again on the Hunter's throat.

Blackthorn clawed at the stranglehold on his windpipe. When he could not loose it, his fingers ploughed furrows in the bloodied sands, hunting another weapon. The Gruagach's broken smile widened.

Blackthorn's hands lost feeling first, then his arms, then his legs. Sparks of light interrupted his vision. A deep quiet seemed to settle over the sanctum, deeper for the agony held silent in his bursting lungs.

He was dying too soon, or with too little resistance—the Gruagach lifted Blackthorn by his neck and shook him. Instead of calling him back to life, the beast wakened fresh torments in Blackthorn's ribs and lacerated shoulder that drove the Hunter on toward death like whips of fire. In his heart Blackthorn stopped cursing his killer, and began to wish the Gruagach's grip were tighter, his blows harder. Pain was the key would open death's door, and beyond it he need feel none. He would have crossed the dark threshold already, if only his geasa did not stand in the way.

It was unjust, his clouded mind railed, unjust that his unfulfilled bonds should even now refuse to let him surrender and die. Unjust entirely that Death would take him all unwilling, and yet grant him no release.

His darkening gaze drifted over his slayer's shoulder. He could just make out the púca's scrawny, naked self crouched at the top of the stairs, but even half-dead, Blackthorn was not so mad as to credit such a sight. Emptiness seared his chest and despair stabbed at his heart, yet if he could have drawn breath, he would have laughed at the ferocious expression he imagined he saw on Reathach's foolish face.

The púca's image blurred and vanished. His sight gone forever, Blackthorn thought. Yet, one last vision came to him before all went dark—the vision of an amber-eyed, silver-furred wolf sprinting from the stairs across the sanctum's angled floor, then flying through the air, hair bristling, teeth bared—a vision of merciless beauty.

Sixty-five

The mouth of the grave gives to the needy

Sayings of the Mothers

Creathna!

His own Name rang in the old Wizard's heart more terribly than the death cries of those his Naming had condemned.

Creathna! Heed us!

Clearly he heard the Mothers' call, but the Name-Sayer of Sliabh Ailp, Wizard of Éirinn, could not bear to answer for the shame that was his.

Once more he bent his gaze to the gray stones at his feet. Once more the master of Márrach bade him lift his eyes and look. Once more Creathna obeyed, followed the pointing finger with his eyes, and spoke a Name. How could he not? Already he had earned Máchail's wrath—and had been warned that only absolute compliance could now spare him the fate the Poet of Teach an Fhásaigh had suffered. A goblin stood ready, axe in hand, should he dare resist Máchail's will, and a black, blood-filled bowl sat by the goblin's foot, waiting for Creathna's head. How could he consider silence, when Márrach's master could take every Name he desired perforce from Creathna's death-swollen tongue?

Máchail pointed again. Creathna looked and saw Nuadhra, the Ó Dubhagán, said his Name aloud, and watched the Chieftain die.

His death was like Cuanna Óg mac Liadhan's before him. Their hearts stopped beating because Máchail had spoken a rann Scáthach's dead lips had once whispered in his ear, and Scáthach's verse said their hearts must beat no more.

Creathna leaned upon the rampart, his eyes following Nuadhra's body as the goblins heaved it over the wall and let it fall to the earth far below. He was dead, but better to die on Márrach's wall than in Márrach's pits with those whose cries Creathna had nightly heard, whose blood had flowed to slake the Shadow King's thirst. This was a death did not imprison the soul, but freed it. This a death an old man might not fear, but welcome.

It could never be his, he thought sadly, peering beneath his snowy brows at Éirinn's betrayer. Máchail would never give it him. The gloved hand was pointing again, at the Ó Briain this time. Art was the great hero's Name.

"Name-Sayer!" Máchail demanded.

I am old, Creathna told himself, and never strong, not even in my youth. And yet . . . my hand already rests upon the wall. A single step, and I am standing where my hand now lies. Who is there swift enough to stop me?

It was easier even than he hoped. Perhaps because his heart was light, he thought, but it seemed to Creathna that he reached the top of the rampart with no effort at all. Máchail's anger shouted behind him, but Creathna was not such a fool as to look back. He hurried on to his next step, the one that took him over the edge of the rampart and out upon the empty air, and that was the easiest step of all.

The color drained from Feargna Óg's face. "Yes," he murmured, then, "At once."

The Necromancer's body became motionless. His unblinking eyes glazed. He grew paler still, white as a ghost.

But, he was a ghost, Meacán thought, then saw immediately she was wrong. Feargna Óg and his ghost were not one. The young Wizard stood alive in the clearing. A flush had returned to his cheeks and he was breathing easily, though more softly than a slumbering dreamer.

His ghost, whiter than the morning mists and as formless, rose from the Necromancer's body and began gliding toward Márrach. And like morning mists, the apparition became thinner, more transparent as it floated away. By the time the shade had reached the edge of the wood, Meacán could not see it at all.

She shivered, not in fear, or not only in fear. It was more than the hollow thunder in the clouds above that made her tremble. It was the morbid desire that possessed her, the longing to know whose soul Feargna Óg's ghost had gone to meet.

Fear was no dark thing to Máchail. He found it shockingly bright, like sunlight that stabs past a lifted curtain into a windowless room. When Creathna threw himself from the wall, all Máchail could do was recoil from the blaze of fear that struck his heart.

An utter coward he had thought the Name-Sayer, too fainting, too feeble for such vigorous bravery. An' the Mothers Saw Creathna's fall—but they must See at last the old fool's dead body at the base of the wall! And they would send for Feargna Óg, the rabbit-faced boy Wizard who spoke more courteously to the dead than to the living. How long before the Necromancer would have the master of Márrach's true Name from Creathna's easily coaxed tongue?

He glanced up at the tower, as if he might spy behind its stones, then cursed aloud his ungifted Sight. Where was the Gruagach with Scáthach's head? A shield of words he must have, a shield no other lesser Poet's rann might broach, despite that his enemies had his Name to twine in the spell.

Though the thick, gray walls daunted Máchail's eyes, the shroud of black storm above the tower gladdened them. He drank in the darkness and it suffused him, overshadowing the glare of foreboding. Not so powerful were the Mothers' Wizards, not so much to be feared. As Fionnghuala's illusions had waned, so were Seamair's gifts failing even now. Shadow was the shield would hide his Name from Feargna Óg's meddling and the Mothers' ken.

He looked again on Creathna. A knot of warriors had formed about the aged Wizard's corpse. One broke away from the others and began running toward the woods, doubtless to carry the tidings to the Queens. A goblin stood in his way, but the runner thrust quickly with spear, and the goblin fell. Barely had he wrenched his weapon from the red-eye's chest before he was running again.

He did not see his danger, for Márrach's champion rode at him from behind. Urchóid's arm came up, lifting Shadow's sword—Máchail marvelled at how the weapon wavered in the wind it made, yet swept down sharp and deadly as any fire-tempered blade to cut across the runner's back.

It was only a common warrior's death, but Máchail was content. The horror of the man's scream in the others' ears, the sight of his flesh writhing back from the shadowy edge of the champion's blade must bring their own dooms upon them all the swifter.

The Necromancer hesitates.

He is uncertain of the way. The shadows bewilder him.

How fares Seamair? Where is the sun? We must lift the darkness that obscures the ghost's path.

She pits her gifts against a chorus of Scáileanna. Liannan's hands clenched. *But even if she succeeds, Márrach's champion will not be daunted by the day. Tadhg! Saileach! Poets all! A rann to break Shadow's sword!*

At the Mothers' call, Ceallach hurried forward, passing Tadhg by in his haste to see the battle. To fight he had come, not to cower in this haunted wood while his Chieftain went warring without him. The Bear of An Clár was even now on Márrach's walls, and Ceallach left behind to swell the ranks of the Poets.

The Mothers gave his modest skills too much honor. 'Twas the Mór-Ríoghain's inspiration had blessed his words that had soothed Aedh Rí Mumhan's madness at the hedge. And last night, his own desperate fear had bidden him call on Brighde's Fire—happily would he have kept silent had a Poet of nobler fame been there to make a truer verse. What could he do that Tadhg of An Chluain Thiar or Saileach of Glas an Mhullaigh could not? Better were he on the field, his spear in hand—

At the edge of the trees, Ceallach stopped and looked with uneasy wonder at the narrow pale of death between the wood and Márrach's bald hill. Had the Queens not commanded his attention to Shadow's sword, still his eyes must have been drawn there, for the piteous screams that echoed around that weapon's dance rose above all other sounds of battle. When a shield was put before it, the terrible blade went through as if the shield, and not the sword were made of shadow. When it met another blade, the lesser shrieked at the touch of the dark elf's sword and trembled in its wielder's hand. And when the Scáil's blade found mortal flesh—

Slay/sword/Scáil—words aplenty sprang to Ceallach's mind, words ringing with sweet alliteration, words hung with meaning and power. None of them did he dare weave to a poem, for none were bright enough to shine on that hideous weapon.

"My skills are no match for a sword conjured from the Dead Lord's realm," protested Tadhg, echoing Ceallach's thoughts.

The younger Poet gave a glad shout, and his fair face lit with joy. "What matter? Cessair is there!"

He saw her clearly, for she had reined in her white steed, and now waited for the dark champion to turn and meet her. The Scáil wheeled with easy grace, his horse lifting his front hooves and pivoting smoothly. The fell sword in his hand separated like puffs of smoke, then drew together again into one long shadow.

Márrach's champion drove his heels into his mount's flanks, and the black horse leapt forward. Gathering himself at a word from Cessair, Fionn raced to meet them. It was magnificent, thought Ceallach, it was poetry. A lethal, black-and-gray wind gusting across the parched earth, a banner of white-gold and silver, rippling under the threatening skies—

Dark and Light swept together like a gale, and if the Scáil's weapon was a storm cloud, Cessair's silver blade was lightning. Dust rose about the horses' stamping hooves, entangling earth and air as the combatants engaged.

Fionn whinnied in protest as his rider pulled him away, but cantered easily up Márrach's hill to where a ragged line of corpses marked the castle's wall. There he turned, ready for his next charge. Márrach's champion galloped toward the woods, slowed his steed, and made a gentle circle until he faced his opponent once again. His horse was eager, but the Scáil held him back, and lifted his lidless eyes to the rampart Ceallach could not see.

Fionn's proud head nodded. He flew down the rise, his feet barely touching the ground. With an eerie cry, the Scáil spurred his horse, and lifted his sword high.

Was he so sure of his stroke, he scorned to keep his side guarded? She would have him, Ceallach exulted, she would have him now. The Scáil was a fool an' he believed Cessair of Cnoc an Eanaigh could miss so inviting a mark. She would cut the dark elf in two—

But Cessair looked away.

As Fionn bore her on to her meeting with Márrach's dark champion, Cessair's helmed head turned to look over her shoulder—her gaze seemed fixed on the empty air above and behind her. A chill snaked up Ceallach's back. Why did the Chieftain not ready her arm?

Cessair set her weight back in her saddle, slowing Fionn with her knees and reining in fiercely, but too late to avoid the Scáil's stroke. Fionn reared, and shifted to catch the blow.

More than mortal the elven steed had seemed to Ceallach. When he screamed, it was as if the Gods had cast out one of their own. The pure, white hide of his neck curled like a dry leaf's edges caught in fire. The exposed sinews of his neck showed red and smoking. Legs churning helplessly, Fionn fell to the ground and rolled on his side, bearing his rider with him. The Scáil's charge carried him on up the rise, but his hissing laugh flowed back down the hill.

Wails, shouts of despair filled Ceallach's ears. They turned to cheers as Cessair pulled herself from under her horse, unlaced her helm and shook loose her glorious hair.

Was everyone mad? Did no one mark, as Ceallach did, how Cessair threw off her gloves and felt along her horse's shaking whithers? Did no one understand why she stroked Fionn's silken mane without once looking down, why she stained her white fingers in the horse's blood before rising to slit his throat mercifully with her sword? Was Ceallach's heart alone wrung with pity, did he alone miss the star-bright fire of her eyes?

"On Cessair, brave Lady!" Tadhg shouted beside him. "Look where Márrach's champion returns!"

"Will you use her so?" Ceallach demanded, finding tongue at last. "Do you not understand that Cessair is blind?"

Sixty-six

Tears of gold the daystar wept
To leave the field that day.
Silver tears the moon let fall
And veiled her face in gray.
Two stars shone on Magh an Rí
Undimmed by clouded night
Two eyes with fame and glory filled,
With battle-joy alight.

The Host of Magh an Rí

Máchail gripped the gray stones until they cut into his flesh. His knees buckled, his vision dimmed. For a moment his exhaustion was so great he doubted his lungs had strength to draw breath or his heart to beat without some respite. With Scáthach's rann and his own adamant will he had blinded the glittering eyes of Cessair of Cnoc an Eanaigh—but it had nearly drained the life from his body to lay his curse on so mighty an adversary.

Strength returned, flowed back to him threefold as he watched Cessair groping sightless along her wounded horse's body, feeling for the place to strike. For once capricious fortune had seen fit to favor him—the rann he had used against her was an old one, a curse Scáthach had made weeks before when Máchail had desired to bring down Ciarán of Latharna. Pure luck it was the Name of Latharna's Chieftain alliterated with Cessair's own. Pure luck Máchail had a spell to fit the moment. Neither her enchanted mail nor her spelled sword could help Cessair now. The champion of Cnoc an Eanaigh was undone.

Márrach's master straightened and gazed over the rampart. The tidings of Cessair's misfortune were being carried from tongue to tongue, the misguided cheers of the Mothers' hosts fading on the shadow-heavy air. Cries of anger and hate, cries of hopeless denial filled Máchail's ears. Music it was to him—Éirinn's Death-Song.

"The Mighty," they called themselves, but Márrach's might humbled theirs. Against Márrach's spells, the Poets' ranna must prove meaningless, the Wizards' gifts unavailing. Under Márrach's shadow, the Kings were impotent, their blood powerless to waken the dead hill to flower. And from the Dead Lord's retribution, not even Éire could offer the Queens sanctuary. Had he feared his true Name on the Mothers' tongues? Their own they would shudder to hear him speak, when Scáthach's head was in his hands.

Patience was his again. Easily he would bide until the Gruagach's return, entertained in his vigil by the despairing litany of Éirinn's defeat and by the spectacle of Cessair's death at Urchóid's hand.

Cessair's blade had keened when it met the Scáil's, and since trembled in her hand. Now it lay steady and obedient in her grasp. Having bathed in Fionn's blood, Airgead was cleansed of fear. Cessair did not need to see with her eyes the crimson of Fionn's courage on her blade, the patterns of death and loyalty running in vivid streaks along its silver edge. Her heart beheld it, and found in the vision a gift of astonishing calm.

Like her sword, Cessair had trembled when struck by the Dark, when cruel words had burst from the shadowy air to rob her of her Sight. The rann had more than blinded her— it had stolen her awareness, her reason, almost her life. Awareness had returned, and reason as well. And 'twas Fionn had died. Cessair of Cnoc an Eanaigh stood living upon the earth, and Airgead was in her hand.

She breathed deeply, for the scent of battle was on the still air—horses' sweat, salt blood, piss, the stink of goblin, the cloying odor of fear. Deeply she listened, for the sounds of battle were in her ears—clashing metal, drumming hooves, trumpeting victory, the rattle of death. Shadows pressed coldly on her skin, but Cessair did not shiver. The taste of defeat was on her lips, but she did not drink the bitter draught. She waited to hear a single horse's coming, a thudding gallop, heavier on the forehooves than the back, for her foe would be riding downhill.

The sounds of horses crowding together came to her, the creak of leather harnesses, the bridles' ring, snorting and stamping. Her ears told her what her eyes could not— Scáileanna had surrounded her. With their mounts they were marking the arena where she was to die. With their gray swords they would keep help from her.

A laugh erupted from one of the encircling Scáileanna, hissing, contemptuous. Cessair waited for his victim's death cry—she would know then which of her folk had fallen. A gasp she heard, and then a moan, but the sounds came from no elven throat. One of Éire's people must have tried to reach her—one possessed of admirable courage, to have dared the ring.

Dying, the brave warrior called out. The voice was young, not a man's, but a boy's. He neither cried for mercy, nor cursed his murderer. Beyond hope or expectation, he began to recite a poem.

> *Called by battle, courage wakes,*
> *Fronts the foe with fearless joy.*
> *An' silver sword slays Fionn's bane,*
> *Sightless eyes will see again.*

Barely could he utter the last line, so hoarse and airless were his lungs, but even so, Cessair recognized the speaker. She called to Ceallach. There was no answer, and she knew the Poet of Tulach was dead.

A war-horn blew lusty and full. Battle's call, Cessair thought, sounding because Ceallach had spoken his rann with his dying breath, and its power was imperative. Her courage soared with the note, as the Poet had promised it would. She heard them now, the hoofbeats of her enemy's horse. She turned to face Márrach's champion, and smiling, lifted her bloodstained sword.

So far the verse had carried her, but for the rest, it was herself and her luck must realize Ceallach's rann. Cessair's smile became a laugh. Long or short a warrior might be, fair or dark, woman or man, but a great warrior was ever lucky, and was Cessair of Cnoc an Eanaigh not one of the greatest warriors ever to lift sword under Éirinn's skies?

Her hand stole to her belt to touch the shamrock Tréfhuilgne had given her at the gates of Brugh na Bóinne. Here was luck better than Sight. The Scáileanna hissed at the sound of her mirth, but Cessair's laughter rang out undiminished.

She knew the champion's distance—could she have come unscathed through so many battles and not be able to judge the nearness of the foe at her back? She waited until the last moment, then danced away from Fionn's still corpse. The rhythm of the pounding hooves hesitated—the Scáil had shifted his weight to redirect his mount, but she had made him ride too close to make the turn with much control.

Though Cessair knew her enemy's sword made no sound in lifting or falling, she was certain the Scáil held it high, believing her defenseless against him. Again she laughed, and not even the Dark that imprisoned her Sight could fetter the joy of it. To live was sweet, but to die no worse, an' she could die fighting.

"Come, then. Come," she whispered, confident the Scáil was near enough to hear her.

She imagined his smoky blade lifting a hand's breadth more, whipping down—

Boldly she leapt toward sounds of the charging Scáil, tossing her sword to her left hand as she moved in, and sweeping it up where the horse's chest must be. She sought the animal's heart, cutting deep, but struck bone. The close, hot scent of blood made her gasp like a lover.

Tugging her sword free, Cessair rushed toward the horse and threw herself against the wounded animal's shoulder. The chill of Shadow's blade caressed her armor, but she had not stopped moving, and only its cold wind touched her.

The dark weapon must have bit into the Scáil's own mount, for the horse screamed in Cessair's ear. He reared, and came down unsteadily, staggered, and reared again. A hoof grazed her arm as she grabbed for the Scáil's leg. On her next try Cessair closed her hand upon the dark elf's boot and pulled his foot from the stirrup.

The Scáil kicked her hard in the shoulder, but could not shake her loose. Surely Shadow's sword was lifting, surely arcing down to cleave her unhelmed head. Before the stroke could fall, Cessair released the Scáil's leg, tossed her sword from her left to her right hand, and drove it up with all her might.

Her goal was the soft spot under his arm where his leather vest was slit to allow his arm free play. Her blade struck solid metal—the studs protecting his ribs, doubtless—but the force of her blow was wicked. She heard a hiss of pain, and her sword lost contact with the Scáil as he pitched in his saddle.

The champion's careening weight was an impossible burden for his wounded mount. Unbalanced, the horse fell to the ground, wild with pain. Between the hissing of the dark elves, the horse's death throes, and the war cries of Cnoc an Eanaigh all filling her ears, Cessair could not hear if her foe was pinned beneath his steed or thrown from him.

Daring the horse's thrashing hooves, Cessair leapt over the animal, and luck again was hers. Her opponent had been thrown, and was just now rising. His movements were too soft to betray him, but the Scáil incautiously drew a sharp breath as he hurried to his feet. To Cessair the sound was clear as a call.

She approached with her own blade whirling, left then right, high and low, a shield of red and silver before her. Were Márrach's champion wise, he would defend awhile, and attack when she tired. Cessair laughed to drive the Scáil's wisdom from him.

"Gray-skinned lackey to a mortal fool," she taunted. "None so blind as cannot See your disgrace!"

More she would have said, but this was enough to draw his blade. He struck from the side, swift and sudden. Cessair's ceaselessly moving sword caught its edge. It was all she needed.

Turning to front him, she parried again and moved to attack, aiming a two-handed blow at the Scáil's head. He stopped her blade with his own, but so had she wished him to do. She had him in arm's reach.

Cessair's right hand left her hilt, her fist swept back-handed hard and heavy across the Scáil's jaw. Her leg snaked between his feet. She kicked side and back, and her enemy was falling.

In an instant she was on top of him, seeking his sword arm. The Scáil heaved under her, fighting her weight and the weight of her armor to lift himself. A chill breeze from Shadow's realm stroked Cessair's skin, the forerunner of the dread sword.

Shivering, she reached her hand out toward the cold wind, and closed her fingers upon the Scáil's wrist. For an instant she threw all of her strength into forcing his sword arm down, then set her boot on it, pinning Shadow's blade to the ground. His other limb she stilled by jabbing with Airgead until it slipped into the joint that hinged his shoulder to his arm, severing his ability to lift it. Swiftly she stood, freed her sword, and thrust the point so deeply into the champion's neck, the hard earth swallowed half the blade.

At first she mistook the golden splendor that filled her for battle's glory. When she knew it for the daystar's glad light, she gazed full upon it, and when she looked away, Cessair's eyes were shining brighter than the sun above.

The certainty that the Hunter's soul was yet unbroken struck Máchail in the same moment as the sun's unblinking eye.

He had believed that when the Spear had snapped, so had the Hunter been destroyed. He had believed that with the Hunt in ruins, Éirinn must fall. He had believed the Dark already the victor, had believed Fate Herself would drive Light from the field.

Plainly he saw his folly. 'Twas Shadow's triumph was assured, not Márrach's. Neither on an ash haft, nor a silver spearhead had Éire's geis fallen, but upon a man's soul. Nothing save time or death would break it.

Máchail's anger cast a shadow in his cold blue eyes. Would he lose this battle because Éire refused to admit defeat? Because She jealously clung to Her last miserable moments as if She might yet prevail? What matter that Bealtaine's sun had not yet risen? What matter that the Hunter yet drew breath? Fools the Gods were, fools the mortals that warred below. Not for hope, but for false hope they fought, for false hope risked life and more than life to bring him down.

"He will never Hunt the Light," he shouted to the bright sky, "never bring the spoils of the Hunt back to Éire. His geis can never be fulfilled!"

Máchail's words were like a child's, full of vehemence, empty of influence. The truth in them did not darken the skies, nor raise his white-eyed champion from Márrach's hill. The shackles were gone from Cessair's Sight, the shadows from Feargna Óg's path, and still the Gruagach was not come.

The curse against Cessair had sapped his will, but Máchail fed it again with bitterness and hate, and bent it upon the Shadow King's sword. By the time he had conjured the weapon to his hand he was pale and shaking. The grim sword steadied him. He hurried down the unshaded stairs and made his way across the sunlit close, and his thoughts were arrows of darkness.

In his sanctum was Scáthach's head. In his sanctum the black moonstone gravid with the spells that guarded the broch. From the one he would wring a poem that his Name could not wound him. The other he would conjure to Shadow's realm. Though the foe might gain the wall, over-run the close, even force the gate and take the gatehouse, yet the Queens' magics would never breach Márrach's tower while the moonstone endured. And who was there bold enough to wrest the gem from the Dead Lord's hand?

That he would find the Hunter in his sanctum as well, Máchail never doubted. There could be but one reason for the Gruagach's poor service.

The Hunter he would kill. Éirinn's spurious hope would die with Conall mac na Caillí, and die this day, not weeks hence on summer's morn. What need had Máchail to wait for time, when he held Death's Shadow in his hand?

Sixty-seven

*'Tis death to mock a Poet,
to love a Poet, to be a Poet*

The Third Triad of Éirinn

Returning life hurt Blackthorn more than his retreating death. All he could think was to get away now the Gruagach's hand had released him. All he could manage was to cough on the unexpected air his lungs took in and to curse his limbs for refusing to obey his will.

As the darkness lifted from his sight, he saw the wolf was no longer flying through the air, but was fastened on the Gruagach's back. His pale eyes sparkled like cracked ice, and his sharp fangs were invisible, sunk in the Gruagach's black shoulder.

Bowing his spine and twisting toward his new attacker, the Gruagach grasped the wolf by his coat. Blood beaded up under the monster's nails as they dug into the wolf's silver-gray fur. The animal's jaws stayed tightly shut, and he rumbled deep in his chest. The Gruagach pulled harder, tearing his assailant from him. The wolf's teeth ripped through the Gruagach's shoulder, and he howled, his voice clear and unafraid. Roaring with pain and outrage, the Gruagach hurled his tormentor across the room. The wolf yelped as he struck the solid stone of the sanctum wall, then slid to the floor without a sound.

The Gruagach was already lunging for Blackthorn, but life was again pumping though the Hunter's veins, his stiff muscles at last responding to his fierce commands. As he shoved himself back and away from the grasping paws, a bolt of sunlight plunged through the open thatch and fell upon the Gruagach's face. The beast froze in the beam, half-standing, half-kneeling at the lip of the ragged hole, his good eye closed against the brightness.

Blackthorn wanted to leap at his enemy as the wolf had leapt, to strike him as the sun-spike had struck. His limbs were leaden, his movements sluggish as a drunken man's. The Gruagach's eye was already open when Blackthorn's boot caught him under the chin. The beast fell back, arms flailing, his body teetering on the edge of the gap. With a violent effort the Gruagach threw himself forward, landing on his belly. His legs slid down into the hole and dangled on the empty air, but his powerful paws grabbed hold of the protruding floorboards. Digging his nails into the uneven wood, he started to pull himself up into the sanctum.

Lying nearly flat on the sloping floor, Blackthorn kicked again, this time finding the Gruagach's blind eye. The beast grunted, but his paw flew up to capture Blackthorn's leg, risking the fall, if he could take his enemy with him. His bloodied claws scraped along Blackthorn's leather boot as the Hunter's leg drove past the clutching fingers and his heel rammed into the Gruagach's wounded shoulder.

As a hand pulls instinctively from fire, as muscles shiver in the cold, so did the Gruagach's claws loose from the splintered floorboard, unbidden, unwilled. His arms and legs raked the air as he fell, but his nails could not catch on the sunlight. The bell's death had been more glorious. No pealing song, but only a mad howl came from the Gruagach's throat as he hurtled to the ground, and when he struck the hard earth, only a small, dingy cloud of dust rose about his suddenly still form.

Blackthorn gave no thought to the Gruagach's dead body on the courtyard floor, or the tale it would tell. The magpie called earnestly, but for once he gave her no ear. He clambered laboriously to steady ground and hurried to where the wolf had fallen.

Reathach sat slumped against the gray stone wall, his eyes

closed, his limbs flaccid. He looked for all the world like a child lost in lazy slumber, but his lids fluttered open when Blackthorn's arm stole gently under his shoulders. His head lolled at an impossible angle as Blackthorn brought him upright. A smear of bright blood colored the gray stone where his head had rested.

"She told me, she did," Reathach said, soft as a sigh. "She said I'd find me courage by the shores of Loch Dearg, but 'twas yourself I found, and thought she'd spoken me false. But sure, an' wasn't it the truth all along? No more a mouse . . ."

Grief stung Blackthorn's eyes and tightened his throat. "What were you thinking, bodach, to follow me here? And what of the oath you swore—"

"I swore to leave when me geis was fulfilled," the púca retorted. "I never said I'd not come back again." The effort of speaking stole the impudence from his reply. "And where would the Hunter of Éirinn be now, I'm sayin', an' I—"

Too many words, carrying his life away as they left his lips.

"Killed I'd be, entirely, I'll not deny," Blackthorn agreed, "had my Death not turned and fled before your fierce courage. And wasn't it yourself destroyed the Gruagach? Not the greatest coward, but the boldest champion of the five kingdoms is Reathach the púca, and so the songs will tell."

A corner of Reathach's mouth twitched to a smile. "Another of the Bards' lyin' tales, folk will say . . ."

Blackthorn bent close to hear.

"No more . . ." the púca whispered. "No more a mouse, but a wolf am I . . . and will be . . . for . . ."

His last breath gone, Reathach's last words went unspoken.

"Forever and aye," Blackthorn finished quietly.

It wasn't true, what he had told the little man. His Death had not fled, only retreated a little way, and was even now returning—His step was on the stair. Yet, of all the lies to which Blackthorn had given tongue, 'twas this small deceit he least regretted.

"You were a fool to follow me," he said simply, speaking the truth now Reathach could no longer hear.

"And you a fool twice over to have come to Márrach at all."

Blackthorn wondered that Máchail had not yet raised his sword. Surely neither honor, nor pity, nor respect for the dead would give Márrach's master pause. Pleasure it must be, pleasure taken in another's sorrow had delayed Máchail's hand.

Now the sword was lifting. The beryls on his enemy's glove glinted in the sun, but day's light shunned the dark blade, and left its shadow intact. Máchail came on slowly, in a line with the stair, expecting his foe would attempt to escape. Ever a poor hunter, Blackthorn thought. He believes he stalks the timid deer, but I the stag to him.

He came to his feet already running. Pain scored his side with every step, but he had not far to go. As Shadow's sword swung hurriedly down, Blackthorn ducked under Máchail's stroke, caught his enemy's wrist, and forced it high. His charge carried them both to the wall. He smashed Máchail's sword arm against the gray rock, ground it on the wall, scraping his own knuckles raw. The gemstones cracked, but his enemy's clenched fingers did not open. Máchail balled his other hand into a fist and drove it into Blackthorn's sore ribs. Together they slammed into the beechwood chest, knocking over the blood-filled pot at its edge. The falling bowl threw a splay of red across the floor, and rang as it hit the ground and rolled.

A black frost of pure hatred rose to cover the blue of Máchail's gaze. An unnatural strength hardened his arm to iron. Blackthorn let go his hold before Máchail could break it, and backed quickly, barely avoiding the silent sweep of Shadow's blade. Turning, he sped for the unguarded stair. His step faltered on the blood-smeared floor, and Máchail was there before him.

Snatching up a wand from the wall, shorter by half than the one the Gruagach had used against him, Blackthorn caught Máchail's first cut upon it. He nearly died then. Shadow's sword went through the piece of wood like a knife through butter, missing his chest by a hair's breadth. He stumbled back, and would have fallen but for the wall. Two wands remained, but even could he reach them, they would be no use against the deadly shadow in his enemy's hand. There was nothing left him but to despair and die. If Máchail's smile had not evinced the same thought, he might have accepted his fate with greater grace.

"Would I had my blackthorn in my hand," he swore.

Ribbons of notes rolled from the magpie's tongue and rippled in the air.

"Be still, old Hag!"

Máchail's command boomed against the tower's stones, but he never shifted his gaze from Blackthorn, and his sword was already raised. What though the magpie sang—an' he could not silence the bird, he would silence the Hunter who had made her sing, and before his desire could be granted.

Máchail's stroke was deadly. Even as it fell, the Wish-Bringer's spell burst into substance and weight in Blackthorn's hand, and Strife there to meet the descending blade.

Máchail aimed another cut. Again Blackthorn parried, and again, each time deflecting Shadow's sword from his flesh. The pale glimmer of light that ran along Strife's edges sparked when it met Máchail's blade. Blackthorn's smile gleamed as the light of his sword blazed brighter.

Máchail's attacks became more deliberate, more savage. Bronze and iron had shattered under the Dead Lord's sword. Even silver Airgead had wailed in pain. He would not suffer this black blade to be silent, but hear her cry as she broke in brittle pieces under his blows.

"Your hope is ill-fated." Máchail filled his voice with assurance and made his words a promise.

He feinted at the wound in Blackthorn's shoulder. A wariness crept into the Hunter's eyes, and his smile tightened. Máchail feinted again, making as if to swing the flat of his blade at the Hunter's side, and was rewarded by Blackthorn's quick move to guard.

"Your wounds will betray you."

Blackthorn spat to ward off Máchail's curse. As his head turned, the master of Márrach lunged, aiming a cut to the Hunter's chest. Blackthorn countered quickly, beat soundlessly on Máchail's smoke-cloud of a blade. Máchail shifted to parry in turn, but instead of attacking, the Hunter turned tail, and ran.

Only a moment, two at most, did Máchail stand easy, enjoying his enemy's flight. Then he saw the Hunter's intent. His pleasure was gone and fury in its place, but still he stood unmoving. The Hunter could not possibly succeed.

Blackthorn slid down the sloping floor toward the open hole in its center, his sight fixed on the fall before him. At the last moment he jumped, tearing his gaze from the deep, sun-filled shaft and forcing his eyes up to the magpie's suspended cage. Midair he spun, his arm swinging. As Strife cut through the bars of the cage, the wickerwork base broke cleanly away, and dropped through the hole in the floor.

Blackthorn's momentum carried him across the gap, but he landed heavily. The boards groaned and bent under his weight. He started to slip down the canted floor.

"Fly, Róisín," he heard Máchail cry. "Fly back to your pools. For all your wishes, my curse is unbroken. Come Bealtaine the Hag you will be evermore."

He jabbed Strife's point into the wooden floor. The first board he tried creaked and split apart. The second held his blade, and he began to haul himself up.

A hiss more dreadful than any Scáil's brought Blackthorn's head whipping around. He saw Máchail racing to where the magpie was perched on a pile of cups, torques, daggers—

Like white veins on black marble, cracks had appeared on the pillar of shadow that had held Máchail's treasures. The cracks were multiplying, widening, and the sorcerer's hoard spilling out upon the floor. Every moment added fresh trinkets to the mound, but the magpie came up almost at once with a small, dark stone in her beak.

Again the hiss of voiceless rage erupted from Máchail's throat. He was nearly upon his tiny foe, but wings are ever swifter than legs, and the magpie's beat furiously toward the sky. In less than a moment she was through the opening in the roof and had disappeared from sight.

Máchail did not look where the bird had flown, but turned on Blackthorn. All Shadow's dark fury fell with his gaze. Cloaked in hatred, shielded by spite, armed with the Dead Lord's own sword, he stood before Blackthorn as the Shadow King's champion. Máchail's shadow fell upon the Hunter where he lay clinging to Strife, and the darkness was not his own, but his God's, palpable and deadly cold. Struggling against the numbing chill, Blackthorn pulled himself higher, freed his sword from the floor, and staggered to his feet.

Máchail came for him, his smile perfect, his blue eyes

impossibly black. He was on him in an instant, his evil blade hammering down on Strife's, and the weight of the Dark was behind his stroke. It made no difference that Blackthorn wanted to stand steady, that he willed his arm to lift and return the blow. The best he could manage was to ward off the relentless shadow in Máchail's hand.

He blocked a cut to his hurt side, then another low to his thigh. Máchail swung two-handed at his neck, and Strife was barely in time to keep Blackthorn's head on his shoulders.

Máchail did not disengage, but pressed harder, forcing Blackthorn back against the cold stones of the wall. The wavering edge of Máchail's blade was only Strife's width from Blackthorn's eyes—he had no way to stop Máchail's fist driving under the swords and pounding into his gut.

He fell, keeping hold of Strife, but unable to raise her against Máchail's next blow. Shadow's sword passed him like a cold wind as he threw himself to the side. The fell blade bit deep into the tower wall. Wood, leather, iron, the Dead Lord's sword would cleave, but Márrach's stones were covered in shadow, and they clung to their own.

Blackthorn came to his knees. He doubted it was worth the effort to try to crawl away, but he crawled anyway, through a puddle of blood, while his enemy fought to free his weapon. He stopped when he found himself staring into Scáthach's green eyes.

His lover's fair cheeks had faded to peeling tatters of gray. Her flaxen hair was matted and browned with dried blood. Death had blackened her lips, but Scáthach's eyes were the color of the sea, and their beauty as deep.

"Máchail is his Name," Blackthorn whispered, so softly only Scáthach could hear. "The right words, mo mhúirnín. They mean everything now, and you promised me."

His sword free, Máchail whirled to find the Hunter's back to him, and he on his knees not five paces away. The fool wasn't moving, wasn't even trying to get away. He was beaten—he feared to look on his death.

Máchail came up silently behind him. His sword was silent too, silent to rise, silent in its descent, yet Blackthorn suddenly lunged away, as if he had heard his death coming. Too late Máchail saw the Poet of Teach an Fhásaigh's head lying on the ground where his stroke must fall. Though he

did his best to turn his blade, his errant blow grazed
Scáthach's cheek.

At the touch of Shadow's sword, Scáthach's hair shriveled
to ash. Her eyes sank away and disappeared into empty sockets. Her decaying flesh withered to thin, curling flakes of
skin, laying bare the white bones beneath.

Máchail followed the Poet's eyeless gaze. Shadow's hissing
rage again poured from his throat. The grinning skull was
turned toward the Hunter, and he standing ready, and grinning savagely back.

Máchail's thrust came quick and bold. Blackthorn's return
was quicker still and forced Máchail to retreat. The sorcerer's
black eyes narrowed, his head lifted like a dog's when he scents
danger. This was not the same enemy a single blow had sent
sprawling to the floor but moments ago. He tested Blackthorn's
confidence with a quick cut to the head, and found himself
falling back yet again. His feet nearly stumbled over a bony
corpse—Máchail spat and kicked the lifeless body out of his way.

Dark anger flamed in Blackthorn's eyes. Cold fear
Máchail would like better to see, and he possessed the means
to call it forth.

"Had I your sword's Name, I would break it." Máchail
smoothed his voice to silk. "As I have only yours, Conall
mac na Caillí, my curse will fall on you."

The Hunter didn't flinch, as Máchail hoped, or even
frown. He laughed.

"You have nothing," Blackthorn answered him. "Not
Conall mac na Caillí, but Vengeance is my Name. Call upon
me, if you dare."

Had his enemy's laugh been bitter or despairing, Máchail
would have relished the sound. The Hunter's laugh was rich
with the triumph Máchail had promised himself, and that he
could not bear.

He attacked, his blows rapid, vicious, precise. With the
Hunter's death he would drive away the glaring doubts that
flamed in his heart. The smallest cut would be enough.

Not a single stroke could he get past the Hunter's guard,
rather the threat of the black sword had him steadily backing. When the Hunter began to chant, his voice keeping
time to the dance of swords, fear's blinding light fell full
upon Máchail's soul.

For each mother's tear Máchail made fall
For each mother's heart Máchail made sore
Ten thousand drops of his unredeemed blood
Shall weep o'er the Hunter's white-edged blade.

When the curse was cast, Blackthorn swung his sword in a whistling arc about him, then drove it down at Máchail's head. So swift his stroke, the white light of Strife's edges could not keep up with the blade, but hung upon the air. Shadow's sword rose to guard. At their meeting, Strife spoke at last. Not a wail, or a moan, but a glad shout she gave, as if all the souls that craved revenge on Márrach's master were crying out upon the blade.

Strife passed through the Dead Lord's sword as if it were no more than an empty shadow, entered Máchail's skull, and drove clear to his heart. A fount of blood gushed from the ruin of Máchail's body, staining the white fire of Strife's edges red.

His enemy was falling before Blackthorn had pulled his sword free. By the time the corpse struck the ground, Máchail's gloved hand was empty. Shadow's sword drifted upon the bright air in wisps of gray smoke, and gradually dwindled to nothing.

In death, Máchail's eyes did not return to their natal blue, but whitened, like a Scáil's. Blackthorn watched them pale, the wine of victory growing sour in his mouth. He had his vengeance, but neither his Spear, nor the woman he loved, nor even a friend to keep him company in his sorrow. He turned away from his enemy's corpse and walked slowly to where the púca's lay crumpled in the sands.

At first he doubted his arms would hold Reathach. Even Strife, that had always given strength to his limbs, weighed heavy in his hand. He could not wish himself stronger—the magpie was long gone—but when he stooped to lift the púca, he found his friend no more burden than a husk autumn's winds had emptied of summer's fruit. Only birds whose bones were hollow were so light in death as Reathach was, only the mists were so pale.

He had barely begun to descend when thunder shook the tower. A rain of thatch tumbled from the roof, the wooden floor rattled. Even the stone steps under his feet trembled.

He had gained the next landing when the thunder rolled

again. This time Blackthorn heard sense in it, and knew it for the Wizard Reochaidh's voice.

"Márrach!" he heard the giant bellow.

The broch groaned in reply. Cracks appeared in the steps under Blackthorn's feet, and in the tower's stones. Spears of light shot through the widening gaps in the wall. He staggered, clasping the púca tighter to him, but his arms were empty. A white mist clung briefly to his bloodstained hands and twined lightly about Strife's blade, then vanished entirely. The stones on his left, those forming part of the broch's inner wall, cracked and fell in toward the courtyard. Blackthorn ran for his life.

The stairs shifted under him. His torn shoulder scraped against the wall before he caught his balance and raced on. As he reached the level of the windows, the tower rocked again. Hope failed him. Even were he not hurt, he'd likely lose this race with Reochaidh's voice. Wounded as he was, he would never win clear of the broch before it fell.

With an agonized grating of rock against rock, large rifts appeared in the roof over his head. A shower of coarse, gray powder fell from the cracks. Blackthorn was already racing for the next flight of stairs. His foot on the topmost step, the tower shook again, tumbling him into darkness. Jagged slabs of stone crashed down from the roof, sealing off the light from above.

He rose slowly, painfully to his feet. Finding Strife by her light, he placed the little courage he had left on the faintly gleaming edge of his sword, and forced his legs on through the shuddering, unrelieved dark.

Reochaidh shouted again. The giant's voice rumbled cruelly against Blackthorn's bones, and a crazed web of golden light appeared on the outer wall. With unhurried grace, the whole edifice broke away from the stairs. Blackthorn had a glimpse of the close before he fell, a sunlit yard teeming with dark panic. Then the stairs crumbled beneath him, and he dropped, a pale, bloody stone plummeting with his gray companions to the hard earth far below.

Sixty-eight

*The gates of death open as wide for the reluctant soul
as for the willing*

Sayings of the Mothers

Meacán peered through the trees and out upon the sunlit battlefield.

We must be winning now, she thought. *We must. The storm is banished, the dark champion slain. The goblins' eyes are wounded by the sun, and the Scáileanna are daunted by the Kings' bright swords.*

But Márrach stands yet unseen, Liannan spoke in her mind, *and so unconquered.*

Meacán squinted at the bright, bare mound, trying to imagine the walls she knew were there. The rampart defied her sight, but she clearly saw a speck in the sky above the hill. The mote grew, sprouted wings, and became a magpie winging toward the woods.

"Look to the skies," she said hoarsely to Fionnghuala.

To her surprise, the Deceiver not only looked up, but leapt to her feet.

"'Look to the skies,'" Fionnghuala repeated wildly. "What mean you, Meacán? The Oak Seer said the same as yourself, but I, not understanding—"

Over their heads the magpie flew, so low Meacán could

hear her feathers beat upon the air. Something dark dropped
from her beak, and the bird called out boldly. Meacán pulled
away—the creature was from Márrach, and what but evil
could come from those shadows?—but Fionnghuala quickly
reached out to catch the bird's present. It fell into her hand,
a round, dark stone. Still calling, the magpie darted up
through the empty branches of the trees and circled back
toward the barren hill.

"What is it?" Meacán whispered.

For her answer, Fionnghuala opened her fist and showed
Meacán a large black gemstone. The Deceiver tossed it high,
and began tapping her fingers against each other, weaving a
net of fire and light in the air before the stone could return
to her hand. Into the web the black stone dropped, and the
strands of flickering runes held it fast. Swiftly Fionnghuala
spun new threads to bind it. As she worked, shadows blacker
than the stone's own hue began to play on the gem's surface.

"Och!" she cried. "A Name, Mothers! Had I a Name, now
could I rend Márrach's veil for you!"

Feargna Óg's ghost, a flicker of white wafting through the
trees, caught the corner of Meacán's eye. No more substantial
than a straggling cloud of mist lingering under the beeches,
the wraith skimmed over the ground toward the Necromancer, raising the hairs on Meacán's arm and the back of her
neck. Briefly the ghost enveloped Feargna Óg's body, then
seemed to sink into him. When it was only himself standing
there, Feargna Óg took a dizzy step toward Meacán and
Fionnghuala.

"Máchail!" he cried. "Not Mac Ailch. His Name is
Máchail!"

Máchail.

The Mothers spoke the Name for all to hear. Feargna Óg's
face flushed with pride and elation.

By the time the Queens reached the grove, Fionnghuala's
hands were busier still, plucking light from the air and twining it into new patterns. Runes she cast in glittering lines,
each a letter of the false hunter's Name.

"Did I not say a spell of illusion masks Márrach's walls?"
Fionnghuala said softly. "To this stone it is bound, by his
Name, and with that Name will I break it."

One after the other the streaks of light flew from her fingertips to the stone. When the last rune reached its goal, slivered shadows of gray and black burst from the jewel. They caught in the Deceiver's coruscating web, and burned.

Clapping her hands, Fionnghuala banished her work. The blazing runes vanished, and the stone dropped into her waiting palm. Lifting her hand, she displayed what she held. In her fingers was a marbled jewel, a tiny, milk-white world, overrun with black rivers.

On Márrach's once-empty hill, Shadow's stronghold stood revealed for all to see. The Mothers' armies stared amazed, or shouted their astonishment at what their eyes beheld.

"One spell I have broken, Mothers," said Fionnghuala, handing the magpie's gift to Liannan. "Many more does the spell-stone yet hold, their shadows beyond my powers to affect."

But not beyond ours, Bochna assured her.

Softly at first, the Queens began to chant in wordless harmony. Their voices grew louder, swelling with determination. The Poets drew near, Tadhg of An Chluain Thiar and Saileach of Glas an Mhullaigh, and though neither spoke aloud, the Mothers' chant became a song.

The leafless arms of the beeches creaked as if a wind were stirring them. No wind, Meacán knew, but the rann on the Mothers' lips, borne into the world by the air that was Éire's breath, the rann was making the trees rattle. When one verse was done, the Queens began another, and when the second had ended, they gave their voices to a third. For every poem the Mothers spelled, a dark shadow on the stone faded and disappeared.

At last Liannan held up the stone and laughed. A pure white moonstone glistened in her hand.

Neither sight, nor rann, nor Wizard's craft can Márrach's walls now daunt! she rejoiced, and Magadh called silently, *Reochaidh!*

The Destroyer stood apart from them, at the edge of the forest, watching the battle. When he spoke, he might have been shouting in Meacán's ear.

"Márrach!" he thundered.

The warriors on the field bent before the power of his voice. Márrach's heavy gate flew open, as if in welcome. Like a fortress built of sand, Márrach's walls began to crumble.

"Márrach!" he roared again.

The great tower shook under the blows of Reochaidh's voice. I should be glad to watch it fall, Meacán thought. I should be glad to hear the Scáileanna wailing and the goblins howling, the sound of Shadow's defeat.

The stones of the broch's outer wall shattered and fell. Huge clouds of gray dust rose over what was left of the gatehouse and rampart. I am glad, Meacán insisted to herself, but turned away. The battle won, and in all the war what had the Dancer done? Wandered lost in Shadow's realm, and returned with a useless Name on her lips. A poor Priestess she had made in the ring of fire, and here stood aside from the battle, watching helpless while others fought and died.

Meacán wandered far from the grove, deep into the trees. She came to a large granite boulder standing in the midst of a tiny patch of day, warming in a broad sheet of sunlight. It was moss-covered, though all else in the forest was bare, and riddled with inviting nooks and crannies. With a long sigh, Meacán sat down and curled her weary bones into a comforting curve of stone.

"I told her to let the rains fall," the boulder said.

Meacán threw herself away from the rock, tripped on her skirt, and fell awkwardly in the dust.

"Shall she fly to Loch nEathach for a mouthful of water?" the mottled stone went on.

A black-and-white shadow flickered in the air over the Dancer's head. 'Twas the magpie come again. As the bird flew to the stone, the boulder stretched and rose. Granite softened to flesh, and then it was no more a rock, but Úna.

The Oak Seer's face was younger than Meacán had ever seen it. The buds were opening on her skirt, young shoots of woodbine wound through her tangled black hair, her staff had sprouted dark oak leaves. Perched on the Oak Seer's shoulder, the magpie sang a tale so passionate, so full, Meacán wondered that such a raucous singer could bring forth such riches.

The bird fell silent, and Úna nodded sadly. Without warning, the Seer swooped down on Meacán like a kingfisher, grabbed the Dancer's wrists, and turned her palms to the sky.

"Don't you wish these hands held water?" she demanded.

Meacán pulled away from Úna's vehemence, shaking her head in confusion. Úna piped like a wren's impatient nestling—urgent, hungry, pleading.

"Hurry. Hurry. Seamair has failed him. Death stops his tongue. Wish, that the Hunter may drink."

"The Hunter?" Meacán fought to understand the Oak Seer's hopelessly tangled words. "What, has Seamair seen Blackthorn?"

"Don't you wish these hands held water?" Úna snarled, gripping Meacán's wrists even tighter.

"Yes!" Meacán snarled back. "As you will! I wish these hands held water!"

The magpie's voice soared, dipped, floated a moment on a bright, high note.

Meacán stared at her cupped hands. Clear, cold water ran over her palms and splashed onto the dusty earth. The magpie dropped from Úna's shoulder to Meacán's wrist, dipped her head once to drink, and darted away through the trees.

"Hurry, you silly goose!" Úna's voice was like the slap of rain on stone. "Hurry, or you'll lose her!"

What was the point of doubting and delaying? Why try to make sense of the Oak Seer's words? Not the mind, but the heart understands the wild, and Meacán's heart for once was wise. For once, and at last, the Dancer did not contest Úna's will.

The magpie was nearly out of sight, and Meacán would soon be without a holdfast. Still, she had danced in the wind a dozen times, and knew the trick. Not her limbs, which never could beat like a bird's wings, nor yet her heavy, earth-bound bones would carry her up. Her thoughts must dance, her hopes must lift her to the heavens. No matter that her heart fluttered fearfully. Creatures of the air were often afraid, but flew none the worse for that. And though she was unsure of her destination, Meacán could now see her path through the trackless sky—on the magpie's black-and-white tail she danced, over Márrach's broken battlement to the ruin of its tower.

The Mothers' host poured through the breach in Márrach's wall and into the close. Bitter the fighting under the sun,

and deep the shadows cast by the walls still standing, deep
enough to hide the Scáileanna and shield the goblins from
the day. It was not an inviting place to Meacán's eyes, but
the magpie dove unhesitatingly into the heart of the gory
confusion and alit on a twisted corpse lying among the
tower's stones.

The sight of her brother's mangled body cast a cold
shadow over Meacán's heart, robbing her dance of flight.
She fell to the ground with jarring speed, caught her balance, and started to run to him, shouting and waving her
arms to frighten away the bird who had perched on his
shoulder. A magpie was but a crow, after all, a battlefield
scavenger in black-and-white plumage.

Hearing the magpie's song, Meacán fell silent and slowed
her step. Not harsh as the scaldcrow's, but gentle as the dove's
was the bird's voice, calling so patiently. Tears welled up in
Meacán's eyes as she climbed over the sharp edged rocks to
reach Blackthorn, but curses were on her tongue. Not for
Márrach, or even Máchail. Meacán cursed Úna, for it was
plain the Oak Seer had sent her too late to her brother's side.

For all the pain that was his in his moments of clarity,
Blackthorn could have laughed at the foolish game Death
and his geasa were playing with him. The fall should have
killed him—when he struck the unyielding earth, his soul
had tried to flee the wreckage of his body and hurl itself into
Death's dark abyss. Straight and true he had dropped into
oblivion, a spider on a string, but like impish children, his
geasa had caught at his thread, yanking him back to pain-
wracked life. As often as he surrendered to the numbing
dark, his unfulfilled bonds cruelly hoisted him back to sensi-
bility. They must soon tire of the game, he thought, feeling
Death tug at him once more. It was only a sack of broken
bones they toyed with, after all.

When next he was hauled awake, soft feathers were
caressing his cheek. Even could Róisín have granted so considerable a desire, Blackthorn found he could not wish for
healing. His mouth wouldn't work, or his jaw open. Breath
came barely in and cut like a knife as it left him. He tried a
simpler word, a smaller favor. He tried to force his lips

around the word "water," but as he was dragged down to unconsciousness once more, he doubted he had made any sound at all.

The next time he rose to awareness, he was certain it would be his last. He had only roused because his geis to Róisín was chirping as an insistent magpie in his ear, and he could not deny her. Gently, painfully, the magpie's beak tapped the corner of his broken mouth, and a single drop of water fell on Blackthorn's tongue.

With all the will left him, Blackthorn struggled to summon the star's last power, to call upon Water. If his efforts to speak brought forth even a moan, his own ears could not hear it. And yet, as the silken strand that held him to life finally broke and Death drew him unresisting into His embrace, the drop on Blackthorn's tongue burst into a sweetness to ameliorate the salt taste of his blood, a sweetness to rival the nectar of Róisín's kiss. In all the world only the water of life could be so sweet, or death's honeyed poison.

As Meacán came near enough to touch her hand to Blackthorn's broken body, a star of throbbing blue blazed at his throat, a blue so pure the heavens might envy it. The light lingered while she wiped her eyes with her hands, lingered while she blinked and stared, lingered while she reached a tentative finger to the brilliant sapphire star. She had barely touched it when the blue flamed to white. Then the light was gone, and all that remained was a tarnished silver pentacle upon a blood-caked chain. She watched the tiny star lift slightly as Blackthorn drew a small breath, and lower again as his air slipped silently away.

Three times Meacán watched the tarnished silver rise and fall before her disbelief swelled into hope. It was more than that Blackthorn breathed. The terrible, impossible angles of his fractured legs were slowly righting into natural lines. His head rolled as his neck shifted to align with his spine, the protruding bones of his arm knit together and lay smooth under the skin. Seeing his other arm caught, Meacán struggled to shift a gray stone from Blackthorn's hand, and when she succeeded, watched his crushed fingers straighten and the cuts on them close.

"Conall," she whispered.

Kneeling beside him, she lifted his head to her lap, startling the magpie to a nearby stone.

"Conall," she called again.

His flesh was cold, his skin ghastly pale, the pulse of his heart too fragile to be the rhythm of a man's life. She wondered that it beat at all. So little of his life's blood was left in his body—it was all spilled on the stones. The magpie sang out, but Meacán shook her head.

"Can he have but a moment left in life?" she asked the bird.

Horse's hooves clattered on the hard stones. Meacán looked quickly to judge if it was friend or foe, and beheld a black steed nearing. Her throat constricted with fear until she saw the horse was riderless, and his bridle was of elven silver. I am a fool, she thought. I imagine evil in every dark thing.

"Eocha!" she called.

He came close and, bending his head low, gently nuzzled Blackthorn's neck. Tears rose again in Meacán's eyes, but when she spoke her voice was steady.

"Will you bear us to Úna?" she asked.

Eocha knelt at once on the sharp stones, but Blackthorn was as heavy as a dead man. Every moment Meacán struggled to get him across Eocha's saddle seemed an eternity to her, and a thousand more passing before she was up behind her brother and riding for Márrach's fallen wall.

She found the Oak Seer not where she had left her, but on the greensward where the Kings Aedh and Eoghan had died, under a shady oak. Flowers filled the tree's spreading branches, dancing in the wind that rustled like careless laughter among the leaves.

Sixty-nine

One for Sorrow, Two for Joy
Three to Marry, Four to Die
Five for Silver, Six for Gold
Seven for the Secret Never to be Told

a rhyme for counting magpies

The longest road out is the shortest road home. So the Mothers often said, but Blackthorn did not find it to be true. Long and difficult his journey to the gates of Death. Longer still the way back.

Mostly he travelled alone, with his geasa to lead him and his memories for company. Sometimes it seemed to him Úna watched his progress, gliding over his path as an owl. He threw a curse at the bird, remembering her betrayal that night long past when the Stag had bent his neck to drink under the alders of An Mhorn Bheag. The owl hooted in derision, and Blackthorn's words drifted away, aimless as thistledown at the whim of the wind.

Through the empty dark, to darker dreams, to a true twilight in the world of the living he passed, and when he could, he opened his eyes.

He found himself staring at the rough-barked bole of an enormous oak, and almost smiled. Well he knew this curve of root and trunk. It had served as his sickbed before when the boar of Sléibhte Mhám Toirc had gored him, and he the young Hunter, overbold in choosing his quarry. And again, when he had met with goblins in An Ghreallach and a wound they gave him festered, it was here he had come to heal.

Then he had been glad to lie in the Mother Oak's lap, glad of the Seer's aromatic salves and bitter potions. Now grief rose, an ache in his throat, for he knew he had been a long time resting in Úna's care, and time had been against him from the start.

He willed himself to his feet and away from the tree. His body obeyed him without complaint—it was whole and well. It was his soul was about to be cursed.

Tomorrow's promise hung on the evening air. It mingled with the hawthorn's voluptuous scent, howled with the baying wolves on the ridge. Every blade of grass poured sweet, heady oil on the fecund ground. Every bud opened wide to the hum of life. Every songbird's throat proclaimed Éirinn's passion. It was Bealtaine. This night was summer's eve.

A sound, or less than a sound, a sense of someone near made Blackthorn turn. Looking back toward the oak, he saw the great tree dwindle to a staff in Úna's hand. The Oak Seer, who grew young and old and young again with the seasons, stood before him now a maiden on the threshold of womanhood. Her skirt was a garden of rose and broom, flowering blackberry vines twined between her breasts and along her arms, cherry blossoms made a garland for her hair. He met her eyes without shame, for Úna's gaze held neither pity nor reproach. The wild is pitiless. The wild casts no blame.

She squatted, then sat unmoving as a stone, and so Blackthorn knew it was his patience Úna desired. As he stood, mirroring her stillness, the shadows lengthened. One by one the forest's colors were lost to the night, and last a liquid glimmer of gold that flowed for an unending moment between earth and sky before surrendering to the dusk.

When gray twilight was in full possession of the wood, Úna's lips parted, and her mouth opened like a falcon's in flight. As well her eyes flashed like a falcon's, and she held the Hunter in her ruthless regard. He would have matched her raptor's gaze, but light was just a memory now, and Blackthorn's eyes bewildered by the shadows. He could not follow her fingers as they reached into the oak wand, but saw her hand come out again holding Strife.

"Who gave you this gift?" she asked.

Blackthorn never hurried to answer the Oak Seer's questions. Her inquiries required no replies. They were spoor to follow, traces she set before a fumbling hunter's nose when he had missed the trail.

He took Strife from her hand, bound it across his back, and considered. Mortal skill had not forged the blade. Dana, perhaps, or Éire Herself might have given the sword to him on high Binn Chuilceach. . . .

"Áine is the giver of gifts," he told her.

As soon as the words had left his tongue, a vision of Brugh na Morna overwhelmed Blackthorn's senses. Screeling pipes filled his ears, perfume clouded his mind, elven dancers whirled before him in a blaze of desperate color. Yet, the Sidhe were nothing, drab as dried bracken beside the exquisite Goddess dancing in the center of their ring. Full-breasted, sun-haired, star-eyed Lady whose Name is Brightness, Áine, giver of gifts—'twas Herself had wintered in Brugh na Morna, and for a moon kept the Hunter of Éirinn at Her side.

He was a thought away from remembering all Áine had told him, when Úna smiled. No ordinary smile, a wolf's grin spread across her face. Her look drove the enchantments of Brugh na Morna from Blackthorn and quickened the beating of his heart. Best he loved Úna when she was one with the wolf. Always it had meant a hunt was before him.

The Seer reached again into her wand, this time bringing forth a smooth, straight length of ash wood. The full moon dallied below the far ridge, but by her light, fanning out above the eastern hills, Blackthorn saw the end of the shaft was ragged, a piece of kindling snapped short on someone's knee. The strips of elk hide that bound the broken point of gleaming silver to the other end of the staff smelled faintly of pine sap and old blood.

This, too, Blackthorn took from Úna. Her face altered subtly as the broken Spear left her hand. Her grin was still wide, but it had become a dog-fox's, quick and canny.

Blackthorn did not fail to notice the change, but neither did he stop to understand it. He had listened with half an ear as the thrush and cuckoo sang farewell to the sun. He had marked the wood mice foraging in the thickets, caught the wind's sigh as it rose to meet the mists. He had heard all the woods declare summer's approach, but it was not Bealtaine's call that compelled him to the edge of the clearing. Summer was coming indeed, riding in like a Queen on the broad back of the sacred White Stag—it was the call of the Hunt Blackthorn could not deny.

The Stag was abroad in the forest. Blackthorn could not see his quarry, or hear his thudding hooves, or smell the musk of the animal's gleaming hide. He did not need his senses to tell him the Stag was running in the wildwood. He was the Hunter, and the white elk his prey. They called to each other. This Hunt was theirs.

Úna had shown him the falcon, but Blackthorn strove instead to evoke the nighthawk's sight and silence, the better to spy the Stag's trail in the moonlit woods, the more softly to glide through the trees. Bears' spoor he found, and heard the beasts grunting in the pleasure of their mating—there at the base of the slope where the stream pooled. He went on, giving them a wide berth. Bear was not his quarry. Red deer froze on the shadowed hill when they felt the nearness of Death, but neither hart, nor hind, nor roe was the Hunter after, and they went on grazing when Death's shadow had passed them by.

He came at length to the hill that had been An Bhrí Mhaol, and after was called Márrach. All the woods were alive with summer's coming, but the knoll was barren still. Barren, but not empty. The ruins of Shadow's stronghold lay stark under the slanted moonlight. In the place that had once been the heart of the broch, the place that Urchóid had challenged him, and the Gruagach died, there Blackthorn found the fresh print of a giant elk.

He let go the owl and called forth the wolf. Bending low to the track, he drew the scent of it into his nose, sifting through the smells of dirt, old blood, and goblin for the one that was the elk's alone. Lifting his head, he scanned the ground for more traces of his quarry's passing, found them and followed them, stalking his prey down the hill, across the valley floor, then up the western ridge.

The Stag had chosen a steep path, and left tracks along it plain as the day. Blackthorn halted at the crest, to test the winds and learn what the Stag had learned—where lay the water, where the spring-wet bogs, where the high wood his quarry loved best.

Swift when he saw his way, slow when the track eluded him, the Hunter came at last to a high knoll, and no track upon it, no spoor to lead him, no sign of where the elk had gone. Throwing himself flat against the damp grasses at the base of the hill, he pressed his ear to the sod until he heard the faint echo of silver hooves pounding the earth. To the north his quarry was running, and north ran the Hunter, to rolling hills thick with gorse, furze, and holly, and groves of smooth, gray-skinned ash. A moonbeam shone on a slim crescent of paler wood, uncovered when the Stag's hoof had clipped an exposed root. The sap was just beginning to rise to the wound—with his quarry so close, the Hunter curbed his haste, daring to go on only as fast as he could go soundless.

A silver spark flashed between the boles of the trees. The Hunter trembled with eagerness, but remembering Reathach, made himself small and crept toward the light quiet as a mouse. Even a true mouse could not be so silent as to reach the Stag unheard, but an' he could get close before his prey was aware of him . . .

The spark kindled under the trees' black boughs, grew to a white flame that danced among the flowering thickets, flickered down the wooded slope, darted over the river. On the far side of the water, the Stag paused and raised his head to taste the air. The wind was changing, and the Hunter changed with it, moving to keep downwind of his quarry—but wind is ever an inconstant ally. The breeze was confused, and shifted to every corner before deciding to blow steadily up from the south. The Stag started, tasting Death on the air, and was away. The Hunter was after him like a hound.

The elk's powerful legs thrust his huge body up the rowan-covered hill swift as a squirrel up a tree, but the Hunter stayed close behind. His quarry would hide, an' the woods gave him cover, would fight, an' he stood at bay, but the Stag was a creature born for flight, and in all the world there was none swifter.

Topping the crest, the Stag lifted his head, brushing his tines against the moon-brightened sky before leaping away. His silver hooves drummed on the forest's floor, beating out the rhythm of the Hunt, and the Hunter's glad cry was the

song to match it. Fleet as an arrow from the bow was his
quarry, but the Hunter was swift as the thought that loosed
it. Tireless as the rolling world the White Stag ran, but the
Hunter was unflagging as the moon that nightly girds the
earth, and would not weary in this Hunt, not an' he must
give chase the length and breadth of Éirinn.

Swift as wildfire the Stag raced though the woods, and the
elk's cunning equalled his speed. He chose paths to daunt
the hound at his heels—devious paths to lead him astray,
dangerous paths to lead him to harm, treacherous paths to
lead him to his death—but the hound would not be
daunted. Through pools of moonlight and darkness the Stag
ran, beneath the star-crowned branches of the trees, across
fen and field, over mountain and under hill, and the Hunter
was his shadow.

The white elk came at last to mountainous country honey-
combed with wooded dingles and flower-sweet glades. He
bounded up a rocky spur, leaving no prints. From the summit
he leapt across a stream-carved cleft to a stone-sided hill,
leaving no trail. Around the hill and down the far slope,
then to a broad stream he ran. He took to the water-path,
following it even through the deep pools until he reached a
narrow, pebble-lined bank at the edge of a thick pinewood.
Climbing from the water, he wound through the trees, and
veiled his light behind curtains of darkness. When the shadowy pines gave way to ivy-bound oaks and elder, hazel and
whitethorns—he went like the wind through the moon-
dappled forest.

At the entrance to a narrow coomb, a may tree stood
guardian. A rill sang from the heart of glade, promising to
ease the Stag's thirst. The rising fogs offered to shroud his
light, the close-woven trees to bar the Hunter's way. The
invitation was irresistible—lowering his rack to pass the
doorward, the Stag picked a path down into the dell.

Though the coomb's inducements were as sweet to the
Hunter as they had been to his quarry, Blackthorn did not
beg admittance of the flowering may. A roebuck or fallow
stag he might chase until their own exhaustion brought
them down. The white elk would run before him forever,
and the Hunt come to nothing an' he had no more cunning
than his prey. Long enough he had run behind—now must

he overtake the Stag, and run before, and lie in wait along the trail.

The hound was gone, and the dog-fox in his place. Soft and sly, the Hunter sprinted along the high rim of the copse. When he had slipped by the front door unseen, quick and canny he stole in the side gate. The watch was awake—voles and owls, bright-eyed weasels, foxes, wolves. Blackthorn put the wind ahead of him and told easy lies to his fellow hunters and their prey. The meadow mouse believed Blackthorn a night-stalker after his flesh and did not betray him, lest he betray himself. The crafty pine marten believed the Hunter no more than a wayward breeze. The owl believed the Hunter was a fox padding after her own prey, but when she went to chase him from her hunting grounds, he was already gone.

At the bottom of the coomb the Hunter found the trap he needed—a steep-sided, muddy escarpment that would refuse the elk's weight and just beyond it, filling the lower end of the dingle, a fortress of wild roses not even the Stag could overleap. And he chose his cover—his lie. He would tell the Stag he was the tall, waving grass that grew on the stream's lower bank. He crouched down, willed his body to stillness, and waited as the shore waits for the returning tide.

The black alders drew their branches through the Stag's tremendous rack and caressed his broad back as the sacred elk made his way to the water's edge. He went cautiously, sniffing the air, but smelled only rose and mint, wet earth and sweet hawthorn. He listened, but heard only the wolves calling to each other, mice scurrying for cover, the careless song of a nightjar from the top of the coomb, and the tall grasses rustling in the wind.

Bending his neck, he dipped his muzzle to the brook, his tines glittering as if they were made of starlight, his coat brighter than the unveiled moon. The murmuring water reflected his glory, but Blackthorn knelt in the darkness that lined the bank, and the Stag drank unafraid.

His crowned head lifted as he looked back over his trail. The Hunter was nowhere to be seen. His spoor was not on the wind, nor his footstep on the path. The Stag turned away, and moved on, deeper into the coomb. The waters danced high over his hooves as he came ever closer to his Death.

Smoothly, soundlessly the Hunter rose from his cover. The Stag bolted, racing for the may tree, but Blackthorn was before him, cutting across his path. The Stag wheeled, bounded to the other side of the stream. The soft earth broke under the Stag's hooves, and carried him back down to the water. Lifting his forefeet, the giant elk pivoted once more and sprang forward, racing downstream. Around the next bend he faced a forest of flowering thorns. Wild roses filled the coomb from one side to the other, and stretched before him to where the sheer, impassable side of the mountain rose to mark the lower boundary of the coomb.

Turning at bay to face the Hunter, the Stag bellowed, shaking blossoms from the trees. Petals drifted down like snow, and the glade fell silent.

As a hawk Blackthorn had hunted, as a wolf, as a hound. As a man he would have made the kill, and himself the only creature in the wild with the right to answer the Stag's challenge. His broken reply dangled uselessly from his hand. A fool he was, and no hunter. To corner a dangerous quarry, and there front him without a chance of bringing him down—such folly turned a hunter into prey, and so it must be now for Blackthorn. The chase had been his, and for that he was glad, but grief was his as well, for the kill was denied him.

He met the Stag's eyes. They were like Úna's, pitiless and wild. Éire's geis blazed in them, a white-gold flame. Blackthorn stood amazed. He had thought to look on his death, but in the elk's fierce gaze, it was not his own death he saw. It was the Stag's.

"I have watched the grinning wolf lick the blood from the deer's throat." The Hunter's voice was soft with understanding. "I have seen the look in the hare's eyes when the fox springs, and the salmon's unblinking stare when the bear lifts him from the water. The mystery was shown me in every kill I made, and I a blind fool not to have Seen it till now."

He lifted his broken Spear. Light from the Stag's tines glinted from the weapon's marred point as the huge animal came forward.

"I thought it was pride in the hunter's heart. I thought it was resignation in the hunted's eyes."

The giant elk was near enough now that Blackthorn could

reach out a hand to the thick ruff of white that draped the Stag's shoulders and covered his chest. He wondered that he could look upon such brilliance, and not destroy his sight.

"It was love in the hunter's heart," he said. "And in the hunted's eyes, as in yours this night, it was assent."

Like a live thing, the Spear leapt from the Hunter's hand. Piercing the Stag's white breast, it buried half its broken length in the elk's deep chest, and rived the heart beneath.

The Stag's roar was like the roar of life in the earth's molten womb, and rang in Blackthorn's ears until there was no other sound in the world. The Stag's pain was like lightning's fury and blasted Blackthorn to his knees. But the Stag's death was a fire, white and hot, and it seared the Hunter's geis from his soul.

Seventy

In the cracks of time 'twixt night and morn
Neither dark nor light holds sway
But peace can be yours when twilight falls
And hope at the dawn of the day

All the folk of Temuir, and many more besides, were crowded upon the wall. Most looked toward Temuir's hill where the Mighty were gathered. They looked to see the Bealtaine fire the Priestesses had called, and to draw some measure of courage from the flickering red flames they glimpsed through the standing stones. Others looked out over the partially restored village to the fields and wooded hills where they longed to be, but dared not go.

Meacán's sight was on the far downs as well, though she stood within the circle of stones on high Temuir Hill. She, too, longed to dance to the places she beheld. Not even the spice of the fire's fragrance could mask the enticing scents the wind carried to the temple from the fertile fields, nor its crackling voice silence the evening song of the forest. Bealtaine was come, and not a soul within Temuir but wished to leave, to run over the moon-bright grass and climb the grassy knolls where the hawthorns flowered. This was a night for drinking honey mead, dancing naked around the fires, running to the flowering wild to make reckless, sacred love until dawn—but in Temuir, as in all the strongholds of the five kingdoms, this Bealtaine eve was a night of grim and wary vigil.

Meacán turned her eyes from the hills. Liannan's head was high as she studied the flames, but her face was grave. All the faces were grave, Tadhg's, the Cailleach's, Reochaidh's, and certainly her own. Only Niall looked glad, but Niall was a King, and looked never more splendid than when he looked toward battle.

Neither Scáil nor goblin can we See, Meacán heard the Maiden's thought clearly in her mind, *but there are shadows enough under the trees to give them cover*.

Shadows enough, Meacán agreed bitterly. Nine years the shadows of night and forest would lie under the Dead Lord's dominion, and give cover to the Shadow King's hosts. Nine years would sorrow and strife mark the turning of the Wheel. Nine years before the Stag would run again and a new Hunter attempt to Hunt the Light.

Meacán's thoughts led inevitably to Blackthorn, but she refused to follow them further. She had seen the ruined Spear the Mothers had brought to the Oak Seer, and never would forgive Úna her wolf's grin as she took it from Liannan's hand. The best she could hope was that Blackthorn slept still, curled in Úna's oak, or that he had died without waking. Wherever the Hunter of Éirinn's soul wandered now, the dawn would break it.

Meacán's tears were hot, but she shivered—the rest of her was suddenly cold. Would it were an evening chill she felt, or a fleeting cloud darkening the moon's face. Would it were, but in her heart she knew it was the coming Dark she felt closing in, the shadows gathering to the Dead Lord's banner.

As she moved closer to the fire, a chill wind blew past her, snuffing the flames. In the time it took Meacán to catch and hold her breath, Darkness overwhelmed all Temuir, from the heavens above to the village below. Her heart rose to choke her, and silence seized her throat, but Meacán's soul cried out in despair.

Not a sound had she made, nor anyone made, when the Mother's fire reared up from the ashes of the pit. A gust of hot wind blew from the flames to fill the temple, warming Meacán's cheeks like the flush of desire. A glad shout rose from the wall, and Ulaidh's King echoed it, shouting with laughter. Meacán stared in astonishment. Still Niall looked splendid, but the glory that covered him was not battle-joy. The flame in his eyes was for Liannan—he took her in his arms, and Meacán laughed too, rejoicing in his passion.

The circle of stones was bathed in silver, and silver jewels shone above—audacious stars, daring to glint in the moon-drowned night. It was the light making her so giddy. It was the wild songs of summer the people were singing from the wall, and their frenzied dance that was carrying them through Temuir's open gates to the fields beyond. More, it was the shadows on the hill—for the Dead Lord had lost his hold on them, and they tempted the Dancer with promises of pleasure and delight.

"How—" she began, but got no further. A gruff voice spoke coaxingly in her ear.

"A flower-wreathed bower I'll build you, fair Lady, a bed of sweet grasses and wild thyme, an' you'll come with me over the hills."

The Bear of An Clár's arm was already about her waist. Meacán laughed and danced away from him, but went only a little way. He hurried to catch her, and she slipped again from his grasp, dancing invisible through the air to the top of the path that led down Temuir's hill. The wound he had of a Scáil's sword on Márrach's wall stiffened the Ó Briain's gait, but it did not pain him, only made him lumber like a bear as he gladly gave chase. Through the streets of Temuir they went, Meacán shrieking with laughter, the Bear rumbling with lust, out the gate and up into the hills.

To the hawthorn-crowned knoll Meacán danced, but there stopped breathless to gather may blossoms into her skirt. She thrust a few in the Ó Briain's grizzled beard, but he wore them with good grace. Like all bears, this one of An Clár was as playful in love as he was fierce in battle.

With Bealtaine's enchantments clouding her reason, Meacán did not think to ask again by what magic the Dark had fled and the Light returned until summer's day was well dawned. Even then, her lover had no answer to give her, save that all Éirinn had shared in the spoils of the Hunt.

*   *   *

As soon as the Hunter left Márrach's hill, the Oak Seer went as a swallow to the haunted rise in the midst of the valley. The birds and beasts yet shunned the place, and the fairy folk as well. Úna walked there alone, but she had Seen the coming dawn, and walked unafraid though the mound was barren and ghosts moaned among the broch's tumbled stones.

To dare the wild and bring the quarry down, to return from the wild, bearing the gift of life—this the hunter's service to his clan. The Hunt was more—those called to Éire's service pursued a greater quarry and it was to Her they must render their kill.

Far-Seeing are the Mothers, and sharper still the Cailleacha's Sight, but only eyes that are wild can follow the Stag's trail. Only Sight untamed can behold the Stag's death.

Úna's bright gaze pierced the night to See the Spear pierce the Light. Shadows rose from the black earth, fell from the sky, flung their dark cloaks over her, over all Éirinn. She roared then, like the Stag was roaring, neither in victory nor defeat, but in the savagery of the kill.

All the Light in the world was the Stag's in the moment of his death, and the world was in Shadow. All the Light in the world was the Hunter's when he had brought the Stag down, and still the world was ruled by the Dark. All the Light in the world the Hunter returned to Éire, and so did Éire return Light to the world once again.

Aengus Óg, walking on Márrach's hill, came upon Úna the Oak Seer weeping like the rain. What heart is so hard the beauty of the wild cannot move it? And Aengus Óg's heart was ever easily stirred. He came to her, and caught her tears before they fell to earth. They glittered with silver moonlight upon his hand.

"Weep not, Oak Seer," he said. "As the Hunter of Éirinn has brought Shadow to Light, so do I bring glorious summer where spring dared not come, as I promised the Lady of Cnoc an Eanaigh."

He smiled and swept his arm in a broad circle, showing her the hill. Pale flowers nodded among tall grass, their perfumes rising on the crisp, clean air. Ivy rustled as mice and voles ran in and out among the stones, disturbing the broad leaves that covered them.

"Márrach no more, but An Bhrí Mhaol again," he said.

"Márrach no more, nor yet An Bhrí Mhaol," she answered. "Brí an Draighin, they will call it. The Hill of the Blackthorn."

Aengus Óg nodded, and to please her caused a blackthorn to grow at the crown of the rise.

"Tarry here but awhile," he coaxed. "Your Hunter has done well. Take some pleasure with me, before the next one comes to find you."

Úna's head lifted, proud as a swan's. "Many the Hunters gone before, many the Hunters to come. None like him. None so bold and cunning, none with heart so true. I have taught them all. I will teach them, every one, but none do I love as I love him."

"You weep for the Hunter, then? He has fulfilled Éire's geis, but Áine's will break him."

Úna's tears flooded her cheeks. "For Róisín Dubh was my Hunter lured to Brugh na Morna until Scáthach was dead and could not help him. For Róisín Dubh did Áine keep the Hunter's Spear from him, that he must seek Inis na Linnte where wishes come true."

"Generous Áine was to the Hunter as well," argued Aengus Óg. "Love She gave him from Róisín Dubh's heart, and a sword unequaled in all Éirinn."

He came closer, to stroke her hair and bring his lips near her ear. The shameless invitation of the flowering earth was in Úna's perfume, the heat of beasts mating flamed under her skin.

"Weep for him, Éire's daughter," he murmured, "but smile on me, for I must have your embrace or go mad."

Úna smiled through her tears. Fairy folk helped her disrobe, untwining the flowering vines from her arms, and plucking the petals from her skirt one by one. They left a rumpled carpet of blossoms about her feet, and ran laughing to make a bower beneath the blackthorn tree.

"Not for my Hunter do I weep," Úna said, letting her Bealtaine lover draw her into his arms, "nor for any sadness. So bright the happiness I See in summer's morn, my eyes are overfull with joy."

Bealtaine

Nine years had Blackthorn borne Éire's geis. Nine years its white flame had burned in his soul. No more a fire, no more his own, yet he bore the geis still. It was a Name on his tongue, cool as the moonlit air and clear as crystal—the Name of the next Hunter. When he called her, the Hunt would be hers, and in her heart Éire's geis would be fire once again.

He dipped his fingers into the patches of moonlight that danced on the rill and watched them cover his hands in hooves of silver. He summoned the pale mists and they clung to his legs and back, molding themselves into the strong muscled body of a gigantic white elk. The stars shone down on him, and when he lifted his eyes to gaze on their light, he lifted a great weight, for a tremendous crown of silver was set upon his brow. While this night lasted, moonlight and starshine and the Bealtaine fires would cloak Blackthorn in the Stag's semblance that he might do the Goddess one last service.

He raced up the trail to the top of the coomb. At his passing the flowering hawthorn bowed in homage and threw petals in his path. South he turned, and east, hooves thudding on the forest floor. The grasses tossed, the trees sighed, the day-birds woke and sang aloud, thinking his light was the coming dawn.

He forded the streams of Eas Aedh-Ruadh and ran on through the glades gold-flowering and the budding woods. He flew past the open gates of Brugh na Bóinne, heard An Daghdha and the Mór-Ríoghain call out his praises in voices rich and harsh. Over the high plains and the low fens he ran, by rivers and lochs, until he came at last to Each-Dhroim when the black sky had paled to gray and the stars were reluctantly fading.

Though he had come from far Ulaidh to Laighin, Blackthorn was barely winded. He stood quietly behind the simple bower where the next Hunter of Éirinn was stirring in her lover's embrace. His voice husky with desire, the lad tried to entice her back to his arms.

"Night lingers, and so its chill. Curl against me, my fair flower, and we will keep each other warm."

"Night is gone, and morning nigh." Laughter, and a mock grunt of pain. "Loose me, you randy bodach. What, will you let summer's sun find me here? An' I bathe not in Bealtaine's dew, no more your fair flower, but an old hag I'll be soon enough."

Next moment she stood outside the little lean-to of branches and leaves, shivering slightly, and giggling, too. Blackthorn should have called to her then, but he stood silent, bound and helpless in chains of geasa. Though his eyes never left the maiden, now disappearing down the path to Each-Dhroim, his Sight was fixed on a memory of far-distant Inis na Linnte, on the Hag hurrying from the night, pulling her filthy skirts from the damp ground and cursing the dew. He heard the young girl's laughter, but it was her words to her lover echoing in his ears—"an old hag I'll be . . ."

Love's geis demanded he fly, and the Hunt's prevented him, and between the two his soul was nearly torn apart.

A single leap and he stood before the next Hunter, blocking her path. He wheeled, roaring her Name.

"Aoife!"

Shafts of gold broke free of the earth and shot across the heavens, transforming gray sky to blue.

"Aoife!"

The girl trembled, but it was not fear in her eyes.

He called a third time and a last. "Aoife Iníon na Mná Feasa!"

And he was away, down the mountain to the valley, hurtling through the sleepy woods. Aoife would try to follow, as he had once followed his Stag, but she would not catch him. Not even his hoofprint would she find. Swift had he travelled to Each-Dhroim, but now his feet scarce touched the ground. If he would save Róisín and his own soul, he must outrace the dawn.

West he ran, keeping pace with the fleeing night, but the impatient day pursued him like a hunter. Beneath his hooves the rolling world turned toward summer. Above his gleaming rack the wheel of stars fled the sun's light. Swift as the wind Blackthorn had flown to Aoife, but the wind he left gasping behind as he raced to Róisín.

He forded An tSláine and An Bhearú, crossed the fair downs of Tiobraid Árann, and when he came to the broad An tSionainn, like Eocha he leapt into its rushing waters and swam for the far shore. Sliabh Bearnach he passed and the Ó Briain's lands of An Clár, and ever the dawn was on his heels.

To Aillte an Mhothair the day coursed him, past the ruins of Lios Chanair. Blackthorn never slowed, but leapt from the limestone headland and flew over the churning, foam-topped waves into the deeps of heaven. Like a shooting star he sped across the skies, leaving a silver trail for the eager sun to follow. Like a shooting star he fell through wisps of cloud to the jagged pinnacle of a solitary island drifting in the vastness of the green-gray sea.

As his silver hooves struck the peak, so did the golden sun. Day overran the mountain's top, flushing the mists from the wooded slopes and stripping Blackthorn of the White Stag's guise. The mists fled the forest in sweeping mantles of white, but night yet clung to the mountain's sides. Slipping dawn's rose and golden snares, Blackthorn ran for the shadows as a fox runs for the thickets and the hounds after him. The fox is sly and leaves no trail, but Blackthorn dragged his hands along the ferns and grasses, and brushed his body against the forest's arms until his clothes and skin were drenched in dew.

As he came in sight of the cave, Dearg bounded from it, his bark torn between welcome and challenge. The dog took up a protective position on the threshold, and the Hag came to stand at his side. Her smile was cruel, her laugh crueler.

"Too late!" she screeched, lifting a long, crooked finger to the east. "Here is summer's day!"

Not even the curse that made her so hideous could make Blackthorn hesitate. He snatched her pointing hand, and held for a loathsome instant a scaly, withered claw in his dew-wet palm. The Hag shrieked and tried to pull free, but he only held her tighter, and drew her out into the brightening air.

When her feet touched the damp ground, the Hag began to fight like a cornered badger. She howled and scratched, and her hound leapt about barking as loud as he could. It was nothing to Blackthorn, for the old woman's fingers had grown smooth and firm in his. Where the Hag's soiled, tattered rags brushed the wet grasses, they melted away into nothing. Where her misshapen toes trod the earth, they grew straight and lovely. Wild with hope, he wrapped his arm around her waist and dragged her down into the dew-soaked lawn.

"A moon you had of me in Brugh na Morna," he prayed desperately to Áine. "Give me now but a little time back, and hold the dawn at bay."

The Hag spat. Blackthorn dodged, and she twisted out of his grasp. He caught her back by her scraggly gray hair and found thick black tresses twined in his fingers. Pressing the screaming, clawing creature into the wet grass, he soaked her rank rags in the dew. They faded and vanished away, and the mottled flesh beneath them bloomed fair and full of life.

How it was she stopped screeching and started laughing, stopped fighting him and lay back to let him wash the ugliness from her face, her arms, her long, slender legs, Blackthorn was never quite sure. Dearg still bounded in a frantic dance about them, still barked and howled in deep excitement, but the Hag was gone and Róisín Dubh, the Wish-Bringer of Inis na Linnte, lay a dew-washed rose in Blackthorn's arms.

Dawn crept quietly to the edge of the grassy ring, transforming the gray, misty clearing to a bed of green, white, and

gold for the lovers to lie in. Blackthorn plucked delicate
dewdrops from the shamrocks and brought them one by one
to adorn Róisín's eyelashes, plucked more to make a beaded
necklace at her throat. He ran his fingers through the wild
rye, then through her hair until each strand was black and
lustrous. He sucked the nectar from long blades of grass and
kissed her ears, her breasts, her lips like roses. Great pleasure
he took, and half the morning, making sure the blessed dew
reached every curve and hidden crevice of Róisín's body.

When the sun was high and the dew burned away, they
slept for a time, Róisín's head against Blackthorn's shoulder,
his buried in the soft pillow of her hair. What Róisín
dreamed she never said, but Blackthorn dreamed of Brugh na
Morna.

When he woke, he kissed her, and told Róisín Áine's
words he had at last remembered.

Let me go, gentle Lady. The Stag calls and I must away.

*Ochone, mo mhúirnín, but stay awhile more. Come, listen to
the pipers play.*

*Sweet Goddess, open the gates of Brugh na Morna. My geis
urges me be gone.*

*And so it will an hour from now. Refresh yourself from my
cup, Blackthorn. My maidens will sing ere long.*

*Giver of Gifts, Bléssed Áine, grant me release that I might
seek my heart's desire!*

*Your heart's desire? Why, go then, and seek it. But be not
amazed, Conall mac na Caillí, if Áine knows the desires of the
heart better than does the Hunter of Éirinn.*

Appendix A

The Wheel of the Year

Days in Éirinn begin and end at sundown. There are seven days in a week, and approximately four weeks in every moon. Though the Wise claim the moon made the first calendar, Éirinn's year is simultaneously measured by two overlapping cycles: the lunar and the solar.

The lunar year contains thirteen lunations, new moon to new moon. Each lunation is named for a sacred tree which, in turn, represents a letter of the Ogham alphabet. Birch (Beith), the first full moon after the winter solstice, begins the year, followed by Rowan (Luis), Ash (Nion), Alder (Fearn), Willow (Sail), Whitethorn (Uath), Oak (Dair), Holly (Tinne), Hazel (Coll), Vine (Muin), Ivy (Gort), Reed (Geataire), and finally Elder (Ruis). Each moon has its own powers, affiliations, meanings, and dangers. Lunar phases are new, waxing, full, waning, or old. New moons are sacred to the Maidens, Full Moons to the Mothers, Old Moons to the Crones. Full moons are times of celebration. In the dark of the moon the Scáileanna and goblins make bold, and so have the Tuatha dé Éireann come to fear it, yet they believe also the dying moon may grant a wish or bestow a secret gift.

The solar cycle reflects the transition of the seasons. The Wheel of the Year spirals endlessly through time, a circle cross-quartered by days that mark the end of one season and the beginning of the next. These days comprise the four great festivals of the year, each celebrated with feasting, song, music, dance, poetry, and lovemaking. The revelry lasts not for a single night, but for a "tide" of thirteen nights and twelve days, linking the solar year to the primacy of the lunar calendar. During these festivals, the gates to the Brughanna are open and the boundaries between the worlds are blurred.

Samhain (SOW in), "summer's end" and the beginning of winter, is Éirinn's New Year. *Imbolc* (IM bowlk), "stirring," acknowledges the waking fires of life within the winter-cold earth. *Bealtaine* (BAHL ten eh), "Bel's fire," is winter's end and summer's dawning. *Lughnasadh* (LOO nuh sah), "the games of the God Lugh," marks the beginning of the harvest season. The stations of the sun, the solstices and equinoxes, while noted, are considered lesser holidays, mere midpoints of the seasons. The winter solstice (midwinter) lies between Samhain and Imbolc, the spring equinox between Imbolc and Bealtaine, summer solstice (midsummer) between Bealtaine and Lughnasadh, and the autumn equinox falls between Lughnasadh and Samhain.

While four seasons are celebrated, The Wise say the Wheel of the Year has but two true seasons, Summer and Winter. Each is ruled by a different sun; Summer's Big Sun shines between Bealtaine and Samhain, Winter's Little Sun between Samhain and Bealtaine. As Samhain and Bealtaine are the hinges on which the Wheel turns, so are they the greatest and most perilous days of the year. Every ninth year, it is on Samhain that the Stag begins to run, and on Bealtaine that the Goddess Éire chooses her new Hunter.

Appendix B

The Mighty are those whose gifts and abilities imbue them with great personal power; the Mothers, the Kings, the Sidhe, the Wizards, and the Poets. Lesser folk of Éirinn armor themselves with nicknames, revealing their true Names only to their nearest kin or dearest friends. The Mighty are known by their true Names, and garner more power and fame to themselves every time their Names are spoken.

The Mothers. A Queen-Mother of Éirinn is a priestess, chosen for her ability to manifest her affinity with the land, and also for her managerial, mediational, and political skills. She trains for the queenship in her years as Maiden, and serves as advisor to the Queen when she becomes the Old Woman.

The Kings. Kings of Éirinn serve the Goddess of the land by serving the Queen. This service is sexual and martial; a King's semen and a King's blood are equally potent. In battle, Kings are possessed by a madness—the mantle of kingship—that makes their blood boil, their skin harden, and fills them with an insatiable desire for the deaths of their enemies. Mantles of kingship fall as they will. Kings may be challenged at Lughnasadh. The contest for the kingship is a battle to the death. Both King and rival are cloaked in their mantles, and the spilling of either's blood is considered a blessing for the land. Should a King die during the year, a successor is chosen at the Games, but as there is no sacred blood to flow, victory in the Games and some sign that the victor possess the royal madness is enough to win the kingship.

The Sidhe. Also called the Tuatha dé Danaan (the People of the Goddess Dana), the Sidhe are the high elves, the elves of the light, the Fair Folk, the Good People. With life spans and understanding far beyond that of humans, the Sidhe have little to do with the Tuatha dé Éireann (the People of the Goddess Éire), but live and love and fight and die in an Éirinn slightly apart from the five kingdoms. Their concerns are rather with their dark counterparts, the *Scáileanna,* with whom they are ever at war. Even so, the doors of their dwellings in the hollow hills are opened at the turning points of the year, and they consider chance meetings with humans fortuitous and significant.

The Wizards. Unlike the Mothers, whose powers come from the invocation of their deity and remain essentially the same from one generation to the next, the Wizards' unique powers are born to them and are theirs alone. Wizards are obstinate, self-centered, and easily angered. Whether this temperamental quirk is intrinsic to the nature of a Wizard's gift or an unfortunate result of their inevitable fame is a matter the Wise have yet to decide. By virtue of their gifts, seven wizards are chosen by the Mothers to serve Éirinn. In return for this service they are given a Wizard's *Sliabh* (shleev), a magnificent dwelling within a mountain, complete with every amenity and servants to tend to their needs and desires.

The Poets. Poets can fashion truth and intent into a *rann,* a spell of words, meter, and alliteration that must realize the purpose for which it was created. Poets are sacred in Éirinn, both honored and feared. Their favor can be a blessing beyond imagining, their displeasure an immutable curse.

Appendix C

BARDS AND BARD-SONGS

Poets are rann-makers, filled with the power of word and inspiration. Bards, like their cousins, the *seanchaithe* (SHAN ukh ee heh), or storytellers, are entertainers. They travel from town to town, bringing old tales and news. As a rule, Bards' songs commemorate events, but occasionally a Bard is possessed by poetic inspiration, what the Tuatha dé Éireann call "drinking from the Poet's cup." Bardic Lore claims that in their last moments, a Bard-Song comes to all Bards—their Death-Song. At any other time a Bard-Song may be disastrous. Silverweed, the Bard of An Dubh-Linn, sang a Bard-Song that was a lament for her dead lover. It broke her heart with grief, and she, too, died. Larkspur, the Bard of Tráigh Lí, unintentionally sent the Mighty of Éirinn to sleep at their Samhain feast. Reed, the Bard of Cluain Meala, sang a love song so potent he was overcome with lustful passion. The most famed Death-Song was made by Shearwater, the Bard of Sligeach. With his lover Suibhne he stayed too long on the heights of Na Cruacha and was overtaken by goblins when night fell. His Bard-Song defied the rules of poetic ranna, (the last stressed syllable of his rann alliterated with stressed syllables preceding it), and left the hill forever cursed.

Appendix D

GEASA

A *geis* (GESH), (plural: *geasa* (GASS uh)), is a magic bond or taboo. A geis may be a task or quest, such as finding a treasure, or it may be a restriction, such as not speaking to men with red hair. It can be one's fate—to become a Poet or to kill a King. A geis may be laid by one being on another, it can fall accidentally on a person through magic or misdirected will, it can be taken upon oneself when a person sees his or her destiny clearly. Only by fulfilling a geis can one be free of it; a broken geis breaks the soul, and neither death nor time nor the mercy of the Gods can ever make it whole again.

Glossary

Airgead (AHR ih gid) "silver"; Cessair's spelled sword.

Alp Luachra (ahlp LOO khruh); a magical creature that can infest people, taking all the nourishment from their food and causing them to be possessed of an insatiable appetite.

Bealtaine (BAHL ten eh); see APPENDIX A.

Bean Sidhe (ban SHEE) "woman of the fairy folk"; an elven woman often Seen in fairy-green washing the bloody clothes of those about to die. Her keening is an omen of death, usually for one of the Mighty.

Bodach (BOH dakh) "scoundrel"; a vulgar person, a churl. Sometimes used as an insult, other times meant more fondly, as a term of commiseration.

Broch (BROKH); a conical tower.

Brugh (BROO); *Brughanna* [plural] (BROO uhn uh); the dwellings of the Gods and Goddesses and of the Sidhe are magnificent halls hidden within the hollow hills of Éirinn.

Cailleach (KAHL yukh); *Cailleacha* [plural] (KAHL yukh uh) "old woman"; grandmother, crone, old hag. (See NAMES)

Crannóg (KRAN og); an artificial island or lake dwelling.

Currach (KUR uh); small, wicker frame boat covered with hide or leather, propelled by bladeless oars.

Each Uisce (akh ISH keh) "water horse"; a fuath that plays its tricks at dangerous river crossings. The *each uisce* tacitly offers a ride across the water. Those who accept the invitation are given a dunking, and often drowned.

Fear Dearg (far DARG) "the red man"; a red-haired, red-complected, red-clothed fairy. Of changeable nature, sometimes the *fear dearg* torments those he encounters with macabre and gruesome pranks, at other times he offers valuable advice and valuable help to those lost in the wild. It is wise to be polite to any flash of red one glimpses in the forest, and should a red man ask to warm himself by your fire, it would be exceedingly unlucky to refuse him.

Fuath (FOO ah) "water sprite"; though many fairy folk detest water and will not cross it, there are a number of water sprites who dwell in the lochs, rivers, and seas and whose chief entertainment is luring the unwary to watery graves.

Geis (GESH); *Geasa* [plural] (GASS uh); see APPENDIX D.

Grianán (GREE uh nawn); a sunny room, a summer house.

Imbolc (IM bowlk); see APPENDIX A.

Lughnasadh (LOO nuh sah); see APPENDIX A.

Mo Mhúirnín (ma VOOR neen); my dear, my darling.

Murúch (MUH rookh); *Murúcha* [plural] (MUH roo khuh); the seal people, who can remove their sealskins, and walk about as mortals.

Ogham (OH um); a runic alphabet given to the Tuatha dé Danaan by Oghma Sun-Face, and later shared with the Tuatha dé Éireann. Ogham is both a written runic language and a manual sign language.

Púca (POO kah); *Púcaí* [plural] (POO kee); shape-shifter. Seen either as a small sprite with human features, or as an animal, most often a horse.

Rann (RAHN); *Ranna* [plural] (RAHN nuh); a poem made to conform to a specific metric and alliterative pattern that gives it power. A spell, a rune.

Rí (REE) "king"

Samhain (SOW in); see APPENDIX A.

Scáil (SKAWL); *Scáileanna* [plural] (SKAW lyun nuh) "ghost, wraith"; the dark elves, so called because of their gray skin and utterly dark eyes. Mighty warriors and magicians, the Scáileanna see themselves as the rightful rulers of Éirinn, and believe their dominance contested only by the Sidhe. Generally, they consider humans beneath their notice, human towns and activities inconsequential. They present a danger only to the wayward wanderer who intrudes in their domains.

Sidhe (SHEE); see APPENDIX C.

Síle na gCíoch (SHEE lyeh nuh GEE ukh); a small female figurine, with her vulva prominently displayed.

Sliabh (SHLEEV); *Sléibhte* [plural] (SHLEYV teh); "mountain"; most sléibhte are simply geographical features. Seven of these mountains, made hollow many long ages ago by the craft and wizardry of Diarmuid the Builder, have become the dwelling places of the Seven Wizards of Éirinn. These are: Sliabh Ailp, Sliabh An Óir, Sliabh Thuaidh, Sliabh Slanga, Sliabh Buidhe, Sliabh Mis, and Sliabh Bladhma.

Tine (TAI nuh) "fire"

Tuatha dé Danaan (TOO uh huh day DAH nun) "the People of the Goddess Dana"; the Sidhe, the elves of the Light.

Tuatha dé Éireann (TOO uh huh day AYR uhn) "the people of the Goddess Éire"; the human folk of the five kingdoms.

Uisce (ISH keh) "water"; also *Uisce Beatha* (ISH keh BAH huh) whiskey, "the water of life."

Names

Aedh Rí Mumhan (EE REE MOO wan) "Aedh, King of
Mumhain"

Aengus Óg (AYNG us OHG); God of life and youth. *Aengus*
means "true vigor."

Aill (AWL) "a cliff"; an elven Chieftain of An Cnoc Gorm,
Aill once wagered with the hero Cearnach mac an
tSeanchaí. He won the hero's right eye, but lost to
Cearnach the pride of An Cnoc Gorm, a marvellous dappled gray mare.

Áine (AW neh) "brightness"; called the "giver of gifts," *Áine*
is a Goddess of abundance, wealth, fecundity, nurturance,
and happiness.

An Daghdha (uhn DAH yuh) "the Good God"; a great warrior, as are most of the Gods, but also a particularly beneficent and reasonable God, a protector of the diverse
peoples of Éirinn, and generous with his favor. The fairy
folk feel especially close to *An Daghdha*.

Aoife Iníon na Mná Feasa (EH fuh ih neen nuh mnah FASS
uh) "Aoife, daughter of the Wise Woman"; the next
Hunter of Éirinn.

Badhbh (BAH eev) "scaldcrow"; one of the three aspects of
the Goddess of Battle. The three named together, *Badhbh,
Macha, and Mór-Ríoghain* is a common expletive.

Beannachán Óg (BAN uh khawn OHG) "young little horned one"

Bochna (BOKH nuh) "ocean"; Queen-Mother of Laighin.

Bóinn (BOYN); the Goddess of Midhe's great river.

Breac (BREK) "speckled, a trout"; the Mariner, once a Wizard of Éirinn.

Brí (BREE) "hill"; the Maiden of Midhe.

Brighde (BREE deh); the Goddess of Fire, and so of beauty, inspiration, love, healing, and art. Imbolc, the festival that marks the beginning of spring, is Her festival. The common expletive *Brighde's Fire* refers to Her sacred fire that has been kept continually burning in Dair na Tintrí since time before memory.

Brónach (BRO nukh); a mighty warrioress, and mate of Cú Ceat, Chieftain of Dún na gCon.

Cailleach (KAHL yukh); *Cailleacha* (KAHL yukh uh)[plural]; "old woman"; the Wise Woman, the sacred Crone. A Priestess (usually a Mother past childbearing age) whose powers of Sight, telepathy, and empathy are fully developed. (See GLOSSARY)

Caireann (KAR in); the Queen-Mother of Ulaidh.

Ceallach (KEL lukh); the Poet of Tulach, in service to the Ó Briain.

Cearbhall (KAR ool); a champion from the lands of Tiobraid Árann, east of the Silvermines. He is called "Broad-Hand" not only because his hands are big, but also because of his custom of felling his foes with a single, open-fisted blow.

Cearnach Caoch mac an tSeanchaí (KAR nakh KAYKH mak SHAN uh khee) "triumphant one-eye, son of the story-teller"; a champion of Ulaidh who won an elven horse in a wager with Aill of An Cnoc Gorm, and rode to great fame on the back of his dappled gray mare.

Ceithil (KEH uhl); a Chieftain so wise, noble, and beloved, her honor grew great as one of the Mighty. She used her true Name, and was called "Queen" by her people.

Cessair (KASS er); the Chieftain of the Sidhe of Cnoc an Eanaigh. The tales of how Cessair learned the arts of war and came by her extraordinary armor of silver mail were long ago lost. A fragment that tells of the forging of her enchanted sword Airgead is still sometimes sung, but the

story is so astonishing, none but doubt that the tale is a
glorious example of how sweetly a Bard's tongue can sing
a lie. For though the song claims Airgead was forged by
the Wizard Cian, the Smith of Sliabh Thuaidh, it is well
known *Cessair* wielded the blade in the battle of Magh an
Rí four generations before the Wizards' Sléibhte were
built. Moreover, the Wise assure us that there has never
yet been a Wizard of that Name.

Ciarán (KEER awn) "twilight"; the Chieftain of Latharna.

Coll (KOWL) "hazel"; a champion of Dún na nGall, left to
defend the fort when Niall departed for Temuir.

Conall mac na Caillí (KON uhl mak nuh KAHL ee) "strong-
like-a-wolf, son of the Old Woman"; the true Name of
Blackthorn, the Hunter of Éirinn.

Conmac (KON mak); a warrior of Cnoc an Eanaigh.

Conn (KON); a guest in Dún na Bó, Conn murdered the
dún's Chieftain, but was himself killed by the man he had
betrayed.

Corann (KOR in); a warrior of Cnoc an Eanaigh.

Cormac Rí Chonnacht (KOR mak REE KHON ukht)
"Cormac, King of Na Connachta"

Creathna (KREH nuh); the Name-Sayer of Sliabh Ailp, one
of the seven Wizards of Éirinn.

Cú Ceat (ku KAHT); Chieftain of Dún na gCon, famed
throughout Éirinn as the Wild Dog of Ciarraighe. He and
his mate, Brónach, lead their people naked into battle.
Those that have heard their war cries say they are like the
baying of hounds.

Cuanna Óg mac Liadhan (COON uh OHG mak LEE han);
the young son of Liadhan, a Chieftain of Laighin.

Dáithí (DAW hee); called "Two-Winds" because of a magic
ring he possessed, giving him mastery over eastern and
western blows. By the power of his ring he journeyed over
the waves to Tír na nÓg while a living man, and returned
to tell his tale.

Dana (DAH nuh); a Mother Goddess most revered by the
Sidhe, who consider themselves Her people—the Tuatha
dé Danaan.

Dearg (JAH rug) "red"; the Hag's hound.

Diorbhal (DER uh vul); heroine of the tale "Diorbhal's Ride."
Diorbhal ended nine years of slavery and hardship for the

people of Mumhain by successfully bringing a message of great import from the Sidhe of Cnoc an Eanaigh to Mumhain's Queen.

Diorchaidh (DER uh khee); Diorbhal's mother.

Diurán (DYUR an); a King of Ulaidh who was spelled to sleep by an elven harper.

Domhnall (DON uhl) "mighty"; the Spell-Maker, a legendary Wizard of Éirinn. Though one of the Seven, Domhnall declined to live in a Wizard's Sliabh, preferring to dwell in his own treasure-filled, spell-laden mountain, Sliabh Coimeálta, called by others, "Domhnall's Keep."

Donnchú (DON uh khoo) "dark hound"; once King of Na Connachta.

Dubhghall (DOOV uhl) "dark stranger"; one of the Sidhe of An Cnoc Gorm. *Dubhgall* once brought the Poet of Teach an Fhásaigh a rare gift, a woven carpet from southern lands beyond the reach of snow and rain. In exchange he received a poem that blinded the God Oghma Sun-Face long enough for *Dubhghall* to steal a magic heifer from the God's sunlit pastures.

Dúr (DOO er) "hard, obstinate"; Meacán's horse.

Eimhear (AY ver); Queen-Mother of Mumhain.

Éire (EH ruh); the Earth Goddess. Humans of the five kingdoms call themselves the Tuatha dé Éireann; the People of the Goddess Éire. The creatures of the wild are also Her children, as is the White Stag. The Hunter of Éirinn bears Her geis.

Eocha (OH khuh); the horse lent Blackthorn by the Sidhe.

Eochaidh (OH khee); the Stone-Eye, once the Wizard of Sliabh Mis.

Eoghan Rí na Midhe (OH wen REE nuh MEE) "Eoghan, King of Midhe"

Fearchar (FAR uh kher); the Flyer, once the Wizard of Sliabh Mis.

Feargna Óg (FARG nuh OHG) "young Feargna"; the Necromancer of Sliabh Slanga, one of the seven Wizards of Éirinn.

Fiach (FEE ukh) "raven"; the harper of Cnoc an Eanaigh.

Fionn (FIN) "white"; Cessair's horse.

Fionnghuala (FIN oo lah); the Deceiver of Sliabh Buidhe, one of the seven Wizards of Éirinn.

Gruagach (GROO uh gakh); servant to the false hunter.

Guibhne (GIV neh); God of smithcraft, and of ale and intoxication.

Laochail (LAY khel); the late King of Midhe, killed on Bealtaine when he was thrown from his horse.

Liannan (LEE an uhn); Queen-Mother of Midhe.

Longaire Rí Laidhean (LONG er uh REE LAH yun) "Longaire, King of Laighin"; *Longaire* means "tracker, pursuer."

Lugh (LOO); a God, often called "Lugh the Long-Armed." *By the Spear of Lugh* is a common expletive, but the Wise debate whether the phrase is meant to refer to his phallus or the sun-spikes he hurls. The festival of Lughnasadh is His—the yearly Games where contests are held, and a King may be chosen.

Mac Ailch (mak EYLKH); the Conjuror of Sliabh An Óir, one of the seven Wizards of Éirinn.

Macha (MAH khuh); the second aspect of the Goddess of Battle. (see above—BADHBH)

Máchail (MAW khil) "blemish, defect"; the false hunter's mother, captured in a raid on Latharna and sold into slavery, so despised the son the Alban raiders' violence forced her to bear, she Named him *"Máchail."*

Maelgorm (mayl GORM); a warrior of Cnoc an Eanaigh.

Magadh (MAH guh); the Queen-Mother of Na Connachta.

Máirín (MAW reen); a legendary robber-maiden, whose looting of Domhnall's Keep and her theft of three golden hairs from the head of the Goddess Niamh are told in her tale.

Manannán mac Lir (MA nuh nawn mak LEER); Lord of the Waves. The white crests of the swells are said to be the Sea-God's white beard.

Marfach (MAR fakh) "deadly, fatal"; a Scáil of Márrach.

Meacán Iníon na Caillí (MEH kawn ih neen nuh KAL ee) "bulb/root, daughter of the Old Woman"; the Dancer of Sliabh Mis, one of the seven Wizards of Éirinn.

Mór-Ríoghain (MOH ree uhn) "great queen"; the third and most powerful aspect of the Goddess of Battle. When warriors hear the Mór-Ríoghain call their Name, they know they will soon meet with death or glory, and likely both. (see above—BADHBH, MACHA)

Muirgheach (MUR ee); a King of Na Connachta who died a royal death on Inis Mór, the largest isle of Oileáin Árann.

Muirne ní Finne (MOR nuh nee FIN nuh); once Queen-Mother of Ulaidh, now the Cailleach of that kingdom.

Niall Rí Uladh (NEEL REE UHL uh) "Niall, King of Ulaidh"; Niall means "champion."

Niamh (NEE uvh); Niamh of the Golden Hair, Goddess of Youth.

Nuadhra (NOO hruh); the Ó Dubhagán (oh DOO vuh gawn), a Chieftain of Mumhain.

Ó Briain (oh BREE uhn); the Chieftain of An Clár, called "the Bear" for his ferocity. His true Name is Art (AHRT).

Ó Súilleabhán (oh SUL ih vawn); a Chieftain of An Daingean (uhn DANG uhn).

Oghma (OH muh); called "Sun-Face." A warrior God, and bestower of the Ogham runes on the Tuatha dé Danaan.

Othras (UH ras) "festering sore"; a Scáil of Márrach.

Racánaí (RUH kahn ee) "brawler"; Niall's horse.

Reochaidh (RUH khee); the Destroyer of Sliabh Bladhma, a giant, and one of the seven Wizards of Éirinn.

Reathach (RAH ukh) "running"; a púca.

Róisín Dubh (ROH sheen DOOV) "the little black rose"; a wizard, also called the Wish-Bringer of Inis na Linnte.

Ruairc (RORK); the Poet of An Fharraige, best famed for two ranna. In "The Death of Donnchú," *Ruairc* Named the hill where Donnchú died "Leacán Ruadh" (red hill), for the King's blood that stained it, and so it has been called ever since. The second rann was *Ruairc*'s poem to repay the hospitality of the Chieftain Canar—the rann that caused fire to destroy Canar's hall.

Ruairí (ROH ree); a wizard, called the Fire-Worker.

Saileach (SAHL yukh) "willow"; the Poet of Glas an Mhullaigh.

Scáthach (SKAW hukh) "the shadowy one"; the Poet of Teach an Fhásaigh.

Seamair (SHA mar) "shamrock"; the Weather-Worker of Sliabh Thuaidh, one of the seven Wizards of Éirinn.

Suibhne (SIV neh); a maid of Sligeach, the Bard Shearwater's lover.

Tadhg (TA yug); the Poet of An Chluain Thiar.

Tréfhuilgne (TRAY il guh neh) "trefoil"; the green-haired God of the shamrock.

Turlach (TOOR lukh); a hero of song whose virility and battle-madness won him the Kingship of Mumhain.

Uisdeann Óg (WHIS din OHG) "young Uisdeann"; an ill-fated lad immortalized in "Uisdeann Óg and the Scáileanna of An Dubhchathair."

Úna (OO nah); the Oak Seer. A prophetess, a shamaness of the Wild.

Urchóid (ER khay) "malice, evil intent, harm"; a Scáil, the champion of Márrach.

Places

Achadh na Liag (AKH uh nuh LEEG) "the field of the flag-stones"

Aillte an Mhothair (AWL chuh uhn WOH er) "the cliffs of Mothar (MOH er)"; limestone cliffs on Na Connachta's western coast.

Alba (AHL uh buh); a country east of Éirinn.

An Baile Meánach (uhn BAL eh MYAW nukh) "middle town"

An Bearnas Mór (uhn BAR nis MOHR) "great gap"

An Bhanna (uhn VAH nuh); a river in northeastern Ulaidh.

An Bhearú (uhn VAH roo); a river in Laighin.

An Bhóinn (uhn VOYN); a river in Midhe.

An Bhrí Mhaol (uhn vree WEEL) "the round, bald hill"

An Bhuais (uhn VOOSH); a river in northeastern Ulaidh.

An Chathair Dhonn (uhn KHAH er GHOWN) "the brown fort"

An Chluain Thiar (uhn khloon HEER) "west meadow"; the dwelling place of the Poet Tadhg.

An Clár (uhn KLAWR) " the plain"; lands of Mumhain, for generations under the stewardship of the Ó Briains.

An Cnoc Buidhe (uhn knok BWEE) "yellow hill"; a hollow hill in southern Mumhain, a dwelling of the Sidhe.

An Cnoc Glas (uhn knok GLAHS) "green hill"; *glas* is a mingling of green and gray, a color of which the Sidhe are particularly fond.

An *Cnoc Gorm* (uhn knok GORM) "blue hill"

An *Cnoc Leathan* (uhn knok LEH uhn) "broad hill"

An *Cnoc Maol* (uhn knok MWEEL) "bald hill"

An *Droim Fiodhach* (uhn drim FEE ukh) "wooded ridge"

An *Dubhchathair* (uhn DOOV kha hur) "the black fort"

An *Dubh-Áth* (uhn DOOV aw) "black ford"

An *Dubh-Linn* (uhn DOOV lin) "black pool"; a village in east Midhe, and also a village in west Na Connachta.

An *Earagail* (uhn YER uh gil); a mountain far in the north and west of Ulaidh, a favorite haunt of Úna the Oak Seer.

An *Fharraige* (uhn AR ig yeh); once the dwelling of the Poet Ruairc.

An *Ghreallach* (uhn GRE lukh) "a miry place"

An *Leacán Ruadh* (uhn LEH kawn ROO) "red hill"

An *Lorgain* (uhn LOR gin) "the shin"; a traders' crossroads at the southern end of Loch nEathach.

An *Meall* (uhn MYAWL) "little round hill"

An *Mhorn Bheag* (uhn WORN VEG); a little river in Ulaidh.

An *Mullach* (uhn MUL ukh) "the summit"; birthplace of Eoghan Rí na Midhe.

An *Ómaigh* (uhn OH mah); a town in Ulaidh, a great crossroads for travellers, Bards, and traders moving east and west.

An *t-Ard Achadh* (uhn tard AKH uh) "the high field"; a small village of Mumhain, and also a broad, high plain south of Béal an Átha Móir. The second is the site of two battles fought between the Sidhe and the Scáileanna in the days of Muirgheach the Lost King.

An *Trá Mhór* (uhn traw WOHR) "big strand"

An *tSionainn* (uhn TSHUN uhn); Éirinn's greatest river.

An *tSiúir* (uhn TOOR); a river in Mumhain.

An *tSláine* (uhn TLAW nyuh); a river in Laighin.

Aonach Urmhumhan (EE nukh OOR woo uhn) "the fair of east Mumhain"; the town's name derives from its yearly midsummer fair when the small village becomes a bustling center of revelry, pleasure, and trade. People come not only from the east of Mumhain, but from all over Éirinn to hear the music, dance, sample the foods, buy the wares, trade the horses, and wager on the races and games.

Ard na Gaoithe (ard nuh GEE) "height of the wind"

Áth na dTrom (aw nuh DROM) "ford of the elder bushes"

Baile an Bhothair (BAL eh uhn WO her) "town of the road"

Béal an Átha Móir (BEYL uhn AW huh MOYR) "mouth of the big ford"

Béal Cú (beyl KOO) "the mouth (delta) of the hound"

Béal Feirste (beyl FERSHT eh); the seat of the Queen of Ulaidh, a large walled port on the eastern coast of Éirinn.

Béal Leice (beyl LEEK uh) "the mouth (delta) of the flagstone"

Bealach Cláir (BAL ukh KLAWR) "the road of the plain"

Binn Chuilceach (bin KHWIL kyukh) "hill of the playboys"; at Samhain, in the Year of the Stag, the Scáileanna overran *Binn Chuilceach*. With the mountain as their base, they kept most of northwestern Éirinn under their sway. Their power was diminished when Cessair of Cnoc an Eanaigh slew the Scáil Chieftain in battle.

Brí an Draighin (BREE uhn DRY in) "hill of the blackthorn"

Brugh na Bóinne (BROO nuh BOY nuh); a hollow hill in Midhe, overlooking An Bhóinn. A dwelling of the Gods.

Brugh na Morna (BROO nuh MOR nuh); a mountain in the wilds of western Ulaidh also known as Mullach an Lia Dhuibh.

Caiseal (KASH uhl); the seat of the Queen-Mother of Mumhain.

Cathair Cheann na Leasa (KAH er KHYAWN nuh LAS uh) "the stone fort at the head of the circular enclosure"

Ceatharlach (KAH her LUKH); the seat of the Queen-Mother of Laighin.

Ciarraighe (KEER ree) "the black people"; in Mumhain.

Cionn Tíre (kin TEER uh); a rocky headland of Alba, to the north and east of Ulaidh.

Cluain Meala (kloon MEH luh) "the meadow of honey"

Clochán na bhFormhórach (KLOKH awn nuh WOR wor ukh) "the Giants' Stepping-Stones"; on the north coast of Ulaidh, also called "the Giants' Causeway."

Cluain na Lárach (kloon nuh LAW rukh) "the mare's meadow"

Cnoc an Eanaigh (knok uhn YEN ee); home of a clan of legendary elven warriors.

Cnoc na Fírinne (knok nuh FEER in uh) "the hill of truth"; so dear is truth to the Sidhe of *Cnoc na Fírinne*, a false-

hood spoken within or upon their hill brings death and
Shadow's curse to the prevaricator. Despite the danger to
humans in terms of lost time and bewildered senses, matters where perfidy is likely—treaties, questions of law—
are often decided upon the hill's slopes.

Cnoc na gCapall (knok nuh GAH pul) "hill of the horses";
the horses of the Sidhe are without equal in the world,
and the herds of *Cnoc na gCapall* are the Sidhe's pride and
joy.

Coill na n-Áirní (kayl nuh NAR nee) "the sloe wood"

Cromghlinn (krom LIN) "crooked glen"; a narrow valley east
of Loch nEathach. *Crom* is also the ancient Name of a
grim and dark God.

Dair na Tintrí (DAR nuh TIN tree) "oak tree of the lightning bolt"; where stands Brighde's temple, a place of healing and inspiration. When the Mothers summon Fire to
do their will, it is the flames of *Dair na Tintrí* that answer
them.

Doire Eile (DER eh EH leh) "Eile's oak-woods"

Dún an dá Éan (DOON uhn daw AIN) "fortress of the two
birds"; in his haste to save his sister from Alban raiders,
the hero Cearnach Caoch mac an tSeanchí rode straight
across Ulaidh, turning neither for wood, nor river, nor the
fort of Dún an dá Éan. His elven mare broached every
obstacle, and overleapt the dún in a single bound.

Dún na Bó (doon nuh BOH) "fort of the cow"

Dún na gCon (doon nuh GUN) "fort of the hound"

Dún na nGall (doon nun GAWL) "the fortress of the
strangers"; originally built by northern foreigners attempt-
ing to establish a foothold in Éirinn, the fortress became a
citadel of Éirinn when King Conchúr (KON uh khur) Rí
Uladh stormed it and drove the invaders out.

Each-Dhroim (AKH rim) "horse ridge"

Eas Aedh-Ruadh (ass ey ROO) "the falls of Red Aedh"; Aedh
was a King of Ulaidh who drowned in the cataract. The
glades along the many streams that run from *Eas Aedh-
Ruadh* are favorite hunting grounds of the folk of Dún na
nGall.

Éirinn (EH rin); the isle of the five kingdoms, and the surrounding seas.

Gaillimh (GAH liv); a large port town of Na Connachta.

Glas an Mhullaigh (GLAHS uhn WUL ee) "green hilltop"; home of the Poet Saileach.

Inis Ceithleann (IN ish KEH lin) "Ceithil's island"; Ceithil's descendants claim it was she first conceived the idea of piling rocks in a loch to build an artificial island, a crannóg. The one she chose for her seat still bears her Name.

Inis na Linnte (IN ish nuh LIN teh) "island of pools"; the home of the wizard Róisín Dubh the Wish-Bringer, an isle that floats freely in the waters of the western seas.

Laighin (LAH yin); the southeastern kingdom of Éirinn. Bochna is Mother and Longaire her King.

Latharna (LA har na); a port village north of Béal Feirste, known for its flint trade.

Lios Chanair (lis KHAN er) "Canar's fort"; a Chieftain Named Canar built a circular earthen fort south of Aillte an Mhothair and overlooking a sheltered bay. A proud man, Canar sought the service of a Poet, hoping to enhance his fame with ranna of praise. He succeeded at last in persuading Ruairc, the Poet of An Fharraige, to dwell with him for a time, but Ruairc's rann fell far short of Canar's aspirations. Displeased with the quality of Canar's hospitality, Ruairc composed a verse declaring the feast before him was fit only for flames to devour. A fire immediately ignited the board, consuming not only Canar's feast, but his entire hall.

Lios Dúin Bhearna (lis dyoon VAR nuh) "gapped fort"; when Canar's fort south of Aillte an Mhothair was destroyed, he built this hall farther north, in the shadow of Sliabh Ailbhe (AYL vuh).

Loch Dearg (lukh DARG) "the red lake"; a small lake in Ulaidh.

Loch Dubh (lukh DOOV) "the dark lake"

Loch Éirne (lukh AYR nyeh); in reality two lakes, the upper a rocky, swirling cauldron, the lower a broader, calmer basin.

Loch nEathach (lokh NYAH ukh); in eastern Ulaidh, the largest lake in Éirinn.

Luimneach (LIM nukh); a port village in Mumhain on the banks of An tSionainn.

Magh an Rí (MAW uhn ree) "plain of the King"; 'twas at the battle of *Magh an Rí* that Cessair, a young elven maiden

of Cnoc an Eanaigh, first took to the field wearing spelled
   silver mail and wielding an enchanted blade, and won
   great fame and glory thereby.

Márrach (MAH rakh); an Alban word. When kine or other
   animals are herded together, driven into a dead-ended
   ravine or defile, then the entrance sealed off by a twisted
   fence of wood and bramble, the resulting enclosure is
   called a *márrach*. *Márrach* may also refer to a maze, to an
   enchanted castle, or it can mean "spellbound."

Méan (MAYN); a river in northeastern Ulaidh.

Midhe (MEE) "the middle"; the middle kingdom, east-central
   Éirinn. *Midhe* shares borders with Ulaidh to the north, to
   the south with both Laighin and Mumhain, and Na
   Connachta to the north and west. Liannan is Mother and
   Eoghan her King.

Mullach an Lia Dhuibh (MUL ukh uhn LEE yuh DOOV) "the
   summit of the black pillar stone"; a mountain in western
   Ulaidh known to the Wise as Brugh na Morna.

Mumhain (MOO wun); the kingdom in the south and west
   of Éirinn. Eimhear is Mother and Aedh her King.

Na Connachta (nuh KAN ukht uh); a kingdom in the west of
   Éirinn. Magadh is Mother and Cormac her King.

Na Cruacha (nuh KROO khuh) "stacked hill"; where the
   Bard Shearwater and his love Suibhne were surrounded
   by goblins and killed.

Oileáin Árann (EH lawn AWR an); a group of three islands
   off the west coast of Mumhain.

Ráth na Saileach (RAW nuh SAL yukh) "the circular fort of
   the willow trees"; though the Bards tell no tale of it, and
   the event is not in living memory, it is common knowledge
   Ráth na Saileach fell to the Scáileanna long ago. Originally
   Named for the proud willows that grew nearby, many now
   Name the place *An Ráth Salach* (uhn raw SAH lukh),
   meaning the dirty or polluted fortress, and fear to go there.

Seanghualainn (shan GOO lun) "old shoulder (of a hill)"

Sléibhte Mhám Toirc (SHLEYV teh wahm TURK) "the
   mountains of the pass of the boars"

Sliabh Ailp (shleev AYLP); a Wizard's dwelling in Na
   Connachta.

Sliabh An Óir (shleev uh NOR) "gold mountain"; a Wizard's
   dwelling in eastern Ulaidh.

Sliabh Bearnach (shleev BAR nukh) "gapped mountain"

Sliabh Bladhma (shleev BLAW muh); a Wizard's dwelling in Midhe.

Sliabh Buidhe (shleev BWEE) "yellow mountain"; a Wizard's dwelling in Laighin.

Sliabh Coimeálta (shleev koh MAYL tuh); a mountain in Mumhain also called "Keeper Hill."

Sliabh Éibhlinne (shleev EV lin uh); in Mumhain.

Sliabh Mis (shleev MISH); a Wizard's dwelling in Mumhain, not far from Tráigh Lí.

Sliabh Slanga (shleev SLAN guh); a Wizard's dwelling in southeastern Ulaidh.

Sliabh Tuaidh (shleev TOO uh); a Wizard's dwelling in northwestern Ulaidh.

Sligeach (SHLEY gukh); a port town in Na Connachta.

Teach an Fhásaigh (TAKH uhn AW see) "house of the wilderness"; when a young girl, Scáthach the Poet, coming upon a fair meadow at the base of Binn Chuilceach, was inspired to make a poem. Once sung, the rann caused her magnificent house to appear at the edge of the field.

Temuir (TEH wer); the ancient Name of the seat of the Mother of Midhe. *Temuir* also refers to the temple on the hill above the Queen's halls, or the village outside her walls.

Tiobraid Árann (TIH bred AW run); lands of Mumhain, east of the Silvermines.

Tír na nÓg (teer nah NOHG) "land of the young"; an enchanted isle to the west beyond the circles of the world, dwelling place of the Gods and the Dead.

Tráigh Lí (traw LEE); a large port town in western Mumhain.

Tuaim (TOOM) "tumulus"; Turlach of Tuaim hailed from *Tuaim dá Ghualainn* (TOOM daw GOO lan; "tumulus of the two shoulders"), the seat of the Queen-Mother of Na Connachta.

Tulach (TUH lukh) "little hill"

Ulaidh (UHL uh); the northernmost kingdom. Caireann is Mother and Niall her King.

Bibliography

An tSuirbhéireacht Ordnáis. *Éire, Eagrán Gaeilge*, Baile Átha Cliath: Rialtas na hÉireann, 1970.

Briggs, Katharine. *An Encyclopedia of Fairies; hobgoblins, brownies, bogies, and other supernatural creatures*. New York: Pantheon Books, 1976.

Burl, Aubrey. *The Stone Circles of the British Isles*. New Haven and London: Yale University Press, 1976.

Edwards, Ruth Dudley. *An Atlas of Irish History*, 2nd edition. London and New York: Methuen and Company Ltd., 1981.

Graves, Robert. *The White Goddess* (expanded and revised edition). Magnolia, Massachusetts: Peter Smith, 1983.

Hogg, Ian. *The History of Fortification*. New York: St. Martin's Press Inc., 1981.

Joyce, P. W. *Pocket Guide to Irish Place Names*. Belfast: The Appletree Press Ltd., 1984.

Ó hÓgain, Dr. Dáithí. *Myth, Legend and Romance; an encyclopaedia of the Irish folk tradition*. New York, London, Toronto, Sydney, Tokyo, Singapore: Prentice Hall Press, 1991.